HOME FROM HOME

Oppressed by the aftermath of September 11th, New York novelist Anna Kovac decides she needs a change of scene. On the spur of the moment, she agrees to a house-swap: her elegant Manhattan townhouse for a villa in Tuscany. Along with two friends from England, Genevieve and Candy, she moves to the picturesque village of Montisi for the summer. Their rural paradise is bliss — until mysterious things start to happen. When her New York architect and friend, Larry, falls from scaffolding to his death, Anna rushes home, only to find that the locks have been changed on her house. Someone appears to have stolen her identity, emptied her bank account, sold her possessions — even abducted her beloved father . . .

Books by Carol Smith
Published by The House of Ulverscroft:

FAMILY REUNION
GRANDMOTHER'S FOOTSTEPS

CAROL SMITH

HOME FROM HOME

Complete and Unabridged

CHARNWOOD
Leicester

First published in Great Britain in 2003 by
Time Warner Books UK
London

First Charnwood Edition
published 2004
by arrangement with
Time Warner Books UK
London

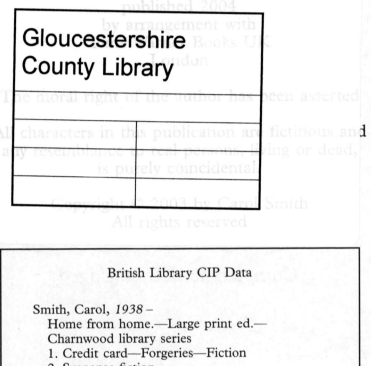
British Library CIP Data

Smith, Carol, *1938 –*
  Home from home.—Large print ed.—
  Charnwood library series
  1. Credit card—Forgeries—Fiction
  2. Suspense fiction
  3. Large type books
  I. Title
  823.9'14 [F]

  ISBN 1–84395–224–6

Published by
F. A. Thorpe (Publishing)
Anstey, Leicestershire

Set by Words & Graphics Ltd.
Anstey, Leicestershire
Printed and bound in Great Britain by
T. J. International Ltd., Padstow, Cornwall

This book is printed on acid-free paper

Acknowledgements

Grateful thanks, as always, to the efficient Time Warner team — my editors, Tara Lawrence and Joanne Coen, and the brilliant sales and marketing people. Also to Jonathan Lloyd, my agent, who goes where I would never have dared to tread.

A big thank you, too, to Charles Chromow and Bob Prinsky, market observers and US financial experts, for giving me the benefit of their professional wisdom. And most of all to Steve Rubin, for sparing so much of his time to show me how to construct a selling synopsis.

Part One

1

The day the world changed, Anna saw it happen. She had taken the Fifth Avenue bus to 57th Street, on her way across town to a breakfast meeting, when the first plane went over, unnervingly low, and she watched the inevitable impact from a distance. Fifteen minutes later, still dazed with disbelief, she and her publisher witnessed the second strike and the ensuing terrible implosion of the twin towers. In that brief space of time civilisation altered. Over three thousand people were lost, many of them vanished without trace. It was to be weeks before Anna would sleep properly again, months before she finally banished the dreams.

She was late with her book, which wasn't going well. A trauma like this was the last thing that she needed. She would lie awake all night with a pounding heart, reliving, over and over, those harrowing images. In the early hours, as the light began filtering in, she would finally lapse into a fitful doze, only to be woken in what seemed like mere seconds by Sadie, demanding breakfast. Sometimes she just gave up and went back to her desk and tried to get on with her work. From her study window, at the top of the four-storey house, she could see a vista of flickering screens. The city that never sleeps was on overtime.

Paige, with her pragmatic lawyer's mind, told

3

her briskly that she was overreacting. It had been a catastrophe affecting the whole world; now it was time to put it on hold and get back to ordinary living. Too much brooding was simply not healthy, a way of letting the terrorists win.

'Not possible,' cried Anna, in despair. Her father had lived through far worse in his youth but throughout her own life she had always felt protected. It was going to take an almighty adjustment before things returned to normal, assuming they could.

'That's the trouble with you creative folk,' said Paige in her down-to-earth way.

'Meaning I'm some kind of spaced-out nut?'

'No, just that you live in your own encapsulated world.' Implying that Anna really ought to get out more. She was fast becoming a hermit.

But the book was like an albatross dragging her down; her imagination simply was not functioning. Not in any positive way; all she could come up with now verged on the sick.

'Give yourself the weekend off and come with us to the country.' Both Paige and Charles worked harder than most yet equally liked to play. Their house in Quogue was the epitome of good living but Anna couldn't spare the time even for that.

'A couple of days won't hurt,' Paige assured her, but Anna dared not ever relax. The tenuous thread of her seventh novel was threatening to disintegrate. And where would she be should that ever happen, with this expensive new piece of real estate to maintain? The movie money had

4

proved a terrific plus but the financial commitment stretched way into the future. She was far too savvy to depend on another movie deal happening again. Living off one's wits proved an endless treadmill and, for some reason she could not fathom, the books got no easier to write.

'It is just that your standards improve,' said Paige, but Anna refused to believe that.

'Once it is finally finished and delivered,' she threatened, 'you'll not be able to get rid of me at weekends.' Tennis and barbecues and lounging around the pool. Cocktails with the well-heeled Hampton set, every sybarite's dream. She and Paige had been friends since their student days, part of a very tight set. The sister, Anna occasionally reflected, that she'd always rather wished she might have had. Their lives had gone in divergent directions yet still, after almost fifteen years, they remained every bit as close. Paige, with her sharp mind and dynastic beauty, had captured the glorious Charles in their final year. No children (no time) but a brilliant marriage and a lifestyle that could not have been bettered.

'Gotta go,' said Paige, as ever in a rush. 'Catch you again on Monday. Don't overdo it.'

★   ★   ★

Sunday lunch with her father had become a sacred ritual, about the only time these days that Anna took trouble with food. She would ride the subway down to Tribeca and walk the last three blocks to his street, to the shabby but spacious

5

family home in which she had been raised. These days it was looking well past its best, with cracks in the masonry and a sagging front stoop. The spindly plane trees cried out for attention and the neighbourhood overflowed with full garbage sacks. There were black kids playing in the street outside and they whooped with delight when they saw Anna.

'Yo, Anna. How're ya doin', man?'

'Good,' she yelled, kicking back their ball. Many of them she had known since infancy; a few were her father's pupils.

George Kovac, in his heyday, had been a world-class musician, solo violinist with the Philharmonic, feted, since the age of nineteen, on concert platforms all over the world. His exit from Poland had been sudden and dramatic; he had had to abandon everything, which meant more than just his money and possessions. Now, recently turned eighty and increasingly arthritic, he had relinquished his international career to teach the local children of the community. His pupils were from deprived backgrounds and without proper schooling; occasionally he discovered one with outstanding musical aptitude. George was a genius at coaxing out that talent, charging them only a pittance for tuition. Putting something back, was how he termed it. Better than sitting on his backside, simply growing old.

'Your dad's an inspiration,' was the opinion of Anna's friends, who would frequently make the trek downtown in order to seek his wise counsel. Shambling and craggy, with thick greying hair and eyes fast losing their power, he still remained an imposing figure who cared more for his neighbours' wellbeing than for his own.

Today she was cooking her mother's chicken paprika, ever a favourite with George. The pans in his kitchen were the ones her mother had used. Occasionally Anna would sneak in a replacement, knowing that he preferred things as they were. The house itself was steeped in memories as though time had stood still. Even the noise from the street outside was muffled by solid brickwork and the heavy drapes that hadn't been drycleaned in years. The dust and aromas of several decades hung in this room undisturbed, as though Anna's mother's presence were still in the house. She had been a beautiful and inspired flautist who had died suddenly and unexpectedly. Now George spent his days, when not actually teaching, slumped in his decrepit easy chair. Like him, it was sagging and had shaped to his angular frame but he fretted if anyone chose to usurp it. It was all that remained of the old life, she supposed. Anna knew enough to leave it alone.

This Sunday, as always, she served lunch in the dining-room, the only time the room was ever used. The rest of the week her father fended for himself, eating in the kitchen standing up. Anna carefully folded the heavy hand-made lace cloth, relic of a distant age when the world had been at peace, and replaced it with a cheerful cotton one from Macys, more practical and easier to keep clean. She set the table with the tarnished silver that had been her mother's only dowry. How little the two of them had had to set

7

up home, yet the love that had lasted through the years burned as brightly since her death. George shuffled in and looked around with approval, then unlocked a display cabinet and selected two of the long-stemmed hock glasses they used for festive occasions. Ceremoniously he uncorked a bottle of wine, placing it on an antique silver coaster.

When Anna carried in the steaming casserole he sniffed appreciatively and virtually smacked his lips. He regularly went through this courteous little charade though she knew all too well that her culinary skills would never be in her mother's class. Her mother, dead these eleven years, had been an exemplary housekeeper. Anna envied the love he still had for her, hoped that some day she might strike lucky and find something like it herself.

'So tell me about the house,' he said, once they were seated and served. Despite his pretended disapproval of the profligate way she was spending, he was secretly proud of his only child who had grown into such an independent spirit. If you've got it, flaunt it, was Anna's philosophy, though her father devoutly believed in that rainy day. Carefully she detailed all the things she was doing, new furniture, new fittings, even some structural work. Nothing, it seemed, was she keeping from the old life. She was like an eager bride-to-be only doing it all on her own.

'Your mother would not approve,' he said, sadly shaking his head, though she saw from the twinkle in his eye that he was only teasing. She had always known, since her earliest years, exactly what she wanted, and putting money into property these days seemed the most sensible investment. Especially now, with the stock market on its uppers. There were endless reports on the financial pages of thousands of solid investors facing ruin. Yet her father couldn't help worrying on Anna's behalf; George, who had arrived in the States with nothing, had always been obliged to scrimp and save.

'But that was then and this is now.' She lived in quite different times. And, due to the excellent education he had given her, came from an altogether more affluent class. 'The movie deal is just a bonus,' she explained, 'like a flukeish lottery win.'

He laughed and ruffled her hair with pride. 'My daughter, the money maven,' he said fondly. 'Just be sure that you don't overdo it. No point running to me when you go bust; I have very little put away.'

'My regular earnings are something quite apart,' Anna explained, not for the first time. 'I promise you, I still have a savings account.' She had loved the Lexington Avenue apartment, but moving to Madison was the ultimate dream. She had always wanted a house of her own and now, fortuitously, had achieved it.

The apple dumplings were another perennial favourite, then Anna cleared the table and tidied up. She made the coffee and carried it into the parlour where George was already settled with the papers. Occasionally she worried about him living here alone but he had been in this house all his married life and refused now to be uprooted. Although this quarter of lower Manhattan was no longer considered very safe, George remained one of its fixtures. Here, at least, he was known and respected, still a commanding force in the community. She trusted to the goodwill of his neighbours to let her know if ever anything should go wrong. As it was, they spoke several times a week and, on rare occasions, she even succeeded in luring him uptown. Since she had paid so much money for a house, his curiosity had been piqued. Not even at the height of his professional career had he earned such a sum.

★　★　★

They listened to a concert after lunch and idly discussed the week. Anna confessed that the book was dragging, that she found it increasingly hard to concentrate. She told him about the flickering screens, proof that her neighbours were sharing her disquietude. All over the city were new insomniacs, fearful of what might come next.

'A lot of my friends are too scared to go out. Staying home has become the fashionable thing.'

George, who had seen his whole heritage destroyed, took each day as it came. His pleasure was derived from the simple things of life; his daily walk to the grocery store, his music, his chessgames, the children and, of course, Anna. He was inordinately proud of his talented daughter, had read each of her novels more than once. His sole regret was that her mother had not lived to witness the flowering of her wonderful talent.

The old grandfather clock in the hall chimed four. 'Pa,' said Anna, 'I really have to go.' She still had a mountain of domestic chores to deal with before she felt she could get back to her writing.

'Take care, child,' he said, seeing her to the door, then stood and watched her walk away until she turned the corner.

★　★　★

Rather than taking the subway all the way, Anna chose to walk from 42nd Street, instinctively averting her gaze from the gap in the skyline left by the missing towers. It was a blindingly hot November afternoon and, since she spent most of her time at a computer, she badly felt the need to stretch her legs. She had forgotten about the marathon. Even as late as this, almost sundown, some runners still straggled by in ragged clumps, cheered on by an enthusiastic crowd, many waving flags. It was like an endless street party, block by block; people in shirtsleeves came pouring out of their doorways, carrying glasses and yelling with zealous enthusiasm. The Stars and Stripes was everywhere, draped over buildings, on the hoods of cars, fluttering from lampposts and fire hydrants. The *Times* had published a fullpage reproduction which was taped to the inside of countless windows. A strange, sad tribute to the thousands who had gone. A moment of unfamiliar patriotism.

By the time she reached home, Anna was

exhausted; thirty-two blocks in this unseasonal heat. And yet the unaccustomed exercise had done her a power of good. Her skin was flushed, her eyes were bright and her muscles had a healthy tingle. She stood on the sidewalk, groping for her key, and felt the familiar pride of acquisition. The front of the building was still covered with scaffolding, from when they replaced the guttering and repainted the cream stucco façade, but the door itself was a work of art, solid oak with a black wrought-iron knocker. She had bought the place off a Japanese bank who had used it solely for corporate entertaining. When they suddenly relocated back to Tokyo, Anna had snapped it up at a bargain price. Here, in this much coveted district, 74th Street between Madison and Park, real estate values had long been sky-high, the more so since what was happening in the stock market. Scared investors were moving their assets fast into bricks and mortar and Anna, by pure luck, was already a jump ahead. This house represented all she had ever wanted. It made her feel positively grown-up.

★   ★   ★

She was at the computer, doing her daily stint, when Larry Atwood, her architect, walked in. Sometimes he got on her nerves with his free use of her key but he always explained that he hated to disturb her. Not that hearing his authoritative voice off-stage wasn't sufficient distraction. She could not resist popping down to see him as he

12

handed out daily instructions to his men. There were four of them, working on separate shifts, and they seemed to have been with her for ever. She had managed to get them to turn down the radio but that didn't deter them from whistling and guffawing. Or stopping for endless coffee breaks, even whole afternoons. They had knocked through the wall between kitchen and breakfast-room, to open up the space that she desired. And the original mouldings on the ceilings had been restored; the house was slowly reclaiming its elegant past. Sadie was in there, with dust on her fur, rubbing her beautiful head against their legs. She was constantly angling for attention, this cat. Anna picked her up and nuzzled her neck.

Larry, for once, was wearing a decent suit instead of his usual jeans and sturdy trainers. Off to a meeting at City Hall, he explained, to do with planning permission for another job. He was an outgoing, laughing man with mackerel eyes; Anna had known him since Yale. And, because of their long-time friendship, he was charging her less than he might. Despite her new-found prosperity, she was grateful.

'Everything on schedule?' she asked. As if.

Larry laughed and nodded. 'Shouldn't be too long now till we finish. I'm sure you can't wait to be shot of the lot of us.'

Anna simply smiled and shrugged and put on a fresh pot of coffee. She knew her role in this all-male commune, would indeed be heartily relieved when they had gone. But she had to admit that their work was first-rate. Step by step, the formerly down-at-heel brownstone was being transformed into a magnificent home. She had lived here now for the past four months and the restoration work had at first seemed unending. She found herself camping upstairs on the upper floors, venturing down only when she knew that they had gone. But out of a cloud of brick dust and confusion, her dreams were taking on substance. Soon she would be able to show it off to her friends. She was dying to know what they'd think of this latest achievement.

'When can I fix the house-warming party?' she asked. 'I don't suppose there's a chance that it might be inhabitable by Christmas?'

'No,' said Larry, calculating rapidly. 'March, at the very earliest, I would guess.'

★ ★ ★

The breast cancer committee meeting was boring and painfully slow. Anna got home at a quarter after nine, wondering why she still bothered. Public awareness was all very well but these days she had far too much else on her plate. It dated back to her journalism days when she'd adopted the charity as a fighting cause. She had produced some impressive results in her time; now it was little more than an irksome chore. Mainly she disliked the overbearing chairwoman, a wealthy Sutton Place divorcee with delusions of grandeur. All they ever did these days was bicker and drink a particularly nasty sherry, of which it appeared she kept an endless supply.

'I guess you've done your bit,' sympathised Paige when Anna, armed with a restorative vodka, rang her that night for a moan. 'They have nothing better to do, those women, than retail therapy and lunch.'

Anna, guilty at her lack of moral fibre, worried that she should not let them down.

'Without me there, and the buyer from Barneys, I reckon they'd very soon come to a grinding halt.'

'You've made your contribution,' Paige reminded her. 'Without you they would never even have got started. Plus you've got a book to finish. You can't do everything at once.'

'Maybe I'll take a sabbatical,' said Anna, not relishing the thought of having to broach the subject. Mrs Kaufman was a formidable woman who rarely stopped talking long enough to hear what anyone said.

'Shall I write you a sick note?' suggested Paige. 'Asking if you can play hooky for a while?'

Anna smiled. 'It's a tempting thought.' She looked at the pileup of reading she had to get through. Slack off for a moment and it overwhelmed her, like leaves at the beginning of fall. There were times when her life resembled an unmade bed and she didn't know how to start straightening it. She was also on the committee of PEN, the international writers' association, of which the AGM was imminent. It was getting too much, her head was spinning. With a further eight months to work on this wretched book.

'What you really need is a vacation,' said

15

Paige. 'I told you, you should have come with us to the country.'

★ ★ ★

Having freshened her vodka and scrambled some eggs, Anna stretched out in the living-room to catch up. The top two floors were more or less complete and this was the room she liked best. Comfortable off-white upholstered sofas set off the Botticelli flowered rug that she had picked up in the summer sales at half its original price. The handsome Roman blinds, which she had duplicated throughout, were in a neutral heavy linen which, though they would be a devil to keep clean, gave the whole place a feeling of summer brightness that never failed to raise her spirits, especially when, like now, she had come home late. She loved the house with the passion of new acquisition and often felt reluctant to go out at all. Everything in the world that she valued was here on these four spacious floors. Upstairs were her workroom and panelled library, next to her elegant bedroom and en suite bathroom. Occasionally she fantasised about pulling up the drawbridge and spending the rest of the winter here alone. She had always been satisfied with her own company, a reason for her continuingly single state.

Sadie, purring like a sewing-machine, draped herself over Anna's knees and graciously allowed her to fondle her ears. Mainly what Anna was ploughing through was junk mail and periodicals, plus a pile of newspapers she hadn't had time to catch up with. Habits died hard and she was still subscribing to several monthlies from her previous life — the *New Yorker*, the *New York Review of Books* as well as *Publishers Weekly*. There had been a time when she could fit it all in but right now her energy was sapped. Were she more strong-minded, she would cancel all subscriptions but then might run the risk of missing out. Now was not the time to sort things out; once the book was out of the way, she would try to tidy her life.

Sighing, she flicked through each wordy publication, pausing to browse the occasional feature; occasionally ripping one out. As she watched the pile of rejects grow, her spirits started to lift. At last, at almost midnight, she was through, with only the *Yale Alumni Magazine* left. There was rarely anything of much interest there these days but she could not always be sure. Skip an issue and she might miss some news, the death or advancement of one of her close contemporaries. And that would never do; Anna was very much a creature of habit. She skimmed through rapidly, planning a leisurely bath. The writing had gone well today, she felt herself slightly less pressured. Her irritation with the breast cancer committee gradually eased away. Paige was right, it was probably time to resign.

Shoving the somnolent Sadie aside, she put on a Schubert piano sonata that usually did it for her. Background music; her parents would not approve, but it bathed her overwrought nerves with exquisite balm. Paige was right, she took on far too much. She had cleared her life ruthlessly in order to write full-time and already it was silting up with more unnecessary clutter. Across the street the screens still flickered and the Stars and Stripes adhered grimly to the glass. Her appetite for this city was waning; even the dull roar of traffic invaded her space.

It was only then, on the brink of switching off the lights, that her eye was caught by the ad.

2

Genevieve Hopkins was waiting for a call. One already several days too late. If he didn't ring by tonight at the very latest, she was bound by foolish convention to turn him down. And that would be a blasted nuisance since she'd spent so much already on the outfit. The frock itself had been relatively simple. Candy had steered her into the charity shop where they'd picked up a nifty little Fifties moiré silk in a flattering hyacinth blue. Candy had an unerring eye for style; unaccompanied, Genevieve never would have chanced it. It was the shoes and bag that had run her into debt even though she agreed that she couldn't have done without them. Four-inch heels that made her totter like a drunk but displayed her slender ankles to perfection. But Hector hadn't rung her yet. And now she was having serious doubts that he would.

She wandered disconsolately around her cluttered house, picking up armfuls of washing from the floor. The boys had been home for the weekend and treated the place like a tip. Since their father had defected with that bitch from Sales and Marketing, they had been steadily growing out of control. It had been almost a relief when they both went off to college, though at times she felt that her life had lost its purpose. She ought to be doing more work on her book; instead she was glad of almost any excuse to postpone the beastly chore. Talk about displacement activity; her enthusiasm for her chosen profession had been on the wane for years. Having to produce a new novel every twelve months had become little more than a yoke she could not duck out of. And, although at first the advances had seemed like riches, these days she could never figure out where the money all went.

David had been a steady provider; she was bound to grant him that. Unimaginative and pedantic though he could at times be, they had nevertheless rubbed along very comfortably together. So that when, three years ago, he had suddenly dropped his bombshell, the fallout had knocked her right off course. He was the only proper boyfriend she had ever really had; the thought of facing the future without him had thrown her into blind panic. Two hungry teenagers meant that she couldn't opt out so, instead, she'd been forced to grovel to the bank, who had helped her work out a rough kind of financial plan. One she found almost impossible to stick to; bills kept coming in that she didn't expect. She would call her agent and anxiously explain and the resourceful woman would as often as not bail her out. A commissioned piece for the *Daily Mail*, a short story for *Woman's Own*, even the occasional charity lunch, though Genevieve was a nervous speaker. One way or other she usually managed to cope. It was precarious living from hand to mouth but still she managed to stumble on and, at least, they hadn't yet had to repossess the house.

Then Hector Gillespie had entered her life,

bringing her sudden renewed hope. She had met him at a private view, been introduced by an acquaintance. He was shorter than she was, with a weighty paunch, but she liked his mellifluous Highland burr as well as his air of authority. He was, by profession, an opera critic with a regular column in a Sunday paper and a row of books to his name. His knowledge and blatant erudition had only added to her insecurity; she was genuinely astounded when he called. Since then they had met sporadically and soon he had coerced her into bed. She didn't find him in the least attractive but needed the affirmation of his desire. If only, she sometimes thought, he would marry her, all this financial roller-coasting could stop.

But Hector was coming up to fifty and had never committed himself yet. Though inclined to pomposity, he was socially presentable and much in demand at events as a single man. He was out on the town almost every night and, she feared, not exclusively with her. There were several women whose names he let slip but she had not yet plucked up the courage to ask who they were. Or whether they were sharing his sexual favours; she rather suspected that they were.

'Ask him,' advised Candy, when she confided her fears over lunch. 'It is always better to know the truth.' She had been a single parent for eight years, was expert at sniffing out phoneys.

'But what if he says yes?' wailed Genevieve, unwilling to face the prospect of life without him.

'Then at least you'll know and can decide

what you really want. I'd dump the bugger if I were you, there are plenty more fish in the sea.'

But bright-eyed Candy, with her beguiling smile, was svelte and silvery as well as ten years younger. She muddled by with her forays into fashion and raised that difficult child all on her own. Genevieve couldn't imagine how she managed. Candy was far more courageous than she could ever be.

She broached the subject as they walked home through the rain. 'How have you managed all these years alone?'

'One day at a time,' said Candy briskly. 'And never allowing myself to feel victimised.' Trevor, her ex, had treated her badly and only stayed in touch because of the kid. She rarely mentioned him any more, felt only irritation when he called. But a boy needs a dad so she allowed him regular access though, over the years, his visits had grown steadily sparser. If she let it bother her, it would doubtless get her down, but Candy was made of sterner stuff than her friend.

'They are none of them worth it,' she said with her bright smile. 'Give me my girlfriends any time for loyalty and laughs.'

Genevieve wished she could share her optimism but never felt wholly complete without a man.

And now Hector was doing his same old thing and not phoning. The gala performance of *Arabella* was something she longed to attend. Not so much for the music as the occasion. In the presence of royalty, the stars would be out in force and Genevieve yearned for a bit of restorative glamour. Hence the new outfit. She was heartily sick of how she looked and wearing the same tired old clothes almost every day. She went to the gym on a regular basis, thus still had the figure for the hyacinth blue dress. It was at the gym that she had first encountered Candy. They had fallen into an easy friendship though Genevieve still knew very little about her. Simply that she found her amusing; life-enhancing in her way.

★   ★   ★

She had never particularly liked this house, not from the day they moved in. It was the first suitable one they had found, early on in their marriage when Genevieve discovered that she was pregnant. Not a natural homemaker, she had simply had to make do and, when a second baby closely followed the first, moving became the lowest of her priorities. Highbury, in those days, before the trendy Blair government, was barely on the fringes of civilisation and even though now it was steadily upgrading, her attitude towards it continued lukewarm. When David defected she had found herself stuck, too poor to make the move to a better neighbourhood. Also, too dispirited; whatever was the point? Alone with her two raucous sons, she felt that she had failed.

Lately, since Hector, she had pulled herself together and even given the outside a fresh coat of paint. But the rooms remained cramped and dark and overcrowded; she had even succeeded in blinkering herself against the garish carpet on the stairs. All the improvements she had once planned to make had faded, along with her dreams. She occasionally saw the disdain on Hector's face on the rare nights he stayed over. Usually she had to go to him, at his bachelor pad in Devonshire Place. With her makeup and toothbrush in an overnight bag, she felt like an ageing call girl. Even worse was returning on the early morning Tube, concealing her rumpled hairdo under a scarf. It wasn't in the least romantic; in fact it made her feel slightly soiled. Candy was right, she really should dump him. But what, if she did, would she do for a social life then? She was a woman of a certain age with children who were virtually grown-up. There was no way now that she could lie about her age, whereas men like Hector, with few commitments, could continue to play the field for as long as they liked.

Genevieve's problem was endemic to her generation; she had launched herself straight into marriage from being a student and thus had zero experience of playing the field. Without a regular partner, she wasn't quite sure how to cope. Most of the long-time friends she had made only ever socialised in pairs. And an attractive unattached woman, even one of her vintage, was sometimes perceived as a threat by the smugly still married. The advent of Hector had provided a new lease of life; somebody wanted her, she was grateful for his attention. He was older, shorter, fatter; all those things. And yet she felt defined by him, no longer just somebody's cast-off.

'Get out there and have some fun and find yourself somebody else.' Candy was always so positive, the reason Genevieve liked her so much. It seemed that she never got miserable herself but bounced back fighting, with a brand-new scheme, if ever her plans went awry. She was an excellent foil for Genevieve, spunky, original and fun.

★ ★ ★

'Love is like a seesaw,' Genevieve's American friend, Anna, was fond of saying. 'When you find your end dipping too drastically, it's essential you kick the ground very hard or else the game is lost.'

'Love is all very well,' said Genevieve wistfully, 'but I'm not at all sure I would recognise it now, even if it bit me on the bum.'

It all had to do with self-esteem, but Genevieve was far from being convinced. Anna was confident and brave and fulfilled and exulted in her independent lifestyle. Somehow she had managed, all these years, never to have had to rely upon a man. She was popular and gregarious yet entirely self-sufficient. Genevieve envied her that endless freedom.

'It comes with practice,' Anna assured her. She had had her own sexual mishaps in her youth. The solitary life was a mindset, she explained. Once you gritted your teeth and took the plunge, it was possible to get used to almost anything. And it gave her the space, so essential to a writer, in which to think and contemplate and read.

'Don't you ever get lonely?' Genevieve asked her.

'No more than anyone else. If you don't have to fit yourself around another person's needs, it is that much easier to accommodate your own. If ever you feel a sudden urge for company, you can always call up a friend, while on nights you are not in the mood for going out, there is nothing to prevent you staying home. No rows, no discussions, no having to find a babysitter. The only person to worry about is yourself. Feet up, mudpack, *The Sopranos* on the TV. You can do what you damn well please and that's what I like.' She neglected to mention the sleepless nights, when her brain was racing overtime and the three a.m. blues set in. Then she would give almost anything for someone at her side, to hold her tight and comfort her and drive the phantoms away. But those moments of total panic were rare and not worth mentioning now. Childhood was something well in the past; she had to fight her battles on her own.

Anna had obviously done a lot of thinking and had things under control whereas Genevieve lived her life almost always on the edge. Jumpy, apprehensive, scared of her own shadow. That was the principal difference between them. And yet, for the past five years, since Santa Fe, the two contrasting women had been good friends. Sharing the same humour, liking the same books; these days they kept in regular touch by email.

★ ★ ★

26

They had met in New Mexico, at a literary convention, the sort of thing at which Anna normally sneered. She had been invited as a prize-winning novelist on a panel of 'celebrity' writers, whereas Genevieve was there at her own expense, part of the regular networking her publishers insisted was essential. Anna's own books were intelligent and well-crafted, attracting good reviews and growing sales. The movie deal was a huge boost to her readership, though she was level-headed enough to know that it might not ever get made. Fashions changed, the studios were fickle, but news of the sale had proved a publicity boost; a 'name' director with a stable of successes and an Oscar nomination in the can. With the chance, maybe, of getting to write the screenplay, a field into which she had always wanted to stray. And then, of course, there was the purchase money. Nobody could quibble about that.

Each had recognised a kindred spirit among the varied and colourful oddballs who hang around on the fringes of such occasions. They were largely failures, which was quickly apparent; real writers, as Genevieve was rapidly finding out, simply do not have the time to spare. These were mainly pathetic wannabes, who either financed their own publication or else hawked around a tired old typescript in the vain hope of breaking through.

'The truth is,' said Anna, with her customary frankness, 'there are very few writers of any sort I can stand.' Bores and pedants, most of them, interested mainly in sales figures and self-promotion, which had very little to do with art or even value for money. They laughed. Genevieve, when she loosened up, became instantly much prettier. The slightly gawky British manner softened into radiance when she relaxed. And, at Anna's anarchic instigation, had sunk several rounds of margaritas. At that stage she was not yet divorced, yet already alarmingly lacking in self-esteem. The extent to which she had been mentally undermined was obvious to Anna and painful to observe.

'Men are very much overrated,' Anna pronounced. 'I have yet to encounter one I could not live without.'

★ ★ ★

Yet Genevieve's novels, when Anna got round to them, were sly and quirky and engagingly fresh, not at all what their rather crass packaging seemed to imply. Genevieve had to be the world's most bashful writer, but that was all part of her slightly wistful appeal. It would be hard, because of their charming insularity, for her books to break into the American market but if even one received critical notice, to Anna's mind the rest should naturally follow. That was the power of word of mouth, her reason for being in Santa Fe. It all boiled down to self-belief and refusing ever to give up.

'Your problem,' Anna was bold enough to say, 'is that they are publishing you all wrong. You are far too good a writer for those sugary girlie jackets.' The so-called 'chick lit' phenomenon was already virtually over. 'You need to be taken seriously up-market and given the real distinction that you deserve. Your wicked humour and sharp observation should be aimed at a far more intelligent readership. Take Nancy Mitford and Barbara Pym. I honestly believe that, properly packaged, your rightful place should be alongside them.'

Naturally, such inspiring words were balm to Genevieve's ears and she tried very hard to believe what Anna was saying. And, indeed, here they were, after all sorts of changes, the firmest of buddies, practically joined at the hip. Anna also had strong opinions about Hector, regardless of the fact she had never met him. She had seen the effect that he had on her friend which, for her, was quite enough. British women could be unbelievably feeble; she could not understand why Genevieve didn't fight back.

'Leave him,' she urged her, unwittingly echoing Candy. 'You are far too good to be messed around in this way.' As long as Genevieve put her life on hold, waiting to see what might transpire with a man who quite clearly did not love her, she stood no chance of ever meeting anyone new. She was like a cab with its meter light switched off, giving out negative signals.

'Be bold,' advised Anna, 'and put yourself about more. You're a great-looking gal with a burgeoning career. It is he who should feel the privilege of knowing you. Who the fuck does the bastard think he is?'

29

Her words, of course, fell as usual on deaf ears for poor Genevieve simply lacked the basic courage. Like now, for instance, hanging around at home, forlornly awaiting a call that would never come.

3

'Get this!' said Anna to Paige next morning, reading it over the phone.

> Italy, Tuscany. Beautifully renovated XIV-century villa, 40 minutes from Siena. Six bedrooms, pool. Easy day trips. In exchange for house/apartment in midtown Manhattan. Four months April – July.

It was signed simply 'Yale grad '78'. Followed by an email address.

'What do you think?' All night she had been turning it over in her mind, considering all the ramifications, wondering if she dared.

'Sounds just what the doctor ordered,' said Paige. 'Why are you even hesitating?' The great thing about being a professional writer was that you could work wherever you chose. No being stuck in an air-conditioned office or fighting the crowds to get home.

'If you guys would come I would jump at it right away. Confess, it sounds like everybody's dream. You, me, Charles, whoever you care to include. We could all of us do with a break in the sun, especially somewhere like Tuscany.'

'I wish,' sighed Paige, on her way out of the door. 'But with all that's going on at the moment? Dream on.' September had thrown the city into chaos. She was finding it hard to

31

keep herself totally sane.

Anna paced the floor, unable to settle. Tuscany in the spring, a dream; right now, there was nothing in the world she could think of that she would rather do. To escape from this oppressive place and finish her overdue book without the nightmares. The only real problem was that she couldn't drive.

'What do you think?' She bounced it off Larry who said he'd come like a shot, if asked.

'I wasn't actually inviting you,' Anna told him sweetly. 'Though in any other circumstances, of course, you'd be at the top of my list. But I'm afraid that, right now, I need you here more. The house has got to take precedence.'

Larry understood that, of course he did. Life would be easier for everyone concerned without Anna hovering, breathing down their necks. Her irritation with their noise and roistering spirits hung like a heavy blanket in the air. From the number of times she popped down to check their progress, he could tell they were ruining her concentration. Without her constant presence there, they could finish the job that much faster. Though it wasn't, of course, his place to suggest it since she was the one picking up the tab.

'If I weren't here,' said Anna, reading his thoughts, 'I reckon your team would be a whole lot happier. But suppose I went ahead with the swap, what would the advertiser think? About having workmen still around. Do you suppose he would mind?' The house, after all, consisted of four spacious storeys. Plenty of room in which to spread out and still not be inconvenienced by the builders.

'If it's not till April, we'll be more or less out of here.' And the swap would be an incentive to hurry them along. With the basement kitchen and dining-room complete, there really wasn't a lot more left to do. Certainly nothing structural, only the finishing touches. Nobody, surely, could be upset by a couple of taciturn painters.

'I'll think about it,' said Anna. It was just too perfect, there had to be a catch. She went to bed wondering whether she dared go ahead.

* * *

Anna's email caught Genevieve on the hop. She had stayed up far too late last night, imbibing too much wine. He hadn't called and she wallowed in mortification, conceding herself unworthy of such a man. While the kettle boiled, she studied the *Daily Mail* with its two-page spread of photographs from last night. There they all were, the glittering and the great, posing on the steps of the opera house. Two lots of minor royalty, Princess Michael and the Wessexes, were pictured regally shaking a sea of hands. Genevieve, still in her scruffy pyjamas, sniffed; the little hyacinth number had gone unworn. She searched for a glimpse of Hector but in vain; he obviously wasn't sufficiently grand to be snapped. Either that or too short, she suppressed a smirk, and wondered who he had taken in her place. One of those faceless women, she had no doubt. Younger and smarter, with a knowledge of opera and plenty of scintillating chat. In his world, she knew, she could not compete and wondered why he had bothered with her at all.

She made the tea and slumped at the table to drink it, gazing despairingly at her untidy kitchen. An old-fashioned airer was laden with football gear; her older boy had come home last night and left her his laundry to be done. It was probably just as well that she hadn't gone out. He had arrived from Nottingham without prior warning, expecting to be fed. Then was off again for an all-night party from which he had not yet returned. At least one of them had an active social life; after all, he was almost twenty-one.

'All right for some,' thought Genevieve glumly, running her fingers through her unwashed hair. Just the sight of her growing boys accentuated her feeling of life passing her by. David was off with his fancy piece, leaving her to clear up the mess at home. It wasn't fair but when had it ever been?

The table was cluttered with all kinds of things: ironing, unwashed dishes and her computer. Unlike Anna, with her pristine and orderly study, Genevieve worked wherever the mood took her, surrounded by a chaotic sea of muddle. But at least it meant she was close to the kettle and could make endless cups of tea without getting up. The telephone rang; it was almost eleven. She knew, as she rose to get it, that it wouldn't be him.

A girlfriend, ringing to commiserate; Genevieve smiled in spite of herself and went to the fridge to fetch the bottle of wine. Which, she

34

found, was more restorative than tea, even at this hour in the morning. She settled down for an intimate natter, telling herself that her writing would just have to wait. Anna worked a disciplined eight-hour day and also very often through the weekend. Her novels appeared regularly, eighteen months apart, usually to rapturous reviews. But, then, Anna led a blissfully untrammelled life, with only that old dad of hers to distract her. And, from all Genevieve had heard about George Kovac, he was every bit as independent as his daughter, an adored friend and confidant to whom she could tell anything, rather than any sort of ageing encumbrance. She sniffed again. Recalling Anna's seesaw analogy, she felt she deserved something much better.

After forty-five minutes of therapeutic chat, during which she drained off the bottle, the friend had to change for a lunch date across town so Genevieve finally switched on the computer. There was little point in dressing, she had nowhere to go and didn't expect her boy back for several hours. His incursions into town had two main purposes, to catch up on his social life and dump his dirty washing. The other boy was every bit as bad but, at least, further away.

Before she returned to her own turgid prose, Genevieve checked her email. Which was when she discovered Anna's message and a sudden gleam of hope came into her eyes.

★　★　★

The email outlined the Tuscan plan and wondered if Genevieve was up for it. Was she ever? Anna didn't need to ask. She had never felt more in the mood for running away. But then, immediately, the doubts came crowding in. Who would look after the house while she was gone and what if one of the boys should suddenly need her? They were both almost adult and living their separate lives but, as a parent, she hated to let them down. There was also the question of cost to be considered; Genevieve was almost perpetually skint. Yet the villa, as Anna pointed out, would be free; she surely couldn't afford to turn it down. The main objective would not be riotous living but to get on with their work in peaceful surroundings, away from the distractions of everyday life plus the noise and pollution of summer in the city. She should think of it as a kind of retreat, monastic if not entirely spiritual.

'I'll call you at noon, your time,' added Anna, which meant more or less now. She obviously knew that her indecisive friend would take more than a little persuading. Yet Genevieve, now that the thought had occurred, seemed the absolutely obvious choice. Even, in some ways, better than Paige since she wouldn't have anyone else in tow. Not that Anna didn't dote on Charles; it was just that drawn-out threesomes rarely worked. Two was much better when it came to a period of time and they got on well, had similar tastes as well as pressing deadlines to be met. Also Genevieve spoke rudimentary Italian and, still better, could drive. Anna was bent on wooing her

36

hard, though fully aware it was likely to prove uphill work. Genevieve suffered from that ultra-British condition of resolutely refusing to have fun.

★ ★ ★

'Provided we stick to a regular work routine,' said Anna, when she made the promised call. 'Think how wonderful it should be. The villa sounds vast, six bedrooms and a pool. Close to Siena, too, which I hear is marvellous.'

'I am not sure I can afford it,' said Genevieve automatically, getting cold feet in her familiar negative way.

'What's to afford? It all comes free, apart from the day-to-day living expenses which we can split between us; it won't be much. Tuscany is notoriously low-cost and airfares are so low right now, you will hardly feel the pinch. Cheaper than staying in London, believe me, and I'm sure that, like me, you could use some R and R.' As well as space from those two loutish lads, though that she didn't add.

'But the house,' protested Genevieve, still not wholly comprehending. She was always uneasy when it came to matters of finance.

'Simple,' said Anna. 'I will do a straight swap.' The point, after all, of the ad.

'You'd allow a total stranger into your home?' Genevieve was amazed. 'How could you possibly bear that?' She knew how obsessive Anna was; the house was all she had talked about for months.

'I've been in it such a short time,' admitted Anna, 'that it hasn't yet truly started to feel like home.' Besides, there were always workmen about and lovely Larry continually dropping by. She could certainly use some rest and recreation herself, and not just from her workload.

'How can you be sure it would be safe?' persisted Genevieve. 'What guarantees would you have?'

'The key thing is, the guy's a fellow Yalie. You can't get much more respectable than that.'

Genevieve continued with her usual feeble wavering, swinging, as if in fever, from hot to cold. Basically she loved the idea, yet was also, though she didn't say it, worrying about Hector. There might be some perfectly plausible explanation as to why he had had to stand her up and hadn't called. Anna succeeded in buttoning her lip. This was one decision that Genevieve could only make for herself.

'Don't leave it too long,' was all she said. 'Or someone else is bound to snap it up.' If they hadn't already, which was more than likely. Opportunities like this were rare. They'd be fools not to grab it right away.

★   ★   ★

A whole week went by and Anna had given up, resigning herself to a long anxious summer in the city. Christmas was fast approaching, with its usual razzmatazz, though this one looked already like being muted. She spent Thanksgiving quietly with her father, during which she told him cautiously of the Tuscan plan. What had seemed like such a brilliant idea faded with every day of Genevieve's silence.

'Do it,' said George, as positive as Paige. 'I tell you, if I were younger, I would come too.'

'You'd be more than welcome.' There was plenty of room and at least, that way, she would not have to worry about him.

He laughed but shook his head. 'You are too kind. But my days for jetting around the world are over.' He reached across and gave her more wine. 'But you should do it while you still can. You work far too hard as it is.'

'And you'd be all right?'

'Of course I would. I am not yet senile, you know.'

But it wasn't that easy if Genevieve wouldn't come. There were very few people Anna knew who had the leeway simply to cut and run and head off into the great unknown on a whim. Most of her friends had regular jobs, with Genevieve, perhaps, the sole exception. And she knew too much to bank anything on her after all these years of close friendship. Genevieve's problem, adorable though she was, was a total inability to fight back. One hostile act and she crumpled into subjection. It was hard to imagine how the British Empire had lasted as long as it had. Anna gritted her teeth and went back to her work. She was still hardly sleeping, or even seeing people, but gradually getting on top of things again. The flickering screens had become less intrusive but everywhere she went she heard the same topic. To the extent that she preferred to stay home. Sadie was so self-centred, she didn't care.

And then, to her amazement, the telephone rang and it was Genevieve, weeping fit to bust.

'He's done it again,' she wailed when she could speak. 'Booked for Bayreuth with another woman because he feels *The Ring* would be wasted on me.'

Anna, scandalised, was also amused. This man really did sound the pits.

'I didn't think the two of you were still speaking,' she said. 'You told me last week it was over.'

'He called and we went to a movie,' admitted Genevieve. Which was when this ugly secret had emerged. Even then, it became apparent, he had not intended to tell her but the other woman, Miriam, had called while she was still there.

'Apparently, like him she's an opera freak.' Probably younger and prettier too.

Anna could not imagine how Genevieve could possibly still be bothered; he sounded such an utter waste of space. But her friend was obviously hurting a lot so she managed to soft-pedal on her comments.

'He's always putting you down,' was all she said. 'It's high time you taught the jerk a lesson. Come to Tuscany and let him stew. Trust me, it's no more than he deserves.'

★ ★ ★

Jubilant that Genevieve had finally made up her mind, Anna wasted no time in answering the ad.

40

She was certain the villa would no longer be available and checked her email every half hour, desperate for a reply. Which, to her surprise and relief, came quickly. A friendly message from one D. A. Sutherland, saying that her house sounded just the job. He needed to be in New York for four months and what she described was exactly what he had hoped for. Safe and central, a perfect match. He didn't even mind about the builders. Provided there was sufficient space in which he could comfortably work, he wasn't fazed. And as for Sadie, he was an animal lover and would enjoy the privilege of having her around.

'He sounds divine!' said Anna to Genevieve, when she called to tell her the swap was going ahead.

'Almost too good to be true,' agreed Genevieve. 'Do we happen to know if he is married?'

Anna grinned; her friend was so predictable. 'I haven't a clue,' she said. 'But I'm afraid that's purely academic anyhow since we're not going to get to meet him. He'll be here in New York while we are there.' She suspected Genevieve was starting to get cold feet and so briskly overruled her. 'See!' she added triumphantly, 'I knew it would all work out. I told you, you can always trust a Yalie.'

Just to make doubly sure, however, since she secretly acknowledged that Genevieve did have a point, Anna checked with Paige. Who efficiently looked him up in the alumni directory for '78 and reported that he was, indeed, there with a

41

rather impressive résumé.

'Hear this,' she said. 'Marine biology, magna cum laude, and also on the rowing team. Brains as well as brawn.' Which reminded her, she had a cousin around that age who had also rowed for Yale.

'Can't do any harm to check him out,' said Paige and dialled the Baltimore number.

Her cousin, Wilbur, was positive in his praise. Now quite a fat cat attorney, he had once been a fun-loving jock.

'*Dan* Sutherland?' he said. 'A terrific guy. One of the all-time greats. A marvellous all-rounder with a first-class brain who might have turned his hand to almost anything. Popular, gregarious, also very well-heeled. He would have made an excellent politician. And he certainly had no problem with the ladies.' He laughed in a slightly suggestive manner but made no attempt to expound. Wilbur was one of those laddish middle-aged men who have never quite left their fraternity days behind. 'Do tell him hi from me if you happen to see him, though I rather think these days he spends most of his time travelling. He became some kind of high-flying photographer doing worthy things for the environment. Why exactly do you need to know?'

Paige explained about the possible house swap and, again, Cousin Wilbur was fulsome in his praise. 'I seem to recall now there was some sort of Italian connection. Tell your friend not to hesitate. Believe me, I'd go like a shot if it were me.'

'Well, that's okay then,' said Anna, relieved,

glad of his reassurance. Now that the plan was starting to take shape, she could scarcely wait to get going. Sunshine and solitude and a peaceful, healthy life; it should certainly make up for the rotten past few months. Once Christmas was over, there were only three months to get through and pleasant anticipation would make the time go faster. She would sort through her summer wardrobe and buy some sharp new outfits, just in case. She had insisted to Genevieve that they were going there mainly to work but wanted, just on the off-chance, to look her best. Her father was right, she should grab it with both hands for he knew, more than most, how things could change.

'Do you reckon we ought to have some sort of a contract?' she wondered, then firmly dismissed the thought. It was fuddy-duddy and out of tune with the casual spirit of this friendly exchange.

'Well, on your head be it,' warned Paige, the cautious lawyer. 'Though I can't deny I would kill to be coming too.'

★　★　★

Candy and Genevieve each had important news. Genevieve went first. Candy was green with envy when she heard about the Tuscan plan. It was a howling February with gale-force winds that rattled the windows and sputtered soot down the chimney. The two hadn't met for several weeks because of the Christmas holidays but now that Hugo was safely back at school, at last Candy had the time for some relaxation. Until

43

half-term; the weeks went speeding by. Sometimes it seemed that the child was on permanent vacation. They sat in the Dôme, nursing their second espressos, unwilling to brave the elements for a while. By mutual consent, they had given up on the gym, at least until the weather was slightly less harsh. Candy, for once, looked exhausted and drained, with mauve shadows under her eyes. Although she would never admit to it, caring for Hugo took it out of her since he never, not for a second, could sit still. Genevieve, who didn't like to pry, marvelled at how Candy coped. At least her own husband had stuck around while the kids were growing up. But Candy had never been married, which must make a big difference. Nor had she ever even lived with Hugo's father. Whatever had happened had not been intended, though Candy would always declare brightly how lucky she was.

'I got my little bundle of joy without having to put up with his dad,' she would say and certainly, for most of the time, she appeared relaxed and content. Hugo's father was some kind of roving reporter who never seemed able to hold down a permanent job. They did not see that much of him, which Candy found a blessing, though there must have been times she could have used some support, especially with that hyperactive child. Genevieve thought wistfully of Hector and how much she was missing him already. At least the trip should act as a diversion and keep her from fretting too much.

Now it was Candy's turn to divulge and she instantly brightened up. 'I showed some of my

44

rough autumn sketches to a buyer from Harvey Nichols. And, after a really short wait, she has told me she likes them.' Colour was returning to her pallid cheeks and, as she talked, her eyes regained their sparkle. Genevieve hugged her with genuine delight, thrilled at this unexpected piece of good fortune. This could be just the leg-up Candy required to put her up there with the other London designers. She had seen some of the beautiful clothes her friend had made and the workmanship was exquisite. If anyone deserved success, it was Candy. As Genevieve knew from her own experience, the creative life is rarely easy. And having to live from hand to mouth, without the security of a regular income, can be exceedingly hard. Even without the additional burden of a kid with learning difficulties.

'If I can get them to her by the end of the summer, they might even give me my own line. Can't you just see it, 'Macaskill Modes'? But tell me more about Tuscany,' Candy begged. 'It does sound the chance of a lifetime.' What wouldn't she give to be somewhere in the sun, with time and space to work on her designs. Genevieve told her about the house and how it had all come about. And when she let slip that her friend in New York was the novelist Anna Kovac, Candy's eyes positively bulged.

'*The* Anna Kovac? I just adore her books. Couldn't put the last one down. And now I am pleased to see that it's going to be filmed.'

Both sank into contemplative silence and Candy toyed with the sugar. 'I don't suppose,'

45

she said cautiously at last, 'that I could come along too?'

Genevieve thought rapidly but could see no reason why not. The house, from all accounts, was vast, and with three of them there, instead of just two, she would feel that much more secure.

'What would you do with Hugo?' she asked, afraid of what the answer might be. Their summer idyll destroyed by that child . . . but Candy quickly reassured her.

'No problem, his father can take him,' she said. 'It's time the idle bastard pulled his weight.' And most of the time he'd be away at his special school. She would fix things so that it would not be a problem.

'I'll have to check with Anna,' said Genevieve. 'I'll get back to you as soon as I possibly can.' She was not at all sure that Anna would want to be bothered by a third person tagging along, particularly someone she did not even know. Anna took her writing very seriously; the fewer disturbances, the better.

But Anna, somewhat to Genevieve's surprise, seemed perfectly relaxed. The more the merrier was how she saw it, provided they all stuck to strict work routines. It was essential that she finish this book and she needed to do a lot of catching up. And so it was fixed for the start of April, with Candy coming to join them later, after the Easter holidays were over and Hugo back at school. Anna and Genevieve would meet at Pisa airport and rent a car to take them to Montisi where arrangements would have been made by Sutherland for them to collect the keys.

46

'So we're not going to get to meet him at all?' said Genevieve, sounding wistful.

'No, as I've told you, we should pass him in mid-air. Which is the whole purpose of the exercise.' A shame because he did sound intriguing, especially so since Wilbur's ecstatic response. This trip, however, was not about socialising, but a quiet retreat in which to catch up on their work. Away from the horrors of city life and the memories Anna was trying so hard to suppress.

4

The scent of sunshine was almost palpable when she stepped off the plane in Pisa. Just the short walk across the tarmac evoked a myriad fragrances of early spring, combined with a sharp new sense of hope in the air. It could be she was imagining it but, for the first time in many months, Anna felt a surge of sudden optimism. They had arranged to meet at the Hertz desk and there already was Genevieve, whose flight had come in forty minutes earlier, looking flustered and preoccupied until she saw Anna and waved.

'I've sorted out the car,' she said, after they had embraced. 'It's only a small Fiat but, I promise you, more than adequate for just the three of us.' She hated the thought of driving in Italy but was determined not to let Anna know. It was only a pity that Anna had not learned; surprising, considering how good she was at almost everything else. Still, soon there would be Candy to help share the load and it could not be remotely worse than the horrors of driving in London.

They stowed their luggage in the neat little car, then Genevieve spread out the map. 'We take the autostrada towards Florence. Then down the main artery to Rome, which has a turn-off at Sinalunga. Montisi is somewhere in that area, slightly, I think, to the south.'

Anna looked at her watch. It should take them the best part of an hour, which meant they would be at the villa by just about five. After sitting on a plane for so long, she longed to chill out and unwind. And sample the famous Toscana wines about which she had read such good things. With Genevieve concentrating hard at the wheel and Anna holding the map, they edged into the stream of traffic and, unexpectedly, Genevieve found herself relaxing. Compared with London's arterial roads, this seemed remarkably undaunting. Which, combined with the balmy weather, snapped her straight into holiday mode. They had pulled it off and now here they were, with a full four glorious holiday months ahead. It was good to be with Anna again after more than a year and a half. She looked thinner but every bit as chic, with a new crease of worry between her eyes, unsurprising after all she had been through. But that sort of detail would keep for later. Genevieve focused on her driving.

'Tell me about Candy,' said Anna after a while. She had folded the map and was now relaxing; the road signs were easy to follow from this point.

'There's really not a lot more to add. She is bright, hugely talented and fun. With a wicked sense of humour.' She always had everyone in the gym in stitches with her off-the-cuff remarks and rapid-fire repartee.

'Sounds good to me.' Ten years younger, Anna also knew, but that ought not to present any problem. Provided she allowed them to get on

49

with their work; not too much larking about.

'So how are things with Hector at present? Did you let him know you were going away?'

'No,' said Genevieve, proud for once. She really cared about Anna's opinion, was scared of appearing too much of a wimp. The truth was, he hadn't been in touch. But the way she was feeling now, in these great surroundings, she couldn't care less if she never saw him again. She peeled off her sweater and rolled up her sleeves and let the pine-laden breeze waft through the car.

'Shall we open the roof?' asked Anna, entering into the spirit.

'Why not?' It was a brilliant day. And they had certainly had more than enough winter this year in London. The sleet had rattled the panes and the wind had howled. It was weeks since they'd last even glimpsed the sun.

So they drew into a lay-by and did just that. The road, which at first was industrialised, rapidly mellowed into open countryside with undulant hills of a smoky purple and the signature cypresses of Tuscany.

'*We're on vacation,*' crooned Genevieve, thoroughly happy, drumming on the steering-wheel and running her fingers through her streaming hair.

★　★　★

Montisi, when they found it, looked enchanting. Pure mediaeval, with a narrow, twisting main street on which, they had been told, they would

50

find Raffaele's trattoria. He was the keeper of the keys who kept an eye on the villa. The sun was already beginning to sink and gild the austere stone buildings with its light. The local inhabitants they passed were mostly dressed in dusty black and some of the men were even leading donkeys. There was a pungent mingled aroma of cabbage and manure and the general earthiness of a country village. Chickens scattered left and right from their wheels. The sinking sun was a great orange orb in the sky. They easily could have gone back in time. It must have remained unchanged for centuries.

'I love it already,' said Anna, delighted, peering at the instructions she held in her hand. And there it was suddenly, round the bend by the twisted fig tree, the trattoria with its faded painted sign. 'Guess this must be it,' she said and they both undid their seatbelts and got out of the car.

Even as early as this there were people in there drinking, mainly gnarled old farm workers with faces as ruddy as the soil. There was a huge brick wood-burning oven in the centre and a forest of bottles behind the bar, mainly of regional wines. Great smoked hams and festoons of garlic hung from the weathered beams. In New York or London it would all be fake but this, without question, was the genuine thing.

'Just smell that woodsmoke,' breathed Genevieve with relish while Anna strode over to the bar.

The man who hastened across to greet her was

stocky but well-built and powerfully muscled, with twinkly treacle-brown eyes. '*Signora*,' he said with a glance of appreciation at her well-toned body and silk designer shirt. Anna shoved her huge dark glasses defiantly up into her hair.

'We are looking for Raffaele Manenti,' she said and saw from his instant smile that they had found him.

'What may I do for you, *signore*,' he asked, offering them seats at the bar. He uncorked a bottle of a rough local wine and handed them each a brimming glass. Then placed in front of them a plate of bruschetta and a bowl of olives. The wine was delicious, with a subtle hint of sandalwood. The shady interior of the trattoria contrasted dramatically with the sinking sun. There was a feeling of somnolent timelessness in the place; the smell of the woodsmoke, the aroma of fresh herbs, the tang of the olives which were stuffed with anchovies. Both of them instantly felt at home; they might have been sitting here for years. Even this man with his warm and friendly smile already seemed unnervingly familiar.

'We are here to pick up the keys,' said Anna, reluctantly snapping herself out of her trance. 'To Mr Sutherland's villa.'

The Italian continued to study her politely, blank incomprehension on his face.

'Signor Sutherland?' she repeated more succinctly, searching through the printed-out instructions for the villa's actual name. '*Casavecchia*. It is somewhere here in Montisi; you must know it. Yours was the contact name that we were given.'

'*Si, signora*. I know it well. And also Signor Sutherland. But he has let me know nothing about the keys. Apart from a brief phone call from his secretary in Patagonia. The line was crackly, I could hardly hear a thing. I confess I was not expecting you so soon.' Actually, not at all, his expression implied.

Anna sighed and looked helplessly at Genevieve. Everything till now had gone so smoothly, surely they couldn't screw up at this late stage. After they had built up such hopes and both had travelled so far. She was tired and hungry and the musky, eloquent wine had gone straight to her head. She longed only to be able to crash out and not have to worry any more.

'He specifically told us to come to you for the keys. He knew we were arriving this afternoon.' He was almost certainly already in her own house; that was the arrangement they had made. She had left him amply provided for, with the keys in the architect's care.

Raffaele shook his head and looked pensive while generously topping up their glasses. 'I have not heard from Signor Sutherland direct. Not for many months.'

'But wasn't he just here?' asked Anna, puzzled.

'Signor Sutherland is only occasionally here. Most of his time he spends travelling abroad.'

'Oh.' This was a hard one. She was now not sure what to do. It had all appeared so clear-cut in that brief exchange of friendly emails. She wished she had some form of tangible proof that they really were who they said. That was the downside of electronic mail, so much had to be taken on trust. She had an urgent desire to talk to Paige and ask what she would advise. How Paige would laugh, but that wasn't important. This could surely be no more than just a minor crossing of wires.

'Couldn't we just stay here and eat?' suggested Genevieve. The enticing smells from the fragrant wood stove were getting to her in a major way. All she had had on the cheapo flight had been an overpriced sandwich.

'But if someone has been in touch with you, then surely it must be okay.' Anna, though weary and disconcerted, was suddenly right back on track.

Raffaele silently polished a glass and made a great show of considering. It was clear to them both he was not being obtuse, merely hedging until he had made a decision.

'*Un momento,*' he said at last, squeezing Anna's shoulder reassuringly. He disappeared into the kitchen at the rear and they could hear him talking rapidly on the phone. Anna looked at Genevieve and shrugged. At last, or so it would appear, something seemed to be happening. And the wine and the ambience were certainly excellent. She felt extremely reluctant to move on.

After a full five minutes Raffaele reappeared, profusely apologising for having kept them waiting. He spoke in rapid Italian to one of his waiters before ushering them out into the street. In his hand he carried a bunch of large iron keys.

It seemed he had decided to believe them.

'I will show you the way,' he said courteously. 'Please follow me.'

He reversed his dusty old battered car out from under the fig tree and led them slowly back down the narrow street, then up a rutted cart track that ran off at a sharp angle. Through fields of tall foliage that looked like bamboo, they bumped along at a snail's pace, to emerge eventually on a kind of plateau with staggering views across a great sweeping valley. Raffaele paused to allow them to catch up, then waved his hand expansively at the view.

'All of this is Tolomei land,' he said. 'The region is known locally as Valdombrone.' His car vanished down another precipitous path and there it was, a carved wooden sign almost hidden by the foliage, informing them that they had reached *Casavecchia*. The path levelled out to a long straight track, sprouting with weeds and summer grasses, at the end of which were a pair of vast gates, chained and solidly padlocked. Raffaele got out and fumbled with the keys, then pulled back one of the gates to allow them through. Genevieve drove past him into a spacious walled courtyard in front of an imposing three-storey villa, painted a pleasing sun-washed terracotta. A double flight of steep granite steps led up to the massive front door and facing the villa from across a well-kept lawn was a smaller building, also terracotta, which, on later investigation, turned out to be a chapel. Fourteenth-century and unrestored, imbued with an aura of sanctity and beeswax. With faded annunciation scenes and even a Latin inscription above the door. This was all so different from anything she knew, and Anna found herself suddenly steeped in emotion.

Instead of expecting them, luggage and all, to struggle up the steep front steps, Raffaele led them to a door round the side that opened straight into the kitchen. The room was vast, with a low-beamed ceiling and burnished quarry tiles upon the floor. It was cool and dark and refreshingly still after all the travelling they had done. It looked untouched through the centuries except that the fixtures and fittings were modern, selected with discreet and admirable taste. There was a great black stove that could cater for hordes and, to Anna's delighted surprise, an American fridge-freezer with an ice machine on the front. Raffaele unbolted the doors to the terrace and they followed him outside. He pointed to a narrow flight of steps.

'Those lead up to the pool.'

In order not to waste more of his time, they left the luggage in the car while he took them on a rapid tour of the house. It was certainly palatial, with six spacious bedrooms, linked in pairs by interconnecting bathrooms, as well as comfortable lounges on each floor. There was even a long, narrow nursery containing a row of small beds. At the bottom of the staircase were a pair of imposing carved doors.

'Signor Sutherland's private quarters,' explained Raffaele. 'I think you will find they are locked.'

'Don't worry,' Anna assured him, getting the

message. 'I promise we will be as good as gold.' She had taken the precaution of locking her own bedroom door though had left her study available in case Sutherland should want to use it. Since he was planning to work from home, she thought he might welcome the space. She had left a note telling him to use her office equipment and not to worry about the phone. In New York local calls were all-inclusive. Besides, he was there as her guest. The best thing about a house swap, she could see, was having small necessities on tap.

Raffaele, on the point of leaving, stopped and turned back to Anna. 'Let me get this straight,' he said. 'You spoke to Signor Sutherland in person?'

'No,' said Anna, 'that is not what I said. We never actually spoke. Everything was arranged by email.' She wondered if he had any idea what she meant. 'Here,' she said, digging out her business card. 'Why not check it out with him direct.'

'No need,' said Raffaele, politely refusing the card, 'I understand he is travelling at present. But do, please, make yourselves at home and anything you need, just let me know. I will arrange for Maria, the housekeeper, to come in. She will let you know where everything is.'

'*Grazie*,' said Anna, relieved, formally shaking his hand. At last, with luck, she was going to get to relax.

*   *   *

The second he left, they were back up the stairs, properly checking out the accommodation. There was so much space, far more than they would need; it wasn't at all easy to make a choice. Eventually, after a lot of thought, Anna opted for the suite on the second floor. It overlooked the courtyard and chapel and a rather quaint circular fishpond, surmounted by a leering, leaping satyr. Here, she reckoned, it should be quieter; here she could set up her laptop by the window and perhaps gain inspiration from the view. Genevieve took the high-ceilinged ground-floor room which opened off both dining-room and terrace. Although less secluded, she loved its lofty dimensions and tall French windows, with filmy drapes that swayed and danced in the breeze. Candy was welcome to the whole of the attic floor. First come, first served; besides, she had younger legs.

They lugged in their bags and dumped them in their rooms, then went back out on to the terrace. The lingering last rays of the sun dramatically streaked the sky with purple and orange. Genevieve went in search of wine and quickly returned, triumphant. A rack in the kitchen was crammed with bottles; provided they kept a note of what they drank, they could always replace it when they left.

They climbed the steps to take a look at the pool. It was discreetly concealed behind thick shrubbery with a magnificent, unimpaired view across the hills. As the sky grew darker, the stars popped out, as brilliant and sharply defined as diamonds.

'Happy?' asked Genevieve cautiously. She still could not quite believe they were here; it always took her a day or so to unwind.

'You bet!' said Anna, beside herself. This had all the signs of turning into one of her more inspired gambles.

★   ★   ★

By the time it was fully dark and the bottle finished they retreated back to the house where the lights were on and enticing smells were wafting from the kitchen.

'*Buona sera, signore!*' said a good-humoured voice and an olive-skinned woman, with a spreading waistline, stuck her head shyly round the door. She was, she explained in her limited English, Maria, here to prepare their evening meal. She indicated that she lived nearby and would send in someone on a regular basis to clean. Cook for them, too, should they ever require it. All they needed to do was let her know.

She lit the candles in the elegant dining-room and, like royalty, the two of them sat down. The meal she set before them was a feast: pickled vegetables, followed by crab ravioli and then a fragrant *ossobuco*, the best either of them had ever had. Maria popped in to say goodnight; the fruit was already on the table and there was cheese and fresh bread in the kitchen. She offered to make coffee but Anna waved her away.

'Go,' she said, 'you have done us more than proud. With food like this on a regular basis, what hope have we of ever keeping our figures?'

Maria laughed and spread her hands wide to demonstrate the way they were likely to swell. She was a handsome woman in, perhaps, her early sixties with the glowing patina that spoke of a healthy life.

'*Buona notte*,' she said, with many nods and smiles. It was clear she was happy that they were there, to breathe back life into this wonderful house.

Anna scrabbled in the dining-room armoire and emerged with a dusty bottle of grappa. 'I'm game if you are,' she said, nodding towards the terrace, and Genevieve managed to find the appropriate glasses. They had both of them been travelling for hours. Yet the magic of this enchanting place already had them in thrall. To think, had it not been for that serendipitously spotted ad, Anna would still be disconsolate in New York and Genevieve in rainy London, fretting.

'To us!' said Anna, raising her glass beneath a bright canopy of stars.

5

'Shopping,' explained Anna over her second cup, sitting at the table making a list. She was already dressed and immaculately groomed when Genevieve emerged around nine, bleary-eyed and virtually comatose. She was wearing cute Viyella pyjamas and her hair looked like a bird's nest. She was never at her best at this time of day.

'I thought you were planning to work regular hours.' Blindly she groped around, looking for something to eat. All there seemed to be were last night's leftovers hence, presumably, Anna's orderly list.

'I've already done two hours,' said Anna. 'I always aim to start no later than seven.' Which, to Genevieve's blurred reckoning, meant three a.m., New York time. Small wonder then that Anna was so successful; she deserved every accolade she got. It might play havoc with her social life but Genevieve had never known her complain. And whatever went on in her private life that Anna wasn't telling, it had to be better than anything in her own.

Genevieve hacked herself a hunk of cheese and broke off a handful of grapes. The sun was brilliant and the terrace doors wide open. She poured herself coffee from Anna's cooling pot and drifted outside, barefoot, to savour the air.

'What do you like for breakfast?' called Anna,

still engrossed in her list. Odd, considering how long they had been friends, that they really did not know each other's tastes. Although they met more or less every eighteen months, they had never, till this moment, even shared. Anna existed on caffeine and aspirin; Genevieve led a more self-indulgent life.

'Glad at least one of us still has some energy.' This morning she felt distinctly shaky; the grappa hadn't helped.

'I haven't been sleeping properly in weeks. I kind of got out of the habit,' said Anna, whose brain was whirring in massive overdrive after her early morning session. It was going so well, she'd been reluctant to leave it, but first things first and the shopping had got to be done. Anna was never comfortable until things were properly sorted. She lived a regimented life of timetables and lists, whereas Genevieve simply muddled along. Talk about chalk and cheese, they were diametric opposites, yet still managed never to get on each other's nerves.

'Cereal will do me. And fruit,' said Genevieve. Beyond that she could not possibly project. She slumped on a warm stone bench in the sun and found herself drifting off again. That huge feather bed had been such a rare treat and the house so silent she could have slept hours longer. Sometime she would have to start thinking about work but not today. She could not remember when she had last had a break, away from the cavilling demands of all those males.

'Somewhere there should be pool furniture,' said Anna, her mind already racing ahead. 'Once we've stocked up with necessities and found out where everything is, we'll begin to get the hang of things and make ourselves properly at home.'

She had left her own place stuffed to the gunnels with every possible item her tenant might need. Food to see him through the first few days, despite the fact that Manhattan supermarkets virtually never close, and the nearest one was only one block from her house. Champagne, well chilled, plus a case of chardonnay; bread and orange juice and eggs. Every necessity she'd been able to think of. Her grandmother would have made him chicken soup; Anna had done the next best thing. There was even expensive shower gel in the guest bathroom, with an extra toothbrush in case he forgot his own. She so much wanted him to love her house, regardless of the fact they would never meet. She just felt she owed him so much and was grateful. To think, if she hadn't bothered to read the Yale mag, she would never have found this paradise. Talk about lucky. One glance at that mind-stopping view was enough. She must be sure to leave him a note.

'Come on,' she said briskly, rinsing out her mug. 'Get your act together and let's go explore.'

*　*　*

Even by mid-morning it was hot and this was still only April. Anna wore stone-coloured chinos with matching shirt, and the delicious raspberry sneakers that had caught her eye in Blooming-dales. Already the worry lines were easing from

63

her face and her bright dark eyes, inquisitive as a robin's, were, as always, fully alert. Genevieve, more conventional, had chosen a sundress over a plain white T-shirt, with serviceable rubber flip-flops on her feet. She carried a wide wicker basket she had unearthed to help transport all those items on Anna's list. As one who actually liked to shop, Genevieve would rather opt for daily excursions, but the super-efficient Anna, who didn't drive, preferred to stockpile and thus save time, plus energy and gas. And, since they were going to be cohabiting so long, Genevieve didn't attempt to argue. It was, as it happened, a major relief to have someone else to make all the daily decisions.

They drove back down the narrow track. Beyond the boundaries of the villa's extensive grounds, the bamboo opened up into acres of vineyards, picturesquely studded with scarlet poppies. The warm, loamy air came wafting through the car windows; there were crickets doing their number in the undergrowth. The heat was rapidly intensifying; they were wise, thanks to Anna, to have made an early start.

'What did he mean, I wonder, about it being Tolomei land?'

'I really have no idea,' said Anna. 'Though I'm sure we will find out.' She loved every aspect of this mediaeval area; felt she had stepped right back in time.

Genevieve parked outside the trattoria and Raffaele saw them and came quickly hurrying out.

'*Buon giorno!*' he cried, with what seemed like

64

genuine enthusiasm. 'Is everything all right with you ladies? How are you settling in?'

'Brilliantly,' said Anna, 'and thank you so much for Maria. She made us feel completely at home. What a gem!'

Raffaele's smile widened and he bowed in acknowledgement. 'Anything at all we can do for you, just ask.' This morning he appeared to be much more at his ease. Whatever doubts he might once have had seemed to have vanished overnight. Which was good. If they were going to be living in this village for four months, they needed as much goodwill as they could get. It was not an acknowledged tourist spot, another big plus in its favour.

'We are off to do a major shop,' explained Genevieve, dragging out the basket.

'Then you must go first to the market,' said Raffaele, 'which is just around the corner, next to the car park. There you will find the finest vegetables and fish that is freshly caught. And after that, Simonetta's general store which should have anything else you could possibly need. And if *she* lets you down, do please let me know. I am here at all times to make your stay memorable.'

His teeth were exceedingly white against his tanned skin and his dark curly hair, clipped close to his scalp, was showing faint touches of grey. He was burly yet fit, with a touch of the gourmet's paunch but, combined with his fighting physique, that hardly mattered. Genevieve found him a fine-looking man. She reckoned him just about forty.

65

'I wonder if he is married,' she said, as they walked in the direction he had indicated.

'Why, do you fancy him?' Anna was amused. At least that might help to keep her mind off the interminable subject of Hector.

'Not especially but he does seem awfully nice.' In two brief meetings, she had already observed, he had been so much warmer than the buttoned-up men who were all she ever met in London.

'That's the Italian male for you. Horny and priapic as a goat. Beware of the Latin lover.'

Anna was scrutinising her list as they found the market and went in search of vegetables. 'I suggest we work from a kitty,' she said, as both made their random selections. A string of fat pink garlic, great handfuls of basil and mint, juicy succulent tomatoes fresh off the vine. 'That way it's easier to keep things straight. Better than having to divvy up every bill.'

Genevieve had no problem with that; besides, it was all unbelievably cheap. She balanced a vast watermelon on her hand then stashed it at the bottom of the basket. If they lived like this she was bound to lose weight; the Mediterranean diet was famously healthy. She was also tempted by aubergines but they wouldn't last long and already they had more than enough. If Anna would allow her to pop down here every day, she could keep them in fresh vegetables all summer.

After they had loitered in the market for a while, they both began feeling hot and thirsty and agreed it was time for a break. They found a café with tables outside, in the shade of a huge plane tree, and settled down for a glass of wine even though it was not yet quite eleven.

'This is definitely the life,' said Anna, feeling the pressures of the past few months beginning to ease away. She was pleased with how the book was progressing and planned to put in more hours after lunch. She had brought from New York a fat folder of research notes and would soon embark on the intricate business of weaving the narrative strands together into a seamless whole. This was the part of the process she liked best, when the first draft was completely sketched out. It was a bit like embellishing charcoal with oils, once the underlying pattern had been established.

'You are amazingly disciplined,' said Genevieve, impressed. 'I sometimes go whole weeks without writing a word.'

'People have different ways of working. There are no hard and fast rules.' This was a subject on which Anna was something of an expert. 'I just find a strict routine works best for me.' She grinned. 'Guess it's because I'm so anally fixated.' Now that she was feeling less oppressed, her attitude to the book was slowly improving. It would be her seventh in just ten years. At last she felt she was more or less into her stride. Learning to write was like anything else, progressive. And the more one did, the better it should become. At least, that was the theory; she was still not entirely convinced. Which was why she was glad to be having this long break away.

'Take it slowly, stage by stage,' she advised whenever she lectured. 'Provided you write even a sentence each day, it will steadily grow, like a scarf. The secret of creative writing is mainly the basic slog of getting it down.' There was no such thing as a muse, she told them, it was you alone facing that empty page. Which made writing such a solitary profession. 'Don't get it right, get it written.' It was a craft as much as an art; she said; those that failed to make it often just lacked the energy and courage. Plus, of course, an iota of talent, but that was something, surely, that went without saying.

They rose reluctantly and wandered on, in search of Simonetta's store. They needed oil and balsamic vinegar, unwilling to use up those that were in the house.

'He's already been more than generous,' said Anna. 'Let's not eat the poor man out of house and home.' Although he was scarcely ever there, she wanted to leave things exactly as they had found them. The villa was magnificent and she felt a sudden urge to meet him and thank him for allowing them to be there.

'Talking of married,' she said, echoing Genevieve, 'I also wonder if *he* is.' Despite the fact there had been no mention of a wife, the villa had a distinctly feminine touch. Even the table linen toned with the plates, something a man would hardly do. Unless, of course, Maria had done the shopping, though somehow her homely image didn't quite fit. Maria was of solid yeoman stock, there was no mistaking that, born and bred in Montisi without a doubt, with a finely arched nose in the Roman style, denoting generations of in-breeding.

'Careful,' said Genevieve, grinning at Anna's lapse. 'You are starting to let your hormones show.'

'Nonsense,' said Anna, 'I was merely wondering. All that marvellous, luxurious space just for a single man.' It was the writer in her, she might have added, always delving into people's lives. The stuff of which her novels were made, accurate first-hand reporting from the front. But she couldn't be bothered, it was far too hot. Besides, Genevieve knew as much as she did.

They also needed other basic staples, like washing powder, soap and kitchen matches. They dawdled along the winding main street, peering into every shop they passed. Knitting patterns, toiletries; basic requirements such as surgical trusses. It was quite astonishing what was on display in a small, back-water village such as this.

'I shall know where to come when I need one,' promised Anna as, laughing, they located Simonetta's store.

It was double-fronted, with a wide-open door behind a beaded curtain to keep out the flies. On the counter was a bacon-slicing machine and the smoky fragrance of ripe pancetta melded with that of some marvellous fruity cheese. Like Bisto kids, they stopped dead in their tracks and inhaled. A handful of shoppers were standing just inside, comfortably chatting and obviously not in a hurry. Life in Montisi was hardly frenzied and they welcomed a new bit of theatre like the entrance of these two newcomers. They smiled and nodded and stood aside while the woman behind the counter positively beamed.

'*Buon giorno!*' she said, with a radiant smile, as if she knew already who they were. 'The ladies from *Casavecchia*. What may I do for you? I hope you are enjoying our lovely village.'

Both smiled and said that indeed they were and the local ladies stopped their chatter in order to try to understand. Anna carefully worked through her list while Genevieve packed things into the basket.

'Any time you need anything,' said Simonetta, 'I can almost promise I will have it in stock. If not, it can be ordered from Sinalunga. I can even have it delivered,' she added. 'Eraldo can bring it on his bike.'

With much smiling and nodding and shaking of hands, they finally succeeded in disentangling themselves. Simonetta, it was obvious, was a kingpin of the village and therefore a valuable force to have on their side.

'Let's treat ourselves to lunch,' suggested Anna, once they were safely outside. 'I don't much feel like having to cook today. Besides, we have already done a full day's work.'

Genevieve laughed in absolute agreement. 'Provided you don't let me pig out on pasta. I don't want to go home looking like a blimp.'

★ ★ ★

Over lunch the conversation drifted predictably to Hector; despite the way he treated her, he was rarely very far from Genevieve's thoughts. Yesterday's fighting spirit seemed to have faded a

70

little and the old wistful note came creeping back into her voice. She admitted that he had not been in touch and that this time she was sure he would not return.

'If he's still seeing other women,' said Anna staunchly, 'then he's certainly no way good enough for you.' Why she held such definite views, she was never exactly sure. She saw things always in black and white and was adept at ending relationships. Let them step out of line even slightly and that, for Anna, was the end. She terminated relationships just like that, allowing them no leeway. Yet, deep in her heart, she occasionally wondered why it should be that she viewed things this way. Everyone, surely, was allowed one mistake; she tried not to be judgemental about her girlfriends. It was possible the secret lay in her parents' close marriage. They had met fairly late, when her father was middle-aged, after indescribable horrors in both their pasts. Looking back, as she often did, Anna realised how lonely life had been as an only child with preoccupied parents with eyes only for each other. And then her mother had died far too young. It was something Anna almost never discussed, a void concealed deep in her soul. Not even to be shared with Genevieve, who tiptoed through life, afraid of her own shadow, too meek to stand up for herself.

And now was saying plaintively: 'I miss him.'

'Why, in particular?' asked Anna.

'He takes me to interesting events. Openings, screenings, cocktail parties. Occasionally first nights.' When no-one more exciting was

71

available; she had few delusions about that.

Anna, irritated, clucked at her. Whatever her secret reservations, she grimly stuck to her guns. If he stepped out of line, then dump the swine. No man was worth so much pain and aggravation.

'Don't be so thoroughly weedy,' she snapped. 'How often do you need to hear it, you are beautiful, talented and *fun*. Any decent man in his right mind should consider it a privilege to be seen out with you.'

'*Signore*,' said a now familiar voice, and there was Raffaele hovering above them. His warm brown eyes simply glowed with geniality. Now *there's* a man, reflected Anna to herself, who looks as though he might have the requisite balls.

'Come on,' she said, as he swept away their plates. 'Let's get back to the villa and find out what's what.'

★ ★ ★

It was mid-afternoon and the place was pristine, with no sign at all of the ravages of last night. The kitchen was scrubbed and the dish towels rinsed and drying. Someone had done a truly immaculate job.

'I think I could easily get used to this sort of life,' said Genevieve. They lugged in the shopping and stowed it in the cool, capacious larder, then went in search of other essentials, starting with the pool furniture. In a basement room beneath the kitchen they unearthed a horde of delights. A ping-pong table, complete

72

with bats and balls, as well as a washer and dryer. And, folded neatly along one wall, a row of garden chairs in plain bleached linen with huge square sun umbrellas to match.

'Very classy,' said Anna, with approval, as they carted them up to the pool. There were also matching cushions for the wooden recliners. Further evidence of a woman's subtle touch.

'I am sure he can't live here alone,' insisted Genevieve. Everything was in such exquisite taste.

'He is a photographer. Maybe he's gay.' Anna enjoyed putting in the boot.

'Unlikely if he spends his life working in the rainforests.' She imagined him as a sort of Indiana Jones. Genevieve had always been romantic.

'Don't be so sexist. You can't ever tell. Men sometimes give you surprises.'

'He is probably trying on all your clothes. I hope he doesn't stretch them.'

'As long as he doesn't frighten the builders. And keeps his mitts off my fur coat.'

'Raffaele said nothing about a missus. But maybe that's just the Italian way.'

'Lord of the manor and all that, you mean. Keeping her firmly out of sight. More likely she accompanies him to the jungle, carrying the cameras, making up the hammocks, sweeping out the tent while he works. If I had a husband who travelled all the time, I'd be damned if I would let him out of my sight.'

'I thought you didn't want one.' Genevieve was amused. Anna often came up with contradictions. Although they were more or less the same age, their life experiences could not have been more different.

'I don't. But I would, if you see what I mean.' The sun was high and the wine had done its work. They changed into swimming things and went back to the pool.

'What we really need,' said Genevieve, 'is hats.'

'Next time we go to the market,' promised Anna, surprised at how thoroughly indolent she felt. All this exertion was having its effect. Two minutes later and both were fast asleep.

★ ★ ★

Later that afternoon, Anna stood at the open window, refreshed, serene and still damp from her shower. As she dried her hair, she gazed across the wide expanse of rolling hills towards the distant mass she knew was Siena. Her lunch, her nap and later her swim had added to her feeling of utter contentment. She felt stretched and rested and unfamiliarly calm; all she was missing slightly now was Sadie. She hoped Mr Sutherland was a genuine animal lover, but he'd hardly have claimed that he was if it wasn't true. And Larry would still be in and out, adding the finishing touches. She knew she could trust him to keep his eye out for the cat. Below her, on the manicured lawn, Genevieve crouched by the pond. It was green and sluggish, with its sinister ancient fountain, and looked as if no-one had cleaned it out in years. There were dragonflies and fat lazy bees; it felt as if time had stood still for a couple of centuries. They had been inside the chapel and admired the faded frescoes. Whoever owned this house in the past had certainly lived well.

'I wonder if there is a ghost?' said Genevieve.

'No way,' said Anna, stamping on the thought. 'The vibes, for one thing, are much too good.' She knew about these things.

'Could be a benevolent one. Here to watch over the house.'

'We already have Raffaele and Maria doing that. We don't want to risk overcrowding.'

Tonight they planned a quiet meal on the terrace, lemon pasta with a tomato and mozzarella salad. They had found a couple of hurricane lamps as well as a drawerful of candles. It was fun being just the two of them, able to gossip and catch up on each other's lives. Although they emailed regularly, it was not quite the same as conversation. Genevieve had her hair wrapped in a towel and was wearing a brief cotton robe. In just one day she was starting to get quite a glow. Colour suited her, she so often looked washed out. She deserved a bit more fun in her life, had been decidedly wobbly since David's defection. Anna had met him only twice, briefly, and privately thought him a bit of a stick-in-the-mud. But a woman accustomed to having a husband must find it exceedingly lonely at times when he left. Hector sounded a nightmare whom she hoped never to meet. Genevieve was far too sensitive for that kind of offhand treatment; she needed someone to encourage her and see her for what she was.

Her hair was dry. Anna unplugged the dryer, then sorted through her clothes for something to wear. She hadn't done any work since lunch but was determined not to slack off. Genevieve hadn't even opened her laptop but, then, her attitude towards her work had always been somewhat lax. Though opposites, they made a great team, got on without any problems. Respected each other's feelings and privacy, even laughed at each other's jokes. There were very few people Anna knew with whom she could comfortably travel. Genevieve was the rare exception; she was really very glad that she had come. In a few days Candy Macaskill would arrive; Anna devoutly hoped she was going to fit in.

6

Candy arrived at the end of the week, in a flurry of baskets and bags. She looked like a rather beguiling gypsy in flip-flops and a home-made patchwork skirt, with a battered straw hat crammed down on her flyaway hair. Genevieve had offered to meet her off the plane but Candy, for reasons of her own, preferred the local bus.

'It makes it more of an adventure,' she explained when eventually she came panting up the track. She stood in the middle of the cool, dark kitchen, spilling her bits and pieces all over the floor.

'I've brought you some home-made lemon curd,' she said, delving into one of her many baskets.

Anna, to her private relief, took to Candy instantly. She was slight and elfin with a cloud of dandelion hair and a wide, infectious smile that lit up the room.

'Candy's an unusual name for a Brit,' commented Anna. 'Though I must say, it certainly suits you.'

'I changed it the second I left school,' Candy confided. 'Couldn't bear the one my parents had lumbered me with.'

'What was it?' asked Anna, intrigued.

'Promise you'll never tell anyone?' said Candy. Anna, hugely amused now, nodded.

Candy, having checked theatrically for eaves-droppers, leaned forward and hissed in mock horror: 'Beryl! Can you imagine being stuck with a moniker like that? I'd have either ended up a suburban hairdresser or else working for the Town Hall.' She did have a point.

She loved the villa and raced all over it like a child, clapping her hands with sheer exuberant joy.

'This place is really ace,' she said, bounding back down the stairs. 'Mind if I take the attic so I can spread out?'

Neither minded; both were happily settled and those steep polished stairs were inclined to be slightly unnerving. Candy's motley baggage was stuffed with sketches and fabric samples which transformed the long, low-ceilinged room into an exotic bazaar. Candy loved it. After sharing a damp crowded cottage all these years with a hyperactive child, so much space and those glorious views were far more than she had expected. She brought her sketchpad down to the kitchen and entertained herself, as the others cooked, with lightning cartoons of the two of them at work. After they had eaten and cleared away, she allowed them to leaf through her impressive portfolio.

'It's not remotely finished yet.'

She was undoubtedly very talented; both of them loved her designs. She had skilfully captured the season's prevailing spirit in her own individual, slightly airy-fairy style.

'These should be a big hit with Harvey Nicks,' said Genevieve, whose favourite store it was.

'And put you on the fashion map in no time.'

'Let's hope,' said Candy, in desperate need of a breakthrough. It was hard to make ends meet with no steady job.

★ ★ ★

She had badly needed this time away though had not been quite sure what to do about her son. Although the school looked after him very well and he only ever came home for occasional weekends, she felt guilty at simply pushing off for four months in Italy without him. Well, three and a half, if she counted the school holidays, though still a lot of time for her to be gone. There was no-one else she could really turn to; her parents were dead and she had no siblings. They were just two orphans of fate. And yet the idea was too good to let go; she was tired and embattled at the thought of all that extra work. Making ends meet on a freelancer's earnings took up most of her energy and the prospect of working with Harvey Nichols was something she must not let go. Not if it killed her; not at this stage. It was a dream she had had for so long. The last time they had had any sort of a break had been two weeks at Butlins in Skegness two years ago when Hugo was coming up for seven. It was not Candy's usual sort of choice at all but another mother had tipped her off and, actually, both had enjoyed themselves very much. There were organised activities every moment of the day to occupy Hugo's attention and wear him out, while Candy was able to relax at last and simply catch up on her sleep. It was bliss. If she could only afford it, she would do it again, but the Italian jaunt was more attractive. She had had to make up her mind fairly fast so, after a lot of deliberation, she had gone against all her natural instincts and picked up the phone and called Trevor.

To say he had been surprised was an understatement. It was months since she last had initiated a conversation and usually ended up cutting him off mid-sentence. But this was a question of priorities and Candy was in no position to take a stand. If she was going to get that portfolio done, she needed not to be running around after the kid. It was that simple. So she had braced herself to be sweetness incarnate and heard herself asking for his help.

Trevor, to give him credit, had reacted graciously. No, he said, he was not too busy nor planning to go anywhere. In actual fact, he had very little to do since the assignment he had been working on for months was very nearly finished.

'He will be at school most of the time,' explained Candy, 'with just the long vacation to be got through. If you could possibly take him then?' She could hardly believe her good luck. For once the man was acting responsibly, almost like a proper father, and furthermore appeared not to mind her having asked.

'No problem,' said Trevor, just as nice as pie. 'In fact, I will really enjoy it. It is time I got to know him a little better.'

When they'd made their arrangements and

Trevor had rung off, Candy had danced a wild tarantella then rushed to tell Genevieve the news.

'He was almost civilised,' she said in jubilation. 'I can't imagine what's got into him.'

'Maybe he's growing up,' suggested Genevieve, though that had never made any difference to David. 'And genuinely wants to bond more with his son.'

'Whatever,' said Candy, 'it means that I can come!' And she had whooped away to rummage through her clothes.

★   ★   ★

Now that they were well and truly into their routines, Anna rose every morning with the dawn. She had imposed a rule, with which Genevieve complied, that they only break for a very brief lunch, then not meet up again till the cocktail hour. After which they were free to do whatever they liked; let down their hair, have fun.

'What about using the pool?' asked Candy wistfully. 'Is that off limits as well?'

'You can please yourself,' said Anna. 'I am only telling you what I've found works best for me.'

Breakfast for Anna consisted of one cup of coffee, which she brewed in a small tin percolator and then carried upstairs to her desk. She had re-established her narrative flow and the book was purring along. By the time she came down at the end of the day she felt energised and fulfilled. Genevieve, who preferred a leisurely breakfast, got up a little later. But, inspired by Anna, she was on the job by nine and managed to stick at it, more or less, until they convened on the terrace for lunch at one. After that, she usually sloped off to the pool to take a lengthy siesta in the sun.

Candy, however, never stirred until noon and often appeared for lunch in her negligee.

'I was up till after three,' she would tell them, yawning. 'I always function best in the early hours.'

She talked to Anna about her books, was a genuine and avid fan. She had read them all with a flattering degree of attention which warmed Anna's heart towards her even more. However ditzy she might seem on the surface, there was a real and original intelligence working beneath.

'It's good for the morale to know someone is actually reading them,' said Anna. 'There are times it can seem like writing into a void.'

★   ★   ★

Candy, to the surprise of the others, turned out to be an inspired and instinctive cook. She would wander around the extensive grounds and return with fistfuls of this and that which she'd then transform, with an apparent lack of effort, into something tasty and unusual.

'It comes from growing up poor,' she explained. 'I am used to having to scrape by.'

Sorrel soup and home-made pesto; she discovered a munificence of herbs growing wild

82

and garnered them carefully so as not to impede their growth. She even occasionally made her own pasta, beating in unexpected flavours that never failed to delight. There were tomatoes staked carefully close to the kitchen door where they caught the early morning sun and, behind the compost heap, neatly planted rows of beets and lettuces. Someone here at some time in the past had been a thrifty gardener and made the most of the resources they had at hand. There were also luscious black figs in abundance which Candy sliced with prosciutto from the market and sprinkled with basil and mint.

'In another life, you might well have been a chef.'

'I have neither the patience nor dedication.'

'I wonder who does the garden?' pondered Anna. They had seen no sign of any sort of outside help. 'And why the vegetables if the villa is hardly ever used?' None of it quite added up.

She asked Maria next time they saw her, waving her hand in appreciation over the neatly staked rows. Maria beamed and nodded with pleasure, then modestly indicated herself.

'I,' she said in her halting English, 'try to keep them watered and weeded and also thin them out. Occasionally Raffaele comes up to dig. We like to keep things nice in case the owner should suddenly return.'

'Does no-one else ever use the house?' It did seem a terrible waste. Maria shrugged and gestured in the air, talking fast in her difficult local patois which even Genevieve found hard to understand. As it happened, Genevieve had

83

popped into the village so Anna could only guess.

'Is the villa often rented out?' she asked. Maria shook her head.

'I think,' said Candy, 'she said something about family. Though who that family is, she doesn't say.'

'They are probably mostly all related in Montisi. In-breeding in these country villages is a fairly usual way of life.'

'But Sutherland isn't an Italian name. I wonder how he fits in.'

'Maybe he has an Italian wife,' said Anna, which made the best sense. Since he had been at Yale, he was obviously not a local, but it could be that he had married into the community.

'Ask her,' said Candy, but Maria just gabbled on and soon they waved and smiled and wandered away. Anna told Candy the little they knew and she entirely agreed about the elegance of the house. As a designer herself, she had a very perceptive eye, had picked up many small details the others had missed. The positioning of the mirrors, for instance, and the super-abundance of softly shaded lamps. The house, though austere, had been furnished for comfort and the kitchen was almost professionally equipped, with rows of bottled preserves upon the shelf.

'I am pretty certain this is not the work of a man. If we took a peek inside his private suite, all would undoubtedly be revealed.'

'We can't,' said Anna, 'we promised Raffaele. Besides, the doors are locked.'

'Coward,' said Candy. 'It's the obvious way. There must be some method of gaining access without having to force the lock.'

'Not that it's any of our business,' said Anna. Sutherland, after all, was in her own house; she hated to think of him snooping through her things. It went against the spirit of the arrangement. She had left everything but her own bedroom unlocked, even her filing cabinet. Trust was the keynote of swapping homes; she was starting to feel quite an expert. She had left a long memo on the kitchen table, detailing everything he might need to know. Telephone numbers for the vet and the maid, the whereabouts of the nearest liquor store, the dry-cleaner, the post office, the subway. She had also provided a metro map in case he used public transport. And Larry's number, should anything go wrong. Though, of course, he could always call her here, which seemed to make better sense.

'We could always ask Raffaele, he is bound to know.' Candy was like a puppy with a bone. Anna detected the gleam in her eye and knew she had mischief in mind.

'What, and look like silly schoolgirls? I don't think so. After all, what difference can it make?' She was ultra-sensitive about personal privacy, especially since her profile had become so much higher. The idea of anyone asking questions about her own life filled her with instant dismay. The thing that stood in Sutherland's favour was that Paige's cousin had known him at Yale. That, to her mind, was the best recommendation, a guarantee of good behaviour.

Candy laughed. She didn't remotely care but got a buzz out of sending Anna up. 'You realise,' she said solemnly, 'that in all probability his wife is now living in your house? Using your dishes, soaking in your bath, inviting the neighbours in for drinks. Stealing the affections of your cat, countermanding the architect's instructions. Don't worry,' she added, 'there's no problem with that. She seems to have excellent taste.'

'Stop!' said Anna. 'You're making me nervous.' The thought had halted her in her tracks. Surely he would have mentioned a wife, wouldn't he, since he was planning to be there for so long? All he had said was that he needed space to work and did not object to the workmen being around. She saw from her grin that Candy was only joking, but that didn't stop her feeling slightly uneasy. She loved the house with such a passion, she hated the thought of another woman there. Illogical, maybe; there were three of them here and yet it was not quite the same. She thought of checking with Larry, then dismissed it. There was no point in worrying about something she could not control. A deal was a deal, she had accepted his terms and, in all honesty, felt that in fact she had come out of it better. Her place was still a building site while the villa was sheer perfection.

★ ★ ★

The market became a favourite venue and pretty soon they were very well known in the village.

Montisi was so far off the beaten track that tourist invasions were rare. The inhabitants were courteous and reserved, with a moving dignity that guaranteed respect. Many of the older women still dressed, head to foot, in black. To begin with, even Genevieve had problems understanding them, found the local dialect hard to crack. But Candy was immediately in on the fast track; smiles and nods worked every bit as well. So that soon they found themselves accepted and knew many of the stallholders by name.

'Hats,' prompted Genevieve, the first time they took Candy there.

'Hats,' agreed Anna, so they made that their first port of call. All sorts of other things lurked within that market. Between the food and vegetable stalls were dotted piles of tablecloths and a garish array of clothes.

'Who buys them?' asked Anna, as Candy fingered through them. Multi-coloured rayon housedresses, styles that might well have come from another age. All they needed were bandannas and mops to do a Fifties' Doris Day act in chorus.

'Real women,' said Genevieve, 'who actually live here and can't afford much for a lesser priority like clothes.'

'This would really suit you,' said Candy, pulling one off the rack. 'Try it on.' It was cotton in a wraparound style, designed to fit all sizes, and did, indeed, go really well with the new healthy glow in Genevieve's cheeks. Cornflowers on a lilac background; over the plain white

T-shirt she wore it was demure, with a soupçon of sauce.

'How much?' asked Genevieve and Anna rapidly calculated.

'Nine dollars. Can you believe that?' she said as Genevieve forked through her purse.

The hats were a riot and they ended up buying two; Candy already had her battered old straw. Anna opted for a jaunty trilby in raspberry cotton that echoed her shoes while Genevieve chose something more flexible in raffia which, gussied up, Candy assured her, might even do duty for a wedding. 'Stick a few cornflowers under the band and you're there.'

Companionably, they wandered on, comfortable in this new threesome.

★ ★ ★

Next on the must list was Simonetta's shop. Candy needed insect repellent and the others more of that wonderful cheese. Also, the pasta was running low and they could use some tins of *ceci* just in case. Besides, Simonetta, they had rapidly established, was the fulcrum of gossip in this village. No expedition into Montisi was complete without dropping in on her.

'You will love her,' said Anna. 'She has a wicked sense of humour and her English is really very good.' Which made a change; in this part of Tuscany few of the natives spoke much English, though the girls were rapidly picking up on the nuances. By the end of the summer they should be fluent, assuming they lasted that long.

It was close to one and siesta time; for once the shop was deserted. Simonetta popped out with her radiant smile and insisted on giving each of them a glass of sweet wine and a biscuit so dry it was almost impossible to swallow.

'It means she likes you,' said Genevieve quietly. 'A local Montisi custom.' She bought the cheese and an armful of beet leaves to make that delectable local soup. In a very short time they were turning into peasants and moving more and more into local fare. Genevieve was secretly pleased. Despite her declarations that she really no longer cared, the weight was miraculously dropping off without effort.

'No junk food,' Anna reminded her.

'Also all those stairs,' added Candy. Plus the long, hot walk back when they didn't take the car and went down to the village for fresh bread. Anna's Spartan regime was certainly working. All three of them were feeling and looking good.

★   ★   ★

'Isn't this pure bliss?' said Genevieve, as they lazed in the early evening out by the pool. Candy was doing her nightly thirty laps, determined to keep up the good work of the gym; not, so it would seem, that she really needed to. In her brief bikini, she looked like a waifish child with her wild Botticelli tangle of seaweed hair. She certainly had a load of energy; just watching her swim made Genevieve feel limp. Anna was silently writing in her notebook; these days it seemed that she rarely let up.

89

As the sun slowly sank, the fireflies appeared, like jewelled Tinkerbells hovering over the grass. From all around them came the fragrance of the *genista*, the bright yellow broom so abundant in these parts.

'Plantagenet,' said Genevieve, out of context. 'That's where it got its name.'

Anna, still scribbling, was not really listening. She had suddenly hit a roll, she said, and needed to get it all down.

'I find,' she said at last, snapping the notebook shut, 'that it helps to leave a paragraph halfway through. Gives your brain something constructive to do, even when you think that it isn't switched on.' Here, she found, she was sleeping like the dead. At last the terrible images were fading.

'You know, I don't miss New York one bit.' Except, of course, for beloved Sadie. 'I wonder how Sutherland is settling in.' Or should that be the Sutherlands? They were still no wiser. There was one thing, though, on which all three were agreed. They could not have felt more at home in his beautiful villa.

'I hope he's as happy there as we are here,' she mused. Pretty soon the work would be done and Larry and his labourers would move on. Part of Anna felt disappointed not to be there to see it finished, though this paradise that she was living in now was effective compensation. The house would be like a birthday present, something to look forward to at the end of four glorious months.

Candy came dripping out of the pool and

perched on the edge of a recliner, towelling her hair.

'Drinkypoos time,' said Genevieve, getting up. 'What do you girls fancy doing tonight about supper?'

★ ★ ★

Since Candy had joined them, they tended to go out more. She was so turned on by the sheer fact of being abroad that it seemed unfair to expect her to stay home and cook. She had never been to Italy before, was overwhelmed by the foreignness of it all. The trattoria had become their favourite hangout, though there were also a couple of other small places nearby. They always got a huge welcome from Raffaele, who in some ways resembled a large and bouncy dog and kept a regular table just for them. He certainly had an attractive personality as well as being an accomplished charmer with his taut, suntanned skin and flirty eyes that occasionally swam with emotion. Italian yeoman stock, earthy and sound. Feet on the ground and eyelashes to die for.

'I wonder if he's married?' said Candy, unaware that she was treading familiar ground. There had never been so much as a glimpse of a wife, unusual in such a tight community. The others told her she had a one-track mind, always on the lookout for a man. He was far too old for her, anyway; she should take her place in the pecking order and wait for it to be her turn. Anna and Genevieve swapped glances; it was fun

91

having Candy here.

'She is probably stuck in the kitchen, poor soul, slaving over a hot stove.' Genevieve, these days, had few illusions about the opposite sex.

'Looking at least ten years older than he does. In one of those voluminous black dresses.'

'With sweat stains under the arms . . . '

' . . . from that stall in the market.'

'Wearing slippers with holes in to ease her aching bunions . . . '

' . . . and with chronic lumbago from the mountains of washing-up.'

'With a bunch of anxious *bambini* at home. Scabies and rickets, you name it.'

Raffaele nodded benignly, enjoying their riotous high spirits, though luckily not quite fluent enough to follow their actual drift. It was a balmy, wonderful Tuscan night and the aroma of woodsmoke was fast going to their heads. They had ordered baked chicken with rosemary potatoes, were growing daily more relaxed about their figures. Especially where their drinking was concerned. Raffaele, without any consultation, brought a litre bottle of the rough local red that had now become their usual. He was amused and happy to watch them having fun. They certainly added some colour to his establishment and helped enliven the rest of his clientele who were mainly farmers and local tradespeople, often with their whole families.

Anna had lately been having exotic dreams. 'Do you think it might be the poppies?' she asked the others. 'Growing among the vines,' she persevered when both of them started to cackle. 'No, really. I'm being serious. Remember where opium comes from.'

She did have a point and the dreams were not only colourful but stayed in her head when she woke, which was unusual, though nightmares, of course, often linger on in the shoals of the subconscious.

'What you're suggesting,' said Candy, giggling, 'is that you're perpetually stoned.'

'If you like, though only mildly.' It was a pleasant enough feeling, she could not fault it; her brain felt remarkably relaxed. Maybe it was simply that she had ceased to worry and her cares were easing away. Her father, when she last telephoned him, had sounded remarkably spry.

'Don't waste your money,' he told her sternly. 'I am perfectly able to cope.'

Genevieve, too, was feeling less anxious since her most recent calls to both her boys.

'*Ma*,' they had said, in perfect echo of each other. 'Why don't you just quit fussing?'

★ ★ ★

That night, when they returned to the villa, they went skinny-dipping in the pool. The moon was full and the water bright silver; they lay on their backs and watched a shooting star. The real lives they had left behind seemed suddenly remote. Anna had finally stopped worrying about Sadie and they hadn't heard a mention of Hector in days.

'Can't we just stay here for ever?' begged Candy. 'I feel as though I have died and gone to heaven.'

7

Time passed and the temperature rose. May came in with a glorious flourish, tinting the lambent scenery with shifting light. The rolling hills turned pink or mauve; depending on the time of day, and distant Siena lay shimmering in the heat like the mythical kingdom of Oz. In the villa the windows and doors stood wide open to encourage the static air to circulate.

'We really must go there one of these days,' said Anna, standing on the terrace in shorts, a glass of chilled wine in her hand. Genevieve, beside her, nodded; Candy had yet to appear. The attic, and now most of the other rooms too, were strewn with a jumble of fabrics and fine ink sketches as the fashion portfolio spread its wings and flew rapidly out of control. Candy, now that she had settled in, was firing on all cylinders; she was certainly very gifted, no denying that. And knowing that Hugo would be safely with his father meant she no longer had that nagging worry. She slept long hours which paid dividends; awake, she was the most delightful company. Anna was happy too with her own steady progress and even Genevieve's book was gathering steam.

They walked around wearing very few clothes, careless of possible intruders. The villa was so isolated that anyone approaching would be seen from sufficient distance that they would have plenty of time to cover up. Not that they ever had visitors at all, other than Rosa, a smiling village girl who came in regularly twice a week to dust and do light housework. She was sweet and willing but apparently spoke no English, which Candy found frustrating. She would have made an ideal spy who could tell them all the things they were dying to know. Genevieve tried talking to her in Italian but either she did not understand or pretended that was so. It was hard to tell.

'Damn,' said Candy, 'we will just have to work on Maria.' Though with her, too, they usually drew a blank.

Occasionally Rosa cooked, which was always a treat. Although they all took turns in the kitchen, it was nice, at times, to be able to sit down to an authentic Tuscan meal, served on the table on the terrace, shaded by a couple of the huge umbrellas.

Candy, when not comatose in bed, spent many hours stretched out topless by the pool. 'What?' she said, the first time Anna approached her, almost as though she were doing something wrong.

'You should be wary of taking so much sun,' warned Anna, the practical city girl. The last thing she wanted to do was nag, but this was potentially slow suicide. But Candy, for so many years deprived of life's little luxuries, blatantly chose to ignore her advice. After years of working so hard just to make ends meet, these minor health scares failed to bother her. Even her frenzied sketching had come temporarily to a halt; all she wanted to do right now was bake her brains and just wallow in the sun.

★　★　★

Paige, despite her horrendous workload, stayed in regular touch with Anna by email, one of the marvels of modern technology, far better than telephones or letters to Anna's mind. Paige had a witty and distinctive turn of phrase that always made Anna crack up. Wry and irreverent, her sharp observations were always bang on target. The city, she reported, was stupendously hot, with temperatures high in the nineties. If it weren't for the weekly bolthole of Quogue, she didn't know how they would ever survive.

'I am beginning to think we made a colossal mistake, not taking you up on your offer and coming too.' But Charles was embroiled in the financial gloom that hung like a pall over the city and Paige, too, had more work than she could comfortably cope with. Normally, by this time of year, things were becoming pretty dead, but the mood in New York was manic and intolerable, with people scared of what might be coming next and seeking ways to ward off further catastrophe.

'I envy you your freedom,' Paige wrote, 'as well as your God-given talent. Being able to do your own thing wherever you choose. Lazing around in your Tuscan paradise while the rest of us poor mortals slowly succumb to the traffic fumes. I hope you get cellulite from eating too much pasta; it isn't fair that you should get off scot-free.'

Dear Paige, still stalwart after all these years. Anna could see her clearly as she had been, that first semester at Yale when they'd roomed together. Paige, with her golden patrician beauty, had dazzled the men in their year but her mind was level and her judgement sound; she had never allowed herself to get carried away. Till the advent of Charles, she had played the field and always kept things light-hearted. And their relationship was still as firm as it had been then; top of the things Anna missed about New York was the regular banter of her closest friend.

'Saw Larry and Phoebe last night,' Paige reported. 'We took your dad to the Philharmonic and they were in the next row. Both looking blooming; because of what's happening business is going really well. People are scrambling to sell off their investments and put the cash into bricks and mortar instead. Larry is experiencing a sudden bonanza. Instinct tells me that his next significant career move might well be into politics. He would certainly make an extremely capable mayor.'

That was a surprise but Paige was usually right. Her naturally delving legal brain picked up clues that others might overlook and Larry, too, had been a close pal since Yale, part of their tight inner circle. Anna was pleased and grateful that they were spending time with her father, it helped to assuage any lingering guilt about leaving him so long on his own. But Paige, along with her other friends, had always adored the old man. He was wise and caring and generous with his time, always prepared to listen and give good advice.

'I wish my own dad could have been like yours,' was one of Paige's regular laments. Hers had been a tight-assed corporate lawyer who, although endowing his children with trust funds and first-rate education, had fallen sadly short on most of the rest. And ended up changing wives at a late age before drinking himself to death.

'Why ever would you need him? You've got Charles,' was Anna's stock reply. She envied the Colliers their solid union, perhaps the best marriage she knew at close hand. She had never, herself, wanted to be tied down yet exulted in Paige's contentment. If she should ever have the good fortune to find a soulmate of her own, she hoped she might one day be similarly happy. But that was something she rarely discussed, not even with her intimates. Anna, at heart, had long been a loner, a cat that walked by itself.

'Any news of my house?' she emailed back. It was all very nice that Larry should be thriving but she hoped not at her own expense. Since he was doing it all at cut price, she wasn't in any position to argue but she worried that Mr Sutherland might be inconvenienced.

'He didn't say,' replied Paige. 'And I confess I forgot to ask. If I find a reason to be in your neck of the woods, I will go and take a peek at it myself.'

'Don't bother,' replied Anna. 'You've enough on your plate as it is.' But she longed to know how things were shaping up. And so she called Larry direct.

'Everything's fine,' he told her breezily. 'We are coming in bang on schedule. With luck, we'll be out of there in a couple of weeks. I must say,' he added, 'that you made a brilliant investment. Have you been keeping an eye on Dow Jones?'

'Not really,' said Anna, who had seen only occasional headlines. 'What precisely is going on?'

'Corruption, corruption, corruption,' said Larry. 'Many of the biggest players are starting to come unstuck. People are panicking and selling off their stock but most have already left it far too late. The party is over but they're only just catching on. Millions have lost their retirement plans.' There was the faintest hint of satisfaction in his voice. He, too, had been shrewd enough to put all his savings into property.

'How's my tenant? And is he coping?' Anna hoped he loved her house as much as she loved his.

'I haven't actually seen him yet. He seems never to be around.'

'Is Sadie okay?' she asked, instantly alarmed, afraid her pampered pet was being neglected.

'Sadie's fine,' said Larry soothingly. 'Always looks sleek and content. And the house itself is in apple-pie order. You'd hardly know that anyone was living there.'

'Is his wife there?' She felt she had to know.

'I wasn't aware he had one. The only person who occasionally drops by acts more like a PA.

100

In and out at the speed of light, sorting through mail and returning calls, too busy even to chat.' Also too snooty, he privately thought. He hadn't warmed to her at all.

For a reason she could not identify, Anna felt oddly relieved. She hadn't liked the thought at all of another woman in her space. But knowing that Larry was keeping an eye on things, meant she could finally relax. She lapsed back into her pastoral idyll, shoving all thoughts of New York to the back of her mind.

★ ★ ★

She awoke with a start in the early hours at the sound of horrendous screeching. Because of the heat, she had left the windows open and thought at first it was coming from her room. Her pulse raced unnaturally fast and she rose in terror. The moon was almost full again and the garden was bathed in brilliant light. Peering cautiously over the sill, Anna could see nothing unusual on the lawn. What sounded like a pack of hyenas voraciously slaughtering chickens or, at the very least, a vixen on heat, was causing no discernible havoc below. Unperturbed, the garden slumbered on. But the noise continued with shattering resonance until, after a while, Anna went back to bed. Her heart was pumping overtime and she found that she could not settle. She would have been tempted to creep down to Genevieve's room if it weren't for those dark, daunting stairs. She tossed and turned, pulling the sheet up high, and eventually managed to

101

drop off again into a fitful doze.

When, as usual, she arose in the early dawn the disturbance had ceased completely. While her coffee was brewing, she stepped outside to watch the sun rise slowly over the hills. The grass was still glistening with morning dew and only the crowing of a distant cockerel disturbed the absolute tranquillity. In New York, all night, she could hear the rumble of traffic, punctuated by sirens and occasionally screams. This was a totally different environment; Anna basked in its peace.

'Frogs,' said Genevieve knowledgeably at lunch, familiar with them from her country childhood. 'In the mating season they certainly do make a racket. Until you know what they are, it can be scary.' She hadn't been able to hear them herself since her room faced in the opposite direction and the walls of the villa were fourteen inches thick, one good reason it had survived intact all these years.

'Frogs?' said Anna, unconvinced. 'Well, show me where they are, then.'

Genevieve knew already. She led Anna triumphantly to the ornamental pond, surmounted by the wicked, leering satyr. Both stared into its murky depths, but beneath the water lilies, nothing stirred.

'They must be sleeping it off,' said Genevieve, disturbing the surface of the water with a twig.

'I wish they'd keep their damn rutting to themselves,' said Anna, though now they had identified the sound, it would not seem nearly so bad. Nature red in tooth and claw or green in libidinous flipper. She grinned. In Manhattan it would have meant murder or worse. She could not begrudge them a little amphibious fun.

★ ★ ★

That night they ate poshly in the dining-room, with candles on every surface. The ancient mirrors, with their tarnished glass, lent a grandeur that was compellingly authentic. If you half-closed your eyes you might almost believe yourself back in the fourteenth century. On occasional evenings they even lit the fire, just to add a homey touch, but the weather at present was so stiflingly hot they welcomed the cool of the huge high-ceilinged room. It was warmer outside on the terrace than in here, even now that it was dark.

Candy had really excelled herself and thrown together an impressive fish stew. She had spent the whole morning poking around in the market while the others were virtuously at work.

'You have got to eat it all up,' she commanded, 'because in this heat it won't keep.' Mussels and squid and a handsome red mullet; she had even discovered some saffron high on a shelf.

'Well, someone certainly appreciates the finer things in life.' She had noticed numerous little gourmet details like that. The quality of the wine was excellent too. No matter how rarely there were visitors here, their host was clearly a perfectionist.

'I wish we could meet him,' she added. It was becoming an obsession. The more they saw, the more they longed to know.

'Leave him a note,' suggested Genevieve. 'Perhaps you can set something up.'

'Candy, you'll be the death of me,' groaned Anna, handing over her bowl to be refilled. At home she rarely bothered to cook and long ago had given up entertaining. Writing was such an absorbing commitment, she seldom felt comfortable away from her screen. Basic things like eggs and cheese could keep her going for weeks.

'You work too hard,' was Candy's comment, passing her the bread. 'You really should try relaxing more, especially while we are here.'

Genevieve pulled a second cork. 'Let's take it up to the pool,' she said. 'But, please, chaps, tonight no grappa.'

Candy gathered up the scented candles and placed them strategically around the edge of the pool. The flickering flames competed with the fireflies and they even found a glow-worm on the steps. It was like entering an enchanted glade, a fairyland of delicate dancing light. With a whoop of delight, Candy ripped off her clothes and dived headfirst into the pool.

'The water's divine, come and join me,' she screamed. 'The last one in does the dishes.'

★　★　★

Genevieve found it hard to open one eye. It was hot and swollen and throbbing like a metronome. She also had a fierce compulsion to scratch — anywhere, everywhere, all at the same time. Something pretty nasty seemed to have stung her in the night. As she cautiously moved, she realised she was covered in abrasions. Horrified, she jerked fully awake, swinging out her legs from under the sheet. Despite the diaphanous mosquito netting, which she'd had the prudence to draw around the bed, the little blighters had still contrived to sneak in. In all, she counted thirty-nine hits, with others that hadn't yet peaked. With her fair complexion, she had always been susceptible; this morning she resembled the Elephant Man. She found Anna in the kitchen, similarly suffering, though her olive skin meant that she had fared less badly. Bright pinpoints of calamine dotted her face like pale measles. And certainly had done little for her mood.

'It was those damned candles around the pool. They must have attracted every bug within range.'

Even Candy was up early too, slathering herself with lotion. 'That's it,' she declared, 'no more skinny-dipping for me. Definitely never again by candlelight.'

★ ★ ★

The heat continued though the itching gradually ceased. They made an emergency trip to Simonetta to stock up with cures and preventatives, and henceforth ensured, before lighting candles, that the mosquito screens were in place. Anna and Candy were unused to country living and Genevieve considerably out of practice. But it did not, in any way, cramp their style nor

105

reduce their general enjoyment. If anything, these minor hitches made them appreciate what they had got all the more. Anna slept like a log these days; even the mating frogs failed to keep her awake. Her brain had cleared, her creative juices were flowing. Her skin was pellucid, despite the disfiguring bites. New York featured less and less in her thoughts as, incidentally, did her house. Or even her father, whom she tried not to call. She did occasionally drop him a postcard but knew how he hated any fuss. She had inherited from him her independent nature and knew when to leave him alone. Too much attention and he started to feel old and she knew that both Paige and Charles were doing staunch duty. She would try to find a way to repay them but that would have to wait until she got back. In the meantime, she must respect his privacy by appreciating this place while she was still here.

★　★　★

Trudging back from the village one morning, laden down with groceries and wine, having recklessly chosen the overgrown shortcut, knee-deep in grass and wild flowers, Anna and Genevieve stopped suddenly in their tracks. It was just past noon and the sun was at its highest. They had opted for exercise instead of the car and now both were hot and exhausted. Also Genevieve was developing a blister and couldn't wait to get home and kick off her shoes.

'What's that?' asked Anna, shading her eyes. A heat haze shimmered in front of the gates; what she saw was more like a mirage. Genevieve was peering too. 'Looks like a bunch of bikes,' she said. 'Surely that cannot be.'

To the right of the gates, the ground swelled steeply upwards, surmounted by a tuft of scrubby trees beyond which rolled the endless verdant scenery with not another habitation in sight. Their villa was the last along the track. What had caught their eye was indeed a cluster of motorbikes, unattended but parked in a tight circle, as if part of some sinister alliance. They counted eleven, which was slightly unnerving; so much for their rural retreat. An involuntary chill ran down Anna's spine and her steps grew instantly more cautious. A lifetime in Manhattan had sharpened her instincts.

'Looks like an invasion from the local Hell's Angels,' she muttered, devoutly hoping that she would be proved wrong. Together they stealthily crossed the lawn towards the villa's main front door which, as always, stood wide open, allowing the breezes to blow through. There was no sound of voices nor movement from within. Everything drowsed in the slumbrous midday heat. No sign of Candy either, though the remains of her breakfast were scattered all over the table and the teapot, when Anna felt it, was still lukewarm. They stowed the shopping, then Anna strolled up to the pool to find out what was going on. And there was Candy, stretched out in the sun, wearing only the briefest of bikini bottoms, hat pulled low, oblivious of the world.

Anna, disapproving, shook her awake. 'You ought to be more careful,' she said. 'You never know who might be lurking around.' She told her about the motorbikes and Candy vaguely remembered having heard them. She'd been half asleep and had taken no notice, assuming that they were simply passing by. Anna advised her to cover herself up while she went to find out what was going on. There were times when Candy resembled a careless child, altogether too laid-back for her own good. Candy pulled on her T-shirt but continued to lie prostrate. She couldn't care less, thought Anna grimly, advancing towards the impenetrable shrubbery, there to protect the pool from prying eyes.

Suddenly she heard a burst of muffled laughter and a frenzied stirring in the bushes and something large erupted right at her feet. For a startled second, she took it to be a large animal but, as it uncurled and struggled upright, she saw it was wearing jeans and a leather jacket. Presumably a local youth, out on the rampage with a cluster of silly-ass friends. Somehow they had managed to crawl through the shrubbery, where they had been hiding and feasting their eyes. Now, with much scuffling and merriment, they all broke cover and raced away back to the safety of their bikes. She shook her head sadly as the engines started to rev and they took off in a cloud of dust. Something, insidiously, appeared to be going wrong. Cracks were beginning to show in their paradise.

8

They did eventually make it to Siena, one weekday morning late in May, when Anna had reached the end of a chapter and the others were suddenly craving a change of scene. For even paradise can occasionally cloy; too much perfection isn't natural. On Anna's insistence, they left at the crack of dawn and were in the Campo in time for a leisurely breakfast before the tourist invasion was properly underway. Candy, still bleary-eyed, was trying hard to shake herself awake but Genevieve did all the driving without so much as a murmur. Candy could take her turn on the journey home, allowing Genevieve to indulge herself at lunchtime. That was the way things usually fell into place; after so many weeks of endless close contact, a workable living arrangement had kicked in. Considering two of them had never met before, the trio was co-existing remarkably well. By now most groups would be spitting and growing mutinous but these three actually liked each other; even more, always the acid test, could still be civil at breakfast.

Already, as early as this, it was hot but they had become acclimatised. They wore short cotton skirts with T-shirts and sandals and, of course, the obligatory hats. Anna was tanned as dark as a native Italian while both the others had achieved a burnished glow. And Genevieve

109

had distinctly lost weight; she was proud of her flatter midriff. How she had achieved it she couldn't imagine, after all the wine and pasta she had consumed.

'Just goes to show that the gym is a waste of time.' She ordered a cappuccino to follow her melon and recklessly stirred in extra sugar. She was far less stressed because she was so much happier and had stopped just grazing on junk food when she felt the need. Also she no longer had to cater for growing boys. They lived simply and healthily on fish and fresh vegetables, the staples of the Mediterranean diet. And, in her heart, she had even stopped hankering after Hector; felt only the occasional passing pang. Spending time with lively, independent women had turned out unexpectedly life-enhancing. She no longer worried about how she looked and went without makeup during the day, though Candy was doing great things for her morale by overhauling her wardrobe. It reminded her of boarding school, which she had always rather enjoyed. In many ways the success of this trip was due to the fact that she was finally discovering she could cope on her own without a man. A slice of wisdom she had picked up from the others; if nothing else, she would gratefully carry that home. And stand it on the mantelpiece, in place of the more usual straw donkey, a memento of a seismic change in her life.

'If we are going to do the Duomo,' said Anna, studying her guidebook, 'we ought to get in there before the crowds. Which means now.'

Obediently they filed after her as she deftly led them by the most direct route. Anna, it seemed, had a natural radar and rarely ever had to consult a map.

★　★　★

Siena was a truly enchanting city which had remained the same, virtually unaltered, since the Middle Ages. Its steeply climbing mediaeval streets were backlit at night like a stage-set, with seventeen separate neighbourhoods, the *contradas*, proudly picked out with their own distinctive colours. The highlight of the tourist season was the legendary horse race, the Palio, which dated back unchanged to the eleventh century. Then the Campo swarmed with spectators and the whole of Siena came out in force, waving banners to cheer on their chosen teams. Family was set against family; the *contrada* always came first in their loyalties. Like the Montagues and Capulets, they would fight to the death for the cause. That, however, was not for a few more weeks. The race took place only twice a year, in early July and August.

'We could always come back,' said Anna with a grimace, 'if you think you can stomach the barbarity.' To her mind the sport rivalled bullfighting in its grossness, involving unnecessary suffering to animals and bringing out the bloodlust of the crowd.

Genevieve shuddered. 'I am not sure that I could.' Somewhere she had read that the horses sometimes died. But the thought of all that pageantry inflamed her curiosity, even though the race itself lasted an unbelievably brief ninety seconds.

'Well, let's at least think about it,' said Candy diplomatically, 'and see how we feel a little nearer to the time.' Siena was less than an hour from Montisi; they had done it today at record speed. And it would be a shame to miss out on its biggest event, especially since they were here for a whole four months. The chances were she might never return, so she wanted to cram in as much as she possibly could. Even if Harvey Nichols should come through, and Candy was by no means sure of it, she had never in her life been flush with money and living as a one-parent family took up everything she earned.

For the next few hours they wandered and admired, soaking up the atmosphere and pausing for regular pit stops. The heat was fierce but they were in no hurry, with plenty of time just to wander and explore and savour the colourful street life at their leisure. Anna's favourite spectator sport was sitting outside at a café table, watching the world go by. It was, she felt, far more educational and rewarding than focusing only on inanimate things and helped to fire her writer's imagination, part of the main purpose of trips like this.

'This place is great,' said Genevieve with longing. A hazy daydream was starting to take shape of one day, conceivably, moving here to live. The climate, the food, the easygoing people, especially the hunky, good-looking men. As Anna was constantly reminding her, writers can live wherever they choose, provided they have a lifeline to civilisation. These days, with laptops and the internet, the world was potentially their oyster. And the flight time from London to Florence or Pisa was now just under two hours. She thought about Highbury, with its polluted, traffic-clogged streets, as well as the terrible weather they had been enduring. The wraith of Hector flitted fleetingly through her mind but she banished it sternly before it could take hold. Thus far, she was coping remarkably well without him. She might just drop him a postcard to rub that in.

★　★　★

'I think I have more or less had it,' announced Anna by mid-afternoon. 'Does anyone mind if we think about heading back?' Her calves were aching from all the uphill walking and they had gutted the city, at least for today. There came a point in sightseeing when you needed to stop before it all merged into one uniform blur. She had friends in New York who would rubberneck till they dropped, while retaining no lasting impression of what they had seen. Along with the millions of Japanese tourists who seemed only ever to venture forth in flocks and saw life entirely through their viewfinders. Snaps and guidebooks served their purpose, but it was also essential to savour firsthand the essence of a place and its inhabitants. The beauty of staying so close to Siena was that they could easily return at any time.

As they slowly strolled back to where they had parked the car, down a narrow side street they chanced upon a truly magical shoe shop. The window was lined with rows of pretty sandals, all in the finest Italian leather, at stupendously reasonable prices. They stood like kids in front of a sweet shop, noses practically pressed against the glass.

'Italian footwear is the best in the world,' said Anna, the shopping connoisseur. Hopefully she tried rattling the door but the shop was now closed until half past four.

'It's siesta time,' Genevieve reminded her. As big-city dwellers, all three of them, they had several times been caught out this way.

'Ah well,' said Anna, philosophically. 'What better excuse could we possibly need for coming back very soon?'

★ ★ ★

'Do you mind if we take in San Gimignano on the way back?' It would mean quite a lengthy detour but Genevieve, avidly studying the map, could see an alternative route that should easily work. And since they were not in any special hurry, sitting comfortably in the air-conditioned car would be a welcome alternative to all that strenuous sightseeing. By the time they got there, they would have their second wind and be ready for another bout of exertion. Neither of the others had any objection, so off they set, this time with Candy at the wheel and Genevieve reading out directions.

114

San Gimignano, just east of Volterra, was one of the most famous Tuscan hill towns. Significant for its dramatic skyline, it was a place that Genevieve was particularly keen to see. According to the book she was reading, recommended by Raffaele, it had reached its zenith in the Middle Ages before the Black Death had decimated its population and power had reverted to Florence. Since knowing Raffaele and listening to his stories, she had become engrossed in the history of the region. He had a way of describing things that made her want to know more. And unlike Hector, who dismissed her as an air-head, the Italian went to considerable pains explaining his heritage to her. Not just in a sketchy way but with all the passion of a natural born teacher. This would be an excellent way of showing her appreciation. A little encouragement could surely do no harm; she was growing increasingly attracted by this warm and eloquent man.

Anna, unaware of all this, gratefully grabbed the chance for a snooze in the car. She had lately been working such long, intense hours that by this time of the day she was pretty much knackered. Softly, as the other two talked, she drifted off and began quietly to snore.

'She's back on the serious narcotics again,' giggled Candy, recalling their opium joke.

'Let her sleep,' said Genevieve. 'She does work awfully hard. And obviously needed this break.' No-one who hadn't been there on the spot could start to comprehend what she must have been through. And, unlike either of the other two,

115

Anna rarely discussed her emotions, preferring to keep her nightmares bottled up.

'It's useless trying to cosset her,' said Candy, who understood from personal experience just how complex these things could be. All those hours spent with doctors and psychiatrists; small wonder that Trevor had eventually wandered off.

'Not too loud,' said the ever loyal Genevieve. Anna had been immensely good to her by talking her through her various problems. Now, if Anna would only allow her to, perhaps she could pay a small part of it back. It was good to see her finally relaxing.

She had, however, overlooked one crucial thing — the effect the spectacle of the towers of San Gimignano was likely to have on her. Anna woke abruptly as Candy pulled into the main drag, looking for a convenient parking space. The sun was starting its glorious descent and the shadows were lengthening dramatically so that the initial impact of what she saw before her hit her like a sudden blow to the heart. She stumbled unsteadily out of the car and simply stood and stared.

'What is it?' asked Genevieve, alarmed and concerned, rapidly grabbing her arm. The colour had totally drained from Anna's cheeks; she looked like a person in shock.

'The towers! I never knew,' she said, appalled by this eerie echo of New York. The tall, imposing mediaeval skyscrapers were legendary in Tuscany, the main reason for the fame of the small walled town. Two, in particular, standing close together, were indeed uncannily like what

Manhattan had lost.

'Once,' explained Genevieve, thinking fast and anxious to make amends for what she had done, 'there were as many as seventy of them standing. You could, according to Raffaele's book, cross town by rooftop as easily as by road. They were built initially as fortifications but also as monuments to their owners' egos. The higher, the better, just like modern city life. Some mediaeval Donald Trump must have been getting his rocks off. Think of it, all that boiling oil just to repel your neighbours. No dropping in for a cup of sugar in those days.'

'I presume they only used extra virgin,' put in Candy to lighten the tone. 'If you're going to be boiled alive, let it be with taste.' She, too, was startled by Anna's extreme reaction, had not, up till now, entirely realised how terrible it must have been to witness the destruction at firsthand. The television coverage had been gruelling enough but how much more horrendous to have been there.

Genevieve gave Anna a spontaneous hug, deeply sorry now that they had come.

'Interestingly enough,' and she read aloud from the guidebook, 'this was also once a centre of banking and corruption.'

As well as the site of some serious Renaissance art so that, by the time they had taken it all in, Anna had regained her equanimity. It was strange, she thought, as they walked back to the car, how history could play such devilish tricks. Those forward-thinking builders from the past had contrived to

117

demonstrate that time was an endless whole with nothing really altering at all.

★ ★ ★

'I'm famished,' announced Anna when they finally headed home. They'd had nothing but snacks to eat all day and now it was very nearly seven. The sun was low and the heat reducing; a welcome breeze was stirring the sluggish air.

'Let's stop off at the trattoria,' said Genevieve, once again taking her turn at the wheel. 'We could all use a break and it's simpler than going home first.'

'Will he be open yet?' asked Candy, but Raffaele's establishment very seldom closed.

'My treat,' said Anna, as they bounced into the forecourt. She felt in urgent need of some space in order to download the day's experiences. In both Siena and San Gimignano, history appeared to have stood still. It would take a while for her brain to adjust and her breathing to resume its natural pace.

The place looked deserted, though the door was, as always, open, and a dusty Land Rover stood outside, a gun tossed casually in the back. A friendly golden retriever came to greet them, head down, tail waving vigorously like a flag. Genevieve gently caressed its ears as the women looked around for some other sign of life. Inside the trattoria it was dark but blessedly cooler. Raffaele was stationed at the otherwise empty bar, drinking with a stranger he didn't introduce.

'*Signore!*' he said, with apparent delight, and

led them through to a shady table outside. He brought them bread and a flagon of wine, then rapidly laid a cloth and awaited their orders. No need to take them through the house specials; they practically knew them all by heart.

'Please take your time,' he said, seeing their indecision. 'I will be waiting inside.' He retreated to the coolness of the bar and his unidentified drinking companion.

'So,' said Raffaele later, once they had given him their orders and he was busy with cutlery and plates. 'How are you ladies getting along? Is everything all right at *Casavecchia*?'

'Fabulous!' said Anna, able at last to relax. 'We are having a really great time. The villa is splendid and so well kept up. It seems such a shame that it isn't more often occupied.'

'We are on our way back from Siena,' said Genevieve. 'A truly enchanting town.' She was going to ask him for more of his stories but unusually, for once, he seemed preoccupied.

'Ought we return for the Palio, do you think? Everyone talks so much about it.'

'I would say so, without any doubt. But will you still be with us by that time?' He seemed puzzled, as though that was not what he had been told, though who he could have been talking to was a mystery.

'For the first one certainly, in July,' said Anna. 'We have the villa until the end of that month.'

'So you have been in touch with Signor Sutherland?' He buffed a knife with a spotless cloth before carefully setting it in place.

'Nope,' said Anna, 'there has not been any

119

need.' Now that she knew that her cat was all right, the last of her niggling worries had faded away. She relaxed in her chair, kicking off both her shoes, imbibing the glorious scents of the summer evening. It would take a lot to beat this place. How glad she was to be here and not in New York. But Raffaele, somewhat to her irritation, seemed very much still on their case. How many times did she have to explain? She wished he would learn to mind his own damn business.

'Tell me,' said Genevieve, adroitly changing the subject, alert to just how short Anna's fuse could be, 'that night we arrived and you showed us the way to the villa, what was the name of the family you mentioned that owns so much land around here?'

'Tolomei,' said Raffaele, suddenly brisk. 'They are among the biggest landowners in Tuscany. You may have seen their palazzo in Siena.' He busied himself shaking out their linen napkins and seemed not to want to pursue the subject at all. Anna's eye briefly caught Genevieve's. She idly wondered what he was not revealing.

The stranger had emerged from the gloom of the bar and now stood quietly listening, drinking his beer. Anna gave him a cursory glance, then took a closer look. He was tall and rangy, dressed in faded denim, his eyes obscured by reflective lenses. Raffaele continued ignoring him completely, made no attempt to introduce him or draw him into their group. A local farmer, would be Anna's guess, remembering the Land Rover and the gun. The clothes might be old yet were

120

obviously expensive. You didn't find tailoring like that in a village such as this.

'*Scusi*,' said Raffaele, 'forgive me for asking again, but how exactly do you come to be staying there?' He slung the cloth carelessly across his shoulder and planted both meaty hands on the table. His liquid eyes were serious for once, all trace of his usual flirtatiousness totally gone.

For Chrissakes, what was it with this buffoon? Inside her head, Anna was once again screaming. *Read my lips!* she wanted to tell him; maybe he wasn't very bright. Why couldn't he let the subject drop? She had told him over and over as much as she knew. Her arrangement with Sutherland had been totally straightforward; if he hadn't bothered to fill Raffaele in, that was not her problem. For all she knew, or even cared, he was merely the keeper of the keys. Like Maria, nothing more than a retainer, paid to do a specific job.

'I swapped,' she repeated, struggling to keep calm, heartily wishing he would go away and leave them to eat in peace. 'Direct with Signor Sutherland by email. In exchange,' she added, 'for my own place in New York. He wanted somewhere to stay for four months. I needed to get away.'

'And you're saying that's where he is now?' Raffaele remained unconvinced.

'As far as I know. That was the purpose of the ad. Why is it suddenly so complicated? What's your problem?'

Raffaele, muttering, went back inside for the food. As he passed, he said something fleetingly

121

to the stranger who drained his glass and followed him into the bar.

Anna, exasperated, raised her eyebrows; it was fast turning into a farce. Only she wasn't finding it amusing, not in the slightest way. First the frogs and then the mosquitoes, followed by the Hell's Angels gang. She had come all this way in search of a retreat and refused to allow irritations to rattle her now.

'Look,' she said firmly when Raffaele reappeared, arms weighted down with their order. 'Why not check it out with him direct? Here's my telephone number in New York.' She handed him the business card he had already rejected.

'No need, *signora*,' he said, mollified. 'I assure you that is quite all right. Forgive me for asking so many questions.' His eyes remained troubled but were now evasive. He wished them all *buon appetito* and finally left them alone.

The food was superb and Anna cooled down. She must not allow things to get to her in this way. She regretted having snapped at him, he was only doing his job, but she did find his constant inquisitiveness very trying.

★ ★ ★

The stranger was waiting with his dog when they walked back to their car, leaning against the Land Rover. Anna glanced at him curiously and he gave a peremptory nod, then stood and stretched and wandered over to talk. He was taller than she had realised at first, with the long easy stride of an athlete, and his skin had that

122

healthy year-round tan which spoke of a life lived largely out of doors. When at last he spoke to her she got a huge surprise; his English was fluent and he had an American accent.

'So what's all this about a house swap?' he asked, as though it were any of his business.

Anna bristled, instantly back on her guard. She'd had more than enough aggravation for one day. There was something about his nonchalant stance that got right up her nose, combined with the fact that he couldn't be bothered to smile. That was the thing about Italian men; despite the charm they so easily turned on, beneath it all they considered women inferior.

'So what's it to do with you?' she snarled, facing him, arms akimbo.

The eyes behind the mirrored lenses continued completely inscrutable. Anna had a sudden urge to knee him sharply in the groin. 'Don't patronise me,' she wanted to shriek. 'Get off my fucking case!'

Instead, she inhaled and buttoned her lip, taking deep breaths to cover her agitation. This hadn't been a good day at all; first San Gimignano, with its horrifying echoes, now this insufferable man.

'I overheard you mentioning that Sutherland was in New York.' He seemed impervious to her worsening temper.

'I guess so,' said Anna, as Genevieve unlocked the car. 'Along with his wife, so I believe. Staying in my house in midtown Manhattan.' Even without the sun it was hot; she wanted only to get home now and into the pool. 'If you're so

123

interested, ask him yourself.' And she thrust the card that Raffaele had rejected into his receptive hand.

'Thanks. I'll do that.' He slid it into his pocket. At last he did smile and his teeth were flawless; despite her fury she noticed that. He clicked to his dog then turned on his heel and abruptly strode away.

★ ★ ★

'Wowee!' said Candy with appreciation, once they were safely out of earshot. 'You know something? That guy's pretty tasty. I certainly wouldn't kick him out of bed.'

'Down, girl!' said Genevieve, sneaking another look as he calmly started his engine and drove away. A fine-looking man, that could not be denied, although sadly way out of her league. Given the choice, she still preferred Raffaele, with his gourmet's belly and earthy Italian charm. Except when he was in a mood, like tonight, when she had secretly found him slightly threatening. There was more to the man than immediately appeared. She wondered what his link was with the stranger.

Anna alone sat silent though inwardly spitting with rage. 'Bastard!' was all she eventually said though she wasn't entirely sure why.

9

'See if you can find me some basil, there's a love,' said Candy, 'and perhaps, while you're out there, some sprigs of oregano and mint.' Genevieve was hovering in the kitchen, having just completed her morning's work. Anna was still invisible upstairs but the sun was well and truly over the yardarm, no argument about that. It was definitely time for a drink. Genevieve glugged the remains of last night's bottle into Candy's eagerly proffered glass. The white was slightly less palatable than the red but drinking red at lunchtime gave them all headaches. Genevieve, wearing her schoolgirlish aquamarine robe, looked burnished and delectable from the sun. Since hanging around all these weeks with the profligate Candy, she had relaxed many of her primmer domestic habits. Candy, up earlier than usual for a change, wore minuscule shorts and a scarlet halter top which she would whip straight off the minute she got back to the pool. The local Hell's Angels, or whatever it was they were, had been back several times since that initial invasion. Anna disapproved of Candy's flagrant exhibitionism, seriously worrying that she might end up with more than she could handle on her own. But there was no stopping Candy, a dedicated sun-worshipper; for as long as it shone, she would soak up as much as she could.

Today, though, it was her turn to make lunch and she was preparing one of her lavish, imaginative spreads. Crostini were baking under the rather slow grill and she was slicing mozzarella and tomatoes, hence her need of the basil. Genevieve trotted obediently into the garden where a riot of untamed herbs grew along the borders. She came back triumphantly clutching a generous bunch and they both inhaled reverently its uniquely pervasive aroma. Basil was surely the quintessence of summer, certainly here in Italy.

'Heaven,' said Genevieve, opening a new bottle then piling up the dishes to carry outside. She had spread a colourful cloth on the garden table and carefully chosen ceramic plates that would tone. Because everything here was in such perfect taste, it lent an air of festivity to even the simplest of meals. Again she found herself wondering what its owners must be like to have created such a mellow and beautiful home. Occasionally she fantasised about some day being part of such a team. Two kindred spirits, working contentedly in tandem to create the manifestation of their dreams. She cringed even to think of that garishly patterned stair carpet and how she had put up with it all these years. No wonder Hector didn't take her seriously; as a homemaker she was a disaster.

'Better summon Anna,' said Candy. 'It is very nearly ready.' She handed over the platter of crostini, topped with ricotta and anchovies and her own home-made onion relish.

'Mmm,' said Genevieve, sneaking a taste then

126

rapturously licking her fingers. 'You really are a terrific cook, Beryl. It's a shame you waste so much natural talent working as a seamstress.'

Candy, grinning, flipped her with the dish-cloth; the sparring between them had become a regular thing. 'If I'd stayed in Watford and hadn't moved on, who can say what great things I might have achieved. Beryl's Beauty Parlour on the High Street, perhaps, instead of Macaskill Modes.' Several difficult babies instead of just the one. Talk about wrong side of the tracks; Watford, though less than an hour from central London, might have been somewhere on the moon.

It was amazing to Genevieve what Candy could achieve with just a needle and thread and a box of pins. She would half-close her eyes and study what Genevieve was wearing, then boldly attack with a sharp pair of scissors and alter it there, on the spot. Someone a little more chicken, maybe, would not have the courage to risk such desecration, but experience during the past few weeks had proved how inspired Candy was. She was working creative miracles with Genevieve's rather tired clothes, purely out of her own good heart and enjoyment of her craft. Plus, of course, her perpetually sunny nature. It would certainly take a lot to rattle Candy.

Anna came down, stretching and rubbing her neck. Too many hours hunched over a computer could do all kinds of permanent damage. But right now the book was on such a roll, she was reluctant even to break for lunch for fear of losing her narrative flow. Genevieve handed her a glass of wine.

'You can't just sit there writing all the time. Allow your brain time to recharge.' Although she, too, was doing her daily stint, Anna's determination continued to shame her.

'Where do you get your ideas from?' asked Candy, tearing basil and delicately drizzling oil.

'The same place you get your fashion designs.' Anna tapped her forehead. 'And yes, you are right, it pays to take a break.' She stretched both arms above her head and arched her spine to relax it.

'I'm dying to read it,' said Candy, leading the way.

'You'll have to wait till September,' said Anna, much pleased. Having a genuine fan around was doing her ego a power of good. Writing was such a solitary occupation, she needed occasional affirmation, especially from a declared non-reader like Candy, whose usual fare was trashy paperbacks.

They sat grouped at the end of the long ash table, surrounded by Candy's feast.

'There's enough here to feed the whole neighbourhood,' said Anna, pouring iced water from an earthenware jug.

'Eat before it gets cold,' advised Candy, handing around the crostini. It was a pleasure for her to cook grown-up food for a change. Hugo only ever fancied burgers and baked beans and other junk food. She wondered fleetingly how Trevor was coping, whether he liked the burden of full-time parenting. She grinned to herself as she tossed the arugula salad and reckoned he would be in for quite a shock. Trevor was not known for his empathy or warmth. He had a brief attention span and would quickly walk away.

'I was thinking about my kid,' she said, 'and how he is finding being alone with his dad.' She chuckled. 'They both have a deal of growing up to do. Each is accustomed to always expecting his own way.' Head-on confrontation; she was enjoying the thought. With luck, they should gain from the experience and it might make things easier at home.

'How come you never married him?' asked Genevieve. She had long been intrigued by Candy's hippy existence and wondered how she had ended up on her own. Not through lack of admirers, of that she was sure; Candy positively radiated charm.

Candy shrugged. 'It was one of those things that simply never happened. Both of us always got our timing wrong.' She wrinkled her nose and thought back through the years to the time, long ago, when she'd fleetingly cared about Trevor. He was a freelance journalist, moving around with his work, while she was at art school, waitressing at night in order to make ends meet. By the time they'd arranged to move in together and she told him about the baby, his ardour was cooling and his interests had shifted elsewhere.

'How do I know it's mine?' he'd dared to say, flicking channels to find the football. They both worked such long hours that they rarely met. It

129

had been her idea to share a place; he had never shown very much commitment.

'Who else's?' she screamed, threatening him with the chip pan, for a moment prepared to do him serious harm. Now she momentarily closed her eyes, forcing the memory back into her subconscious. By the time Hugo was born, Trevor had been long gone. She had not heard from him again for several years. That was the last time she had shown serious emotion except where her baby was concerned. Ever since, all her love had been channelled towards the kid; no-one was ever going to hurt her so much again.

'Did you ever regret it?'

'Not for a second.' About that Candy was adamant. Yes, there had been a few hard times when she had worried about paying her bills, but somehow, through courage and sleight of hand, she had usually managed to stay afloat. And, despite the problems of Hugo's slight affliction, she had loved every single moment of bringing him up.

'Didn't you ever want children, Anna?' said Candy. It was something she never talked about.

Anna shook her head. 'Guess I've just been fortunate,' she said. 'And never been troubled by my biological clock.' So many women of about her age went into a last-minute panic, suddenly feeling their chances slip away, prepared to make terrible compromises in order to reproduce. Anna had never experienced that, perhaps because of her happy family background. She had grown up knowing herself totally loved, even

130

though somewhat isolated.

'Also, at your age,' she said to Candy, 'I had more important things to do with my time.'

'More important than sex? Surely not.'

Anna laughed. 'Of course not, idiot. But I wanted a proper career.' She had worked as a journalist, like Candy's ex, but unlike him had really done very well. Freelance commissions from major magazines until, one day when she felt herself ready, she had bravely settled down to write her first book. It was a solitary life but one she had never regretted. Creating whole scenarios brought its own reward. She certainly hadn't felt the lack of tiny pattering feet.

'But, then, there are always your books,' said Candy kindly. 'You have done your bit for posterity. Your name is bound to live on.'

Anna flicked an olive at her. 'Thanks a bunch,' she said.

'Who knows, one day your prince may still turn up,' said Genevieve romantically. 'I wonder how you will feel about things then.'

Anna shrugged. She still had dreams, the main one of which had been that elegant house. 'I'll be sure to let you know when it happens,' she said. 'Though it would have to be a really special guy to come between me and my vocation.'

'And you always have your cat,' added Candy with a smirk. 'All that is really missing is a rocking chair.'

'And a shawl. I suppose I could knit one,' said Anna, entering into the spirit. She loved these two women, was grateful they had come. Could not imagine settling back to total isolation.

'I wouldn't want to be without my boys,' said Genevieve, without much conviction. Everyone laughed. The conversation was beginning to get serious; time to lighten up. Candy disappeared back into the kitchen and returned with a massive water melon which she proceeded to hack into wedges. The fruit and vegetables here were stupendous; it would be hard to readjust to bland supermarket fare.

They lolled around and drank more wine, replete yet still reluctant to clear up. Anna kept nibbling at the leftover *crostini* and Candy urged her to finish the lot as she didn't want to have to chuck them out.

'You always make too much,' complained Anna. 'It is turning me into a glutton.' But she grabbed another slice of the thickly encrusted toast and ate it with keen relish.

The sound of a distant engine caught their attention and all three fell silent, listening to its approach.

'Sounds like somebody coming here.' But who in the world could it be? It was slightly too early for the harvesting of olives and most of the local farmers kept well away.

'Not those bloody motorbikes again.' But this was, quite clearly, only a single engine. There was a crunching of gravel in the villa's forecourt and they all got up and went to take a look. An ancient taxi had pulled up outside and out of it was climbing a short, portly figure, wearing a ridiculous panama hat and carrying a huge striped golf umbrella. He was talking in rapid Italian to the driver who was struggling with an alarming amount of luggage.

'Aha,' he said archly as he turned and saw them watching. 'I thought I'd drop by to see how you girls are behaving.' He paid the driver with a handful of loose change and the man drove off in obvious disgust.

★　★　★

Hector Gillespie, for it was he, having pecked Genevieve awkwardly on the cheek, lunged at Anna with out-thrust hand, in the manner of a paunchy garden gnome.

'I surmise that you must be the famous one,' he said, with a cultivated Scottish burr. 'Certainly, if you can afford to rent this place.' He chuckled as though he were wit incarnate, a man exceedingly pleased with himself. Anna and Candy simply stood there speechless. Both, they found out later, loathed him on sight. He was even worse than either had expected, a caricature of all they had imagined. Genevieve, flushed with guilt, babbled incoherently. It was clear she had not been entirely honest; how else could he have known where she was staying? She must have forgiven him for Bayreuth but not had the courage to tell them. This, thought Anna, they did *not* deserve, especially since they were supposedly here to work.

Formal introductions were made and Hector carried in his bags, followed by Genevieve, clutching his hat and umbrella. She shot the others a stricken glance that met with a total brick wall. It was her mess entirely, she would have to sort it out, with the least amount of disruption to their harmony.

Hector, impervious to the prevailing froideur, continued to prattle on. 'Now don't you go worrying your pretty little heads about making me feel at home. I am perfectly willing to doss down with Gen, until you can sort out something a little more permanent.' Sharp, alarmed glances passed between all three but Hector was having a very thorough look round. He wandered into the dining-room and studied its dimensions with approval.

'Well,' he pronounced, greatly satisfied, 'there is certainly more than ample space.'

'Get rid of him!' hissed Anna behind his back. 'What the hell does he think he is doing here?' How *dare* he. She had noted, inconsequentially, that his nostril hairs were ginger, matching the jaunty little beard that looked as though it were glued on. Doubtless, beneath the baggy flannels and unflattering sage green sweatshirt, his body was covered with a similarly unappetising pelt. Also, she noticed, he walked with a slight limp.

'I can't,' wailed Genevieve, knowing him all too well; this man, so expert at caustic putdowns, possessed the fine-tuning of an ox. It wasn't as if he ever listened, and she *had* been guilty of sending that ill-judged postcard. But now that she saw him again, up close, the slight wistful feeling that occasionally assailed her had vanished without trace. Compared to Raffaele, with his warmth and charm, the pallid Hector could not even start to compete.

That night Genevieve insisted on doing the cooking. Hector was too tired, she explained, to feel like going out. He was on his way back from Bologna, where he had been covering a music festival, and thought he would surprise her by turning up unannounced. Also, she admitted, he was faddy about his food.

'I'm afraid he won't eat garlic,' she warned them, thereby instantly ruling out most of their favourite dishes.

'How can that be?' asked Candy, astonished, 'when he bangs on about being such an international foodie?'

Genevieve was suitably embarrassed. 'Something to do with his Scottish upbringing,' she said. 'His Morningside mother convinced him early on that garlic was vulgar as well as not quite nice; only for peasants and foreigners. The ones who breathe in your face on the Tube during rush hour.'

'Silly mothers raise silly children.' It endorsed everything that Anna had ever thought.

Genevieve settled conservatively for macaroni cheese and a plain green salad. Despite her irritation, which she found hard to suppress, Anna magnanimously opened some rather good wine, while Candy set the dining table with tall red candles in elegant holders to go with the linen napkins that matched exactly. By the time she had finished, the room looked enchanting. With one accord, the ladies retired and decked themselves up to the nines.

135

Not so Hector, who emerged in the same crumpled clothes, oblivious of the niceties of life. He located Sutherland's excellent sound system and worked through his collection of opera CDs, clucking derisively at his taste in recordings. Then disappeared into Genevieve's room and returned with a handful of his own.

'The man is clearly a philistine,' he sneered. 'Presumably tone deaf.' And proceeded to blast them with selections of his own which prevented any attempt at conversation.

'How could she do this to us?' groaned Anna. After all the years of such close friendship, she could not believe they had been reduced to this. Candy, equally appalled, merely shook her head. She considered saying, to cause a bit of mischief, that her personal favourite was *HMS Pinafore*, then decided the ploy was bound to misfire. The man, besides being a boor, was also a fool. And simply not worth the effort.

Hector took the head of the table, as though it were his rightful place, and lavishly poured the wine that Anna had opened. Genevieve, from habit, served him first, and he started to dig in right away, not bothering to notice that the others were still waiting. After he'd lengthily pontificated on the aria that was playing, from a little-known opera by Massenet that none of them had even heard of, he finally switched his attention to them, though not with any apparent degree of interest.

'How is the book?' he asked Anna dismissively, as though she had only ever written the one, then proceeded to ramble on over her reply which was, as it happened, monosyllabic.

'I know how it is with you ladies,' he said archly, squeezing Genevieve's knee. 'You and your wee potboilers, you take it all so seriously.' He beamed benevolently round at them, while Candy spluttered into her wine, and held out his plate to Genevieve for seconds. Anna noted, with savage satisfaction, that he had a glob of cheese sauce stuck in his beard, while Candy was trying heroically not to laugh. Eventually, as was bound to happen, Hector's eye lit upon her. He liked her daring décolleté and gilded aureole of puffball hair. Also, as Anna had already observed, she was ten years younger than they were.

'And what do you do, young lady?' he asked, wiping his face with his napkin.

Candy stared innocently back at him with wide, ingenuous blue eyes. 'I'm afraid I'm a humble dressmaker,' she said. 'I cannot compete with these two.'

'Never you mind,' said Hector benevolently, helping himself to more salad. 'There is far too much emphasis placed these days on the education of women. It is quite sufficient to be decorative, my dear.' And he leaned across and gallantly patted her arm. 'And handy with your needle, too. It should make you an excellent wife.'

Candy, for one long moment, sat transfixed, then pushed back her chair and made a dash for the kitchen. Anna joined her, on the pretext of fetching more wine, and they both stood hugging each other, shaking with mirth. If he weren't so dreadful, it would be even funnier, but how would they ever survive his presence here?

10

Hector expected a full cooked breakfast which it fell to poor Genevieve to prepare. Fruit and flakes weren't enough for him, he needed lots of protein to sustain him.

'No wonder he's so flabby,' remarked Candy. 'He really should be severely cutting down.'

'Maybe he'll have a coronary,' said Anna. Which would be an effective way of getting shot of him.

Genevieve had to abandon her daily routine of starting work at nine. Along with breakfast, he demanded the morning paper, so one of them had to fetch it each day from the village. Hector, needless to say, didn't drive, though Anna was in no position to fault him for that. It seemed he was determined to be as disruptive as he could. He would wander around in a disgusting old bathrobe, allowing glimpses of his corpulent belly, playing his awful opera CDs and noisily rustling the newspaper. Candy escaped him by staying in bed, while Anna got up even earlier in order to make herself scarce. Genevieve would stand miserably at the stove, listening to a litany of complaints. The Tuscan sausages were not up to scratch, he liked his eggs to be sunny side up and not flipped over in the pan. She was sent on a hunt for coarse-cut orange marmalade and then for English-style bread. He had also brought with him some Earl Grey tea which he noisily slurped as he lingered on over the crossword.

'Ask him when he's leaving,' prompted Anna.

'I can't,' said Candy. 'Besides, he'd never take the hint.'

It was no use relying on Genevieve who seemed to be firmly back under Hector's thumb. The more he complained, the more she visibly wilted. Gone was the new joie de vivre she had lately been displaying. He disapproved of what Candy had done to her clothes, considered the hems too short and the necklines too low. And was totally impervious to the fact she had lost so much weight or that her skin was now glowing with health.

When he'd finally finished eating, leaving Genevieve to clear up, Hector would disappear upstairs, newspaper in hand, and lock himself in the bathroom for half an hour. He would then swap bathrobe for baggy shorts and waddle up to the pool for a soak in the sun. A man that shape should never dress that way but Hector was oblivious of taste. His paunch slopped grotesquely over his belt; his legs were white and, as Anna had guessed, covered in thick sandy hair.

'Gross or what?' whispered Candy, stifling her giggles, though she did take exception to his invasion of her territory, especially since he had a rasping snore whenever he nodded off. If anything good had come from his intrusion, it was that she no longer sunbathed topless; in fact, spent less and less time around the pool but moved her recliner defiantly on to the lawn.

'Utterly vile,' was Anna's chilly pronouncement. He no longer had even the power to make her laugh.

★ ★ ★

Weary of lying alone by the pool, and suffering from a virulent case of sunburn, Hector, waiting to be fed, slipped on his disgusting bathrobe and shuffled off to explore. He had been all over the villa already, peered into everyone's rooms, tuttutting at Candy's extravagant waste of space and the tip-like chaos of the attic. Luckily he was up there on his own or they might have detected the covetous glint in his eye. This space, remote from the rest of the house, would be just the place for him to settle and get on with some work of his own. He still had the Bologna festival to write up and was also drafting a book on Berlioz. He liked it here, it was comfortable and handy. He might stay on until the women left. But being in with Genevieve, though having its obvious attractions, seemed not to be working out too well. She had been out from under his control too long; he would have to rein her in. He blamed the influence of the other two, especially Anna, whom he found unacceptably abrasive. He had never much cared for American women, who were bossy and over-assertive. He would think up some way of displacing Candy. She could do her little doodles somewhere else.

He slip-slopped down the highly polished stairs and out of the main front door which faced the chapel. Genevieve, since it was almost

141

lunchtime, was out there, harvesting herbs. Hector shuffled across the lawn and she, guilty at the way she was avoiding him, laid her cuttings in a shady corner and followed him inside. The frescoes, which she had looked at before, were, on closer scrutiny, pretty magnificent. Though they were faded and, in places, patchy it was amazing how, after all these centuries, so much still survived intact. Hector put on his reading glasses in order to study them closer. She knew from experience how pedantic he could be. With luck, he might remain in here for hours.

'Must get back to the kitchen,' she said blithely, attempting to push her way past him. 'I will call when lunch is on the table. It shouldn't be very long.'

'Look at this,' said Hector, ignoring her, pointing at a faded coat of arms. It was blue and silver, in the shape of a shield, sporting three crescent moons. He peered even closer, standing up on his toes, attempting to decipher the ancient Latin. '*Mutare vel timere sperno*. It would appear,' he said grandly, 'that whoever once lived here was connected with nobility.' Some sort of dwelling had been continuously on this land right back to the Middle Ages; Hector was impressed. He possessed a strong streak of rampant snobbery that extended even beyond his musical tastes.

Over lunch he raised the subject again and all of them mentally groaned. It seemed they could never sit down to eat without a thundering lecture from this bore. If only he'd just shut up and enjoy the view and be grateful for the food they put before him. But, despite his gastro-nomic claims, he never seemed even to notice what he was eating but rattled on, often with his mouth full, until he had driven them away.

'Let him take his turn in the kitchen,' Candy had often suggested. But Anna, not liking the thought, resisted; so far it was the only room he hadn't yet invaded. The longer they could repel him, the better. That was her point of view. Besides, she would bet five bucks on Hector not even knowing how to boil an egg. She had encountered men like him before and saw right through his façade.

'How's your Latin?' he asked them now, eager to score further points with his erudition.

'We don't do Latin in the States,' said Anna.

'And I left school at fifteen,' added Candy.

Everyone looked hopefully at Genevieve, who just shrugged. 'We'll check it out with Raffaele,' she said, glad to be able to bring him into the conversation. 'He's lived here all his life and is bound to know. He owns the trattoria in Montisi,' she explained, 'and is also, in a way, our landlord. We can ask him next time we go there.'

Hector, in his usual boorish way, ignored her and, without pausing, continued to hold forth. Roughly translated, the motto read: *I scorn to change or to fear.* Whoever's it was sounded suitably autocratic. He very much liked the idea of such grandeur, would seek out someone with appropriate education, perhaps the lord of the manor himself. Which was not at all a bad idea; he brightened. It was simply a question of tracking the fellow down.

143

After a few more days of lolling around, Hector began to revive. Having recovered from the excesses of Bologna, his passion for Italy, combined with his natural greed, made him start to feel restless confined to the villa. By that time normal channels of conversation had almost completely dried up; if any of the three of them ever ventured to voice an opinion, Hector always expected the final word. Anna and Candy were heartily relieved when he announced a sudden need for an excursion. Though, it transpired, for one evening only; he was bent on showing Genevieve a good time. At first he suggested that she drive him to Siena but that, as Candy pointed out, meant she wouldn't be able to drink. Hector scowled. He hated having his wishes thwarted yet was also reluctant to appear a spoilsport in front of the other two women. He had a high opinion of his own eligible status and had Candy down as a possible stand-in next time a gap occurred in his social calendar.

'Why not go to the local trattoria?' suggested Candy wickedly. Genevieve looked appalled but couldn't deny him. At least that way they would get to talk to Raffaele and Hector could ask him first-hand about the fresco.

Hector looked deeply condescending. 'I very much doubt that there's anything in this backwater to match my usual culinary requirements. You must remember, I'm a widely travelled man.'

Genevieve, unguardedly, leapt to Raffaele's

defence. 'I think you'll find that you're wrong,' she said, realising just too late what she had done. Hector, who always knew better about everything, cocked one quizzical ginger eyebrow at her.

'And is it recognised by Michelin?' he asked — to him, the ultimate test. Genevieve had to admit that she'd no idea.

'But the food is brilliant,' she said, her colour rising. Hector's silent glance spoke volumes; he simply left the room.

'Don't let him get away with it,' Candy exploded the moment they heard his footsteps up the stairs. 'Most of the time he treats you like a servant. Who the fuck does he think he is? And why on earth do you let him get away with it?'

'I'm sorry about him,' said Genevieve helplessly. 'I didn't for one moment think he would come.' It had been a whim, a private revenge; she wasn't accustomed to having such tactics work.

'Well, now he *is* here,' said Candy firmly, 'do what you can to make the best of it. See that he spends some money on you for a change.' Not just money, time as well. Instead of treating her like an unpaid skivvy; it was disgraceful how much he took for granted. So far he'd shown no intention at all of even contributing to his keep. And when it came to things like clearing the dishes, Hector was never to be found.

★   ★   ★

'You're quite sure you won't come with us?' asked Genevieve hopefully as Hector settled himself in the car without bothering to open her door. Tonight he had made a bit of an effort and was wearing a tan jacket with a clean white shirt and a pink and green striped bow tie.

'Garrick Club, you know,' he had explained while he was dressing but Genevieve couldn't care less. And nor, she was certain, would the others either. Such petty snobbery was terribly out of date.

Anna and Candy, standing meekly in the driveway, mutely shook their heads. They could barely contain their muffled delight that Hector, after all these days, was actually leaving the premises. They had all sorts of secret indulgences lined up, starting with a leisurely swim and followed by Candy putting highlights in Anna's hair. After which they planned to watch *Terms of Endearment*, Candy's favourite ever movie, which she'd serendipitously discovered upstairs in Sutherland's eclectic video collection. And Anna had elected to cook tonight, in celebration of their brief reprieve. Neither could wait to see him go and get on with the business of the evening.

'I don't remember ever disliking anyone quite so much,' Anna said as they cheerfully waved them off.

'Poor Genevieve,' said Candy, suddenly doubtful. 'Maybe we should have gone with them after all. He treats her so badly all the time, constantly putting her down.'

'By this time in her life,' said Anna, 'she

146

should be able to stand on her own two feet.' Forget what Hector might think of the trattoria, she wondered what Raffaele was likely to make of him. Despite his occasional moments of detachment and the cautious suspicion she had sometimes seen in his eyes, Anna, the professional observer, watched with absolute fascination Raffaele's growing interest in Genevieve. Her own life might be sterile at the moment but Anna had known passion in the past. She'd put money on it; she recognised the signs. If only Genevieve weren't so bashful.

'I confess I'd love to be a fly on the wall,' she said. 'To witness the clash of the Titans.'

'Godzilla versus King Kong, are you suggesting?'

'I was thinking more Godzilla versus Mighty Mouse.'

★   ★   ★

Genevieve was looking particularly fetching tonight. Raffaele was hurrying forward to greet her when he took in the hovering presence of Hector and practically stopped in his tracks. What was this? A new development he had not expected. All his Italian virility took charge even though he remembered that he still didn't totally trust her. The orders he was getting from elsewhere particularly warned him to be wary of these women. Something very definitely was wrong. Until it was sorted he had to tread very carefully.

'*Signora*,' he said, regaining his composure

147

and courteously including Hector in his bow.

Hector, eschewing Genevieve's regular table, was looking around for something more remote. 'Far too noisy,' he loudly announced, ignoring Raffaele totally as he stalked away to the furthest, darkest corner. Genevieve, embarrassed, gave Raffaele an apologetic shrug but had no other choice than to meekly follow her escort. The restaurant was three quarters full, with the satisfied hum of contented diners quietly enjoying their food. Several of them, already known to her, greeted her with affection and Genevieve acknowledged each one with a wave and a smile. Hector's expression grew ominously darker. How dare this woman possess a life of her own.

Raffaele, after a suitable pause, presented himself at their table, pad in hand, to run through the evening's specials. This was the part that Genevieve usually liked best, savouring his mellifluous Italian that made the food sound even more enticing than it was.

'Tonight, *signor e signora*,' he began, allowing the words to roll sinuously over his tongue, 'we have seafood bruschetta made with mussels and clams, ricotta and thyme tortelloni with fava bean sauce, and grilled pork ribs, Florentine style.' He beamed at them both expectantly, pencil poised. 'And then, of course,' and his tone grew more seductive, 'we have today's *sopra tutto*, spaghettini with lobster sauce.' He kissed his fingertips expressively and rolled his eyes heavenwards:

Genevieve sparkled, her absolute favourite, but

Hector appeared to be only half-listening, his eyes still glued to the printed menu, deaf to the eloquent recital.

'I will certainly have that,' said Genevieve, salivating at the thought. 'With an onion and tomato salad, please. On the side.'

Raffaele, signifying his approval, rapidly scribbled it down. Then turned expectantly to this man he had not met before who seemed to be taking the menu extremely seriously.

'Is the pasta nice and fresh?' asked Hector, ignoring the fact that Raffaele owned the restaurant and treating him condescendingly, like a waiter.

Raffaele stared, for a moment nonplussed. 'For this dish the pasta is factor-made,' he explained, deferential though less so. 'As is the custom in this part of the world.' Normally he might have swivelled his eyes; out of deference to Genevieve, he resisted.

'Bollocks,' said Hector rudely, 'it is simply cutting corners. Everyone knows that pasta should be freshly made.'

'Actually, Hector,' ventured Genevieve timidly, wondering as she said it how she dared, 'in Italy, for certain dishes, dried pasta is the norm.' The fashionable fresh stuff, once so popular in trendy delis, had now virtually vanished from the shelves. The famous Italian chefs stuck to their guns; factory-made was what they recommended for many of their most popular classical dishes. Especially seafood, where the grainier texture liaised more successfully with the sauce.

But Hector was having none of it. He hated

not to be right. 'And what about the carp?' he asked with suitably heavy sarcasm. 'Is *that* fresh?'

'*Si, signor*,' said Raffaele, deadpan. Genevieve secretly squirmed. At that precise moment she'd have given anything at all to be able to spirit herself home.

Hector demanded to see the wine list, ignoring her protestations that the house wine was really good. She had, after all, sampled it often enough, though wasn't inclined to admit that to him. He was always implying that she drank too much, though his own intake could hardly be called abstemious. He hummed and hawed and flicked through the many pages, then once again summoned Raffaele to the table.

'Don't you have anything French?' he enquired. Raffaele looked totally disbelieving while Genevieve wanted to bury her face in her hands.

'*Signor*, the wines of Toscana are among the finest in the world.' A glint of dislike was now evident in Raffaele's eye, though Hector was far too self-involved to observe it. He continued to ponder aloud and change his mind then, just as Genevieve was beginning to despair, eventually settled on a bottle of chianti classico. Genevieve was quick enough to glimpse the disdain on Raffaele's face.

* * *

The evening was a nightmare from start to finish. Even after the food had been served, Hector continued critical and allowed his opinions to resonate round the room. The tortelloni were too salty, the fish was too bland, while the granita was over-chilled and hurt his teeth. Genevieve kept sneaking glances at her watch, wondering what the others were doing now. She saw them stretched out on the vast upstairs couch, glasses in hand, engrossed in that marvellous film. But anything had to be better than this. Hector, as he guzzled his food, was pontificating about Italy, flecks of fish adhering to his beard. She hated him with a sudden intensity for his rudeness towards Raffaele. Talk about letting the side down; she could have cried. Eventually, to her immense relief, Hector called loudly for the bill and Genevieve made a dive for the washroom in order not to witness him settling up. She had meant to ask Raffaele about the frescoes but that would have to keep for another day. If, that was, she ever dared come here again. Right now she wasn't sure.

They drove home in silence. The roads were deserted and in just a few minutes they were back at the villa's gates. Lights were on all over the house; Genevieve's spirits leaped: the others were still up.

'We're home,' she called, as they entered through the kitchen where everything was clean and tidied up, with a tantalising lingering whiff of garlic in the air. She climbed the stairs rapidly, hoping to shake off Hector, and found them, as she'd expected, on the couch. The television, however, wasn't on; they were just sitting, quietly talking. At Genevieve's entrance, both looked up and she saw, with a sudden jolt of shock, that

151

Candy had been crying.

'What's up?' she asked, in genuine alarm, crouching on the floor in front of her and taking hold of her hands. Candy's nose was red and raw and the whites of her eyes bright pink. Beside her there was a scrunched-up letter, apparently the cause of her distress. Genevieve, receiving no answer, looked at Anna who, with an almost imperceptible head shake, warned her to tread very carefully. But Genevieve cared too much to hold back; over these past few weeks of close proximity, her feelings for her friend had immeasurably deepened. Candy had always been a fun companion; feisty, optimistic and brave. But now she was something much closer than that, as dear to her as a sister. Genevieve couldn't bear to see her cry. It was frighteningly out of character.

'I'll tell you tomorrow,' mouthed Anna so Genevieve, taking the hint, left the room.

'What seems to be the problem with the poor wee lassie?' asked Hector, hovering behind her in his crass, overbearing way, set to stick his nose in and undoubtedly cause Candy more distress.

'Nothing that need concern you. She's just upset.' Genevieve had become uneasily aware of his growing interest in Candy. Here he went again, up to his same old tricks. When would she ever learn? She pushed past him quite roughly, in a flash of sudden anger, almost making him lose his balance and fall.

'And now I'm off to bed,' she announced. 'Goodnight:'

152

11

The letter had arrived by a roundabout route, brought by a postman on an ancient rusty bike all the way from Sinalunga. Candy, laughing gustily as Anna simmered the sauce, had carelessly ripped it open, registering only that it came from Hugo's father. Doubtless one of his smug reports, to let her know how well they were getting along. Slowly the laughter drained away, along with all the colour from her face. Anna, distracted by her sudden silence, glanced up curiously from the stove.

'Candy, what is it?' she asked in alarm, instinctively turning down the flame.

Candy said nothing, was reading the letter again, then silently handed it to Anna. When she spoke, she was choking with so much emotion that she almost couldn't get the words out. 'The bastard's getting married,' she said. 'To someone he's only just met.'

Anna, scanning the letter, was perplexed. She had distinctly had the impression from Candy that the whole thing was way in the past. 'Is that such a bad thing?' she enquired. 'I thought you no longer cared.'

'You are missing the point. Read on,' said Candy wildly, raking fraught fingers through her puffball hair. 'This woman, whoever she is, is seven years older. And yes, you've got it, keen to start a family right away.' She began to cry, in

153

great gulping sobs, and Anna put an arm around her shoulders. 'They want to adopt Hugo formally and give him what Trevor terms 'a stable home'. The nerve of the man after all these years. When he hasn't even kept up his child support payments.'

'Hold it right there,' said Anna. 'Calm down. It surely can't be that bad.' No-one could take a child away from its mother, not one as meticulously caring as Candy. She went on reading. The sinister part, the bit that had got to Candy, was that the bride-to-be was a solicitor, specialising in family law. Candy had been solely responsible all these years for raising the child on her own but the cold fact was that a father also had rights. And this woman would know all the legal loopholes. No wonder the bastard had been so compliant when she'd swallowed her pride and asked him to look after Hugo. He had never shown very much interest before; he must have had this up his sleeve all the time.

'I've got to go home.'

Anna poured them each a glass of wine and they sat down at the table. 'There's no point in doing anything hasty,' she said, 'until you know the full facts of the situation.' A married couple might feasibly score points over a single parent but she still refused to believe that they could win. Not when the child was as young as Hugo and had special needs. Perhaps they could reach some sort of a compromise, starting with a calm discussion between the three of them. Paige would know, was at the very least the sort of person that Candy should talk to, assuming that

British and American law were more or less the same — she would know this too. Later perhaps she would call New York. Email was fine for gossip and chat but this looked too serious for that. With a sudden pang, Anna realised how much she missed her, her wise and capable best friend.

'I'd best start packing. I hope I can get on a flight.'

'Slow down,' said Anna practically. 'You don't even know where they are.' Which was true; the letter had taken longer than usual to reach her. Trevor and Hugo were off on a fishing trip, somewhere unidentified in the heart of Wales. 'Why go home and be miserable on your own when nothing can happen, in any case, till they return?'

It made much more sense for Candy to remain here, with two supportive companions to prop her up. Also Anna knew in her heart that, selfish or not, she relied on Candy to prevent her from doing Hector serious harm.

★　★　★

'What we all need,' said Anna next morning, when Genevieve had at last succeeded in getting Candy to see sense and stay, 'is a little retail therapy. We deserve it.'

They were sitting out in the garden, drinking coffee. Hector was still incarcerated upstairs. Anna, for once, had taken time off from her writing in order to help cheer up Candy but Genevieve, who had been through it all herself,

155

was able to add hard facts to Anna's cool logic. When her husband had left her for another woman it had all been cut and dried. Apart from the shock — she had not seen it coming — things had been sorted out with remarkable ease. He paid the school fees; she kept the house. They hadn't ever needed to talk to lawyers. But that was another illustration of Genevieve's overly submissive nature; she quickly saw all kinds of good reasons for blaming it on herself. If she had only been a better wife, if she hadn't let herself go; even perhaps if her novels had been more successful. And if she didn't spend her days at the kitchen table, writing books that were rarely ever reviewed, then David might not have lost interest so soon and looked for someone he could be more proud of.

Candy began to laugh. She loved it when Genevieve started to put herself down, she did it even more effectively than Hector. 'Yeah, yeah,' she said, the old twinkle back in her eye. 'And if you hadn't needed to put food on the table and insisted he go out to work, he would never have met her in the first place. Right?'

'Let's go to Siena,' said Anna suddenly, remembering the shoes. Hector had been banging on all week about wanting to see the sights. Although it would be an almighty pain to have to take him with them, they were going to have to endure it some time and could frighten him off from tagging along by saying they were going there purely to shop. 'We can drop him off at the Duomo,' she said, 'and let him do his own thing.'

They were all agreed. No time like the present; each felt the need of a change of scene. When Hector finally emerged, on his way to the pool, they informed him of the Siena plan but said he could stay at home if he preferred. Naturally he wasn't going to do that.

'You might have told me before I got dressed,' he grumbled, but went back inside to put on street clothes and shoes.

* * *

'Do you remember where it was?' asked Genevieve, as she parked.

Anna had a rough idea; her homing instinct was as acute as ever and it was definitely somewhere in this neighbourhood. They said their goodbyes to Hector and watched him walk away, guidebook and newspaper under one arm, reading glasses strung round his neck on a cord. He had left the golf umbrella behind but still wore the foolish hat. Anna and Candy had given up pretending; what a ridiculous figure he was. They both had a hearty laugh at his expense and Genevieve, somewhat guiltily, joined in too. It was still living purgatory having him in her room; she was thinking of suggesting that he move upstairs to the nursery because of his ceaseless snoring.

'How on earth have you managed to stick him all this time?' asked Candy, genuinely baffled. 'The man's a buffoon, not remotely in your league. I can't see how you could possibly ever have fancied him.'

157

Genevieve gave her a watery smile. 'I suppose I was just grateful for his attention.' Not that he'd given her much of that, at least from what she had told them.

'If we're lucky, we'll manage to lose him at lunchtime too,' said Anna. They had simply said they would doubtless see him around. Siena was a very small town, most of it grouped round the Campo. Otherwise he knew where the car was parked and that they planned to leave no later than four. There was plenty to keep him occupied with all those galleries and churches. It was a glorious day and Candy was feeling much brighter. Ideal conditions, in fact, for a bit of a binge.

★　★　★

They located the shop without difficulty and this time found it open. They stood and drooled, as they had before, then wasted no more time and went inside. Anna could suddenly feel her money burning a hole in her pocket; in the window she saw at least three pairs of sandals she felt she could not live without. It was months now since she had last been power-shopping; the events of September had totally killed the urge. But now she found the old craving creeping back and could not wait to get spending. It would still be summer in New York when she got home and, by that time, she would be up against her deadline. She might as well stockpile now while she had the time. Besides, these sandals were quite unbelievably cheap.

158

'Can you believe it?' she said, wriggling her toes, admiring the gilded thongs with their intricate roses. 'Less than fifty dollars a pair. I think maybe I will take them in all colours.'

Genevieve laughed, enjoying her extravagance. Sometimes she felt that her friend had too little fun. And on Anna's tanned feet, with their immaculate toenails, the sandals certainly did look delicious. 'Go on,' she urged. 'What have you got to lose? It is, after all, only money.' And Anna, at this point, was particularly flush though no-one could deny that she had earned it.

They had them also in silver and pink, again both in Anna's size. She tried them on and paraded around and the smiling saleswoman, comfortably overweight, applauded and encouraged her.

'*Bellissima, signora!*'

'What do you think? Should I take all three pairs?' The others chorused their approval. 'At least they should see me through to Labour Day.'

She handed over her Visa card and the woman took it away. They had lived so frugally since arriving in this country, it would scarcely make a dent in her credit balance. She wondered what other treasures she might find, now that she had revived her retail habit. She had bought a pair of the most exquisitely cut pants last time she was in Rome. It was possible that in Siena, too, she might find a similar bargain. Certainly it was worth a look; at least they had plenty of time.

'Leather's the thing,' said Genevieve knowledgeably. 'Just as it is in Florence. Also, fancy stationery.'

'And yummy *panforte*,' said Candy with relish; they had passed a shop window packed full of it. 'Rich and sinful, like Christmas cake. Divine!' She would take some home for Hugo, she decided, which immediately brought on a mini attack of the blues. Poor little mite — but the others had helped her to rally. No-one was ever going to take him away; she would make certain of that.

'*Signora*.' After a lengthy pause, the woman had returned. She still had Anna's card in her hand and a flicker of discomfort on her face. There was, she explained in her halting English, a small problem. Visa were refusing to accept the card, saying that it was over its credit limit.

'Not possible,' said Anna impatiently. This card she kept solely for foreign travel and she knew for a fact it was fully paid up. 'It has to be some mix-up at this end.' Italy was hardly known for its efficiency. 'Please try again.'

The woman obligingly went back to the phone but with the same result. When Anna spoke direct to Visa, they politely refused to honour her purchase because she had insufficient funds.

'But it's a gold card,' she protested, 'and I pay it off every month.' She'd been raised to be meticulous about such things.

'Perhaps,' said the woman, now deeply embarrassed, 'the signora has another card she could use?'

Anna, whose mood had radically changed, shook her head. Genevieve offered to lend her the money; they could easily settle up once they got home. But Anna's enthusiasm for shopping had evaporated. Something needed fixing that could not wait.

'Come on,' she said urgently, 'let's get out of here. I must return to the villa right away and find out what the hell is going on.'

'Don't you have your cellphone?' asked Candy.

'Yes,' said Anna, 'but I don't think it will work for an overseas call. Besides, I don't have the Visa number. Let's go.'

★ ★ ★

They located Hector, still dawdling in the Duomo, and hustled him, protesting, to the car. Having finally succeeded in making it to Siena, he hugely resented being made to leave so soon, before he was even halfway round the Cathedral. It was packed, he told them, with so many important works of art, that he could happily have spent several days there, just browsing. Richard Wagner, apparently, had been so bowled over by the splendours of the Duomo that he had even thought about setting *Parsifal* there. Hector had, after all, just been in Bayreuth and was always keen to share the fruits of his knowledge.

'Look, for instance,' he said dramatically, 'at that monument over there.'

'No time,' snapped Anna, panting to be off, certainly not in the mood for one of his lectures. He could always stay on in Siena, she told him curtly, and find his own way home.

'But I've made a startling discovery,' he said,

161

strutting with self-importance. 'At least allow me to show it to you while we're here.' Fuss, fuss, fuss; where would it ever end? He knew all too well what women were like; she had probably simply forgotten to mail the cheque. The downside of this Italian jaunt was having to shepherd all three of them. 'That monument is to the Tolomei family and, guess what, it is their coat of arms that also adorns the frescoes in our chapel. Blue and silver with three crescent moons. Even the Latin motto is the same. It would appear we are living on Tolomei land,' he said, as if talking about royalty.

'We knew that already,' snapped Anna, heartily sick of his intellectual posturing. Sick, too, of his deep inherent snobbery which kept on popping up.

'According to my guidebook,' he went on, 'the family claims direct descent from the Egyptian pharaohs, the Ptolemys. Almost certainly apocryphal, I would think, but nonetheless a charming theory. Ptolemy the First, so the history books tell us, ran Egypt like a business, strictly for profit. Whereas the Italian Tolomeis have been bankers for generations. Interesting how it all fits.'

'Cleopatra,' said Candy suddenly, surprising them all. 'My kid just did her at school,' she explained. 'The dozy mare married her brother.'

'As they all were inclined to do in those days.' Hector was not yet prepared to relinquish the limelight. 'Later she moved on to Julius Caesar, immortalised by the Bard.'

'Can't we please get going,' said Anna. 'If

you'd just stop yapping and showing off.' The longer they stood here, the worse things might become. She needed to talk to Visa without further delay.

'Now, now, children,' said Genevieve placidly as they all piled into the car. But Hector was already into one of his mammoth sulks while Anna stared grimly out of the window, trying hard not to panic.

★ ★ ★

The Visa office in New York could not have been more helpful. When Anna called and explained the situation they checked her personal details first, then took a look at her account.

'No, ma'am, there's no mistake,' said the woman eventually. 'Your credit limit is twelve thousand dollars and you've over-spent by seven hundred.'

'But I haven't been using the card,' protested Anna. 'Where were these payments supposedly made?'

All of them in New York or its vicinity; the woman went through the list. Groceries and jewellery, expensive computer equipment. A two-thousand-dollar payment to Louis Vuitton. Someone had systematically cleaned her out. She was appalled.

'But I haven't even been in the States. Not for a couple of months.'

'And you still have the actual card in your possession?'

'Yes,' said Anna. 'Right here. In my hand.'

After another lengthy pause, during which Anna was put on hold, the woman returned sounding guarded and slightly less apologetic and said there was nothing further she could do.

'What the hell do you mean?' asked Anna, enraged. 'Someone has clearly stolen my credit card details. Aren't you going to put a stop to it? This is a disgrace.'

'I'm afraid it's beyond our jurisdiction. According to our records, all these purchases were made in good faith. You are saying you still have possession of the card; is it possible that another family member also has access to it?'

Anna, always quick-tempered, now lost her cool entirely. 'No!' she shouted. 'I demand that you cancel it. I will cut the damn thing up.' And not renew it, was what she meant, as if the woman would care.

The line went silent for another few minutes, then Anna was asked for her confidential password. Luckily that was something she knew; the same as the one for her computer. But the woman told her it was incorrect. She no longer had the requisite authority to cancel her own credit card.

★ ★ ★

Next Anna tried ringing her own home number but found the machine was not on. The phone just rang and rang but nobody answered. She tried it again at intervals all afternoon, then gave up and called Larry instead.

'Hi, babe!' he said, surprised to hear from her

164

again. 'How are things going over there? What's the weather like where you are? Over here it's as hot as Hades.'

Anna, never one for idle chitchat, came rapidly to the point. She explained what had happened with her credit card and that she urgently needed to contact Sutherland. 'What's going on with him?' she demanded. 'He never seems to be there.'

Larry admitted that he still hadn't met him. Maybe he was travelling a lot. 'You are surely not suggesting,' he said, 'that this has anything at all to do with him?'

'I have to consider everything,' said Anna. 'And nobody else, other than you and your team, has legal access to my house.' Which included her personal papers; she shuddered. And everything else she possessed.

Larry begged her not to get upset. These days this kind of financial scam was becoming run-of-the-mill. It didn't require any special expertise to get hold of someone's credit details and fake a duplicate card. A waiter, a salesperson, an order placed over the phone; theatre tickets, flowers mail order, magazine subscriptions. The opportunities for fraud were manifold and getting worse all the time. The internet gave out regular warnings not to divulge such information. Also, since Anna styled herself with just her initials, A.L., it opened the card up to use by either sex. Slowly her pulse returned to normal. Larry was right, she must not be paranoid. These months in paradise had dulled the edge of her usual city smarts. Why would a

165

man of such obvious prosperity feel the need to indulge in petty theft? Besides, he was highly educated, magna cum laude from Yale. Too intelligent to believe that he wouldn't get caught when he was the only real suspect.

'How's Sadie?' she asked, slowly calming down, hoping her darling was not being neglected. If he was only rarely there, then who was feeding the cat?

'Sadie's fine,' Larry reassured her. 'Sleek and healthy and obviously much-indulged. He clearly *is* there enough of the time. It is just that we never get to see him. And there's always that female sidekick I mentioned before. Girlfriend or employee, I am still not quite sure. But she seems to be doing a perfectly competent job.'

'Or wife,' prompted Anna.

'Or wife, perhaps, though somehow I really don't think so. Next time I see her, I'll be sure to ask, if only to put your mind at rest.'

All this made total sense to Anna; Sutherland was, after all, a photographer who had wanted this house swap for a definite period because of something urgent he had to do. Of course he would have a PA with him, if only to hold the fort while he was out on the job.

And the good news was that, true to his earlier promise, Larry would be gone by the end of the week.

12

Life at *Casavecchia* was more or less back to normal. Larry's reassurance did make sense. Anna now accepted entirely that she had merely been the unlucky victim of a purely random crime. Hector kept urging her to go to the police but she couldn't see, at this stage, what they could do, not while she was still in Italy. She would have to wait till she got back home and could have a face-to-face with the Visa people. And she could not return until the four months were up because of the terms of the house swap. At least she now had the security of knowing that an automatic lid had been put on her losses. Since the card was well and truly over its limit, no-one could use it until it had been paid off. She also had the comfortable awareness that her bank account was in better than usual shape, soon to be even more enhanced by a further injection of movie money. It took more than a thief to bring her down, now that she was over the initial shock. Despite the vast expenditure on the house, which seemed to go on for ever, she had never before in her life been this solvent. Her tension eased, she got on with her book which continued to glide along.

Candy, through Anna's intervention, was also in much improved spirits. The wonderful Paige, who invariably came up trumps, had produced a relevant legal expert who had succeeded in putting her mind at rest. No court in the world, he assured her over the phone, would give custody to an absentee father who had never been anything more than just part-time. So Candy had abandoned her plan of curtailing her trip and was once more hard at work on her designs. The ones already completed were magical and inspired; the portfolio for Harvey Nichols would soon be ready.

'Just think,' said Genevieve, poring over the sketches, 'soon you'll be up there on the catwalk with the stars, rubbing shoulders with Naomi Campbell, too grand for the likes of us.'

'What are you going to spend it all on?' asked Anna.

'Food,' said Candy, 'and shoes for the kid.' She was far too canny to start counting chickens, certainly not at this early stage. The fashion business was notoriously cutthroat. She had heard too many bad stories.

Genevieve was less under Hector's thumb and rebelling. Since she had banished him from her room because of his reverberative snoring, she was able to reclaim some independence and not be quite so much at his beck and call. These days she insisted he at least fix his own breakfast, although she continued to be responsible for bringing in the food. As well as doing the clearing up; he left the kitchen in a right old mess, but they still had the wonderful Rosa to come in and clean.

'I also have a book to finish,' Genevieve reminded him. 'With a deadline every bit as pressing as Anna's.' She managed not to listen to his predictably scathing riposte; so much time spent here with just the others had toughened her up considerably.

So Hector sulked and riffled through Sutherland's music collection, sneering at his limited operatic knowledge. Anna succeeded in closing her ears but insisted he turn down the racket while she was working. She hadn't come here to be blasted by sound; a writer needed silence in which to think. The man persisted in rubbishing their host, while all the time behaving boorishly, with no consideration for anyone else. With luck, he might soon become bored and move on, though so far showed little sign of doing so. He still sprawled inelegantly out by the pool and his pasty complexion had turned an unsightly brick-red.

'I cannot imagine what you ever saw in him,' became Anna's regular refrain. 'The man is pompous and boring and obtuse.' Controlling, too, though she wasn't going to say that. Anna could be stern but was rarely unkind and Genevieve had already put up with enough.

Genevieve had, though, to concede that Anna was right. 'I guess I must have been desperate,' she admitted, remembering the time when her confidence hit rock bottom and she believed no man would ever admire her again. Her husband had dumped her for someone much younger, leaving her alone with just the kids. Hector's timing, just that once, could not have been improved on. She'd been cheered and flattered when he first came on the scene, whereas now the sound of that braying, dismissive voice had seriously started to grate. If she heard one more mention of Maria Callas, whom he always referred to reverently as '*La Divina*', she thought she might at last be tempted to tell him where to shove it.

★ ★ ★

Still, Hector was now installed in the nursery where, at least, he had a choice of beds. Despite his angling for Candy's attic, he had been firmly relocated to the floor below, in the long, narrow room that was usually the province of kids. That was clear from the four little beds, with their nursery lamps and matching candy-striped covers. And the huge walk-in closet at the end of the room in which they could stash all their toys. There were jigsaws and boardgames in piles on the shelves as well as *Winnie-the-Pooh* and *The Wind in the the Willows*. It seemed that the Sutherlands had spared on no detail. It was good to imagine this friendly house alive with the chatter of little voices.

'Presumably the Sutherlands have children of their own.' There was nothing to suggest that this wasn't so. Except that Raffaele and that chilly, blank-eyed stranger had made no mention at all of any appendages.

Hector, with a deep lack of grace, had carried his lumpy bags upstairs and spread things all over the room. Whatever bad thoughts he had about Candy, his habits were slovenly in the extreme. He left a pile of unwashed shirts and socks for Genevieve to deal with. Rosa, she knew, would have willingly done it but she saw no reason to lumber it on her. Men like Hector viewed women as facilitators, especially ones less fortunate than themselves or who simply did not happen to share a language. Except that Hector's Italian was fluent so that was really no excuse. It was like being back with her two idle sons. Genevieve now heartily regretted ever having sent that ill-judged postcard.

Now, at least, she could sleep at night and so could Candy and Anna. The motorcyclists had not returned, the frogs had gone quiet, their season presumably over. Peace ruled once more in *Casavecchia*. Even the mosquitoes left them alone.

★ ★ ★

'Look what I've found,' said Hector, bursting in on Anna. 'In a trunk at the back of the nursery cupboard.' Anna rested her wrists on the edge of the keyboard and silently prayed for forbearance. No doubt another of his snobby discoveries. Time must be hanging heavily on his hands. She glanced up at him with a questioning expression, then focused with interest on what he was clutching: a girl's straw boater with a blue and yellow ribbon, lovingly wrapped in tissue paper.

'Good heavens.' She held out her hands for it and turned it round and round. It had obviously been worn quite a lot but probably not for a while. It was hard to imagine why anyone would have kept it. Not in a country place like this where it could have no possible use. Doubtless

171

an echo from somebody's past, preserved for sentimental reasons. It might have been lying there for years. 'What else did you find?' she asked.

'Come up and see,' said Hector, leading the way.

He had hit the nursery like a mini tornado, his things were piled on all four beds. The cupboard door now stood wide open, as did the trunk he had found. Anna peered into its tidy depths, already disturbed by Hector. Neat pleated skirts and blue flannel blouses, sensible knee-length games shorts. Plus, in the corner, a battle-scarred lacrosse stick. Boarding school gear from a time machine, completely out of place in rural Tuscany.

'I found it under a pile of old curtains. I was moving things around,' he said, 'to make room for my own stuff.' It was just like him to go snooping where he shouldn't but Anna was nonetheless intrigued. The more they discovered about the Sutherland ménage, the more fascinating it became. Maybe there was a daughter too who went to school in England.

'Do they still wear that kind of uniform?' asked Genevieve when the others came up to witness Hector's find. 'I am sure it's all terribly out of date. Isn't it jeans and T-shirts these days with jogging outfits for games?'

'I wouldn't know,' said Candy, who had left her secondary modern at fifteen. 'But the workmanship is so exquisite it must have cost someone a bomb.'

'I wonder why they kept it, whoever they were.

172

You would think it would do better in a charity shop.'

Candy was now digging discreetly under the layers and came up bearing a filmy white silk dress, with beautiful hand-worked embroidery on the sleeves.

'Confirmation dress,' said Genevieve. 'I would love to know how long it's been hidden here.'

'Well, at least the moths haven't found their way inside. They are obviously better mannered than the mosquitoes.'

'Do they even have moths in Italy?'

'I can't see why not. Provided they can survive in all this heat.'

'Put it all back,' said Anna uncomfortably, feeling that they were trespassing where they shouldn't. 'And cover it carefully with the curtains again. We don't want Sutherland, when he does return, thinking we have been prying into his secrets.' She shot an accusing glance at Hector, who remained impervious. She hated the thought of any stranger fingering through her own private things, was glad she had thought of locking her bedroom door.

'I must get back to work,' she said. 'I'll catch up with you at lunch.'

★   ★   ★

'Any further thoughts?' Anna asked, as Candy hacked slices of bread.

'Only that there's a whole history here. Which, when you consider the age of the house, isn't remotely surprising.' It made Candy feel oddly

173

comfortable to know that the house had once led a normal life. Apart from the immaculate accoutrements, it did seem strangely lacking in personal things. No family photographs, no pictures, no books apart from the ones in the nursery. Not even old signs of a pet. Nothing at all to give any sort of clue as to what its owner's tastes might be, other than of the very best.

'I suppose if he's almost never here, there's no point in leaving stuff lying around.'

'Which seems such a waste of a beautiful house. He could rent it out through the tourist season and make an absolute killing.'

'Not if he's connected to the Tolomeis.' Hector was still puffed up about that. 'They are one of the most powerful families in these parts. I would love to know how close the connection is.'

'I meant to ask Raffaele,' said Genevieve, cringing to remember that terrible evening. They had kept away from the trattoria ever since; she could not bear the thought of a similar confrontation. If only Hector would get the message and leave, but he seemed to have dug himself in. He was writing his column and phoning it through without a care in the world.

'Next time we go to Siena,' he said, 'I am going to look for that palazzo.' And undoubtedly ask himself in there for tea; Hector had that sort of brazen cheek.

'Maybe they'll beg him to stay,' muttered Candy. 'How could anyone possibly resist his natural charm?'

★ ★ ★

Seated peacefully one morning at her laptop, Anna was idly hunting for a word. One of the things she liked most about the writing game was that it stretched and finely tuned the mind. Her latest indulgence was the dictionary on disk; she spent endless contented hours just browsing through it. It might slow her progress but she felt it improved her style. The reviews of each new book bore witness to that.

Something odd started happening on the screen. A block of text she had been polishing for hours suddenly, without obvious reason, disappeared. One moment she was working on it; the next, the screen went blank. Anna cursed and fumbled around, trying to figure out what she had done wrong. When typing fast, as she knew from experience, it was possible to strike the wrong key and throw everything else out of kilter. But this new laptop was state-of-the-art and therefore, supposedly, foolproof. She was careful always to save text as she went along and also to do a full backup after each session. Yet the missing paragraphs had completely vanished; were not even in the recycle bin. Maybe the batteries were running low, though the usual warning had not appeared on the screen. And, since she was mostly plugged into the mains, that shouldn't, in any case, happen.

She rapidly closed all her files and logged off, then checked that the power was on. But when she re-booted, that chunk of text was still missing, which was doubly frustrating since she'd been making such progress and knew that her morning's output had been especially good.

175

Once lost, it was hard to re-create without damaging her narrative flow. After all these years regularly using a computer, by now she ought to know what she was doing. And then, in front of her disbelieving eyes, it started to happen again. Another two pages simply melted away as though the machine possessed a will of its own, a malevolent one at that. Some outside force was manipulating her cursor. Stunned, she watched it move across the screen.

'Genevieve!' yelled Anna, now thoroughly rattled. 'Get up here fast and tell me what's going on.'

★ ★ ★

Genevieve hadn't a clue and neither had Hector, which did not, of course, stop him pontificating at length.

'As a lifelong Luddite,' he said with smug satisfaction, 'I don't trust any form of gadgetry but still dictate my column over the phone.'

Anna could do without his interference; she wished he would leave them alone and go jump in the pool. What was happening here was seriously unnerving. Were it not for the fact that they were stuck in the heart of nowhere, she would call the helpline and seek professional support. The last thing she needed was for the hard disk to crash, not at this vital late stage of the book. She had to admit that Hector did have a point, not that she would ever let him know. At least with an old-fashioned pen and paper you knew you were relatively safe. Too many writers

176

she'd heard of had lost whole chapters; one, whose computer had been nicked from his house, an entire book. If that should ever happen to her, she doubted she would be able to go on. Just the thought of having to do so much rewriting made her feel positively faint.

'I can't even print it out,' she groaned. She always travelled light, without a printer. She could usually borrow one, if ever the need arose, though presumably not in a rural backwater like this. She did at least have the backup tapes, for which she was profoundly grateful. And a rough early draft on the main computer, which she hoped was not affected by what had just happened.

'What exactly do you mean?' asked Genevieve, hovering bemusedly behind her. Despite the fact that she used a laptop herself, her grasp of computer know-how was pretty sketchy. Anna, whose knowledge of cars was nil, was nonetheless forever updating her technology. She found it fascinating, and the better it was, the more she enjoyed her daily grind.

'My two computers are networked,' she explained. 'This one and the main one in New York. Which means that, before I go anywhere, I plug them together and they synchronise. Everything there is instantly updated, including my address book and diary. It is hugely handy and saves a lot of effort. And when I get home, I repeat the process.' Computer science could occasionally be a headache but, when it all worked, definitely simplified things.

It might be worth a quick call to New York to

check with her technical advisor. The least he could do was reassure her, since his was the brain that had created the system. She clicked on her on-screen address book for his number but was unable to access it. Instead, a blocking message appeared, informing her that the address book was currently in use. 'Another user' had it open and was working with the file. Anna would just have to wait.

'I don't believe it!' she said, profoundly shocked. The nightmare was rapidly worsening. Something was happening that she did not understand and starting to scare her profoundly. She double-clicked on her other files, all with the same result. Her financial spreadsheet, her biographical details; most frightening of all, her online bank balance. They all flashed up the same stark message. Access to them was denied.

'What exactly does that mean?' asked Genevieve, way out of her depth.

'It means,' said Anna grimly, through clenched teeth, 'that somebody, using my main computer, is snooping through my files.'

Somebody in New York was what she meant. Somebody in her house.

* * *

She tried repeatedly to get through but the line continued busy. She guessed the handset was probably off the hook. Meanwhile her files remained inaccessible. Whoever was reading them was certainly taking his time. Sporadically, she also tried Larry but never with any success.

178

In New York it was still only mid-afternoon; someone by now should pick up. Although Larry was usually working on site, he ran his tight business from home, aided by his efficient wife, Phoebe, who did all the paperwork.

'Call the cops, why don't you?' again urged Hector, but what exactly did he think she was going to say? That someone to whom she had given her keys was using her home computer? A total stranger whom she had invited in and told to help himself to whatever he liked? There might still be some sort of rational explanation, though Anna was at a loss to imagine what. In frustration, she scrolled through a list of her files to remind herself what was there. A chill ran through her as she read her meticulous notes. She had annotated all her credit card details, including their separate PIN numbers, and also thrown in, as an added bonus, her Social Security number.

'Don't you have a secret password?' Even Genevieve knew that you should.

'Indeed I do,' said Anna sharply. Which only added to the mystery. Nobody but her knew what it was. Sutherland could use the computer for general purposes but supposedly not access her personal data. After a couple more agonised hours, slowly, one by one, the files became free. She ran through them rapidly, skimming their contents. Most of the details of her personal life were laid out succinctly on the screen. She had always been proud of her innate tidiness; could not have made things easier had she tried. The last one to clear was her online bank account which now she opened with fingers that positively shook. The final tranche of the movie money had been due at the beginning of the week, paid in direct by Warner Brothers according to contractual terms. She had meant to check it but somehow never had. Now she registered, with total disbelief, that her current credit balance stood at zero.

Her anguished cry brought the others running. They found her white-faced and in shock.

'I can't believe it. He has taken all my money. The bastard's cleaned me out.'

★ ★ ★

If Anna thought things could not get worse, she was wrong. After countless futile attempts to reach Larry, the phone was eventually answered by a faltering voice she barely recognised.

'Phoebe?' said Anna doubtfully. Perhaps she had got the wrong number. There was no reply, just laboured breathing, then words were spoken quietly in the background and a stranger's voice came on the line.

'Who is this please?' The voice was male though not one that Anna recognised.

'Is this the Atwood residence?'

'Who is it wants to know?'

'It's Anna Kovac. Calling from Italy. Will somebody, please, tell me what's going on?'

There followed a muffled conversation, then Phoebe took over again, her voice so distorted it was hard to make out what she said. She sounded like an old or demented person. Or one in the grip of profound and disabling shock.

'Phoebe? What's happened?' asked Anna, in sudden terror.

There was a long fraught silence until Phoebe could find the words. 'It's Larry,' she said at last. 'He's dead,' sounding as though she still could not quite believe it.

'Dead?' repeated Anna, not entirely comprehending. The line to New York was crackling and not at all clear. She could not believe she had heard correctly, it had to be a mistake.

'Dead,' repeated Phoebe, beginning to cry. 'He had an accident.'

'What sort of accident?' It made no sense. He had sounded so bouncy and full of life the last time they had spoken, only days ago.

'He fell,' said Phoebe, still quietly sobbing. 'They were taking the scaffolding down.'

The scaffolding. Oh God, her house. 'And what exactly occurred?' He couldn't be dead, not exuberant Larry, always so full of life. Anna had known him since her student days.

'Nobody knows for certain. He must have slipped. Somebody called the police.'

'Somebody in the house, you mean?'

'I don't know.' Phoebe was clearly devastated and confused; Anna really didn't like to press her. She whispered platitudes, then rang off, too stunned to take in all the implications.

'That settles it,' she announced to the others. 'Now I have to go home.' To attend the funeral, to be with Phoebe. To try to make sense of what was going on. Most of all, to track down the elusive Mr Sutherland and finally confront him face to face. For a moment she thought about calling her father; childhood habits die hard. Then remembered in time that he was now old and frail. She didn't want to risk alarming him unduly.

★ ★ ★

The drive to Pisa was balmy and delicious, with the glorious high summer foliage resplendent whichever way they looked. On a happier occasion, they would have driven that much more slowly in order to savour the scenery to the full. Sun-baked stone farmhouses with terracotta roofs; olive groves cut into steep climbing terraces and a strange golden light illuminating the trees against an undulant backdrop of misty purple. Anna was far too upset to take it in. The Tuscan scenery she had found so inspiring had suddenly entirely lost its allure. She was full of grief and all she could think about was this nagging worry that had to be resolved.

Genevieve had loaned her some cash for the trip which, with her traveller's cheques, just covered the airfare. She hadn't bothered with buying a return ticket in case she decided to stay on. Again, the writer's life was flexible. She had half-thought she might move on to Florence or Rome. In New York, she had the security of knowing she still had a separate savings account with just enough put away to see her through until she had sorted things out. Rationally, she knew that it had to be a blunder. Somebody at the bank had screwed up royally. The movie company could just be in arrears; perhaps there was a fault on Anna's phoneline. But until she knew the truth, she couldn't relax.

'Stay in touch and let us know what happens,' said Candy and Genevieve when they hugged her goodbye. Despite the drama, they were also intrigued. 'Promise you'll let us know the minute there's news.'

Candy had agreed to stay on at the villa, at least till they knew when Anna was coming back. There were six weeks of the house exchange still to go and Hugo and Trevor had not yet returned from their trip.

'We always have Hector to take care of us,' said Candy, in a clumsy attempt at levity.

But Larry was dead and Anna's money all gone. Things surely couldn't get any worse than that.

Part Two

Part Two

13

Anna arrived in New York in the late afternoon and took a yellow cab straight to East 74th Street. The evening rush hour was already in full swing and the traffic predictably snarled up. She writhed with impatience on the bumpy back seat, willing the driver to go faster. This one was taciturn and some sort of foreigner. His silence was welcome since she had no desire to talk. The city was sweltering and smelled strongly of tar and scorched rubber; the contrast with the fresh Tuscan air practically made her choke. Even within the cab, her throat felt gritty. Eventually, after what seemed like hours, he made a right into Madison Avenue and pulled up in front of her house. She was travelling light, with only a single bag, and the laptop suspended from her shoulder. Distractedly, she paid the driver, then turned to take a good look at her pride and joy.

With the scaffolding down, the building appeared pristine, better even than Anna had dared to hope. Larry's team had worked miracles. The stucco exterior had been cleaned and repainted a brilliant, luminous cream and all the long sash windows were freshly washed. The windowsills had been re-pointed and the ancient scroll mouldings restored. And the handsome oak door, which Larry had recycled from a building site in Brooklyn, provided a suitably elegant finishing touch. Despite her current preoccupations, Anna's heart swelled with satisfaction. For a work of art such as this had she slaved all these years. She ascended the short flight of steps from the sidewalk and hesitantly rang the bell. Her heart was beating unnaturally fast; she dreaded any sort of altercation. Nothing happened, so she tried again, three short buzzes in a row. At this time in the afternoon, the odds were against anyone being at home, but she would not consider trying to enter without first giving proper warning. She might be the owner but he was the approved tenant; they had an informal agreement to that effect. Again nothing happened, so Anna tried the knocker, listening to it resonate through the house. A sound that sonorous should alert even the hard of hearing, but Anna instinctively knew there was nobody there.

She put down the laptop and scrabbled for her key, then took a deep breath and inserted it into the lock. She wasn't quite sure of the correct protocol but had travelled all these miles and was too het up to care about splitting hairs over details like that. Something decidedly fishy was going on; her sole concern right now was to find out what. And if her tenant happened not to be at home, then that was hardly her fault. She owned the house and had the right. Now was not the time for niceties. Too late it occurred to her that she probably should have called Paige. Having her lawyer along would have made it more official.

She tried to twist the key again, then realised it

was resisting. She pulled it out and inspected it closely, assuming she had selected the wrong one. But this was unquestionably the key to the main front door; the other two on the ring were just for the dead bolts. Someone appeared to have changed the locks; she was pretty certain that it wouldn't have been Larry.

She shifted her attention to the right of the door and tried peering through the first-floor parlour window. Her handsome linen Roman blinds were uniformly three quarters closed, designed to conceal the interior from passers-by as well as from the searing effects of the sun. She pressed her face close to the sparkling glass and adjusted her vision to the dimness inside. Then froze with shock at what she did not see. It seemed that all the furniture had gone. Her pictures and ornaments had disappeared too, even her clock from the mantelpiece. Emotion as powerful as an electric current coursed through Anna's veins. Something unbelievable had been happening in her absence. Her instinct to return had been spot on.

She retreated rapidly back down the steps and tried the basement door, which led into the kitchen. With the same result — it was firmly locked and she did not even possess the relevant key. Those locks too had been replaced, as had the iron grilles. She stepped back further on the sidewalk to examine the upstairs windows. Everything looked in impeccable repair but the house had the slightly neglected air of having been recently abandoned. Surprisingly, in this oppressive heat, not a single window was open even a crack. And then she saw it, on the second floor, the real estate agency's board. For a second she wondered if she had come to the wrong address, even checked the number to make quite sure. Then fished out her cellphone and dialled the agency's number on the board, only to get a recorded message saying that the office was closed for the night.

So then she sat on the steps and called Paige, her fingers almost too tremulous to make the connection.

'Anna?' said the alert, familiar voice, unleashing in her a torrent of emotion. She tried to explain but could not find the words. All she could do now was helplessly blub. And she had no idea what had happened to Sadie. The thought of her pet alone and abandoned practically broke her heart.

'Grab a cab,' ordered Paige with her customary efficiency, 'and get yourself over to my office right away.'

* * *

Paige sat serenely in her leather executive chair, the sunlight pale and ethereal on her hair. Even on a day like this, not a detail was out of place. Her neat linen dress displayed not a single wrinkle, her nails were shaped to a sensible oval and immaculately and expensively French polished. A secretary appeared with two glasses of iced water and Anna collapsed on the stylish cream sofa as though punctured by a pin. Which was, in effect, more or less what had happened.

The air had been effectively knocked right out of her.

'Run it all through again slowly,' instructed Paige, handing her a box of tissues. 'When precisely was it that you first suspected anything was wrong?' Nothing had been mentioned in recent emails. There was no way Anna would not have turned to her first.

'Not really until the computer played up. Though I did find it odd that he seemed never to be there when he'd been so awfully keen to make the swap.'

'And you never got round to meeting him in person?'

Anna shook her head. 'It wasn't ever really feasible,' she explained. 'He was there and I was here. We were timed to pass in the air.' *Besides, he was a Yalie.* The words hung between them but remained unspoken. This was no time for 'I told you so's'. Anna was obviously much too shattered. And the situation did look bad. She was right to be so concerned.

'And what about the credit card fraud? Do you think that could have been part of the same scam?' It certainly looked so; too much of a coincidence. But again Anna shook her head.

'I really can't tell you. I seem to be losing my marbles. I no longer have any idea of what's going on.' And what about Sadie, what had become of her? A house, at the best of it, was bricks and mortar; an animal was supposedly for life. (*Get one from the animal shelter.* She remembered her father's advice. But she had spotted this kitten in a fancy Madison Avenue

191

shop and fallen in love on the spot. *You get what you pay for*, she had tried to explain but she knew that, in some historic way, she had radically let him down. Though Sadie had become a great favourite of his, *the only grandchild he was ever likely to have*.) Now Anna brushed away her tears and tried to put a good face on it. A cat, however precious, was only a cat. Look what those people had gone through in September.

'So why didn't you email me about the credit card fraud?' Paige was only being professional but there was just the slightest hint of hurt in her eyes.

Anna, getting it immediately, was embarrassed. 'I talked to Larry,' she told her lamely. 'And he convinced me that everything was all right.'

There was no need for Paige to say anything at all; besides, she loved Anna far too much. She insisted that she come home with her and ushered her into a cab. Charles wouldn't mind, he was hugely fond of Anna, and they had a luxurious guest suite.

'Just waiting for you,' said Paige, pulling down the blinds and turning on the air-conditioning full force. She opened a row of empty closets, equipped with dozens of padded hangers trimmed with minuscule lavender bags. There was bluebell oil on the edge of the tub and chocolates next to the bed. Anna, who normally might have made fun, embraced Paige in a long and silent hug.

'Just for one night,' she agreed reluctantly,

hating, as always, to impose, but Paige was adamant she stay for as long as it took; what else, after all, were best friends for? Or, indeed, lah-di-dah spare rooms. With luck, it would all turn out to be just some minion's colossal fuckup though, privately, her lawyer's brain was far from believing that so. For someone as smart and streetwise as Anna, this situation should never have come about. She remembered how down and depressed she had been; perhaps, for once, she had not been thinking quite straight. But now was no time for recriminations; the milk had been well and truly spilt. They had to get fast to the root of the problem and put in some speedy damage limitation before it got any further out of hand.

'What now?' asked Anna helplessly, after they had got her safely settled. Charles was home and mixing martinis; Paige had phoned for a Chinese takeaway. Anna's energy had been well and truly sapped. All she really wanted now was to sleep.

'First thing tomorrow, we're calling the real estate people and after that we will talk to Visa and the bank. In the meantime, try not to worry too much. There has to be some logical explanation.' Paige was always so gloriously upbeat. One of the many reasons that Anna loved her.

'Can't we do anything now?' asked Anna as she paced the Colliers' spacious living-room. 'Break a window? Force our way in? Call the firefighters to cut through the bars on the windows?'

'No,' said Paige practically, taking her hand.

'Anything like that would be a disaster. All you've got going for you, right now, are your rights. Break the law and you'll be in more serious trouble.'

'But it's my house.'

'I know, but it has to be proven. Just because somebody else broke the law does not automatically put you in the clear. These things, I'm afraid, have to be done in the right way. Trust me.' She laughed. 'I'm a lawyer.'

'Do you want to call your dad?' Paige asked later, once they had eaten and cleared away.

'No,' said Anna, quite positive about that. 'I really don't want to worry him at this stage.'

Paige nodded. She loved and revered the distinguished old man and saw him as often as she could. But she had noticed how, in recent months, he had started to look that much frailer. Anna had always been the pivot of his world and he was bound to feel he had somehow let her down. Best to leave him until things were properly sorted, when Anna's sudden return could be viewed as a treat.

★ ★ ★

First thing next morning, Paige rang the real estate office and got put through to the relevant person, a woman with a distinct attitude problem who seemed strangely and immediately on her guard. Yes, she agreed, the house was on the market, in fact she had already had an offer. She seemed uneasy to be talking to a lawyer and constantly on the verge of hanging up.

'Really?' said Paige, astonished. 'How can that be? Without the knowledge of the owner, Anna Kovac?'

The woman grew suddenly even more uptight. 'I'm afraid I don't know about that,' she said. 'All I can tell you is that we have the necessary authorisation.'

'May I ask who from?' Paige was at her silkiest and Anna could see she was right into her stride. Though a beautiful woman who cared much about life's luxuries, beneath the velvet glove was a fist of steel. She might equally have made it on the stage or, indeed, as a model. Instead the brilliant scholar had chosen the law. She flashed Anna an encouraging smile and slowly the burden of worry began to ebb. Paige would fix things; that was her special talent. Anna was grateful to have her taking charge.

'That is classified information,' said the woman, beginning to sound distinctly disconcerted. 'I am not empowered to tell you any more. Have you called to make an offer? I'm very busy.'

'Ask her about Sadie,' hissed Anna, before she could hang up, desperate to find out whatever she could.

'Can you tell me the whereabouts of the owner's cat?' said Paige. 'A pedigree lynx-point Siamese who was left in the care of the tenant.'

'I know nothing about a cat,' snapped the woman, who clearly could not have cared less. 'Now, if you'll excuse me, I have to go.' And rudely, without allowing Paige another word, she hung up.

'How could they sell my house without my knowledge?' Anna, after a proper night's sleep, was starting to bounce back.

'They can't. Don't worry. It will all come right in the end. But there's nothing to stop someone putting it on the market.'

'But how could they get away with it? Surely the agency should demand some proof of the vendor's identity.'

'Correctly, yes, but often they don't bother. Think about everything you have heard about real estate sharks. A bunch of shysters all competing in a very cutthroat market. What do they care about legal rights; they are in there solely to make a rapid killing. Provided you have the keys and obvious possession, it is not the business of the agency to dig deeper or to demand any proof. Not until a deal is agreed; then it becomes more tricky.'

'What would happen in the event of a sale?' Anna was trying to remember. It was only months since she had been through the process herself but so many things had intervened, her recollection was hazy.

'They need the deeds, which should be in the owner's possession. That, they are bound to find, is the stumbling block. Without them, they cannot go ahead. What,' Paige added, 'as a matter of interest, did you do with yours?'

'At first they were with the bank, as security, but then, when the movie deal went through, they let me have them back. Now I keep them safely in my study, locked inside the safe.' At which she groaned. Along with everything else,

196

that they would have removed.

'We will cross that bridge when we come to it.' Paige briskly brushed it aside. Though she tried not to show it, her heart was sinking. With every new piece of information, the situation was growing that much more complex.

Next Paige talked to the Visa office, explaining that she was Anna's lawyer. When she gave them the details of Anna's account they obligingly looked it all up. But the answer, depressingly, remained unchanged. She was way beyond her credit limit. There was nothing more at this stage they could do until she had paid it off.

'Right,' said Paige grimly, reaching for her purse. 'Now we are going to the police.'

★　★　★

The precinct was crowded and depressing. Paige and Anna had to wait their turn and were there for over an hour.

'Can't you pull rank?' muttered Anna frantically, still obsessing about the cat.

Paige shook her head. 'The very last person the cops respect is a lawyer.' Her smooth blonde hair was swept neatly into a coil. She looked as demure as a socialite at a charity lunch but inside that elegantly coiffed head existed a razor-sharp brain. She laid delicate fingers on Anna's wrist and exhorted her to stay calm. 'They have to go through the correct procedures. I am only sorry it is taking so much time.'

The duty sergeant, when it was finally their turn, looked weary and unkempt. He had obviously been working a very lengthy shift and was badly in need of a shave. When Paige started speaking, he produced a mountain of official forms which he laboriously started to fill in. The questions he asked seemed trivial in the extreme, with no apparent relevance to Anna's case. She shot Paige a glance of pure agony; this was obviously getting them nowhere and while they were stuck here, sorting out all this crap, anything could be happening to her cat. Paige conveyed to her silently that the man was simply doing his job, the questions purely routine. When they got to the details of the invasion of her computer, he raised cynical eyes and stared levelly at Anna.

'How come just anyone could access your files? Don't you use a password for security?' *Puh-lease.*

'Of course I do,' said Anna, stung. His assumption was making her mad, not to mention feel stupid. What sort of fool did he take her for? He seemed to be suggesting it was somehow her fault. This was the last thing she needed right now, some smart-ass cop poking fun at her. 'I use the name of my cat,' she said. Straightforward and easy to remember.

Theatrically, the cop covered his eyes. No doubt she listed her PIN numbers too? At Anna's sheepish nod, he groaned and sadly shook his head. 'Lady,' he told her wearily, 'you women are all the same. Name of partner, name of pet. It's virtually routine.' He looked as though he were contemplating ripping up the forms until Paige rose suddenly to her feet and imperiously took command.

'Sergeant,' she told him, 'we have wasted enough time.' They needed some kind of investigation fast. She handed him her business card and watched as the penny slowly dropped.

'Come on,' she said crisply, steering Anna towards the door. 'We have far more important things to do.'

★　★　★

Back in Paige's office the two of them took stock. It now seemed fairly pointless to wait for the police to intervene. They were overburdened and slow-witted, plus far from sympathetic. Anna said she suspected that a man like that duty sergeant resented a woman like herself, independent, educated and obviously well-heeled.

'Or I was,' she wailed, recalling her vandalised account.

Paige made an appointment to talk to Anna's bank but the manager couldn't fit her in until the following week. 'We have to do something instantly,' she said. 'Let's start by proving that the house is legally yours before they go ahead and conclude a deal. The least it will do is save time.'

'But how?' said Anna, again in despair. 'My papers were all inside. Without access, why should anyone ever believe me?' She had lived there such a very short time, she had not even got to know her neighbours. With a plummeting heart, she thought of her fancy new filing

199

cabinet; fireproof, rustproof, immaculately in order, finished in tasteful antique-looking wood to blend with the rest of the room. Only, alas, not locked; not that that would have made a difference. In any case, she assumed the house had been systematically swept clean. All her possessions would have been removed, including any relevant legal papers. If only poor Larry had not been killed. His death seemed suddenly sinister. She had tried calling Phoebe, who was still in no state to talk. All she knew was from that one brief conversation. He had apparently lost his footing and fallen. Nobody had witnessed it first-hand.

She told Paige about the woman who had been there, PA or girlfriend, Larry had not been sure. 'I am now beginning to wonder if it might have been his wife. That would make most sense, don't you agree?'

'I hadn't realised there was a wife. You never mentioned that before.' Paige had always had a shrewd suspicion that Anna rather hoped Sutherland might be single. She had been so delighted when the swap was arranged, had been perfectly willing to accept his credentials on trust. She remembered her cousin Wilbur's remark about Sutherland having no trouble with the ladies. It might be worth calling him again to find out what else he knew.

'I didn't think there was at first but now it seems to make sense. The villa is done in the most exquisite taste with all the fixtures and fittings exactly matching. Also, there are signs of children. Well, a daughter at least.' She told Paige about Hector's discovery in the nursery, out-of-date clothing that had probably been there for years.

'So you think his wife might be with him in New York? In which case, where is she now?'

'She presumably set up the sale and they've both headed for the hills.'

'So it's another case of *cherchez la femme.*' Paige became instantly thoughtful. Though it really did not advance things in any way. They still had no idea what was going on nor where the elusive Sutherland might be.

'What about the previous owners? They must have a record of the sale. After all, you paid them a load of money. They must have hung on to the papers for the IRS.'

Miserably Anna shook her head. 'I bought it, remember, from a Japanese bank.' They had used it solely for corporate entertaining and sold in a hurry when they relocated. Anna, who had happened to be in the right place at the right time with sudden huge money in her account, had been lucky enough to buy it at a snip. Certainly they must have kept legal records, but she did not know where they had gone. Back to Tokyo was all they had said. She hadn't been interested at the time.

Paige remembered the occasion only too well. At the time of the purchase they had celebrated in style, rejoicing at Anna's propitious luck. She put a supportive hand on Anna's shoulder and implored her not to lose heart. It was early days yet, they had only just started. They would unravel these problems one by one and then take appropriate action.

'Why not call your dad,' she suggested, 'and go spend an evening with him.' He'd be thrilled to see his daughter back and she need not fill him in on too much detail.

'I might just do that,' said Anna slowly. At least it would help to take her mind off things.

14

Somewhat to Anna's surprise, her father appeared not to be there. She tried him at nine and again at eleven and then at one, when he would normally be having his lunch. She was mildly concerned. It was not like him to be out for so long, certainly not a whole morning. He taught his pupils in the front parlour at home and rarely walked further than the single block to the grocery store on the corner. It could be that he had a doctor's appointment or was out playing chess with a friend. She would try him again at a later hour, though remained cautious about alarming him. He did not, she reminded herself, even know that she was back and his life, after all, was his own. Like her, he was both independent and strong-willed. She had always been thankful for that.

Once Paige and Charles had departed for work, Anna's insecurities crowded in. She felt she ought not to impose on them too long, despite their generous insistence that she should stay. She was far too fond of both of them to risk damaging the friendship, calling to mind the old adage about fish and house guests. Luckily she still had enough in her savings account to pay for a modest hotel. As soon as she got her old energy back, she would make appropriate arrangements to move on. Meanwhile, feeling the need of some loving kindness, she called her former neighbour,

Colette O'Connor. They had been through a lot together, over the years, and Colette's door was always ajar, a fact well-known throughout her neighbourhood. She was an East Side social worker with a keen sense of community and one of the warmest hearts that Anna knew.

Not today, however. As soon as she registered that it was Anna on the line, Colette's voice became distinctly guarded. There was no effusive shout of delight at her friend being home prematurely. No invitation to come straight over and catch her up on the trip. Rather, Colette sounded positively evasive as she quickly muttered something about her workload.

'I'm afraid I can't talk to you now,' she said, as coolly polite as a stranger. 'All sorts of important things have come up. I have to go.'

Stunned, Anna stared at the abruptly silent phone, then slowly replaced the handset in its cradle. Could it be that her paranoia was really taking hold or had she just been well and truly snubbed? By someone she had considered a trusted friend and part of her innermost circle. She would have called Paige but hated to disturb her. Instead, she poured herself another cup of coffee and started ringing round the rest of her friends. All of them intimates who normally would have cared; none of whom seemed any more to give a damn.

★ ★ ★

'What's going on?' she asked Paige later. 'I'm beginning to feel like Rip van Winkle, returned after twenty years, yet nobody cares.'

'You've been overstretching your brain,' said Paige, as always brisk and to the point, with little room in her soul for sentimentality. Considering how close they had always been, in character they were actually quite unalike. Anna, the dreamer; Paige, the pragmatist, yet the very best of friends since their student days. Paige had been working so hard herself, she had largely dropped out of the social scene. Though their circles of friends overlapped quite a lot, she had not been keeping up. Life for the past few months had been fraught, with little room in it for fun or entertainment.

'I am sure you are just imagining it.' Most New Yorkers, especially now, had their own preoccupations. Anna, for too long, had been living a dream. Normal people, Paige reminded her, had real jobs with regular hours. None of this lying around in the sun, awaiting inspiration from the muse.

Anna grinned. Paige always had had the knack of being able to cheer her up. On things like that were true friendships really grounded. She was doubtless being solipsistic again, writing was such a solitary occupation. Just because her own life had changed was no reason she should expect any special attention. She might have chosen to skive off for the summer but reminded herself that others had not. Soon they would start returning her calls, she was sure. They could not know what a crisis state she was in.

Anna told Paige of her plan for moving on.

She could not, with any conscience, intrude any longer. Here, on the affluent Upper West Side, was wonderful for a while but she needed a space of her very own in which to get on with her writing. Just one modest room would be quite enough; she had to be alone for her concentration. Paige protested but Anna stood firm. There was a small, slightly drab hotel near where she lived that looked both innocuous and respectable. She had often passed it and been curious to see inside. Besides, it was on Madison, close to her house.

Paige, getting it immediately, withdrew her objections. 'You can always come back to us if you get depressed.' Tomorrow she had the meeting with the bank; with luck, very soon she could solve all Anna's problems and enable her at last to return to Tuscany.

★ ★ ★

Anna tried her father again but he continued not to answer. She thought about dropping in on him, then chided herself for being over-fussy. Nothing annoyed him more than being nannied and he had raised his daughter in exactly the same mode. She would wait a few days, until things were a little calmer, and then go round and surprise him. Cautiously, she phoned Phoebe instead and received permission to drop by.

The Atwoods lived in a new apartment complex that Larry's firm had helped to construct. Phoebe opened the door with red-rimmed eyes and stood with Anna for a long emotional moment, locked in a wordless hug. Eventually Phoebe pulled away and led her into the spacious open-plan room. She offered refreshment but Anna wasn't staying; really just wanted to check that she was all right.

'I still can't believe he's gone,' said Phoebe, nervously picking at the tissue in her hand. 'Whenever the phone rings, I expect it to be him, and still find myself setting the table for two.' In just a week she had lost ten pounds and her normally glossy hair was lank and greasy. Their children were grown and away at college; Phoebe faced a bleak future on her own. 'It's just not fair,' she said, crying again. 'Everything in our lives was going so well.'

Anna awkwardly patted Phoebe's hand and wondered if she really should have come. But the nagging question refused to go away; she had to find out exactly what had happened. 'Tell me about the accident,' she said. 'That is, if you can bear to.'

Phoebe had no objection. In a way it was a relief to be able to talk. 'I keep reliving it in my mind, though actually nobody saw it, not first-hand. The men had been taking the scaffolding down and were piling it on to their truck. Larry was up on the second floor, doing his mountain goat act.' Despite her grief, a pale smile lit her eyes. 'He always was a buffoon.'

'And then he fell?'

'Just like that, without warning. All anyone heard was his cry.' His dying cry was what she meant.

Anna digested this. 'Yet someone called the police, you said?'

Phoebe nodded. 'Though they still have no idea who it could have been.' A neighbour, maybe, though none had yet come forward. Or, alternatively, somebody in the house. It had happened so quickly, all had been confusion; he was dead on arrival at the hospital. Phoebe began visibly to fade again so Anna hugged her and quickly took her leave. There were questions still that needed urgent answers but she felt she had already exceeded her welcome.

'Take care,' she said gently, giving Phoebe another hug. 'And let me know if there's anything I can do.' She felt guilty; if it hadn't been for her house, Larry would still be alive. And that, even more than anything else that had happened, hardened her determination to fight on.

★   ★   ★

She moved her few belongings into the Caledonian Hotel, where she tried to revitalise her writing schedule. But sitting all day in a gloomy, shuttered room — especially in this terrific heat — proved not to be conducive to much work. She missed the freshness and shifting light of Tuscany as well as the constant freedom to wander at will. Most she missed the company of the other two, which surprised her even more than she would have guessed. Anna, from choice, had always been a loner, but she'd grown accustomed to their lively camaraderie and constant light-hearted banter. Even Hector, in retrospect, was just a bit of a goon; were she to bump into him right now, she might even give him a hug. All things were relative, after all, and he had provided some welcome light relief. She couldn't stop thinking about Larry's horrible death and whether it had been an accident after all.

* * *

Paige had her meeting with the bank, which turned out to be less than constructive. They had no idea how the account had been cleared and the manager was reluctant to discuss the matter. All he could confirm was that the money from Warner Brothers had been paid in, then withdrawn again in slightly under a week. The signatory had been A. L. Kovac; everything had appeared to be in order. Frustrated and furious, Paige called Anna and the two of them met for an after-work drink in the bar of the Plaza Athenee. It was mid-July and the city was stifling. Anna, now accustomed to pure country air, felt almost light-headed from the heat.

At first Paige made a feeble attempt to gloss over the gravity of the situation, then had to admit she felt seriously out of her depth. She still hadn't made any progress at all and now the bank, too, was being deeply disobliging. She ran a list of points past Anna to see what she might have overlooked.

'You checked your online balance, right?'

Anna nodded. 'Yes.'

'And the last time you did that, there was money in the account?'

Another nod. 'As it happens, quite a lot.' She had been surprised but then had never been very good at keeping up to date with her current earnings, particularly since nowadays most incoming money was paid straight into the bank.

'With another tranche due shortly from Warner Brothers?'

'Due at the start of the week.'

'And now it would seem to have disappeared, though the bank confirm it was temporarily in there. Long enough for them to have registered it. Someone succeeded in siphoning it off, using your family name and initials. What they can't explain, and neither can I, is how that could have been done without your PIN number. Or, indeed, your personal passcode calculator to which nobody else but you should ever have access.'

There was a shifty pause during which Anna looked uncomfortable. She knew all too well what was coming next.

'Oh no,' said Paige, reading the expression on her face. 'Please don't tell me what I think you are going to. I don't believe it. I can't cope.' Theatrically, she thrust her head into her hands.

So Anna had to confess. 'You know how bad I have always been with figures. I find it so much simpler to stick to just one.'

'Of which you keep a note on your computer . . . '

'So that I won't forget it.'

'But what about the passcode calculator?'

asked Paige, once she had taken this in.

'I keep it safely in a drawer of my desk. Alongside my cheque-book and paying-in book. That way, I know where they are.'

'And you didn't bother to take them with you?' Or think of locking the drawer? Not that, in the circumstances, that would have made a lot of difference.

'I couldn't see any point. I travel light.'

They drank in silence. What more was there to be said? Paige, for the moment, seemed to have run out of questions. Anna was feeling exceptionally dumb, but none of this had occurred to her before. As why, indeed, should it with a totally trustworthy tenant, whose credentials she had even bothered to check? With a member of Paige's family, no less, though that was something she wasn't about to mention. There was nowhere the blame could be laid except squarely with her.

'It has got to be Sutherland,' Anna said finally, 'without the slightest shadow of a doubt. A fool I may be but not to that extent. He set it up from the start, that is obvious now. But how are we ever going to pin him down? He appears to have got away with it and now apparently vanished.'

She had taken to wandering past the house, hoping for some sign of occupation. But the real estate board was still on display, though whenever she tried calling the agency, no-one was ever available to talk. Neither, unsurprisingly, were the police coming through. Paige felt she was banging her head against a wall. The trouble was that at this time of year, most of the

211

people who mattered were out of town. She hoped it wouldn't drag on until Labour Day.

And then Anna was struck by a colossal realisation, the obvious trump card they had somehow overlooked. She had not been thinking clearly for days or else she could not have missed it. She stared at Paige with bulging eyes, then started to chuckle in a faintly manic way.

'What?' Paige was not in a mood for levity; she felt she had seriously let Anna down.

'Think. He may have pinched my house and drained my bank account but look what I have gained in return. He has not left me entirely empty-handed.'

'The villa.' Paige could have kicked herself but these were harrowing times. Like Anna, she had been scarcely sleeping for days.

'The second I get home, I am calling Montisi.' All Anna's energy came surging back. They could smash through those solid locked doors, if necessary, and likewise batter the truth out of Raffaele. Someone in that village had got to know something. They were all in it together, she'd be willing to bet.

★　★　★

'There's a guy at the bar who keeps on staring over here,' said Paige as Anna waved frantically for the bill. Anna distractedly followed her gaze to where a group of well-dressed men were standing. The one who had been showing interest was immaculately turned-out, with the dark and saturnine looks of a movie star. Aware

212

of Anna's attention, he turned away and buried himself in conversation with his friends.

'Johnny Delano!' said Anna with joy, rising impulsively and making a beeline for him. 'Where have you been hiding?' she asked, giving him a hug, and Paige, from across the room, observed his sudden apparent unease. He returned Anna's hug, however, then introduced her to the group.

'Anna Kovac, famous novelist. One of my all-time favourite people.'

Anna brought him over to meet Paige. A former neighbour, she explained. Johnny was a TV director who had lived in her previous building, though she hadn't seen him since the move, almost eight months ago.

Paige, diplomatically, had to go. 'Catch you later,' she said, giving Anna a meaningful look.

'Can we talk?' asked Anna urgently. There were things, she realised now, that she felt Johnny might know. He obligingly fetched his drink and settled into the chair vacated by Paige.

'Am I glad to see you,' said Anna, from the heart. They had been good pals for a number of years. He was slightly younger but dead attractive and, like her, highly creative. Together they made an excellent team and also shared a zany sense of humour. She realised how much she had missed him.

'Who's the blonde bombshell?' He rarely missed a trick.

'Unbelievably, my lawyer. I can't believe that your paths haven't crossed before.'

'So what's the problem?' asked Johnny,

relaxing, though his dark eyes still flickered uncomfortably.

Anna shrugged, at a loss to know where to begin, but Johnny fetched her another drink and she soon found herself pouring out her woes. It was a relief to be able to run things through and, at last, get them into perspective. She left out nothing and Johnny was transfixed; he listened until the end without interrupting.

'And you let this stranger into your house, just like that?'

Anna nodded, still feeling a fool. She no longer had anything to say in her own defence. She didn't even mention that he was at Yale.

'But what I need to find out from you,' she said, recalling the purpose of this drink, 'is what the hell is the matter with all my friends?' None of them seemed to want to know her any more, apart, of course, from Paige, who didn't count. She saw immediately she had scored a direct hit. Johnny shifted awkwardly and gazed silently into his glass. So she hadn't been paranoid at all; there really was something wrong. She patiently waited until he was ready to talk.

'Well, my darling,' he said at last, looking her straight in the eye, 'I can't pretend that we weren't all a tiny bit shocked.' Anna stared back blankly and allowed him to struggle on. She hadn't the faintest idea what he was saying. 'I mean, a deal's a deal — and well done you — but doing the dirty like that on your own father? I'm afraid we all feel that you acted somewhat shabbily. You have to admit such behaviour wasn't quite kosher.'

'What the hell are you talking about?' asked Anna, after a stunned pause. This appeared to have nothing at all to do with her current situation, though it was clear to see that Johnny was upset and that there were tougher things to follow.

'So soon after 9/11,' he continued. 'It's hardly what might be called patriotic.'

'Stop!' said Anna, frustratedly, on the point of giving him a shake. 'Tell me what you are on about. I really don't have a clue.' She sensed something even worse was coming and steeled herself to withstand another blow.

This time Johnny heard her and filled her in. Shortly after she had left for Italy, indecently soon in the opinion of her friends, her father had been moved to a retirement home and his house, the family home in which she'd been raised, immediately put up for sale.

'*What?*' screamed Anna, almost crazy with disbelief, but Johnny doggedly ploughed on. An odd time, they had all agreed, to be selling property in Tribeca, when prices had plummeted to rock bottom and nobody had any money any more. Added to which, and he was sure she would see their point, they all felt that fine old man deserved far better. Failing he might be, but not to that extent; he was still in pretty good nick for a man of his age. He surely couldn't have many more years. Could she not just have curbed her greed and waited for time to take its natural course?

For a moment Anna thought she might throw up and clamped her hand to her mouth. The horror of Johnny's story overwhelmed her. There she had been, worrying about something as trivial as money, when all the while her father had been abducted. And she hadn't known because she hadn't called him. Selfish, as ever, to the last.

'Help me!' she said feverishly, clutching at Johnny's arm, and saw in his eyes, to her immense relief, that finally someone believed her.

15

'I have to find him. Fast,' said Anna, almost inarticulate with distress. They were sitting in Colette's cheerful kitchen, with its familiar pine table and bright enamelled mugs, and Colette was stroking her hand. Thanks to Johnny's persuasive charm, her former neighbour had at last accepted her story and was making up for her recent coldness with Irish coffee and sympathy and hugs. All of which Anna needed in abundance. She, more than anything, regretted that she had not been quicker off the mark. If only she had bothered to check up on her father the day she first failed to reach him on the phone, she might have discovered a whole lot sooner what had been going on. Not that they knew very much even now. Only what Johnny had already explained, that the house, apparently, had been placed on the market and George had disappeared.

'Where did you get the story about the home?' asked Anna, still finding it hard to take in.

'One of those street kids,' said Colette. 'I happened to drop by on a Sunday night with free-range eggs from my sister's farm and found the place deserted and boarded up.' The budding ball-players had filled in the rest. They had witnessed the old man being helped into a car and were told by his female escort that he was moving into a home for his own safety.

Somewhere in upstate New York, they thought, but weren't too clear about the details.

'Shame,' one of them had said, with real regret. 'He was a great old guy and always looked out for us.'

'Naturally,' said Colette, 'I assumed that woman was you. Though now I realise I should not have jumped to any such conclusion. Especially since, at that time, you were travelling overseas. My fault, guess I just wasn't thinking too straight, it has been one hell of a year. Plus, I love you enough to confess, my judgement was clouded by anger.' George Kovac, a star in his own right, had always had his fan club. And had spent considerable time with his daughter's friends.

Tears clouded Anna's eyes again; she could still not quite believe what had happened. Who in the world could possibly wish a man like her father harm? Stealing her money and her house, she could see, was possibly fair game, part of the grabby society they now inhabited. But latching on to an unworldly old man? That was despicable beyond belief. Even forgetting his horrific past, all George had ever done was delight millions of music lovers until, when by his own perception his faculties had started to wane, he had passed on his gift to poor kids just for the love of it. George, in everyone's opinion, was a saint. Anna had always felt proud to be his daughter.

'So who was this woman?' asked Colette, splashing more Irish courage into their mugs. Someone who must have known Anna was out of the picture or else she surely would never have dared to attempt such an outrageous ploy.

'I really have no idea,' said Anna. 'Though the only person Larry reported ever seeing in my house was female. PA or girl-friend, he never found out, not as far as I know. All he said was that she was super-efficient and taking good care of the cat. That was all I needed to know. Until Sadie, too, disappeared.' The tears returned and Colette consoled her. The only good to have emerged from the whole wretched business was that Anna had regained the respect of her friends, now full of apologies, genuinely contrite, keen to do what they could to help make amends.

'Now,' said Anna, brushing away her tears, 'I am starting to think she was much more involved than that. It occurs to me that she might have been Sutherland's wife; his wife or whatever, and fellow conspirator. Doesn't that make better sense? It is obvious now I was set up from the start. And whoever did that also went after my father.'

'How would they know about your father if they didn't even know you?' It was a fair question; Colette had a point. But Anna reminded her of the rest.

'Once they had access to my home, they could find out whatever they liked.' All those neatly labelled files, the whole of her life laid bare. If only she hadn't always been so damned tidy; anally fixated again.

They sat in silence, absorbing all this. Put so bluntly, no-one could disagree.

'I doubt it was specifically aimed at your father,' said Johnny, after a while. 'More, I would think, just a predatory bid to gain possession of his house.' Effective, too; it had already been sold. They had established that fact though, once again, not the identity of the vendor. Somehow someone, while Anna was out of the country, had tricked George into signing his property rights away, then presumably kidnapped him as well. It was growing more sinister with everything they learned and Anna was seriously worried about her father's safety. Organised street crime, she had read about that, though never to this extent. The city supposedly had been cleaned up since the mayor had introduced zero tolerance, but clamping down on drug dealers was one thing, corrupt financiers quite another. These days the papers were full of cold-blooded swindles, much of it targeting the elderly and infirm. Luckily for Anna, she had good friends. Without them she did not know how she could have coped.

'First thing tomorrow, I promise you,' said Colette. 'I am going to pull rank with the social services and find out exactly what has happened to your dad.'

* * *

It took her precisely two days to locate him. During which period Anna collapsed in over-whelming anguish and remorse and spent long hours lamenting with Paige over what could have triggered this horrible sequence of events. She

220

believed neither in God nor superstition, yet something in her stars was decidedly awry. She could work very hard and replace the stolen money, not that that even mattered in the scale of things, but in no way could she ever replace her father or her family home. In some way, its loss meant more than the loss of her own. It was the house in which she had spent her happy childhood, the backcloth to her parents' solid marriage, the secure environment that, she supposed, had made her who she was.

'I have been very selfish, I see that now,' she said. 'I should never have even considered being so long away. Had I stayed in the city and kept my eye on him, none of this would have ever happened. What sort of daughter must I be and what is he thinking now, wherever he is?' Assuming that he was still alive; they all steered clear of that one.

'A good one,' said Paige firmly, who knew her better than most. 'The daughter he raised to be clever and independent and succeed in a brilliant career. You know how proud he has always been of you. He wouldn't have you any other way.' No unsuitable marriages for Anna, nor messy divorces or children that hadn't been planned. And she had always been there to keep him company; less like father and daughter, more like real friends. George Kovac had much to be thankful for. And would not, for certain, be blaming her now. Whatever.

'But we don't have any idea where he is or whether he has come to any harm.' Anna frenetically paced the room and chewed at the corner of a cuticle. Usually she was immaculately groomed but the façade was lately wearing thin. Any more time and she might crack altogether and then whoever it was would have finally won.

'Try not to worry,' said Paige, who was worrying too. 'I am confident that Colette will find him.'

Charles was mixing them more martinis, not that that helped very much. The theft of the house as well as most of Anna's assets had seemed, at the time, the worst thing ever. But now the abduction of her father too had eclipsed even that. Whoever had been responsible for such a cruel and malevolent act had to be very dangerous indeed.

And the finger pointed at one person only, the mysterious and elusive D. A. Sutherland. Nobody else was even remotely in the frame, no matter what credentials he might have produced. Anna flinched now to recall her own naïveté, tossing aside any caution because they had both been at Yale. What a sucker she had been; he would have spotted that instantly when she eagerly responded to his ad. A sitting duck, a woman on her own, one no longer in the first flush of youth. With, furthermore, a recent financial windfall that had not gone unnoticed in the press. A natural target for a ruthless conman.

'Don't beat up on yourself,' said Paige. 'There is no way you could have known. Everyone these days is turning out corrupt. The worst thing lately, so Charles was just telling me, is that even Jack Welch, everyone's business hero, now admits he had his nose in the corporate trough. The world has changed a lot in the past year. We are none of us as innocent as we were.'

'I still should have known,' said Anna stubbornly. 'And not let this happen to my dad.'

As it was, she was relying on Colette's professional contacts to find him and help to bring him safely home. Paige's natural first instinct had been to involve the police but Colette had persuaded her, at least pro tem, to hold off until she had followed less official channels. After a lifetime in the social services, she knew what they were up against. And even though the process might be lengthy, she preferred initially to deal with the devil she knew.

'You won't achieve anything,' she finally convinced Paige, 'by rattling the cages of authority. I should know after all these years of constantly fighting red tape. I promise you, I won't waste time. I would just rather start by trying to fix things my way.'

Paige initially was set to argue, then saw the flickering hope in Anna's eyes. So, against all her lawyer's killer instincts, she grudgingly conceded to Colette. They had never been particularly close but both adored Anna and put her happiness first. That and, of course, her father's wellbeing. The old man was very dear to both of them.

At the end of two days Colette called in triumph to announce he had been located in White Plains. At the Park Residential Clinic for the Elderly, where he had been living for several weeks. Within minutes the three of them were on the road, heading towards the turnpike, Paige at the wheel, Colette with the map and Anna fretting silently in the back. She feared what her father must think of her for permitting this to have happened. After all the atrocities he had lived through in his life, now it must seem that he couldn't even trust his own daughter.

The street, when they found it, was dingy and run-down, the house colonial and shabby. A pair of old armchairs with sadly sagging springs lay abandoned on the porch, surrounded by a tribe of feral cats on the lookout for a meal.

'Now, leave it to me, girls,' instructed Colette, grabbing her briefcase determinedly and heading across the street. 'There is no point trying to frighten them with the long arm of the law. Someone, undoubtedly, was merely doing their job.' Which was always the answer with government departments; the buck was for passing on.

Paige, with admirable restraint, held back, though was set to put the frighteners on people should things not go according to plan. But Colette was accustomed to this sort of situation and greeted the buttoned-up woman who answered the door as though they had known each other for years. She briefly explained that they were here to visit Mr Kovac, and, when she had convinced her that Anna was really his daughter, the woman doubtfully made an internal call. After a brief discussion with whoever answered the phone, she indicated that they should follow her. It was obvious that Colette's air of calm authority, combined with the badge she flashed, had got them inside. This was a professional who knew what she was doing. Even Paige was impressed.

'Be careful what you say to him,' the woman warned as they trudged up the stairs. 'He is inclined at times to become confused and we don't want him getting upset.' She led them up a couple of flights that stank of urine and disinfectant, then punched out a code on an electronic door which opened to admit them. 'Security,' she explained to Anna, seeing the expression on her face. 'To stop them wandering off. At this stage in their lives, I'm afraid, we have to accept that they are little more than helpless children.' It was not an image that fitted Anna's father but now was not the time for any dissent. They had found him, that was the only thing that mattered, and soon, with luck, she would be taking him home.

The corridor was narrow and harshly lit. Identical doors bore cards with handwritten names; right at the end was one that read 'G. Kovac'. A nurse in a white overall ushered them in and stood, alertly attendant, at the door. And there he was, in a tiny cramped room, in a chair jammed between the washbasin and bed, wearing striped pyjamas that Anna had never seen and an institutional-looking navy blue robe.

'Dad,' cried Anna, rushing to hug him, appalled when he instinctively recoiled. His hair needed trimming and his fingernails were dirty. He looked like a refugee. He was obviously bewildered and not at all sure where he was. When Anna gently questioned him, all he knew was that some woman from social services had turned up on his doorstep one day. She had flashed some sort of identification, then insisted on being admitted and, after a cursory inspection, had declared the house structurally unsafe. Unless he vacated it instantly, she told him, she could not be held responsible for his safety. At any moment, the roof might well cave in; it was as crucial as that. She would make arrangements to move him, she had said, to temporary accommodation that was safe. Paige flashed Anna a complicit glance. It was becoming clear how the scam had been effected. Of course he had signed the papers on the spot — the woman had insisted — and since his only kin, his daughter, was currently travelling abroad, he had docilely gone along with what she wanted. Anything for a quiet life. Which, Anna had to admit, was George to a T. He had never had any interest in possessions.

Eventually things were sorted out and the matron agreed, reluctantly, to let him go. Whatever it was that had happened had not been her fault. There had been some sort of a misunderstanding; Anna was willing to leave it at that. Colette, who obviously knew her stuff, produced the necessary paperwork and soon they were able to pack his things and leave. While Anna was helping him into his clothes, Paige produced her business card and took the matron aside. How, she wanted to know, had this situation come about? Who, exactly, had brought him in and what had been her story? Seeing that Paige was not out for an instant conviction, the woman cast her mind back.

'She said she was a lawyer, acting for the family who were abroad. He was growing forgetful, they were worried about him. It was supposed to be just an interim stay until they could make a permanent arrangement.'

'And who was to be responsible for his bills?' demanded Paige. It could not be cheap to keep him here, no matter how down-at-heel it might appear.

'Standing order with the bank,' said the woman. 'It had all been set up by proxy. There was a family trust that would soon take over, or that's what this lawyer said.'

Paige and Anna exchanged a swift glance. Gradually the pieces were slotting in.

'I don't suppose she left her card?' The matron shook her head. 'She said she'd be back in a couple of days. We never saw her again.'

'Can you remember what she looked like?' Paige was almost panting with excitement.

'Slim and dark and stylishly dressed. I remember thinking how young she was to have such a responsible job.'

'Let's get out of here,' said Anna, guiding her father to the stairs. She wished she had somewhere to take him back to other than her dismal hotel.

'Don't even give it a thought,' said Colette. 'He is coming home with me.' The least she could do for Anna, after such a treacherous breach of faith, was provide the poor man with a comfortable haven until they could sort something out. And, with luck, repossess his house. Paige was already on to that.

With her father now safe and being properly cared for, Anna at last got round to making that call. She found Genevieve and Candy on the verge of not getting on, bored and starting to be edgy with each other, suffering from incipient cabin fever. The barn of a house was all very well but unnerving now with just the two of them in it. Neither had ever quite adjusted to the night sounds of nature in the raw and it didn't help that their rooms were so far apart.

'Don't you sometimes miss Oxford Street?' Candy had asked Genevieve wistfully. Genevieve nodded. There were occasions when she could have killed for a burger or an afternoon at the sales. Even, perhaps, some bracing London rain, though she hardly dared admit it, it seemed so ungrateful.

'Hi!' said Candy, relieved to hear Anna's voice. It was after ten and they were thinking of turning in. Genevieve was still lingering on the terrace, sipping wine by starlight and watching the fireflies. The pungent aroma of genista hung heavily on the night air and there seemed to have been an invasion of crickets, sawing away in the trees.

They had at last succeeded in ridding themselves of Hector, who had flounced off to Florence in a huff. When Anna asked the reason for his departure, all Candy could do was giggle. She checked that Genevieve was safely out of earshot, then carried the phone into the kitchen and closed the door.

'He made a pass at me,' she hissed, 'and didn't like it at all when I batted him off.' Hector, who saw himself as a dashing Lothario, was unaccustomed to rejection. His standing as an opera critic gave him a puffed-up self-importance that didn't sit well with his squat, ugly body or his almost fifty years. He was used to women flattering him and listening with respect to his pronouncements. When Candy simply crumpled up with mirth, his pride, not to mention his ego, had been hurt. So, aware that Genevieve was no longer under his thumb, he had saved whatever face he had left and departed.

'Good riddance!' Candy had said, as his taxi drove away. 'Do you think you'll continue to see him back in London?' Despite her amusement, she had loyally not said a word. If Genevieve wanted to abase herself, it really wasn't any of Candy's business.

'I hardly think so,' Genevieve had replied, pulling a face. 'Somehow, I can't think why, he has lost his allure.' It was her turn to laugh now, at the thought of his pomposity, though that was not the main reason for her decision. Secretly, all she could think of these days was the handsome, hunky Raffaele whose smouldering eyes and curly black hair had the power to make her breathless. They were more or less sure now that he was unattached but having Hector in constant attendance certainly hadn't helped. She looked forward to being able to eat at the trattoria again.

Now she poked her nose round the door to find out what was going on.

'It's Anna,' said Candy, passing her the phone and automatically reaching for the grappa. These days, any excuse would do. It was certainly high time that Anna returned.

'What's up?' asked Genevieve, glad to hear Anna's voice. They needed her back to organise things and help keep them both on the level. Since she had been gone the days had seemed to drag and neither one was working as hard as they should. Even the absence of Hector had simply served to diminish their fun. Without his comical presence to deride, much of their childish humour just fell flat.

'Too much to tell you now,' said Anna, 'but I need you to do some urgent detective work.' It was vital, she told them, that they found out all they could about their mysterious and very much absent host. 'Dig up everything you can,' she said, 'no matter how trivial it might seem. Talk to Maria and Simonetta; someone has to know where the bodies are buried. I need to get all the dirt I can before he does any more damage. Bribe or batter, whatever it takes, just so long as you winkle out the truth. This man, I am certain, is a dangerous criminal whose activities have to be stopped and the only weapon we have, so far, is his house.' Which ought to be sufficient to barter but hers was worth a lot more. She asked them to force their way into his locked quarters and sift through his possessions. And, while they were at it, look out for his computer. She would fight him with his own weapons if she could.

'Surely he'll have it with him,' said Genevieve, who was rarely parted from hers.

230

'Maybe,' said Anna, 'but it's still worth a shot.' Anyone who could so effectively pillage her system had to be some sort of technological wizard. Her mind went back to Raffaele's friend, the arrogant stranger with the coolly mocking eyes, who had asked so many questions then walked away. She was now convinced they were all in it together, probably part of organised crime, even, maybe, an offshoot of the mafia. She had never entirely trusted Raffaele despite Genevieve's growing adoration. He was too effusive, too anxious to please; altogether too nice. Though she had noticed the steely glint in his eye, which was how her suspicions had been raised. Someone in New York, it seemed, had murdered Larry in cold blood. Although it was not yet proven, it did seem likely. And until the police came up with something definite, all of them had to watch their backs.

'One more thing,' she said, before finally ringing off. 'Find out all you can about Sutherland's wife.'

16

Paige and Charles Collier were sitting at dinner in a neighbourhood restaurant on the Upper West Side, around the corner from their spacious eighth-floor apartment. Paige, these days, seldom ever cooked; it was one of those mundane things she had given up. Time spent together had lately become so rare, they relished these evenings alone, just the two of them. Charles, a banker, had been following Anna's plight with very nearly as much interest as his wife.

'Tell me,' she asked him now as she picked at her salad, 'what in particular would motivate anyone to act quite as ruthlessly as that?'

'Greed,' replied Charles promptly, not even having to think since he'd witnessed so much in the course of his business life. 'You wouldn't believe what people will do for money.' Especially now with the stock market so insecure. Financial disasters were thick in the news. Hardly a day went by without some new corporate skulduggery being uncovered.

'But why would he take it all?' she said. 'The house, her assets, even the family home? It does seem rather excessive to leave her with nothing.' Beneath the steel veneer, Paige was softer than she liked to pretend and resolutely believed in fair play.

'Precisely because he could,' replied Charles. 'No point in leaving anything behind. This

232

particular perpetrator knew exactly what he was up to. A professional conman, would be my guess, who has undoubtedly done it before.'

Paige ate in silence as she pondered this point, then wondered aloud how Anna had been selected. Could she have just been a random choice or was she specifically targeted?

'Think about it, it can only have been random. He couldn't have known she would even see the ad.'

'He must have had loads of other replies,' said Paige. 'It sounded unbelievably enticing. So why pick Anna out of all the rest? Simply her rotten luck, do you suppose?'

'Newly renovated townhouse in a highly desirable neighbourhood. Plus he will have found out that she lives alone.' They had, after all, exchanged emails about the swap. And Anna had foolishly trusted him because of Yale.

'And,' added Paige, 'she is now becoming quite famous. Is it possible he could have heard about the movie deal?'

Charles shrugged; in these areas anything was possible. 'Richer pickings is what you are suggesting. With a scam like this, nothing would surprise me.' The rogue was sounding more unscrupulous by the second; the measure of what poor Anna was up against. Wall Street was in turmoil, the Enron scandal on every front page. It was almost safer to keep money under the mattress than risk one's hard-earned savings in the markets. Anna had been well advised to put hers into property, though no-one could have imagined that this would happen.

Paige shuddered, unusually fastidious for her. 'He has to be stopped before he does any more harm. Where do you suppose he has stashed the money and how come he got away with it?' She was still frustrated that she hadn't tracked him down and that the bank was continuing to block her.

'Offshore account most probably,' said Charles. 'Somewhere safe where it can't be got at. As soon as he's bled her dry, he will disappear.' Which rather seemed to have happened already; to date there had not been a single sighting.

'We can't allow that,' said Paige with determination. If only the damned police would get up off their butts. 'But if he's disappeared,' she suddenly added, 'how is he going to handle the sale of the house? Putting it on the market is one thing; all he needed was proof of residence plus a great deal of gall.' And a shady realtor without too many scruples who could not be bothered to check on his true credentials. 'But what will happen if a deal goes through and money has to change hands?'

'That will be the crunch point,' said Charles. 'It will be interesting to see what happens then.'

'It does seem possible,' said Paige a little later, 'that he may never actually have been around at all. Nobody seems to have seen him or even heard his voice. What precisely do we know about him? Zilch. Except that he's a photographer, constantly on the move.' Which, now she came to think of it, could well be no more than a cover.

'Except that,' Charles reminded her, 'he's a former classmate of Cousin Wilbur. Who seemed to think the sun shone out of his ass.' It might be worth another word with Wilbur, in case he had anything to add.

'What would be his purpose, I wonder, in wanting a foothold in New York? It wouldn't appear to fit in with his way of life.'

'Money,' said Charles. 'Look at the real estate values. Apart from California, the highest in the country.' And, in these uncertain days of a totally bearish market, investors who had been heavily scorched were putting their savings elsewhere. Property was the investment of choice; not a lot could happen to bricks and mortar though even that, since 9/11, was not as safe a bet as had always been thought.

'So, assuming he was in it for what he could steal, how come he ran the risk of losing his own home? What's to stop Anna simply confiscating it? I can't see he'd have any comeback under the law.'

Paige paused while the waiter delivered their main courses, rare steak for Charles, a filleted plaice for her. She leaned across and filched one of his French fries; slim though she was, she remained a covert trencherman.

'Unless,' she said slowly, with a flash of sudden insight, 'the Tuscan villa isn't his at all.' Their eyes met as they absorbed this possibility. Slowly the disparate pieces were starting to fit. 'The only person that anyone has seen is the woman at Anna's house. Who Larry said had been looking after the cat.'

'And Anna now thinks might be Sutherland's wife.'

'Though that does seem a little too obvious.' If the police were less lethargic, they would be in there, rounding her up. Except that now she appeared to have vanished too. Whenever they passed, the house was bolted and barred, with never any sign of even a light.

If only poor Larry hadn't died. It was all so annoyingly frustrating. Paige longed to talk to Phoebe Atwood, though felt it still wasn't quite the time.

'What about Anna's cleaner?' she said suddenly. 'How come none of us thought of talking to her?'

★   ★   ★

Anna, of course, should have come up with that one herself. She had neither been sleeping nor keeping her eye on the ball. She cursed herself when she got Paige's phone call; Consuela had been with her eleven years and had come with her to the brownstone when she moved. Anna had paid her in advance for the full four months. She should be there, cleaning and keeping an eye on things, so where had she got to now? Finally galvanised into doing something constructive, Anna set off on the bus to East Harlem to track Consuela down. She located the house without any trouble, in a long narrow row with fire escapes at the front.

Consuela, when she opened the door and saw her, burst into tears of relief. 'Oh Miss Anna,' she cried, clutching her in her arms, 'I simply didn't know what I should do. The woman told me I was no longer required. I didn't know how to reach you.'

Anna hushed her and followed her inside where she was watching a TV gameshow with her grandchild. The little girl, with pink bows in her hair, placidly shifted to the far end of the sofa, leaving the women to talk.

'What can have happened to Sadie?' was Anna's first question, but Consuela just miserably shook her head. 'I don't know, Miss Anna, she seemed fine last time I saw her, stretched out nice and comfy on your bed.'

'And this woman, what was she like? Can you describe her?'

'Slim and dark. Polished manners and very good clothes. I think she was somebody's secretary, she had that air. Brisk and contemptuous, too grand for the likes of me. Could hardly be bothered to give me the time of day.'

'What was she doing in the house? Apart from feeding the cat? Did she appear to be living there? And keeping an eye on the builders?'

'I don't think so, Miss Anna, she didn't even take off her jacket. She was opening the mail and listening to messages, always in a hurry.'

'You don't think she could have been Sutherland's wife?' Now that Anna had got that idea, she was finding it hard to dislodge. It would help to account for all sorts of weird things, them working together as a pair.

Consuela considered. 'I really don't think so. Though I can't exactly say why. She didn't seem interested in the house, was merely doing her job. And she hardly took notice of the cat at all, which surprised me.' Sadie was one of the friendliest creatures. A person would need a heart of stone not to pet her.

'And you didn't get her name?'

Again Consuela shook her head. 'I found it very hard to understand her.'

'Look,' said Anna kindly, after some thought. 'I want you to know, the job is still yours. Whoever she was, she had no right to dismiss you. The problem is, I no longer have a house or anything else for you to clean. You should still have some money in hand. If not, I will let you have more.' She promised to stay closely in touch and let Consuela know as soon as the problem was fixed.

On the doorstep they hugged again and, when Anna was gone, Consuela privately called on Our Lady, beseeching her to find the missing cat.

★   ★   ★

Paige was interested to hear about Consuela, so far their one and only possible lead. She was still hesitant about intruding on Phoebe but at last legal inquisitiveness overcame her finer feelings. It was several weeks now since Larry's death and still the cops hadn't bothered to be in touch. Time to put a bomb up their backsides, starting with checking with the widow. Paige dropped by on the pretext of a sympathy call but Phoebe was unable to add to the little she had already told Anna. There had been an accident, he must somehow have lost his balance. The police appeared to have gone cold on the case.

On an impulse, Paige drove down to Baltimore to talk to Cousin Wilbur. He was gardening when she got there, late afternoon, portly and flushed, with a baseball cap on his head.

'Paige!' he said, embracing her heartily. 'What a wonderful surprise.' She had called from her cellphone to say she'd be passing through. Her legal brain was too cautious to let it seem urgent; until she knew what she was dealing with here, she was playing her cards very close. They walked, arms linked, across the immaculate lawn and he mixed them each a cocktail in the conservatory. Orchids and geraniums surrounded them in pots. The heady, earthy smell was quite exotic.

'Not too strong for me,' warned Paige. She did not want to risk getting booked; potentially disastrous for her career. She also needed to keep a clear head. Wilbur might be kin to her but she had not yet ascertained where his loyalties lay.

'So what brings you to this neck of the woods?' He lowered himself into a basket chair which creaked in protest at his weight. Gone was the one-time athletic jock; he was little more now than just a complacent attorney. Family money had provided this pile; all his children had been at private schools. Nancy, he explained, was off at a charity fundraiser. He seemed to be very content with his lot and none too curious about Paige. Which was just as well.

After a spot of idle chat, catching him up on

the news, Paige steeled herself to cut to the chase without giving too much away. This could turn out to be the breakthrough she'd been seeking, but lawyerly caution held her back. Even within the family, she would not risk showing her cards, not to a one-time crony of Sutherland's without first discovering whether the two were still close.

'Tell me,' she said, after a suitable interval, aware that she should soon be taking her leave. The traffic at this time of night would be heavy. She didn't want to risk alarming Charles. 'Some time ago you mentioned Dan Sutherland. I think you knew him at Yale.'

'Sure,' said Wilbur, freshening his drink. 'A great guy, Dan. I've forgotten how you know him. It is years now since the two of us last met up.'

'Oh, he's just a friend of a friend,' said Paige vaguely. 'I was wondering if you knew where he might be now.'

'I do know he's almost always on the trot. Fellow always did have vagabond shoes. I admire that sort of inexhaustible energy, just thinking about it these days makes me feel tired. Very bright indeed, is Dan, with a sharp, original mind. Might have turned his hand to practically anything.'

'Instead of which he settled for taking snaps.' Paige could not keep the irony out of her voice. To her mind, photography wasn't a manly job but then, perhaps, she was thinking of Cecil Beaton.

'Only on a very superior level. He's won a lot of international prizes and has lately become

240

something of a media star.' It could just be fraternity solidarity but Paige had rarely heard such praise from her ultra-conservative cousin. Interesting.

'And you've no idea where he might be now?' Her patience was starting to wear thin. What a silly old buffer he had become, with his amateur potting and over-noxious cocktails. And yet he was only a few years her senior, barely middle-aged.

Wilbur sat and scratched his head, oblivious of Paige's irritation. 'You could try *National Geographic*,' he suggested. 'Or some of the other big glossies. If they have him on assignment, which one or other of them is almost bound to, they ought to be able to tell you where he is.'

'One last thing,' said Paige, preparing to leave. 'Do you happen to know if he is married?'

Wilbur looked startled. 'Not that I'm aware of and it's the sort of thing that the alumni mag would certainly have picked up. Mind you,' he added, 'it's been years since I saw him. Who knows what the fellow's been up to in that time. I would just be very surprised if he'd got himself hitched. Dan always was pretty much of a loner. I doubt if anything's changed.'

Paige kissed him and muttered her thanks and apologies but said she really must be off. Sent her love to Nancy and the kids and hoped they could all meet up before too long. Wilbur walked her to her car and watched as she buckled up.

'My regards to Charles,' he said. 'Oh, and Dan Sutherland too, when you finally catch up with him.'

It took her less than a morning to track him down. Wilbur was right; he was with *Geographic*. Currently on assignment in Patagonia, where he'd been for more than a year.

'You mean he hasn't been working in New York?'

'No, ma'am,' said an obliging young woman. 'Not as far as I know.'

'And do you have a contact number?'

'Not one I can give out. When he needs us, he calls. It's as simple as that. Dan is very much his own boss.' Plus, of course, there was email but that often did not work, not when he was in transit through the rainforests. There were months on end when he was out of touch altogether, some of the areas he worked in were that remote.

'I can always take a message and pass it on.' The girl seemed genuinely keen to be of help.

Paige thought fast then told her it wasn't necessary. The truth was, she wouldn't know what to say to him even if she could. It seemed she was back at square one again except now she knew for certain he wasn't around. Nor, apparently, had he been all year, not since before the exchange of houses, which really didn't make sense. She wanted to bang her head on her desk. She felt as though she were trying to wade through mud.

17

'His wife!' echoed Candy, after Anna had rung off. 'Where did she get the idea that he's even got one? And how come she found that out in New York? I thought all the action was supposed to be happening here.'

'Dunno,' said Genevieve, equally in the dark. 'I suppose there's always a chance that she's tracked him down. In which case she's a meanie not to have let us know instead of just giving instructions for breaking and entering.'

'I think that right now she's got other things on her mind. She did sound awfully rattled.' Anna had filled them in quickly about her father but was in too much of a rush to talk very long. Things appeared to be hotting up on her side of the Atlantic. They would do whatever they could to help her out. Besides, since Hector left, they had time on their hands. First they had to interrogate Maria, who came in every Tuesday to supervise the housekeeping. It would not be easy since her English was so poor and, whenever they asked too many questions, a veil dropped over her eyes. But they would persist and try to charm her. And also chat up Simonetta, who seemed to know most of the village gossip and had once worked as an au pair in Enfield, of all places, the reason her English was so good.

When Anna called a couple of days later, she found both Candy and Genevieve in a state of giddy excitement. They had taken to amateur sleuthing like true pros, any slight tensions that might have built up having dissipated with the fun of this new game. Each clamoured to talk to Anna first; Candy, being quicker, grabbed the phone. Maria had dismally failed to come through, pleading the Fifth Amendment, 'non capito', but Candy had finally, after many patient hours, succeeded in picking the lock to Sutherland's rooms.

'Dressmaking scissors make an excellent burglar's aid,' she gleefully reported, 'though you do need a steady hand.' Luckily by now the grappa was finished and they were leading a slightly more sober life.

'So what did you find?' They had Anna on tenterhooks. This could be the crucial break-through she was after.

'We haven't dared go in there yet,' said Candy, lowering her voice. 'Didn't want Maria sussing what we were up to.' Maria was still in the kitchen, cleaning the stove, but soon, with luck, would be off to the market to shop.

'Be careful,' warned Anna, though she wasn't quite certain of what. Just longed to know what they'd find behind those locked doors. Progress at last and not before it was due; perhaps they would crack the mystery now in one throw.

'Don't worry,' said Candy. 'We'll ring you as soon as we can. Bye, Maria,' she called out loudly and stood with Genevieve, watching her walk away.

They left it a good five minutes, just in case,

then cautiously twisted the heavy wrought-iron door handle.

'Bluebeard's cave,' hissed Candy, still in a whisper. 'Maybe we'll find what's left of his other victims.'

★ ★ ★

Another vast corporate scandal had broken, close on the heels of Enron. The news, as well as the financial pages, was covering it in minute detail. Two top executives of a telecommunications giant had surrendered voluntarily to the FBI and were photographed throughout the media being led away publicly in handcuffs. Later both were released on personal bonds, respectively of two and ten million dollars. The Bush administration was doing its stuff by trying, as publicly as it could, to stamp out corporate crime.

'What exactly is this all about?' asked Paige. Finance was Charles's department. Although she kept her eye on the headlines and knew just how shaky the stock market was, she was far too engrossed in her own massive overload to have followed it in any special detail. That, as she was fond of telling their friends, was her reason for marrying Charles.

Charles accepted another cup of coffee and glanced up from the newspaper he was reading. It was a quarter past seven and they were having breakfast. Both would be in their offices by eight-thirty.

'It is part of a series of law enforcements aimed at prosecuting corporate lawbreakers and protecting the savings and pensions of Joe Public.' Seeing the cynicism on Paige's face, he grinned. Neither one of them, by any stretch of the imagination, could be described as Republican.

'But what is it really about?' persisted Paige, suddenly tuning in. All these weeks she had been brooding on Anna's misfortunes and now it would appear to be happening to other people as well.

'It is nothing especially new,' explained Charles, 'but the chaos wrought by what happened in September hasn't exactly helped.' So many small businesses had been totally decimated, their records completely destroyed. It was a bit like London after the Blitz only this had all occurred in just fifteen minutes. Apart from the on-the-spot looting in the streets, it gave leeway for other, far more serious crimes. All sorts of charlatans had been taking reckless chances. The Security and Exchange Commission was working overtime.

'These guys,' said Charles, indicating the headlines, 'are not necessarily corrupt but victims of a tightening administration. It is more to do with politics than fraud. A sign of the current vulnerability of the White House.' A reflection, maybe, on the President.

What they had done, he tried to explain as concisely as he could with one eye on the clock, was create hundreds of 'special purpose entities' designed to raise debt through an outside company and keep it off the books, while also not losing control of the assets. They hired a bunch of so-called banking experts and gave them the chance of investing in these assets, fobbing it off as 'partnerships' to the big guys. That way they could conceal liabilities and, in some cases, create paper gains. And the banking experts were set to clean up, provided they had nerves of steel. That, in a nutshell was it, said Charles.

'Some of them are just kids,' he added. 'Late twenties to early thirties, often chancing their arm just for the hell of it. With impeccable pedigrees and expensive educations, cashing in on their fancy WASP connections. Investment advisors, they call themselves, and basically what they do is this. They build up a client base for whom they invest money — often, in order to appear more authentic, adding a percentage of their own. Then, after a suitable interval, they siphon off most of the funds to a personal account and stash it somewhere safe where it can't be touched. It is, pure and simple, white-collar crime and they richly deserve to get caught. Fastow, for instance, who allegedly screwed up Enron, faces up to a hundred and forty years in jail. Hence the current involvement of the SEC. Situations like this are popping up like mushrooms. Everyone seems to be in on it right now.'

'Well, I suppose it is preferable to bombing Iraq.' All these issues were very much in the news. Paige, not normally sentimental, silently blessed her stars for Charles as well as her rock-solid marriage. But, concurrently, her mind was embarking on an intriguing new avenue of possibility. It came to her like a nuclear blast and left her with a rapidly heightened pulse rate. Suppose there was something that you badly needed to hide, what better way could you possibly choose than simply to disappear? In the devastation of the terrorist attacks, thousands of innocent people had vaporised. It had made a huge tragedy still more insupportable for the relatives who felt that they could not yet grieve. It could be months, if not years, before things were finally sorted and even then a lot would be based on guesswork. The ideal cover, she suddenly perceived, for concealing all manner of crimes.

'Don't you know someone in the SEC?' she asked casually as she stacked the dishwasher.

'Yes, Dave Kelly. But what's that to do with this?'

'And what precisely does it do? The SEC, I mean.'

'In a nutshell?' He laughed; this looked like turning into a full-blown seminar. She was going to make him late if he wasn't careful. 'The Securities and Exchange Commission is an agency of the federal government, charged with keeping an eye on the securities business. It sets the rules for the brokerage firms and investigates any violations. Anything else you need to know now that won't keep until tonight?' He glanced up at her with narrowing eyes. 'What is your devious little mind up to now?' And saw from her bland smile that she wasn't telling.

'Just a hunch,' was all she would say. 'I promise I'll fill you in once I've figured it out.'

'You always were a Miss Marple manquée. You picked the wrong profession.'

*　*　*

The huge oak doors swung silently inwards and Candy and Genevieve stepped cautiously inside. Sutherland's quarters were dignified and sparse, with long shuttered windows leading out on to the terrace. The light filtering through the closed slats was dim but they dared not run the risk of opening them for fear of attracting attention from outside. No matter what Sutherland might have done, his private rooms were supposed to be off limits; Raffaele had made that abundantly clear and they did not want to risk his disapproval. The suite comprised a vast, high-ceilinged room, with two smaller ones leading off it. It was more spacious than an average townhouse, demonstrating how huge the villa actually was. Ancient frescoes in faded terracotta were still faintly visible in the plaster. One entire wall had been fitted with shelves, crammed to overflowing with learned-looking books. And opposite the windows hung an imposing portrait in oils, of a dark jowly man in uniform and medals, which dominated the room.

'Crikey,' said Candy, peering up at it in alarm. 'I wonder who this old geezer is? He looks like a general, Mussolini perhaps. I don't think I'd care to have him on my case. Certainly not watching me all the time.'

Genevieve, too, felt discomfited by the

portrait's staring eyes, as if its subject knew they ought not to be there. She looked around for possible clues that might be of use to Anna, but couldn't see anything remotely intimate that could give them any sort of insight into the man. The suite looked as if it had been closed up for years, and was pervaded by a smell of ancient mustiness. In the corner, close to the terrace doors, was a vast mahogany desk, with a light box on it and stacks of shiny photo boxes. Next to it stood an antique plans chest which proved to hold negatives and prints; drawers and drawers of folders of them, all neatly labelled and dated. And above them, on the wall, a framed certificate — *Wildlife Photographer of the Year. D. A. Sutherland. 1998.* But no sign at all of anything private, nothing that Sutherland would not want a stranger to see. No trace, either, of any computer, nor even a telephone port. Even the old-fashioned telephone extension turned out not to be connected.

'That's really weird,' said Genevieve, 'considering this is his home. Not to have a computer modem nor anywhere obvious to plug one in. For someone who endlessly travels the world, it does seem oddly archaic.'

'Especially since his exchange with Anna was done entirely by email.'

Genevieve crossed to the bedroom doorway, where she saw filmy white mosquito netting looped above the bed. Again, that lingering aroma of decay, though everything had been meticulously dusted and polished. Maria had obviously done a stalwart job, keeping it all in immaculate order, though it must be a thankless task if the owner was so seldom here. Talk about loyal servitude: she was clearly one in a million. Which made it seem unlikely that she did not know more than she said. How to subvert that loyalty was the problem.

Genevieve opened the vast carved wardrobe, half-expecting a body to fall out. But all she found was a faded bathrobe that looked as though it hadn't been worn in years. Candy was rifling through the chest of drawers, which contained nothing more interesting than old sweaters and socks, with a gentle sprinkling of mouse droppings. No giveaway clues of any kind here, nothing to tell them more about the man. No framed photos nor personal knick-knacks; not a single thing to indicate that he was even coming back.

The bathroom was cavernous with a great claw-footed tub and black and white marbled tiles upon the floor. The old-fashioned lavatory tank dripped away relentlessly, causing a lengthy rust mark down the wall. There wasn't so much as a toothbrush on display, nor even a bar of soap.

'Surely he can't have taken everything to New York?' The less they found, the weirder it became.

'Unless, of course, he was planning not to return. A one-way ticket to the promised land to take up permanent residence in Anna's house.'

'And then sell it on?'

'At a mammoth profit before disappearing back to the jungle again.'

'But who would ever abandon a villa like this?'

'It's like the *Marie Celeste*,' said Candy, still whispering. 'Come on, let's get out of here. It's starting to give me the creeps.'

★   ★   ★

Anna was disappointed when they told her they had found virtually nothing. 'There must be something you overlooked. Everyone, surely, leaves some sort of a trail.' She seemed to be running around in circles, like a hamster in a wheel, while all the while that man remained dangerously at large, doing who knew what more damage without restraint. The world was falling fast into anarchy. She read it in the papers every day.

'You could try looking at his photographs,' she said, though what use that would be she didn't know. Any clue to the secrets in his life might give her the ammunition she required.

'You haven't seen how many there are. Stacks and stacks of boxes, going back years.'

'Full of rainforests and conservation areas.' At least, if what Paige's cousin had said was true.

'We still haven't spoken to Raffaele,' said Genevieve hopefully, willing Anna to give them the nod to proceed. Because of Hector, it was ages since they'd seen him and she was starting to suffer keen withdrawal pains. She yearned for his warm, admiring smile and the glint of libido in his eye. He was like a breath of Italian spring after an icy London winter. He, more than anyone, made her feel truly sexy, something she had been starved of for far too long. Anna hesitated then told her to go ahead. At this stage, she really had no other choice, yet still felt in her gut that they shouldn't trust him. But, face it, she had reached the bottom of the barrel. Almost anything now was worth a shot.

'Be careful,' she warned, 'and don't let him know too much.' They must not risk playing into the hands of the enemy.

★ ★ ★

'You'd not believe some of the stuff that is emerging,' said the SEC man, Dave Kelly. His shirt was wrinkled, his hair unkempt, he had not slept properly in weeks. In the aftermath of September 11th, the country's financial systems were all up the spout. The strain he was under was clearly visible and there was the glint of fanaticism in his eye. He was seeing her purely as a favour to Charles and Paige was suitably grateful. She had dressed with even more than her usual care, in a teal blue suit that had cost a small fortune, and her silver-blonde hair was drawn tightly back into a knot. The epitome of the no-nonsense lawyer, she was endeavouring to conceal her mounting excitement. After all these weeks spent chasing her tail, the gleam of a possible breakthrough was finally dawning. It was something that Charles had inadvertently said. About how to conceal illicit earnings.

'Things are coming to light that were hitherto unsuspected.' Dave Kelly ran his hands through his hair, the fever in his eyes as manic as hers.

'The general mayhem has provided cover for more than one case of quite unbelievable fraud. Even the FBI are now involved, though I beg you, please, not to breathe a word. Soon there may well be a major announcement. Heads in positions of power are likely to roll. The government is heavily implicated. You would not believe the half of it,' he said.

Paige's well-tuned antennae pricked up. 'You mean even bigger than Enron?' she said. 'Surely not.'

Dave Kelly looked at her and blinked and she knew she had got it in one. The whole world now knew the extent of the Enron collapse and that the SEC had filed a civil lawsuit against the Chief Finance Officer, seeking damages for defrauding Enron investors.

'Things,' she added carefully, intensifying the charm, 'unconnected with the terrorist attacks?'

Now he nodded, quite unsuspecting. Paige was the sort of lady he rarely encountered. Her beauty and razor-sharp intellect stunned him. He could not see what danger he was in.

'Criminal things that might have surfaced months ago, had not many of the records been destroyed. How we are going to sort it all out, I really cannot imagine. All we've uncovered so far is the tip of the iceberg. At least, that is how it appears as things stand now.' Again his hands went clawing through his hair and she noticed that his fingernails were chewed. This man was hurtling towards the end of his rope; it could surely only be a matter of time. She could not afford to let that happen, not before she had

254

milked him for all he was worth. Paige thought fast and took a gamble, which was part of her stock in trade.

'Tell me something,' she asked him. 'If you had just succeeded in stealing huge amounts of cash, where do you suppose you would put it in order to be safe?'

He looked at her long and hard without replying. He might be fraught and on the edge of infatuation but he certainly wasn't a fool.

'I don't suppose,' she added carefully, 'that you'd let me look at your records.' Nothing ventured, nothing gained and, in the end, she invariably got what she was after.

He stared at her, profoundly shocked, snapped back to reality by her outrageous request. 'You know I can't do that,' he virtually spluttered. 'I'd be out on my ear in record time. Our work in this department is subject to Grade-A security. At the very least, I'd be facing criminal charges.'

Paige fluttered her lashes and switched on her little-girl charm; the things she would occasionally stoop to all in the name of duty. 'I can see you are busy,' she said sympathetically, 'so I'll be off. Thanks again. You really have been a great help.' You don't know how much.

'I wonder,' she added, as he walked her to the elevator, 'if we could meet again sometime, perhaps when you're not quite so pressured?' Her clear blue eyes were entirely without guile and he was suddenly acutely conscious of her perfume. One second was all it took and she had him hooked.

Even despite the accolades, they were unpre-
pared for the quality of the pictures. The sky, for
once, was overcast and it was still too early for
supper, so they had crept back into Sutherland's
rooms and obediently went to work on the plans
chest. Genevieve felt distinctly uncomfortable at
Candy having forced the lock, even though it
had been done with her total collusion. She was
nervous that Maria might suddenly return and
report their bad behaviour to Raffaele. 'No time
like the present,' she said. Once they had
completed their task, she knew she would find it
easier to sleep.

They decided to leave the negatives alone,
despite the convenient presence of the light box.
This was photography of the very highest order;
they must not risk doing any damage. Instead
they each grabbed a handful of yellow folders
and spread the glossy prints across the desk. And
what prints they were; they were both astounded.
No wonder he had won all those awards. Rare
animals, exotic birds, waterfalls and mountains.
A whole lost world captured in exquisite detail, a
permanent record of things fast becoming
extinct. The debate about photography not being
art was in this case demonstrably groundless.

'What are we actually looking for?' asked
Candy, after a while. She could have spent hours
slowly sifting through the prints, so impressed
was she by their excellence. This man,
Sutherland, whatever his moral character, was
possessed indisputably of a truly staggering

talent. With work of this calibre, what reason could he have to steal? Still things failed to add up.

'Don't really know,' said Genevieve, equally affected, hating to have to tear herself away. 'Anything, I suppose, germane to the question of why he might have treated Anna in this way. Though I cannot see where conservation fits in, particularly since it means travelling most of the time.'

'He must be incredibly brave,' said Candy. 'It has to be dangerous work.' No lounging around in a cushy studio, posturing and chatting up models. He was out there in uncharted territory, possibly risking his life.

'Look at this crocodile!' Genevieve was appalled. With its scheming eyes and malevolent grin it looked close enough to the camera to swallow it whole. You could see every wrinkle of its leathery hide and the way its tail was thrashing about in the water.

'All he needed was one false step . . . ' said Candy with ghoulish relish.

Genevieve shuddered. She was not an outdoors person. Though was mesmerised by the brilliance of it all.

They went on looking, but failed to unearth anything they could reasonably call a lead. It was getting late and Genevieve was hungry and wanted to tart herself up before going out.

'Time to stop,' she said, shifting the folders of slippery prints, succeeding only in knocking them all over the floor.

'Shit!' said Candy, on her hands and knees.

'Now he is going to know we've been in here snooping.' She tried to slide them back into their files and make some semblance of order. With luck, he wouldn't notice that they were no longer in strict date order, although he was clearly such a pro, that didn't seem very likely.

'Don't worry, by the time he finds out we three will be long gone.' Genevieve's eye was caught by the corner of an envelope jutting out from beneath the desk. It must have dropped from one of the folders. She bent to retrieve it and, as she picked it up, out dropped a handful of black and white prints, stylish and very atmospheric. Their subject was a striking young woman, glancing up from repotting geraniums as if caught unawares. It was a memorable face with bold dark eyes and heavily accented brows. Her thick, lustrous hair was artfully tangled and piled loosely on top of her head. It was difficult to tell, from the deliberately grainy texture, precisely when the pictures had been taken.

Genevieve caught her breath in triumph. 'She looks a bit like Elizabeth Taylor. I think we may have found her,' she said.

18

'Goodness,' said Simonetta when she saw the photographs. 'Where on earth did you get hold of these?' She carefully wiped her hands on her apron to take a closer look. Candy and Genevieve were instantly embarrassed, not wanting to reveal what they had been up to. They had dropped in on their way to the trattoria because Candy was out of tissues. It was seven-thirty, the shop would soon be closing, but the usual coven of garrulous old ladies was in there, chattering away. They passed the pictures from one to the other, clucking and sorrowfully shaking their heads. One, the oldest, dressed in black from head to foot, solemnly made the sign of the cross.

'Who is she?' Genevieve asked nervously. There was a distinct chill feeling of everyone closing ranks. She regretted ever having brought the subject up. They had certainly not expected this sort of reaction. All eyes turned to Simonetta, the only one among them who spoke English. She just shrugged. Clearly something was bothering her, it was not at all like her to be so unforthcoming. But the heavy-lidded eyes were guarded; she failed to meet Genevieve's gaze.

'Raffaele is the one to tell you, if he feels that you should know. It is something he rarely talks about any more.' She took Candy's money and

259

rang it up on the till, then returned to the conversation she had been having. In fast Italian that they could not remotely follow. It was clear they were being deliberately shut out.

'Go easy on him,' said Simonetta as they left. 'It is something he may still not be able to handle.'

'Well,' said Genevieve, the moment they were outside, 'I wonder what in the world *that* was all about.'

'Raffaele's dark secret, from the look of things. Maybe it explains his apparent single state. Some private sorrow from the past that no-one will discuss, though, obviously, no secret in the village.' The woman in the photographs had clearly been something special. Not quite a traditional beauty, better than that. A sharp intelligence combined with a siren's smile. There was something about her brilliantly lucid eyes that positively sucked you in.

Genevieve experienced a powerful shaft of jealousy. She was mad to have even dreamed that he might be unencumbered, not a man as attractive as that and certainly not at his age. Every bloke she ever encountered came with a load of emotional baggage and Raffaele was the best she had come across yet. She wondered when the photographs were taken. From the stylised black and white grainy texture, it was not at all easy to tell. This year, last year; even, perhaps, decades ago? The way the woman was dressed certainly offered no clues. She was wearing a low-cut peasant blouse, revealing more boob than was strictly necessary. Genevieve instinctively hated her. She was already wrecking her dream.

'Maybe she was his mother,' suggested Candy, aware of Genevieve's sudden shift of mood.

'Maybe,' said Genevieve miserably. She could not bear to think that Raffaele's heart might be taken, yet it was pretty silly ever to have assumed that not to be the case.

'Are you going to ask him?'

'I don't know. Let's wait and just play it by ear.'

★ ★ ★

Raffaele, when he saw them walk in, looked almost as though he were relieved. It had been so long since he had last seen them that he'd worried he might have scared them off, which was not what he was intended to do. *Keep them under close surveillance.* The instructions had been more than clear. These foreign women who had invaded the villa had not found Montisi accidentally but were part of a convoluted plot. Or so his associate believed. But looking at them now, as they fluttered in the doorway, it was hard to believe that they were not as straightforward as they seemed. The taller one, Genevieve, looked particularly sensational and familiar regret flooded Raffaele's chest that he'd been ordered to keep well away. She was wearing a diaphanous delphinium blue dress, made for her by Candy in just two sessions. Her legs were long and slender and tanned, her toenails expertly buffed. She had shed more pounds which suited

261

her well. Raffaele, at heart, was a true romantic but his purpose now was to find out as much as he could. He hurried across the restaurant to greet them.

'*Signore!*' he breathed with his faintly unctuous charm, then led them both to their regular corner table. As he pulled out Genevieve's chair and helped her to settle, Candy could not suppress an involuntary twinge of discontent at being so blatantly ignored. Genevieve certainly deserved brownie points for having finally had the guts to get shot of Hector but all this overt attention from a man as fanciable as Raffaele was secretly starting to stick in her craw. Genevieve did look good in her new creation but Candy was prettier as well as ten years younger. *Hello!*

On this particular evening the restaurant was relatively quiet so Raffaele fetched a bottle of wine and joined them, uninvited, at the table. It was a golden opportunity and one that he must not miss. Without their more forceful American friend, he hoped to be able to elicit more information.

'And where have you been since I saw you last? Enjoying yourselves, I hope.'

Genevieve, remembering their recent spot of burglary, flushed in sudden confusion and dropped her fork. As Raffaele stooped to pick it up, Candy frowned and rapidly shook her head. *Don't go giving things away*, was her meaning. *You could hardly look more guilty if you tried.*

'Just lounging around the pool,' she said. 'It's a shame to waste a second of this glorious weather.' Despite Anna's warnings about too much sun, Candy had almost perfected a beautiful tan. Raffaele smiled politely in agreement but his eyes kept returning to Genevieve. *Oh well*, thought Candy, *I suppose I can't complain*. Romantic involvement was the very last thing she was after at the moment. Her mind returned to Trevor again but she tried to suppress the thought. If he really was set on stealing her kid, there were no lengths to which she wouldn't go to stop him.

'What do you ladies do when the sun goes down? Those nights that you don't come here?' He could not believe they were simply on vacation, not for as long as four months. Surely no women on their own who were not extremely rich could find the time for so much idleness. Raffaele was a man who had worked hard all his life and disapproved of others not doing the same. He had been told to monitor their comings and goings and find out who they had really come here to see.

'I'm a writer,' said Genevieve, who had told him before, 'and so is our other friend, Anna. Candy here is a brilliant fashion designer, putting together her new collection for a very prestigious London department store.' She beamed proudly at Candy who looked a touch embarrassed. Surely this lusty Italian male would not be interested in that. 'It may not appear so, but all three of us are working really hard.'

'So how did you first find *Casavecchia?*' That recurring question again.

'Anna saw an ad in a New York magazine.

From someone keen to go there for four months. Mr Sutherland, in fact, as you already know. Are you saying you haven't checked it out with him?' It all seemed most confusing; nothing added up. And something in Raffaele's tone sounded almost accusing.

'And will there be anyone else joining you here?'

Genevieve shook her head. 'There's bags of room but that's the whole point. We all needed peace and quiet in order to work.'

'Hector was an aberration,' put in Candy, 'but I'm pleased to say that now we've got shot of him.'

Raffaele's stern expression eased and he grinned. He had made no bones about disliking the arrogant Scot, though courtesy had prevented him speaking his mind. Not his business who they hung out with, but he had always been convinced that Genevieve could do better. But right now his mind was on more serious things. He needed some information to make his report.

'Signora Anna,' he said. 'Where is she tonight?'

'New York,' said Genevieve, suddenly radiant, turned on by his physical presence. She sensed he liked her though was too shy to show it. She wondered what she could do to egg him on.

But Raffaele was not in the mood to flirt. A guarded look had entered his eyes. 'New York?' he repeated, apparently startled. 'Why, if I may ask, did she cut short her stay?'

'Trouble,' said Candy cautiously, shooting Genevieve a glance, wondering just how much it was wise to divulge. But Anna had asked them to find out all they could and now seemed an ideal opportunity for some delving.

'And will she be coming back soon?' he asked.

'We certainly hope so,' said Candy. 'We miss her a lot and are finding it very hard to cope without her.'

Raffaele, preoccupied, put down his glass untouched and disappeared precipitately into the kitchen. Startled by his unexplained mood swing, Genevieve and Candy quickly conferred.

'What do you think?'

'I really don't know.'

'Should we, do you suppose, risk raising the subject?'

'What's there to lose?' Anna had requested it. 'The worst he can do, I imagine, is throw us out.'

When Raffaele, after a lengthy absence, finally returned, Candy slapped the photographs on the table and boldly asked him to tell them who it was. Predictably, Raffaele's face turned a paler shade and, when he picked them up, his hand was trembling.

'Where did you get these?' he asked her sharply, all trace of his former benevolence totally gone.

'We found them in the villa,' said Genevieve, not wanting to go into detail. 'And wondered if she might be Sutherland's wife.'

'Wife? What wife?' His voice was suddenly hostile. 'Daniel has no wife. And neither have I.' He passed one hand quickly across his eyes, then handed back the photographs. 'Put them back where you found them,' he said, 'and leave the matter alone.'

265

Anna had an uncomfortable awareness of possibly being stalked. It was not in her nature to feel so jumpy but the horrendous happenings of the past few months had managed to undermine her in many ways. She spent her days quietly at Colette's, writing and keeping her father company. Since the disruption of his life, his teaching had gone by the board. She had written a personal note to each of his pupils, explaining that he was temporarily indisposed, though in her heart she had a sinking feeling that for George this could well be the end of the line. He seemed older, frailer and still very much confused. All he could tell her about his abduction was that some unknown woman from social services had whisked him away. Who she was, he had no idea; he could not begin to describe her. His feisty independence had gone. Which, on top of everything else, was another bleak burden for Anna.

Usually they ate early, as soon as Colette got home, then Anna returned to her lonely hotel room to try to get on with her writing. Work on the novel was only limping along since, these days, she found it so hard to concentrate, but her pressing September deadline loomed large and now she had to rely more than ever on the delivery payment that would be due. No more winging it and trusting to the bank's benevolence should she fail to come in on time. No matter what else might be on her mind, she could not now afford to slack off. Colette, true to form, had come through with flying colours, with all the warmth and moral support she had unfailingly given in the past. The rest of the inner circle were rallying too. They were deeply contrite that they had ever thought badly of Anna, were doing all in their power to help make amends. Whatever else might be wrong in her life, she now knew for certain she could rely upon her friends.

Though not, so it appeared, on the police, who continued not to return her calls. All she had in the world was on the line, yet still she could not get them to take her problems seriously. Their inept indifference was making her crazy. Luckily Paige was very much on the case. She was pursuing a whole new avenue of her own which, for the moment, she was not divulging to Anna. Too many of her leads had proved false. She did not want to risk disappointing her again.

So life for Anna had become very restricted and she longed to be back in Tuscany with the girls. The happy memories of those glorious carefree days had now receded as if they had never been. Only the knowledge that they were still there, actively searching, brought any kind of solace to Anna's soul. The last she had heard, they were planning to tackle Raffaele. She hoped that, between the pair of them, they would get him to spill the beans. She still believed he was guilty as hell, despite all that beguiling Italian charm. Where men were concerned, Anna remained hard-headed. It took more than a sunset and a pair of empathetic brown eyes to get beneath her skin.

267

She made a point, on her way home from Colette's, always to detour via 74th Street to check if anything had changed. The feeling of being followed continued but never, when she turned, was there anyone there. It was still the height of summer and the air was humid and stifling. The streets of Manhattan were dry and parched and the traffic fumes suffocating. The terrible devastation that had destroyed life as it had been was gradually mellowing into recent history. The fires of Ground Zero had long been extinguished and the city was emerging from its mourning. People were slowly beginning to come to terms though not, of course, to forget.

The house, whenever she passed it, looked empty and forlorn. It broke her heart to see it like that after all her ambitious plans. One evening she noticed that the board was down, which meant, she assumed, that they must now have a firm offer. But when she called the real estate office, again they refused to talk and were positively rude when she attempted to force the issue. They would not even listen to her story, virtually accusing her of being some sort of impostor. She had no rights; they knew nothing about her. It was not her name on the title deeds though they also refused to divulge whose it actually was. She handed the whole thing over to Paige who was working on serving a writ. Everything legal dragged on for so long; Anna felt herself on the edge of despair.

On this particular evening she was standing, as she so often did, across the street behind a tree, as furtive as if she had no right to be there.

Twilight was gradually creeping in and she was feeling more than usually despondent. What, she wondered, was the point of working so hard, only to have everything snatched away? The lights were off, the windows shuttered, no flicker of life there at all. She wondered again what had happened to Sadie and intense emotion surged through her. In some ways, the loss of her pet was the worst thing of all. Apart from missing Sadie's intelligent company, she felt she had seriously let her down. And the thought of that beautiful pedigree cat loose on the New York streets was driving her crazy.

From deep in the shadows, she experienced again the feeling of being watched. She swung round quickly but the street was deserted; even the traffic had thinned out. She waited another forlorn few minutes, then wearily trudged on to her dreary hotel.

'Get a grip,' she ordered herself severely. The last thing she needed now was to start feeling spooked.

★ ★ ★

He called two days later, sounding somewhat apprehensive. Women like Paige were way out of his league but he had been unable to dislodge her from his mind.

'I know it's short notice but is there any chance you could manage that lunch today? Only there's something in my office you might find of interest.' He knew he ought not to but, what the hell, he was smitten by her translucent

269

porcelain beauty. Also she was a lawyer from a blue chip firm, married to a highly reputable banker. It was not beyond the bounds of possibility that she might even be able to help him in some way. That, at least, was how he kidded himself. After so many months of unendurable pressure, he was reduced to clutching at straws.

'Great!' said Paige, though with a sinking heart. She had not expected him to come through quite so quickly. Fortunately she was adept at coping and a little light flirtation could do no harm. She agreed to meet him in a restaurant in his building, after which it was up to him how things panned out. The thought of Anna's anguish spurred her on. They were more, far more, than just lawyer and client.

★ ★ ★

Genevieve sounded unusually subdued when she called. Normally, because of the time difference, they left it for Anna to make contact first but today she had something she needed to get off her chest. In the past few days, since the departure of Hector, Genevieve's voice had sparkled with happiness so that Anna, disregarding her own miserable situation, had been pleased when it dawned that her friend might be falling in love. Well, good for her, she deserved some sort of break. In the several years since they had first met she had been having a rotten deal. First the husband and then that dreadful man. It was time something magical finally worked out for her despite what Anna might privately think about Raffaele. But, crooked or not, he was certainly appealing and a million times preferable to Hector. She would keep her mouth shut and her fingers firmly crossed that all would eventually work out.

Genevieve, however, was solidly in the dumps and feared her budding relationship might be over. She described how they had discovered the photographs and also the reaction of the women in the shop.

'They acted as if she were the Antichrist,' she said. 'One even made the sign of the cross. Whoever she was, they were not about to discuss it. Even Simonetta wouldn't talk.'

'So what did you do?'

'We took them to Raffaele. And that was our biggest mistake.'

Anna could hear the quaver in Genevieve's voice and sensed she was getting close to tears.

'He was positively rude when we asked him who she was, virtually told us to mind our own damned business. Said we should put them back where we found them and leave the matter alone. And then he went into the kitchen and that was that. He only came out when we paid the bill and even then was barely civil. Whatever it is we have stumbled into, we clearly should not have been messing with Sutherland's photographs. There's a lot going on that we simply don't understand.

'Oh, by the way,' she added, 'Sutherland isn't married, so there goes your theory about him being there with his wife. Raffaele isn't married either but it was more than clear that the woman in the pictures means a great deal to him. Means or meant; I am certain she is dead. Which is pretty macabre, when you think about it. It seems that I'm playing second fiddle to a fucking ghost.'

'You can't know that for sure,' said Anna, though it certainly did look that way. Clearly there was some mystery surrounding the woman which no-one in the village was ready to share. 'I'd just hang in there and see what happens. But better not go back into Sutherland's rooms.'

It had been worth the try but again they had drawn a blank. Why did that no longer surprise her? Anna confessed her own fears about being followed but also conceded it was probably just in her head.

'Take care,' she said. 'I will call you as soon as there's news. Paige is on another new trail but refuses to let me know what it is. I think she feels I have been through enough. And, you know something, she's dead right. And please don't worry about upsetting Raffaele. Behave as normal and I'm sure he will soon come around.' Genevieve was so gentle and sweet. There was no way he could stay mad at her for long.

★   ★   ★

'Take a look at that,' said Dave Kelly, his barely suppressed excitement making him sweat. His hand was shaking like a hardened junkie's, he looked like a man in urgent need of a fix. He

272

moved aside to allow Paige to study his screen. She read the list and was instantly skewered by a sharp adrenalin jolt that felt like hope.

She raised an enquiring eyebrow at him. 'What exactly is this?'

'A list of the companies that had offices in the twin towers. Not just the big ones, like Cantor Fitzgerald, but everyone in the financial world who lost staff.'

'Why are you showing me this?'

'I am not exactly sure. You will see that, apart from the tax department, almost everyone else was a bond trader.'

Her theory again; how smart of him to have deduced it. Maybe he wasn't such a klutz after all. She glanced around for the water-cooler, checking to make sure it was nowhere in sight.

'I wonder,' she said at her most feminine and appealing, 'if I might possibly have a glass of water.'

'Sure,' he said, delighted to do her bidding, and disappeared obediently down the corridor.

Swift as a cobra, Paige struck and, within seconds of his leaving her alone, was rapidly working his printer. By the time he returned with a paper cup in his hand, the printout was safely in her purse. What he did not know he need never fret over, though she had a shrewd instinct he knew more than he let on. Unethical, maybe, but she was a lawyer who had been fumbling in the dark for far too long.

They chatted for a further few minutes, then Paige made her pretty excuses and said she really must go. She thanked him profusely for giving her lunch and promised that next time it would be on her. *Fat chance*, she thought as she hailed a cab. The one good thing about gullible men was that they were so easy to manipulate.

19

It was early morning and the streets of Montisi were deserted. Simonetta, in a flowered pinafore, was sluicing the pavement directly in front of her shop. Candy, for once in her life up with the lark, had bravely volunteered for breakfast duty and was down in the village, stocking up with supplies, while Genevieve lazed on in bed. Simonetta, putting aside her pail, greeted her with her usual radiant smile.

'*Buon giorno!* You're up early,' she said. 'It looks like being another glorious day.'

Candy followed her inside, inhaling the powerful aroma of freshly ground coffee. 'I'll take some of that,' she said, 'and also a chunk of the pancetta.' She picked out some figs and a box of fresh farm eggs and lined them up on the counter. When she did make the effort, she enjoyed this time of day, with the sky a limpid pinkish blue and the cuckoo spit still on the grass. She took a gamble on Simonetta's mood. 'I guess we boobed where the photos were concerned. I hope we didn't offend you.'

'Not at all,' said Simonetta, slicing the pancetta, 'it was just a bit of a shock.'

Candy thought quickly and wondered if she dared. 'I am also afraid that we might have upset Raffaele.'

'Don't worry about it,' said Simonetta rather too fast, revealing that she obviously already knew. 'It's just something he's going to have to learn to cope with. All of us, in fact.'

'I assume that means she is dead?'

Simonetta nodded. 'It hit the whole village very badly.'

'Especially Raffaele?'

She nodded again. At which point, to Candy's intense irritation, one of the gnarled old harpies came hobbling in. No point now in even trying to continue. She would simply have to wait for another chance. She paid, picked up her groceries and left. On the short drive home she thought hard about what she should do and decided not to say anything to Genevieve, who was depressed enough as it was, poor thing. No point in making her feel worse.

★ ★ ★

Time passed and still Paige sat on at her desk, engrossed in the purloined list. In addition to the big names Dave Kelly had mentioned, there were fourteen single-spaced pages of them. Mainly bond traders, some of them one-man shows, whose offices had been in the World Trade Centre. If her latest theory held any substance at all, one of these names might be a cover for something considerably more sinister. The Enron chief had used characters from *Star Wars* in order to cover his tracks.

She remembered what Charles had explained to her at breakfast; the concept of off-balance-sheet partnerships. If a company structured a special borrowing arrangement, in which the

276

obligation to repay failed to appear on its statements, then it could reduce the liabilities shown on the balance sheet. The investors would never see the transaction; only the phoney brokerage statements. And by the time they discovered the truth, much of their money would be gone, magicked away by the crooked trader and stashed in a secret account. Most of this was gobble-degook to Paige yet she was starting to get the gist.

A faint draught fluttered the air behind her where the door to the stairwell stood ajar and, looking up at the clock, she realised just how long she had been there. It was Friday night and growing late; everyone else would be gone now. Soon she too would have to be off; in thirty minutes' time she was meeting Charles. She ran her eye down the list again, on the lookout for something unspecified. The name she had expected to find was Sutherland; instinct told her that he had to be somehow involved. The little about him that they did know all seemed to fit; his silence, his evasiveness, the fact that he worked mainly abroad. Yet now it seemed that he might have been stalking Anna; Paige was still at a loss to understand how. There were still a lot of missing pieces but a picture was slowly emerging, if incomplete.

The facts remained indisputable. Anna had innocently answered an advertisement, suggesting a home swap from April to July. She had checked out the references and done it in good faith, exchanging her own extremely valuable property with a stranger who had hailed from the same alma mater. It had all seemed perfectly cut and dried at the time, regardless of Paige's initial misgivings. But Anna, in some ways, was that much more trusting; Paige admired her for that. Next she had had trouble with her credit card which someone had run well above its limit and, after that, all the money from her bank account had mysteriously vanished without trace. Then she had found that the house was on the market and her father had been temporarily abducted while his own house was peremptorily sold. The money from that had never been recovered. This had to be organised crime. Paige, after all her weeks of fruitless research, was now convinced that the secret lay in this list. If she could only establish that one missing link, she would be able to turn it over to the FBI.

That draught again and the feeling that someone was out there. She glanced around but the light was no longer on. Just a couple more minutes and then she'd be off. She stapled the pages together. She wondered if Charles would be awfully cross if she worked through the weekend.

* * *

Simonetta lived above the shop, with a balcony crowded with flowering plants and a cheerful, melodious canary in a wicker cage. She was busily watering as Candy passed beneath and found herself suddenly drenched.

'Oi!' she shouted. 'Are you trying to drown me?' Luckily she was wearing her versatile hat.

Simonetta peered through her phalanx of brilliant foliage and laughed when she saw what she had done.

'*Vieni!*' she said, beckoning, beaming with delight. 'Please come up here and have a glass of wine. I am sorry if I have made you wet.' It was almost lunchtime and business, for once, was slow. Candy, returning from the market, needed no second invitation. Genevieve, for a change, was actually working; it would do her good to be left in peace for a while. They had shaken down to a new routine, more relaxed than Anna's but nonetheless effective. Besides, there were things Candy was keen to find out and now seemed the perfect opportunity. She wanted to ask more about the woman in the photographs but sensed she would have to work round to it. So she began with something relatively safe.

'Have you always lived in the village?' she began as Simonetta bustled around, pouring wine into tiny fluted glasses and arranging the sweet, dry biscuits on a plate.

'Since I was three years old,' she said. 'My grandparents were from Siena.' Presumably the boundaries of her universe until she grew up and mysteriously landed in Enfield.

'And how on earth did Enfield come about?' asked Candy, impressed by women who radically changed their lives.

Simonetta shrugged expansively. 'God moves in mysterious ways,' was all she would say.

'But you ended up back here?'

'I had no choice. My father died and my mother needed help in the shop. Besides, by then

I had seen the world and was ready to settle down.' Simonetta's wide grin was irreverent and infectious. It did not appear that she had suffered too much.

'Yet you never married?' Candy was curious, despite her own rebellion in that department. Simonetta, though not a beauty, was fun with lively intelligent eyes.

'No-one asked me,' she said with a chuckle. 'And here, in Montisi, there isn't a lot of choice.'

Which brought them neatly to Candy's main agenda. 'Tell me about Daniel Sutherland,' she said.

'Daniel, ah, what a lovely man. One of the most generous I have ever known. He'd do anything for anyone, especially if they're in trouble. Would give away the shirt off his back if need be.' A faraway look came into Simonetta's eyes and her expression perceptibly softened. 'I have known him most of my life, you know. We grew up together in this village.'

'Here?' said Candy, taken aback. 'We sort of thought he must have married into Montisi.'

'Daniel, alas, is not the marrying kind.' She made no attempt to conceal the regret in her voice.

'But with a name like Sutherland and educated at Yale . . . '

'His mother was the Contessa di Valdombrone. She married the Count when Daniel was just a child and he raised him here as his step-son and presumed heir. Daniel and Raffaele have always been close; they are, after all, step-cousins.' Then, observing Candy's growing confusion: 'Raffaele is the nephew of the Count.'

It was a lot to digest but explained a good few things. She would have to go away and think it all through.

'You should have seen them as young men,' said Simonetta fondly, 'forever up to mischief of some kind. Once they even competed in the Palio, sporting the family colours, carrying the flag. They were both so handsome, all the women were crazy about them. And yet, in all those years, unbelievably, they managed never to fall out.' It was clear, from the sudden slight quaver in her voice, that neither had she been entirely immune.

'So *Casavecchia* was part of his inheritance?' They had assumed it was something he had bought.

'*Si, si*, it is part of the Tolomei estate.' Simonetta obviously thought Candy knew more than she did.

And now she was definitely out of her depth. Her look of total bafflement made Simonetta laugh. 'The Contessa's husband and also Raffaele's uncle was the Count Ildebrando Tolomei di Valdombrone.'

It was not entirely the dry biscuit that made Candy choke; she needed to get away as fast as she could. It was siesta time for Simonetta and Genevieve would be waiting for her lunch.

'I've got to go,' said Candy, draining her glass. 'Please may we do this again some other time?'

★   ★   ★

Charles Collier had been waiting a full twenty minutes; the concert was scheduled to start in fewer than ten. He looked repeatedly at his watch as he paced the concrete plaza. It was not like his wife to cut things quite so fine. Lately, he knew, she had been hugely preoccupied, trying to sort things out for the wretched Anna. Five more minutes and he'd leave her ticket at the box office. He did not want to risk missing the opening Dvořák. His mobile rang and he answered it impatiently. He had had a taxing day himself and was anxious to unwind.

'Sorry, honey,' said Paige, 'I am on my way. I'm just at Columbus Circle, crossing the street. Be with you soon.' She sounded hugely excited. '*Wait* till you hear what I think I have stumbled upon — '

She was interrupted by a sickening screech of tyres and a violent scream before the phone went dead. Charles shook it in bewilderment, for a second not comprehending, then threw himself into the heavy traffic, in reckless disregard for his own life.

★ ★ ★

Emboldened by all she had learned from Simonetta, Candy persuaded Genevieve to return with her to the trattoria that night. They had kept away since the incident of the photographs, scared of once more inciting Raffaele's wrath. They still didn't have the full picture, only that he had suffered a bereavement with which he was trying hard to come to terms.

282

A look of relief crossed his face when he saw them; he hurried across and took both of Genevieve's hands.

'*Signora*,' he breathed, 'I had started to worry. I'm afraid I spoke to you harshly last time we met.'

She squeezed his hand. 'It doesn't matter. We were interfering where we had no right to be.'

Raffaele, relieved, gave her an affable smile. 'Soon I will tell you everything,' he promised.

While he was getting their order, they conferred. Should they press their advantage while the going was good? Candy thought definitely though Genevieve was cautious. She feared to invoke that coldness again in his eyes. But Anna, in New York, continued to suffer. Their first priority must surely be to do what she had asked.

So once the food was on the table and Raffaele, still beaming, hovering, Genevieve plucked up the courage to ask him about his relationship with Sutherland. Simonetta had been talking, she explained. They were both intrigued to know more about their mysterious absentee landlord. Raffaele hesitated, his eyes inscrutable, clearly struggling with powerful inner conflicts. But Candy was gazing at him with spellbound attention while the candlelight threw a halo round Genevieve's head. He could not resist these two lovely English ladies and felt in his heart he probably could trust them. So he eased himself comfortably into a chair, loosened his tie and embarked upon his story.

Daniel's mother, Alicia, was a society beauty

from San Diego who had married Daniel's father while still in her teens.

'It was — how you say it? — a true love match. One look and for them that was it.' He kissed his fingers expressively, the embodiment of the sentimental Italian. A frisson of excitement flickered down Genevieve's spine. The plain-speaking earthiness of this man, especially after Hector, made her giddy.

The couple settled in Colorado where he worked as a mining engineer. They were blissfully happy until, when Daniel was five, his father was killed in an aircrash in the Rockies and the feckless Alicia, unable to cope alone, soon after remarried a much older man. Raffaele's uncle, Count Tolomei, owner of most of the land in these parts. Genevieve's eyes met Candy's. It must have been his portrait they had seen, though they dared not let Raffaele suspect they'd been in there snooping.

The Count raised Daniel as his son and heir but died when Daniel was fifteen, leaving the bulk of the estate to Alicia and *Casavecchia* to Daniel.

'Plus an expensive education in the States. I tell you, he looked upon him as his son. Daniel is as close to me as a brother. We grew up together as children in this village. There is nothing in the world I wouldn't do for him. Or, indeed, he for me.'

One by one the pieces were slotting in; slowly it was starting to make sense. It explained the strong bond between the two men and the fact that, in Raffaele's eyes at least, Sutherland was

284

something of a saint.

'So where is he now? That's what we need to know.' Enough of all the sentimentality; the urgency was sharp in Genevieve's voice. She sat up straighter and her cheeks were becomingly flushed. If he doesn't crack now, thought Candy, amused, then he's tougher than he would appear.

'You tell me. You said New York,' said Raffaele, instantly back on his guard. 'His work means he moves around all the time. Often we have no contact for months though he knows I am always here, should he ever need me.'

'How much time does he spend here altogether?' asked Candy.

'Very little,' said Raffaele, 'which is sad. Only when it fits his busy schedule.'

'But he was here in November,' Candy persisted. Which was when the ad appeared and it all began.

Raffaele calculated then shook his head. 'I would say it's at least a couple of years since Daniel last set foot in *Casavecchia*. His occasional visits are always very rushed and even then he only comes if there's something that urgently needs fixing. He has been in Patagonia for months, before that in Nepal. It's the life he chose though it's sometimes hard on those of us who love him.'

Silently they absorbed this information, then Genevieve made a bold decision. She hesitated to incur Raffaele's wrath, yet felt the time had come to spill the beans. Nothing would be gained by prevarication; the situation was far too serious for that. She leaned across and gingerly touched his hand.

'There's something you ought to know about,' she said.

Briefly, choosing her words with care, Genevieve filled him in. She told him everything that had happened so far, beginning with Anna seeing the ad, right up to the callous abduction of her father. The credit card fraud, the missing text; most of all, the cold-blooded theft of Anna's house.

'I am afraid your saintly Daniel is a crook who has ruthlessly preyed on our friend.'

Raffaele's eyes were suddenly icy. 'How do you figure that?' he said.

'Because,' said Candy, leaping in, 'he's the only person with legal access. No-one else has the keys to Anna's house. Not now the architect is dead.'

Raffaele stared blankly, as if not comprehending, so Genevieve started to run it all through again. But Raffaele silenced her with a curt gesture. His charm had vanished along with his good humour.

'The architect is dead?' he repeated.

'Yes, I was certain you would know that. He had a fall.'

Candy was starting to grow impatient but Raffaele looked as though he had seen a ghost.

'*Scusi*,' he muttered and bolted from the room. They heard him in the kitchen, frantically phoning.

* * *

286

By the time Charles got there a crowd had gathered and all he could see through their legs was a flash of teal blue. They told him an ambulance was on its way but, from the expressions of the nearest spectators, he grimly surmised it was probably already too late. He pushed his way through them to where she was lying, on her back with her hair all unpinned. He wanted to cradle her in his arms but knew he had to wait for the paramedics. Instead he picked up her bloodstained purse and silently cursed the relentless ambition that had snatched his darling from him so abruptly and far too soon. Since college he had only ever had eyes for Paige; she had been the whole focus of his life.

'Hit and run,' said a sympathetic bystander. 'Guess the poor lady never really stood a chance.' But Charles, in his heart, remained unconvinced. He knew from their discussions of the securities frauds that something underhand had been going on. And his beautiful, head-strong, impetuous Paige had done her usual thing and leapt straight in. For once, however, and it broke his heart, she had unknowingly been batting way out of her league.

20

Right around the corner from where Anna was staying was a basement café in which she occasionally ate. Today being Saturday, she dropped in there for brunch. For once she had left her father alone with Colette. There were times when she felt that she badly needed space. Too much was presently weighing on her mind for her to be any sort of company. She had brought the newspaper and intended to read it but found herself with zero concentration. At six that morning she had been awoken by the phone — Candy and Genevieve, bursting with news, eager to fill her in. They did their customary double act, passing the receiver back and forth while they told her all about their evening with Raffaele. Culminating in his unexpected exit without so much as a word of explanation.

'It was all most odd,' said Genevieve plaintively. 'Suddenly his attitude totally changed.'

'It was when we let slip about Larry,' chimed in Candy. 'He disappeared to make an urgent phone call.'

'And never came back.' Which had really upset Genevieve. More had been hanging on that one contrived meeting than she cared to admit.

Now Anna sat and contemplated all the underlying implications. She had asked the girls to continue their good work while, at the same time, exhorting them to be careful. The more convoluted it all became, the more potentially dangerous. No-one knew for sure what it was they were embroiled in but it was wise to remember that Larry had ended up dead. And, despite their belief that he was a good guy, she feared they might have played straight into Raffaele's hands. Words like mafia flitted through her brain; something positively shady was going on. It all boiled down to two basic facts: someone had been responsible for the crimes and still none of them had yet encountered Sutherland.

She was mopping up her eggs Benedict and looking around for more coffee when a man descended the stairs from the street and halted in front of her table. Since he was effectively blocking the light — the restaurant was gloomy and the stairway unlit — all Anna could make out was that he was tall.

'Mind if I sit here?' he asked casually, even though the place was far from full. Then, without even waiting for a reply, he plonked himself down on the opposite chair and asked a passing waiter for coffee and toast. Because the street door was temporarily open, all Anna could make out was his silhouette.

'Well,' he said calmly, removing his mirrored shades. 'Finally I have succeeded in tracking you down.'

★   ★   ★

The eyes, which she had never seen before, were as tawny and probing as an eagle's, but the teeth were familiar the moment he smiled and reached across the table to offer his hand.

'Dan Sutherland,' was all he said, as the waiter brought his coffee, then he relaxed and waited for Anna to react.

For a full sixty seconds she was frozen with disbelief, then the anger boiling inside her began to erupt. He had the gall to sit there, invading her space, as though it were the most natural thing in the world. This man, who had methodically sucked her dry, appeared now to be offering the hand of friendship.

'You've got some damned nerve,' she spluttered, once she had regained the power of speech, seriously wondering whether to call the police. But, since the chances of them ever showing up were minimal, she might as well take the time to hear him out. It was, after all, their first real encounter, aside from that single brief brush in Tuscany. Then his manner had been supercilious when he had coldly and rudely grilled her about the house. She also remembered, with a dart of sudden alarm, the gun in the back of his Land Rover. He had not even deigned then to tell her who he was; now it seemed he was offering some sort of a truce.

She bit back her rage; there was little point in fighting. She could always change her mind and summon help. Besides, she was curious to hear what he had to say. Whatever his story might be, it had better be good.

'How did you find me, in any case?' No-one

outside her tight circle knew where she was staying.

'I have my ways.' He tested his coffee and then his toast arrived. He took his time before answering her question. 'Sooner or later you were bound to show up. So I hung around your house and simply waited. And, speaking of nerve,' and now his voice grew colder, 'what the fuck were you doing in my house?'

Anna was too surprised to answer. How dare he try to grab the moral ground. 'Why didn't you tell us who you were?' she came up with feebly. 'What was it with all the cloak-and-dagger stuff?'

Another long pause while he considered her thoughtfully. 'There were reasons,' he eventually said.

'What kind of reasons? You knew who we were. It had all been covered by email. Your secretary even called Raffaele from Patagonia to tell him we were on our way.'

'I have no secretary,' he said.

Silence again and, again, deadlock. They seemed to be going round in circles.

'I had to be certain.' He stirred his coffee. 'When Raffaele called, I came straightaway to find out what the hell was going on.' He looked at her with those clear perceptive eyes and suddenly, for no reason she understood, Anna started to feel slightly less embattled. Despite the fact that his story didn't add up, she believed that he wasn't lying.

'You thought we were trespassers?' she suggested.

He nodded. 'And why not? You had no right to

291

be there. The villa is private and has been shut up for years. The only people who ever go there are personal guests of my own.' The smile had gone and now his eyes were flinty. His face was stern with a strong and resolute jaw. Like cats preparing for a fight, they sat rigid and sized each other up.

Until, unnervingly, he started to chuckle. 'You must admit, it does have its farcical side. Don't worry,' he added, in a gentler tone. 'Raffaele has brought me up to date. It seems we have both been the victims of a trickster. Let's call a truce, at least for the time being, and exchange what information we both have. You, so I'm told, have lost everything whereas I am hot on an entirely different trail.'

He picked up both bills and paid the cashier, then courteously escorted her into the street. It was clear, from the easy way he took control, that he knew exactly where she would be heading. His stalking must have been more thorough than she had known; no wonder lately she had started feeling spooked.

'Look,' he said outside her hotel. 'There are things I have to do that can't be postponed. Could we, perhaps, meet up later for a drink? It is vital that we put all our cards on the table.'

Gradually Anna felt her anger abating. His suggestion was, at the very least, constructive. She had been through so much in the past few weeks, she no longer had the heart to keep on fighting. All she wanted was some sort of resolution. And something about him made her feel she could trust him. Despite all the evidence to the contrary, in person he came over as absolutely straight. Why, if he weren't, would he have bothered to track her down? The very least she could do, she supposed, was give him the benefit of the doubt.

'Come here at seven,' she said, mollified, and watched while he scrawled down her number. She was drawn by his unnervingly steady gaze that seemed to see into her soul. He was lean and fit and, yes, attractive, with the sort of permanent tan that came from an outdoor life. A feeling of cautious hope swept through her. Maybe, after all, it would be all right.

Until she entered the lobby and saw Colette, white and shaking, clearly waiting for her.

'Anna,' she faltered, coming forward with arms outstretched, and Anna was overwhelmed with sudden terror.

'Dad?' she whispered, not sure she could face the answer. She didn't believe she could handle anything more.

Colette shook her head. 'It's Paige,' she said.

And Anna knew, without having to ask, what had happened.

★ ★ ★

So now New York's finest were belatedly on the job, keen to discover the identity of Paige's killer. For murder it had been, of that there could be little doubt. Eyewitness accounts simply did not tally with a straightforward traffic accident. The driver had swerved up on to the sidewalk and sent her flying as she waited to cross the street, then vanished into the rush-hour traffic while a crowd of horrified bystanders looked helplessly on. Who, the police were keen to know from Charles, might conceivably have wanted to kill his wife? The only answer he could logically come up with was that she was, by profession, a criminal lawyer. Until he looked in her purse and found the papers.

For the moment, he decided not to tell the police; he wanted to think things through before he did. Shock meant he wasn't entirely rational; he turned to Anna instead. They clung to each other in their inconsolable grief, unable to believe that such a thing could have happened. They'd been friends for as long as he had known Paige; since their second year at Yale, in fact, though Charles had been at Princeton and two years older. After all these years, they felt as close as family. It wasn't a lot of comfort but it helped.

'Whatever I do,' swore Charles, fists tightened, 'I will get the bastard responsible for this.'

He showed her the slightly bloodstained pages, now also spattered with his tears. 'These are top-security SEC documents which Paige should never have been allowed to see.' Let alone carry away in her purse; there were so many questions without answers. What she had been up to, he still didn't know; bitterly regretted that she hadn't told him. 'She said she thought she had a hot new lead and got me to introduce her to Dave Kelly. My friend at the SEC,' he explained. 'They met up a couple of times.' Many men, blessed with a wife as glorious as Paige, might have felt the occasional twinge of insecurity. Not

Charles Collier; nor had he ever. One of the many reasons that Anna had always envied their marriage.

He wondered if he should talk to Dave, though hated to implicate Paige. On the other hand, now that she was dead what could it possibly matter? Lawyers were hardly known for keeping their noses clean and Paige had always been one of the best — probing, insightful and thorough.

'So she didn't discuss it with you in any particular detail?'

'Only ever peripherally, though I knew it had something to do with your case. She told me she'd fill me in when she'd worked things out.' That was his feisty, unstoppable wife, always prepared to go that extra mile. Tears came flooding back and he started to weep. The two of them had only ever had eyes for each other. What on earth was he going to do with the rest of his life?

Anna hugged him and waited until he was calmer. Her mind was fixed on the SEC and Dave Kelly.

'You think he might have given her some sort of tip-off?'

Charles shrugged. 'I really can't say.'

'So go and talk to him instantly. Find out everything he knows. If you want, I'll come with you.' She held out her hand. For the first time in all the years she had known him, Charles looked on the brink of cracking up.

★   ★   ★

Dave Kelly, as Charles had rather feared, could not tell them very much more. He was shattered, of course, by the news of Paige's death, but also completely at a loss to imagine what conceivably might have triggered it. When Charles produced the stapled pages, he explained it was something he had wanted her to see.

'Strictly against the rules, of course, but I had a gut feeling she might be able to help me.' He had been hugely impressed by her agile brain and obviously formidable intelligence. He ran through her theory, which coincided with his own, that someone was using the September devastation in order tactically to disappear. 'The first time we talked, I thought she was being overfanciful but then I received details of everyone who was missing, along with the companies they ran. Some large, like Cantor Fitzgerald, some small; one-man shows that had only recently been set up. Among the jumble of them on that list, there's a chance one's a cover for a shady operation.' Which was why the SEC had become involved.

'Sorry,' said Anna, 'you have lost me completely.' Maths had always been her very worst subject at school. Her own particular talents lay in a different area of her brain, one of the reasons she had never learned to drive.

Charles explained briefly about special purpose entities and the gangs of small brokers linked to corporate fraud. It all went back to Enron, he said, whose recent demise had dramatically blown the cover on all types of corporate skulduggery, previously unguessed at.

'Paige believed that the person who swiped your money might have ploughed it back into a bogus account and used it as bait to attract bona fide investors.'

'So what's with the list?' She still didn't quite understand. What had been Paige's fascination with those names?

'I had been through it so many times,' admitted Dave, 'and it still didn't make any sense. But because she appeared to have reached similar conclusions, I gambled on allowing her to see it.' He caught Charles's eye and gave him a guilty grin. 'Well, you knew Paige,' was all he said.

She had acted so swiftly, he had been impressed and had never let on that he knew. Another thing Charles understood completely; the only way to control her had been always to let her have her head.

'The last time we spoke, she sounded excited.' Charles well recalled the jubilation in her voice when she called to tell him that she might have found a new lead. And then the screeching of brakes and she was dead. He furtively wiped his eyes to stop the flow.

'So what exactly had she discovered?' asked Dave. 'I confess that I am still in the dark.' He suppressed his dream of that longed-for third meeting when she would have explained it succinctly over lunch.

Charles sniffed and shrugged. He didn't know either. A penalty of loving a maverick woman.

'Here, let me,' said Anna, grabbing the list. What they were saying made no sense to her;

perhaps a fresh eye might throw some new light on the matter.

It took her three minutes of intensive skimming before it simply leapt off the page. Tucked away near the end of page fourteen, a bond company listed simply as 'Ptolemy'.

The blood started hammering wildly in her ears. 'Got it, that's him!' she almost shouted. 'That's Dan Sutherland, I know I am not wrong.' There was no other person it possibly could be.

21

'Why don't we simply turn him in?' Charles was
visibly panting for a fight. 'I will slice off his balls
and stuff them down his throat if ever I get my
hands on the fucking bastard.' Nothing he could
devise would be bad enough for the man who
had cold-bloodedly run down his wife and for no
reason that Charles could understand, which was
infinitely worse.

Anna felt much the same but more controlled.
She put her arms gently around his neck and
rested her cheek against his chest. He was
hurting so much it was painful to observe but
she was suffering too. Emotionally she agreed
with him but first they must think things
through. Larry and Paige had already died; this
was not a children's game they'd become
involved in. Dan Sutherland, for all his apparent
honesty, now looked like being the dangerous
killer they had initially taken him to be.

A man who could look her squarely in the eye
only hours after murdering her best friend had
to be deeply unscrupulous and also very
probably deranged. They must not run the risk
this time of allowing him to slither off the hook.
If they turned him over to the cops right now,
the chances were he would slip through their
demonstrably incompetent fingers. Before they
could shop him, they needed hard evidence
which could only be achieved from another

meeting. That was how Anna reasoned, at least; reluctantly Charles agreed.

The original appointment had been cancelled because of Paige but Anna had rearranged it for two days' time. She knew that might appear to be a bit on the callous side but Paige would have been the first to urge her on. She had done so much and now she was dead. They owed it to her not to bungle things now. Anna explained to Charles, as gently as she could, exactly what it was she intended to do. He thought about it, then nodded agreement. Any sort of action was better than none.

'Mind if I tag along?' he asked. 'I feel so pathetically useless.' Until the autopsy was out of the way, time hung heavily on his hands. He could not face the bank nor being at home on his own. Paige had been the sum total of his life; they had not even bothered to have a family. He was feeling murderous since their meeting with Dave but rational enough to acknowledge that Anna was right. Despite all the pointers that appeared to incriminate Sutherland, they must tread very warily to ensure that he didn't get away. Softly, softly, catchee monkey. That was the only way to play it.

'Do come,' said Anna, 'I could certainly use some backup.' It would give him something to focus on and her the reassurance of having him there. A man as dangerous as Sutherland was not the kind of opponent to face alone. Anna was slightly scared but also intrigued. She could not equate the man she had met with the monster that lay beneath.

300

She had fixed to meet him for drinks at The Mark so Charles came by and they strolled up Madison together.

'I can't guarantee my behaviour,' he warned her. This was, after all, the man who had ruined his life.

Gently Anna took his hand. 'Let's hear him out first and then make up our minds. We can always call in the cops if we decide to. But first we really need to hear what he has to say.'

It was hard to imagine what story he could come up with. She worried about its effect on Charles, who at Princeton had been a pretty nifty wrestler.

★ ★ ★

He was taller even than Anna remembered when he rose from a corner banquette to greet them. He was wearing jeans and a battered leather jacket and, without the shades, looked much more human. A camera case was on the bench beside him; even in circumstances like these, he was obviously always on the job. She made the introductions without explaining who Charles was, nor his reasons for having come along. No point in making him suspicious at this stage; a friend, was all she said, and left it at that. Despite the recent ravages of grief, Charles Collier was still a fine-looking man. She was proud to have him there at her side.

'So now, where were we?' asked Sutherland briskly, once the waiter had taken their orders and gone. 'Talking about this fictitious house

301

swap.' He pulled out a palmtop computer and flicked to his notes.

'And the way you have ruined my life,' flashed back Anna, instantly on the offensive. Something about the very maleness of the man always succeeded in getting her hackles up. Last time they'd met he had ended up charming her but that was before what had happened to Paige. Now she hated him unequivocally. It was he who, by placing that fateful ad, had started off this whole horrible sequence of events.

Charles, beneath the table, kicked her foot. Trading insults was not constructive and so far, to his huge surprise, he was favourably impressed. This gaunt-faced stranger with the world-weary eyes had the air of a man of some distinction. Despite the agony in his heart, Charles's pent-up belligerence subsided. Let them hear him out and then decide what the verdict should be. The drinks arrived, creating a minor diversion, then Sutherland resumed his interrogation. Charles could see, from the glint in his eye, that he was taking Anna more seriously than she might think.

'Tell me,' said Sutherland, sipping his bourbon. 'Why do you suppose I would ever have considered allowing total strangers into my home?' Money's no object was implicit but unsaid. This man could afford the finest hotels.

'Because you needed four months in New York.' That's what the ad had said.

'For Chrissakes, I am a *wildlife* photographer. Hardly my natural territory, wouldn't you say?'

'But I didn't know that,' said Anna, flustered,

302

still spoiling for a fight. 'It just seemed the ideal arrangement at the time. Me to Italy, to finish my book, you to Manhattan, presumably on a job.' She remembered vividly how depressed she had been, wanting only to quit the city of sorrows and hide herself away in some rural retreat.

'And it never occurred to you to check?' He might as well have had the shades back on, his eyes had become so inscrutable.

'I did that,' she said, 'with Paige's cousin.' Charles supplied the name. 'Who thought you were an A1 guy. Told us to tell you hello.'

The corners of Sutherland's mouth quirked slightly. He was laughing at her again. After all she had been through, the misery he had caused, she couldn't believe that he still wasn't taking this seriously. Because of him she had lost two dear friends, her house, all her money as well as the family home. She was destitute with nowhere to go and he still didn't even know about the cat. This was no moment for levity; she was on the verge of losing it altogether. Charles again touched her foot beneath the table, silently begging her not to give way now. Far too much was riding upon it and this man was beginning to intrigue him.

'You are claiming that you never placed that ad?' She tried to get a grip on her emotions.

'Damn right,' he said forcefully. 'Finally you get it. And now you seem to suggest I have stolen your house. I spend most of my time on the far side of the world and have only come here now because of Raffaele.'

'Raffaele? He called you?' Anna was startled. So the two of them had been in contact all the time. Another deception, her instincts had been right. They never should have trusted that fawning Italian.

'You bet. He keeps an eye on my affairs and has my best interests at heart. And, therefore, instantly alerted me when you ladies first blew into town.'

'But he told us he never knows where you are,' said Anna, suddenly feeling rather foolish.

'He lied.' The eyes were clear and now disconcertingly amused. For the first time she noticed the scar across his cheek, something that had been much more than just a scratch. 'Look,' he said in a gentler tone, seeing how upset she had become, 'I'm as keen as you are to get this whole thing sorted. It seems someone must have been taking my name in vain and that I cannot allow. Yet no-one apparently has ever encountered that person. Doesn't that strike you as odd?'

'Just your secretary.'

'I told you, I don't have one.'

'Nor a wife?'

He shook his head.

'So who is this woman?' Who had fired Consuela, checked the mail and been boldly in and out. Who might have been there when Larry died and possibly called the police. Who was solely responsible for losing the cat, of that Anna had little doubt. And taken her father, on false pretences, to a run-down retirement home in White Plains before disposing of his house? If

304

she wasn't in some way connected to the scam, then who in the world could she be? The woman from the real estate agency? They had only ever talked to her on the phone. Or any of the countless others who had acted to stop Anna sorting things out and left her practically destitute and alone. She lowered her eyes, on the brink of tears. It was much too painful to go on.

'That,' said Sutherland calmly, ordering another round, 'is exactly what we are here to try to figure out.'

Charles, now totally absorbed in it all, was fast coming round to respecting him. He had come here today in a mood to break someone's head but instead had been unexpectedly won over. This man, with his calm demeanour and rock-solid confidence, impressed him more by the second. All the signs were that he was innocent, or why else would he be here at all instead of on a flight back to Patagonia?

'It is even worse than you think,' he said, after careful deliberation. He owed it to Paige to show his hand in order to catch the hare that she had started. 'There have already been two unnecessary deaths. We must not run the risk of any more.'

'Two?' said Sutherland, obviously taken aback. 'I had only been told about the one.' He seemed genuinely startled and concerned; Charles was certain now that he couldn't be faking.

'My wife,' said Charles, 'was killed yesterday. Apparently on the brink of a major breakthrough.'

'Your wife? The lawyer?'

Charles nodded.

'I am so sorry,' said Sutherland, reaching across and briefly touching his arm.

Anna watched all this with fascination. He appeared to be totally sincere. If not, then he must be a brilliant actor. In order to save Charles the ordeal of giving details, she now stepped in and told him about Larry and then Paige. Two senseless accidents in the space of just a few weeks. The odds against it happening to close friends had to be infinitesimal.

'So you think they were murdered?'

'I am positive,' said Anna. 'Although, so far, we have no actual proof. The only reason, by the way, that we haven't yet called in the cops.'

Sutherland listened attentively. A small nerve started ticking at his jawline and it looked as though his blood was draining away. When he spoke again, his voice had dropped much lower. He seemed to be talking primarily to himself. 'I thought we were dealing with just theft and deception. I honestly didn't know things had gone quite this far.'

Anna, alert to his sudden mood change, was shocked to realise she found him disturbingly attractive. At any other time . . . but that was not why they were here. She was still working up to lobbing her hidden grenade.

'Tell us what you know about Ptolemy,' she said, watching closely for his reaction.

His gaze remained level, without so much as a flicker. 'I have not the slightest idea what you're talking about.'

'Ptolemy, as in the Pharaohs,' persisted Anna.

'Cleopatra and all that stuff.'

There was a sudden brief flash of recognition which was just as instantly snuffed out. Anna would swear before a court of law that he knew precisely what she meant. There followed a long pause, while he swirled the remains of his bourbon, putting his thoughts together before he replied. She had got him; she felt her adrenalin rising. Actor or not, she knew that she now had him nailed.

Eventually he looked up at her and his eyes were as clear and unwavering as before. Amber, she realised, was their actual colour; they seemed to change with the nuances of light.

'I think what you are referring to,' he said, 'is the fanciful local legend in Siena that the Tolomei family dates back to Ancient Egypt. Not true, of course, although they have been around for some time. Their forebears were bankers and that is what they are now. Bankers and landowners and pillars of the community. The rest, alas, is just a lot of baloney. I would love to believe that my relatives had been kings.'

He grinned and suddenly looked boyish and much younger. The shadow had faded from his eyes. 'But you still haven't told me what all this is about?' His bewilderment, she would have sworn, was genuine.

So, encouraged by a nod from Charles, she plunged in and told him the rest. About Paige's incursion into SEC records and her search for a phoney corporate name, one that might lead to the perpetrator of all that had happened to Anna. Ptolemy had seemed to ring instant bells but Sutherland was shaking his head. 'Nothing whatever to do with me, though I'd love to hear more some other time.' Here he looked pointedly at his watch. 'Pretty soon I am going to have to go. So may we, please, now cut to the chase?'

His sudden brisk mood change startled Anna but Charles took over the narrative. He explained about Paige's investment theory and where she believed Anna's money had gone. Sutherland listened with rapt concentration, asking a few perceptive questions and entering notes into his palm pilot. He then brusquely snapped it shut and rose to his feet.

'You have both been a lot of help,' he said, 'but now I have to go. There is something I need to do that cannot wait.'

'Hang on,' said Anna, struck by a sudden thought. Something about this man still didn't quite add up. 'If you're not actually working in New York, how come you are here at all?' *Geographic* had seemed unaware that he had left Patagonia.

He slung his camera bag over his shoulder then paused. For a moment he stared at her with those clear inscrutable eyes as if wondering how much he could trust her.

'I am looking for someone,' he said.

22

The sea was flat and almost white in the hazy afternoon heat. Genevieve, paddling at the edge of the surf, was glad she had remembered to bring her hat. Raffaele, in shirtsleeves with his pants rolled up to his calves, laughed as he waded beside her. They were like two kids on a Sunday-school outing, willing it never to end. His muscular arm was tight around her shoulders; she was keenly aware of his body's urgent heat and the musky aroma of masculine sweat heightened her own visceral excitement. She knew exactly what he had in mind, it was what she yearned for too, but this was neither the place nor, indeed, the time. The Hector memories must first be cauterised and that was not going to happen overnight. Added to which, anticipation is very often the greater part of seduction. For the first time ever, with her new-found confidence, she was prepared to string it out for as long as it took.

They were at Castiglione della Pescaia, thirty minutes' drive away. Raffaele had, after weeks of procrastination, eventually summoned the courage to ask her out.

'*Bellissima*,' he had pronounced with approval when he'd turned up at the villa to collect her. After several months in the open air, she had truly blossomed and was looking quite stunning. Candy, in her generous way, had run up yet another of her effortless creations, this time in heavy embroidered cream cotton which did wonderful things for Genevieve's tan. Beneath the demure straw hat, her hair was heavily sun-streaked and healthy eating had made her even more svelte. Raffaele took one look and visibly melted; it was clear he wanted to ravish her on the spot. Since his cousin, Daniel, had been on the phone he had come to the welcome conclusion that he could trust her. And now wanted only to make up for lost time. Not for nothing had Raffaele been born Italian.

'Now, behave yourselves, children,' Candy had said, mockstern. 'Don't do anything that I wouldn't do.' She felt a shade wistful as she waved them off, then climbed the steep stairs to her studio and her drawings. The fashion portfolio was very nearly done and she knew in her gut that it was good. Inspired, in fact; the others had raved and assured her that Harvey Nichols were bound to snap it up. Soon she would have to face going home to sort out the stark realities of life. Trevor was still looking after the child. There had been no more news of his wedding plans and she was privately hoping that they might yet fall through. A man in his forties with a commitment phobia could scarcely be considered a good marriage bet, not for a woman several years older, anxious to settle down.

She still had occasional nightmares when she considered all the implications. No other woman must ever be allowed to meddle with the upbringing of her son. Yet love appeared to be

310

suddenly all around her, or so it certainly seemed from where she sat. The light of desire in Raffaele's eye could scarcely be misconstrued and she had never seen Genevieve looking more incandescent. She felt a pang, which was loneliness, and wished that Anna would come back. The role of third wheel was not one she was cut out for, though the last thing she would ever do was begrudge a friend genuine happiness. Especially after the horrors of Hector, it was the very least that Genevieve deserved.

It was interesting, Candy thought, as she sat by the window and sketched, the amount of emotional rubbish even intelligent women would put up with. Forceful women with lives of their own could turn into putty in the hands of a domineering male. Although she had had to raise Hugo on her own, she had never experienced a moment of regret. Yes, it was tough and she had often been scared but would not have wanted it any other way. Anna and Genevieve were opposite poles but Candy fitted somewhere in between. She could not have borne to be without her son, yet hated the concept of needing to rely on a man. Anna had made a huge issue of staying single, boasting that she had never experienced a maternal urge in her life. Genevieve, on the other hand, was an entirely different animal. She essentially needed male approbation to boost her confidence and make her sparkle, to oil the wheels of her everyday life.

She resembled a Japanese paper flower; her petals only unfurled when they were watered. Seeing her now with the clearly besotted Raffaele was seeing her at her very best. How she had ever put up with Hector, Candy would never understand. But until Raffaele slashed his way through the thicket, the odds had been that the relationship would have dragged on. Genevieve just wasn't strong enough not to jump at Hector's whim the next time his diary had a sudden vacant slot and he needed a stopgap date. She shuddered to remember his puerile pass; he was the absolute worst type of British male. The notion of even being touched by him continued to make her skin crawl.

She thought about Anna, marooned in New York when all she wanted was to be back here with them. The terrible events that were happening in her life were way beyond all logical comprehension. Whatever it was she was up against was taking a frighteningly darker turn. With two fatal accidents so close together, the situation had become exceedingly alarming. Candy hoped Anna was being careful and not doing anything too rash. Anna, in turn, had warned her to stay on her guard and keep an especially beady eye on Raffaele. For all that romantic Italian charm, she still could not quite bring herself to trust him. Anna probed deeper than superficial sex appeal and something about him made her slightly uneasy. He was almost too friendly and anxious to oblige, yet look what had been happening since the house swap. Total disaster; the decimation of all she had owned. She still could not believe he was not involved.

'Something most definitely doesn't add up,' she had said when she called the previous night.

Genevieve was in the kitchen fixing supper, and didn't even hear the telephone ring. 'Please don't alarm her. Just keep your wits about you.' She described her two meetings with Sutherland, omitting the fact that he had disturbing eyes. Nor did she bother adding that she found him unnervingly attractive. Candy had seen him for herself and she was nobody's fool.

★   ★   ★

Before they paddled, he had treated her to lunch, a four-hour idyll on a sun-drenched terrace overlooking the sea. The innkeeper, part of a tight fraternity, had welcomed them both with elation. The food, none of which appeared on the printed menu, was the best that Genevieve had ever tasted, each dish personally and lovingly selected by the landlord, especially for them. From a basket covered by a fresh linen cloth, he produced his pièce de résistance, a knobby excrescence, covered in black warts, looking like an ancient and gnarled potato. Raffaele applauded and reverently sniffed it while Genevieve watched him curiously.

'Tartufo!' he exclaimed delightedly, passing it over for her to sniff too, then handed it back to its owner. One of the rarest of treats, a summer truffle, to be thinly shaved over a bowl of fine angel hair pasta. 'The food of the gods,' Raffaele declared, omitting to mention its famed aphrodisiac powers. After that, lobster fresh from the ocean, rushed from the barnacled pot to the restaurant's stove. Served with a crisp green

313

salad and tiny potatoes and a generous dollop of garlic mayonnaise.

'Only perfection for such a beautiful lady,' said Raffaele, kissing her hand, and Genevieve experienced a small shiver of excitement as she saw the unabashed longing in his eyes. But that, she reminded herself, would simply have to wait. First there were far more urgent things that had to be sorted out.

'Go on with your story,' she said, gently withdrawing her hand.

Raffaele, duly rebuffed, did as bid and continued his narrative.

★　★　★

On the death of her second husband the Contessa had panicked, unable, or so she believed, to manage without a husband. First time round she had married straight out of the school-room and barely had any single life at all. She had walked down the aisle with Ildebrando within months of becoming a widow and had grown accustomed to being indulged like the pretty, headstrong girl she essentially still was. Daniel was off in the States by that time and only ever came home for the long vacations. There was ample money but very little to do, with far too much empty time on her hands. She found the forbidding palazzo in Siena cavernous, chilly and austere. Also stuffed with priceless antiques that continuously made her nervous. This was no life for a woman of her age, not yet into her forties. Alicia was unwilling to dress in black and resign herself to a permanent back seat along with the other Italian widows who clustered like crows on a chimneypot. She had loved her husbands, both of them, but still had a lot left to give. To hell with propriety, all she really wanted was to get back out there and dance.

And dance she did, more than she ever could have dreamed, when, in less than a year, she married again. She hoped the Tolomer family would forgive her but she was not yet of an age to commit social suttee. This time the pendulum swung right back and she opted for somebody younger. Julio was handsome, in a swarthy Mexican way, and twenty-seven years to her thirty-nine. An unusual choice after her first two husbands, he was, by profession, a dance instructor on a cruise ship. Alicia met him in a bar in New York where she had gone for a spot of remedial shopping. Later she declared it was love at first sight.

'To begin with they were happy,' said Raffaele. 'He made her laugh and she really liked to dance.' Because of the money the Count had left her, pursuing pleasure presented no restrictions. She closed up the palazzo and moved to Rome, to a vast apartment close to the Spanish Steps where they entertained as lavishly as royalty. Her friends in Siena viewed Julio with mistrust, recognising the charlatan he eventually turned out to be. He was sleek, he was charming, with oily slicked-back curls and a smile as meltingly seductive as a fallen angel's.

'Alicia was infatuated,' said Raffaele, looking

315

back. 'My uncle had left her secure and well off but now she was crazily in love.' His brown eyes softened as he recalled how she had been, a giddy girl in a spin of excitement, thrilled at last to have found her handsome prince.

'And Daniel? Where did he fit in? What did he think of him?' It could not have been easy for a boy that age to acquire such a youthful step-father. Genevieve thought of her own two sons. At least she had never done anything like that to them.

'Daniel was sixteen and inclined to be judgemental. Luckily, though, he was still away at school.' Raffaele, for the moment, was being unusually discreet. The fact of the matter was that Daniel had loathed Julio. He had scarcely known his own father, who had died when he was just five, but had learned to revere and trust the man who had made him his surrogate son. To lose him too, at such an impression-able age, had helped mould the loner he was now.

'And then this bounder appears on the scene. I think you can imagine how he felt.'

Genevieve, looking back to her own failed marriage, empathised with someone she had once thought a crook. All they had gleaned about the elusive Mr Sutherland had added up to a totally ruthless man. Yet now this warm Italian, whom she trusted more and more, was throwing a whole new light on the situation. Despite what lingering reservations she still had, she was more than willing to put her trust in Raffaele.

316

'He suffered,' explained Raffaele gravely, 'yet was powerless to intervene. Imagine, a sensitive youth of that age having to watch his mother's descent into hell. Right in front of his eyes when he was there. They danced, they squandered, they threw expensive parties and Daniel saw his heritage being eaten away. Not that he cared particularly, money has never impressed him, but Alicia, always so fearless and independent, was suddenly in thrall to a petty tyrant. The dancing master, with his foppish, elegant ways, was bit by bit revealing his monstrous side. Not unexpected to Roman society but devastating to her only son.' Daniel took after his father, he explained, basically serious though worldly-wise and a bit of a puritan at heart.

The innkeeper, beaming broadly, was back at the table, anxious to find out how they were liking the meal.

'*Magnifico*,' declared Raffaele in a way she had learned to expect.

'*Bene, bene*,' said their delighted host, satisfied that his honour was not at stake, and brought them a basket of summer fruits and a plate of chocolates.

'As the years went by, the money began to run out. Daniel, having graduated well, elected to stay in the States. He felt he no longer had a proper home here apart, of course, from *Casavecchia*, but his chosen career involved him in a vast amount of overseas travel and there wasn't very much scope for him here in Italy. I kept an eye on the house for him and occasionally some of us used it. He has always

317

been very generous in that way but what else would an unmarried man be doing with a villa of that size?

'And then one day, out of the blue, Alicia returned, having been dumped by Julio. He had gone through her fortune, found himself a younger woman and disappeared as mysteriously as he arrived. Sadder, wiser and considerably more cynical, she rented out the palazzo to make ends meet and took up refuge in *Casavecchia*.'

'Rented out the ancestral home?' Genevieve's heart went out to her. She understood all too well how she must have felt. No wonder *Casavecchia* was so exquisite and had such a feminine touch.

'All she had left to lean on was Daniel. Plus, of course, her daughter.'

'Her daughter?' Genevieve was doubly surprised. The story was growing more complex with each new revelation. 'So Daniel has a sister?' she said. Odd that had never been mentioned before. All sorts of facts about Daniel's family were now beginning to emerge.

Raffaele's face clouded; for a moment he went silent. 'A half-sister, Mercedes,' he explained. 'Child of the villainous Julio who disappeared.' Mercedes, he told her, was seventeen years younger than Daniel, with her mother's looks and wayward streak but also a strong dose of her father's instability.

At this point, he looked curiously contrite; it was not, indeed, his nature to speak ill of anyone.

'She was inclined to be wild and headstrong at times,' he said, 'but Daniel always adored her.

Me too,' he admitted, a touch self-consciously, 'though she rarely even gave me the time of day. To her all I was was a slightly besotted older cousin, there to give her treats and keep her amused but not to be taken seriously.'

'What did she do?' asked Genevieve curiously. There was clearly a lot that he was still holding back.

'Investment broker. Incredibly bright. She moved to New York the moment she graduated from Stanford.'

That sudden silence again which was not at all like him. Genevieve looked at him with suddenly dawning concern. 'What's the matter?' she asked, struck by his expression, all her maternal feelings out there in force.

'That we don't know where she is right now. Daniel hasn't heard from her since September. Naturally he has had to assume the worst.'

Genevieve got it instantly. 'The woman in the photographs?'

He nodded miserably. 'I'm afraid I made a bit of a fool of myself. Though that was all over a long time ago.' He thought for a while and a tender smile crossed his face. 'You should have known her in her heyday,' he said. 'She was, as they say, a regular piece of work.'

What a truly terrible situation. Genevieve was at a loss to know what to say. 'And her mother?' she asked, after a moment's pause.

'Dead these past two years,' he said. 'She married a fourth time and retired to Palm Springs. She remained a great beauty right to the end, well into her late sixties.'

'So at least she won't be worrying about her daughter.'

'That,' said Raffaele sombrely, 'is the only blessing.'

23

Anna was finding it increasingly hard to sleep. The hum from the archaic air-conditioner in her hotel room gave the illusion of being in an engine room but the alternative was worse: she had tried that too. In temperatures of almost a hundred, New York was not a comfortable place to be. In Tuscany she had grown used to sleeping with the covers off and the windows wide open, though only when the mosquito screens were in place. Here, if she opened the window even slightly, the dull roar of Madison Avenue traffic permeated her dreams. She tossed and turned and tried hard to drop off but her brain remained stubbornly acute. She was thinking obsessively about Dan these days and whether or not he could be trusted. Although, logically, all the evidence weighed against him, both she and Charles were inclined to believe that he was, almost certainly, telling the truth. He seemed like a man who would not stoop to lie; if arrogance could be considered a virtue, in his case it worked in his favour. Charles, who had every reason to mistrust him, had, against all the odds, been completely won over.

'The guy's sincere. I'd put money on that. He seemed to be genuinely shocked when he heard about Paige.'

'Not just faking it?'

'Absolutely not.' The confrontation seemed to

have stimulated Charles; the hopeless, lacklustre look had gone from his eyes. Once more he was back at his fighting best, committed to bringing Paige's killer to justice. Which, since they now agreed it wasn't Dan, meant they were back where they had started, depressingly at square one. 'So where do you suppose he was racing off to?'

'I haven't a clue,' said Anna. He had left within minutes of the Ptolemy revelation, while claiming absolute ignorance of the matter. Regardless of which, she strongly suspected that there were things he was deliberately suppressing. She and Charles had stayed on at The Mark and eaten supper, while trying to analyse everything that had been said. Neither had taken notes, which she now regretted. She remembered Dan's small, efficient palm-held computer into which he had punched out his notes.

'You think he was telling the truth about the house swap?' That story, even despite their change of heart, still sounded somewhat contrived. Who else but Dan could have placed the ad, with the certain knowledge that the house would be empty and that Raffaele was the holder of the keys? And what had stopped Raffaele simply standing his ground and summoning the local *polizia*? Instead of which, he had conferred with Dan who had graciously permitted them to stay. All Dan had done was drop by to check them out, then left without even telling them who he was. Odd behaviour, to put it at its mildest, in view of all the things he was now claiming. He could, just as easily, have evicted them on the spot. He wasn't what one might call a welcoming man.

'In theory, practically anyone in the village could have set it up,' said Anna. In a small, tight-knit community like that, everyone always knew each other's business. Except that almost none of them spoke English and, even then, just a few uncertain words. 'And why,' she added, 'should any of them want to? Swap Dan's sumptuous villa there in order to live in New York?'

'Greed,' said Charles promptly, his standard reply. People would do almost anything for money. A smart opportunist, with a knowledge of what was what, might easily have done it simply to make a killing.

'But how would they know about the Yale connection? Or, indeed, the alumni magazine?'

Charles thought carefully but failed to come up with an answer, the more so because he didn't know Montisi. He knew equally little about Dan Sutherland, only that he now trusted him which, with Charles, went a long way. He hadn't rocketed to the top of a banking career without an understanding of human nature. They sat on in silence, pondering this equation, both uneasily suspecting that the answer might be staring them in the face. If only they could figure it out without having to wait for Dan.

'They are not all peasants,' said Anna, considering, calling to mind the ebullient Simonetta. Her English was pretty fluent; for a time she had lived abroad. She made no secret, so Candy reported, of her ongoing passion for

Dan. The sole strike against her had to be her high profile. If she ever happened not to be in the shop, the whole of the village would know. Unless, of course, she had some sort of accomplice. Which brought them neatly back full circle to where they had first come in.

'Guess all we can reasonably do now is wait,' said Charles. 'I am sure he will let us know as soon as there's news.'

* * *

So here Anna lay, in her stuffy hotel room, unable to blank her mind to those probing eyes, tawny as a jungle cat's. Intelligent and insightful, Dan had a way of looking at you as though seeing more than you cared to let him know. He was tall and lean and obviously fit, with a physical presence, she was well aware, that rarely failed to turn heads. She was faced with an unpalatable truth, one that shook her to the core. Against all her more rational instincts she was falling under his spell. It was years since she'd felt this way about a man or, indeed, anything at all. One moment she was resenting him for his acid superiority, the next fervently praying, like a besotted adolescent, for the telephone to ring. She liked the bone-crunching firmness of his handshake and the way he fired straight from the hip. She also liked the disconcerting way he looked at her which made her feel jittery inside. There was nothing too complex about Dan Sutherland; what you saw was precisely what you got.

'A real man' was what they would have said in the old days. Someone straight and dependable who would always be there for you. A dream, maybe, from a Fifties movie but, nonetheless, still seductive. If she didn't allow her intellect to take charge . . . but Anna Kovac was an extremely bright woman who had always preferred to be in control. Unlike Paige, but that was a different matter. Despite the fact they had roomed together and been best friends from the start, Anna had always been cautious about commitment whereas Paige had known her own mind and gone right for it.

★ ★ ★

They buried Paige on the hottest day of the year. Anna recalled now the stultifying heat and the limp bunch of freesias, Paige's favourite flower, that she had somewhat ineffectually dropped on the coffin. She'd been driven out there in a stretch limousine, provided and insisted upon by Charles, to the small upstate village on the edge of the Hudson River where Paige had spent her childhood years. Anna had always been happy here, loving her roommate's mother as much as her own. Paige's father had mainly been absentee, stuck in meetings in the city or jetting around the world making loads of money. Before the ceremony she walked the perimeters and Paige's dogs, remembering her well, had slunk up beside her and licked her hand for comfort. Why had it had to happen to Paige, so beautiful, so clever and so nice? She stood on the edge of the river and finally cried. Paige, who was perfect; Paige, her best friend. Paige who had only died in the course of duty. If it hadn't been for this horrible mess, Paige would still be alive and thriving today.

Anna turned, and the dogs did too, to retrace her tracks back to Paige's mother's house. The funeral crowd was already gathering; even from this distance she could pick out a host of familiar faces.

'Anna,' they said, coming forward to greet her, kissing her and smothering her with hugs. Anna, the valiant; Anna, the best friend. Anna who was becoming slightly famous, and but for whose existence Paige might still be alive.

Charles found her sobbing against the boathouse wall. Having seen she was missing, he had also absented himself. 'What?' he asked, as he gathered her into his arms and, in the same spirit, she had finally broken down.

'Is it my fault?' she asked him, soaking his shirt with her tears. 'If it hadn't been for my problems, would Paige still be alive?'

'Hush,' he said, the valiant Charles, stroking her hair to calm her. 'If you hadn't been around all these years, who knows what might have happened to Paige.'

On that note he had left her, striding away, head held resolutely high, to shoulder the coffin and face the future alone, a strong man who had lost his reason to live. Anna stood and watched him go and wondered, as she occasionally did, whether she had, after all, seen all of the picture.

'Anna darling,' said Paige's mother, leaning a

lavendered cheek against her own. 'You know there was no-one she loved more than you. I am only grateful that you were there at the end.'

But I wasn't, thought Anna, *I was somewhere else entirely. Worrying about my own petty problems, uncaring of the safety of my friend.*

★   ★   ★

Meanwhile there was the book still to finish and her father's affairs to sort out. In the weeks since his rescue he had perceptibly rallied and some of the old fighting spirit had filtered back. There was no room in Colette's cramped apartment for him to be able to resume his teaching, apart from which, she didn't possess a piano. It was time he made plans to move on but, where to? Both he had his daughter remained destitute and homeless; nothing seemed to have changed for a number of weeks. Anna made numerous trips to Tribeca to try to establish the situation with his house. As Colette had reported, it was heavily boarded up, with a property developer's sign on prominent display. Instant action was obviously called for. It was vital that the demolition programme be stopped before they brought in the bulldozers. Paige had been trying to impose an injunction; Anna had no idea how far she had got.

She chanced dropping in on Phoebe for advice, praying she wasn't being too intrusive. Phoebe, through Larry, knew most of the building trade and was glad to have something to take her mind off her grief. She was adamant that, in principle, there was no legal way they could just go ahead and demolish the house without formal authorisation, though few of these cowboys paid much attention to the letter of the law. Phoebe, pleased to be useful again, made a few calls that endorsed all Anna's fears. This so-called developer's reputation was, put at its mildest, fairly shady.

'No honest contractor would buy property in such circumstances. An old man coerced under heavy duress into signing bogus documents.' Phoebe's old spunk was back there in a flash; she had washed her hair and was even wearing makeup. 'I'd love to help you,' she volunteered, 'I could certainly do with the diversion.' Too many empty hours alone in the state-of-the-art duplex were threatening to drive her slightly batty. The problem, once the children had left home, was the much-talked-about empty nest syndrome. Sure, they would visit but it was not the same as having an ongoing solid, caring marriage. Sometime in the future, maybe, Phoebe and Charles should get to know each other better. For two decades, since they had all been at college, they had merely been peripheral friends. But not until after a decent interval, they still had their grieving to go through. Anna filed a mental aide memoire to get them both together over dinner. But only when, she reminded herself with a jolt, she had a home of her own in which to do it.

With Phoebe behind her, she confronted the developer and warned him, in no uncertain terms, that an injunction was imminent. She then went to see Paige's law practice partners who reassured her that this was indeed the case. For the present the property could not be touched. It was up to Anna, as its owner's daughter, to take the next legal step.

★ ★ ★

All this took time, which came as a relief, since it helped to stop her thinking too much about Dan. In any case, realistically, she knew him to be a lost cause. He lived his life thousands of miles away and would doubtless go back there as soon as he was finished with whatever it was he had come here for in the first place. Anna had managed to remain single all these years by always being the first to walk away. There had been endless admirers, she was blessed with many friends and almost never felt the lack of male company. But as soon as any relationship showed signs of even slightly changing gear, Anna was off in a cloud of dust. Despite the advice she doled out to her girl-friends, she was never capable of heeding it herself. She swore by the joys of the single state, mainly because she lacked the courage to change it.

But over the years she had watched the Collier marriage with openly envious eyes. What Paige had achieved was what Anna would have liked; more than a lover, a soulmate too, someone to share her secrets and her hopes. Paige and Charles had been the ideal couple, always an inspiration to spend time with. Their dinner parties were legendary in New York; once Paige decided to quit the kitchen, she had fallen back instead on stylish caterers. Leaving her free to talk to her guests and ensure that everything went smoothly. Anna, accustomed to being on her own and out of the habit of entertaining, now had to face a crucial truth. Regardless of her growing success, beyond the superficial, she was lonely.

★ ★ ★

She kept in almost daily contact with Genevieve and Candy, updating them with what was going on. Which, at the moment, was precisely nothing. There had not been another word from Dan; for all she knew, he might even have left New York. There was no real reason why he should have said goodbye. If, as they now believed, he had done no wrong then, equally, he owed her nothing. She had lost her home, her money and her cat and Charles had lost his wife, but what was any of that to do with him? He, on the other hand, was letting her friends stay on in his villa and, as of now, had not asked them to leave.

Genevieve sounded on top of the world, deliriously excited about Raffaele. They still hadn't done it but it was only a matter of time.

'To travel is often better than to arrive,' said Anna cynically. There she went with her homilies. What did she know, anyhow, about the mechanics of love?

Candy's portfolio was virtually complete and Hugo was due back from his fishing trip. Soon she would have to return to the real world. Their summer idyll was almost at its end.

'But not before I get there,' pleaded Anna. She hated the thought of their threesome breaking up.

'I will stay here as long as I can,' promised Candy. 'Provided you hurry up and sort things out.'

★　★　★

So she worked on her book and worried and dreamed about someday being with Dan. She reflected on his chosen lifestyle, saw him as a latter-day Thoreau. A man of money and education who had opted instead for simplicity. She envied him his driving sense of purpose. All she had ever achieved was a handful of novels.

'I think you may be in love,' said her father shrewdly. 'When you feel the time is right, I hope you will permit me to meet this man.' His daughter was the most precious thing he had; all he cared about now was that she be happy. She had done so well in her writing career but it was time she found something more. Living and working alone was not good; she needed to widen her perspectives. She was a good-looking woman with a bright intelligence and a talent far greater than she thought. She needed to get out into the world a bit more and live a properly fulfilled life.

'I'm too old,' said Anna, though secretly, in her heart, she felt like a foolish kid. If Genevieve could find happiness with Raffaele, then she wanted some of it too. Though how to achieve it, she no longer knew. She had never been any good at making the running. And Dan remained a complete enigma. She knew almost nothing about his life except what he'd volunteered.

She sat in her stuffy hotel room and fretted. None of the bad things had yet been resolved. She felt life was passing her by.

24

And then, just as she was on the brink of losing all hope, he called.

'Meet me tomorrow at your house,' he said. 'Four o'clock. Be there on time.'

'Why?' she asked.

'You'll see,' he said.

'Can Charles come?'

'That's up to you.'

Anna flew into a fervour of excitement and checked the wardrobe to see what she had to wear. Since she had only brought with her that single bag, she had very limited choice and now no money with which to indulge herself further. The weather was still uncomfortably hot so that, in the end, it had to be the linen safari suit he'd already seen. She would have to make do with sponging and pressing it; she could not risk the hotel messing it up. She pined for the Sienese sandals she hadn't bought, settling instead for a pedicure. It made little difference in any case; he was hardly likely to notice how she looked.

'What do you suppose he is up to?' asked Charles.

'I really have no idea.'

As Dan had requested, they arrived there on the dot and this time found the house abuzz with people. The blinds were up and the windows open while the door had been left on the latch. For the first time in weeks Anna mounted the front steps and cautiously crossed her own threshold. Dan appeared to be acting host. He came forward to greet her and welcomed her into the main parlour. She glanced with approval at the expertly restored plasterwork, although it still wrenched her heart to see that all her possessions were gone. Empty, the room looked far larger than before, with its walls of palest apricot and highly polished wood floors, though without the sofas and the Botticelli rug it seemed to have lost its personality.

Rather to Anna's surprise, Dan placed a slightly proprietorial hand on her shoulder and steered her round to meet the other people. The frumpy woman with thick pebble lenses turned out to be Esther Feldman, the real estate agent, while two of the suited men were lawyers, there at Dan's request. A black man, tall with distinguished grizzled hair, was simply introduced as Mr Roberts. He remained in the background watching the proceedings. Someone from Larry's building firm, Anna guessed.

'I wanted you here,' said Dan to Anna, 'to witness the closing of the sale.'

She stared at him in blank astonishment but all he did was smile. It fell to Esther Feldman to explain. 'Mr Sutherland is the purchaser of the house.' Her eyes, behind the thick lenses, were uneasy. It was clear she knew now exactly who Anna was and remembered her own brusque rudeness on the phone.

Anna noticed, with quiet satisfaction, the smear of fuchsia lipstick on her teeth. One thing now, though, was instantly clear: this was not the mystery woman who'd been seen in the house.

'May I please know what the hell is going on?' Charles was suddenly growing truculent. He did not like the look of this at all, more fishy business to sort out. Dan, however, held up one hand in a mollifying gesture, begging him to be patient.

'All we need now,' he said to Esther Feldman, 'are your formal instructions as to where the money should be paid. I'll deposit cash in the vendor's account as soon as you give us full details.'

Charles, with a sharp inhalation of breath, gripped Anna's elbow in sudden comprehension. He was there way ahead of her, saw what Dan was up to. His admiration for him grew even more. Esther Feldman, flustered and out of her depth, scrabbled in her briefcase for her notes. Everyone stood and quietly looked on until she produced the appropriate piece of paper.

'Here,' she said, proffering it to Dan. 'The details of the offshore account and the trading company's name.'

Dan held out his hand for it but Mr Roberts was in there first.

'I'll take that, thank you,' he said to her courteously, flashing his FBI badge.

Everything else was a blur of confusion which Anna, later, found hard to recall. Hands had been shaken and documents signed and then Dan had handed her the keys.

'Yours,' he said, with the same quirky smile. 'I can only apologise for taking so much time.'

★ ★ ★

'So now you have to tell me everything,' said Anna. 'Leaving out nothing, please.' They were dining at Jean-Georges to celebrate and Anna had rashly splurged her remaining dollars on something chic and nifty from Armani. Charles had been invited too but pleaded diplomatic fatigue. Anna still ached for him, the way he was grieving, and knew he was in no mood to socialise. Still, he was pleased for her, on more than one front. He had always seen something not apparent to her, the light of admiration in Dan's eye.

Dan went pensive as he crumbled his bread. 'It is very, very complicated,' he said.

'No hurry. Take your time.' She was cautiously happy to be here with him, even though she still wasn't sure that she could trust him. There was a lot he hadn't yet clarified; she hoped he would do that now. For the occasion he was wearing a conservative dark suit with a blue shirt that accentuated his tan. Cleaned up, he was a remarkably handsome man. Anna still couldn't quite believe her luck. Or the fact that he genuinely seemed to like her; the world-weary cynicism was gone.

He savoured the excellent wine he had chosen and gave it his full consideration. 'I'll tell you something about the rain-forests,' he said. 'They don't do a lot for one's palate.'

Bit by bit, throughout the excellent meal, he filled her in on what had happened. The FBI, he could now reveal, had been on the case all along. And even had an informed idea of who might have murdered Paige and Larry, though that

336

they had only come to recently, in the light of new information. There was still a lot of checking they needed to do.

'Wait,' was all he would say at this stage. Anna must learn to be patient. Despite his good humour at the joyfulness of the occasion, trouble still lurked in his eyes. Eventually, when the plates had been cleared, he gave her his absolute attention. 'You certainly deserve to hear the whole story, though it isn't going to be easy. I am sorry I couldn't be more honest with you from the start.'

He was working in Patagonia, where he had been for several months, when the events of September 11th had occurred. He had watched the devastation, along with the rest of the world, then placed an urgent call to his sister, who lived in Brooklyn Heights.

'Her apartment is right on the promenade, facing the foot of Manhattan. Since her office was in the World Trade Centre, all she had to do was cross the bridge.'

He called as soon as he heard the news but there hadn't been any answer. It was almost nine-thirty; she'd already have left for work. But when he then tried her direct office line, all he got was static. So he hopped on a plane to New York right away and went straight to her apartment. 'I pulled a few strings with *Geographic*,' he explained. 'The airlines were all snarled up.'

Anna stared at him, aghast with horror. This was worse than anything she could have imagined. 'You found nothing?' she asked, with her hands to her mouth.

Dan simply shook his head. 'Worse than that. I found her passport, in her desk alongside her chequebook. Unwashed dishes in the sink, the newspaper still on the mat. And apparently none of her personal things missing. I checked as far as I could. No-one from her building who survived remembered having seen her. I could only surmise she was there when the terrorists struck.'

'I am so sorry,' said Anna in a whisper, unable to imagine what he must have been going through. Losing her house and her money had been bad but this was a million times worse.

Dan stared into the middle distance and a warmth she had never seen before came slowly into his eyes. 'Mercedes,' he said in a far gentler voice, 'always was something of a rebel. She was seventeen years younger than me so I really helped to raise her. My mother found her a bit of a handful; she was always running wild. From the day she was born, I looked upon her as my special charge.' The baby sister he had always longed for arrived just a little too late.

'By then I was off at school in the States but I saw her whenever I came home. She loved *Casavecchia*, considered it partly hers, though my step-father actually died some years before she was born.'

'The Count?' questioned Anna.

He nodded. 'Ildebrando. He was like a real father to me. If he hadn't died suddenly when I was fifteen, things would have turned out quite differently. I, I suppose, would be managing the estate. And Mercedes would never have been born.'

★ ★ ★

He paid and they left and went back to her dreary hotel. Now that the house was hers again, she would shortly be able to move in. First, however, there was the question of furniture. The FBI were still hot on its trail though Anna strongly doubted that it hadn't been immediately dispersed. Still, now that they had frozen the offshore account, soon she should have her money back and be able to replace it. She could hardly believe it, it had happened so fast, and she owed everything to Dan.

'Go on,' she said as he poured them both a nightcap and they settled on the cramped sofa which smelled of stale ash. 'What happened next?' His story was enthralling though she hated to see the pain in his eyes as he told it. This was his little sister he was describing, whom he had spent the best part of a year believing dead.

'What happened next was the FBI. They called without warning while I was staying in her apartment, still frantically trying to locate her.' It was one of the biggest heists in history, millions coolly filched from her clients' accounts. She was always exceedingly bright, he explained, with the beauty and panache to carry it off. Plus the expensive American education, paid for by Ildebrando's legacy. 'My mother sent her to Andover, then on to Stanford Business School

339

when it became obvious how good she was with figures.'

'And before that to boarding school in England?' asked Anna, suddenly getting it.

'St Mary's, Sherborne. But how could you possibly know that?'

Anna flushed with embarrassment. She remembered Hector's exuberant triumph as he'd burst in on her, while she was trying to work, brandishing the school boater. 'One of our houseguests discovered her trunk. He really had no business to look inside.'

Dan smiled, quite unconcerned, his mind back in the past, immersed in a sea of memories that had suddenly come rushing back. 'That was my mother all over,' he said. 'Hoarding things in case of a rainy day. Though Ildebrando left her so well off, she need never have had another financial worry. Not until she married Mercedes' father.'

Back to the present. Anna was still curious. The past they could resurrect some other time. From the things he had hinted at and the way he was looking, it seemed there might be other occasions for that.

'So you think she may yet be out there somewhere?' Why else would the FBI still be on the case? They had found the money and were extraditing it. They could surely have called it a day.

'Now I do, after all that's been happening to you. Only Mercedes knows enough to have engineered such a sting. Including the fact that I am almost always travelling and often incommunicado for months at a time. Without a passport, it's unlikely she's left the States but since the whole scam was set up by email, that won't have presented much of a problem.'

'Why do you think she did it?'

'Very simple. My guess is that, once she saw her office building collapse, she recognised a perfect chance to disappear entirely. The Feds had been on to her for months and were rapidly closing in. It could only have been a matter of weeks at the most. In some ways, she was very lucky. She always was an opportunist. Got that from her father, I suppose.'

'So why the house swap?' It still wasn't clear.

'Think,' said Dan, as though he had known her for years.

Anna, usually so bright, was puzzled. She had never pretended that maths was her strongest suit. Any discussion of finance left her reeling; even Charles had given her a headache when he tried to explain the workings of the SEC. 'All I know about money,' she explained, 'is when it is there to spend.' Which reminded her of the credit card theft, presumably also Mercedes.

'If she's disappeared, presumed to be dead, she no longer has an identity. Right?' No passport, no checking account, not even a home. The Brooklyn apartment had now been sealed by the FBI.

Light dawned and Anna began to nod. Of course, how obtuse could she be. 'So she needed to steal one from somebody else? Preferably youngish and female and single.'

'With a fancy address in Manhattan. Right. When you answered the ad, she must have felt like a pig in clover.'

Anna sat silently and thought it all through. What a brilliantly devious plan. 'She must be exceedingly clever,' she said.

He grinned. 'It runs in the family.'

'So why immediately sell the house?'

'It could only ever be a stepping stone. In four months' time you were going to come back and then the shit would have really hit the fan. She needed the house to sell it on and establish a new identity in the States. And she would have succeeded if it hadn't been for Raffaele, who alerted me just in time. By the way,' he added, 'to answer your earlier question, that's what I've been doing in New York.'

'And in Italy?' He had turned up unexpectedly. Anna still remembered the frost in his eyes.

'To suss you out. Raffaele called and I came right away. Both of us hoped you might lead us to Mercedes.'

'So you thought that she and I were in league?'

'It made sense. So we had to check. Remember, at that time, we still thought she was dead. Your arrival was the first spark of hope we had had.'

'And Raffaele was in love with her?'

'Briefly, a long time ago. He always did have too big a heart. I guess he's probably over it by now.'

I hope so, thought Anna, thinking of

Genevieve. She seemed finally to have run out of questions.

'I'm so very sorry,' she said and gripped his hand. 'It seems that both of you must have been through hell.'

25

The sunset was spectacular with a pinkish-golden light that irradiated the darkening hills with its glow. The main thrust of summer was gradually petering out. From now on it would be woodsmoke and chillier evenings.

'This is Tuscany at its most impressive,' said Dan, his arm resting lightly on Anna's shoulders. 'Now you can see precisely where the Renaissance painters got their inspiration.' The colours at this time of year were luscious; deep, reverberant and vital. Like the crude poster paints she remembered from school; the exuberance of Titian and Caravaggio.

Many things had happened in the intervening weeks, not the least of which was that Anna had finished her book. It was safely in her publisher's hands which meant an abrupt change of pace. No more leaping out of bed at the crack of dawn for that first shot of energising coffee. These mornings she lingered on beneath the duvet; now she had more important things on her mind. For she and Dan were fast becoming an item, to the extent that he'd put off his return to Patagonia. They had started dating and he'd then invited the whole lot of them back over here.

They were out on the terrace for the cocktail hour, this time formally as Dan's guests. Candy with Hugo; Genevieve with her boys. Even

George Kovac had been persuaded to come. Maria was preparing a gala dinner to celebrate their reunion while Dan and Raffaele danced gracious attendance as hosts. For the first time in years, the villa was full and, from the satisfied smile on Maria's face as she bustled about in the kitchen, creating magic, it was clear she felt that at last it was filling its proper potential. It had stood neglected for far too long. That must not be allowed to happen again.

'Any changes you care to make, feel free,' Dan had said indulgently. 'It could do with a female touch.'

'Nonsense,' said Anna. It was far too soon. Besides, she couldn't see that it could be improved. The Contessa, Dan's mother, had had excellent taste and Maria had worked miracles all these years, keeping it up to scratch. Provided they came here as often as they could and also threw it open to their friends, *Casavecchia* should have a new lease of life with all the cobwebs of memory blown away for a far more positive present. Whoever could have guessed, when she had recklessly answered that ad, that Anna would ever end up here with an open invitation.

They'd had many discussions, in the past few weeks, about how their separate careers might interact. *Have laptop, can travel* had long been her boast. Now she was going to try putting it to the test. There were projects on which a photographer and writer could successfully and profitably liaise. It would be a challenge she would gladly welcome. She had worked far

345

too long on her own.

'You could always try an adventure novel,' said Candy, the pulp fiction queen. 'Perhaps become a female Wilbur Smith.'

'Or,' cut in Dan crisply, 'write an *Oscar and Lucinda* and win the Booker Prize.'

Anything seemed possible now. Life was opening up. As long as I am with him, thought Anna, nothing else really matters. She would follow Dan wherever he went, do what he wanted to do. She looked at him, slouched elegantly against the terrace wall, head bent, listening intently to her father, and felt that her heart might implode with happiness. It was all due to Dan that George was here at all, though he had come with the minimum amount of protest. George had made remarkable strides since the snatch and was almost fully restored to health and fitness. He liked this man with the taste to be courting his daughter, admired his vision and stalwart old-fashioned values. He saw, from the way Dan's eyes followed her around, that this latest suggestion that they try working on joint projects was not altogether altruistic. Both had succeeded brilliantly on their own and both were pretty set in their ways. There had to be more to it, he hoped that was so; it would be nice for Anna to have someone to care for her as well as he had done himself. Not that Anna needed looking after any more; she had been her own woman half her life.

George's own future had also been arranged. He was going to move into Anna's house, under the surveillance of Consuela. This was a perfect solution for Anna, since in future she'd be travelling so much. The house, restored to its state of perfection, cried out for a permanent tenant. And the music lessons could now be resumed for those children whose parents would allow them to come uptown. Colette was putting out feelers for more; the house fell within her catchment area. Dan had donated a Steinway baby grand which took pride of place in Anna's study.

'I hope it won't get in the way of your work,' worried George, hating the idea of imposing.

'No problem,' said Anna, who had grown to prefer the laptop. She could write wherever she liked in the house, which sometimes improved inspiration. '*Mea casa, sua casa.* That's what families are about.' She liked the idea of her father living there, of having him to come home to whenever she could. She had spent so much money and time doing it up and wanted him to share its harmony. At heart she remained the intense little girl who had always sat on her daddy's knee. Now she had two men to spoil her but that was okay. It would not be too hard, she felt, to get used to that.

★　★　★

Dan also took it upon himself to sort out the business of George's house. It turned out the developer had bought it in good faith so that, now that the FBI had frozen the offshore account and George would be getting the purchase price back, they might as well let him

347

keep the house. Anything else would involve lengthy litigation and Dan was against George being harassed in that way. His twilight years should be happy and serene, with his music, his pupils and his family around him.

'They are going to knock it down,' lamented George. 'Almost forty years of my life.' It had been his first foothold on American soil after he had left everything else behind him. Here he had brought his beloved bride; here he had raised his daughter. He would miss the immigrant community a lot, though could always pop back downtown for his regular chessgames.

'But where you are going is so much nicer,' coaxed Anna. Safer, too. With Colette and Johnny on hand should he ever need help. No more threats of a retirement home. Anna and Dan would ensure he was taken care of for the remainder of his life.

And then something truly miraculous had occurred. Consuela had turned up on the doorstep of East 74th Street one day holding Sadie in her arms. The real Sadie, cautiously purring, not just a lookalike. Consuela had, through the cleaning ladies' grapevine, succeeding in locating her at last. She had been found, wandering collarless, by a neighbour on the block who had taken her in and asked around but failed to come up with any leads. Anna was relatively new in the area; few people knew that she even had a cat. Sadie was sleek and looked well-fed and entirely at her ease. She had regarded Anna with her customary hauteur before stalking around the house, tail held high, and imperiously demanding food.

'She looks fit as a fiddle,' said Anna, overcome, though she took her in for a checkup, just to make sure. The neighbour was telephoned and profusely thanked, then granted perpetual visiting rights for life. 'I think she will probably get a kitten of her own,' Anna told Consuela. 'The vet has a list of the top few breeders and she has clearly now become addicted to Sadie.'

'Nice of her, then, to let her go,' said Dan. 'And good to know there are still some decent people in this city.'

'Everything's working out so well,' whispered Anna, hoping the future might be similarly bright for her friends.

★   ★   ★

George and Hugo instantly bonded and spent hours together in earnest conversation. The child, just turned nine, was an unexpected delight, with his mother's unstoppable energy and infectious grin. His latest enthusiasm, encouraged by his father, was collecting and preserving rare bugs. Rural Tuscany proved to be an exciting new hunting ground. Often they would be seen wandering off together, the tall, stooping man with a shock of iron grey hair, escorted by the lively child with his newly bought butterfly net. They would put what they caught into sterile screw-top jars and Hugo would industriously label them.

'That boy's considerably brighter than people give him credit for,' George told Anna when

349

Candy was not around. 'Which is often the case with children with special needs. I've a shrewd suspicion he might turn out to be musical. I'd certainly love to have the chance to find out.'

Which was not, as it might have seemed, so very far-fetched. When George told Candy she whooped with delight and confided her next daring plan. The completed portfolio had been an instant success. The buyer from Harvey Nichols loved it and offered her a contract on the spot. Macaskill Modes would actually just be called 'Candy' and aimed mainly at the late-teen shoppers swarming in every high street. Anna, remembering the buyer from Barneys who sat on the breast cancer committee, offered to introduce them some time if Candy were ever in New York.

'Bring Hugo over in the holidays,' she said. 'You can always stay in my house. I know Dad would really enjoy having him around. Look how well they get on.'

It would also put distance between Hugo and his own father, not entirely a bad thing. A wedding was still scheduled but no date had yet been set. Hugo told Candy that they were constantly rowing.

★   ★   ★

Genevieve's two lanky sons were tossing a frisbee on the lawn. They were almost men, with their hairless, concave chests and brightly coloured bead necklaces round their throats. One was sporting a David Beckham haircut and a tiny

350

tufted beard that he'd soon shave off. Their manners were acceptable though their laughter often loutish. Their mother had made a passable success of trying to bring them up. At night they would usually go off to the village, where they had found the centre of Montisi's social whirl. Not exactly bright lights, big city but a certain improvement on staying at home with their ma.

Ma, in any case, had little time for them now. Her full attention was focused these days on Raffaele. She was thinner, prettier, more vivacious than in years and, they both agreed, looked ten years younger. Not that they'd ever let her know but secretly they were proud. Their father's new wife was a bit of a nag; it was a great release to come over here and slob about uncontrolled.

Raffaele was organising a lunchtime barbecue, having closed the trattoria for the day. 'Unheard of,' said Dan, with his endearing quirky smile, rapidly cuddling Anna in the kitchen.

'Do you think he loves her?' Anna was still concerned. Genevieve was such a fragile plant, she could not bear to see her let down again.

'Undoubtedly,' said Dan, 'as never before.'

'But Mercedes . . . '

' . . . is in the past,' he said, stopping any more questions with a kiss.

★　★　★

Maria had spread the long garden table with an immaculate white linen cloth and chosen matching ceramic platters that set off the food to perfection. Raffaele was cooking while Dan did the carving. They made an unbeatable team.

'You can see they grew up together,' said Anna. 'As coordinated as skaters.'

'It is like a wedding reception,' said Candy, not without an element of wistfulness.

'Your turn will come,' said Anna and Genevieve in unison. Candy had much to achieve before she settled down. Besides, she was ten years younger.

The feast was consumed and the speeches made. And Raffaele had another surprise up his sleeve. Maria, it now turned out, was his mother. Sister to Ildebrando and the lynchpin of the family. Between them they ran the estate for Dan, which was why she kept such a careful eye on the house. And explained the loving tending of the garden. She had always hoped he would come back.

In a perfect world, thought Candy whimsically, Maria should really marry George. Then, at last, they would all be part of the same family.

Which reminded her: 'Whatever happened to Hector?' And was unanimously ordered to shut up.

★ ★ ★

It was evening now and the sky was sprinkled with stars. Everyone, having had their siestas, was out on the terrace again. Dan discreetly led Anna away to take her on his favourite cocktail walk. Each of them carrying a glass of wine, they followed the path that bordered the firefly meadow, a fairyland of shimmering light, enhanced by fragrant *genista*.

'All right?' he asked her, his arm around her shoulders, and Anna silently nodded. She had never, in her lifetime, felt more fulfilled; her heart was bursting with hope. The future, she felt, held the answer to all her dreams, dreams that till now she had never allowed to surface. She had convinced herself she was best off on her own. Now, at last, she admitted she might have been wrong. Perhaps her theory about the poppies was truer than she had believed. Certainly something was making her feel giddy, though her glass was still almost full.

Above them, in the brilliant sky, a shooting star streaked across the heavens and they watched it together, in companionable silence, her head resting gently against his chest.

'Are you thinking about Mercedes?' she asked.

He nodded and she felt how tense he was. 'There is something I haven't told you yet, that I wanted to keep till the others were not around. Early this morning I had a call from Bob Roberts. They think there's been a sighting of her in New Mexico. Nothing definite but they are still on her trail. He has promised to keep me informed.'

'New Mexico?' said Anna, puzzled.

'Her father, Julio, is Mexican,' Dan reminded her. 'When he left my mother he headed home. He had spent most of her money by then and went rapidly to ground.'

'So you think she is trying to cross the border. Without a passport?' said Anna.

'There are ways and means. And one thing about my sister, she has never lacked initiative.'

'One final thing that's been puzzling me.' She hated to upset him more but it was something that had been bugging her for days. 'Why Ptolemy if the Count wasn't even her father?'

Dan laughed. 'Mercedes was always a vain little thing and fancied herself as looking like Cleopatra.'

Anna hugged him and he responded but she saw that his eyes were sad. And so she silently clung to him and they went on watching the night sky. This woman she had never met had nearly wrecked her life and her father's and murdered two of her closest and dearest friends. And yet, without Mercedes, Anna would not have met Dan. It was a hard one to figure out; she would leave it till later.

'I am sorry you never knew her,' he said, obviously reading her thoughts. 'Though now, of course, I am hoping you never will.'

And, hand in hand, they retraced their steps to join the riotous gathering on the terrace.

We do hope that you have enjoyed reading this large print book.

Did you know that all of our titles are available for purchase?

We publish a wide range of high quality large print books including:
Romances, Mysteries, Classics
General Fiction
Non Fiction and Westerns

Special interest titles available in large print are:
The Little Oxford Dictionary
Music Book
Song Book
Hymn Book
Service Book

Also available from us courtesy of Oxford University Press:
Young Readers' Dictionary
(large print edition)
Young Readers' Thesaurus
(large print edition)

For further information or a free brochure, please contact us at:
Ulverscroft Large Print Books Ltd.,
The Green, Bradgate Road, Anstey,
Leicester, LE7 7FU, England.
Tel: (00 44) 0116 236 4325
Fax: (00 44) 0116 234 0205

Other titles in the
Charnwood Library Series:

FALLING SLOWLY

Anita Brookner

Beatrice and Miriam are sisters, loving but not entirely uncritical; each secretly deplores the other's aspirations. Their lives fall short of what they would have wished for themselves: love, intimacy, exclusivity, acknowledgement in the eyes of the world, even a measure of respect. Each discovers to her cost that love can be a self-seeking business and that lovers have their own exclusive desires. In search of reciprocity, the sisters are forced back into each other's company, and rediscover their original closeness.

THE LADY ON MY LEFT

Catherine Cookson

Alison Read, orphaned when she was two years old, had for some years lived and worked with Paul Aylmer, her appointed guardian. Paul, an experienced antique dealer whose business thrived in the south-coast town of Sealock, had come to rely on Alison, who had quickly learned the trade. But when he had asked her to value the contents of Beacon Ride, a chain of events was set off that led to the exposure of a secret he had for years managed to conceal. As a result, Alison's relationship with Paul came under threat and she knew that only by confronting the situation head-on would her ambitions be realised.

FLIGHT OF EAGLES

Jack Higgins

In 1997 a wealthy novelist, his wife and their pilot are forced to ditch in the English Channel. Saved by a lifeboat crew, they are returned to land at Cold Harbour. But it is the rediscovery of a fighter pilot's lucky mascot — unseen for half a century — that excites the greatest interest at the disused airbase. The mascot's owners, twin brothers Max and Harry Kelso, were separated as boys and found themselves fighting on opposite sides when the Second World War broke out. They were to meet again under amazing circumstances — and upon their actions hung the fate of the war itself . . .

ON BEULAH HEIGHT

Reginald Hill

They needed a new reservoir so they'd moved everyone out of Dendale that long hot summer fifteen years ago. They even dug up the dead and moved them too. But four inhabitants of the dale they couldn't move, for nobody knew where they were — three little girls, and the prime suspect in their disappearance, Benny Lightfoot. This was Andy Dalziel's worst case and now fifteen years on he looks set to re-live it. It's another long hot summer. A child goes missing, and as the Dendale reservoir waters shrink and the old village re-emerges, old fears and suspicions arise too . . .

ME AND MY SHADOWS

Lorna Luft

This is the autobiography of Lorna Luft, a remarkable woman and singularly talented performer. Often highly amusing, sometimes harrowing — but always candid — it is the inside story of one of the world's most famous showbusiness families. Lorna Luft, the daughter of Judy Garland and producer Sid Luft, and half-sister of Liza Minnelli, grew up in the hothouse of Hollywood screen royalty. It is the story only she could tell, not only as first-hand witness to events others have only speculated about, but also of coming to terms with her mother's, her own and her family's patterns of addiction.

QUEERING CHRIST

BEYOND JESUS ACTED UP

ROBERT E. GOSS

THE
PILGRIM
PRESS
Cleveland

For David:

in thanks for his love

The Pilgrim Press
700 Prospect Avenue, East
Cleveland, Ohio 44115-1100
www.pilgrimpress.com

Printed in the United States of America on acid-free paper

07   06   05   04   03   02   5   4   3   2   1

Library of Congress Cataloging-in-Publication Data
Goss, Robert.
    Queering Christ : beyond Jesus acted up / Robert E. Goss.
      p. cm.
    Includes bibliographical references and index.
    ISBN 0-8298-1498-1 (cloth : alk. paper)
    1. Homosexuality – Religious aspects – Christianity.   I. Title.
BR115.H6 G67 2002
230'.086'64 – dc21

                                2002070225

CONTENTS

FOREWORD

When Father Bob Goss was trying to discern whether to choose his priestly vocation or his husband, Frank, he might have felt isolated. In fact, he is part of a great Catholic tradition of those who have found God and ministry serving not only those oppressed by society but those persecuted with even greater zeal by the church itself.

There is a lost generation in the Roman Catholic Church, lost not to themselves but to the institution. Born in the preconciliar church and nurtured in the optimism of the Second Vatican Council, these are the dreamers and activists who lived to see the church try to grow into the liberating body that Jesus and the reformers who came after him always intended. As children, they listened with rapt attention to the gospel stories of love; they intuitively fastened on the stories of liberation and the principles of justice embedded in the scriptures. What a parochial school it would have been if they had all been there at once, some as teachers, some as students! A few linger on the margins of the institution while others have left it entirely, and they represent a vast number of people who, formed by the church's best impulses, have now grown beyond it. Their consciences have guided them as surely as Jesus was guided by the Spirit into the wilderness, as surely as God led the people of Israel from bondage in Egypt. Their commitments to exploring the twin issues of gender and authority have rendered them dangerous and unacceptable to the Roman Catholic hierarchy, but some beautiful part of them will always be part of the religion of their ancestors.

History will show that Boston College professor Mary Daly led the exodus when she became the first woman to preach in the Harvard University Chapel on November 14, 1971. She invited the women present to leave the service, disavowing the patriarchy of both Catholic and Protestant Christianity as irredeemable. She modeled the unthinkable: it never occurs to many Catholics to actually leave the church, so carefully indoctrinated against spiritual individuation are we from an early age. Daly created a doorway through which others have left the church, or have been compelled to leave it. Her subsequent struggles for tenure at the Jesuit-run Boston College were a portent of how hard the church would fight to punish and silent its dissidents, particularly its most threatening wayward children, the gender dissidents, who call into question its teachings on the role of women and on sexuality.

Here are just a few other names, inheritors of a tradition initiated by Pope John XXIII and actualized by Daly's bold action: feminist ethicist Mary Hunt, creation spirituality innovator and now Episcopal priest Matthew Fox, gay theologian and former Jesuit John McNeill, founder of New Ways Ministry and Sister of Loretto Jeannine Gramick, founder of the avowedly sex-positive Body Electric School of Massage and former Jesuit Joe Kramer, and most importantly for this essay, another former Jesuit, the emblematic priest to the unchurched and the postchurched, theologian, scholar, and activist Bob Goss.

As Mary Daly began with _The Church and the Second Sex_ in a distinctly Roman Catholic theological and social location and then progressed to the post-Christian _Beyond God the Father_, so Goss began an indigenization of gay and lesbian liberation theology ten years ago in _Jesus ACTED UP_ and is now in _Queering Christ_ changing the boundaries of feminist and queer liberation theology, creating an entirely new discipline. Goss appreciates gay and lesbian apologetics, but in these essays he leaves that pursuit forever in the past. No longer content to reform Christianity, he seeks now to reinvent it, while still honoring its historical roots. There is no doubt that what he does is queer theology or liberation queer theory; the reader is left to wonder if it is still Christian.

Let's briefly consider the content of the chapters in the first section of the book.

This first group of essays contains the most challenging material in the collection and might well have been subtitled "Sex with God." Just as the title _Jesus ACTED UP_ brilliantly associates the name of the first-century reformer Jesus with the late-twentieth-century HIV/AIDS activist groups that called themselves "ACT UP," so in this section Goss expresses the discourse of lesbian, gay, bisexual, and transgender sexuality with decidedly Christian theological language and categories. At times theoretical, at times confessional ("Each Sunday morning [Frank and I] made sexual love, followed by eucharist at the dining room table for the two of us" [22]), Goss argues from both personal experience and a provocative analysis of the intersection of sexuality, gender, and authority.

I think of this section as developing the theme "sex with God" because Goss incorporates an awareness of the divine into his own sexual practices to the extent that God becomes the subject of his sexual attentions, to a degree rarely articulated with such candor by the Christian mystics. It is also about "sex with God" because he suggests that no part of the sexual enterprise is remote from God's participation. In this sense, God is Goss's constant companion in sex, and, by implication, God participates in all of our sexual activities. We accompany Bob from childhood to seminary and ask with him these compelling questions: "Why does God hate the body? Why were the Jesuits and other Catholic religious rejecting the body? Why have Catholic attitudes and practices refused sensuousness and the pleasures of the body?" (12). Later, Goss observes that the rejection of religion does not adequately prepare one to fully embrace and enjoy sexuality, since "both the puritan and the libertine fail to integrate the body into a spiritual path" (14).

In this insight lies the greatest value of Goss's synthesis. The secular queer theorist will be as challenged, and as enriched, by this material as will be the orthodox Christian theologian. In the first essay, the collection's central thread is found: "Sexuality is a symbolic means of communication and communion; it expresses our human need to connect physically and spiritually. This drive for connectedness in sexuality and spirituality would enable me to understand not only their interconnections but also their connections to justice" (15). This — not a crash course on denial of the body as a source of divine revelation and on vocational guidance — should be the substance of seminary curriculum. How did a religion that proudly proclaims that the "Word is made flesh" become so alienated from the body? Goss tells a personal story that epitomizes the crisis that sex-positive theology provokes in Christianity.

Goss also demonstrates in the opening essay the contradiction that is never adequately resolved in the book or in conventional christology. He blithely overlooks the male character of Jesus: "Embodying prayer or engaging in erotic prayer has a long tradition in Christian mysticism where Christ is experienced as a male lover or as a female lover" (18), while also stating, "I finally admitted to myself that I loved Jesus because he was a male and that it was OK to love Jesus passionately and erotically as a man" (17). This might well work for some gay men and some heterosexual women, but it won't work for many lesbians, like the minister who commented years ago in the Metropolitan Community Church, in a statement that resulted in her being tried for heresy in the fledgling MCC movement, "The point of my being a lesbian is that no man is my lord and no man is my master." In this regard, it would do both Goss and the MCC good if he romanticized queer churches somewhat less throughout the text.

Christology is really the issue at the heart of this book. His second essay is perhaps the most gender-dissident in the entire collection and should be required reading for every seminarian, Catholic or Protestant, male or female. In "Catholic Anxieties over (Fe)male Priests" he does his finest work. One wonders why Catholics would prefer the most inferior male clergy to the most qualified female clergy candidate — but this seems to be precisely the church's preference. As I write this, the Catholic archdiocese of Boston is being torn apart by revelations that Cardinal Law simply moved pedophile male clergy from parish to parish, claiming that he was following the prevailing custom. Here Goss pulls back the curtain and displays what feminists have been saying all along — that the all-male, often homosexual, clergy epitomize the authoritarian structure that sanctifies both sexism and homophobia on an institutional level. These are the questions begged by the initial chapters: If Christianity relinquished its obsession with a male Christ, and if it purged itself of both sexism and homophobia, would it still be recognizably Christian? This is the groundwork for the next chapter.

"Finding God in the Heart-Genital Connection" is Goss's paean to Joe Kramer, another fellow former Jesuit, whose work as a theologian could only be appreciated by a sex-positive spirituality that is difficult to imagine in conventional Christianity. Goss has written here the definitive appreciation of Kramer's work, which doesn't appear anywhere in queer religious or secular writing. Because of his own background Goss is able to perceive the value of Kramer's work to groups of people who rarely, if ever, converse. He again draws on both the personal and the professional, and the result is a unique contribution historically and theologically: "I have known Kramer since the days we were both Jesuits. His spirituality is Ignatian, and within that spirituality, he has promoted a sexual praxis that has impacted thousands of gay and bisexual men in integrating their sexuality and spirituality. We share a vision of finding God in sexuality. It is time for the theologian and the sexual shaman to engage in the messiness of intercourse" (57).

If you've had your mind and your spirit stretched this far through the book, you're ready for the next essay, where Goss again goes somewhere that Christian theologians have hitherto been afraid to go — to and even into the sacred bodies of people with HIV. As a modern medical phenomenon, HIV/AIDS continues to be uniquely religiously stigmatized. There are more people with HIV alive now than ever before, and as I write, the U.S. government is flat funding and in some cases reducing federal funds for HIV care through the Ryan White CARE Act. More people die daily from HIV/AIDS than died in the World Trade Center, and yet our government, while pledging billions of dollars for a war against terrorism, has pledged a paltry 500 million dollars over the next three years to the Global Fund to Fight AIDS coordinated by the United Nations.

This is the context in which Goss writes "Is There Sex in Heaven?" The only Christian ethicists writing on this topic have done so judgmentally. The Catholic Church counsels against the use of condoms while millions die; Goss takes us into the bedrooms and backrooms in order to understand why gay men have unprotected anal sex. He even invites us into his own decision making process, telling the truth about his own carefully nuanced decisions to have unprotected sex under particular circumstances. The ability to disclose, the ability to be candid, the ability to be compassionate, these qualities must be at the heart of both sexual ethics and public health. This essay will have credibility and authority with the HIV-infected as well as the HIV-affected. I say this as one of the former, and I almost always feel alienated or scapegoated in treatments of the topic of HIV prevention written by the HIV-negative. Goss is the first HIV-negative religious writer on this topic who has made me feel like a worthy participant in this discussion in which we all have a stake.

In the final essay of this section, Goss once more pushes beyond the usual framework of discussion and brings a refreshing level of candor to the discourse on gay and lesbian marriage. Finally in this debate we see the difference between the carefully orchestrated conversations calculated to win unreflective straight allies to the notion that gays just want marriage like everybody else and the discussion as it actually takes place in queer circles. This is the essay that "sexuality commissions" should be reading alongside the materials both pro and con that have been produced on this subject by a largely heterosexual authorship. While sexual orientation is not ontological, a GLBT (gay/lesbian/bi/transgendered) social location does influence the presentation and content of relevant material, and in this essay we see vintage Goss. He is a theologian, historian, and ethicist; he is a pastor, priest, and counselor. And his own story threaded throughout the book makes the best case for the recognition and validation of the complexity of GLBT relationships.

In subsequent chapters Goss makes the case for the positions he takes in the first five chapters. He incorporates a bisexual, transgender, and otherwise gender-fluid sensibility to an unprecedented degree in his own work and, in many instances, in the works of his peers, to whom he always pays appropriate and comprehensive tribute. Queer people know something about a queer Christ, queer scriptures, queer theology. Queer theorists need queer Christians, and queer Christians need the critique that only the secular queer theorists can provide; even Goss's beloved MCC hasn't begun to queer itself to the extent that Goss's thoughtful work demands.

Before he died, Goss's first husband, Frank, made him promise two things: "I want you to go into teaching; I think that you will be a good teacher. Secondly, I want you to fall in love again" (26). This book is proof that Goss kept these promises. Goss has fallen in love again, and not only with his new husband, David. The book also reveals his love for God, for the church, for Jesus, for HIV-positive bodies, for sexuality, and for the queer communities that he continues to serve through his vocation as writer, activist, professor, and priest. Someday each of these essays will be the topic of a separate book, and each of these essays will certainly spark other authors to write their own groundbreaking contributions. Until then, let *Queering Christ: Beyond Jesus ACTED UP* be a kind of salon where many voices meet, no longer in apology, but to plan the revolution.

Jim Mitulski

PREFACE

We speak of God as love but are afraid to call God lover. But a God who relates to all that is, not distantly and bloodlessly, but intimately and passionately, is appropriately called lover. —Sallie McFague[1]

Sexuality is clearly a political issue in our society and in our churches. The issues of the bedroom have not been restricted to the bedroom but have been extended into the realm of public debate, social policy, political struggle, cultural regulation, and even violence. The religious right — conservative and fundamentalist factions within the Catholic, Protestant, and Mormon churches — has attempted to extend its restrictive control of bodies to the bedroom, transgressing any consideration of privacy rights through ballot initiatives, the dissemination of hateful propaganda, electing candidates to school boards who will roll back multiculturalism, and virulent opposition to same-sex marriage. Its opposition to sexual minorities is interwoven with a long-standing opposition to gender equality and the reproductive rights of women. At the heart of the opposition of the religious right, there is an incredible fear of human sexuality, needing to tightly regulate it through a politics of sexual shame, exclusion, and legislation.

The politics of sexual shame have dominated Christianity nearly its whole history to justify a misogynist and erotophobic theology that failed to acknowledge the original blessings of sexuality and human beings. Contemporary Christians have hardly achieved a cultural puberty around sexuality when they try to contain it and put it back into a bottle, especially over issues of sexual and gender diversity. Coming from diverse erotophobic traditions within Christianity, many religious people — including many queers — have been damaged around the issues of sexuality and gender. Over the last decades, queer Christians have created cultural spaces for themselves, exchanging the unfreedom of our closets within churches for the limited freedom of cultural and spiritual ghettos.

---

1. Sallie McFague, *Models of God in an Ecological, Nuclear Age* (Philadelphia: Fortress Press, 1987), 130.

These spiritual ghettos became denominational groups, base communities, churches, and networks of resistance crossing denominations. These groups presented translesbigays with unexpected freedoms, hopes, and dreams, for they gave them places where they could be fully aware of their own oppression and heal themselves from years of religious abuse. These ecclesial spaces provided queer Christians places where they could discover the blessing of their sexuality, could dream dreams of freedom for all, and could hope to liberate other Christians from heterosexism and erotophobia. There Christian translesbigays experienced healing of the self-hatred of closets and cultural erotophobia; there they experienced their own goodness, lovableness, and the original blessing of their sexuality. They learned to work to integrate their sexuality and spirituality. Queer churches, base communities, or counter-communities have become sexual communities, and they have become the matrix where new Christian sexual theologies are emerging.

The reenvisioning of queer sexuality includes a thorough reembodying of queer spirituality. Reembodying queer spirituality leads to a redefinition of the divine to include the erotic dimensions of queer love and lives. Thus, the liberation of queer sexuality and the liberation of God from erotophobia are interrelated and have become an ongoing project for this century. The reembodying of queer spirituality involves not only freeing our sexuality from narrow regulations but also freeing God from traditional antisexual theological constructions.

Queering Christ represents nearly a decade of reflection as a queer Christian theologian. It was a decade of transitions for me: the loss of a lover, a new lover, finishing my dissertation at Harvard University, publishing *Jesus ACTED UP*, leaving the Catholic Church and joining the Universal Fellowship of Metropolitan Community Churches (UFMCC) as clergy; prospecting for a full-time, tenure-track position and being constantly turned down because I was heterosexually challenged; and finally securing a full-time, tenure-track position where I could be myself. The book reflects a decade of tremendous personal change and growth as a queer theologian.

Queering is a method that I use theologically. As a verb, "to queer" means to spoil or interfere with. If the theological system is already spoiled, spoiling the spoiled system to make it more inclusive of folks disenfranchised from Christianity is a good. This book is divided into four areas that I queer: sexuality, the Christ, the Bible, and theology. These form the quadrants of my spirituality that aims at the queer reconstruction of Christianity, and they reflect a life that aims to integrate the depths of spirituality and sexuality with a practice of justice. Much of the explicit material on justice does not appear in this volume but is reserved for the sequel to *Jesus ACTED UP.*

I start off the book with an autobiographical chapter because my social location is especially important for understanding my particular sexual theology. Sexual theology involves always the texts of our lives. My own life provides me with a basic text from which I begin my theological reflections. My social location is certainly that of a gay male — one who has grown up in heterosexist and misogynist Catholic culture and has grown beyond some of those nascent prejudices to become feminist-identified and a queer, sex-positive theologian. I experience many privileges of being a white, middle-class male, albeit a lesser cultural male because I do not conform to heterosexist masculinity. There are many men and women who suffer far worse from the cultural system of compulsory heterosexism and gender fundamentalism that privileges males, whiteness, able bodies, and the upper classes. I weave narrative details from my own life within some of the following essays. Though my life forms the basic text for my study and understanding of sexual theology, it is neither normative nor prescriptive for any others. It may elucidate some of the theological themes in the following chapters, and it may help those who comprehend my journey to find traces of God's erotic grace within my own life.

Certainly, my studies with the Jesuits and ordination as a Jesuit priest have exercised a deep impact. I have lived Jesuit spirituality for more than thirty years, most in a queer, unorthodox fashion. Chinese feminist and queer-positive theologian Kwok Pui-lan invited me to speak at the Episcopal Divinity School (EDS) on queer sexual theology. My own alma mater, the Jesuit Weston School of Theology, shares facilities with EDS. It saddened me that no Jesuits came to the lecture because of the control exercised by the new generation of theological and sexual inquisitors. In "Catholic Anxiety over (Fe)Male Priests," I explore the recent flurry of books on the Catholic priesthood as a gay profession. I argue that Catholic priests perform a fe(masculinity) and that the real issue may not be a gay priesthood as much as a misogyny or fear of women that might expose the true gender deviance of Catholic priests as (fe)males. Priests are battered wives and need to break out of the cycles of ecclesial abuse. While many queer Protestants have placed authority in the traditional biblical passages that supposedly condemn homosexuality, many queer Catholics place authority in the clergy and the magisterium of the Catholic Church. I attempt to destabilize the authority of Catholic priests and bishops by exposing the contradictions of a gay priesthood that is fearful of women and yet duplicates feminized performances of masculinity. There is much that is good within Catholic Christianity, but there is also much that is violent and hate-generating.

Several years ago, I delivered a paper on the ethics of barebacking to a group of theologians at a professional gathering, a conference of the American Academy of Religion. I was very nervous because the topic of barebacking — condomless sex among gay men — is controversial. I asked the question: Are there any ethical circumstances for barebacking? To my surprise, the paper was well received. I placed it online for discussion by gay men and found many positive responses in airing the discussion. It touched a number of core issues for gay men that have remained undiscussed and for which there need to be safe places for dialogue.

Ever since I met him at Tea Dance at the Boat Slip in Provincetown in 1977, Joe Kramer has remained a friend. I have followed his career in transitioning from the Jesuits to becoming a professional sexual practitioner, helping thousands of gay and bisexual men get in touch with their bodies. What I like about Kramer's sexual praxis is his work to create alternative masculine sexual expressions that run counter to masculinist ideologies of sexuality. I dialogue with Joe in an attempt to create a constructionist theology rooted in sexual praxis with the hope of transforming male sexuality from its violent associations to a totally embodied sexuality. I look at the utopian conclusions of Kramer's sexual praxis and raise the possibility of new constructions for a Christian sexual theology. If we can change the sexual praxis of men from violence to full-body sexual enjoyment and love, then maybe we can begin to change our violent society.

One of my principal theological endeavors has been to articulate the value of queer relationships and families. I worked with Amy Strongheart to produce the anthology *Our Families, Our Values: Snapshots of Queer Kinship* (1997). That volume brought a variety of authors from differing social locations to discuss the notion of families. The 2000 U.S. census indicates that there are at least 1.2 million same-sex households and families in the country. The move to legalize same-sex marriage and recognize queer families has precipitated a backlash to block such recognition. Conservative Christians have used arguments that our relationships are not procreative, restricting sexuality to heterosexual marriage and reducing marriage to the biological function of procreation. I develop a notion that Catholic moral theologian André Guindon first proposed by his application of the idea that same-sex relationships have a sexual fecundity or procreation. I show how same-sex and transgendered relationships and queer families express an actual procreativity and a metaphorical procreativity. Traditional Christian arguments falter if the notion of procreativity is not restricted.

My decision to enter the Jesuits and become a disciple of Jesus the Christ — a decision made many years ago, as a teenager — has established a foundational and freeing relationship in my life journey for over three decades. That relationship has matured and expanded in positive explorations around christology, and I have included three essays to articulate various trajectories of my own spirituality and evolving christology. The first essay takes up the history of male homodevotionalism to Jesus. I and many other men attracted to men throughout Christian history have understood Jesus as one of us. The construction of an erotic Jesus attracted to other men has formed a template for understanding the original blessing of my own sexual attractions toward men. This essay provides a genealogy of homoerotic resistance to the erotophobic christology of the asexual Christ or even the recent heterosexual construction of Christ.

In addition, I have included a chapter from *Jesus ACTED UP* on the Queer Christ. It is my favorite chapter in the book, and it provides the reader with some glimpse into the growth of my christology if it is compared with the following chapter on the Bi/Transvestite Christ. The Queer Jesus has led me to the Queer Christ. As I continually try to understand the protean and inclusive dimensions of Christ, I engage a Latina theologian, Marcella Althaus-Reid, who constructs the Bi/Christ. I accessorize the wardrobe of Christ to include the Transvestite Christ in an attempt to understand his inclusiveness, his attempt to identify with all peoples. For me, the Trans/Christ must be mirrored in the images of folks who pass over from one gender into another just as the Christa is within women.

The battle for truth about queer sexuality has focused on churches' use of the Bible to exclude translesbigays. The churches have promoted six texts that spur contempt for queers by so-called moral and respectable people; thus, they are guilty of promoting a climate of violence. In 1998, two men tortured and crucified Matthew Shepard on a fence in the midst of the touting of a number of ballot initiatives that were antiqueer and anti-same-sex marriage. The battle for the Bible is a struggle to deflect textual and social violence. Textual violence has murdered the souls of many queer Christians and provided legitimacy for antiqueer violence.

I worked with Mona West, UFMCC clergy and senior pastor at the Cathedral of Hope, a mega–queer church of over three thousand members in Dallas. We produced and coedited an anthology on reading the Hebrew and Christian Scriptures from translesbigay perspectives. In "Overthrowing Heterotextuality — a Biblical Stonewall," I trace the development of the queer community from a negative apologetic over those six texts of violence misapplied to queers to a variety of readings of the biblical texts from "outing" scriptural characters to "befriending the text." Befriending the text encompasses reading the scriptural text from a variety of queer social locations. These strategies have become commonplace in queer synagogues in their Sabbath teachings or in queer Christian denominations in their Sunday preaching practices, and they provide the spiritual and erotic energy within these communities to transform Christianity.

Queering theology is the subject of the last two chapters. Christian theology has been a malestream and heterosexist practice that has maintained a kyriarchically structured church. Only in the last several decades has theology admitted the voices of women and people from other social locations. Transgression is a queer as well as theological method to remind the queer community how tentative our theologies are. They are never fully inclusive and must remain alert to the hetero as well as the gay/lesbian orthodoxies from which we theologize. In this exploration, I raise the question of transgressing my earlier boundaries of gay and lesbian to include bisexual, transgendered, and a variety of hybrid identities. Gay/lesbian neoorthodoxies, whether cultural or theological, need to be transgressed to include more voices. Queer theory has rightly stressed the nature of postmodern sexualities and identities: how fluid sexual identity is and how we need to pluralize the cultural notions of masculinity and femininity. The emergence of bisexual and transgender movements in the last decade as well as of Asian American, Latino/a, and African American theological voices has begun to exert theological influence. As I supervise a doctoral thesis on transgendered theology and a senior thesis on the same subject in a religious studies department, I am very aware of the vector of my theological expansion over the last decade and the need to maintain such openness to inclusiveness. Queer theologies may never be entirely inclusive but must be open to the possibilities of a new generation of queer thinkers who will queer our theological systems. As I answer the numerous e-mails of undergraduate, divinity, and graduate students working on queer theses, I am aware that the future queer theologies offer critical and transformative possibilities for overcoming the erotophobia embedded within Christian churches and may transform Christianity from a predominantly violent religion to once more being a nonviolent practice with transformative social possibilities.

The last chapter attempts to forecast the future of a queer Christianity. One of the best ways to forecast future developments is to analyze the development in the last three decades. It helps to predict some trends in the future but does not take into the account the chaos of queer innovation and novelty. Perhaps there is a need to develop a Christian chaos theory to forecast the novelties of the coming century. Or it may be that queer Christian sexual theology may be the chaos that disrupts the nearly two thousand years of Christian erotophobia and violence. There is a queer storm brewing at the margins of Christianity. It is gaining momentum, strength, and energy from our heart-genital connections. The last thirty years formed the first onslaught of the hurricane, and we are now in the eye of that queer hurricane. The next generation of queer theologians will unleash such a storm with the winds of truth, love, nonviolent practice, and justice to shatter the oppressive, violent, and erotophobic paradigms of Christianity. The storm threatens to shake the foundations of Christianity by creating a Sexual Reformation that will change Christianity to sex-positive and inclusive paradigms that connect sexuality and spirituality.

I asked Reverend Jim Mitulski, former UFMCC pastor from the Castro District of San Francisco, to write the foreword. He served the San Francisco community for many years through the height of the AIDS pandemic. Jim serves on the local board of the Center of Lesbian and Gay Studies in Religion and Ministry at the Pacific School of Religion. I welcome his critiques and value his insights as challenges for my theological growth, for constructed theology, especially queer theology, needs to be connected to hybrid contextualities of people's lives and the queer community. Otherwise, queer theology will duplicate what I despise about heterosexist and masculinist theologies, abstracted from human lives and with little connection to culture. His reflections provide a postmodern foil and dialogue partner from the heart of queer San Francisco. I thank Jim for his input and his continued commitment and his service to the queer community. He models for me the best of queer spiritual practice.

I want to acknowledge the support of the MCC of Greater St. Louis, my home and community of faith. Its faith journey witnesses what a church can do when it cares about people. It is an organization that undergoes ongoing healthy growth in loving service. My spouse David has provided me with his love and God's erotic grace; he keeps me grounded in everyday life. Other thanks are extended to Deanna Erutti; to my students at Webster University; to my theological colleagues; and not the least to George R. Graham, editorial director at The Pilgrim Press, for his insights; and to The Pilgrim Press for its daring to blaze the market with prophetic titles that aim to make this world a better and more just place to live. *Ad maiorem Dei gloriam!*

--- PART ONE ---

QUEERING SEXUALITY

ONE

OUT OF THE CLOSET
AND INTO THE STREETS

From the first orgasm, and in every orgasm since, I have sought that ecstatic moment, and its allure still colors so much of my life. I seek out its possibility, feel its approach, surrender to it, and the rigid sense of self to melt deliciously as it rises within me, letting myself be caught up in this juicy passion that draws me toward it. There is aloneness in this, as I close my eyes and go deeply into my experience of pleasure and let the ecstatic flow become all that I am. There is a deep solitude in the drinking of this water.

—Michael Kelly[1]

Over fifty, I look back at my life with its currents, eddies, and streams to find traces of God's imprint and directionality. Oftentimes, I felt pulled by strong currents. Sometimes I was able to swim against the current, and other times I just floated with the current, wondering if the undertow would finally overwhelm me. God pulled me, carried me, and strengthened me to answer the call to become an intimate life partner. My story is certainly not hagiography, but it is woven with theological themes reflected throughout my writings and rooted in my life choices and practices. For me, it is a love story between me, Jesus, and other people. Jesus evolved from a friend in childhood, to lover, and to the Queer Christ calling me out of the closet into the streets as an activist priest.

From my earliest memories as a child, I always felt different and could not name my feelings. I loved boys as a boy. When I read Homer's *Iliad*, I found myself moved by the emotional depth of Achilles' relationship with Patroculus. In class, my teacher pointed out the virtue of their friendship. Friendship! Yes, they were best friends, but there was more than friendship. There was a passionate connection between the two

---

1. Michael Kelly, "Christmas, Sex, Longing, and God: Toward a Spirituality of Desire," in *Our Families, Our Values: Snapshots of Queer Kinship*, ed. Robert E. Goss and Amy Adams Squires Strongheart (New York: Harrington Park Press, 1997), 69.

Greek men. Here was the model of passionate love between two men, and something in me intuited that I was like Achilles and Patroculus. It was the first same-sex model of love in my youthful world. I intuited that this love story somehow named me. But guilt kept me from fully investing much energy beyond the natural explorations of boys with boys.

I was raised with the normal Catholic guilt about sex. It could well have been Presbyterian, Baptist, Lutheran, or Greek Orthodox guilt. All the churches have perfected their rituals and social mechanisms for transmitting guilt about the body and sexuality: Sunday school, catechism classes, sermons, ritual clothes, and the encoded negative messages about sexuality communicated by families and religious specialists. The ritualistic, educational, and social structures of churches communicated a negative morality about the body and sexuality. It encouraged a regimen of bodily control and a vigilance for any sexual feelings. My terror of the body and sexuality was intensified by Catholic education and familial silence about sexuality.

I remember my mother, after Mass one Sunday, at the altar rail undergoing a pre–Vatican II purification rite called "churching." She was purified from the recent birth of my sister, and the rite of churching enabled her to be readmitted to communion. She was purified from the "curse of Eve," the pain of childbirth and the vestige of concupiscence. The message was quite clear to a impressionable lad: sex, birth, and women are impure, dirty, and sinful. I noticed that my father did not have to undergo any churching rite. Only my mother participated in such a rite of cleansing; fathers were privileged. I noticed other women frequently going to the altar rail for this churching rite. Catholic Christianity had encoded quite specific messages about sexuality and impurity to me as a child of five years. A ritualistic message communicated was that women were certainly not equal to men. Women and childbirth were impure. Sexuality was to be feared; it was dangerous. It could lead you away from God; it definitely barred you from God's grace.

The earliest public discourse on sex that I engaged was the practice of confession, and it was certainly not the healthiest form of discourse on sex for a Catholic youth. Confession served to reinforce and underline Catholic values on sexuality, symbolically restoring sinful individuals to the community. It created personal anxiety about all types of sexual misconduct. The elements of the Catholic sacrament of penance as practiced in the form of confession from 1216 into the present consist of private confession of sins, contrition, absolution, and satisfaction for sins. The priest has the power to forgive sins because he represents

Christ. The confessional box maintains a class distinction of power between priest and the penitent, and it is the authority of the priest to absolve sin that gives him power over the penitent to shape the direction of his/her life. Through the confessional, the priest is able to shape values, reinforce guilt, and maintain control over the penitent.

The confessional was the dark box where God's surveillance was intensely encountered, and it required that I speak the truth about sexual feelings and actions. The Catholic confessional provided a model of surveillance in which the father confessor intervened in the family, and Catholic control was extended over human sexuality. For many Catholics, the confessional did not deny or silence sexuality but rendered it expressible and controllable. The ritual of the confessional box was an instrument of terror for pre–Vatican II Catholic youth. You entered in secrecy into a dark closet to speak the truth about sin to God's representative on earth. For confession to work, the penitent had to specify the exact number and circumstances of each mortal sin. If you lied or held back on truth, your confession was invalid. Your sins not only would be unforgiven but would be compounded by your lying to God. I did not realize until later how the dark confessional closet created the closet in my own life. It closeted my deepest sexual feelings and longings.

The confessional became a spiritual "panopticism" (literally, "seeing everything") where God's surveillant gaze focused on you.[2] God sees all your actions; God knows all your deepest feelings and impure stirrings. God's surveillance created a culture of guilt and anxiety. I remember a nun who described the last judgment. She described how everyone would know all the disgusting sins that I committed. "Your sins," she said, "will be placed on a big movie screen where all can see your lack of love for God." This image terrified me as a youth. Everyone would see my sexual feelings and see how much of a sinner I was.

Puberty introduced a terrifying dimension into my struggles with body and spirit. My genitals were the devil's and my playground. No sin was more terrifying to confess to the priest than "I had impure thoughts," and all pre–Vatican II Catholics can testify to the terror of confessing such thoughts. As a youth, feelings and thoughts were often conflated in my own mind. This reflected the state of Catholic catechismal practice, for relishing an impure sexual thought could be as mortal a sin as the actual commission of a sexual act. Mortal sins in those days could be

---

2. See the discussion of panopticism in Michel Foucault, *Discipline and Punish* (New York: Vintage Books, 1979), 195–228.

committed in thought, word, and deed, and they were a sure gateway to hell.

Fortunately, the priest seldom asked me about the content of those impure thoughts and just asked me the perfunctory "How many times?" I would actually have preferred death to telling him about the content of those secret male desires that were pulsing in and through my body. They were "dirty," dirtier than the thoughts of some of my childhood friends whose feelings and thoughts centered on girls. I was different because my feelings and thoughts were centered on my male friends. I was terrified of being labeled a "faggot." I was one of the 10 percent, and I did not understand at the time what it meant to be attracted to other males. There was no one to talk about these deepest feelings that God saw and condemned.

I remembered asking God to take away those impure thoughts, sexual feelings, and attractions to male friends. These recurrent thoughts and feelings, I believed, would lead me straight to hell. I was convinced that I was destined for hell. Hell was the place of punishment of mortal sinners like myself who lacked the inner discipline to control their sexual impulses. Later in high school when I read James Joyce's *Portrait of the Artist as a Young Man,* the scene where the Jesuit priest vividly describes the torments of hell repeated my childhood experiences of nuns and priests who lingered on the punishments of hell for mortal sinners. I felt like young Stephen Daedalus, terrified of hell, and I was convinced that my sexual feelings would lead me there.

The only strategy that I devised in my childish head to escape the torments of hell was to collect and accumulate indulgences. A good Catholic response! For Catholics, indulgences were time off from the punishments of purgatory. As a confused youth, I thought that indulgences might be also used as parole time from an eternity of punishment in the flames of hell. If God was just, God had to recognize some good in me despite my mortally sinful, sexual desires. God would reward me, I hoped, with time out of hell for the good that I did. So I worked to accumulate indulgences in the tens of thousands and hundred of thousands of years. I tried to accumulate plenary indulgences (full parole from purgatory) but was always uncertain whether they could be applied to parole from hell. I only hoped that indulgences would offset my sexual urges.

As puberty arrived, I experienced my first orgasm with all its terrifying feelings of pleasure and guilt. I learned to masturbate with neighborhood boys in ritual circle jerks; the older boys demonstrated how to masturbate. I imitated their actions, and my first orgasm felt wonderfully pleasurable. So I practiced masturbating by myself and with others. The downside of what appeared to be pleasurable was the accompanying Catholic guilt. Nothing that pleasurable came without a price. God saw me masturbating, and it was after all a mortal sin to touch yourself that way. Confessing impure acts to the priest was even more difficult than confessing impure thoughts. The confessor would ask further probing questions. "Alone or with others?" If I said alone, the confessor would ask what I did. I begrudgingly would tell him. He would lecture me how much God loved me and how much I disappointed God with my sin. Christ died for me because he loved me and wanted to save me. Priests were experts in making you feel guilty. I turned away from Christ's love, and I felt guilty. The priest gave me ten Our Fathers and ten Hail Marys for my masturbatory sins. The confessor would often instruct me to pray to the Virgin Mother of God for help in fighting impurity.

If I confessed impure acts with others, the confessor would make me rehearse all the particular details of the impure acts: "With whom? What did you boys do? How many times?" Some priests were more attentive to these sins than others. I did not understand at the time why they were so interested. Sometimes I felt their anger directed at myself, and I was too young to realize where their anger originated and what "transference" was. I only knew that Christ's representative on earth was angry with me or disappointed in me. I loved Christ, and this priest spoke in the name of Christ. I left those weekly confessional sessions dejected, depressed, and thoroughly guilt-ridden. I knew that I could at least receive communion the next day and perhaps for the next several days without engaging in the mortally sinful act of self-pleasure. I could love Christ purely for a couple of days.

Despite my sinfulness, I sensed that Jesus loved me. He was a friend, a companion. And I genuinely loved him and felt his presence. I always felt a dissonance between the Jesus I knew as a companion and friend and the Jesus represented by priests and nuns. The church, however, represented him as the crucified savior who would judge all transgressions. Sexuality and the church's portrayal of Jesus were at war within me. Who would win control over my body? The church's Jesus would win temporarily. Instead of making myself sexually attractive to other males, I overate and gained weight. I made myself unattractive, and my sexuality remained dormant through high school, with occasional slips.

Oftentimes, my erotic urges were channeled into prayer. I loved Jesus and wanted to follow him. I wanted to be at one with him. What I really wanted to do was to make love with him but was too guilt-ridden to admit this to myself. In the quiet of prayer, I felt a gentle call to follow him. Growing up Catholic, I knew that I was not attracted to women and not interested in marriage. The only options that seemed available were religious life or the priesthood. My erotic desires and feelings for males contributed but were the not sole reason for my becoming a Jesuit priest.

Lifeless bodies, crucified bodies

I entered the Jesuits as emotionally conflicted and guilt-ridden as St. Paul. I intuited that we shared a common thorn in the flesh. Paul felt tremendous guilt and shame that produced a self-loathing and low self-esteem that I understood only too well: "Wretched man that I am! Who will deliver me from this body of death?" (Rom. 7:24). I struggled with the same body self-loathing and what I now understand as internalized homophobia. Paul understood his thorn as an invading agent, and protection was only possible by the powerful action of God (2 Cor. 12:7–9). The thorn caused him inner turmoil and anxiety. The thorn is described as a body ailment (Gal. 4:13). Paul possessed, I thought, a condition like my own, one he considered as incurable. It was a condition of inner war that caused him scorn and self-contempt. In chapter 6, I will speak more in depth about Paul's homoerotic devotion to Christ and the subsequent tradition of Christian homodevotionalism to Jesus the Christ.

Rather than seek marriage as an outlet for his passion, Paul sought a relationship with Christ. I would understand within a couple years of Jesuit novitiate, or what I like to describe to friends as boot camp, that Paul's personal unrighteousness was replaced by the righteousness of God. He repressed his homoerotic feelings into a homoerotic relationship with Christ. The Pauline closet was the prototype of the Catholic clerical closet, and most Catholics are unaware how true this psychological dynamic is within Catholic religious orders and priesthood. That a sizable majority of religious and priests are gay is too hard for them to fathom.[3]

The battle for control over my body intensified through my college years and my years in the Society of Jesus. Ignatius of Loyola wrote "that everyone of those who live under obedience ought to allow himself to be carried and directed by Divine Providence through the agency of the superior as if he were a lifeless body which allows itself to be carried to any place and to be treated in any manner desired, or as if he were

---

3. See Mark Jordan, *The Silence of Sodom: Homosexuality in Modern Catholicism* (Chicago: University of Chicago Press, 2000). For examples of the staunch denial mechanism, see Dennis O'Brien, "Evidence Anyone?" *Commonweal* 33, September 8, 2000, 33–35.

an old man's staff which serves in any place and in any manner whatsoever in which the holder wishes to use it."[4] His instructions are directed
to young men committed to following Christ and cultivating mystical
experiences. Ignatius's notion of obedience aimed to create and shape
bodies completely submissive to the will of their superiors and the authoritarian church. His metaphors for the ideal Jesuit as a "lifeless body"
and "an old man's staff" encapsulate a military metaphor of the ideal
soldier in the hands of his commander. The ideal Jesuit was to cultivate
a submissive body by repressing passions like St. Paul.

When I started Jesuit novitiate (or boot camp), I immersed myself
in the residual body-negative attitudes and practices of mortification
preserved by the Society of Jesus from its medieval origin. I was committed to ascetic practices and disciplines to master "creature comforts,"
those material things that kept us unfree. I was training myself within
a military model to live simply and to become a soldier for Christ. The
more intense that my prayer became, the more I prepared myself to
follow and serve Christ. I lost forty pounds through fasting and exercise
during a thirty-day retreat and subsequent months. Though ostensibly
fine-tuning my body for the rigors of ministry, I was also unconsciously
making myself attractive to Christ.

As a young and impressionable novice, I was introduced to the *flagelium,* or the whip. There were nights in which the novice master or
his assistant would place a sign reading *hoc nocte,* which means in Latin
"tonight," on the bulletin board. The sign indicated that you were to
whip your body with the *flagelium,* a rope with knotted chords. I took
flagellation seriously since I was young and naive, just out of high school.
I was there to dedicate my life to God and the service of God. I would
strip down naked and whip my shoulders and back in devotion to and
love for Jesus. I never drew blood but left bruises on my shoulders. The
Roman soldiers whipped Jesus, crowned him with thorns; they spat at
him, stripped him, and crucified him. That Jesus died for me only intensified my piety. Passionately, I whipped myself in identification with Jesus
and in love for him. I wanted to share the sufferings of the man I loved.
Sometimes, looking back, I wonder if flagellation was not a form of masturbation. My Jesuit piety promoted an erotic identification with Jesus.
Some former Jesuit friends have told me stories of becoming sexually
aroused while flogging themselves. I can now see how Father Raymond
Bertrand, my novice master, fostered a homoerotic relationship with the

---

4. Ignatius of Loyola, *The Constitutions of the Society of Jesus* (St. Louis: Institute of Jesuit
Sources, 1970), 248–49.

imagined naked body of Jesus writhing in pain on the cross. He often spoke of being embraced and loved by Jesus from the cross. He spoke in very tender terms of God's love for me.

In prayer, I imagined a naked Jesus as a muscular, handsome bearded man embracing me and became sexually aroused. I envisioned burying my face in his hair-matted chest, and I found myself fighting off sexual fantasies. Catholic asceticism aimed at repressing sexual impulses, maintaining flaccid penises, and creating lifeless bodies, but Catholic piety stimulated an erotic love for Jesus. Catholic asceticism introduced a monastic discipline of the flaccid penis while Catholic piety transformed ascetic practices into an erotic stimulation of the penis. Only several years later was I able to sort out this contradiction between the asceticism of the flaccid penis and a piety stimulating the penis.

For Sts. Paul and Ignatius, the flesh was the enemy. Ignatius Loyola often whipped his body severely or stood in a river in the middle of winter up to his chest to tame his passions. From conversations with my novice director, I often had the impression that Ignatius invented the cold shower. The body was the site of temptation and sexual pleasure, the gateway that Satan could use to tempt me away from God. Hair shirts, itchy woolen shirts worn under your T-shirt, were abolished by the time I entered the Jesuit novitiate, yet the body-deficit or body-mortified attitudes were still in place during this formative period. In the novitiate, we had several bizarre Jesuit priests who took all the body-deficit practices very seriously. There were rumors that one scrupulous and humorless priest used a hook to hold his genitals while washing them with a brush to avoid ever touching them. These instruments were abolished before I entered the Jesuits.

Another instrument to torture the body was the "chains" (*catenulae*). It was a chain-link device with barbs and spikes turned inward, very much like barbwire fence. The chain was worn around either the upper thigh or the waist under the belt. The barbs pricked the flesh but normally not enough to break the skin, only irritate the affected skin. When the novice master or his associate placed the sign *cras mane* (tomorrow morning) on the bulletin board, it indicated that you were to wear the chain the next morning for penance.

We still had other domination-submission rituals to create lifeless bodies. We lived in a large institutional building where daily schedules were rigidly controlled. We took our meals together, prayed and studied together, worked together. The only times that we were apart and away from the gaze of others were when we were in our cubicles. A custom book of rules for conduct was designed to control bodily demeanor and shape the celibate body. These rules regulated our demeanor and everyday behavior. We had to walk calmly, upright, never giving the appearance of rushing. Our eyes were always cast down, especially when walking in public lest we see a seductive women or in my case a handsome man. Our eyes were downcast when speaking to a superior. How often I stared at other novices' crotches while literally obeying the rule of modesty of eyes!

Our speech was to be edifying and never frivolous. We were never to keep our hands in our pockets lest we touch and stimulate our genitals. We prayed in rigid kneeling postures, a medieval gesture of submission of a vassal to his lord. We were never to be alone with another Jesuit novice. The custom book, a book of communal regulations, read "never two, always three" (*numquam duo, semper tres*). We were assigned in groups of three for outdoor recreational walks. The custom book regulated against what were called "particular friendships"; we were to love everyone equally. Finally, we were never to touch one another (*noli tangere*). These and other rules aimed at creating submissive, obedient, and sexless bodies. The more that I tried to repress sexual feelings, the more intense they became.

The body must be denied; it must be disciplined, bound, and restricted. The body must be abused in the name of self-conquest and spiritual transcendence. The ascetic self is disembodied and fragmented; it is split from the body. The separation of the self from the body has had tragic results. It degrades the body and degrades human sexuality in particular. Bodily spontaneity is feared and denigrated. Embodiment is seen not as mediating spirit but as blocking spirit. The regime of bodily mortification to produce the ascetic self numbs the person to the bodily issues of compassion and justice. It is a regime similar to anorexia nervosa, sharing characteristics with asceticism of severe restraint, bodily retention of fluids, and sexlessness. Sociologist Bryan Turner has pointed out the parallels of anorexia to religious asceticism. Like the ascetic, the anorexic tries to control the interior world through a regimen of fasting and starvation. The female anorexic attempts to suppress menstruation and adopt a permanent childlike body and attitude. Through fasting and a corporal regimen of bodily discipline, the ascetic becomes sexless.[5]

One morning I left the chapel from morning visit while still wearing the chain. A novice friend violated the novitiate rule *noli tangere* (don't

5. Bryan S. Turner, *The Body and Society: Exploration in Social Theory* (New York: Basil Blackwell, 1984), 193–97.

touch), grabbed me, and picked me up around the waist. I screamed! The chain painfully broke the skin around my waist. My body was punctured. The event left me questioning the value of the chain and the mortification of the body. Why does God hate the body? Why were the Jesuits and other Catholic religious rejecting the body? Why have Catholic attitudes and practices refused sensuousness and the pleasures of the body? Through most of its history, Catholic Christianity has attempted to negate the body by torturing or deadening human feeling. Asceticism fears the body and its pleasures; it grows from a strict dualism between body and soul. Catholic Christianity generally felt that it was necessary to deaden the body and its affectivity for the spirit to flourish and live. Some ascetics derived pleasure from bodily torture or the endorphin high from the rush of physical torture or deprivation. For some religious, bodily torture led to sexual arousal. I understood asceticism as making myself a better instrument in Christ's service.

My questioning began a process leading me to affirm that God created my body as good and holy. I took God's incarnation seriously: "And the Word became flesh and dwelt among us, full of grace and truth" (John 1:14). If God was embodied, I thought, then the body must be a vehicle of grace and truth. The body was not a sensual obstacle to the moral and religious life; it was a vehicle to connect with God. How ironic that the very religion that believes in the incarnation of God has consistently been negative to the human flesh. Pete Gardella writes: "We have treated the body as a thing to be sanctified, controlled, and directed toward a transcendent goal. But human beings can neither sanctify nor escape from their bodies. We began to regard the body as inferior when we began to sin; yet the capacity for passion may be the means of salvation."[6]

After the Jesuit novitiate, I discovered a number of other Jesuits who valued the body as the locus of grace and truth and who were less accepting of the indoctrination of lifeless bodies. They were less pious and perhaps a little more jaded and cynical of the anti-body piety and rhetoric. Many of us mocked and joked about those anti-body attitudes. Humor helped us all survive and not take the body-deficit piety so seriously. The anti-body rhetoric of medieval Christianity was changing or lessening as the full reforms of Vatican II were implemented in the So-

---

6. Peter Gardella, *Innocent Ecstasy: How Christianity Gave America an Ethic of Sexual Pleasure* (New York: Oxford University Press, 1985), 161. On Christianity's problematic relationship with the body, see Lisa Isherwood and Elizabeth Stuart, *Introducing Body Theology* (Cleveland: Pilgrim Press, 1998), 52–77.

ciety of Jesus. The body was now becoming the site of grace, full of new dangers.

Finding God in my sexual experience

Little did I realize that there were many men in the Jesuits and Catholic priesthood like myself, not attracted to women. As a youth I perceived priests as men who had learned to control their passions through heroic struggle. Entering the Jesuits was for me like a kid going into a candy store, or what Joe Kramer describes as "homosexual heaven."[7] Most of the men were like myself, and there was a subaltern network of Jesuits engaged in sex with one another. I would learn to become sexually mature. I entered the Jesuits initially imitating St. Paul, repressed and fearful of my homoerotic feelings yet sublimating them in my love for Jesus. My own internalized homophobia blocked me from self-love and truly loving other men, including Christ.

Body-deficit spiritualities manifest body loathing and provide a horizon for the hatred of bodies and the need to control bodies. One of the pervasive fears in American culture is that of the human body. Bodies have been understood as dangerous to the spiritual quest. The life of the body and the life of the spirit have remained incompatible for religious specialists. Countless Catholic religious and clergy were asked to take a vow of chastity or celibacy to do what was unnatural, the elimination of passion. Normal sexual passion was described as lust. Even though many may have never committed any sexual acts, many religious and priests felt as guilty as if they had carried on torrid sexual affairs with Christ. The dualism between body and spirit took its toll upon them. Many resorted to alcohol to deaden the erotic urges of the body; others created alternative strategies to keep their bodies alive to passion and sensuality.

Despite my vigilance against bodily urges and masturbation during boot camp, I never could quite live up to the idealized self of a Jesuit that all novices attempt to cultivate. Our repressed and tightly controlled bodies rebelled on feast days. When we had the opportunity to escape the tightly regimented daily order, we left bodily discipline behind and fell prey to our homoerotic longings for touch and love. Cultivating a lifeless body, I suffered a touch deficit. Like many, I desired touch and emotional intimacy.

---

7. David Guy, *The Red Thread of Passion: Spirituality and the Paradox of Sex* (Boston: Shambhala, 1999), 208.

Oftentimes, another novice would ask if I wanted a back rub. The first time I agreed, I naively did not realize that a "back rub" was a euphemism for a sexual encounter. Human touch and love are real needs, and ascetic rigor in developing a "lifeless body" goes against our human nature. Young babies need physical touch to survive. Of course, I felt guilt-ridden from these experiences. Later I noticed a pattern that emerged with other Jesuit sexual partners. I call it the "Gee, I was drunk last night and don't remember what I did" syndrome. This denial mechanism allowed some of my Jesuit sex partners to deny their human need for sex and love, bodily affection and warmth. This denial mechanism distanced sexual partners from you until the next encounter, and the cycle of human need for intimacy, covert sex, and tremendous guilt and shame would repeat itself. It offered the pretense of celibate, lifeless bodies.

When I later talked to other Jesuits, I learned that these acts of bodily resistance to the ascetic discipline of the body were more widespread than I ever imagined. I discovered that a fellow novice well respected for his rigorous piety and Marian devotion was promiscuous. His room had a door to a fire escape on the second story, and that fire escape had stairs to the ground level. That fire escape carried an incredible amount of male, non-Jesuit traffic for sexual encounters. He was certainly not untypical. This puritan-libertine syndrome rejects the body. The puritan comprehends the body as an obstacle to religious experience while the libertine reduces the body to pure pleasure. One deadens the body through nonuse, the other by overuse. Both the puritan and the libertine fail to integrate the body into a spiritual path. Both fears and obsession with the body depreciate the body and sexuality as a potential site of the sacred. Both devalue the world: one by rejection, the other by consumerism. The puritan shuts out deep sexuality from religious experience while the libertine shuts out deep spirituality. The paradox is that deep sexuality and deep spirituality overlap, and it is difficult to attain depth in one without the other.

Such sexual experiences — though institutionally frowned upon — countered the traditional dualist theologies and practices that opposed the body against the spirit. A number of Jesuits mentored me to a sexual and a spiritual maturity. They taught me that the erotic was a meditative gateway to the sacred. The body was not to be deadened by austere practices of self-abnegation but enlivened by its affectivity and even sexuality. The body was sacramental, the locus of revelation and the site of spirit. I began to experience the connection between body and spirit, sexuality and spirituality. I engaged in meditative sex, becoming mindful of its deep connection to God and harnessing the sexual energy into interconnectedness with the people and the world. I came to know Christ in my most intimate relationships. I realized that orgasmic bliss had many of the subtle qualities of intense, sublime, nonconceptual contemplation of Christ.

More importantly I began to heal the split between my spiritual self and my bodily urges. I began to tackle the internalized homophobia within me that blocked spirit. The erotic is the embodiment of the spirit's spontaneity. To eradicate sexuality would be, for us as bodily persons, to permanently block the spirit. Sexuality, I realized, was neither destructive nor peripheral to my spirituality, for sexuality is intimately involved in the center of human life. Sexuality is a symbolic means of communication and communion; it expresses our human need to connect physically and spiritually. This drive for connectedness in sexuality and spirituality would enable me to understand not only their interconnections but also their connections to justice.

During my theological studies in preparation for ordination to the priesthood, I found many more Jesuits open to sexual encounters and love-making. Jesuits in training, priests, superiors, and spiritual directors taught me how to love men. They mentored me into human love and justice. I look back at the period of my theological studies when individual Jesuits taught me a great love of humanity, justice, and the sexual love of men. I integrated my deep experiences of sexuality with my prayer and with my work for justice. I worked in a leper colony in India and in Mother Teresa's House of the Dying Destitute in Calcutta. I experienced death firsthand, and I remember seeing Christ's eyes in a dying man's face. I knew only a few words of Bengali, and I held him as he died. His death in my arms was as intimate as any sexual encounter with another man. Washing and caring for dying men in the House of the Dying Destitute became an embodied experience of touching and caring for Christ. I saw Christ's face among the poor, the sick, and the abandoned. These experiences have remained graces through my life and imprinted the directionality of an erotic spirituality connected to justice issues. If I love Christ, then I must commit myself to love his presence in people in need.

Embodied spirituality became for me the recovery of bodily sensuousness and openness to life. The separation of self from the body results in egocentric behaviors, bodily degradation, and punishment. It is a joyless and fruitless struggle to overcome the body in pursuit of spirit. I recovered my body from the insidious addiction of dualism so ingrained within Christianity since the second century. Treatment for my own body hatred began with discovery of my own body, massaging, touching, and becoming aware of it. I pursued Tai Chi, dance, yoga, self-sexuality, Zen meditative practices, psychotherapy, and ministry to the dying. I rediscovered embodiment and discovered openness to reality. I learned that my body was transparent with spirit, filled with a zest of life, and filled with sexual desire for men. My body was less an obstacle to prayer and more a gateway for prayer. My body became the means for expanding my connections to people and God.

My sexual/spiritual awakening took place within the Jesuits. I woke to the goodness of the body and the beauty of the spirit. Deep sexuality and deep spirituality are woven into the energy system of body and spirit. My relationship with Jesus the Christ was evolving. My journey in bodily recovery was transforming me from an imitator of a repressed St. Paul into the Beloved Disciple. The physical description of the Beloved Disciple's head on the breast of Jesus at the Last Supper attracted me. Like many gay Christians, I always intuited that Jesus and the Beloved Disciple not only freely expressed their love physically but also celebrated it sexually.

I found confirmation of my call to priesthood and service in my awakening to embodiment. I found the eucharist to be a significant part of bodily love. It began to take on a homoerotic dimension. Jesus said, "This is my body which is given to you." Eating Jesus' body and drinking his blood were physical acts of participation, intercommunion, and sexual love-making. I was falling in love with Jesus in a new and erotic way.

Coming out: erotic conversion

Jesuit spirituality provided a framework of prayer and rational examination of my feelings about being gay; it provided me with the resources to "come out." These spiritual resources involved finding God in all things: including sexual experiences, the focus on Jesus and following him in discipleship, and a Christian vision of love and justice. These spiritual resources placed me on a collision course with my own self-image and closetedness. They were vital to my coming out and the integration of my sexuality and spirituality — once the erotophobic Christian ideologies were removed, the other resources were able to become powerful tools for recognizing the original blessing of sexuality.[8]

---

8. See my article on the damaging effect of closetedness to one's spirituality and the need to come out and come out to God: Robert E. Goss, "The Integration of Sexuality and Spirituality: Gay Sex Prophets within UFMCC," in *The Spirituality of Men: Sixteen Christians Write about Their Faith*, ed. Philip Culbertson (Minneapolis: Fortress Press, 2001), 200–217.

After ordination as a Jesuit priest in a parish in Oswego, New York, I remember, vividly, one morning celebrating the eucharist for the parishioners. While in devotional prayer at eucharist, I envisioned Jesus in meditation and felt sexually aroused. My initial feelings of sexual arousal triggered a residual internalized homophobic reaction. I felt guilt over my erotic arousal for the man, Jesus. Then, a feeling of wonder and of beauty mixed with erotic excitement swept away the internalized homophobic mechanism that I developed so well as a Catholic child. This erotic arousal for Christ became a quantum leap in my spiritual life; I finally understood the connection between deep sexuality and deep spirituality. I finally admitted to myself that I loved Jesus because he was a male and that it was OK to love Jesus passionately and erotically as a man. I came out to God and named myself gay. It was more than just coming out as gay; my spiritual journey and my sexual journey were really one path.

This envisioning or what I understand as a form of lucid dreaming or imaginative envisioning at eucharist was a profound experience of what Catholic spirituality calls "infused contemplation," that is, the self-communication of God to a person in prayer. It had a deep impact both on the directionality of my life and on how I would view the eucharist. The eucharist and the erotic became thoroughly enmeshed in my spirituality.

I analyzed my sexual feelings that summer in specific examinations of conscience and continually thought about the experience of infused contemplation in prayer. I spoke with my spiritual director to discern the movement of God's Spirit in my prayer. I also masturbated, allowing myself to make love with Jesus in prayer and contemplation. Contemplation is a meditative envisioning of God in image or symbol. It has some of the qualities of a lucid dreaming and free association without blockage. These added erotic energies deepened my meditative experience and coming to love myself.

My technique of meditative prayer was to envision Christ with me and experience him as a lover. Scott Haldeman, Betty Dodson, and Joe Kramer argue that masturbation can be spiritual and can become a form of transcendental meditation.[9] Masturbation can harness fantasies and

9. See in this volume "Finding God in the Heart-Genital Connection." Scott Haldeman speaks about meditative sex and masturbation in "Bringing Good News to the Body: Masturbation and Male Identity," in *Men's Bodies, Men's Gods: Male Identities in a (Post-)Christian Culture,* ed. Bjorn Krondorfer (New York: New York University Press, 1996), 111–24. Betty Dodson, *Sex for One: The Joy of Selfloving* (New York: Crown Trade Paperbacks, 1987), 120–30. Joe Kramer has produced a number of videotapes on masturbation, connecting it to spirituality. See also Guy, *Red Thread of Passion,* 201–22; and David A. Schulz and Dominic S.

sexual energy. When prolonged, it can stimulate and extend pleasure. When fantasies are focused into making love with Christ, the experience opens itself to a fundamental and profound consciousness of God. My visualizations of Jesus were certainly explicit, erotically envisioning various forms of making love to Jesus the Christ. I had sexual intercourse with Jesus. Sometimes he was the top, and sometimes he was the bottom. My relationship with Christ was mutual and deep. Jesus became the first male lover with whom I felt thoroughly comfortable. It was a natural progression for me to move from being a companion of Jesus to becoming a lover of Jesus and then to falling in love with a man.

God is neither male nor female, but the presence of God in contemplation can evoke either female or male imagery. Embodying prayer or engaging in erotic prayer has a long tradition in Christian mysticism where Christ is experienced as a male lover or as a female lover. The Christian mystical tradition is primarily bisexual and homoerotic because God has been traditionally envisioned male. This is apparent in the visionary writings of late medieval mystics such as Hadewijch, Hildegaard of Bingen, Teresa of Ávila, and John of the Cross, among many others in Christian history. In spiritual direction, I also have found that some women pray to Christ with their bodies and experience orgasm in their communion with Christ. Sexual ecstasy frequently accompanies spiritual ecstasy, and both may involve orgasmic release. For me, erotic prayer propelled me to a new intimacy with Jesus the Christ, a new awareness of my interconnections with humanity and nature, and a new level of discipleship. Later in life, my theological goal has been to articulate a sexual theology that encompasses the integration of sexuality and spirituality, various configurations of relationships, the interconnection of love-making and justice-doing, and eros as revelation of God.

When I applied the rules for discernment of genuine religious experiences to my erotic contemplation, it met all the criteria for what was traditionally understood as infused contemplation. I experienced a profound goodness and rightness in my contemplative love-making with Jesus the Christ, and I came to accept my gayness as Jesus the Christ of God accepted my erotic feelings of love. That summer in Oswego, New York, I glimpsed a small portion of the fullness of the erotic grace of God and the grace of being born gay. I had yet to understand what the full implications of being a gay priest in the Catholic Church were and was far from understanding what it meant to be a queer priest in exile.

Raphael, "Christ and Tiresias: A Wider Focus on Masturbation," in *Enlightened Sexuality: Essays on Body-Positive Spirituality*, ed. Georg Feurstein (Freedom, Calif.: Crossing Press, 1989), 215–41.

Little did I realize what the erotic grace of God was preparing for me in the coming months!

Both the sexual drive to bond with another human being and the contemplative yearning for union with God have a common source in eros.[10] I allowed my prayer to become sexual, abandoning narrow self-images to discover who I really was in the presence of God. I envisioned making love to Jesus, felt myself become sexually aroused, and climaxed in an orgasmic union with Jesus the Christ. That Jesus became my deep sexual partner in prayer felt right. I could no longer keep the erotic presence of God in the closet, and God came out in my life in an orgasmic explosion of interconnectedness of love and justice. I felt that my life had been like a shamanic vision quest to seek the sacred knowledge of my life. I found that answer in the interconnections between the divine and the human, the spirit and the body. Thus, I first "came out" and admitted being gay to Jesus the Christ. It would take a few more months to come out to other Jesuits and to friends. I began to name myself and my erotic desires for Christ. I had become the Beloved Disciple and knew Jesus the Christ as my gay lover.[11]

Coming out and religious conversion have some strong parallels. My life was forever changed. I realized that erotophobia and homophobia alienated me from the most creative and loving power of the universe. God was at the root of my deep sexual longings. I made authentic connection with the source of my erotic power and my vocation to priesthood. I moved from fear toward joy, a desire to authentically connect with other men and love women, humanity, and the world. What bound me to God was not secretive but the public love of Christ and love of men. The sacred embodied the human experience of love among sexual partners. Could we become an open community of sexual love? I was not sure at the time but became more convinced later of the tribal sexual connections and sacred bonds that gays celebrated.

The closet serves as a control of desire; it restricts sexual desire to the furtive and the secretive. Following Christ meant becoming who I am in connection with other men and humanity. The clerical closet is only acceptable for those who want to rise within the closeted hierarchy of Catholic religious power and privilege. My refusal to pretend to be heterosexual would mark me as deviant in the eyes of my closeted

10. Kelly, "Christmas, Sex, Longing, and God," 61–76; see also Michael Kelly, *The Erotic Contemplative*, 6 vols. (video) (Oakland, Calif.: EroSpirit Institute, 1994).

11. Robert E. Goss, "The Beloved Disciple: A Queer Bereavement Narrative in the Time of AIDS," in *Take Back the Word: A Queer Reading of the Bible*, ed. Robert E. Goss and Mona West (Cleveland: Pilgrim Press, 2000), 206–18.

contemporaries. I spoke the gay truth about Catholic priests and religious. My coming out meant my stepping into the light as a target of
violence and exclusion. It also meant that I entered what was socially deviant and closed doors open to me as a white, straight-appearing priest.
Openly gay, sexual priests are dangerous to a closeted church and hierarchy. As long as you keep the secret of the closet, you are safe. Or
as a Jesuit superior said to me, "As long as you did not become public
or settle down with anyone, you could be promiscuous." What God was
doing was grooming me to become open as both priest and lover, and
this would lead into an institutional collision.

Both priest and lover: a journey into exile[12]

I met a Jesuit, Frank Ring, five months after ordination, and we instantly
fell in love. Frank was studying at the Jesuit Weston School of Theology
while I was enrolled in my first year of graduate school at Harvard.
Frank was handsome, sensitive, spiritual, fun, full of life, and committed to issues of social justice. He was excited by his vocation to justice.
We were growing in love and intimacy. We engaged in erotic prayer and
love-making. Our sex was eucharistic, intensely passionate, and intensely
spiritual. During our sessions, I felt Christ in a way that I only experienced in my solitary erotic prayer. I felt Christ in our love-making and
did not want to give it up.

Ten months after we met, we spent a week in Provincetown. We had
been apart for the summer, and in Provincetown we began to explore
the possibilities of leaving the Jesuits and moving in together. Frank was
not ordained, and leaving the Jesuits was a less difficult decision for him.
In fact, he had already come to that decision prior to starting theological studies and wanted to use the time to test his decision. For me, it was
far more complicated. I always wanted to be a priest, and now I knew
that I was deeply in love with this guy and wanted to spend my life with
him. I didn't know how to put that together with God's call to priestly
service. So I began a three-month discernment process with a spiritual
director. Frank did likewise. I prayed each day for Christ's guidance on
how I could be both priest and lover. Christ answered me one Sunday
afternoon during a meeting with other same-sex couples in the fall of
1977. Frank and I were facilitating a group of gay and lesbian couples
who wanted to develop communicative resources to sustain their inti-

---

12. On this subject, see Robert E. Goss, *Both Priest and Lover* (video) (Oakland, Calif.:
EroSpirit Institute, 1994).

macy. Frank and I worked with them and planned to adapt the Catholic marriage-encounter model to lesbian/gay couples. We facilitated a number of such encounters for gay/lesbian couples, and I blessed many of their marriages or unions as a Catholic priest.

During the meeting, I felt Christ saying, "Celibacy was a church-made rule. Follow me into exile; become both priest and lover. I will lead you places never imagined." I told Frank after the meeting that I intended to leave the Jesuits, and I told him what I felt Christ was saying to me. We went to a Dignity mass and then returned to my residence. We went up to my room, and Frank lay on the bed and said that he needed about fifteen minutes of silence. I watched him on the bed. I wanted to spend my life with him, and I hoped that he did not turn me down. I said to Christ, "You got me here; you better help me." After what seemed to be the longest fifteen minutes, Frank asked me, "Can we name the dog after my father?" A month later, we blessed and exchanged rings in a private service for ourselves.

We attempted to leave the Jesuits quietly, and two friends from Dignity/Boston generously threw a shower for us. It was completely practical since we had only our clothes and books to move into an apartment. The shower was a dinner and party, a little too campy for me at the time. There were several gay Jesuits at the party who were on the phone that very evening to friends across the country. News of our leaving together turned out to become a major scandal. Several months later we heard the rumors circulating about how two Jesuits, a priest and a scholastic, left together, how the Jesuit rector at the theology school married us, and how the Jesuit community threw a wedding reception for us. The story still persists even today in Jesuit lore. Many of our closeted Jesuit friends distanced themselves from us for fear of being identified with us as gay.

Coming out has public consequences. I left as an unlaicized priest, refusing to go through the process of invalidating my call by Christ to serve as a priest. My Jesuit superiors applied intense pressure to me to go through laicization, a paper procedure to try to invalidate the ordination or to render it dormant. Reluctantly, I said, "I agree if the reason for my leaving was a sacramental homosexual marriage." I knew too well that the Vatican Congregation for the Clergy would never release me from ordination for that reason since it would amount to a Vatican recognition of homosexual marriage. My family took to my leaving the Jesuits and moving in with Frank in a gay relationship very hard. For a number of years, communication with my family was strained. Loss of Jesuit friends and family was the price paid for coming out and following

Christ into exile. Christ called me to a more authentic witness as a gay man who was a lover and priest. I recognized that Jesus was already out there at the margins of society and not in the church. In exile space at the edge of society, I found Christ in my lover and the gay/lesbian community, and I began with Frank to create our family of choice.

We formed a family with an extended network of close friends. The model for our relationship and even our extended family of friends was the Jesuit model of friendship and community. We formed an openly gay, Christian community of apostolic love. Our community remained inclusive of those who were alienated and harmed by the churches.[13] For fourteen years, we prayed, made love, supported ourselves, founded a business, created Food Outreach (a major AIDS service organization), and worked in various ministries for the queer community. The Jesuit ideals of prayer, generous service, and justice-love infused our household. Our own love-making and prayer empowered our apostolic community of love; and our love spilled beyond ourselves as a couple to reach outside in service to others.

Each Sunday morning we made sexual love, followed by eucharist at the dining room table for the two of us. Both sexual love and eucharist were intimate and sacred moments of love-making. In our love-making, each of our ego-walls dissolved. We choreographed fused bodies in an ecstasy of pleasure and prayer. In sexual ecstasy, we celebrated deep love and deep spirituality. When one's body and mind are joined meditatively together in love-making, the sexual/spiritual potential moves beyond the ordinary orgasmic threshold of both partners into a new dimension of reality. There was a sense of oneness with each other and a deep sense of Christ's presence in a dynamic energy flow embracing our bodies. There was a letting-go and a surrender to rapture that transported us into a meditative realm of consciousness where boundaries dissolved and where the body of Christ was experienced in intimate touch, taste, smell, play, and so on. There were times that I saw Christ's face within Frank's face as I penetrated him in intercourse. As I was penetrated I felt penetrated by Frank and Christ. As I tasted Frank's body, I tasted Christ's body. We experienced a ménage à trois and the inclusionary love of God.

We made love and extended that sexual love into our weekly celebrated eucharists. Both were intense experiences of love-making with God. There is no more intense spiritual experience than to make love with your lover and see Christ's face in your lover's face while in the

---

13. See in this volume "Challenging Procreative Privilege by Queering Marriage."

throes of passion. The letting-go was carried into our prayer around the table as we broke bread and shared the cup of Christ's love. The communion intimacy was found equally in the bedroom and at the altar. We embodied love as God embodied love for us in word and sacrament. Eating the consecrated bread and drinking the wine were as intense communion as our intimate love-making. How could I not taste Frank's body and life force in the body and blood of Christ?

Was the journey into exile as priest and lover worth the pain? I say emphatically, "Yes!" No matter what the Jesuits, the church, family, or friends thought of our union, it was holy. It had love-enhancing and justice-enhancing effects. From the very beginning, the following of the Christ was fundamental to our union and household. As we built our lives around love-making, we grew in our sense of ministry. Our passionate yearnings for each other did not enclose ourselves selfishly, as some critics stereotype gay relationships, but turned us outward to engage in our communal obligations to follow Christ. We grew in compassion as we learned to live passionately and act justly with each other. Such a mode of living strengthened our resolve to be compassionate to others in need. Love-making channels passion and energizes action toward justice.[14]

Though we did not adopt the current procreative strategies of having or adopting children, I would describe our union as metaphorically procreative. Our procreative sexual love spilled over into apostolic service to God's people. The more we experienced the passionate love for each other and the presence of the risen Christ in our love-making, the more we felt the need to share our love with others. Our love-making in bed and at the table freed us to serve others in need. Passion was transformed into compassion. We took into our household ministry the throwaway people of our society, the developmentally disabled, alienated gays and lesbians, and people living with the painful realities of HIV illness. We created an apostolic community of love for the marginalized and the disenfranchised.

Hospitality is a tremendous ministry when it imitates the table fellowship that Jesus practiced in welcoming outcasts, the poor, women, and the ill. For us, hospitality became the compassionate welcoming of unexpected strangers into our household and into our lives. As AIDS devastated our circle of friends, we involved ourselves in forming a Christian base community of HIV-positive people, lovers, friends, and care providers. Along with several friends we pulled together in the midst

---

14. Robert E. Goss, *Jesus ACTED UP: A Gay and Lesbian Manifesto* (San Francisco: HarperSanFrancisco, 1993), 167–68.

of our intense grief and pain over the ravages of AIDS. We became a wounded community, a human quilt of prayer to grieve, resist the ravages of HIV, love one another, and sustain our compassionate outreach. Our love gave us energy for compassionate outreach and sustained a commitment to justice.

Such procreativity in our relationship is not atypical in the translesbigay community. I personally know hundreds of couples who have expressed their love in compassionate outreach in volunteer services to the larger community or in a passionate commitment to work for justice. Their love overflows into the hundreds of AIDS service organizations, volunteer services outside of the translesbigay community, and the struggle for civil rights.

HIV comes closer

When Frank was diagnosed as HIV-positive, my ministry catalyzed into AIDS and queer activism. For some time prior, the genocidal indifference and hostility by an array of public institutions against HIV-positive people and the increased incidences of violence against queers and women had affected me. Too many of my friends had died of HIV complications, and too many of my friends had been the targets of violence, harassment, and discrimination because of their sexual orientation or gender. My intensified ministry was a natural evolution of our covenant for justice-love in commitment to the work of ACT UP and the gay/lesbian civil rights movement. I wanted to do something to change the injustice of AIDS apathy and queer discrimination. In anger, I joined the justice groups of ACT UP/St. Louis and Queer Nation. Within Queer Nation, seasoned lesbian activists mentored me in direct-action techniques in the spirit of the nonviolent civil disobedience of Rosa Parks, Gandhi, Martin Luther King Jr., the Berrigan brothers, and others. Several of the lesbians in Queer Nation/St. Louis were seasoned veterans involved in the African American civil rights movement, the antiwar movement, the women's movement, and queer civil rights struggles.

Anger born of love empowered my activism.[15] I was angry at the discrimination Frank experienced from society, the Catholic Church, and the medical and the local AIDS bureaucracy. Anger has been the root of many of the writings of queer activists and theologians. It is a holy and just anger born out of solidarity with loved ones and which moves

---

15. On anger, see ibid., 144–45, 177.

to a commitment of justice-doing. Anger empowers my theological writings and my activism; queer liberation theology, like its Latin American antecedents, is praxis-centered or activist. If theology is not strategically and practically oriented toward human liberation, it is a waste of time and energy. Queer liberation theology is written and practiced in the struggle not only against misogyny, homophobia, heterosexism, and AIDS-phobia but also against a wider array of social oppressions including racism, classism, militarism, and ecological domination. Already immersed in critical feminist and gay/lesbian theological writings, I wrote *Jesus ACTED UP: A Gay and Lesbian Manifesto* in four months. I argued that Christianity was not the enemy of the queer community. Rather, the churches are the enemy. Gay/lesbian theology was too apologetic; it did not challenge institutional Christianity and its violence. I wrote a political queer liberation theology reflecting the developments of queer and AIDS activism in our community. I believe that queer Christian theology has to be dissident, political, proud, erotic, defiant, and activist. It has to center on justice-love.

I wrote *Jesus ACTED UP* with passion and anger. Even today, I am acutely aware while rereading sections of the book that it was born from passionate love-making. I was only too aware of how the churches had promoted violence against translesbigay people. I saw Christ's face within Frank's as HIV ravaged him and as AIDS service bureaucrats treated him as a victim. Similar to contemporary queers, Jesus lived on the margins of political power but threatened the heart of the political order. He died for God's coming reign. Jesus lived God's love and justice in his solidarity with the oppressed and the marginal. God was active in Jesus' inclusive practice, vision, and death. God identified with Jesus' political practices and death, and God raised Jesus as the Christ of the oppressed of history. Solidarity was a key ingredient in my queer theology. Solidarity is the dynamic and compassionate identification with another person or social group, and solidarity with the oppressed leads to holy anger and to a passion for justice-doing. I found the bedroom as the best training site for prayerful solidarity with other people because solidarity is the erotic drive to make compassionate and just connections with those who are oppressed and suffering. Solidarity is making erotic connections with lover, community, and the world, and Christ is in the midst of those erotic connections. Deep spiritual, sexual love-making helped us learn about justice-love and grow in solidarity. When I saw Christ in Frank's face, it became easier to envision Christ's face within another. It was easy to become a buddy with a difficult person living with AIDS because I saw Christ's face within him. I could cook breakfast and

clean for him even when he was unappreciative or hostile. It was easy
to serve food at the Arlington Street supper program for the homeless
and pass out condoms to the teenage male street hustlers. I saw Christ's
face in the homeless and the hustlers.

What the Jesus movement experienced on Easter was the explicit revelation of God's dynamic and liberating energy at work. Jesus' solidarity
with the throwaway people of his society led to his death, and God transformed the lethal silencing of Jesus' death into liberation. God said no
to the silencing and acted up against human violence. On Easter, God
came out for justice-love for all oppressed peoples. Easter thus communicated God's erotic and compassionate solidarity with queers and their
sufferings.

Frank's death: numbness of body and spirit

On Easter 1992, I participated in the organization of a "Stop the Church"
action at the Catholic Cathedral of St. Louis. A hundred activists staged
a peaceful demonstration to reclaim Easter for people living with AIDS,
queers, and women. Three crosses were carried in front of the cathedral
during the Sunday service. Frank had several reservations about the
demonstration and did not participate in the action. But he came to
the protest to offer support from the sidelines, and he participated in
the kiss-in at the end of the action. Eight weeks later many of those same
activists were in that same cathedral for Frank's funeral.

I knew that Frank's T-cell count was less than two hundred; he easily
tired. His liver was severely damaged. On my birthday, we celebrated my
mailing off the first draft of my dissertation to my directors at Harvard
University by going out to dinner. When we came home, we took a
bath together and poured ourselves a glass of wine. Frank said to me,
"Robert." I knew it was serious because he called me Robert only when
I did something wrong or when he had something troubling to discuss.
"Two things that I want for you: I want you to go into teaching; I think
that you will be a good teacher. Secondly, I want you to fall in love again."
I did not realize at that time that Frank had been concealing his real
condition from me because he didn't want me to worry. In a computer
file several days later, I found a funeral service that he designed for
himself. His last act of love was to try to free me to carry on with my life
and to love again.

I started to cry. I didn't want to hear those last words, and he tried
to console me. We made physical love for the last time in that bath-
tub. I experienced pain in the depths of love-making; we were being

pulled apart by a disease that I had no control over. I wanted to be with him always; I wanted to share his pain and death. We experienced one another's pain in a dance of tears and prayerful love-making. We desperately joined our bodies in one spirit while the disease was ripping us physically apart. That night was as painful as the day two years previously that Frank was diagnosed HIV-positive and myself as negative. I wanted to be HIV-positive, and my survivor's guilt sometimes overwhelmed me. I prayed silently to Christ to take me with Frank.

Next day Frank vomited up more blood than I could ever imagine. I was really alarmed and drove him immediately to our physician. In our physician's office, he vomited again, filling up a quarter of the wastebasket. I looked at our physician's face, and I knew then that this was the beginning of the end. He was hospitalized in intensive care. We filed his living will and the durable power of attorney into his medical chart. Two nights later Frank was placed on a respirator against his wishes in his living will and without my permission. I fought with the hospital and internists over the decision to place him on a respirator for five days. Finally, when I threatened legal action, the hospital moved Frank into a private room with the respirator. I sort of slept at his bedside — I couldn't really sleep with the pounding sound of the respirator and knowing how Frank hated the respirator. I felt that the hospital and doctors raped his body. I massaged his heels with lotion since they were bruised and bloodied from his pushing up on his heels to fight against the respirator. The hospital staff took him off the respirator, but he continued to live. That night in the late hours, he woke and asked me what was happening. I said, "My love, you are dying. I will always love you." He said, "I love you." Those were the last words that he would speak. I got him home next day for hospice care and to die in our bedroom with our dogs around him. Three days later he died while I was with him. I kept a promise to him that I would be there for and with him when he died.

Frank was a pious Irish Catholic. As an altar boy, he had gone to mass for the first Friday of nine consecutive months. According to Catholic tradition, this meant that you would not die without the benefit and presence of a priest. Frank often joked that I was his priest and my presence with him was the result of his youthful piety of making the nine first Fridays. I was there with him as I promised.

Six hours after Frank's death I received a phone call from my sister-in-law. She told me my brother Bill had just died. He died of the same complications as Frank. I couldn't believe my ears, for the situation sounded like some Greek tragedy. Somehow I believed that Frank was there to greet my brother and help transition him from this world into the next. My close friends were there for me through the funeral, and some were prepared to go to assist me if I faltered when I got up to tell some of the story of Frank's life unknown to all but myself. I had to tell how generous Frank had been in answering Christ's call to compassionate service.

Throughout that summer, I was numb from grief at Frank's loss. I remember that I cared little about living. My friends helped me through my grieving and survivor's guilt, providing me a safe space to rebuild my life. What did it mean to be HIV-negative at a time when lovers and friends seroconvert and die from the ravages of HIV? Gay men do not discuss this taboo topic because it is too painful to address. What does it mean to be a survivor in a house that is now empty? Eric Rofes has aptly described survivor's grief as posttraumatic stress syndrome.[16] I was suffering from such grief. Like many of us, I have lost hundreds of friends to HIV. My numbness and grief over Frank's loss were so intense that I was at risk of seroconversion. I no longer cared what happened to me. I felt that I would eventually seroconvert, and I actively worked at it. If it weren't for loving and caring gay men who could feel my pain, I would now be HIV-positive. I felt like Mary Magdalene or the Beloved Disciple after Jesus' body was buried and prior to resurrection joy. Somewhere buried in my subconsciousness were glimmers of faith and hope. I still loved Christ and Frank deeply, but I was severely challenged by overwhelming numbness and grief.[17] Friends stood by me when I felt abandoned by my own family and Frank's family.

My in-laws had taken possession of Frank's body and buried him in a family plot without acknowledging his spousal relationship of sixteen years. I had celebrated the holidays with them for eight years and was welcomed in all family gatherings. I had mistakenly viewed myself as part of Frank's family. Death and grief do strange things to families, intensifying dysfunctional family dynamics. Frank's death from HIV had affected his family of origin's relationship to his family of choice. They abruptly broke off all contact with me and denied the reality of what was at the time the most long-term relationship of all our siblings. The final painful erasure of our covenanted relationship was underscored in the AIDS quilt that his mother had designed and assembled. The names of all his relatives — including those of divorced spouses of his

---

16. Eric Rofes, *Reviving the Tribe: Regenerating Gay Men's Sexuality and Culture in the Ongoing Epidemic* (New York: Harrington Park Press, 1996), 47–52.

17. Goss, "The Beloved Disciple," 206–18.

siblings — were included on the quilt panel. There was no mention of his life partner of sixteen years. Their erasure of our relationship was complete. I dedicated *Jesus ACTED UP* in memory of Frank to keep our passionate love alive.

Loving again: life goes on

My grieving had begun the day that Frank was diagnosed seropositive. It continued for the next two and a half years. There were no protease inhibitors available prior to his death, and the antivirals had limited effect on the virus. The progression of HIV into the last stages has an emotional roller-coaster effect upon those living with HIV and their loved ones. Grief and hope pervaded our prayer together as we tried to face the uncertainties of HIV together. One of Frank's greatest gifts of love was that he freed me to love again. I also would add that the ménage à trois spirituality that placed Christ in the midst of our love-making kept me open to love again.

At the end of the summer after Frank's death, I began to recover from the depths of grief. I found I was able to celebrate Frank's life and smile at very vivid memories of our life together. The pain of loss was still in the background, but I was able to foreground much of our past love and celebrate it in prayer. I regained the sense of Christian mission and was determined that I would never abandon my brothers and sisters who were HIV-positive. I would continue to work for justice with ACT UP. Final copyediting on *Jesus ACTED UP* kept me busy while I also finished my dissertation for my mentors at Harvard University. I was coming back into a resurrected focus. I found myself engaging in self-sexuality, remembering love-making with Frank and Christ. Prayer included a reclamation of my own sexuality. Through sexual prayer, I reaffirmed my belief in the living God and the life that Frank now shared with the resurrected Christ. I now realize that reclamation of sexuality is absolutely integral to personal healing, survival, and a vision for justice-love in the time of AIDS.

Five months after Frank's death I met David at Mom's, a leather bar. We initially became sexually intimate without any expectations. Healing for me included a recovery of a healthy sexuality. I certainly was not looking for any relation beyond friendship. I did not want anyone to replace Frank, and no one could replace him. Actually, David and I were both well defended and not looking for an intimate relationship. He was badly bruised from a broken relationship, and I was recovering from my own grief. But we mutually slipped under each other's defenses and discovered something more than an intimate friendship. I found the sacred connection or flame in our ecstatic love-making. Our eucharist sex became a community that included the presence of Christ and vivid, loving memories of Frank.

One of the extraordinary qualities about David is his loving ability to give me the space to continue to love Frank and to love him as well. I have not met many individuals who escape jealousy. One of the first things that David did as we became serious was to visit Frank's gravesite by himself and to speak with him. He won my heart. He has not expressed the slightest jealousy, never objecting to pictures of Frank or to my ongoing feelings. David further assisted me through the grieving process, for his love has been an extraordinary gift of inclusive love. He has, in fact, encouraged me to create a quilt panel memorializing Frank's family of choice, and I completed the quilt in anticipation of the full display of the AIDS quilt in Washington, D.C., in 1996.

Frank and David have taught me the inclusiveness of Christ's love, and their procreative love empowered me as a priest-lover into uncharted territories. Sexual passion, compassion, and justice-love are procreatively interrelated in a holistic spiritual practice. My commitment to compassion and justice continued to express itself in my teaching, mentoring, activism, and ministry.

Both erotic contemplative and queer freedom fighter

My Jesus-centered spirituality has concentrated not just on the sexual dimensions of our love relationship but also on imaging the particular life-events of Jesus and his prototypical practices of God's reign. Catholic spirituality has traditionally stressed the imitation of the life of Christ. Unfortunately, this imitation has been based on a distorted image of Jesus filtered through an anti-body and antisexual lens. For me, the "imitation of Jesus" can be compared to an open-ended paradigm fostering a vision and commitment to liberative transformation. I do not attempt to retrieve and repeat the archetypes of Jesus' practices but reconfigure them into novel paradigms for liberation.

Imaginative solidarity actuates the personal identification with Jesus, who, in turn, remains in solidarity with the oppressed and marginalized of his society. Queer Christians reconfigure Jesus' prototypical actions into their own actions for liberative transformation. This reconfiguration is not only a spiritual experience of connecting with Jesus on a quest for personal perfection but also a passionate identifying born concretely from love-making extended to others. Solidarity includes an imaginative reading and contemplation of Jesus' ministry. Whether or not we are ever able to prove that Jesus was sexual with either Mary Magdalene or the Beloved Disciple, in order to counter the erotophobic forms of Christian practice that now dominate in the early twenty-first century we must assume that God has not only become flesh but also sexually active. Imaginative solidarity with Jesus means active prayer of the Gospels.

Queer Christians recognize the same negative stereotypes and social rituals of hatred directed against themselves in stories about Jesus' conflicts with oppressive social groups and institutional power relations. In reading the gospel stories of Jesus from their own perspective, queer Christians build up their personal identification with Jesus' actions of God's reign. They repeat the open prototypes in their own lives, addressing the exigencies of contemporary homophobic/misogynist oppressions. Queer Christians discover that the God Jesus preached is, in fact, also the God of queers. These texts when prayed, contemplated, or imaginatively envisioned empower queer discipleship in following Jesus the freedom fighter.

Contemplative solidarity critiques bodily indifference through compassionate connections on a personal level with other human beings. The dynamism and energy of queer love-making reconfigure the prototypes of Jesus' justice-actions and transform them into liberative actions for sexual justice. When we pray the Gospels, we need to envision ourselves in the text. It is easy for me to read the Johannine passage about the Beloved Disciple and Jesus' mother at the foot of the cross. How often I have witnessed this in hospital rooms when a gay man with AIDS commends his lover to his mother and his mother to his spouse in a final act of love. I hear my own story configured within the story.

The recovery of the dangerous queer memories of Jesus and his sexuality transforms my Christian practice into a new and dangerous memory. As I retrieve the historical Jesus, I discover an activist advocating an egalitarian vision of God's reign. Jesus was just as dangerous to the hierarchical, exclusive, privileged, and gendered network of religious/political relations of power in first-century Palestine as twenty-first-century queers and ACT UP are to the Catholic hierarchy. The clerical aristocracy of the Temple labeled Jesus' activities as socially perverse or deviant just as we are labeled as "intrinsically evil" and "objectively disordered."

As queer Christians reconfigure the prototypical actions of Jesus in our own lives, we can also make ourselves dangerous to the network of exclusive, hierarchical, misogynist, homophobic, and racist power relations. Jesus' vision of the freedom and the transformation of God's reign becomes particularized in our own struggles for erotic self-affirmation, love, and freedom.

Toward a sexual reformation

For some folks, changing churches can be as difficult as coming out. Because I was culturally and theologically conditioned as a Catholic, my decision to change churches was made over the course of a couple of years. The continual social hatred of the Catholic hierarchy played a significant role in alienating me. In 1986, a letter from Cardinal Ratzinger in Rome labeled gays/lesbians "intrinsically evil, objectively disordered." In 1987, the U.S. bishops' pastoral letter that allowed for use of condoms for preventing AIDS was repealed. The actions of Catholic hierarchs — such as Cardinals Law and O'Connor — forced a repeal of the original letter and promoted an atmosphere of violence toward queers.

Once in a public lecture I spoke about the closetedness of Catholic clergy and the number of gay clergy. A person from the audience noted, "If there are so many gay priests and bishops, why is there such opposition from the Catholic Church? Are gays hurting gays?" I answered, "Yes, we are frequently the worst oppressors of ourselves." Systemic violence from the Roman Catholic Church has continued to promote an environment of violence, targeting the queer community and attempting to strictly regulate and restrict sexual pleasure.[18]

I found myself alienated from the more conservative elements within Dignity. In the 1970s and 1980s, Dignity had been a lifeline and source of resistance to the violence of the Catholic hierarchy. It went into a spiraling decline in the 1990s. When I returned to Boston to finish work on my dissertation at Harvard, I asked the Boston chapter if I could celebrate a memorial mass for Frank. Frank had been president of that chapter for a couple of years, and we both served that chapter for seven years. I had been chaplain and chair of the Liturgy Committee for seven years. The Liturgy Committee and Board of Directors vetoed my proposal based on the title of my book — *Jesus ACTED UP.* The book had not been released yet, and the title upset the conservative elements of Dignity/Boston. How could Jesus and ACT UP be connected? Dignity members wanted to remain Catholic in all ways except for their sexuality. Issues of inclusionary language, social justice, racism, and women's

---

18. In *The Silence of Sodom,* Mark Jordan has documented the social-cultural mechanism for the violence of the Catholic Church toward queers.

inclusion in ministry were of little concern to the membership. It had become a gay Knights-of-Columbus-style organization.

For many translesbigay Christians, their churches have betrayed God's gift of sexuality and continue an erotophobic agenda of violence. Many queer Christians have moved out of their denominational churches as the only way to experience God's liberating grace.

I reached the conclusion that the Catholic Church as an institution was necrophilic, for it was creating dead bodies and dead spiritualities for queer folks. It continues to crucify good people in the name of Christ: women, queers, gay priests, and people living with HIV. Queer Catholic voices were prophetically intermittent to nonexistent. My discipleship in following Christ led from the Catholic Church to considering entering the Universal Fellowship of Metropolitan Community Churches (UFMCC). In 1968, Troy Perry founded the UFMCC as an alternative to the established churches. The UFMCC is unlike the mainline denominational groups or independent churches in that it is a postdenominational church, representing and blending the diverse traditions of a number of Christian denominations. Mainline translesbigay denominational groups place doctrinal adherence at the center of their churches. They differ with their denominations in the area of sexual orientation. UFMCC is a postdenominational church in that it does not start with the principle of doctrinal adherence but rather begins with doctrinal diversity, allowing for a wide range of ecumenical interpretations of doctrine and a blending of a variety of worship practices. It is an ecumenical church not afraid to wrestle with social justice issues of racism, class, and sexism. It is a church in the process of developing a sexual theology that could challenge the established churches. The UFMCC was denied membership in the National Council of Churches. While the UFMCC meets all the ecclesial requirements for standing as a member communion, the Eastern Orthodox members of the NCCC, among some other denominations, threatened to leave the council if the UFMCC was admitted.

The Metropolitan Community Church (MCC) in St. Louis impressed me. It was a welcoming community in contrast to Dignity/Boston. The church had less phobia about Jesus as a prototype of an ACT UPer. I became friends with Rev. Brad Wishon, pastor of MCC of Greater St. Louis. He drew me into a number of workshops and events with MCC. When Troy Perry came to St. Louis, we participated in a civil rights demonstration together. In a lunch afterward, I was struck by the deep faith and commitment that Troy had to justice-love. I was impressed by his genuine humility. He was not there to impress me or anyone else but to bring people to Christ. Troy reminded me of the best of what I learned of Jesuit spirituality and commitment to justice. I entered UFMCC and began the process of transferring my clergy credentials to it. It took a year, during which time I had the opportunity to look at the UFMCC more closely and make a final decision. In 1996, twenty years to the day of my ordination as a Jesuit priest, the UFMCC reaffirmed my original ordination, my call to service. I found a Christian home in my journey into exile where I could write as a queer theologian and mentor future clergy and laity into a vision of justice-love. After more than seven years in the MCC of Greater St. Louis, I have to state that it is the healthiest Christian community that I have ever experienced.

Most churches have an impoverished theology of sexuality that has lent itself to gender and sexual oppression. They have betrayed God's gift of sexuality and gender by refusing to bless queer relationships, recognize our families, or grant us ordination. Queer liberation theology leaves behind the bankrupt theologies of sexuality of the churches and challenges them to recognize their betrayal of God's gift of human sexuality in all its diversity. The implications of queer theory in the reformulation of a Christian theology of sexuality are profound and exciting. Queer theologies no longer attempt the dead-end route of various Christian theologies of sexuality but reconstruct theology within a sexual paradigm. Sexual and gender diversity provides a new paradigm for reinvesting the dead doctrines and practices of an erotophobic, gender-rigid Christianity. Queer sexual theologies have begun to concentrate on several questions: how sexuality and spirituality are connected; the fluidity of sexual identity and gender constructions; sexual relationships; rereading the biblical texts and the Christian tradition from a queer perspective; how spirituality and sexuality affect our attitudes and practices toward God, self, and neighbor; how the church relates to sexuality/gender in mission, worship, sacraments, and rites. The integration of sexuality and spirituality is the fundamental challenge set before queer Christians, who can assist in the sexual reformation of Christianity and the recovery of sexual pleasure as a positive part of embodied living.[19] The recovery of sexual pleasure can begin to pacify the violence that has become embedded in Christian doctrines and practices due to a thorough erotophobia and heterosexist construction of the

<hr>

19. See James Nelson, "Reuniting Sexuality and Spirituality," in *Christian Perspectives on Sexuality and Gender,* ed. Elizabeth Stuart and Adrian Thatcher (Grand Rapids, Mich.: William B. Eerdmans, 1996), 213–19; Marvin Ellison, "Sexuality and Spirituality: An Intimate — and Intimidating — Connection," in ibid., 220–27.

sex-binary system.[20] Queer theology comprehends gender, race, homophobia, class, ethnicity, and disability as shaping our sexuality in addition to our sexual desires. All these factors contribute to our constructions and experiences of human sexuality, and no single location is capable of speaking for all other social locations. Queer theology has the potential to unite people over a range of genders, sexual orientation, races, class, physical abilities, and ethnicity.

As a queer theologian, I prepare queer Christians for the next millennium and their mission to become theological troublemakers or prophets who will shake the theological roots of other Christian communities and challenge them to undertake a more inclusive theology of sexuality and justice-based sexual theology. Queer sexual theologies will remain troublesome and even provocative for churches with their impoverished theologies of sexuality. Can queer churches become "open and affirming" of heterosexuals without the tokenism many queers now experience in many open and affirming congregations? Can we envision the full inclusion of heterosexuals at our table? Can we assist the churches in overcoming their erotophobia?

My vision and mission of justice involve healing the split between sexuality and spirituality within the Christian churches and assisting those churches to rediscover God's gift of diverse sexualities/genders. My mission is the sexual and gender reformation of the Christian churches, but it is derived from a passionate, sexual love of Christ. What I hope you receive from this narrative of my journey toward sexual wholeness is that sexuality and spirituality are not opposites, but the single reality of the erotic grace from God and toward God. When you have "just good sex," realize God also has just good sex.[21]

20. James Prescott, a neuropsychologist, claims that in cultures where sexual pleasure is disvalued, there is a high incidence of violence, and in cultures where sexual pleasure is valued, there is a low incidence of violence. See James W. Prescott, "Body Pleasure and the Origins of Violence," *Bulletin of the Atomic Scientists* (November 1975): 10–22.

21. I borrow the wonderful term "just good sex" from Mary Hunt. See Mary Hunt, "Just Good Sex: Feminist Catholicism and Human Rights," in *Good Sex: Feminist Perspectives from the World's Religions,* ed. Patricia Beattie Jung, Mary Hunt, and Radhi Balakrishnan (New Brunswick, N.J.: Rutgers University Press, 2001), 158–73.

TWO

CATHOLIC ANXIETIES
OVER (FE)MALE PRIESTS

*The "feminine" excess is forgiven or expected because they [priests] are
officially "unsexed." As modern eunuchs, they are permitted to take on
the stereotypes of women.*
                                                        —Mark Jordan

*The priest already occupies a socially degraded position by virtue of his
social femininity. He is further disembodied, neutered by ecclesiastical fiat
and social usage.*
                                                  —Edward Ingebretsen[1]

In *The Silence of Sodom,* Mark Jordan writes, "In the empire of closets
that is the modern Catholic Church, no one knows more than a few of
the compartments. The church is not one big closet. It is a honeycomb
of closets that no one can survey in its entirety."[2] Jordan's book is one
of several recent books that speak about the Catholic priesthood as a
gay profession, but he goes even further than other books by examining
the rhetorical strategies used to deflect public awareness from the fact
that clerical culture allows homosexual boys one way of being gay in
the Catholic Church.[3] His claims find validity within my own life and
the lives of many other young men who grew up in seminaries and
religious communities in the Catholic Church, realized that they were
not attracted to women, and were ordained to the priesthood.

Catholic culture provided me a prestigious alternative to heterosexual
marriage: religious life and the priesthood, a homoerotic subculture

---

1. Mark Jordan, *The Silence of Sodom: Homosexuality in Modern Catholicism* (Chicago:
University of Chicago Press, 2000), 199; Edward J. Ingebretsen, " 'One of the Guys' or
'One of the Gals'?: Gender Confusion and the Problem of Authority in the Roman Clergy,"
Theology and Sexuality 10 (March 1999): 85.
2. Jordan, *Silence of Sodom,* 89.
3. In support of Jordan's claims of a homosexual clergy, see Garry Wills, *Papal Sin:
Structures of Deceit* (New York: Doubleday, 2000), 5–6 and 192–203; Elizabeth Stuart, *Chosen
Gay Priests Tell Their Stories* (London: Geoffrey Chapman, 1993); Donald B. Cozzens, *The
Changing Face of the Priesthood* (Collegeville, Minn.: Liturgical Press), 107–10.

36

where my passions for theology, the intellectual and artistic life, social service, ritual, and mystery could be quenched. It was a haven
for many who failed at cultural masculinity and who searched for ambiguous forms of masculinity. For me, the Jesuits provided a cultural
environment that continued the best aspects of an all-male prep school
but without the presumptions of cultural masculinity and heterosexuality socialized by mandatory sports. The Catholic Church has been
unable to bear witness to the truth about the sexual orientation of
many of its clergy and religious. Clerical closeting is a problem, Jordan
maintains, because of the chilling silence and sanctions that the institutional church imposes on any open and honest conversation about
homosexuality.

I want to read Jordan's work in light of an essay, " 'One of the Guys'
or 'One of the Gals'? Gender Confusion and the Problem of Authority in the Roman Clergy," by Edward Ingebretsen.[4] Ingebretsen's article
raises questions about institutional rhetoric that genders the priest, and
thus his article complements Jordan's work. For example, while Roman
Catholic canon law has traditionally required that a priest be capable of
procreation as a male, its ideology has simultaneously gendered priests
female, placing them in an untenable liminal state of being both male
and female. Ingebretsen notes that Catholic priests are gendered "female" in the rhetoric of marriage, such as being the "brides of Christ,"
and the general culture attribution of the feminine to men in religious
roles. In his book on the Catholic priesthood, Donald Cozzens writes a
chapter on the masculinity of Catholic priests while the former Jesuit
rector Michael Buckley raises the question, "Is this man weak enough to
be a priest?"[5] Both authors recognize the masculinity of Catholic priests
certainly does stand outside of heteronormative notions.

I would argue that what we have here is an alternative practice
of masculinity, perhaps best described as a female masculinity or a
(fe)masculinity, a gender crossing at odds with current cultural heteromasculinist ideologies. Clerical culture provides the social matrix for
alternative performance of masculinity that confuses and even subverts
the gender categories of heterosexist society behind closed doors. I
will explore the gender-bending of priests, discuss a homosexual clergy,
and finally offer some theoretical observations for institutional Catholic
anxiety.

---

4. Jordan writes as a gay Catholic theologian, an outsider, while Ingebretsen makes his
observations as a gay priest within a Catholic religious order.
5. Ingebretsen, " 'One of the Guys,' " 71–87.

Finding a wife or becoming a fallen women

Mark Jordan writes,

> In Seville, where sodomy persecutions were left to civil authority, a
> Jesuit active as a prison chaplain between 1578 and 1616 noted the
> high incidence of sodomy in the religious orders and the diocesan
> priesthood. He reports the view that Jesuits rarely sin with women
> because they can so easily find partners among their students or
> novices.[6]

Some traditions never die, even after centuries! As I mentioned in chapter 1, shortly after my ordination, I met Frank Ring, another Jesuit, and
we fell in love. Our story, as I described in the previous chapter, has
remained a part of Jesuit recreational talk and lore for some time, particularly the events around the wedding shower that two gay friends,
Matthew and Joe, threw for Frank and myself on Valentine's Day 1978,
an event that included a wedding cake with two construction workers
embracing. The rumors and stories about the wedding shower became
so infamous that I received a stern warning from the Jesuit provincial,
who was swamped with calls and protests over the wedding by numerous
Jesuit priests. He warned me I had to remain celibate.

Many Catholic priests in America, Jordan claims, participate in a culture colored by gay tastes, and the camp wedding shower was not lost
on Jesuit culture. The elaborations on the story of the wedding shower
provide more insight into Jesuit gay subculture than the two of us being in love. The story was exaggerated and embellished for a number
of social-political reasons, including the turmoil of changes in the post–
Vatican II church in the late 1970s. While the stories became more blown
up in the retelling in Jesuit recreation rooms during cocktail hour, the
obsession with the story says much about the lives of those Jesuits who
rehearsed it with delight and horror. Homosocial organizations — like
the Roman Catholic Church and the U.S. military — use homophobia
to police and regulate the sexual lives of their members. We had committed publicly what some had covertly engaged in and what others had
covertly wanted to do.

The notion of a priest marrying a young Jesuit scholastic, though
Frank and I were only three months apart in age, played on the trans-
generational sexual fantasies of priests for younger men. When several
months later I attended a heterosexual wedding of a laicized Jesuit priest

---

6. Jordan, *Silence of Sodom*, 126.

who was a teacher and mentor, I heard from Jesuit friends that Frank and I had appeared on BBC television. We had become public, fallen Jesuits, stigmatized by our public sexual lives while other Jesuits, who were covertly sexual, remained honorable within a closeted and punitive system for those who betrayed the secret. Stories were embellished, and the Jesuits attempted damage control by conducting a witch hunt to remove gay scholastics to prevent future recurrences.

A gender-bending matrix

Eve Sedgwick has observed that male desire is perpetrated by a trinity of conditions: homosocial consent, the regulation of homophobia, and the promotion of misogyny.[7] Homosocial consent is the conscious complicity to participate in homosocial organizations, their brokered rules, and their unwritten taboos. In the church, this trinity of social conditions provides the circumstances for the creation of a culture of clerical camp that supports alternative gender-bending in seminaries, rectories, and male religious communities, yet these social conditions perpetuate patriarchy with homophobia and misogyny. Clerical homosocial consent agrees to the unwritten rules of the Catholic Church: "Don't ask, don't tell. Don't get caught in a public scandal." Homosocial consent, institutional allegiance, the threat of expulsion, and silence provide the complex social dynamics of the Catholic priesthood and its hierarchy that prevent public disclosure of the reality of gay priesthood.

Many homosexual Catholic boys intuit that they are not attracted to heterosexual marriage. Two of the options for those homosexual Catholic youth are entering religious life or the priesthood. Eve Sedgwick noted, "Catholicism in particular is famous for giving countless gay and proto-gay children the shock of possibility of adults who don't marry, of men in dresses, of passionate theatre, of introspective investment of lives filled with what could, ideally without diminution, be called the work of fetish."[8] When Catholic youth enter religious life or the priesthood, they assume a prestige and status within the Catholic community with the added benefit of an all-male environment where their homosexual desires can covertly be explored and where an alternative masculinity is accepted as normative.

Mark Jordan aptly places Catholic clergy and seminarians in a transgendered role: "When it comes to clothes, we assign Catholic priests

---

7. Eve Kosofsky Sedgwick, *The Epistemology of the Closet* (Berkeley: University of California Press, 1990), 1–27.
   8. Ibid., 140.

to a mixed or third gender. We have been taught to indulge them as if they were the stereotyped trophy wife of the distant suburbs."[9] It is a culture where men wear dresses, homoerotic rituals are performed, and aesthetic desires are appreciated. In many houses of formation and seminaries, residents are encouraged to develop their aesthetic interests rather than athletic pursuits. Mark Jordan writes well about the campiness, homosexual aestheticism, and the gender-bending found in rectories and religious houses. He is correct in pointing out that seminaries and clerical culture are breeding grounds for future "ecclesial divas."

There are homoerotic rituals to mark the transitions from secular life to seminary culture and even the progression into clerical and/or religious vocation: vows, promises, and ordinations. These reinforce loyalty and homosocial consent of compliant and passive men who sacrifice a public queer persona for a Jekyll-Hyde life. For example, I knew a pastor of a Catholic parish in Fairfield County, Connecticut, who had an apartment, a lover, a totally different persona, and a different name so he could live a gay life in New York City on his days off.

In his writings and talks about priesthood, John Paul II encourages candidates for the priesthood and priests to model their lives after Mary, yet in his encyclical *Priestly Ordination* (*Ordinatio Sacredotalis*), he maintains that women cannot be ordained as priests.[10] Because the function of women is ordained as caregivers, Edward Ingebretsen writes, "Proponents for the ordination of women sometimes forget the fact that putting a Roman collar on a woman only further complicates her performance of social gender by entwining it within the complex weaves of another system of gendered authority."[11] Although priests may not be real men by the narrow cultural norms of masculinity, they cannot be biologically women either. Women are feared not because they provide a sexual distraction to the divine or threat to priestly vocation but because they threaten Catholic priests with revelation of their gender transgressions and performances of (fe)masculinity.

Women must be kept out of cloisters and rectories to maintain this homosocial bastion because they also present a threat in revealing that the clergy is not a heteromasculine institution. Ingebretsen notes the terrible secret of the church's misogyny: "In the current ecclesiastical lockup women cannot be permitted to become priests because that

9. Jordan, *Silence of Sodom*, 199.
10. John Paul II, *Apostolic Letter on Reserving Priestly Ordination to Men Alone* (*Ordinatio Sacredotalis*), May 22, 1994.
11. Ingebretsen, " 'One of the Guys,' " 82.

would make apparent what is in fact the case — that, at least according to public appraisal, there are women priests already."[12] Thus women are excluded from the priesthood not because they pose a castration threat but rather because they might expose priests, not as real men but as feminine men.

Gay men find themselves attracted to the all-male clergy, with its flowing vestments and baroque chasubles, decorated with lace and crushed velvet. The clerical environment is thoroughly queer, even transgender. Many young seminarians, and even old conservative gay Catholic friends, often dress up the Infant of Prague, an image of young Jesus anatomically unsexed, in lacy copes, camp liturgical drag, and a gold crown. It may be the equivalent of gay men playing with Barbie or Ken dolls, or symbolically it may have deeper psychological self-representations, portraying their vocational desire of being the infant dressed in ornate vestments, a desire reenacted in cassocks and baroque chasubles. At liturgy, they represent Christ (*alter Christus*) to the community. Gay priests may be failed men, yet they still have a sacral status that allows for their deviant performance of masculinity.

Clerical culture fosters an aestheticism often wrapped in misogyny, ritualism, and ornateness. Seminaries and religious orders are filled with aesthetically sensitive and effeminate young men whose tastes in liturgy and theology range from neoconservative to antimodern. Jordan notes: "'Effeminacy' is not an attribute of a subset of priests. It characterizes the highly visible actions required of all priests. These queer actions become camp not just through deliberate exaggeration, but because they are punctuated by loud assertions there is absolutely nothing queer about them."[13] They may not be visible to the Catholic public that has been socialized to think of the queer actions of priests as sacred, but they are readily visible to queer folks, growing up and fully adult. The misogynist clerical culture allows for a flourishing culture of show tunes, gender-bending, and campiness. It allows, for instance, and outspoken homophobic cardinal to have allegedly sung Judy Garland tunes with two young effeminate seminarians as they swayed to and fro, walking down the steps while at a diocesan priests' conference at the Park Plaza Hotel.[14] Anywhere else such behavior would be deemed "queer," for it certainly crosses the boundaries of heteronormative masculinity in a

---

12. Ibid., 86.
13. Jordan, *Silence of Sodom*, 186.
14. Reported by a florist friend, who was delivering flowers to the Park Plaza Hotel in Boston and walking behind the cardinal.

Judy Garlandesque fashion. It was recognized by a friend who witnessed it and by other queers for what it was, gay gender-bending camp.

Yet such Judy Garlandesque or diva performances are typical of Catholic prelates and their sycophantic circles of closeted clergy. Consider the recent "Spice Girls" controversy in Melbourne, Australia, when the epithet was coined among Catholic priests and made public to describe the inner circle of clergy around then Bishop George Pell, now archbishop in Sydney. Closeted priests supported Pell's policy of denying communion to openly queer Catholics, and Mary Helen Woods, a close friend of Pell, made these remarkable observations about the Spice Girls:

> They love their ceremonies and they love their incense and they love dressing up, and if they want to describe that inner circle as the Spice Girls, I can sort of see where the comment's coming from. . . . I don't see it as a sexual thing at all — I just see it as, if you like, a power thing. People are attracted to a powerful bloke, they tend to be a bit girlie about it and I don't mean gay, I mean girlie.[15]

Most dioceses have their own rendition of the Spice Girls — flamboyant, closeted, and feminine.

Diocesan seminaries and religious houses of formation have traditionally been bastions of misogyny. Presuming that students have heterosexual attractions, seminaries and religious houses control female distractions and temptations by creating a segregated male society. Many seminaries and religious houses set up cloisters, boundaries of living space where women were not allowed. In past times, when women violated male cloister, the space had to be reconsecrated. Cloisters spatially defined women as impure and threatening; they were perceived as sources of temptation and sin. Numerous hagiographic accounts of male saints glorified the lack of male interest in women as virtuous, or when they spoke of male desire or temptations, they identified sexuality and sexual temptation with Eve and all women.

While clerical culture promotes men living together without women, it has another major effect: creating performances of alternative masculinity among seminarians, or gender-bending. Patterns of heterosexual behavior are tightly regulated to secure celibacy, and the success can be measured by the subversion of heteromasculinity through the promotion of homosocial patterns of living. Within this homosocial environment

---

15. In Ashleigh Wilson, "Pell to Weed Out Gay Priests," *The Australian*, May 14, 2001.

guarding against heterosexual desire, seminarians and clergy create and perform alternative masculinities. Some seminarians call each other by pet or even girl's names. During my theological studies for ordination, I lived with a group of New York Jesuits who were sharp-tongued, misogynist, gossiped a lot, and often called Jesuit friends "girlfriend" or female names. I have found similar behaviors and patterns among the circle of drag queens that I know in St. Louis.

Traditional Roman Catholic theology supports the concept of the priest as the liturgical impersonation of Christ. In his liturgical role, the priest is perceived as another Christ. Though modern Catholic artistic depictions of Jesus may be feminized, fair-skinned with rosy cheeks, the Catholic laity is programmed to understand Christ as sexless. Thus the traditional identification of Christ with the clergy becomes a theological block and psychological denial of the possibility of a homosexual, noncelibate clergy. How can "father" be gay? How can so many priests have died of HIV illness?[16] Yet the denial remains a staunch assertion of Catholic faith along with the dogmatic assertion of the sexlessness of Jesus. Church pronouncements condemn homosexuality, and such public theological hatred deflects suspicion from a homosexual, gender-bending clergy and reinforces faithful denial of the Catholic laity. This theological and psychological logic is deeply flawed but effective in keeping the laity in a state of sexual denial.

This alternative masculine culture promotes cross-dressing, a heightened aestheticism, and gender-bending behaviors. The aesthetics of clerical cross-dressing remains both imitative of the gender codes and at the same time subversive of their heterosexual deployment. I jokingly refer to cross-dressing in vestments as "liturgical drag," but there is a lot of truth to the subversiveness of the cross-dressings of priests and seminarians in the performance and pageantry of homoerotic rituals of celebrating the Lord's Supper. Catholic liturgical culture has fostered some extremes among seminarians and priests, competing with fancy frocks, lace, and baroque vestments. Drag shows take place in churches and cathedrals where ritual pageants occur on as grand a scale as at the Miss Gay America pageant.

Church ritual has remained a suitable stage to perform homoerotic ritual. When a priest lifts up the bread, he changes the host into the body of Christ with his words and intentions. Intimately touching the body with affective love and devotion, he distributes the body of Christ

---

16. Judy Thomas, "AIDS in the Priesthood," *Kansas City Star,* January 29, 2000 (*kcstar.com/projects/priest*).

to the laity to be ingested, an act of erotic consummation. Mark Jordan notes how the act of consecration of the eucharistic bread elevates the image of the priest who lives as a failed cultural male: "And the priest at the altar possesses no longer just his own dangerous and despised body, but the body of Jesus. He possesses it by making it, and he possesses it by impersonating it. The priest holding the consecrated wafer has become Jesus holding his own consumable and divine body."[17]

There are two not-so-veiled symbolic configurations at work in the psyche of the priest. Whereas John Paul II uses the theological rhetoric of Mary as the model for ideological virginity to sustain a celibate priesthood, the priest, like the figure of Mary, through his ritual repetition of liturgical formulas, gives birth to Christ's presence on the altar. Mary the Mother of Jesus ironically becomes the model for the priest. The priest represents Mary in his subaltern identity, but simultaneously he elevates himself as Christ and his own gender status as he inserts the host into the mouths of the faithful. He inserts his own body into the mouths of the communicants; the distribution of communion becomes an act of sex as the communicants take Christ into their mouths. I deem this multiple personality disorder "the Mary-Christ syndrome." It is full of gender transgressions and contradictions within the heteromasculinist gender system.

Moreover, there is a real tension within the clergy between those who would like to be more out as gay and those who do everything to keep the issue of clerical sexuality and, in particular, homosexuality out of the public light. These are different and competing styles of homoerotic cultures. Members of both clergy groups, I might add, have suffered heavy casualties from HIV illness. Traditionalist homoerotic clergy are often "rubric queens," who are fascinated with the smells and bells of liturgical worship, its drag, and the orthodox performance of rites — maintaining female exclusion from the altar. In contrast, modern gay clergy have been pastorally sensitive to queer Catholics — very conscious of the queer exodus from an abusive church, trying to quietly change attitudes, celebrating eucharist for outlawed groups such as Dignity or lawfully sponsored outreach groups, quietly blessing same-sex unions, and fighting the ever-increasing move of the hierarchy toward the right. Those clergy who have become public about their sexuality or opposed

17. Jordan, *Silence of Sodom*, 207. John Paul II echoes a similar sentiment: "Thus he [the priest] feels led to give himself to the faithful to whom he distributes the Body of Christ" (John Paul II, "The Eucharist Is at the Heart of the Priest's Spirituality," June 9, 1993 [*www.sjbrcc.org/jp2preu.html*]).

the hypocritical theological homohatred have been forced out of the active priesthood.

"Fallen women" and wives engaging in secret affairs

Along with many others, I was socialized in the arts of cruising within Jesuit recreation rooms, an environment of sharp wit and humor, theatrical performances, repartee, and campiness. Combine this environment with alcohol, and there is a potential for an erotic linking up with another man. There are similar patterns of male behavior in gay bars: drinking excessively, male banter, some discreet cruising, and an occasional offer of a back rub. As I mentioned earlier, offers of backrubs, as I discovered in conversations with ex-seminarians and former priests, were universally a euphemism for a sexual encounter. In the Jesuits, I was mentored to an erotic love of men through these encounters. Many of these encounters were moments of grace, intimate human encounters of men in love with Christ and with one another. The terrible encounters, however, were with those Jesuits who denied that it ever happened the next day and kept themselves at a distance from their complexes of guilt and shame. I remember having ecstatic, wonderful sex with a Jesuit in a swimming pool. We both longed for male intimacy, touch, and love. His homophobic piety would be triggered on occasions like these; thus he would coldly respond to me as a stranger the next day, a pattern often duplicated in anonymous sex. But several weeks later, he would creep into my room late at night for another dose of guilt and shame.

Ed Ingebretsen notes the strong parallels between openly gay priests and fallen women:

> The priest already occupies a socially degraded position by virtue of his social femininity. He is further disembodied, neutered by ecclesiastical fiat and social usage.... [T]he gay identified priest, not unlike the "fallen woman," becomes caught up in the operation of a socially punitive narrative that presumes a ravenous, all-sexualized life.[18]

Symbolically, misogynist institutional Catholicism identifies the openly gay priest with the abject fallen woman. The gay priest's social femininity is extended to the ravenously sexualized woman. But this is also true of Catholic priests who have been laicized and married to women. They are treated as fallen women and are instructed to sit in the back of churches

---

18. Ingebretsen, " 'One of the Guys,' " 85.

while attending mass. Frank and I became "fallen women," gaining notoriety and endowing a lore about possible same-sex unions among Jesuits. We were neither the first nor the last Jesuits to become a fallen couple.

While the traditionalist group, at least at this point in time, hold all the power, they are not necessarily celibate, only more circumspect in their sexuality and covert in their liaisons. Traditionalist priests may not frequent the gay haunts for anonymous sex, but they sleep their way up the corporate ladder of the Catholic hierarchy. On Halloween at a gay bar, I met a lay gay man dressed in the baroque garment of a bishop with his lace surplice. As I joked that I was the real thing, an ordained but unlaicized Catholic priest, I discovered some interesting facts from our conversation. The layperson dressed in a bishop's costume was a "rubrics queen," a master of ceremonies for an auxiliary Catholic bishop. He was like a number of Catholic seminarians I have known over the years. Enamored with his bishop's drag, he relished telling me tales about participating as a master of ceremonies at the National Conference of Catholic Bishops' mass, sleeping with clergy and a bishop, gay backrooms for anonymous and conflicted sex, and absolution before receiving communion. He candidly spoke about the sexual life of his bishop and his own. The "faux" bishop in Halloween drag was mimicking and parodying his Catholic bishop in cycles of anonymous sex, guilt, and sexual shame within a homoerotic ritual of closeted devotions, sex, confession, and a public façade of celibacy. He mimetically repeated patterns from closeted role models and divas.

Institutional Catholicism has fine-tuned the rhetorical strategies of compartmentalization and deniability to prevent widespread insight into the homoerotic nature of its clergy and leadership. The real closet of the Catholic Church is not homosexuality, but the exclusion of women and the failure to value what is gendered as female. It is the closet of alternative masculinities and fear of female gender-bending. Catholic male anxieties of the penetrated (fe)male (the feminized male) need to be addressed, for if the church is able to uproot its institutional misogyny, then it may live at peace with a queer and noncelibate clergy.

Catholic male anxieties: the penetrated (fe)male

C. S. Lewis once wrote, "God is so masculine that in Him we are all feminine."[19] Religious men have been often been suspect of their per-

---

19. Quoted in Mark Muesse, "Religious Machismo: Masculinity and Fundamentalism," in *Redeeming Men: Religion and Masculinities,* ed. Stephen Boyd, W. Merle Longwood, and Mark Muesse (Louisville: Westminster John Knox, 1996), 98.

formances of cultural masculinity. Religious men and celibate clergy
are less than "macho" men because they do not define themselves by
heterosexual sexual encounters. German anti-Semitism portrayed Jewish males as feminine, even claiming that Jewish men menstruated.[20]
Catholic priests are public failures of heteronormative male gender in
a culture where religiousness is equated with the feminine and where
masculinity is equated with male sexuality and dominance. Catholic religious and priests wear cassocks and vestments; these forms of archaic
clothing are perceived as feminine. They are clerical drag, ornate dresses
and skirts. This deficiency of masculinity is intensified by the patriarchal
assertions of the maleness of God. In a binary system of belief, the maleness of God becomes problematic for fundamentalist and conservative
Christian males by rendering them subservient and feminine to a male
God. In other words, if God is the top, religious men are the bottoms;
they are penetrated men, passive men without full male status. They are
like women penetrated by heterosexual males.

The recent writings of Howard Eilberg-Schwartz have raised questions of how the feminization of religious males by a masculine God has
produced male anxieties about the blurring of gender boundaries and
underlying fears of homoeroticism.[21] In *God's Phallus,* Eilberg-Schwartz
develops a thesis that the father God of Judaism and of later Christianity legitimized male dominance but that it also destabilized notions of
masculinity:

> The primary relationships in Israelite imagination were between
> a male God and individual male Israelites, such as Moses, the
> patriarchs, and the prophets.... Men were encouraged to imag-
> ine themselves as married to and hence in a loving relationship
> with God. A homoerotic dilemma was thus generated, inadver-
> tently and to some degree unconsciously, by the superimposition
> of heterosexual images on the relationship between human and
> divine males.[22]

God's maleness was, thus, problematic for Hebrew men when the scriptural tradition speaks about God's marriage to Israel (Hos. 1–2; Jer. 2:2)
or God's sexual intercourse with Israel (Ezek. 16:8), who is imagined
as a woman. God's maleness feminized Israel, the collection of Hebrew

---

20. Ibid., 89–102; Daniel Boyarin, *Unheroic Conduct: The Rise of Heterosexuality and the Invention of the Jewish Man* (Berkeley: University of California Press, 1997).
21. Howard Eilberg-Schwartz, *God's Phallus* (Boston: Beacon Press, 1994).
22. Ibid., 99.

males. Eilberg-Schwartz uses the story of Noah's nakedness to demonstrate a general Hebrew anxiety of not subjecting a father to a male erotic gaze (Gen. 9:25). Ham gazes upon Noah's nakedness just as he would gaze upon a woman's nakedness and experience sexual desire. His male gaze has feminized Noah by making him the object of sexual desire, and this masculine gaze at other men is unacceptable within ancient Hebrew gender codes. Hebrew anxieties over the "womanizing" of males is reflected in the biblical taboo of homoeroticism in the proscriptions against anal intercourse (Lev. 18:22; 20:13) and in the stories in Genesis 19 and Judges 19. Penetrated males disrupt cultural codes of masculinity based on male penetration of females. (Chapter 9, below, unpacks the humiliation of penetrated males in these tales of rape.)

Eilberg-Schwartz uses the Noah story as a hermeneutical strategy to explain why God's body must be veiled and how ancient Israelites did not depict or imagine God's male body, particularly his sexual organs and facial hair. For example, in Exodus 33:21–23, God allows Moses to see only his back, neither to view his face nor his sexual organs. It is similar to Ham's brothers, Shem and Japheth, who walk backward in order to avoid gazing upon their father's nakedness. The veiling of father God's body is a necessary strategy to preserve the male conceptualization of deity and to preserve Israel from becoming feminized and thus preserving its male identity and status.

Eilberg-Schwartz's notion of collective male anxiety about the paternal images of God may provide us with a key to Catholic institutional terror of modern homosexuality, its misogyny, and even the primal psychological need to maintain an asexual Christ. Mark Jordan hints at a similar trajectory of interpretation when he writes, "Male homosexuality must always be particularly threatening to men in a religion of the God who has assumed a male body. It threatens to resexualize our relationship with Christ, hence our life in God."[23]

In the past, what disturbed John Chrysostom about males engaging in sex with other males was that it overturned gender hierarchies and norms. He wrote, "I maintain that not only you are made into a woman, but you cease to be a man."[24] Chrysostom expresses a quite contemporary feeling of misogynist male Christian anxiety about men who act like women. Such males are colloquially "bottoms" or penetrated males, penetrated like women and lacking full male status. I would suggest that Chrysostom expresses a fear common to male clerical anxieties

23. Ibid., 205.
24. From *In Epist. Ad Rom.* 4.2.3, in app. 2; quoted in John Boswell, *Christianity, Homosexuality, and Social Tolerance* (Chicago: University of Chicago Press, 1980), 157.

within contemporary Catholic Church leadership, religious life, and the diocesan priesthood.

Theological traditions originating in the Deutero-Pauline letter to the Ephesians identify the church as the "bride of Christ."

Medieval Christian bridal mysticism, based on the Song of Songs and prevalent monastic spirituality, was and is still used in the formation of Catholic priests and members of many religious orders. This bridal mysticism comprehends the soul as female, as the bride, and Christ as the bridegroom. For centuries, Catholic priests have been encouraged and formed to seek an erotic consummation as brides of Christ, as in the Song of Songs: "Let him kiss me with the kisses of his mouth" (Song of Songs 1:1). Priests in training were formed spiritually and encouraged to see themselves as "brides," to be penetrated and kissed by the bridegroom. How many gay seminarians and priests fantasized themselves in the arms of Christ or in the enviable position of French kissing Christ, something the medieval mystic Rupert of Deutz reports?[25] The biggest secret for the Catholic laity is that they already have a married clergy theologically and spiritually; their priests are the "brides of Christ."

Comparative religious historian Jeffrey Kripal felt estranged as a heterosexual male during his Catholic seminary years from the homoeroticism of Christian medieval bridal mysticism; he notes that within such a mystical tradition, "heterosexuality is heretical."[26] John Paul II's writings on priestly spirituality often imagine the priest celebrating eucharist as consummating a marriage with the bridegroom. The eucharist becomes an act of erotic love-making in his convoluted writings about priesthood.[27]

For nonmonastic religious orders like the Jesuits, bridal mysticism had little direct influence in the formation of priests. Ignatius of Loyola, however, developed a strong devotion to Mary while developing homosocial bonds of fealty in following Christ the military leader and lord. The Jesuits developed a spirituality of "military toughness" and mobility in service of the church, but their novitiate formation had a strong Marian flavor. Mary was often held up as an example of obedience to God,

---

25. Bernard McGinn, *The Growth of Mysticism* (New York: Crossroad, 1992), 330–32.

26. Jeffrey Kripal, "The Marriage of Heaven and Hell: On the Heresy of Heterosexuality in the History of Mysticism," unpublished paper; it will appear as the introduction to Jeffrey Kripal, *Roads of Excess, Palaces of Wisdom: Eroticism and Reflexivity in the Modern Study of Mysticism* (Chicago: University of Chicago Press, 2002).

27. John Paul II writes, " 'This is my body.... This is the cup of my blood' " — he [the priest] must be profoundly united to Christ and seek to reproduce Christ's countenance in himself. The more intensely he lives in Christ, the more authentically he can celebrate the eucharist" ("The Eucharist Is at the Heart of the Priest's Spirituality").

the primary stress of an order that takes a fourth vow of obedience, a marriage vow, to the pope.

During my years in divinity school, I remember the banter and jokes in the Jesuit recreational room about women. Women provided a threat to the pattern of all-male life. Thus, the phobic fantasy was that women were after Jesuits to divert them from vocations. In my time in divinity school, women at the Jesuit Weston School of Theology provided little erotic interest to the Jesuit students, but they were certainly threatening. But I believe that fears of my then-Jesuit contemporaries were more about themselves because of their feminine performances of masculinity and their exploration of minority expressions of masculinities. The need to exclude women was perhaps motivated by the threat of revealing their own gender transgressions and their fears of repercussions from a narrow binary gender system.

The real threat to the Jesuits of the wedding shower thrown for Frank and me was our betrayal as brides of Christ. We became fallen women, divorced and remarried, making clerical marriage public and muddying the metaphor of brides of Christ. These brides were no longer passive, silenced, or secretive since we revealed our sexual versatility, breaking the ecclesial and cultural gender codes. We had become grooms as well as brides of Christ, with a clearer appreciation of our gender transgressions and the appropriation of traditionally feminine roles in a household. By being penetrated males and taking on cultural female roles, we disrupted the secret of Catholic clerical life and challenged the public gender codes of what real men are.

Catholic tops: aggressive bishops and cardinals

Homosocial organizations arrange their identities and energies to limit the performative ranges of feminine masculinity and use homophobia publicly to deflect suspicion. While Catholic priestly (fe)masculinity has provided an alternative to the cultural performances of heteronormative masculinity, no bishop or cardinal could ever be accused of making Catholic Christianity more masculine. The Catholic hierarchy maintains a fe(male) hierarchy among the clergy in what is certainly a top-down or top-bottom hierarchy. The priest can safely occupy a socially degraded position of (fe)masculinity as long as he plays by the unwritten rules: "Don't tell, don't be visible, and don't get caught in a scandal."

For example, there was a Jesuit priest at Holy Cross College who got drunk with the son of an official, and they found themselves in bed together. As recounted by my inside Jesuit sources, the two were so drunk that they were unable to do anything. Though the Jesuit community defended the drunken Jesuit, Rome forced his expulsion from the order. He broke an unwritten rule, "Don't get caught in a public scandal." Catholic hierarchs will look the other way as long as an event does not demand their attention or public attention, thus requiring disciplinary action.

I believe that Mark Jordan's primary thesis is correct: Catholic ecclesial concern with homosexuality is not really about the laity but about homosexuality within the priestly ranks. The Vatican is not concerned with theology, only control of a clerical crisis that has begun to reach epic proportions in the American Catholic Church. As priests came out in the 1970s and the 1980s, church leaders became alarmed, precipitating a modern-day Peter Damien, Cardinal Ratzinger, to write several letters against homosexuality.[28] The traditional system of pleasures (aestheticism, ritualism, intellectual and artistic pursuits, safe-space to express an alternative masculinity, etc.) functioned to solicit voluntary submission. Jordan correctly writes, "Gay priests and religious are formed in the pleasures of submission to male authority. Who can be astonished, then, that sexually active gay clerics and ex-clerics seem so often to prefer the leather or S&M cultures?"[29] Gay priests and religious submit to their bishops as wives to their husbands. Many priests enjoy the masochism of submission to a Catholic top while defiant and out priests are stigmatized as fallen women, no longer obedient to their hierarchical husbands. Catholic hierarchs are as patriarchal as Promisekeepers, only within a homosocial environment.

This strategy is no longer working except with a select group of conservative seminarians and priests. The Catholic hierarchy has switched its tactics to a rhetoric attacking homosexuality publicly with Vatican letters, ecclesial policies, and monies to fight against same-sex marriage and queer civil rights. This rhetoric is invested in keeping a passive and obedient priesthood.

Mark Muesse has characterized a hypermasculinity among fundamentalist and evangelical male leadership as stemming from fear of the body, competitiveness, aggressiveness, and a strong individualistic ideology.[30] It attempts to project a "macho religiosity," to compensate for a cultural equation of religiousness with femininity. This religious "machoness" is

28. Joseph Cardinal Ratzinger, "Letter on the Pastoral Care of Homosexual Persons" (1986); Ratzinger, "Some Considerations concerning the Catholic Response to Legislate Proposals on the Nondiscrimination of Homosexual Persons" (1992).

29. Jordan, *Silence of Sodom,* 218.

30. Muesse, "Religious Machismo," 90–95.

characterized by misogyny, an internalized homophobia, and a low tolerance of ambiguity. Fundamentalist leaders set up a worldview in binary
oppositions, reinforced by the binary power relations inherent within
traditional Christianity around gender, the body, and sexuality. Their
worldview negates competing visions of Christianity, sexuality, the body,
and gender by assigning them to the feminine, the sodomite, and the
demonic.

While Muesse is addressing fundamentalist and evangelical Christianity's leadership, who are attempting to keep women under control, there
is a parallel with the Catholic bishops and cardinals who, driven by their
positions of dominance and hegemonic (fe)masculinity, attempt to keep
their priests neutered and passive through a variety of ecclesial fiats, internal rewards for silence, and brutal punishments delivered to those
who do not comply. Though they do not employ the unsophisticated
fundamentalist language of the demonic, they employ the philosophical language of "intrinsically evil, objectively disordered." The Catholic
hierarchy has formed unholy alliances with the Christian Coalition and
the Mormon Church to financially support the Knight Initiative in California (2000) that defines marriage as one woman to one man, to fight
to repeal civil unions in Vermont, and to fight other ballot initiatives.
Its aggressive theological statements and social policy are primarily directed to the Catholic priesthood to prevent a competing queer culture
that would attract its current and future priests. Its greatest sin may
involve compelling closeted priests to enforce such violent homophobic policies, for that promotes a significant amount of self-loathing and
self-violence. This is a violent policing of a homosexual clergy, who are
expected to continue the spiral of violence against one another and the
Catholic queer populace.

Conclusion

One could cast a TV series like *Queer as Folk* about seminary life and
the covert networks of priests and their lovers. It would certainly have
the campiness, melodrama, the love stories, the break-ups, the heart-
felt tragedies, and perhaps even the sexiness of the Showtime series.
The next best thing to a series was the British documentary "Queer and
Catholic," produced by a gay former Dominican friar, Mark Dowd, which
aired in London in May 2001. The program sensationalized the fact
that seminarians from the prestigious English College in Rome, where
elite English candidates train for the priesthood, have cruised gay bars
and parks and that priests in the college often call one another by girl

names. While the Vatican is trying to develop new strategies for weeding out homosexual seminarians, some Catholic leaders are now arguing that sexual orientation is irrelevant to the Catholic priesthood since candidates are required to be celibate. The Catholic Church is deeply confused and conflicted about homosexuality (and I would add, sexuality in general) and gender. Its theological positions about women and homosexuality, conflated with Vatican statements of absolute authority, find contradiction within the ranks of its prelates and clergy.

Eve Sedgwick writes, "Closetedness is a performance initiated as such by the speech act of a silence."[31] American Catholic denial mechanisms are firmly entrenched, with a finely tuned rhetoric of sodomy that sets up a symbiotic top/bottom relationship between Catholic bishops and religious leaders and priests. Fear and complicity have become tools for a deadening silence that kills the spirit by refusing to allow Catholic priests to explore publicly alternative masculinities and integrating their sexuality with spirituality in healthy practices. While other minority masculinities such as dyke masculinity or female-to-male transsexuals destabilize the fundamentalist system of binary gender, priestly (fe)masculinity has not threatened the binary gender system. Refusing to be a heterocultural man may express that one is, in some sense, a (fe)male, yet the clerical refusal to be a man is wedded with a deep misogyny. It performs an oppositional (fe)masculinity that has not realized its full potential in signifying that femininity is a lack of masculinity but represents a range of being in the world rich with novel expressiveness and tonalities. The more publicly that Catholic priests distance themselves from their misogyny, the more their (fe)masculinity can become a resistance to the homosocial structure of the Catholic Church. Then the possibilities of real change can take place.

When I speak to closeted Jesuits and priests, genuinely committed to their ministry but quietly and fearfully opposed to the current regime of terrorism, I find similar feelings to women in abusive relationships with men. These priests are not fallen women but remain battered fe(males). Recently I spoke to a priest, terrified to speak publicly against the rhetorical violence of institutional Catholicism against homosexuality. "What can I do if I am expelled from the priesthood? I am sixty years old and have no Social Security for retirement. I'm trapped. . . . I can't do otherwise." Vatican terrorism is alive and vindictive of all vocal opposition on the matter of homosexuality.

Some may see the camp mockery of femininity as an insult to women,

---

31. Sedgwick, *Epistemology of the Closet*, 3.

but I read and perceive it quite differently. I read clerical (fe)masculinity as I comprehend males performing female drag, with one exception. Whereas clerical drag has at its core a fear and hatred of women, queer female drag has a subversive potential to destabilize the gender constructions of heterosexist culture, creating gender-benders and gender inversions. It has political potential to destabilize our rigid gender codes and widen the cultural definitions of masculinity and femininity, for male identification with women in drag is resistance to cultural masculinity. Clerical (fe)masculinity needs to heal its fear of women and come to appreciate the giftedness of the wide range of feminine performances. Then it can become prophetic, challenging gender fundamentalism.

I am currently an openly queer clergy in a church, the Metropolitan Community Church of Greater St. Louis, affiliated with the UFMCC (Universal Fellowship of Metropolitan Community Churches), where approximately 52 percent of the clergy are women and where the majority of clergy are gay, lesbian, bisexual, and transgendered. I accept my "butch" masculinity and my (fe)masculinity; the fluidity of these gender expressions is integrated into my life as a form of public resistance against cultural gender fundamentalism. While I accept some of Mark Jordan's critique of MCC, there is one positive thing that MCC may provide — hope to queer Catholics and clergy.[32] It is the hope of what some features of a nonhomophobic church might look like. I practice a queer Catholic spirituality in exile, without internalized homophobia and misogyny. The MCC of Greater St. Louis and many other MCCs have provided a home for many exiled Catholics who have found healing and hope from the ravages of institutional misogyny and homophobia. The staff of the MCC of Greater St. Louis is predominantly female, and I feel at home with the wide range of masculine and feminine performances of gender on staff. It is refreshing and freeing. As the MCC grows and merges with other churches in the twenty-first century, it may continue to provide a safe haven for exiled Catholics and support the struggles of queer Catholics and clergy against institutional terrorism. A number of MCCers, including myself, joined queer Catholics such as Father John McNeill and other Catholics in the arrest action at the National Catholic Basilica of the Immaculate Conception, protesting the Catholic bishops in their recalcitrant stance on homosexuality.

Although there are particular instances of individual and institutional misogyny among some clergy with the UFMCC, it is also a church where gender-inclusive language is normative, where a variety of ex-

---

32. Jordan, *Silence of Sodom*, 253–56.

pressions of cross-gender identifications are celebrated as natural, and where the integration of sexuality and spirituality is practiced. There is little communal anxiety over a butch dyke, a transvestite male, a leather man, a stone butch, a male-to-female or a female-to-male transsexual clergy, or any other fluid expression of gender. Perhaps the UFMCC models the type of church that queer Catholic clergy and laity can only dream of becoming: openly queer, nonmisogynist, inclusive, and gender-transgressive.

THREE

FINDING GOD IN THE
HEART-GENITAL CONNECTION

*Healing the male heart, I think, has to do with being freer with our bodies,
especially around other men.* —Joe Kramer

*Erotic power is incarnate in heart. It binds the life-giving, healing heart of
ourselves with each other, if we possess the courage to claim it. For courage
itself wells from the heart. And heart enhances erotic power through our
connections to others. Searching for connections is the heart's search to heal
suffering and brokenness. Hearts live in erotic power, the power of our
loving each other at the depths of our being.* —Rita Nakashima Brock[1]

In an e-mail posting by Meta, a science and religion list service, Jay
Johnson's article "The Possibility of Sex as a Christian Spiritual Practice" was sent out to subscribers. Johnson, an Episcopal gay theologian,
asks the question, "Can sex contribute to Christian spiritual practice?"[2]
Without abandoning Christian theological tradition — indeed, working
from Augustinian and Thomist theological traditions — Johnson suggests a constructive theological return to the importance of the body, the
incarnation, and recovery of the erotic as a longing within us for God.

In a pastoral course in sexuality during my studies for ordination, I
took *The Joy of Sex* and compared it to *The Spiritual Exercises* of Ignatius of
Loyola. I argued in that paper that both were "how-to" manuals for intimacy and that sexuality and spirituality were integrally interconnected
for any religious path. As I pursued theological and graduate studies in
comparative religion, I relegated my sexual practice to my personal life
and only later began to reflect upon my sexual practice for my queer

---

1. Joe Kramer, "Sexual Healing: Healing the Heart-Genital Split in Men," in *Sex and
Spirit: Exploring Gay Men's Spirituality,* ed. Robert Barzan (San Francisco: White Crane Press,
1995), 36; Rita Nakashima Brock, *Journeys by Heart* (New York: Crossroad, 1991), 45.
2. Jay E. Johnson, "The Possibility of Sex as a Christian Spiritual Practice," e-mail
posting by Meta 140: More Sex, Wednesday, September 15, 1999, *metalist.org.*

writings. Johnson's question of the recovery of sex within a constructionist theology points to the serious deficiency inherent in Christian
theology. By failing to incorporate a sexual praxis, Christian theology has
remained an accomplice in promoting a politics of shame and guilt to
regulate sexuality within very strict orthodox boundaries. I want to pose
Johnson's question slightly differently: Can sex contribute to Christian
spiritual practice and, in turn, to theology? A radical constructionist
answer must be grounded in a sexual praxis that is transformative of
male-sex to full-body orgasm, connected to justice, and eschatological
enough to configure both the depth of fidelity and the nonexclusivity
of God's love. Present-day male theologians need to embody their theological constructions of human sexuality within a sexual praxis that
explores the full range of experience of what Joe Kramer describes as
the heart-genital connection.

What I intend to do is to interrogate the sexual praxis and thought of
Joe Kramer. I have known Kramer since the days we were both Jesuits.
His spirituality is Ignatian, and within that spirituality, he has promoted
a sexual praxis that has impacted thousands of gay and bisexual men in
integrating their sexuality and spirituality. We share a vision of finding
God in sexuality. It is time for the theologian and the sexual shaman to
engage in the messiness of intercourse; thus, I want to engage Kramer's
sexual praxis toward configuring an erotic Christianity. This is, of course,
a partial vision since my focus is entirely on male sexual experience,
but it is a first step in constructing a gay erotic Christianity. I want to
interrogate three themes in Kramer's sexual practice: (1) balloon sex,
(2) the heart-genital connection and full-body orgasm, (3) and dear
love of comrades. These will provide the jumping-off point for further
theological reflections.

Joe Kramer

Joe Kramer has been described as "Whitman's Child," a masturbation
virtuoso, sex priest, sex magician, masseur, trainer of sacred intimates,
sex educator, retreat master, and erotic prophet. Kramer is certainly a
video producer and a sexual entrepreneur. He has been featured in
the gay popular press such as *LA Weekly, The Advocate, Out Magazine,
Celebrate the Self: The Magazine of Solo Sex,* and other publications such
as *Screw Magazine* and *Tantra.* He was interviewed in Mark Thompson's
best-selling book, *Gay Soul.* Christian La Huerta's *Coming Out Spiritually*
and Toby Johnson's *Gay Spirituality* look at Kramer's contribution to gay
spirituality. Most recently David Guy's *The Red Thread of Passion* placed

Kramer among a sexual lineage of Walt Whitman, D. H. Lawrence, Alan Watts, Marco Vassi, Carol Queen, and Juliet Carr as "pioneers on the boundaries of sex and spirituality."[3] His few writings have appeared in *White Crane,* Robert Barzan's *Sex and Spirit,* and in my own coedited volume *Our Families, Our Values: Snapshots of Queer Kinship.*[4]

Kramer is the founder of the Body Electric School, which provides educational instruction to bodywork professionals, sacred intimates, and erotic choreographers. He is the director and founder of EroSpirit Research Institute, described as a "queer" think tank dedicated to "researching erotic, spiritual wisdom."[5] Kramer produced his first award-winning video, *Fire on the Mountain,* an instructional video on techniques of solo-sex. Then he embarked upon the Gay Sex Wisdom series that included interviews with erotic choreographers, a theologian, AIDS activists, gay contemplatives, sexual healers, and sex teachers. The series included author Andrew Ramer, Michael Kelly's six-video series *The Erotic Contemplative* (endorsed by psychotherapist and author John McNeill and myself as a profound attempt at the integration of gay sexuality and spirituality), a video talk by myself, and Kramer's *Sex Monasteries.*[6] On the jacket cover of Kramer's *Ecstatic Sex, Healthy Sex,* the late queer theologian Robert Williams endorses the audio tapes, "Joseph Kramer has done pioneering work in sacred sexuality. It is exciting, wonderful, and healing."[7]

Joe Kramer has conducted workshops and classes on erotic touch, massage, sexual pleasure, and instructing men how to become sacred intimates in the vortex of gay spirituality, San Francisco. For nearly two decades Joe Kramer has been promoting a thoroughly erotic spirituality and practices for gay and bisexual men. Thousands of men have participated in these classes to enhance and prolong orgasm, to get in

3. Mark Thompson, ed., *Gay Soul: Finding the Heart of Gay Spirit and Nature* (San Francisco: HarperSanFrancisco, 1994), 169–82; Christian La Huerta, *Coming Out Spiritually: The Next Step* (New York: J. P. Tarcher, 1999), 106–8; Toby Johnson, *Gay Spirituality* (New York: Alyson Books, 2000), 175–77; David Guy, *The Red Thread of Passion: Spirituality and the Paradox of Sex* (Boston: Shambhala, 1999), 201–22.

4. Kramer, "Sexual Healing," 32–36; Kramer, "Making Love for the Whole World to Feel: Four Erotic Rituals for Gay Men," in *Our Families, Our Values: Snapshots of Queer Kinship,* ed. Robert E. Goss and Amy Adams Squires Strongheart (New York: Harrington Park Press, 1997), 181–96.

5. See *www.erospirit.org/temp/opening.shtml.*

6. There are thirteen volumes to the Gay Sex Wisdom series. There are video talks by Andrew Ramer, Jim Curtan, Jim Mitulski, Michael Kelly, Joe Kramer, Robert Goss, Tim Updike, and Keith Hennessy. The Gay Sex Wisdom series is a good barometer of popular gay sexual praxis and spirituality.

7. Robert Williams quoted on the audiotape jacket of *Ecstatic Sex, Healthy Sex,* produced by EroSpirit Institute, Oakland, Calif.

touch with their bodies, and to integrate sexuality and spirituality. The résumé of Kramer's work is far more extensive than that detailed in my brief opening. This essay provides a genealogical analysis of what cultural critic Michel Foucault has called the "union of erudite and local memories, which allows us to establish a historical knowledge of struggles and to make use of this knowledge tactically today."[8] Few theological essays have ever analyzed a praxis of sexuality as explicit and graphic as Kramer's sexual praxis. Joe Kramer, I maintain, claims that sex can be a Christian (and many other traditions as well) spiritual practice.

"Balloon sex"

Kramer's emphasis on the male penis might trigger alarm bells for feminists and feminist-identified males, conjuring Norman Mailer–styled notions of patriarchal sex and spirituality. Kramer does make such statements as, "The cock is the male symbol of the divine," but such statements are immediately followed by a balanced assertion like: "Actually the divine is symbolized by both male and female."[9] His language about male genitals is far from phallocentric; it is, I would suggest, a thoroughly queer appropriation of masculine sexuality. He is equally subversive of male heterosexist and gay phallic ideologies — the cordoning off of sexuality to maintain male performance, the identification of sex with power and violence, or erotophobic/homophobic ideologies. He queers male sexuality with what is traditionally understood as female sexuality. I will explore this theme a little later in this essay.

Kramer's Irish Catholicism was significant for the development of his sexual praxis and spirituality. He speaks of how Catholic notions of mortal sin afflicted him in his teen years:

> The Catholic Church helped me because it was a mortal sin to masturbate. I figured, if it's a mortal sin, maybe even after coming, I would just keep stroking, so it would only be one mortal sin. So I learned multiple orgasms. The other thing that the repressiveness of Catholicism did was to bring God and sex together in my mind. God cared every time I had sex. Later on, once I got rid of the guilt, I realized that the God space, the religious space, was intimately tied up with sex. This was a part of what spirituality meant to me.[10]

---

8. Michel Foucault, *Power/Knowledge* (New York: Pantheon Books, 1980), 82.
9. Kramer, "Sexual Healing," 32.
10. Guy, *Red Thread of Passion*, 207.

Despite his Irish Catholic guilt and shame, there was awareness of the convergence of spirituality and sexuality; it was the Jesuits, or what Kramer describes as a "homosexual heaven," who nurtured this insight and prepared him to find spirituality within his sex/body-work.

Moreover, Kramer describes what many of us would call phallocentric male sexuality as "balloon sex." Balloon sex is the excitement that is localized in the genitals, a pleasure that does not move anywhere beyond the genitals. Balloon sex is addictive and compulsive. In the *Windy City Times,* Kramer writes, "The problem is that our conventional Western approach to sex in itself is bad sex. It is geared to getting off and then falling asleep."[11] It is the way many men have sex, focusing on the excitement and the satisfaction of rapid limited pleasure: "Balloon sex actually shuts off other energy centers, because it tightens the body. It doesn't allow energy to flow, and it isn't healing."[12] Male sexual acts are focused on specific acts, involving excitement, erection, penetration, and ejaculation. A partner is incidental or may be an occasion of getting off. Ejaculation involves getting rid of sexual feelings and pleasure quickly. Joe Kramer notes how boys learn to begin to masturbate secretly and quickly at night: "It is an act that takes place quickly, is entirely genital, and — because it involves limited satisfaction — needs to be repeated. And repeated. Picture that same boy grown up now, haunting bath houses or massage parlors."[13]

The male tendency to localize pleasure genitally and rapidly has had tragic effects on men because it has contributed to the male inclination toward an instrumental understanding of sexuality and a sexual praxis where the male genitals are separate from the body. Thus this tendency gives males a phallocentric consciousness separate from embodied pleasure, and the tyranny of ejaculation becomes a driving motivational force. Psychiatrist John Stoltenberg speaks about the consequences of men who separate genital pleasure from body pleasure: "Real men are aggressive in sex. Real men get cruel in sex. Real men use their penises like weapons in sex. Real men leave bruises. Real men think it's a turn-on to threaten harm."[14] Violence and excitement often become fetishized in a masculinist praxis of sex.

One could easily argue how Christian theology and erotophobia have

---

11. Joe Kramer, "Male Sexuality: Ecstatic Sex, Healthy Sex: Six Steps to a Full-Bodied Orgasm Every Time," *Windy City Times,* June 23, 1988, 142.

12. Guy, *Red Thread of Passion,* 206.

13. Kramer, cited in ibid., 203.

14. John Stoltenberg, *Refusing to Be Man: Essays on Sex and Justice* (New York: Penguin Books, 1990), 350.

contributed to males' separation of their genitals from their bodies — St. Augustine, after all, seemed to think that his penis had a mind of its own, acquiescing to lust and concupiscence. Augustine injected into Christian history a distrust of sexuality and sexual pleasure. He was certainly not the first Christian writer to distrust sexuality and sexual pleasure, but he had undue influence upon Catholic and Protestant Christianities. Augustine made the distinction between sex for the purpose of procreation and sex for pleasure. This was based upon his view of humanity's fall in the garden. Before the fall into sin, Adam was able to control his genitals and could propagate without lust, but God meted out a punishment to fit the fall: "Man has been given over to himself because he abandoned God, while he sought to be self-satisfying; and disobeying God, he could not obey even himself."[15] Augustine had to admit that sex for procreation, as long as it is confined to marriage, was potentially good since God had willed human procreation and humanity had the need to survive.

For Augustine, one of the effects of the fall was the problem of male erections. Spontaneous sexual desire was proof of original sin. Thus, the penis does not obey a man's will, for it is under the control of lust. Augustine writes:

> For as soon as our first parents had transgressed the commandment, divine grace forsook them...and therefore they took fig-leaves and covered their shame; for though their members remained the same, they had shame now where they had none before. They experienced a new motion of their flesh, which had become disobedient to them, in strict retribution of their own disobedience to God.[16]

For Augustine, lust defies the power of the will and dominates the genitals. The pleasure of sex disturbs a man's mind, for sexual pleasure assumes power over the whole body. Orgasm overwhelms male reason; thus, sexual pleasure must be contained, regulated, and controlled. Michel Foucault offers this insight on Augustine:

> The famous gesture of Adam covering his genitals with a fig leaf is, according to Augustine, not due to the simple fact that Adam was ashamed of their presence, but to the fact that his sexual organs were moving by themselves without his consent. Sex in erection is

---

15. Augustine, *City of God,* trans. Marcus Dods (New York: Random House, 1950), bk. 14.24.

16. Ibid., bk. 14.13.

the image of man revolted against God. The arrogance of sex is
punishment and consequence of the arrogance of man. His uncontrolled sex is exactly the same as what he has been toward God —
a rebel.[17]

The legacy of Augustine has led to the tragic consequence of institutional Christianity divorcing sexuality and spirituality, an alienation of
sexual pleasure from the body, and promoting a climate of male violence. In cultures where sexual pleasure is devalued, there are high
incidences of violence.[18] This has necessitated my exploration of the
correlation of erotophobia, masculinist ideology, and violence within
Christianity in a future sequel to *Jesus ACTED UP.*

Thus, Christianity developed its spiritual practices and theologies to
surround sex in a web of shame and guilt. The tragic consequence is that
men succumbed to phallic myths of power and that they localized sexual
pleasure to the region of the genitals, rather than attempting to sustain
sexual pleasure and spreading it throughout the body. The containment of sexual pleasure to the genitals motivates men to seek pleasure
as often as they can. The commodification of sexual pleasure has led
males to organize and obtain quick pleasure, package sex, control and
market sex. Sexual gratification takes place as aggression, domination,
conquest, success, and humiliation. A phallic ideology of masculinity
is suffused with the Christian practice of cordoning off sexuality from
spirituality and of quick gratification, often identified with violence and
domination. Male fascination with the phallus is about power. Male theological fascination with the phallus is about keeping women and lesser
males from social, religious, and political power.

                                                                    •

The heart-genital connection and full-body orgasm

Two metaphors give us clues to the implicative horizon of Kramer's sexual praxis: the heart-genital connection and full-body orgasm. Kramer

---

17. Michel Foucault, "On Genealogy," in *Michel Foucault: Beyond Structuralism and Hermeneutics,* ed. Hubert Dreyfus and Paul Rabinow (Chicago: University of Chicago Press,
1983), 370.

18. Joe Kramer put me in touch with an essay, "Body Pleasure and the Origins of Violence," by James Prescott. As noted above, Prescott, a neuropsychologist, claims that in
cultures where sexual pleasure is disvalued, there is a high incidence of violence, and
in cultures where sexual pleasure is valued, there is a low incidence of violence. See
James W. Prescott, "Body Pleasure and the Origins of Violence," *Bulletin of the Atomic
Scientists* (November 1975): 10–20.

uses them synonymously in his talks and video tapes. Through his theological education at the Jesuit School of Theology at Berkeley, Joe
Kramer is familiar with feminist theological discourse on mutuality, but
perhaps the greatest influence of women on his praxis comes from sex-
worker and sex-performer Annie Sprinkle, a woman Kramer says is "the
only woman I've had sex with in twenty years." I remember visiting Joe,
and he showed me a video, *Sluts and Goddesses: The Video Workshop,* that
features a sex-performance of Annie Sprinkle experiencing an orgasm
for more than five minutes.[19] As a male, I was in awe of her abilities and
admittedly envious of her ability to sustain a five-minute orgasm. It was
not localized to her genitals but was a full-body orgasm. In amazement
I watched her body writhe in full pleasure. It is what Kramer describes
as the heart and genitals being reconnected and spreading pleasure
throughout the body. Kramer's sexual praxis aims to subvert men from
their localized orgasm to full-body orgasm and to bring that orgasm
within a communal context, the social context of the heart.

For Kramer, most Western men suffer erotophobia, guilt, and alienation from their bodies. Christian erotophobia has also contributed to
male patterns of balloon sex with its politics of sexual shame and guilt.
Kramer assists men in recovering bodily connectedness through massage
techniques:

> As a masseur, I have noticed physical constrictions in clients' bodies
> and found the major areas of tension and dis-ease are in the heart
> and the genitals — in men much more so than in women. The
> heart and the genitals I call the places of love.... When these two
> places are connected, magic starts to happen and we enter into a
> divine place.[20]

Kramer notes that "massage is meditation on your body."[21] It com-
bines bodily awareness with mind-relaxation techniques. Buddhists have
called this style of meditative practice "mindfulness." The Zen Buddhist teacher Thich Nhat Hanh uses mindfulness to de-escalate violence
within oneself for the practices of nonviolence and peacemaking. Nhat
Hanh speaks of mindfulness as contemplating the body in the body:
"Contemplating body in the body means that you should not look on
your body as the object of your contemplation. You have to be one with

---

19. Annie Sprinkle, *Goddesses and Sluts: The Video Workshop* (Oakland, Calif.: EroSpirit
Institute).
20. Kramer, "Sexual Healing," 33.
21. Ibid., 35.

it."[22] Kramer's use of massage techniques to bring about male mind-fulness of the full body, I would suggest, has a similar effect to Thich Nhat Hanh's use of mindfulness — diffusing the violence of balloon sex within males and generating a sexual connectedness to the body and others. For years, Joe Kramer incorporated popular Taoist and tantric practices of breathing exercises and relaxation techniques to assist men in becoming aware and mindful of their bodily tensions, and therefore, to counter the temptation of balloon sex: "Balloon sex is an act of tens-ing until you pop. But a tense body cannot feel, so many men don't know what full-bodied sexual pleasure is like."[23]

Kramer attempts to subvert balloon sex by teaching men how to masturbate in a prolonged and pleasurable fashion. He coined the word "soloving," from the words "solo" and "loving," in substitution for the word "masturbation."[24] Kramer observes, "[Wilhelm] Reich believed that masturbation was a perversion because there was no love object. I thought, no love object? Wait a minute. Masturbation involves the most important love object of all."[25] Masturbation can become an act of self-love, in the best sense of the word. In an interview with Jeff Kirby, Kramer notes that he adopted the Cherokee erotic instructor Harley Swiftdeer's term for masturbation, "heart-pleasuring."[26] Heart-pleasuring is a self-love that, when placed in the context of full-body orgasm, enables a man to relearn fully embodied sex — thus connected to his own heart, others, the world, and God.

Joe Kramer's goal is to teach men to masturbate, not out of compul-sive drives of balloon sex but in order to move localized genital pleasure to full-body pleasure. He attempts to divert men from immediate ejacula-tion and sexual gratification through massage and touch. Kramer writes: "The more of me I massage, the more of me feels good. Stimulating touch creates an electrical vibration which circulates through the body, building to the ecstatic feeling called a full body orgasm. It is important to note that this full body orgasm is different from ejaculation."[27]

For Kramer, authentic orgasm is always full-bodied; ejaculation is never the goal itself but a means to full-body pleasure. In his audio talk

---

22. Thich Nhat Hanh, *Being Peace* (Berkeley, Calif.: Parallax Press, 1987), 39.
23. Guy, *Red Thread of Passion*, 216.
24. Kramer, "Making Love," 185.
25. In Guy, *Red Thread of Passion*, 214–15.
26. Jeff Kirby, "Erotic Empowerment: Healing the Heart-Genital Connection." This was an interview with Joseph Kramer conducted by Jeff Kirby in the late 1980s. Joe Kramer gave me a photocopy of the interview. It was in a San Francisco paper that went out of business and whose name he could not remember.
27. In Guy, *Red Thread of Passion*, 211.

Ecstatic Sex, Healthy Sex, Kramer outlines six natural steps to introduce oneself to healthy sexual praxis. These include cultivating an alive body, relaxation of tension, breathing consciously, taking time, body mindfulness, and movement and shouting.[28] These six techniques, Kramer claims, lead to a full-body orgasm. He teaches men to use their bodies ecstatically through masturbation and touch, introducing techniques for genital and body massage in meditative mindfulness. These are bodily exercises to stimulate mindfulness and subvert the tyranny of immediate ejaculation. Too many men focus on ejaculation as the goal of masturbation or sexual encounters and work toward that goal. His massage techniques subvert such quick and compulsive male excitement — transforming it into bodily enjoyment. In a conversation, Kramer stated to me that the goal of his sexual praxis was to train men to transform excitement into bodily pleasure, "to ride it into bliss and enjoyment." Thus, Kramer's techniques divert the drive from genital orgasm to full-body pleasure, and one of the significant consequences for Kramer is that this throws men into a state of transcendental experience where they make connections to God, partner(s), and life.

The more I study the sexual praxis espoused by Kramer, the more I find a strong parallel with Jeffrey Hopkins's book *Sex, Orgasm, and the Mind of Clear Light,* where Hopkins provides a gay variation of Gendun Chopel's *Tibetan Arts of Love.*[29] For the tantric Buddhist, the question is how to spread orgasmic bliss without ejaculation to a whole-body ejaculation and to the mind for the purpose of enlightenment and compassionate action. In the Highest Yoga Tantra, compassion is referred to as the "bliss of orgasm without emission."[30] It parallels Kramer's notion of the heart-genital connection, and both combine yogic techniques to make such a link between male sexual pleasure and the body.

Likewise, Kramer mentors his male students to a sexual praxis with a variety of yogic techniques in order to spread sexual bliss throughout the whole body. He connects healthy sexual praxis with the heart and uses massage techniques to spread pleasure throughout the body. Kramer writes, "Touch the way you like to be touched. Touch the way you touch best and the way you think this man would like, but always remember that the man who is being touched is in charge of his massage."[31] Erotic

---

28. Joe Kramer, *Ecstatic Sex, Healthy Sex,* audiocassette tape produced by EroSpirit Institute, Oakland, Calif.

29. Jeffrey Hopkins, *Sex, Orgasm, and the Mind of Clear Light: The Sixty-Four Arts of Gay Male Love* (Berkeley, Calif.: North Atlantic Books, 1998).

30. Ibid., 102.

31. Kramer, "Sexual Healing," 35.

bonding is based upon honoring the person before you; it includes mutuality; Kramer intuits the connection of spreading sexual bliss through
the body with the heart. The heart symbolizes this reembodying sexual
praxis. He writes:

> Most women are more parasympathetic; they're more relaxed, and
> that's why they can have multiple orgasms and go much longer.
> The heart is involved with the parasympathetic, which includes
> things like getting a soothing massage or lying in a hot tub or
> cuddling with a lover. Men have to learn the skill of integrating
> the parasympathetic more.[32]

Kramer describes two important elements lost in balloon sex: connection to the full body and connection to the full social context of
love-making. Solo-sex can be reembodied into a full-bodied orgasm,
breaking with the patterns of release-oriented ejaculation. To love yourself is to connect yourself to life. For Kramer, solo-sex can have the
context of self-love, meditative spiritual practice, and the communion
of saints.[33] Kramer's notion of the heart-genital connection remains
underdeveloped in his writings; he has not developed the connections of
sexuality to justice and compassion that feminist theologians and tantric
Buddhist practitioners make. Sexual love-making needs to find its source
within the spirituality tradition and reconnect to the meditative tradition
of Christianity. The failure of Christianity was its failure to value sexual
pleasure, a gift and a created good.

In *Our Families, Our Values,* Episcopal priest Leng Lim describes the
battle he waged against his body and erotic feelings after years of Christian fundamentalism, reparative therapy, bodily shame, and familial
pressures to be heterosexual. He attended a retreat of the Body Electric
School, designed by Kramer to explore alternative ways of being erotic
and to search for personal healing of the painful alienation of sexuality
from spirituality. Leng Lim writes:

> Two pairs of hands warm, gentle, and firm touched me on my heart
> and genitals, and I was gently rocked from side to side. "Open your
> hearts and genitals, say yes to life and love." I shuddered at the
> words. As the warm oil was spread along the sixth chakra, I found
> myself drenched in powerful sensations of pleasure. Strong hands

---

32. Ibid., 34.
33. In a "queer beyond egroup," I made the suggestion that masturbation involves the
communion of saints. It involves more than myself. Kramer responded enthusiastically to
this notion.

kneaded my aching muscles, so long untouched — and my aching heart, so long yearning. I took another breath and let out a long moan. The battle for integrity was almost won.[34]

Leng Lim found healthy self-acceptance, integrity, and an uncontainable home of erotic energy through the body-work exercises that Kramer incorporated into the Body Electric classes and retreats. His essay is a testament and witness to the need of body-work for Christians and especially the male clergy with their erotophobic heritage. Making the heart-genital connection may be important not only for clergy but also for theologians who write about sexuality from their abstract theoretical frameworks and continue to promote religious abuse in their theologies of sexuality. Connecting the genitals to the heart can save men from damaging masculinity while revealing that sexual experience can be filled with numinosity. Sex is neither divided from full-body experience nor separated from the sacred. By incorporating meditative techniques, holding on to sexual pleasure, not ejaculation, is the goal. This has the potential of assisting gay/bisexual men to identify with women and realize their deep connections to the body. Just as feminist and womanist theologies have recovered the centrality of the body for theology, gay/bisexual theologians can recover the body as the site of the sublime, the sacred. Making connection to the body becomes an organic theological value. Making interconnections with women, the oppressed, the marginalized, and the earth becomes the erotic matrix for theological discourse. The heart-genital connection channels and sustains erotic energy by healing the split that virulent masculinist ideologies have created.

The mind-heart-genital connection is where my theological practice begins since that is the site of God's Spirit. Theology generally focuses on the mind, a speculative construction of truths. When the mind is the locus of theology, it is abstract, stressing spirit over the physical or principles rather than lived experience. When the heart-genital connection is the site of theological reflection, it makes compassionate connections. Seldom does theology focus on the genitals except in a negative or restrictive fashion. This is apparent in the sparse Christian writings that connect orgasm to spirituality. Seldom does theological practice emerge from the connections of the mind, the heart, and the genitals. The erotic brings passion to theological practice. Recent feminist-womanist,

---

34. Leng Leroy Lim, "Webs of Betrayal, Webs of Blessings," in *Our Families, Our Values,* 236.

African American, queer, and Third World theologians make these passionate connections. Indigenous gay theologies must make passionate
connections in a similar fashion.

"Dear love of comrades"

Kramer, however, is not without his critics. There been individuals in
the gay community and among gay scholars who perceive his workshops
and retreats as excuses for sexual orgies. I would counter such criticisms
with the notion that Kramer is promoting eschatological sexuality with
a transformative impact upon men's sexual praxis, introducing them to
the sacred dimensions of sexuality, and providing a safe space for men to
discover sexuality as nonviolent, healing, and connected to their bodies.
Where do men find a space for sexual self-discovery from the years of
shame and balloon sex? This space is created within workshops and
retreats for men. This need introduces the role of community or the
"dear love of comrades" into male sexual praxis. Here Kramer comes
close to what feminists like Carter Heyward have envisioned as the role
of the erotic in creating a just community or what Mary Hunt describes
as "just good sex."

Kramer patterns his notion of the beloved community after his experience of Jesuit community. He describes the Society of Jesus as
"homosexual heaven," a monogendered society of men where the gestalt
of male bonding and spirituality was imprinted upon his consciousness
within a subterranean network of Jesuit sexual liaisons and mentoring.[35]
The importance of his time in the Jesuits consistently appears in his
biographical accounts and interviews. Kramer writes,

> My experience in the Jesuits taught me that the denial of the gifts
> of sexuality is a denial of God's grace. My rejection of my special
> way of loving was the "sin against the Holy Spirit...." I had no
> choice but to leave the Jesuits. My life's commitment then became
> a journey to find or to co-create a community of men whose justice-
> doing and love-making were gifts for the world.[36]

His Jesuit experience of an erotic male-bonded community provided the
seeds for his erotic work and his vision to create a beloved community
of men who would celebrate Whitman's "body electric" in erotic rituals

---

35. Guy, *Red Thread of Passion*, 208. The Jesuits have been a training ground for erotic
spirituality. See also "Out of the Closet and into the Streets," in this volume.

36. In Guy, *Red Thread of Passion*, 182.

and imaginative celebrations. Jesuit spirituality trained him to find God in all experience, including in his own sexual experience. The Jesuits mentored Joe to an erotic spirituality and within an "erotic" community. Jesuit spirituality inculcated a sense of mission and service to the world in Joe, and it taught him to dig deep into himself to discover his gifts and develop these talents in service to the world. This has had significant impact on his mission to mentor men to bodily recovery of the heart-genital connection. But it also created a mission to move beyond the workshops, retreats, and networks of male bonding to form what he terms "sex monasteries." Perhaps I would characterize Joe as an erotic evangelist with a utopian vision of teaching men how to masturbate for the love of the world and to make erotic connections with others.

In his video talk *Sex Monasteries,* he mentions his study of various groups who lived together in an open sexuality: the Oneida community, Centerpoint in New Zealand, and the Short Mountain Collective of the Radical Faeries.[37] These were sexual egalitarian or utopian communities, experimenting with alternative patterns of sexuality that challenged the organization of society along rigid hierarchies of gender.

Kramer primarily envisions an erotic religious community of gay/bisexual men (but not exclusively male) based on rituals of sex. He outlines four such rituals in *Our Families, Our Values.*[38] Such a community could focus on the energies of body, sex, service, art, meditation, and justice-doing. Such utopian communities could be organized around particular religious traditions such as Buddhism and Christianity; such communities could be organized around mutual interest such as holistic health, art, and activism. They would remain training grounds for men to relearn new patterns of embodied sexuality:

> What I've created is a social context in which men can have an erotic experience outside of their normal patterns that they have learned — with people that may not even be their type. Normally, eroticism stays within the same riverbank, the same rut, from the time of puberty. What I give them is a safe, playful, different approach to sex, a different way of running energy in their bodies, an opportunity to have a new experience, something different. Even though they may not know it, people really want to experience things differently; letting go of our desire to control everything is really refreshing.[39]

37. Joe Kramer, *Sex Monasteries,* video produced by EroSpirit Institute, Oakland, Calif.
38. Kramer, "Making Love," 181–96.
39. In La Huerta, *Coming Out Spiritually,* 106–7.

Kramer's notion of erotic monasteries or communities envisions multiple patterns of sexuality, threatening advocates of exclusive pair-bonded monogamous relationships. I have discovered that queer former Catholic religious — male and female — comprehend the style of erotic, religious community envisioned by Kramer in his chapter in *Our Families, Our Values.*

Debate occasionally rages in the queer community over marriage versus polyamory. For many queer Christians, it is too easy to allow for single sexuality as a dating pattern moving in the direction of marriage. Many gay men sleep with their partners before dating and developing a committed relationship. What troubles many is the possibility of new configurations of relationships beyond single or pair-bonded relationships.

Kramer's view of communal sexual relationships opens up new configurations of sexual relations. Many gays openly critiqued gay marriage as building upon a heterosexist and culturally constructed institution of marriage. Christianity has often defended marriage on the basis of rearing children and the containment of lust. While I believe in the giftedness of same-sex (pair-bonded) relationships to the Christian community, I wrestle with Joe's notions of communal variations and the current debate on polyamory.

For example, feminist theologian Elizabeth Templeton hopes that Jesus was correct when he said that there is no marriage in heaven, a statement he made in answer to a question from a Sadducee. The Sadducee refers to a woman who has married six times and asks, "In the resurrection, whose wife will the woman be?" (Luke 20:33). Jesus answers, "those worthy of a place in that age and in the resurrection from the dead neither marry nor are given in marriage" (Luke 20:35). Templeton writes, "For it seems to me that, however we envisage the state of redeemed existence, in or out of time, it cannot be properly envisaged as a place of excluding relationships."[40] Templeton envisions the grace of marriage as a "microcosm of the mutual solidarity between God and creation, which generates a commitment through thick and thin, and for which we depend on resourcing from a lover deeper than even our natural instincts."[41] Marriage traditionally insists on the exclusiveness of forsaking others. While the depth of pair-bonded relationships may mirror the depths of God's infinite grace and commitment to us, does

---

40. Elizabeth Templeton, "Towards a Theology of Marriage," in *As Man and Woman: Theological Reflections on Marriage,* ed. Susan Durber (London: United Reform Church, 1994), 17.
41. Ibid., 16.

it preclude other confirmations from mirroring other aspects of God's love? Can polyamory reflect the breadth of God's inclusive love while faithfulness in a committed pair-bonded relationship represents God's faithful love?

Elizabeth Stuart's provocative essay "Sex in Heaven" suggests that Christians might best examine sex at present not by looking back at past traditions and formulations but by looking eschatologically at sex and sexual relationships.[42] Such "dangerous memories" of the future might shatter our fundamentalist models of sexuality, gender, and sexual relationships — creating open space to affirm the blessings of pair-bonded relationships as well as other polyamorous configurations. Kathy Rudy, likewise, has dared to argue that public and even communal sex can be unitive within the Christian vision of human sexuality.[43] She suggests that gay promiscuous sex could be modeled after Catholic religious communities.

Finally, I value Joe Kramer as a sexual practitioner and as a dialogue partner in my sexual theology. To construct an indigenous theology, gay male theologians need to allow themselves to experience the full range of their erotic desires. Like Leng Lim, we might benefit from getting naked together and participating in training sessions at the Body Electric School. Joe's sexual praxis reminds me to ground my theological constructions within a matrix of the heart-genital awareness that harnesses my theological imagination with a compassionate heart and erotic energy in the total project of love-making and justice-doing. Love-making and justice-doing are the means of transforming what is not yet part of God's reign into a culture of justice-love. As a gay theologian, I live rooted in my erotic life, weaving three strands together: erotic contemplative, lover, and passionate freedom fighter. If theology does not envision or contribute to a culture of justice-love, then it is something other than theological practice. A sexual theology, like an erotic Christianity, encourages love, compassion, solidarity, mutuality, forgiveness, peace, social justice, and a commitment to life.

---

42. Elizabeth Stuart, "Sex in Heaven," in *Sex These Days: Essays on Theology, Sexuality, and Society*, ed. Jon Davies and Gerard Loughlin (Sheffield: Sheffield Academic Press, 1997), 184–204.

43. Kathy Rudy, "Where Two or More Are Gathered: Using Gay Communities as a Model for Christian Sexual Ethics," in *Our Families, Our Values*, 197–216. For Rudy's full argument, see Kathy Rudy, *Sex and the Church* (Boston: Beacon Press, 1997).

FOUR

IS THERE SEX IN HEAVEN?

If biological survival is considered the essential purpose of human life, then motivations to engage in unprotected sex — which assuredly offers the possibility of shortened life — will be understood as pathological. If the possibility of other essential values and purposes are accepted, values that are not about longevity but about the content or quality of life, then unprotected sex might not be considered pathological. —Walt Odets[1]

The term "sex panic" has recently entered queer vocabulary, but according to gay historian Allan Berube, sex panics have occurred during politically conservative times for the last century.[2] Berube defines sex panic as "a moral crusade that leads to crackdowns on sexual outsiders."[3] For nearly three years, the sex panic debate has flared up into a full-scale civil war among specific segments among the gay and lesbian communities in New York City and has spread to other cities. The debate rages over issues such as public sex, police entrapments, closures of sex clubs, commercial sex establishments, circuit parties, and queer sexual culture. The war has been aired in several books, in the *New York Times*, at the 1997 and 1998 NGLTF (National Gay Lesbian Task Force) Creating Change Conferences, over the Internet, in two issues of the *Harvard Gay and Lesbian Review*, in *Lingua Franca*, on an episode of the popular show *ER*, and certainly at many gay cocktail parties.[4]

The debate has its roots in the development of neoconservative gay male figures — such as Bruce Bawer, Andrew Sullivan, Michelangelo Signorile, Larry Kramer, Gabriel Rotello, Rich Tafel of the Log Cabin

---

1. Walt Odets, *In the Shadow of the Epidemic: Being HIV-Negative in the Age of AIDS* (Durham, N.C.: Duke University Press, 1995), 205.
2. Allan Berube, "A Century of Sex Panics," in *Sex Panic!* (November 1997): 4–8.
3. Ibid., 4.
4. Gabriel Rotello, *Sexual Ecology* (New York: Dutton, 1997); Michelangelo Signorile, *Life Outside* (New York: HarperCollins, 1997); Eric Rofes, *Dry Bones Breathe* (New York: Haworth, 1998); Michael Bronksi, *The Pleasure Principle* (New York: St. Martin's Press, 1998). See Caleb Crain, "Pleasure Principles: Queer Theorists and Gay Journalists Wrestle over the Politics of Sex," *Lingua Franca* (October 1997): 26–37; *Harvard Gay and Lesbian Review* 5, no. 2 (spring 1998) and 5, no. 3 (summer 1998).

Society, and others — whose voices not only dominate *Out Magazine* and the *Advocate* but are mainstreamed into the *New Republic,* the *New York Times,* the *Washington Post,* the *Nation,* NPR (National Public Radio), *Newsweek,* and many other media forums. These gay voices speak of a "postgay" epoch when the gay movement will essentially be over as the movement is remade into a straight image. Such a degaying vision is not too surprising when we look at American politics with the emergence of postfeminism and black conservatives. While I may agree with some of their individual points on same-sex marriage and have performed a number of such marriages myself as clergy, I am alarmed by their consistent attacks on postmodernism, queer theory, and gay sexual culture. Such attacks have also been at the heart of the general cultural conservative assault on postmodernism, women's studies, queer theory, African American studies, and cultural studies. For example, Gabriel Rotello has commented, "Queer theory seeks to overturn society's traditional views on sex and sexuality."[5] Rotello does not want to accept the full consequences of queer theory, for it remains too anarchic for him and with troubling consequences.

For postgay voices, the legacy of Michel Foucault, Judith Butler, Eve Sedgwick, Michael Warner, and many others promotes an absolute relativism that comprehends liberation as promiscuity. Thus they have attacked the sexual culture created by the queer liberation movement, sustained by not only sexual activists and academic theorists but also many other segments of the queer community. Such postgay critics have narrowed their focus to public health issues of sexual promiscuity, launching a moral purity crusade to expose a frightening new problem: unprotected and multipartnered gay sex. The postgay critics are reminiscent of the unlikely alliances of the late 1980s feminist antipornography movement with the religious right.

Rotello's book *Sexual Ecology* attempts to regulate gay sexual behavior based on an ecological model. His book is the culmination of the trajectory of the piety of safer-sex campaign, begun in the mid-1980s, and it retains its moral tone. Rotello argues that gay men form an ecological niche for the breeding and spreading of HIV. Thus, he hammers away at the "condom code," the accepted belief that condoms can prevent HIV transmission and preserve the sexual liberation started by Stonewall. Rotello depicts the condom as a "technological fix," a futile effort at prevention to stem the spread of HIV, an effort that fails to address

---

5. In Dinitia Smith, "Queer Theory Entering the Literary Mainstream," *New York Times,* January 17, 1998.

the real issue of the gay male norm of multiple, concurrent partners participating in anal intercourse. He demands a rethinking and regulation of sexual behavior by gay men as a community, asking them to abandon multipartnered sexual intercourse. Neoconservatives unambiguously and too simplistically condemn such behaviors rather than trying to compassionately understand gay men's need for condomless sex. For example, Rotello narrates his witnessing an act of unprotected anal sex at Zone DK: "I witnessed a sex murder/suicide last Thursday night.... I don't know if an actual death will result from the act we witnessed, but I consider it a murder/suicide because the imperatives of AIDS tell me I must."[6] His rhetoric "murder/suicide" is inflammatory, full of moralism and indignation, hyberbolic, similar to the rhetoric from the religious right. For Rotello, the one act of unprotected anal sex is equated with the contraction of HIV; then he equates that one act of unprotected sex with death. His representation is certainly alarmist, if not simplistic. Like Andrea Dworkin, who calls for women to permanently close their thighs to men, Gabriel Rotello calls for gay men to close their buttocks to other men. But is this condemnation realistic? Do Rotello and other critics understand the psychosocial and spiritual importance of anal intercourse for gay men? I will explore the phenomenon of unprotected sex emerging within segments of the gay community. I am neither engaged in an apologetic for unprotected anal intercourse, nor am I upholding the neoconservative critique of such practices as reckless. I want to suggest that there are some spiritual issues involved in some gay men participating in unsafe practices and ask whether their behaviors may have some ethical defense. I also want to end with some observations about the dangers and the loss experienced by gay men.

"Riding bareback"

Infection rates among gay men have not declined in the last three years. A small minority of HIV-positive and HIV-negative gay men have begun to write and publicly speak about the need to engage in unprotected

---

6. See Redick's response to Rotello's comments: "Then, this one act of unprotected sex is presented not only as 'proof' that public sex venues are the site of HIV transmission but also as evidence of the immorality of 'some gay men' who practice promiscuous sex. In this way, the location of sexual practices is conflated with sexual behavior, and public sex becomes equated with unprotected sex, which then results naturally and inevitably in death" (A. Redick, "Dangerous Practices: Ideological Use of Second Wave," in *Policing Public Sex* [Boston: South End Press, 1996], 102).

anal sex, or, in the gay idiom, "skin-on-skin" or "barebacking." Bare-backing chat rooms have sprung up on the Internet as well as bareback parties, bareback seminars, and bareback clubs.[7] Gay men are making very conscious decisions to "ride bareback" and risk exposing themselves to HIV. Columnist Michelangelo Signorile brought the issue of bare-backing to national prominence with a 1997 column in *Out* magazine.[8] He claims that the number of gay men barebacking is small but grow-ing. It is impossible to gauge how many negative or positive gay men choose to engage in unprotected sexual intercourse, but the numbers are growing, to the alarm of HIV preventionists and the CDC (Centers for Disease Control). Barebacking threatens what Gabriel Rotello has labeled as gay sustainable and survivable sexual ecology.

What motives within our communities drive gay men to find the life of seronegativity less important at this time? Is it the pursuit of dangerous sex — as witnessed by dangerous liaisons in the oval office? Signorile further observes that the condom code breaks down because of what he calls the "theologies of the circuit parties and the cult of masculinity."[9] He believes that the recent generation of protease inhibitors, the cult of masculinity, and a variety of other cultural reasons have fueled the breakdown of the condom code. Gabriel Rotello, a more outspoken critic, is opposed to the gay culture of unbridled, multipartnered sex; he does not believe that condoms really work. In all his writings, he neither has anything good to say about gay anal sex nor seems to understand its importance to many gay men. This is a serious flaw in his proposal to construct a gay ecological culture.

The recent writings of Eric Rofes and Walter Odets list some of the complex psychosocial reasons why gay men are motivated to engage in unprotected anal intercourse:[10] the use of mood-altering substances, the new generation of protease inhibitors, the development of a post-exposure treatment or the morning-after drug treatment, the desire to break sexual conventions, the need for dangerous sex, survivor's guilt, love and intimacy, internalized homophobia, or the failure to see the number of deaths. I would add the feeling of immortality by gay teens

---

7. See the Xtreme Sex website: *www5.onramp.net/~tmike/xtremesex/xtreme.html.* There are dozens of "listservs," chatrooms, and websites that have sprung up overnight. It does not seem that the sensationalism surrounding the barebacking phenomenon has produced these. Rather it seems that it has triggered discussion of unspoken sexual practices already engaged in by many gay men.

8. Michelangelo Signorile, "Bareback and Reckless," *Out* (July 1997): 36–40. See also Signorile, *Life Outside,* 127.

9. Signorile, "Bareback."

10. Odets, *In the Shadow;* Rofes, *Dry Bones.*

and young adults, whose rates of seroconversion are increasing at alarming rates. From his clinical practice, psychologist Odets observed that a gay man in good mental health might willingly risk in engaging in unprotected sex. Many gay men are barebacking for no other reason than it holds significant meaning in their lives even with all its incumbent risks. Are they willfully and proudly risking their lives for the better orgasm? Or as the *San Francisco Chronicle* headlined about a gay fringe: "Healthy men are seeking unprotected sex with HIV-infected men, for the erotic thrill of communion with the deadly AIDS virus."[11] My discussions with men in St. Louis point to the fact that even in the heartland, gay men are barebacking for a series of differing reasons too complex for this exploration.

In the midst of a highly charged debate with screams of "sex fiends," "lunatic fringe," and "brainless" by neoconservatives and "condom Nazis" by sex activists, barebacking has been condemned and sensationalized by the media. I will suggest that barebacking has spiritual dimensions for some segments of the gay community. Rofes and Odets have done an adequate job in articulating the psychosocial reasons for barebacking but have left unexplored any spiritual dimensions.

Spiritual dimensions to barebacking?

Some gay men are talking about consciously choosing to engage in unprotected sex for none of the above factors. In a 1994 column in *Out,* Signorile relates a personal incident in which he met a Navy officer,

> a classic gay hunk, tall and masculine, with a buzzed haircut, razor sharp cheekbones, a body of granite, and a Texas drawl. I'll make you see God tonight, he promised me, trying to coax me to go home with him. It didn't take much for me to realize I needed a religious experience.[12]

Without any thought, Signorile engaged as the recipient in unprotected anal sex, even employing the metaphor of religious experience for his act. His confessional column was reprinted in the op-ed pages of the *New York Times.* On the other hand, queer theorist Michael Warner spoke of a series of unsafe encounters where "the quality of consciousness...was like impulse shoplifting."[13] Signorile and Warner, I need to observe,

---

11. S. Russell, "Russian Roulette Sex Parties: Rise in Gay Fringe Group's Unsafe Practices Alarms AIDS Experts," *San Francisco Chronicle,* January 29, 1999.

12. Signorile, *Life Outside,* xxxi.

13. Crain, "Pleasure Principles," 29.

are on opposites sides of the sex panic debate. Signorile subsequently explored the pressures and values leading gay men to abandon the condom code in his book *Life Outside,* while Warner seroconverting has become a spokesperson for "responsible promiscuity." As a sex activist and founding member of Sex Panic! Warner defends gay sexual culture while advocating and supporting HIV prevention efforts. He maintains the rights of gay men to make decisions for themselves.

In the article "Riding Bareback" in *POZ,* seropositive sex activist and writer Stephen Gendin penned,

> A year and a half ago at a conference, I heard a talk by a really cute positive guy on the fun of unsafe sex with other positive guys. He was beautiful, the subject was exciting, and I soon ended up getting fucked by him without a condom. When he came inside me, I was in heaven, just overjoyed. I'd had unsafe sex before, but never intentionally. Those experiences were guilt-ridden because I worried during the sex and afterward — about exposing my partner to HIV.[14]

A letter to the editor condemned Gendin's confession as a "kamikaze sex code" and as "selfish, specious musings."[15] Yes, Gendin was participating in what perhaps many have been conditioned to or would label as "kamikaze sex," but is that all that is occurring here? Let me give a few more examples before offering some explanation. Former porn star Scott O'Hara speaks of a "viral communion" in unprotected sex:

> Feeling a man's dick inside of me, condomless — that's when the sex becomes spiritual in its intensity. Communion, in the truest sense. Integral to that closeness is the knowledge that he intends to leave a piece of himself inside me; his cum, like the sex itself, has a psychological value, beyond anything physical. Recognizing that power is one of the ways I defy this virus, I believe in exchanging bodily fluids, not wedding rings.[16]

For O'Hara, the risks of unprotected anal intercourse have a spiritual value that have more compelling power than death itself. Is this the heroism of a modern-day sexual outlaw? Or is it just reckless irresponsibility? Or are there any other explanations?

14. Stephen Gendin, "Riding Bareback," *POZ* (June 1997): 66.
15. Henry Wallengren, letter to the editor, *POZ* (August 1997); Robert Marra, "Bareback and Reckless," *POZ* (August 1997).
16. Scott O'Hara, "Viral Communion," *POZ* (November 1997): 69.

There are some significant elements lost in the rhetoric of the emotional debate between postgay voices and Sex Panic! Spirituality includes body, sexuality, and self. That sexuality is intrinsic to our experience of God as men and as gay men should hardly be surprising to us, though erotophobic religion has tried to separate sexuality from spirituality. Sexuality expresses ineffable meanings between people that cannot adequately be expressed in any other fashion. This may be one of the gifts of gay spirituality to erotophobic religious traditions. Many gay men view sexuality as a necessary and authentic part of their spirituality, for sex brings not only group solidarity but also a sense of transcendence.[17] The power of sex is a strong drive (and I might add a spiritual instinct) within gay men. Former *New Republic* editor Andrew Sullivan, who envisions himself as the public spokesperson for the new right in the gay community, writes about the spiritual power that sexual experience contains for him, enough to risk seroconverting:

> Sexual experience, from the beginning, seemed to me almost a sacrament of human existence, a truly transforming experience in the adventure of being human; an insight into both what love may possibly be and what death almost certainly is.... And to physically invade another person, and to be invaded, to merge with another body, to abandon the distance that makes our everyday lives a constant approximation of loneliness, these experiences have never ceased to save me. Far from seeing them as a simple negation of spirituality, I instinctively found them to be windows into it.[18]

For many gay men like Andrew Sullivan and myself, spirituality involves loving sexually, and they find authentic meaning embodied in their passions and their loves. Gay men are willing to risk their health for the sake of a viral communion that encompasses elements of a transcendent spirituality of sexuality, and for some gay men, seroconversion becomes a means of solidarity or fitting into the gay male community.[19]

---

17. Robert Barzan, ed., *Sex and Spirit: Exploring Gay Men's Spirituality* (San Francisco: White Crane, 1995).

18. Andrew Sullivan, *Love Undetectable: Notes on Friendship, Sex, and Survival* (New York: Alfred A. Knopf, 1998), 57.

19. In an editorial entitled "Choosing HIV?" Aiden Shaw writes about how he wanted to become HIV. "I romanticized AIDS: It was tragic and saint like, rebellious and dynamic. So nothing felt so deeply right as having sex I was told not to, doing it in a way that was dangerous and knowing....And so I got HIV, as I'd wanted. I laughed when I was told. It was a relief. Everything fell into place" (Aiden Shaw, "Choosing HIV?" *POZ* [November 1997]: 51).

Sex activist Eric Rofes has argued that anal sex is what gives meaning to who you are as a gay man.[20] His comments have a significance that deserves further probing. Many gay men understand and experience anal sex as being as important as vaginal sex to heterosexual men. It has interpersonal, psychological, and spiritual meaning for gay men. Anal penetration, so stigmatized by the term "sodomy," horrifies many heterosexual men. In his provocative essay "Is the Rectum a Grave?" Leo Bersani notes that AIDS has reinforced the heterosexual association of anal sex with self-annihilation and death.[21] Bersani further contends that gay sex, especially anal sex, has not only a subversive potential to parody the notion of "machismo" but also the potentiality of shattering male subjectivity in a "*jouissance* of exploded limits."[22] He writes, "Male homosexuality advertises the risk of the sexual as the risk of self-dismissal, of losing sight of the self, and in so doing it proposes and dangerously represents *jouissance* as a mode of *ascesis*."[23] Gay men find an effacement of the boundaries of self, an ecstatic disruption of self that Georges Bataille has linked to the heart of mysticism and eroticism.[24] This *jouissance* ("pleasure in orgasm") in anal intercourse represents an important element in the spirituality of many gay males, for it effaces self-boundaries in a communion open to spiritual possibilities for gay men.

Men lying joyfully on their backs with their feet ecstatically in the air or in a variety of receptive postures arouses fears among heterosexual men, but for gay men, it signifies receptivity, trust, intimacy, vulnerability, and spirituality. Anal sex carries profound human as well as spiritual meanings. Penetrating another man or getting penetrated by another are powerful, intimate, and spiritual experiences. Though necessary, HIV prevention efforts and educational campaigns have often had the effect of pathologizing anal sex without any serious discussion or understanding of how valuable or meaningful it may be for gay men. The pathologizing effects of risk-management campaigns and the denial of

---

20. Eric Rofes was quoted in the *San Francisco Examiner*: "There is a dawning realization that gay men are engaging in unprotected anal intercourse not because they're drunk, or due to self-hatred, but because sex is a meaningful act.... Sex acts are a major part of what constitutes your identity.... [A]nal sex was seen as an expendable act" (in David Dalton, "Sex Panics: Gay Group Think Promotes Murderous Irresponsibility," *San Francisco Examiner,* January 12, 1998, A 23).

21. Leo Bersani, "Is the Rectum a Grave?" in *AIDS: Cultural Analysis, Cultural Activism,* ed. Douglas Crimp (Cambridge, Mass.: MIT Press, 1988), 222.

22. Ibid.

23. Ibid.

24. Georges Bataille, *Eroticism, Death, and Sensuality,* trans. Mary Dalwood (San Francisco: City Lights, 1986), 104.

speaking about the human importance of the exchange of bodily fluids have impacted the sexuality as well as the spirituality of gay men.
The exchange of semen is often experienced as a vital expression of
intimacy; for gay male relationships it becomes a signifier of powerful
intimacy and human connection, a defiance of the procreative privilege
of normative heterosexuality, and an expression of our freedom. One
barebacker stated:

> There's no better way to bond with a man than to give or receive
> sperm. A lot of bottoms take it into their bodies and keep it as
> a way of remembering the sex. They want to feel it inside them
> and keep experiencing that closeness. It's a physical expression of
> intimacy.[25]

The exchange of seminal fluids does carry the risk of infection, and in
the earlier pre-protease era it carried the possibility of death. But safe
sex has exacted a heavy toll on many gay men. Walt Odets reports a
client explaining, "In sex, touch is the most important thing to me, and
that means skin. That's how I connect to another person. I find this
whether I'm getting fucked or doing the fucking. It's almost the same
thing to me: no skin, no connection."[26] Robert, HIV-negative, spoke
honestly about his sexual relationship with his HIV-positive lover Mark:

> Well, Mark and I mostly have safe sex and sometimes we don't. I
> am more into fucking without condoms than he is — he is trying
> to protect me mostly — and when we do it, it is so powerful and
> important for us....Sex for me is about — I'm talking about sex
> with someone I love — is about holding back nothing, about being
> completely into your feelings and into the other person and his
> feelings.[27]

Here Robert speaks of holding nothing back, sharing completely with
his lover. He is consciously willing to risk infection for the sake of sexual union. Health professionals and clergy, I believe, must take the
statements of the above men into serious consideration.

Are there elements of an authentic spirituality in these statements?
Theologian Richard Hardy writes, "Authentic spirituality...destroys the
body-spirit split to engage us in a life which values and enhances

25. Michael Scarce, "A Ride on the Wild Side," *POZ* (February 1999): 4–5
(*www.thebody.com/poz/features/2_99/bareback.html*).
26. Odets, *In the Shadow*, 196.
27. Cited in Richard Hardy, *Loving Men: Gay Partners, Spirituality, and AIDS* (New York:
Continuum, 1997), 201–2.

bodiliness and interrelationship."[28] Safe-sex campaigns proscribed the exchange of body fluids. But what is the cost to gay men? Do health officials really understand what anal intercourse means for gay men? Do gay clergy understand the felt need of gay men to bareback? My brother, who was HIV-positive and heterosexual, and his wife found it an emotional burden to use condoms. Something in sexual love-making was lost.

Unprotected sex may also embed primal desires to love another man in ways that feel powerful, intimate, and spiritual. I would argue that Robert is speaking about the spirituality of love-making that renders protected sex less important than the risk of contracting the HIV virus. For many gay men, anal intercourse is an important expression, even a spiritual expression, of intimacy. The intimacy of ejaculating in a partner leaves tangible, albeit transient, evidence of intimacy, connection, and a profound exchange. Except for gay erotica, gay men have not spoken or written about what it means to ejaculate into another man or to experience the ejaculation of a partner within you. I would argue that the taboo of theological silence must be broken, and the subject must be openly discussed. To my knowledge, Jeffrey Hopkins and Michael Kelly are the only gay men to speak and write about the integration of anal intercourse into spiritual practice.[29] There is room for much more theological exploration of anal intercourse within the spirituality of gay men.

With the risk of self-confession, I will use myself as text, not place myself as judge. I lived with a man for sixteen years in a wonderful relationship. When we were both tested for HIV in 1990, Frank tested positively while I tested negatively. Mixed antibody status created a crisis for both of us. Frank dealt with living with HIV while seronegativity was personally difficult for me. I was deeply conflicted by being uninfected; perhaps it was proleptic survivor's guilt and anticipation of surviving him. I grew up Catholic, and I know what guilt is. However, it was more than guilt, for I wanted to share Frank's fate. I bonded myself in a covenant, giving up my active ministry as a Jesuit priest. I desired to be in solidarity with him. Though Frank generally refused to engage in condomless sex with me, I was only too willing to engage in condomless sex.

---

28. Ibid., 29.

29. Jeffrey Hopkins, *Sex, Orgasm, and the Mind of Clear Light* (Berkeley, Calif.: North Atlantic Books, 1998); Michael Kelly, *The Erotic Contemplative,* 6 vols. (video series) (Oakland, Calif.: EroSpirit Institute, 1994).

Let me candidly speak about the spirituality of our love-making. We found God in the midst of ecstatic sex or our love-making. Anal intercourse disrupted the boundaries of ourselves; we felt the spiritual charge of the love of God in the *jouissance* of our bodies entangled in pleasure and choreographed in a union that embodied transcendent possibilities. We both resented condoms; they formed a latex barrier to personal and spiritual communion that we so often felt in condomless love-making. Barebacking had been part of our spiritual prayer and our union from its very beginning. I certainly longed for viral communion with Frank, to share his fate. (Only intimate lovers, I believe, can understand that last statement.) He maintained a Christian ethic born from a lifetime commitment of social responsibility "not to harm" and his loving care for myself. I was willing to engage in unprotected sex for the sake of love.

There were, however, special occasions when we negotiated unsafe sex. I initiated discussion and prayer, and we applied Ignatian rules of discernment, the contemplative tradition that shaped our spirituality.[30] We discerned after much prayer and discussion over several months that unsafe sex was a necessary and an all-encompassing part of our spirituality of love-making. Sexual union was integral to us as fully functioning individuals and as a couple, and it was vital to our religious experience of God. We made a conscious choice to engage in unprotected sex to sustain our union and our experience of God, and those were moments of deep spiritual love, trust, vulnerability, and giving. Those moments of unprotected love-making were treasured moments that I carry still with me. It was undertaken within a rational process of discernment and prayer. It was negotiated, premeditated, and consensual. Critics would brand such practices as reckless and foolhardy, yet we were fully aware of the risks to both of us. Thus, I understand the statements about finding spiritual transcendence and communion with a lover, and I maintain even ten years after Frank's death the right to make a rational decision to place myself at risk. While he generally worked out a loving concern for my survivability, I worked out an ethic of solidarity. There were times we compromised our stances out of love for another, and if you wonder, I am still HIV-negative. If I had seroconverted, I was prepared to assume the full consequences for my actions of love-making. I was willing to

---

30. John McNeill defines the discernment of spirits: "To discern spirits is to listen to our own hearts. Our God dwells within us, and the only way to become one with God is to become one with our authentic self. If any action we undertake brings with it a deepening of peace, joy, and fulfillment, then we can be sure what we are doing is right for us. To be able to discern spirits we must have made a total commitment of ourselves to God and be willing to do whatever God asks of us" (John McNeill, *Freedom, Glorious Freedom* [Boston: Beacon Press, 1995], 20–21).

risk everything, life included, for the man that I loved and for whom I gave up active ministry as a Catholic priest and friends. It was not a difficult decision, for it was the same decision that I made years before to generously give my all to God, and part of that call was to give my all to my lover.

Ethics of barebacking: some exploratory thoughts

Are there any ethical principles for justifying barebacking? In an article in *POZ*, Michael Scarce gives a set of guidelines for gay men who intend not to use condoms for anal intercourse. These are meant as noncondom strategies to reduce harm for "sex without limits, a lack of critical thinking and short-sighted hedonism."[31] They are not meant as ethical guidelines for barebacking. Sexual risk or going bareback is nothing new to gay men, for it is an ethical choice that both HIV-positive and HIV-negative gay men, monogamous couples, and couples with mixed antibody status have faced for many years within the AIDS pandemic.

Gabriel Rotello argues for a gay sexual ecology to keep infection rates low in the gay community. I would characterize his ethics as the "rhetoric of communal survivability." He calls for the curtailment of the number of casual partners and advises abandonment of anal sex entirely. But one of the failures of his ecological ethics is his reduction of sexuality to the biological facts while gay sexuality is much more than biology. Neither does Rotello adequately address the psychological, sociological, or spiritual contexts of gay male sexuality; nor does he address the importance that anal sex has for gay men.[32] Rotello glosses over the emotional, psychological, and spiritual needs of gay men whose feelings of love for their partners lead them to engage in unsafe intercourse. His advice to abandon anal sex (including anal sex with condoms) and promiscuity entirely, I believe, expresses an internalized homophobia (if not a form of biological fundamentalism). What would be the reaction if he encouraged African males to abandon sexual intercourse with women? How realistic a proposal would that be?

Rotello locates the spread of HIV in the gay ecological ethics of communal survivability, but is survival the end-all of our being? Can we base an ethical response on such communal survivability without further comprehending the complex motivations of gay male sex? Rotello's proposal appears to me ethically flat because his understanding of human

---

31. Scarce, "A Ride on the Wild Side," 10.
32. Rotello, *Sexual Ecology*, 27.

sexuality is reductionist. He might have offered a more cogent argument if it was based on individual responsibility, a phenomenological analysis of gay sex, and the responsibility "not to harm." Because these elements are missing in his arguments, his work lacks the ethical persuasiveness that it might have. Don't get me wrong! I believe that there is some merit to Rotello's basic argument, minus the rhetoric and the media publicity promoted by his media stunts in a New York bathhouse with photographers and the counter-reaction of Sex Panic!

Let me explore a possible ethical solution. Clinical psychologist Walt Odets presents a position that counters Rotello's ecological rhetoric of gay communal survivability. Odets notes how the desire of some gay men not to survive implicitly threatens the shared social descriptions of reality that allow an optimism about a personal and communal future. Odets speaks of culturally sanctioned deaths, described as altruistic rather than pathological, such as the captain going down with the ship, the soldier who runs headlong into enemy fire to save a friend, or doctors and nurses at risk during times of communicable, fatal plagues: "That the gay man, profoundly identified with his community, often feels such allegiances and identifications is understandable. The experience of a loving partner with HIV powerfully interacts with the social identification in this regard and intensifies the importance of feelings of identification and allegiance."[33] That partners may feel a stronger commitment to solidarity with spouses with HIV is nothing new. That they feel it is important to engage in condomless love-making can be an ethical decision; they do not behave according to an ethics of survivability. Could this be an ethic of solidarity and love?

Sometimes communal survivability is an insufficient reason for ethical behavior. While I was in high school, the Vietnamese Buddhist monk Thich Quang Duc, a young Buddhist woman named Nhat Chi Mai, and other Buddhists immolated themselves, and I still remember those acts. I was shocked by such an extreme disregard for their own lives, and I wondered whether they were like the early Christian martyrs who resisted the Roman state. These Vietnamese Buddhists immolated themselves in order to awaken people to the violence of the Vietnam War and to educate people for peace. The Buddhist monk and writer Thich Nhat Hanh understood their actions as a powerful and compassionate attempt of Buddhists to reach the hearts of people. Certainly, these actions challenged my own teenage ethic of survivability, but their extreme actions shocked me to resist and demonstrate against the war. Thich Nhat Hanh

---

33. Odets, *In the Shadow*, 207.

writes, "Every action for peace requires someone to exhibit the courage to challenge the violence and inspire love. Love and sacrifice always set up a chain reaction of love and sacrifice. Like the crucifixion of Jesus, Thich Quang Duc's act expressed the unconditional willingness to suffer for the awakening of others."[34]

Love and sacrifice may take many compassionate forms of responsibility and irresponsibility. Some may argue that survivability is the all-encompassing ethic, but it certainly wasn't an ethic that Jesus espoused when he knowingly went to Jerusalem and acted up in the Temple. There were more compelling reasons than survivability that brought Jesus to Jerusalem.

Survivability may not be the highest value for some, and the desire to risk death for a greater value of love and solidarity threatens Rotello's utopian ethic based on a personal and communal future. While Odets presents an understanding of gay men who place themselves at risk, there are some points that might be arguably raised about the ethics of barebacking. I want to juxtapose Rotello's ethics of survivability not with sexual rebellion but with those gay men who participate in unsafe sex for a genuine need for spiritual transcendence and love.

I would argue for an ethic of "negotiated risk," but with some qualifications. Though some gay men espouse an ethic of solidarity and love as compelling reasons to ride bareback, I believe that it is necessary also to speak of responsibility, negotiated safety, and decision making. As an HIV-negative person, I have the right to expose myself to HIV just as I may choose to use drugs or drink or attempt a dangerous stunt. There is always a risk to sexual (as well as spiritual) experience, and some gay men have acted ethically when, fully aware of the consequences of their decision, they have ridden bareback. I maintain that the choice is an individual decision, and one needs to consciously weigh the risks for each sexual encounter. There may be mitigating values that compel some gay men to consciously judge that personal and spiritual reasons for engaging in barebacking can have greater weight than an ethics of individual responsibility and avoiding harm to others. Barebacking may be a conscious, rational, and even spiritual decision for a variety of reasons, but the reasons need to be personally compelling. For example, my current spouse of nine years and myself do not use condoms in our love-making. Theoretically, should David or I engage in sex with some-

---

34. Thich Nhat Hanh, *Love in Action: Writings on Nonviolent Social Change* (Berkeley, Calif.: Parallax Press, 1993), 43.

one outside of our relationship, it would be certainly irresponsible to participate in condomless anal sex with one another.

But do HIV-positive men have the right to expose HIV-negative partners to the virus? It is often claimed that HIV-positive men may reinfect or superinfect one another with more virulent strains of HIV and thus put themselves at greater risk. For HIV-positive and -negative gay men, there is generally the individual responsibility "not to harm," not to harm themselves or others. Using condoms is the safest way of having anal intercourse, a realistic harm-reduction strategy that Rotello proscribes. For my spouse, Frank, the responsibility not to harm or to put me at risk was a value that he generally maintained. As I mentioned earlier, it was only in honest discussion and discernment — involving why I personally felt the need to engage in barebacking and why he did not want to put me at risk for HIV — that we brokered a solution. Though he despised the latex barrier as much as I did, he understood my reasons and shared a number of them. We arrived at a compromise: we engaged in unsafe sex on special occasions, but Frank would not penetrate me without a condom. It was a form of risk management, weighing possibilities and probabilities. For both of us, it was a moral decision; it was sane, certainly consensual, and definitely spiritual. It was certainly not safe, but the relationship values that brought us together some fourteen years earlier were celebrated in a depth of love. For some folks, our actions were reckless; for us, they were the results of the demands of a love grounded in penetrative engulfment. And I have no regrets over the decision that we made.

Postscript

It is over two decades since the CDC reported the first outbreak of HIV among gay men. Bareback chat rooms and websites have emerged in the years since the discovery of combination therapies. The latest reports alarmingly indicate rising rates of HIV infection among young gay men. While I argue for ethical decision making in barebacking in this essay, barebacking is a real issue that confronts the gay community currently. Until HIV-prevention efforts allow gay men a forum to speak about the real value, *jouissance,* and the loss of condomless anal sex, there will be no sustainable prevention.

I believe that queer church groups have the opportunity, if they can let go of any residual erotophobia and moralism, to provide safe space for gay men to come together and openly discuss the issue of barebacking. Gay men need a safe-space place (1) to discuss the reasons they will or will not participate in barebacking, (2) to explore truthfully and openly negotiate risks to themselves and to others, (3) and to discern God's guidance in their actions and moral decisions. There have been no forums or support groups for men to speak about the slippage in their sex practices except in the barebacking chat rooms, in condemnatory articles in the press, or in scattered statements by out barebackers. Where can gay men speak about these issues and their feelings? It is politically incorrect to carry on these discussions.

Many gay men, both HIV-positive and HIV-negative, need to have a space to grieve the loss of unprotected sex and dream of a day when they can once again engage in unprotected anal sex. I believe that the queer churches have the opportunity to create such space and support groups for gay men to discuss the range of issues and counter the internalized homophobia and the moralism that do not brook any discussion of condomless sex.

The contrary gay moralist Andrew Sullivan wrote about a personal accident in unsafe sex, describing the relief of finally having real sex and breaking a barrier.[35] He has often castigated gay men for their reckless behaviors of barebacking, but the power of unprotected anal sex is so intense that Sullivan himself was discovered soliciting barebacking sex or what he has called "real sex" on the Internet.[36] The issue is so compelling and so powerful for gay men — whatever their ideological backgrounds — that reintroducing the dimension of spirituality and discernment into the ethical storm may help gay men to better negotiate their risks. When I read Sullivan's description of unprotected sex in *Love Undetectable*, it stands in contrast to his deliberate decision to solicit men on the Internet for barebacking sex. Maybe I resonate with Sullivan's words: "There was so much joy in it and so much sadness that it is difficult to express what it was that we actually felt, and since it could not be put it into words, we did not put into words. There are times when only bodies can express what minds cannot account for."[37] The pain of survival in the midst of death expresses a profound grieving that can only find solace in breaking the condom barrier for intimate touch. God, I believe, is incarnate in those deepest moments of truth, pain, grief, and love.

---

35. Andrew Sullivan, *Love Undetectable: Notes on Friendship, Sex, and Survival* (Washington, D.C.: Knopf, 1997), 60.

36. Michelangelo Signorile, "Virtually Reckless: The Contradictory Faces of Andrew Sullivan," *LGNY,* May 26, 2001.

37. Sullivan, *Love Undetectable,* 60.

FIVE

CHALLENGING PROCREATIVE PRIVILEGE BY QUEERING FAMILIES

Sexuality is part of our behavior. It's part of our world freedom. Sexuality is something we create. It is our own creation. . . . We have to understand that with our desires go new forms of relationships, new forms of love, new forms of creation. Sex is not a fatality; it's a possibility for creative life.

—Michel Foucault[1]

The second wave of queer liberation has concentrated on the right to marriage and family. This new emphasis on marriage and family rights has placed translesbigays on a collision course with religious extremists' family-values campaigns and their adept use of a procreative norm to judge queer unions. The Netherlands has recognized same-sex marriage while many other Western countries — Canada, France, Germany, Switzerland, and the Scandinavian nations — offer some version of civil unions. Only the State of Vermont in the United States offers the recognition of civil unions to same-sex couples. More than twenty-five thousand U.S. companies, universities, and municipal governments offer domestic-partner benefits.

In a fund-raising letter, Beverly La Haye, president of Concerned Women of America, wrote, "Radical homosexuals in America today do not want to be simply left alone. Instead they have a hidden agenda to legally force you and every other American to accept their depraved lifestyle."[2] The Christian right's worst fear was realized in the 1990s. In May 1993, the Hawaii Supreme Court ruled that the state's refusal to issue civil licenses to three same-sex couples under the state's marriage law violated the constitutional guarantee of equal protection. The Hawaii Supreme Court ruling led to a firestorm of legal activity and

---

1. Cited in Didier Eribon, *Michel Foucault* (Cambridge, Mass.: Harvard University Press, 1991), 315.

2. Cited in Sara Diamond, *Not by Politics Alone: The Enduring Influence of the Christian Right* (New York: Guilford Press, 1998), 156.

grassroots activism during the next couple years to defend against the legalization of same-sex marriages in other states. The Christian Coalition and the Mormon and Catholic Churches poured monies into a ballot initiative to block same-sex marriage in Hawaii. By 1996, fifteen states passed bills that denied legal recognition of same-sex unions. Rev. Louis Sheldon and the creators of the video *Gay Agenda* produced another video, *The Ultimate Target of the Gay Agenda: Same Sex Marriage,* that was sent by many of the organizations of the Christian right to state legislatures and the U.S. Congress. The consistent theme of this video was that if same-sex marriages are legalized, then heterosexual monogamy and the traditional family would end.

In the heat of the 1996 election, the U.S. Congress passed the Defense of Marriage Act (DOMA), which permitted states to bar same-sex marriages and defined marriage for federal purposes, such as for the IRS, as the union of a man and a woman. The Christian right intended to make this the primary issue of the presidential election, but President Clinton signed DOMA to make it a nonissue — an action he took in the midst of his extramarital affair with Monica Lewinski. DOMA attempted to nullify the impact of any ruling by the Hawaii Circuit Court or any state court that might hold that same-sex partners were constitutionally entitled to legal recognition.

Queer marriage challenges the moral universe of many conservative Christian churches, challenges everything that they hold sacred and everything upon which their power rests. Keith Fourner, executive director of the American Center for Law and Justice, counters:

> Homosexual marriage directly attacks the family, which is the most vital cell in society. The family is the first government, the first church, and the first school. We must not allow this vital cell, the rock upon which society is built, to be inculturated with a perversion that will destroy it, and with it the future of our children and grandchildren.[3]

Compare Fourner's use of family rhetoric with that of Reverend Gino Concetti, a staff theologian for the Vatican daily paper *L'Osservatore Romano* and spokesman for the pope. In anticipation of the Dutch government's recognition of same-sex marriage, Concetti wrote:

> Homosexuals are naturally incapable of assuring the paternal and maternal image with which a child has need to grow up healthy and

---

3. Cited in ibid., 171.

balanced. . . . In modern society, there's already an army of children who are suffering because of the disintegration of the family. With adoption by homosexuals, that army will be destined to grow.[4]

Both Fourner and the Vatican spokesman irrationally argue that children will be harmed by the recognition of same-sex marriages. However, psychological studies of children of queer parents have demonstrated that they suffer no adverse effects.

Translesbigay people are openly relating, raising children, and demanding official recognition of their partners as spouses. The current push for domestic partnerships, civil unions in Vermont, and marital rights challenges the narrow definition of family as two biological parents who are legally married with children. Interestingly enough, less than 20 percent of the U.S. population are part of families that meet that definition.

In California, the Mormon Church, the Catholic Church, and the fundamentalist churches have formed an unholy alliance to actively contribute millions of dollars to support Prop 22, an anti-same-sex marriage measure by state Senator Pete Knight (Republican, Palmdale). The Protection of Marriage Initiative states simply that "only a marriage between a man and a woman is valid or recognized in California." While California does not recognize same-sex marriages, the Knight initiative attempted to make any such recognition harder. The same unholy coalition between the Catholic hierarchy and the religious right contributed monies and ecclesial support to the Nebraska ballot Initiative 416, also called the Defense of Marriage Amendment. It amends the Nebraska Constitution to say that only marriage between a man and a woman is valid and that civil unions and domestic partnerships are not valid. The measure was overkill and punitive, for it also hurts the children of queer parents by denying them medical insurance benefits.

These defense initiatives have culminated in a proposed ten-year campaign to amend the U.S. Constitution to deny translesbigays legal recognition of their unions. On July 12, 2001, conservative scholars and religious leaders, including black ministers, held a press conference to announce an initiative to pass a proposed Twenty-Eighth Amendment to ban same-sex marriage. Such a proposed amendment would overturn local and state statutes that allowed civil unions of same-sex partners, their adoption of children, and their right to be foster parents. It would

---

4. "Vatican Paper Decries Promotion of Homosexuality," *CWNews* (December 1996) (*www.cwnews.com/browse/1996/12/3270.htm*).

also deny the extension of domestic partnership benefits to same-sex couples.

Narrow definitions, whether from the Christian political right or from antifamily queers themselves, marginalize a number of families in America: singles, single parents, divorced and remarried persons, extended families, ethnic families, and all other families of choice. The emergence of same-sex unions in the late 1970s and early 1980s pushed queer couples in the direction of family roles and the creation of families. For gay men, AIDS may have accelerated the emergence of pair-bonded relationships. The Right to Marry Movement has begun the work of mainstreaming the idea of equal marriage rights, and it has broader social implications for foster-parent adoptions, custody and visitation, and second-parent adoptions. It is intimately connected to the queer movement for family rights and recognitions.

The Christian churches use procreativity as a weapon to argue theologically against the acceptance of same-sex relationships and, by extension, against the formation of queer families. The procreative bias of Christianity and its imprint on Western culture dissociate queers from family by defining us as outside of procreativity. While rejecting the nuclear family as normative for all, queer folks undermine the idea of family as a biological kinship unit, as well as the notion of procreativity. Queering procreativity is a deconstructive process for expanding and redefining family in ways that maintain our rights to difference, equality, family, and sexual partnership. Queering families, moreover, has more biblical precedents in the Hebrew and Christian Scriptures than the notion of traditional family values.[5]

Procreative privilege

Most Christian churches identify homosexuality with unadulterated pleasure, threatening the traditional Judeo-Christian view of marriage and family and violating the procreative norm of marriage. Part of the difficulty lies in the separation of pleasure from procreation. This separation results from the Christian separation of eros from agape and the subsequent devaluation of sexual love-making as a value in itself in favor of reproduction. Conservative Christian critics of domestic-partnership legislation and ecclesial blessing of same-sex unions view

---

5. Robert E. Goss, "Queering Procreative Privilege: Coming Out as Families," in *Our Families, Our Values: Snapshots of Queer Kinship,* ed. Robert E. Goss and Amy Adams Squire Strongheart (New York: Harrington Park Press, 1997), 8–12.

the primary purpose of marriage as procreation. Since translesbigays participate in nonprocreative love-making, they cannot marry and participate in the procreative purpose of marriage. Same-sex unions are unfit to bless because they do not conform to the procreative norm of marriage, an openness to produce children. The Evangelical Alliance in the United Kingdom has recently extended this line of argumentation to the opposition to transsexual marriages, whether same-sex or opposite-sex unions. The Evangelical Alliance fears that the recognition of transsexual marriages within the European Union will subsequently be incorporated into British law.[6] For traditional Catholic theology, homosexuality renders the connection between the unitive and procreative aspects of sexuality arbitrary. Moreover, some Catholics argue that same-sex marriage is "hostile to the regeneration of the female body and to the symbolism of social regeneration in which the body is necessarily linked and has, historically, given rise."[7] This point of view stresses women's unique capacities to create life and the procreative function of marriage, but ultimately this perspective supports patriarchal notions of marriage, failing to respect women's reproductive choices, control over their bodies, and their call to ordination.

Procreativity is the central symbol of Christian marriage, and the linkage of sex, marriage, and procreativity provides the foundation for the moral condemnation of homosexuality. It becomes the basis for interpreting the covenant theologies of the Hebrew and Christian Scriptures.[8] Procreativity also forms the central norm for judging same-sex unions as not meeting the conditions of marriage and queer families as deviating from traditional families. While society and churches have a vested interest in stable, committed relationships for the rearing of children, they refuse to recognize same-sex unions can be procreative and different-styled families can be procreative expressions of love. Their restrictive definitions of marriage and family exclude many configurations of relationships and families.

Procreationism is a Christian theological reduction of the purpose of human sexuality to reproduction. It disdains all forms of sexual

---

6. Jonathan Petre and David Bamber, "Transsexual Weddings Are Condemned," electronic telegraph (May 14, 2000), no. 1815 (*www.pfc.org.uk/news/2000/ea-dt1.htm*).

7. Jean Bethke-Elshtain, "Against Gay Marriage," *Commonweal*, November 22, 1991, 686.

8. Chris Glaser, "Are Gay Unions Christian Covenants?" in *Caught in the Crossfire*, ed. S. B. Geiss and D. E. Messer (Nashville: Abingdon Press, 1994), 132–40. Contrast with the claims in J. Stott, "Homosexual Partnerships: Why Same Sex Relationships Are Not a Christian Option," *Involvement* (1995): 215–24.

expression except penile-vaginal intercourse within heterosexual marriage. One evangelical theologian, Thomas Schmidt, writes, "We cannot understand homosexuality, then, simply as a variant of sexuality along the lines of childlessness or celibacy. It is an expression of sexuality contrary to heterosexuality, involving opposing views of the interdependent values of reproduction, complementarity, and responsibility."[9] For Schmidt and many other Christians, queer sexuality proclaims an independence from the procreative model of marriage and thus threatens the traditional Christian definition of family.

It is ironic that the early Jesus movement, originally an antifamily movement, has become the defender of the nuclear family, for which many conservative Christians claim a biblical basis. The family-values debate is a bogus argument attempting to incite and excite opposition to alternative families. In her history of families over the last two millennia and the making of modern families, Rosemary Ruether observes, "Family values is a misleading and partisan term, used by groups that champion a particular model of family — specifically, one based on male headship and female subordination."[10] Family values represent partisan politics and ideologies that support male hegemony and orthodox heterosexuality.

The current debate pits the traditional family values of the Christian political right against what it labels as "antifamily" forces. Underlying the debate on traditional family values is the fallacious assumption that queers and families are mutually exclusive groups, set apart without any overlap. Many churches render our families either invisible or abominable. In a wider cultural context, the Christian right has made a programmatic attack on working women; reproductive rights; and the families of ethnic and racial minorities, queers, and the poor, under the slogan of "traditional family values." Their arguments promote an antisexual mentality, obscured by the rhetoric of "family values."

The Christian right suspects that we are subverting the nuclear family, which is the building block for a theocratic society. Most churches claim that the family cannot survive the open social presence of gays, lesbians, bisexuals, and transsexuals. In the 1980s, gay historian Dennis Altman wrote the following about the real threat: "It is homosexuals who are prospecting the frontiers of new possibilities. The growing

9. Thomas E. Schmidt, *Straight or Narrow* (Downers Grove, Ill.:, InterVarsity Press, 1995), 51.

10. Rosemary Radford Ruether, *Christianity and the Making of the Modern Family* (Boston: Beacon Press, 2000), 3.

preoccupation of society as a whole with sex, the collapse of old beliefs and standards, means that the very outlaw status of the homosexual
makes him or her a model of new possibilities that has meaning for
others."[11] Queer folks expose the myth of the nuclear family as the only
model of family, and their attempts to resignify the family engenders an
incredible threat because they defy the customary assumptions about
what constitutes family and pluralize the notion of family.

Just as procreative privilege is used to define and restrict marriage,
so it is used to define and restrict what constitutes a family. In *Bowers v.
Hardwick,* Justice Byron R. White concludes, "No connection between
family, marriage, or procreation on the one hand and homosexual
activity on the other hand has been demonstrated."[12] Justice White erro-
neously bases his legal decision on what he considers the long-standing
procreative traditions of marriage and family within Judaism and Christianity. Thus, procreative privilege underpins the Christian notion of
marriage and family, but it is widely construed for heterosexuals and
narrowly applied to deny the social and religious standing of queer
relationships.

Procreationism thus becomes the political doctrine of traditional family values. It refuses to understand any variant of sexuality outside of
marriage. Most Christian churches refuse to understand homosexuality
as a variant of sexuality along the lines of childlessness or celibacy.
Churches sanction the marriage of infertile heterosexual couples or
couples who intend to remain childless, and so they are logically incon-
sistent when they use the doctrine of procreationism to deny the legal
and ecclesial recognition of same-sex couples. Many married couples
who practice some form of birth control do not believe that they must
be open to procreation each time when they engage in love-making.

For many conservative Christians, queer sexuality is an expression
of sexuality contrary to heterosexuality, offering an opposing view of
the independent values of reproduction, complementarity, and responsibility. Personal fulfillment and the reduction of human sexuality to
pleasure are often used as charges against queers who are accused of
not engaging in procreativity and thereby of violating or becoming independent of the creative designs of God. This charge results from a
narrow procreationism that restricts procreativity to biologicalism and
the literal reproduction of human life. Human sexuality is far more than

---

11. Dennis Altman, *The Homosexualization of America* (Boston: Beacon Press, 1983), 172.
12. Cited in Kath Weston, *Families We Choose: Lesbians, Gays, Kinship* (New York:
Columbia University Press, 1991), 208.

the biological connection of bodies. Procreationism is not procreativity, for procreativity, I will argue, includes human reproduction but is not limited to it. It includes notions of social reproduction, renewal, and transformation.

Protestant arguments for limiting the definition of marriage result from a notion of complementarity of the sexes and its conflation with the biblical norm of covenant. Catholic arguments on marriage, on the other hand, are primarily drawn from a natural-law tradition of human sexuality. That tradition maintains the plumbing theory of sexual organs: the penis in the vagina is the natural form of sexual intercourse because the sexual organs "fit" and were intended for that purpose. Protestant and Catholic arguments for limiting marriage suffer from literalism: a biblical fundamentalism or natural-law literalism. Both fail to understand either the metaphoric quality of biblical traditions or the metaphoric dimensions of human sexuality. Both fail to grasp the metaphoric and inclusive dimensions of human procreativity within sexual love-making.

I do not dispute the value of families or Christian marriage and their procreativity, but I advance the argument for blessing same-sex unions (as well as transgendered unions) and welcoming queer families by broadening the notion of procreativity. To charge that same-sex unions are unable to transmit life does not mean that they are neither life-affirming nor life-producing. Translesbigay unions, however, can be covenants that are just as loving as the unions of heterosexual couples. Heterosexual unions are not the only covenanted relationships that are procreative. In fact, same-sex unions can be procreative and regenerative and deserve the social recognitions of marriage and family afforded heterosexual couples by the churches. Procreativity is not a heterosexual privilege, and the Protestant notion of biblical covenant and Catholic natural-law theology can be widened to include queer procreativity. For years translesbigays have formed committed, stable relationships. Now they are demanding official recognition for their unions, domestic-partnership benefits, parenting, adoptions, and custody rights to children. These are timely topics of justice for the churches, calling them to revisit how they stand on queer Christians and their families. Queer folks have a basic right to intimate life just as they have the basic right of conscience.[13]

---

13. David A. Richards, *Identity and the Case for Gay Rights* (Chicago: University of Chicago Press, 1999), 155–60.

Same-sex unions as covenants

Christian ethicist Karen Lebacqz notes the inadequacy of the traditional Christian emphasis on sexuality as procreative and unitive. Christianity has condemned all sexuality outside of heterosexual marriage; this condemnation includes both single heterosexual and translesbigay persons. Lebacqz has widened the normative Christian understanding of human sexuality to include the God-given purpose of sexuality as vulnerability:

> Sexuality has to do with vulnerability. Eros, the desire for another, the passion that accompanies the wish for sexual expression, makes one vulnerable. It creates possibilities for great joy but also for great suffering. To desire another, to feel passion, is to be vulnerable, capable of being wounded.[14]

"Appropriate vulnerability," for Lebacqz, becomes a means for Christians to comprehend the singled and coupled sexuality of all sexual orientations:

> Vulnerability may be the presentation for both union and procreation: without a willingness to be vulnerable, to be exposed, to be wounded, there can be no union. To be "known," as Scriptures so often describes the sexual encounter, is to be vulnerable, exposed, open. Sexuality is therefore a form of vulnerability and to be valued as such. Sex, eros, passion are antidotes to the human sin of wanting to be in control or to have power over another. "Appropriate vulnerability" may describe the basic intention for human life — which may be experienced in part through the gift of sexuality.[15]

Appropriate vulnerability for Lebacqz underscores the human capacities to be affected and be deeply affected by one another. Appropriate vulnerability reflects the covenant metaphor of the Hebrew Scriptures for mutuality and intimacy, inclusive of the eros for communion and the eros for procreation. For Lebacqz, any sexual action that violates the norm of appropriate vulnerability is wrong. Rape, the use of sex as a weapon, child molestation, coercive sex, addictive sexual behaviors, unloving sex, and so on, shut down eros because vulnerability is unequal, coercive, or destructive. Therefore, unequal vulnerability is wrong because it reduces sexual actions to an expression of power over someone. Feminist writers like Carter Heyward, Marie Fortune, Christine Gudorf,

---

14. Karen Lebacqz, "Appropriate Vulnerability: Sexual Ethics for Singles," in *Sexual Ethics and the Church: A Christian Century Symposium* (Chicago: Christian Century, 1989), 21.
    15. Ibid.

Mary Hunt, and Elizabeth Stuart have developed similar lines on mutuality, justice-doing, right-relating, and friendship for comprehending Christian sexual relations.[16]

Lebacqz's link of a singles' sexual ethic to appropriate vulnerability has applicability to queer sexuality. In fact, she acknowledges such an application to same-sex couples: "Gay and lesbian unions, long condemned by the church because of their failure to be procreative, might also express appropriate vulnerability."[17] Appropriate vulnerability marks the sexual covenants between opposite-sex and same-sex partners. Forging a sexual covenant includes the covenantal elements of mutuality, love, justice, and compassion. Lebacqz stresses the relational primacy of the covenant that the Protestant reformers comprehended as companionship and that more recent Catholic theology has understood as the unitive function of marriage. Companionship or the unitive dimensions of marriage exist in same-sex couples as well. They may also exist in other than pair-bonded relationships, but this is not the focus of this essay.

The Presbyterian Special Committee on Human Sexuality develops the important notion of justice-love as the principal norm for evaluating sexual relationships:

> To do justice-love means seeking right-relatedness with others and working to set right all wrong relations, especially distorted power dynamics of domination and subordination. Embracing the goodness of our sexuality, of our erotic desire for wholeness and connectedness is, therefore, a godly gift to us. Erotic power, rightly ordered, grounds and moves us on, gently yet persistently, to engage in creating justice with love for ourselves and all others.[18]

The Presbyterian committee attempted to reclaim a passionate biblical spirituality that could embrace gender and sexual justice as a Christian ethic of empowerment and wholeness. The notion of justice-love emerges from the root biblical metaphor of covenant, and it becomes a vehicle for criticizing patriarchy or its manifestations of misogyny,

---

16. Carter Heyward, *Touching Our Strength: The Erotic as Power and the Love of God* (San Francisco: Harper & Row, 1989); Marie Fortune, *Love Does No Harm* (New York: Continuum, 1995); Christine Gudorf, *Body, Sex, and Pleasure* (Cleveland: Pilgrim Press, 1994); Kathy Rudy, *Sex and the Church: Gender, Homosexuality, and the Transformation of Christian Ethics* (Boston: Beacon Press, 1997); Mary Hunt, *Fierce Tenderness: Feminist Theology of Friendship* (New York: Crossroad, 1991); Elizabeth Stuart, *Just Good Friends: Towards a Lesbian and Gay Theology of Relationships* (London: Mowbray, 1997).

17. Lebacqz, "Appropriate Vulnerability," 22.

18. *Presbyterians and Human Sexuality: The Report of the Special Committee on Human Sexuality* (Louisville: Presbyterian Church, 1991), 9.

homophobia, and transphobia. Justice-love is a criterion that can equally be applied to all Christian sexual relationships.

Justice, compassion, and love signify the creative presence of God's reign, and any notion of covenanted sexual love between partners needs to include the elements that signify the presence of God's reign. Theologian Dorothee Soelle relates human sexuality to God's reign: "The greatest project I can name is the quest for justice, what Jesus called building the kingdom of God. Hunger for justice is part of the love energy that is set free in sexual relations."[19] Genuine sexual love opens the hearts and minds of lovers to other people in need, and this is what Jesus meant by God's reign. Christian ethicist James Nelson arrives at a similar conclusion when he notes that the "incorporation of our sexuality into God's reign means expression in acts shaped by love, justice, equality, fidelity, mutual respect, compassion, and grateful joy. These are criteria for covenant that apply regardless of one's orientation."[20]

Same-sex unions are frequently without the conjugal stereotypes and hierarchies found in heterosexist (not heterosexual) marriages; they are egalitarian, representing what Elisabeth Schüssler Fiorenza has called the "discipleship of equals." Same-sex unions can be life-giving, loving, just, mutual, tender, sensual, nurturing, cooperative, creative, and compassionate. Therefore, Christian same-sex unions can be both prophetic and sacramental. In *Jesus ACTED UP*, I wrote:

> The blessing of same-sex unions represents the *basileia* (God's reign) practice of solidarity; it recognizes the union as sexual praxis, sexual action committed to God's reign. *Basileia* practice starts with the couple's commitment to love, solidarity, and God's justice-doing, and it extends outward to the base community and those in need of God's justice. *Basileia* practice accents the creative mutual love that is the primary focus of coupling. Their lovemaking becomes erotic power sharing in service of God's reign. It attempts to integrate pleasure as a positive component of erotic union. Their love-making also represents the practice of God's reign in an inclusive discipleship of equals, shared resources, and table service. It practices an oppositional *basileia* model of relationship, contrary to the hierarchical political model of heterosexist marriage.[21]

19. Dorothee Soelle, *To Work and to Love: A Theology of Creation* (Philadelphia: Fortress Press, 1984), 133.
20. James B. Nelson, *Body Theology* (Louisville: Westminster John Knox, 1992), 62.
21. Robert E. Goss, *Jesus ACTED UP: A Gay and Lesbian Manifesto* (San Francisco: HarperSanFrancisco, 1993), 138.

Queer Christians and Jews reconstruct the biblical accounts of the covenant made between Jonathan and David and Ruth and Naomi as applicable to their unions. These covenantal narratives between same-sex couples are the most-often-read Hebrew Scriptures used in Jewish and Christian rites for the blessing of same-sex unions. Biblical scholar Mona West's recent reading of the Book of Ruth moves beyond the typical reading of same-sex unions as pair-bonded, covenanted relationships. Ruth, Naomi, and Boaz adopt procreative strategies, manipulate the inheritance laws, and adopt the Jewish traditions to create family. West writes:

> Ruth, Boaz, and Naomi provide our community with an example in which we have been creating families through our history as gay, lesbian, bisexual, and transgendered people.... Certainly, there are ways we in the queer community manipulate laws to overcome the barriers that deny the legality of our relationships. We also work the system to make our relationships more permanent and secure. We do this through domestic partnerships that allow us such benefits as health insurance, accident and life insurance, housing rights, and the use of recreational facilities. We take each other's last names, buy homes together, make wills, give durable power of attorney for health care and finances — all in the face of an ambiguous legal system that discriminates against us. Ruth, Naomi, and Boaz probably would be proud of the ways in which we continue to follow their strategies for creating family and having our relationships blessed.[22]

West writes from her social location as the senior pastor of the Cathedral of Hope, the mega–queer church with over three thousand members. The Cathedral of Hope has blessed same-sex unions and welcomed all configurations of queer families.

Catholic theologian André Guindon also points to Ruth and Naomi as the patron saints for the procreative strategies of same-sex couples. Their story becomes very appropriate, especially given the artificial insemination strategies frequented by queers. Ruth is looking for a legal inseminator to present a child to Naomi, with whom she made an earlier spousal covenant.[23] With Naomi's guidance, she seduces Boaz into a levirate marriage to become pregnant with a child. Upon the birth of

---

22. Mona West, "The Book of Ruth: An Example of Procreative Strategies for Queers," in *Our Families, Our Values*, 57–58.

23. André Guindon, *The Sexual Creators* (Lanham, Md.: University Press of America, 1986), 180 and 201 n. 117.

the child, the village women acknowledge Ruth's son as her covenanted partner's son, declaring, "A son has been born to Naomi" (Ruth 4:17). The two women risk everything within a patriarchal structure to create a family visible only to other women. There is a poignant parallel to contemporary situations where same-sex couples have had to develop procreative strategies to have children and to keep low social profiles so that the patriarchal state may not take away their children.

Christian same-sex unions can express what Lebacqz calls "appropriate vulnerability" or represent God's gratuitous reign in the midst of our society. Lebacqz's notion of appropriate vulnerability opens itself to wider notions of social procreativity. Appropriate vulnerability expresses solidarity with the biblical God who is author of sexual fecundity and justice-love. Both opposite-sex and same-sex couples have an equal opportunity to express the procreativity of the Creator God. Such procreativity takes on numerous social and cultural shapes. It expresses a connectedness with God. Procreativity may refer to the literal renewal of the earth through human reproduction or reproductive strategies of renewing society, or it may also refer to the contribution of inclusive love and justice to change the world into God's reign.

The healthy model of covenanted relationships in the Hebrew Scriptures is primarily expressed in the image of the God who makes a covenant with the weak, the helpless, the troubled, or the alienated. God remains faithful and steadfast to Israel, a small and insignificant nation, as a covenanted spouse or loving parent. The metaphor of covenant encompasses God's passionate desire to be a loving companion to Israel; it enfleshes a divine eros — God's creative energy and passion for loving connectedness, companionship, and justice. The biblical notion of covenant requires a general discussion of procreativity, both on biological and metaphorical levels.

Same-sex unions as naturally procreative

Historically, Catholic and Anglican theologies of sexuality invoke natural law as the unwritten law embedded in creation. These natural-law theologies are often nothing more than biological reductionism and fail to open sexuality to its nonliteral dimensions. One of the most creative Catholic moral theologians in the twentieth century was André Guindon, who contextualizes sexual relationships within the notion of sexual fecundity. Sexual fecundity includes the dimension of the Christian tradition that is understood as procreativity and much more. Guindon does not reserve the notion of human sexual procreativity primarily for heterosexual marriage, but applies it to celibates and gays/lesbians. He explores the possibility that gay/lesbian (and I would include transgendered people and bisexuals as well) sexual language can be procreative or fruitful for the human community. Guindon shifts his discussion from homosexuality as acts to gay/lesbian speech, and the context of fruitful sexual language provides the criterion for comprehending queer sexual language as fruitful:

> With the human fecundity approach, we focus on the task of each individual to grow, through the sexual language, into a whole self. Hence, in the case of gays and lesbians, the main ethical issue lies in their willingness (or unwillingness) to achieve the truth of their existence by creatively expressing themselves in the light of their living options, and by wisely discerning appropriate means. If the moral task consists in making one's own truth or in making sense of one's own life, then we are finally coming to grips, in this approach, with the crucial question of an ethical project for lesbians and gays.[24]

Guindon does not dismiss the capacity of gays/lesbians to communicate sexually but points out a deficit in the lack of other-sex feedback:

> To be fruitful, sexual relationships between human beings presuppose both sameness and differentness. . . . Fecund sexual relationships between human beings, then, also presuppose differentness, that whereby the other is really other. Otherness is the basic condition of real mutuality. The other is, by definition, one who is different from myself, therefore one who may unsettle me, disturb me, astonish me, challenge me. Conflict, its negotiation through interaction and reconciliation, is the very law of moral development. . . . Yet, the other's otherness in the male-female sexual dialogue carries within it a potential for self-discovery in one's male-female humanity which is not present in the same-sex otherness of the other.[25]

The other's otherness challenges each partner in his/her assumptions about the opposite sex. Same-sex relationships, according to Guindon, run the risk of gradually losing the sense of mystery of the other with its differences, conflicts, and negotiations. Here Guindon's arguments fall very short of a promising development in moral theology.

---

24. Ibid., 163.
25. Ibid., 168–69.

If Guindon had had the opportunity to do an in-depth exploration of same-sex relationships and interview various partners, he would have discovered that there is a strong sense of the otherness within each partner. Otherness is not gender-specific but partner-specific. Couples, whether they are opposite-sex or same-sex, always run the risk of losing a sense of otherness when intimacy breaks down. Life partners in same-sex relationships will often describe their growth in friendship, intimacy, and community. They also recognize the need to give each partner the space to be himself or herself. The actual lives of same-sex couples break down the traditional arguments of otherness and biological complementarity. The failure to recognize a wide range of gender expressions and diversities becomes a hindrance to understanding the psychological notions of otherness and the complementarity of partners.

Guindon points out the need for queers to adopt three developmental moral strategies to compensate for what their sexual language does not automatically foster. First, queers need to learn and dialogue from different voices. They can form close friendships across gender boundaries and sexual preferences; however, they may not be able to decode the sexual language of the opposite sex. Guindon acknowledges that the dialogue between the sexes does also contain nonsexual components and modalities, and he argues that it is healthy to expand one's world of experience to include relationships with nongays/lesbians. However, he fails to understand the close warm relationships that develop between heterosexual women and gay men or the relationships of lesbians with heterosexual men. The dialogue between sexes may well be more advanced and developed in some modalities within the queer community than within some parts of the heterosexual world where sexist gender roles often dictate the relationships between men and women. Some queers actually have a greater ease dealing with transgendered and intersexed folks, differences often threatening to heterosexist men.

Second, for Guindon, many queers need to break some of the dysfunctional elements of ghetto existence to develop an inner identity and ego-strength. Queer group solidarity has offered cultural space where many translesbigays have come to accept their sexual orientation and recover from the damage of a homophobic society. Though I generally agree with the need to break out of ghetto existence, I suggest it is for reasons of social transformation and survival of the queers from the violence of religious extremists.

The third relational strategy consists in openness to growth. Openness to growth requires authenticity and integrity; it requires "coming out," making queer sexual praxis a visible presence in the world. Guindon notes that the last remedial moral strategy is equally applicable to heterosexual people. Heterosexuals also need to learn to dialogue with the different voices of gays, lesbians, bisexuals, and transgendered people, and they need to come out of their own patriarchal patterns of gender hierarchies and homophobic oppression.

Guindon admits that same-sex couples "who remain in a partnership generally do so by the strength of their mutual love and dedication and because of a highly qualitative, relational sexual fidelity."[26] He recognizes that same-sex couples can represent gratuitous love:

> Gay (lesbian/bisexual/transgendered) persons whose sexual language is fruitful in faithfulness to a partner, in forgiveness toward their enemies, and in compassion for the oppressed have indeed mastered the art of sexual love in a way which can only build the Christian community. They celebrate love with a gratuity which testifies to the fact that their love is indeed Christian love.[27]

Guindon has expanded the notion of sexual fecundity from a literal definition of procreation to a metaphorical procreativity. He challenges the traditional misreadings of God's invitation to participate in creation as literal biologism. Giving birth to offspring is only one of the many procreative possibilities. Forging a sexual covenantal relationship is also validated by the inclusiveness of its love, its capacity for compassion, and the promotion of justice. Christian ethicist James Nelson follows a similar line of thinking in locating religious meaning in sexual unions: "Sexuality is a sign, a symbol, and a means of our call to communication and communion. . . . The mystery of our sexuality is the mystery of our need to reach out to embrace others both physically and spiritually. Sexuality thus expresses God's intention that we find our authentic humanness in relation."[28]

Procreativity includes not merely the creation of children but also service and creative endeavors for humanity. Human procreativity includes the elements of trust, solidarity, and right-relatedness. For Guindon, the sexual fecundity of a couple, whether heterosexual or homosexual, can include compassionate ministry to the disenfranchised, involvement in an AIDS service organization, volunteer outreach, the struggle for civil rights, and the fight for justice. Dorothee Soelle, likewise, extends human procreativity beyond social life: "The earth is a sexual planet, and

---

26. Ibid., 176.
27. Ibid., 179.
28. James B. Nelson, *Embodiment: An Approach to Sexuality and Christian Theology* (Minneapolis: Augsburg Press, 1979), 18.

we affirm it being good in celebrating the true richness of the human being in loving and making love. We are erotically connected with the world."[29] Human procreativity participates as well in the creation and renewal of the natural world; it also includes environmental justice.

Translesbigays can express a life-affirming vision of sexuality, gender, and freedom. Queer sexual praxis must obviously enjoy a certain amount of visibility to have a social impact. This means that Christian same-sex couples need to be out of the closet to be procreative, to have an impact upon the Christian community, and to challenge society to change. When closeted same-sex relationships are blessed, can they reach their procreative potential in witnessing God's presence to the community? Closetedness does not preclude procreativity; it only narrows and restricts the sacramental potentiality.

Contrary to any implications within Guindon's arguments, I would maintain that same-sex fecundity is not second-rated to heterosexual fecundity. The novel tonalities of queer sexual language provide a critique of dominant cultural meanings of sexuality and gender. Modeling a relational parity, Christian same-sex unions can critique relations that are patriarchal, despotic, abusive, and dysfunctional. Healthy same-sex unions tend to be egalitarian, cooperative, flexible, mutual, sensual, and communicative of the justice-love of the biblical witness. These covenant relations build up the Christian community and provide the foundation for transformational social change into God's reign. Queer unions provide a signpost of cultural change whereby cultural inclusion and diversity replace exclusionary patterns of sexual and gendered power relations. They can be open signposts of what the Hebrew Scriptures envision as covenant or of the community envisioned in Jesus' practice of God's reign.

Queer procreativity: families of choice

Translesbigay people are openly seeking church blessings, raising children, and demanding civil recognition of their partners as spouses. The narrow definition of family as two biological parents legally married and with children marginalizes a number of families: singles, single parents, divorced and remarried couples, extended families, and families of choice. Same-sex couples fall in the category of families of choice but often participate in other forms of families just listed. They remain in partnership through dedication, mutuality, love, and commitment

---

29. Soelle, *To Work and to Love*, 134.

despite social adversity and pressures. There are no legal or ecclesial bonds to hold same-sex couples together, except the daily commitment or the loving choice to stay together. Same-sex couples, like all healthy couples, grow as they work to sustain intimacy, honesty, and open communication.

Those deliberate commitments of same-sex couples have also included the decision to raise children and create families of choice. Today, same-sex couples are raising children in a variety of circumstances and through a variety of means. Gays, lesbians, and bisexuals are just as capable of procreation as are heterosexuals, and many same-sex couples choose to have children. Transsexuals may have children from a prior relationship or marriage; adoption and foster-care options are nonexistent for transsexuals in most states. Queer couples have adopted a number of procreative strategies to produce and raise children and to create families outside the narrow definition of the traditional family. This decision to raise children and create family is what Guindon has characterized as sexual fecundity. It is what the Christian tradition has identified as procreation. This decision for procreativity extends the love-boundaries of the couple to include children.

Anthropologist Kath Weston speaks of families that queers "struggle to create, struggle to choose, struggle to legitimate, and . . . struggle to keep."[30] Queer new families may or may not live within a household. The complexities of queer families of choice are represented by intentional and cultural variables, for such families and households often vary in composition, organization, and representation from heterosexual families and households. They vary according to gender, age, class, ethnicity, and sexual orientation. Queer families consist of household relationships and relationships extended beyond the household: lovers, children, and friends. They can include the choice of biological relatives as well. What characterizes these relationships for the most part is that they are chosen. In opposition to the defined notions of a biological family, choice offers the opportunity to re-create and invent the family as a pluralistic phenomenon without the tyranny of normativity, the power dynamics, the hierarchical assumptions, and the rigid gender stereotypes.

Those deliberate commitments of queer singles, couples, and extended families have also included the decision to raise children and further create families of choice. That queers make a choice to have children runs counter to some Christian theological and cultural notions

---

30. Weston, *Families We Choose,* 212.

of families. However, many queers are rearing children in a variety
of circumstances and through a variety of means. Children are often
conceived or adopted after queers have come out. This forces us to
reconcile queer identity with actual procreative practice. This reconcil-
iation of identity with procreativity challenges the assumptions of those
heterosexuals who claim procreative privileges for themselves and attack
queers for nonproductive hedonism. Sexual pleasure and procreativity
are exclusive to neither group.

Many translesbigays have custody or share custody of their own children through a former heterosexual marriage. Estimations of lesbian
parents range between 1 and 5 million, and the estimations of gay parents range from 1 to 3 million.[31] The American Bar Association estimates
that there are 8 to 10 million daughters and sons of lesbian and gay
parents.[32] We have no statistics on bisexual and transgendered families.
Transsexuals often lose their parental custody or coparenting rights in
the process of their gender transformation. There are also many lesbian
and gay parents who have lost custodial rights to their children in certain states. A gay parent may share joint custody of his children with
his former wife while the spouse of the gay parent often becomes a co-
parent. Sexual procreativity is shared in these parental and coparental
families. To procreate, some lesbians have sought out gay men who were
prepared to be coparents.

Queers do not undertake procreative strategies unless they really
want children and are committed to rearing them. There are no ac-
cidental children. Some queer singles, couples, and extended families
have adopted procreative strategies of producing children through reproductive methods such as artificial insemination, in vitro fertilization,
surrogate motherhood, or sexual intercourse. A lesbian doctor friend
has informed me that there are currently some thirty-seven ways of producing a child without male-to-female sexual intercourse. Most of these
strategies challenge conventional understanding of producing offspring.
Some lesbians have become parents through artificial insemination,
while female or lesbian friends have willingly become artificially insemi-
nated with the sperm of gay singles or couples to produce their children.
Sometimes individuals and couples form a household in which to raise
children. I know two gay lovers and two lesbian lovers who have had
their first daughter through artificial insemination. They share custody

---

31. Jonathan Mandell, "Gay Couples — the Changing Face of New York — Higher
Incomes, Better Educated," *New York Newsday,* June 22, 1995, A1 and A7.

32. Cited in a pamphlet published by COLAGE (Children of Lesbians and Gays
Everywhere), undated, San Francisco.

and responsibility for the rearing of their daughter within two adjacent households. Some bisexuals have engaged in sexual intercourse to produce children. Parents and surrogate parents form extended families involved in the raising of the children.

Some queers may choose to become foster parents while others have adopted the so-called throwaway children of our society: crack-cocaine addicted children, HIV-positive babies, mentally or physically challenged children, children of color, and Third World children. Individual, coupled, and extended families of all sorts have initially involved themselves in foster care and then decided to adopt children. Often adoptions are interracial, adding further social complications. Many white parents of black children include friends of color as extended family to preserve the racial and cultural heritage of their adopted children. There are too many unwanted children within families and within the foster care system. The positive decision of same-sex couples to raise children provides a foundational basis for describing their families as families of choice.

Some couples are compelled to take a low profile within the queer community in order to adopt. The desire for children is stronger than active and visible involvement within the queer community. Some gay men and lesbians have legally married in order to adopt children and create extended families. These same-sex couples have consciously created homes where children can share the benefit of their love and nurturing.

Religious extremists and some state courts have raised questions whether queer parents serve the child's best interest. Same-sex parents, however, differ little than their heterosexual counterparts, contrary to the propaganda of the far right. Queer parents are as capable of being good parents as heterosexual couples. Sexual orientation of parents has nothing to do with the orientation, the welfare, and the development of children. Charlotte Patterson concluded from the results of thirty different studies on the children of gays and lesbians: "There is no evidence to suggest that psychological development among children of gay men or lesbians is compromised in any respect relative to studies among the offspring of heterosexual parents."[33] The sexual orientation of parents has no adverse effect on the psychological and moral development of children. The models of equality between same-sex partners may, in fact, be conducive to the development of healthy models of parenting and gender equality.

---

33. Charlotte Patterson, "Children of Lesbian and Gay Parents," *Child Development* 63, no. 5 (October 1992): 1026.

Metaphorical procreativity

André Guindon also speaks of the sexual fecundity of same-sex couples who do not adopt procreative strategies to extend the love of their relationship through producing or adopting children. It is consistent with his thought that celibate folks can also express a sexual fecundity. Thus, he acknowledges that same-sex couples without children can be productive and fruitful in the same way of celibate sexual fecundity: "Contrary to many other groups, the North American homosexual community represents a sense of shared values and willingness to assert sexuality as part of the whole of life. Their sexual fecundity does have a characteristic social exposure and should contribute to society's own renewal."[34]

For Guindon, sexual fecundity is further characterized by humanizing social interactions that contribute to society's renewal. While Christian tradition frequently makes a distinction between the ability to make life and the ability to nurture that life, it has rigidly limited the notion of procreativity to the first and not extended it to the latter. Parenting is not just a biological act, for in observing my queer friends with their children, I have seen that parenting is a complex psychological and spiritual process of nurturing, loving, and being there for children. Procreativity takes on the metaphorical dimension of social nurturing and transformation, for procreativity must be placed within the frame of social responsibility. I extend it to include the nurturing and transformation of society and world, included in a tapestry of notions and praxes of inclusive love, hospitality, and social justice.

Queer sexual praxis, however, must be visible and out of the closet if it is to have social and cultural impact. Sex draws us closer to a partner, but it also draws couples out of themselves to become closer to the human community, the world, and God. I would further qualify Guindon's notion of sexual fecundity as contributing to society's renewal. This idea is implicit in his writings, and I suspect that he would concur with my grounding queer fecundity in justice-love, working for cultural change and social justice for all peoples. Sexual fecundity involves more than social renewal; it involves the redemption of society or the transformation of society into God's reign. As I've noted earlier, theologian and feminist activist Mary Hunt has stressed that good sex is "just good sex"; it is pleasurable, uncoerced, and community-building: "Just good sex . . . is community building as a specific antidote to the couples trap or other privatizing moves. Perhaps, the intuition that it was meant to be procreative is not entirely wrong, only partial in that just good sex

---

34. Guindon, *Sexual Creators*, 182.

is really part of creating a new network of relationships that emerge from all relationships."[35] Hunt is correct to point out that couples can trap themselves in their own love; they may contain their love to the relationship only and not let their love spill out into a new network of relationships that work for social justice and the renewal of the world.

Same-sex couples frequently experience the need to share the fruit of their love with others. Their love needs to include others and work for their social welfare. It moves from the sense of communion with another person to the wider framework of community and God. The more that Frank and I experienced the love of one another, the more we were free to follow the outflow of our love to serve others in need, create a major AIDS service organization, and shape a sharing center for HIV-positive people. As I've said above, we took into our household the throwaway people of our society, the developmentally disabled, alienated queer folks, and HIV-positive people. We created a community of love for the marginalized. Nurturing and social care for others are the result of sexual love-making. They can also lead to a commitment to social justice, to renew the world and work to overcome social injustice. This dynamic has occurred in my relationships and those of many other queer Christians. The sexual relationship between Frank and I fostered a commitment to social justice and the hope of changing people's lives and world into a more just society, the society envisioned by Jesus in his message about God's reign. These were the fruits of our erotic life together while it also witnessed to injustices of society and church refusing to recognize its sanctity. It witnessed publicly to relational creativity and social procreativity, supporting positive, healthy role models of Christian relationship.[36]

I personally know hundreds of long-term, stable queer couples who express their love in compassionate outreach in volunteer services to the larger community and/or in a passionate commitment to work for justice. Their love procreatively overflows into AIDS service organizations, volunteer services outside the queer community, and the struggle for civil rights. Their love gives birth to compassionate outreach, a commitment to justice, and what the biblical metaphors describe as God's covenant or reign.

---

35. Mary Hunt, "Just Good Sex: Feminist Catholicism and Human Rights," in *Good Sex: Feminist Perspectives from the World's Religions,* ed. Patricia Beattie Jung, Mary Hunt, and Radhika Balakrishnan (New Brunswick, N.J.: Rutgers University Press, 2000), 172.
36. Rudy reflects on my notion of procreativity and hospitality; she considers it as expressing the "unitivity" of sexuality; see Kathy Rudy, *Sex and the Church,* 126–27.

Excursus: transgendered procreativity

A fellow MCC (Metropolitan Community Church) clergy from Chicago told me about the significant numbers of preoperative and postoperative male-to-female transsexuals who stood up as fathers for the Father's Day celebration in the welcoming climate of his church. The UFMCC (Universal Fellowship of Metropolitan Community Churches), the Quakers, the Unitarian-Universalist Church, and pockets within the Episcopal (Anglican), Methodist, and the Presbyterian Churches are dealing with the issues of transsexuality with pastoral sensitivity. Some, like the UFMCC and the Unitarian-Universalist Churches, bless transsexuals' unions.

The conservative and fundamentalist/evangelical churches maintain that monogamous, heterosexual marriage is the only form of marriage and that only a man and a woman can marry. Because of their gender fundamentalism, they claim that transsexual relationships are not Christian marriages and affirm that transsexuals are defying God's created order by refusing to accept biologically born gender and by changing their given gender. These churches actively oppose transsexuals changing their birth certificate to reflect their gender change. Even when clergy can legally marry two males, one partner biologically born male and the other a female-to-male transsexual, they oppose the sexual love-making of these partners because it is not open to procreation. The arguments against same-sex marriage are also directed toward transsexual unions.

The emerging transgendered movement, including gender-benders, intersexuals, and transsexuals, does not focus on the issue of sexual orientation, and yet it is not totally unrelated. Transgendered folks suffer from the same system of gender fundamentalism that targets lesbigays because they violate heterosexist norms based on rigid notions of masculinity and femininity. Gaytrans males and lesbitrans females experience the same cultural homophobia as gays and lesbians. While there may be some differences between transgendered people and lesbigays, there is much that links transgendered folks to the queer movement.

Many of the same arguments for the procreativity of same-sex couples without children could be used in defense of the recognition of transgendered and transsexual unions. Many transsexuals are parents from previous relationships or have adopted procreative strategies. Their transgendered unions are metaphorically procreative, reflecting God's covenant. The above arguments support transgendered Christian marriage.

--- PART 2 ---

QUEERING CHRIST

SIX

CHRISTIAN HOMODEVOTION TO JESUS

Christianity's greatest taboo [is] Christ's sexuality.   —Leo Steinberg

Christ was crucified naked, but I think it is pious to believe that his shameful organs were veiled for decency.   —Johannes Molanus[1]

I remember a conversation with a friend at a restaurant at the Lake of the Ozarks in the heart of the fundamentalist Bible Belt. We talked about the humanity of Jesus. We secured the attention of nearby diners, who were more riveted to our conversation than their own mealtime conversations. To be human for us meant to be sexual. Sexuality was a part of God's creation and a means for beginning to understand love and the love of God. Working out of an acceptance of the full humanity of Jesus and sexuality as part of the incarnation, we explored taboo questions for many Christians: "Did Jesus fart?" We went further into forbidden Christian sexual questions: "Did Jesus have an erection? Did he have wet dreams? Did Jesus have an orgasm?" Of course, we did not go far enough and ask: "Orgasm with whom?"

Early Christianity understood Jesus as remaining unmarried, and he became a model of celibacy for elite Christians and more recently a model of compulsory heterosexuality for contemporary fundamentalist Christians. Jesus has remained a symbol of asexuality for Christian sexual puritans. For nearly two millennia, elite Christians kept Jesus and sexuality totally apart from each other in order to maintain their purity agenda. Sexual puritans have surrounded human sexuality with prohibitions, regulations, and restrictions. The denial of human sexuality within spirituality is damaging to the human spirit because it alienates Christians from their own sexual selves and from their own bodies. This has led to impoverished theologies of sexuality and Christian violence

---

1. Leo Steinberg, *The Sexuality of Christ, in Renaissance Art and in Modern Oblivion* (New York: Pantheon Books, 1983). Molanus is quoted in Richard C. Trexler, "Gendering Jesus Crucified," in *Iconography at the Crossroads,* Index of Christian Art Occasional Papers, vol. 2, ed. Brendan Cassidy (Princeton, N.J.: Princeton University Press, 1993), 114.

against those who stray from married, heteronormative sexuality for procreation.

It is tragic that a sexual Jesus disturbs the Christian image of God while a cruel Father justifying social hatred and violence does not. Hardened dogmas born from Christian patriarchal erotophobia have not only emasculated Jesus but also dehumanized him. To think of Jesus having sexual desires violates the sexless image perpetuated by church theology. To think of Jesus having sex with the Beloved Disciple or with Mary Magdalene places us outside of most churches. Most biblical scholars uncritically accept the textual and theological constructions of a non-sexual or celibate Jesus. If we stand outside of the gospel texts and bring an erotic reading to the texts, we ask questions hardly ever imagined by heterosexist biblical scholars.

In this chapter, I will briefly examine the silencing of the sexuality of Jesus and how Christian men attracted to the same sex have read Jesus as a homoerotic template for their spirituality.[2] The essay is a genealogical exploration meant to recapture the sacred eroticism within Christianity, albeit Christian homodevotionalism to Jesus.

Silencing Jesus' sexuality

The creedal formula "Jesus is like us in all things, save sin" has been frequently understood to refer to sexuality. Christianity has too often equated sin with sexuality. Protestant and Catholic writers construe the fall or original sin of humanity as sexual; for many contemporary Christians, a sinless Jesus is a sexless Jesus. A sexless Jesus, however, masks the Docetism of mainline Christianity that maintains that God appeared only in the humanity of Christ. The underlying premise is that God became human but not sexual.

During my theological studies for the priesthood, I read Bishop John A. T. Robinson's *The Human Face of God,* and the book had a profound impact upon me by restoring the full humanity of Jesus to my own theological perspective. Bishop Robinson pointed out that most people today think of Jesus as sexless and thus not really human: "To think of Jesus as having had sexual desires of any sort has seemed to offend against his purity.... Consequently, the church has appeared to

2. For example, Robert E. Goss, "The Beloved Disciple: A Queer Bereavement Narrative in a Time of AIDS," in *Take Back the Word: A Queer Reading of the Bible,* ed. Robert E. Goss and Mona West (Cleveland: Pilgrim Press, 2000), 206–18; James Martin, " 'And Then He Kissed Me': An Easter Love Story," in ibid., 219–26.

present him as sexless."[3] Robinson concludes his speculation about the sexuality of Jesus with this assessment: "Of course, there is no answer. The Gospels are not there to answer such questions. It is, however, a good question to ask ourselves, to test our reaction."[4]

Until recently, I agreed with Robinson's conclusion about the question of Jesus' sexuality. Does the lack of evidence guarantee that Jesus was celibate and nonsexual? Why are the canonical Gospels silent about Jesus' sexuality? Many religious traditions in the Greco-Roman world portray savior figures who are promoting sexuality or rejecting sexuality completely. Does the apparent silence of the Gospels on Jesus' sexuality indicate that it was not an important issue? Or are there compelling reasons for the silencing of Jesus' sexuality?

The fear of the body and sexuality in first- and second-century Christians led to the social construction of the celibate Jesus. The beginnings of such sexual negativity can be seen in the writings of Paul and his sexual asceticism.[5] For many body-negative spiritual writers and theologians in Christian history, the question of Jesus' penis or sexuality was a forbidden subject, too blasphemous to be raised. A second-century Christian theologian, Clement of Alexandria, noted "the reason that Jesus did not marry was that, in the first place, he was already engaged, so to speak, to the church, and in the second place, he was not an ordinary man."[6] Augustine of Hippo would never have allowed himself to think either that Jesus had an erection or that he masturbated or had a wet dream, all of which are normal male adolescent experiences.[7] Because of his fall to sin, Adam experienced an involuntary erection when seeing Eve naked.[8] For Augustine, the experience of fallen sin was that the male genitals were independent of rational control and subject to passion, infected with concupiscence.

Early Christianity maintained that Jesus adopted celibacy though there is no substantial historical evidence for this save scriptural silence and the projections of Christian ascetics and elite who withdrew into celibacy and monasticism. Sexual activity was the province of the laity, whose

---

3. John A. T. Robinson, *The Human Face of God* (Philadelphia: Fortress Press, 1973), 64.

4. Ibid.

5. On Paul's sexual asceticism, see Elizabeth Edwards, "Exploring the Implications of Paul's Use of Sarx (Flesh)," in *Biblical Ethics and Homosexuality: Learning to Scripture,* ed. Robert Brawley (Louisville: Westminster John Knox, 1996), 75–80.

6. Clement of Alexandria, *Stromata* 3.49, in *Alexandrian Christianity*, vol. 2, trans. J. Oulton and H. Chadwick (Philadelphia: Westminster Press, 1954), 40–92.

7. Augustine, *City of God,* trans. Marcus Dods (New York: Random House, 1950), 14.22.

8. Ibid., 14.16–17.

duty was to procreate, but it was not for the religious elite. Abstinence from sexual coitus became the norm for Christian love and the understanding of Jesus as the perfect human. Thomas Aquinas maintained that Jesus assumed all the bodily defects due to sin. He was subject to death, hunger, thirst, and all such human needs. Aquinas argues that although Christ assumed the bodily defects due to sin, he possessed all the grace and the virtues most perfectly, controlling any taint of concupiscent appetite or sexual drives.[9] Christian churches today cannot imagine a sexually active Jesus; evidence for this is their protests against the movie *The Last Temptation of Christ* and the play *Corpus Christi*.[10]

Were there erotophobic currents that affected the portrayal of Jesus in the four canonical Gospels? How much of the canonical gospel sources were edited to portray a theological image of Jesus suited for the Roman Empire?[11] How does this affect the image of Jesus as nonsexual? The Gospels carefully tried to depict Jesus in the best light to Greco-Roman readers, who would have been suspicious of anyone crucified by the state. Revolutionary elements of his teaching such as the inclusion of women as disciples were thus downplayed for the audiences in the Roman Empire, for Paul and the gospel writers certainly wanted to be assimilated into the Roman world. All attempts to reconstruct Jesus' sexuality and his teaching on sexuality need to recognize that the narrative accounts have been filtered and edited through a screening by each evangelist. It is similar to the Log Cabin Republicans who try to represent the gay community in the most positive fashion so its members can fit into society. They edit out the least desirable information of queer lifestyle.

Jesus' sexuality, likewise, and his teachings on sexuality would have been downplayed to present him as an example of what the Greco-Roman citizens would have understood as a moral teacher. For Paul, Jesus is certainly devoid of sexual desire and is an exemplar of self-mastery. Underlying Paul's theology of self-mastery is his notion of Christ as the enabler of the restored and disciplined self.[12] Paul's contemporary

---

9. Thomas Aquinas, *Summa Theologica* 3, q. 14, a. 4; q. 15, a. 2.

10. The movie was adapted from Nikos Kazantzakis's *The Last Temptation of Christ* (New York: Touchstone Books, 1998). I read it while I was a Jesuit scholastic and loved it because it restored erotic feelings to Jesus. See Terrence McNally, *Corpus Christi* (New York: Grove Press, 1998).

11. Mark's Gospel was written during or toward the end of the Jewish-Roman War (66–70 C.E.); the other canonical Gospels were written in the decades after the war. In all four canonical Gospels, the authors shift the blame for the death of Jesus from the Romans to the Jews. The image of Jesus was whitewashed to diffuse the scandal of his political execution. Only slaves, bandits, and rebels were crucified.

12. Stanley K. Stowers, *A Rereading of Romans: Justice, Jews, and Gentiles* (New Haven: Yale

Philo of Alexandria presents Moses as an example of a Jewish sage of self-mastery: "Moses puts off emotion loathing it as the vilest thing and the cause of evils, above all denouncing desire as like a destroyer of cities to the soul which must itself be destroyed and made obedient to the rule of reason."[13] Philo of Alexandria describes a Hellenized Moses as a man of God three times; he modifies notions from the Hellenistic divine man (*theios aner*) or miracle worker and exercises considerable freedom to portray Moses to Hellenistic readers. While Philo carefully wants to portray Moses as part of the human-divine encounter, he does not want to deify Moses.[14] For Hellenistic Jewish Christianity, the divine-man motif stands behind the gospel miracle traditions of Jesus. The Christian usage points to the real possibility of the canonical evangelists sanitizing the portrayal of Jesus for a Greco-Roman audience. Could not that same aretological apologetic that Philo uses to represent Moses' mastery of sexuality also be at work in the gospel silence about Jesus' sexuality and the attempt to present him as a miracle worker and as a Moses-archetype within Hellenistic Jewish Christianity? Part of the issue is the antisexual and patriarchal environment in which the Christian Scriptures were formed.

The silence of the Gospels about Jesus' sexuality is deliberate. Traditionally Christianity has argued for Jesus' celibacy. Is this really the case, or is it a process of representing Jesus as a sage or divine man? The Jewish scholar Geza Vermes takes Jesus' celibacy for granted and speaks of "prophetic continence."[15] Others contextualize Jesus' celibacy with that practiced by the Qumran community. For many past and contemporary Christians, the idea of a Jesus engaged in sexual relations with another or others is too blasphemous, challenging his divinity.

I think we can reasonably assume that Jesus' sexual relationships were as scandalous as his political message or his practice of calling women to a discipleship of equals with men. Some heterosexual writers like William Phipps provide arguments for Jesus as a Jewish rabbi and

University Press, 1994), 42–43. There are sexual ascetic strains of Judaism represented by Philo and the Qumran community. See David Balch, "Backgrounds of 1 Cor. VII: Sayings of the Lord in Q, Moses as an Ascetic Theios Aner in II Cor. III," *New Testament Studies* 18 (1971/72): 351–64; Daniel Boyarin, *A Radical Jew: Paul and the Politics of Identity* (Berkeley: University of California Press, 1994), 158–79.

13. Philo, *De Specialibus Legibus*, 4.95; Stowers, *A Rereading of Romans*, 59.

14. Carl R. Holladay, *Theios Aner in Hellenistic Judaism* (Missoula, Mont.: Scholars Press, 1977), 103–98; Barry Blackburn, *Theios Aner and the Markan Miracle Traditions* (Tübingen: J. C. B. Mohr, 1991), 64–69.

15. Vermes is the first author to admit the weakness of his arguments about Jesus' celibacy. See Geza Vermes, *Jesus the Jew: A Historian's Reading of the Gospels* (London: Fontana/Collins, 1973), 100.

as married.[16] His married Jesus promotes the contemporary value of monogamy and heterosexuality. What I find important about Phipps's arguments is that Jesus' sexuality was central to his ministry and life. Biblical scholar Robert Funk writes about the conclusion of the Jesus Seminar on the issue of Jesus' sexuality:

> The Fellows of the Seminar were overwhelmingly of the opinion that Jesus did not advocate celibacy. A majority of the Fellows doubted, in fact, that Jesus himself was celibate. They regard it as probable that he had a special relationship with at least one woman, Mary of Magdala.[17]

After examining the scriptural witness, gay writer Tom Horner proposes that "it is a good thing that nothing can be proved [of Jesus' sexuality] on the basis of the evidence we have. My reason is that Christ can remain what he has always been: a Man for All People."[18] For Horner, ambiguity means universality. Elizabeth Stuart particularizes the question of Jesus' sexuality in his subversive passionate friendships, but she does not admit that he expressed himself sexually in those passionate friendships.[19] Nancy Wilson attempts to deshame the fact of Jesus' sexuality by proposing that Jesus was bisexual in his orientation and in his actions. "To deshame Jesus' inherent sexuality, to acknowledge that feelings and fantasies were a normal and natural part of his experience of being human, being male, is one way the Christian church can help to begin to deshame its own members."[20] Jesus' sexuality opens the doors for speculation about its directionality or directionalities.

Most Christians deny Jesus' sexuality or a christology that integrates a value of erotic pleasure. Are our imaginations really stretched to contemplate a sexual Jesus? Are we so erotophobic that we continue proclaiming an asexual Jesus? Such dogmatic assumptions about an asexual Jesus from the silence of textual evidence have been destructively applied to persecute and oppress. While there is theological promise for Stuart's location of Jesus' sexuality within passionate friendships, I do not agree with her reticent conclusion of a nonsexual but passionate Jesus. Nancy Wilson's proposal holds for me the most merit of a historical

16. William E. Phipps, *The Sexuality of Jesus* (Cleveland: Pilgrim Press, 1996), 104–5.
17. Robert Funk, *The Five Gospels* (New York: Macmillan, 1993), 220–21.
18. Tom Horner, *Jonathan Loved David* (Philadelphia: Westminster Press, 1978), 126.
19. Elizabeth Stuart, *Just Good Friends* (New York: Mowbray, 1995), 170–73.
20. Nancy Wilson, *Our Tribe: Queer Folk, God, Jesus, and the Bible* (San Francisco: HarperSanFrancisco, 1995), 147.

reconstruction of Jesus' sexuality. It is as realistic a possibility as the celibacy model.

For many Christians, the scandal of the incarnation is not that God became flesh but that God became fully human and actively sexual. It is imperative for us to retrieve the directionalities of the sexuality of Jesus. If my analysis is too speculative from the textual hints, I err in trying to recover from the violence of the Christian portrayal of Jesus as non-sexual and from the Christian fall to violence. Jesus' sexuality certainly is a template for the healthy appropriation of sexuality by Christians. It forces us to deal with our own erotophobia, and we cannot recover from sexual shame and self-hatred when the primary template of Christian experience has been used to reinforce the notion of sexuality as sinful.

Throughout history, many men and women have intuited a sexual relationship of Jesus with Magdalene or with the Beloved Disciple. Both the Beloved Disciple and Mary Magdalene have been highly suggestive, even erotic, models of love-mysticism for male and female Christians. Their variable constructions of legends, history, and meaning have impacted Christian love-mysticism. Both the Beloved Disciple and Magdalene have physical attributions that played on Christian imaginations.

The Beloved Disciple has a tactile, physical attribute. At the farewell meal, the Beloved Disciple's head is resting on the chest of Jesus (John 13:23). The physical intimacy of that scene has played on the homoerotic imaginations of Christians through the centuries. Many queer Christians have perceived an erotic friendship and passion in their relationships with Jesus. They were attracted and felt a special kinship to a passionate and sensual Jesus. Were these sexually intimate relationships? Our particular focus is on the hint of an erotic relationship between Jesus and the Beloved Disciple and on how men who are attracted to men have understood that relationship.

The mysterious youth in Mark and the Beloved Disciple

Some claim that Jesus was in love with or sexually intimate with two or possibly three men: Mark, the Beloved Disciple, and Lazarus. In Mark 14:51–52, there is brief mention of a young man who was accompanying Jesus at the time of his arrest: "Then the disciples all deserted him and ran away. Among those following was a young man with nothing on but a linen cloth. They tried to seize him but he slipped out of the linen cloth and ran away naked." The youth remains unnamed, but tradition identifies him as Mark, the author of the first written Gospel. This story has worked on the imagination of men attracted to the same sex for centuries. Why was this youth in the garden with Jesus so scantily clad? Was Jesus arrested in the midst of finding sexual comfort and intimacy with him? Was this the sexual baptism that the later Secret Gospel of Mark implies?

The Beloved Disciple in John's Gospel remains unnamed. Some, like Elizabeth Stuart, have argued the Beloved Disciple is a literary fiction, symbolizing "perfect intimacy with Jesus."[21] Vernard Eller, on other hand, arguing from the textual material, has proposed that the Beloved Disciple was Lazarus.[22] Biblical scholar Sjef Van Tilborg views John's portrayal of the relation of Jesus and the Beloved Disciple as the pederastic relationship of the older male as lover (*erastes*) to the beloved younger male (*eromenos*), similar to the relation depicted in Plato's *Symposium*. This pederastic relation of older male to younger male was an educational model in the Greco-Roman world of the first century C.E. There is reluctance among biblical scholars to entertain the classical pederastic model for the Beloved Disciple. Van Tilborg writes,

> The reason that scientific exegesis did not connect the relation of the teacher Jesus to his Beloved Disciple with this typical educational background is, probably, that sexuality is present in the majority of the concerned texts, either explicitly mentioned or at least not far off. The love for the *pais* in the context of education and training has sexual connotations in Greek and Hellenistic thought and action which cannot be brought in line with the a-sexual text of the Johannine Gospel.[23]

From the first century into our present era, Christian men attracted to men have viewed the Beloved Disciple as a cipher for homoerotic passions and homodevotionalism to Jesus.

In a monastery near Jerusalem, biblical scholar Morton Smith discovered a textual fragment of a letter from Clement of Alexandria

---

21. Stuart, *Just Good Friends*, 171.
22. Vernon Eller has identified Lazarus as the best of all possible candidates for the Beloved Disciple while James Charlesworth has more recently argued for Thomas the Twin. See Vernon Eller, *The Beloved Disciple: His Name, His Story, His Thought* (Grand Rapids, Mich.: William B. Eerdmans, 1987); James H. Charlesworth, *The Beloved Disciple: Whose Witness Validates the Gospel of John* (Valley Forge, Pa.: Trinity Press International, 1995). Michael Carden points out that the Acts of John reinforces the intimacy of the Beloved Disciple: "It states that after the resurrection Jesus appeared to John three times to prevent him from getting married." See Michael Carden, "Queering the Bible" (1995) (*http://student.uq.edu.au/~s101014/5SODOM.html#sodom5*).
23. Sjef Van Tilborg, *Imaginative Love in John* (Leiden: E. J. Brill, 1993), 79.

describing and quoting the Secret Gospel of Mark.[24] The fragment of the Secret Gospel appears to know the Johannine tradition of Jesus raising Lazarus from the dead. Jesus raises a youth from the dead and then initiates him through sexual union into a secret baptism:

> [T]he youth, looking upon him, loved him and began to beseech him that he might be with him. And going out of the tomb they came into the house of the youth, for he was rich. And after six days Jesus told him what to do and in the evening the youth comes to him wearing a linen cloth over his naked (body). And he remained with him that night, for Jesus taught him the mystery of the kingdom of God.[25]

Smith argues for the plausibility of this tradition, going back to the secret teachings of Jesus himself, teachings later developed by a libertine group within early Christianity. Smith asserts,

> From the scattered indications in the canonical Gospels and the secret Gospel of Mark, we can put together a picture of Jesus' baptism, "the mystery of the kingdom of God." It was a water baptism administered by Jesus to chosen disciples, singly and by night. The costume, for the disciple, was a linen cloth worn over the naked body. This cloth was probably removed for the baptism proper, the immersion in water, which was now reduced to a preparatory purification. After that, by unknown ceremonies, the disciple was possessed by Jesus' spirit and so united with Jesus. One with him, he participated by hallucination in Jesus' ascent into the heavens, he entered the kingdom of God, and was thereby set free from the laws ordained for and in the lower world. Freedom from the law may have resulted in completion of the spiritual union by physical union. This certainly occurred in many forms of Gnostic Christianity; how early it began there is no telling.[26]

Smith speculates that the Carpocratians (and other Christians) baptized in the nude. The implication of the baptism is erotic. In his letter to Theodore, a priest, Clement writes, "But 'naked man with naked man,' and the other things which you wrote are not found."[27] The implication

24. Morton Smith, *Clement of Alexandria and the Secret Gospel of Mark* (Cambridge, Mass.: Harvard University Press, 1973); Smith, *The Secret Gospel: The Discovery and Interpretation of the Secret Gospel according to Mark* (New York: Harper & Row, 1973).
25. Smith, *The Secret Gospel*, 52.
26. Ibid., 113–14.
27. Ibid., 17.

of the statement is sexual. Did Jesus perform a nocturnal baptismal rite for the youth that he raised from the dead?

Smith's publication of his findings created a firestorm of criticism and a backlash against him because he was prophetically playing by the rules of scholars two decades later — considering authentic Jesus material outside of the canon — and, more seriously, suggesting that Jesus engaged in homosexual practices with his male disciples.[28]

Conservative biblical scholars discredited the discovery and attacked Smith personally. Some scholars claimed that Morton Smith had a vested interest in justifying his homosexuality while others accused him of fraud or forgery. Several reputable scholars took Smith seriously, including one of my own teachers, George MacRae, a Jesuit biblical scholar at Harvard.[29] John Dominic Crossan, likewise, believes that the textual fragment was part of Mark's Gospel but was later expunged because of the libertine interpretations of the Carpocratians.[30] It may be a generation or more before Smith's discovery will be appreciated against a hostile ecclesial and intolerant scholarly climate that is invested in keeping Jesus "sexless."[31]

What is significant for our discussion is how early in Christian history Jesus became associated with male erotic feelings and attractions. Whether the Secret Gospel was originally in Mark's Gospel or was an early addition from a libertine Gnostic tradition in the second century is irrelevant for our discussion. Jesus initiated a young man into homoerotic love and the higher secrets of God's reign. The Secret Gospel of Mark represents an alternative tradition of male homodevotionalism to Jesus that has countered the dominant sexless constructions of Jesus. Today, gay men have reclaimed the text for themselves and Jesus as a paradigm for male same-sex relationships.

---

28. See the excellent article on the history of the controversy sparked by Smith's discovery: Shawn Eyer, "The Strange Case of the Secret Gospel according to Mark: How Morton Smith's Discovery of a Lost Letter by Clement of Alexandria Scandalized Biblical Scholarship," originally published in *Alexandria: The Journal for the Western Cosmological Traditions* 3 (1995): 103–29. *Alexandria* is edited by David Fideler and is published by Phanes Press. A more popular article on the Secret Mark is Hank Hyena, "Was Jesus Gay? A Search for the Messiah's True Sexuality Leads to a Snare of Lusty Theories," *Salon Magazine*, April 10, 1998 (*www.salon.com/feature/1998/04/cov_10feature.html*).

29. George MacRae, "Yet Another Jesus," *Commonweal* 99 (1974): 417–20.

30. John Dominic Crossan, *The Historical Jesus* (San Francisco: HarperSanFrancisco, 1992), 429–30; Crossan, *Four Other Gospels: Shadows on the Contours of the Canon* (Minneapolis: Winston Press, 1985).

31. It has been less difficult for openly gay males to accept. See, for example, Robert Williams, *Just as I Am* (New York: Crown Publishers, 1992); Will Roscoe, *Queer Spirits: A Gay Men's Myth Book* (Boston: Beacon Press, 1995), 246–47.

The apostle Paul

When I read Paul's writings, I find that his devaluation of the flesh is a generalized phobic defense against his own particular fleshy inclination. What was that inclination? Bishop John Shelby Spong argued anachronistically that Paul was a gay male. He writes,

> Paul felt tremendous guilt and shame, which produced in him self-loathing. The presence of homosexuality would have created this response.... Nothing else, in my opinion, could account for Paul's self-judging rhetoric, his negative feeling toward his own body, and his sense of being controlled by something he had no power to change.[32]

For Bishop Spong, Paul's misogyny and his refusal to marry paint a picture of a man conflicted with homosexual desires. Spong, in my opinion, is correct to point out misogyny as a clue to Paul's internal conflict, for misogyny and internalized homophobia are deeply intertwined. Yet the bishop was not the first to raise the suggestion about Paul's homosexual orientation. In his psychological study of Paul, biblical scholar Gerd Theissen raised the same question of sexual orientation prior to Spong's popularization; it was already a question discussed in German biblical scholarship.[33] Furthermore, the famous twentieth-century British scholar C. K. Barrett commented on Paul's argument for men to wear short hair and women long hair in 1 Corinthians 11:13–15: "It does seem probable that horror of homosexualism is behind a great deal of Paul's argument."[34] For Paul, men with long hair and women with short hair are indicative of homoerotic behavior that subverts the gender code and the hierarchical organization of society. American biblical scholars, specializing in Paul, tend to be for the most part white, male heterosexuals, and this may explain the reticence of the scholars to take up European scholars' observations about Paul's sexually repressed attraction to men. Such discussion disprivileges heteronormativity within the biblical academy.

---

32. John Shelby Spong, *Rescuing the Bible from Fundamentalism* (San Francisco: HarperSanFrancisco, 1991), 117. See Spong's whole argument on pp. 115–27.

33. Gerd Theissen, *Psychological Aspects of Pauline Theology*, trans. John Calvin (Philadelphia: Fortress Press, 1987), 26; Hermann Fischer, *Gespaltner christlicher Glaube: Eine psychoanalytische orientierte Religionskritik* (Hamburg: Reich, 1974). See a dated but psychoanalytic profile of Paul by a scholar reasonably well versed in biblical historical criticism: S. Tarachow, "St. Paul and Early Christianity," *Psychoanalysis and the Social Sciences* 4 (1955): 223–81.

34. C. K. Barrett, *A Commentary on the Second Epistle to the Corinthians* (New York: Harper & Row, 1973), 257.

During his lifetime, Paul was forced to repress his latent tendencies toward homoerotic desire and expression. In 2 Corinthians 12:7–9, Paul speaks about "his thorn in the flesh." Some scholars argue that this refers to disfigurement. For example, a contemporary gay scholar, Dale Martin, takes it as a reference to physiological ailment. However, the great Pauline scholar Arthur Darby Nock observed, "The point of difficulty for him perhaps lay in sexual desire, of which he speaks."[35] Paul's ailment is a source of embarrassment and shame. Paul calls his affliction a messenger of Satan, and he believes that God allows it to afflict him to keep him humble.

In 2 Corinthians 12:9, where he maintains that his strength is completed in weakness, Paul understands his weakness as an invading agent. The apostle is certainly full of self-loathing when he writes, "Wretched man that I am! Who will deliver me from this body of death?" (Rom. 7:24). Paul expresses the pain of many translesbigay Christians coming out of abusive churches. Gerd Theissen recognizes a psychological projection mechanism in Paul in Romans 2:1, where Paul says that we condemn in others what we do ourselves.[36] This gives a new twist to the interpretation of his condemnation of homoeroticism in Romans 1:25–26; it is what he fears the most in himself.

Paul can be of significance for those contemporary closeted Christians struggling with their own sexual attractions, for Christ plays a significant role in Paul's restructuring of his self-perception and coping with sexual attractions. Christ became the resolution of his feelings about his attraction to men, not in some modern ex-gay fashion of repression and change of sexual orientation. Rather Paul sublimated and channeled his erotic feelings into a relationship with Christ. He resolved his sexual attractions by channeling them into a relationship with one man, Jesus the Christ. Paul can safely express this attraction to a man as mystical union with Christ: "It is no longer I who live, but Christ who lives in me, and the life I now live by faith in the Son of God, who loved me and gave himself for me" (Gal. 2:30). The Pauline solution of sexual attractions toward the same sex found a resolution in a mystical union with one male — that is, Jesus the Christ replaced many males. This did not remove Paul's sexual attractions toward males but channeled his sexual feelings toward Christ while surrounding himself with younger males in his various missionary journeys. While in the seminary, I real-

---

35. Dale Martin, *The Corinthian Body* (New Haven: Yale University Press), 167–68, 53–55.
36. Theissen, *Psychological Aspects of Pauline Theology*, 241.

ized that I too channeled my sexual feelings toward Christ in prayer and imaginative fantasy while surrounding myself with young men.

I realized this struggle in Paul as I struggled with my own homoerotic feelings toward men and Christ in the seminary. For me, the Pauline closet (though an anachronism) became a prototype for the clerical closet. As I've discussed earlier, through much of Christian history, men and women who were attracted to the same sex entered religious life. They found a homoerotic love relationship with Christ or found a justification for the love of other men or women. Many men often repressed their sexual feelings for other men and channeled their homoerotic feelings into their love relationship with Jesus the bridegroom. They found a resolution, perhaps not completely, of their homosexual attractions in a graceful relation with Jesus the Christ and found self-acceptance and love within that relationship.

The Middle Ages

John Boswell was not the first scholar to point to the homoerotic dimensions of the spirituality of the Cistercian abbot Aelred of Rievaulx (1110–67).[37] Boswell treated Aelred as representative of clerical tolerance toward homoerotic experience, launching a heated debate on the subject of Aelred's homoerotic experience and spirituality.[38] It is clear from Aelred's autobiographical writings that he had a sexual experience with someone at the Scottish court of King David. He writes in typically medieval Christian language about his sexual experiences as a time when "a cloud of desire arose from the lower drives of the flesh and the gushing of adolescence."[39] Aelred struggled with his sexual desires in the form of masturbation and sexual attraction to his fellow monks. He took cold baths, rubbed his body with nettles, and fasted. Aelred's homoerotic attraction was transferred to his contemplative practice. Brian McGuire writes, "Aelred's attraction to other men led him to desire for a physical

---

37. Brian Patrick McGuire, *Brother and Lover: Aelred of Rievaulx* (New York: Crossroad, 1994); McGuire, "Sexual Awareness and Identity in Aelred of Rievaulx (1110–67)," *Cistercian Studies* 45, no. 2 (June 1994): 184–86.

38. John Boswell, *Christianity, Homosexuality, and Social Tolerance* (Chicago: University of Chicago Press, 1980), 221–26; Boswell, "Homosexuality and Religious Life: A Historical Approach," in *Homosexuality and the Priesthood*, ed. Jeannine Gramick (New York: Crossroad, 1989), 3–20. For criticism of Boswell's thesis, see Michael M. Sheehan's review of Boswell's book in *Journal of Ecclesiastical History* 33 (1982): 438–46; see also McGuire, *Brother and Lover*, 140–48.

39. Boswell, *Christianity, Homosexuality, and Social Tolerance*, 222; see also McGuire, "Sexual Awareness," 201.

union with the male who was the great love of youth."[40] Surrounded by the handsome boys of the monastery of Rievaulx, Aelred struggled between sexual temptation and sexual longing for Christ. In their beautiful faces, he experienced Christ. As abbot, Aelred fostered affectionate bonds among monks, going against centuries of traditions against particular friendships and vigilance against erotic friendships between monks. Our focus will center on his erotic contemplation of Christ, not on his sexual affair at the Scottish court or his physical love for the monk Simon. Aelred developed a sensuous spirituality that harnessed his erotic energies and desires with his contemplative practices and everyday life with his fellow monks.

Aelred's contemplative visualization of the spiritualized body of Christ indicates how he channeled his sexual attractions into his spiritual practice. In *The Mirror of Charity,* he identifies with Mary Magdalene. Mary comes to Jesus with all her sexual sinfulness, anointing his feet with oil and kissing him. Mary's tender and affectionate centering on Jesus' body becomes a way of speaking about Aelred's own attractions to the desirable body of Jesus. Aelred completely identified himself with Mary Magdalene and her caresses of Jesus' feet. McGuire observes that "for Aelred, this approach to the body of Christ is not just a means to excite love and devotion: it is a response geared to his own identity, a replacement of his own body and the bodies of any beautiful lovers with the incorruptible body of Christ, risen from the dead."[41] The body of Jesus was available to him in the sacrament at the altar, in his contemplative practice, and in his love of other monks. In the handsome monks of Rievaulx, Aelred experienced the spiritualized body of Christ. He sought physical and spiritual contact with the beautiful flesh of Jesus, and his physical attraction to male bodies was incorporated into his spiritual attraction to Christ.

In "Jesus at the Age of Twelve," he meditates on the disappearance of Jesus from his parents for the three days: "Where were you, good Jesus, during those three days? Who provided you with food and drink? Who made up a bed for you? Who took off your shoes? Who tended your boyish limbs with oils and baths?"[42] Aelred fantasizes massaging and touching the male body of Jesus. He fantasizes kissing Jesus:

> For I think that the grace of heaven shone from that most beautiful face with such charm as to make everyone look at it, listen to

40. McGuire, "Sexual Awareness," 201.
41. McGuire, *Brother and Lover,* 121–22.
42. Cited in ibid., 35.

him and be moved to affection. See, I beg, how he is seized upon and led by each and every one of them.... Each of them, I think, declares in his inmost heart, "let him kiss me with the kiss of his mouth" (Song of Songs 1:1). And to the boys who long for his presence but do not dare to intrude on their elders' confabulations it is very easy to apply the words, "Who will grant me to have you as my brother, sucking my mother's breasts, to find you outside and kiss you?"[43]

Aelred uses the sensuous language of the Song of Songs to describe the relation between Jesus and those who loved him. He has been socialized through bridal mysticism to take the feminine role as the bride of Christ, a role familiar to many Catholic priests and religious. He dwells in his meditation on the youthful body of Jesus in all of its physical attractiveness. His previous homoerotic experiences, which he had outside the monastery and perhaps within as well, fuel his erotic imagination and contemplative prayer. His spirituality, his prayer, and his practice focus on tasting Jesus in the sacrament, seeing him, kissing him, massaging and embracing him.[44] "Jesus at the Age of Twelve" remains one of the classic statements of the Cistercian "passionate love of Christ" (*amor carnalis Christi*).[45] Aelred had a strong sense of loving Christ physically and homoerotically. He sought to touch and kiss Jesus with his body, mind, and soul. Aelred understood the relationship of Jesus to the Beloved Disciple as a marriage, providing an authority for his close and intimate relations within the monastery.[46]

Another example of mystical longing for Christ is Rupert, abbot of Deutz (ca. 1075–1129), who had a series of erotic visions of Christ.[47] He longed to merge with Christ, desiring to die and be with him. In a vision of the Trinity, Rupert envisioned two old men and a beautiful youth. The beautiful youth was Christ, the two older men the Creator and the Holy Spirit. The beautiful youth kissed him. When the three figures departed, Rupert noticed that he was naked, and he rushed back to his bed.[48] His visions are definitely homoerotic; he does not envision himself or his soul as feminine, as often is the case in Cistercian love mysticism. At another time, Rupert dreamed a vision of Christ where he exchanged glances with the Savior. Rupert was invited to the altar, where he deep

---

43. Cited in McGuire, "Sexual Awareness," 213.
44. Ibid.
45. Bernard McGinn, *The Growth of Mysticism* (New York: Crossroad, 1992), 319.
46. Boswell, *Christianity, Social Tolerance, and Homosexuality,* 225–26.
47. McGinn, *The Growth of Mysticism,* 332.
48. Ibid., 330.

kissed Christ. It is the tradition of "being kissed by Christ and kissing
him" so prevalent in monastic spirituality: "I took hold of him whom
my soul loved (Song 1:6). I held him. I embraced him. I kissed him for
a long time. I felt how deeply he appreciated this sign of love when in
the midst of the kiss, he opened his mouth so that I could kiss more
deeply."[49] Here the bridal mysticism used in the formation of monks
and priests for centuries gives shape to a mystical, erotic experience
with Christ. It results in contemplative sex with Christ.

The Renaissance: exposing the genitals of Jesus

Along with very virile representations, early Christian art represented
Jesus as an androgynous figure, without a beard and effeminate. In his
study *The Clash of the Gods,* Thomas Matthews writes,

> Christ in Early Christian art often showed a decidedly feminine
> aspect which we overlook at our own risk. It is not the unan-
> swered but the unasked questions that undermine discourse and
> give an unbalanced slant to an entire field. Whether or not ade-
> quate explanations can be found, it is particularly important that
> this issue be raised in connection with Early Christian images, for
> once this feminine aspect of Christ had gained an acceptability,
> later artists, whether in the Middle Ages or beyond, felt free to
> exploit it without apologies.[50]

The androgynous representations of Jesus in early Christian art raise a
whole series of questions about the masculinity of Jesus. In comment-
ing on the above quotation, Frank Leib provocatively comments, "From
the beginning, without knowing it, Christians have been worshipping a
homosexual as the perfect man."[51] Along with the textual longings of
men attracted to Christ, Christian visual arts have long had a profound
impact in fueling Christian homodevotionalism. Men attracted to men
have gazed upon images of Christ with a homoerotic gaze and erotic
longing. This is particularly the case of Renaissance art.

Leo Steinberg's *The Sexuality of Christ in Renaissance Art and Modern
Oblivion* reproduces 250 of nearly 1,000 instances of art that display the

49. Cited in ibid., 332.
50. Thomas Matthews, *The Clash of the Gods: A Reinterpretation of Early Christian Art*
(Princeton, N.J.: Princeton University Press, 1995), 121.
51. Frank Leib, *Friendly Competitors, Fierce Companions: Men's Ways of Relating* (Cleveland:
Pilgrim Press, 1997), 188–89.

genitals of Jesus. The focus in these reproductions, Steinberg claims, is the "showing of the genitals" (*ostentatio genitalium*):

> The rendering of the incarnate Christ ever more unmistakably flesh and blood is a religious enterprise because it testifies to God's greatest achievement. And this must be the motive that induces a Renaissance artist to understand in his presentation of the Christ child, even such moments as would normally be excluded by considerations of modesty — such as the exhibition or manipulation of the boy's genitalia.[52]

Steinberg comments on these artistic showings of Jesus' genitals: "the evidence of Christ's sexual member serves as the pledge of God's humanation."[53] God has shown vulnerability in becoming human, and the "showing of the genitals" evidences for the Renaissance audience the humanity of God's self-abasement.

Steinberg's thesis has not gone unchallenged, for medieval historian Caroline Walker Bynum has challenged Steinberg's notion of sexuality, arguing that the Renaissance artistic gaze is on the physicality of Jesus, not necessarily on the genitals.[54] Though Steinberg leaves unexplored the significance of Jesus' sexuality, Bynum comprehends Jesus' genitals in the devotional movement toward the physicality of medieval women. Arnold Davidson, on the other hand, criticizes Steinberg for his use of the word "sexuality," which denotes the modern concept of identity. Davidson suggests the replacement of the word "sex," denoting gender.[55]

In *Closet Devotions,* Richard Rambuss challenges Bynum's critique of Steinberg's work.[56] Rambuss reads Steinberg intertextually with an article, "Gendering Jesus Crucified," by Richard Trexler.[57] Trexler argues, "not completely unlike other gods, Jesus, whether in image or in the vision made of him, might physically seduce his devotees."[58] He engages in late medieval and early Renaissance discussion of the need to place the loincloth upon the crucified Jesus to prevent male devotees from becoming sexually aroused. Same-sex devotional gaze was a problem recognized by premodern authors.

52. Steinberg, *The Sexuality of Christ,* 10.
53. Ibid., 13.
54. See Caroline Walker Bynum, *Fragmentation and Redemption: Essays in Gender and the Human Body in Medieval Religion* (New York: Zone Books, 1992), 79–117.
55. Arnold Davidson, "Sex and the Emergence of Sexuality," in *Forms of Desire,* ed. Edward Stein (New York: Routledge, 1990), 89–132.
56. Richard Rambuss, *Closet Devotions* (Durham, N.C.: Duke University Press, 1998).
57. Trexler, "Gendering Jesus Crucified," 107–19.
58. Ibid., 108.

Eve Kosofsky Sedgwick, one of the pioneers of queer theory, addresses the naked images of Jesus in English literature:

> And presiding over all are the images of Jesus. These have, indeed, a unique position in modern culture as images of the unclothed or unclothable male body often *in extremis* and/or in ecstasy, prescriptively meant to be gazed at and adored. The scandal of such a figure within a homophobic economy of the male gaze doesn't seem to abate: efforts to disembody this body, for instance by attenuating, Europeanizing, or feminizing it, only entangle the more compromisingly among the various modern figurations of the homosexual.[59]

Richard Rambuss has suggested that Sedgwick's observation of compromising entanglements of male same-sex desire as they are woven around the image of the Christ's body can be found in the Renaissance poets such Richard Crashaw, John Donne, George Herbert, and other seventeenth-century poets.[60] Rambuss concentrates his discussion on Crashaw's erotic poems about Jesus' crucifixion. Crashaw intensifies his rapturous gaze on the nude, penetrated body of Christ, and he conceives the wounds of Jesus as so many mouths to kiss and so many eyes to shed tears. On the erotic dimensions of Crashaw's religious poetry, Rambuss concludes, "And presiding over the whole is the naked body of Jesus. Around this body accrues a sensuous, even sexy thematics of ecstatic rapture, of penetration and its attendant spurting streams."[61] Rambuss suggests that there is a homoerotic dimension to the metaphysical poetry of John Donne, Richard Crashaw, and Thomas Traherne. Christ is named implicitly, if not explicitly, in the poetics of homo-devotion. In fact, Traherne offers himself to Christ: "His Ganymede! His life! His joy!"[62] Traherne comprehends himself being ravished by Christ as Jupiter ravished Ganymede. Traherne understands himself as Christ's boy, Christ's bottom or Ganymede. Rambuss notes that Ganymede is seventeenth-century slang for "any Boy, loved for carnal abuse, or hired to be used contrary to Nature to commit the detestable sin of Sodomy."[63] No wonder I took to the metaphysical English poets in high school! I

---

59. Eve Kosofsky Sedgwick, *The Epistemology of the Closet* (Berkeley, Calif.: University of California Press, 1990), 140.

60. Richard Rambuss, "Pleasure and Devotion: The Body of Jesus and the Seventeenth-Century Religious Lyrics," in *Queering the Renaissance,* ed. Jonathan Goldberg (Durham, N.C.: Duke University Press, 1994), 253–79.

61. Ibid., 279.

62. Rambuss, *Closet Devotions,* 54.

63. Ibid., 54.

sensed an erotic kinship in their love of Jesus the Christ and fantasies of ravishment in John Donne's poem "Batter My Heart." Richard Rambuss quotes from Francis Rous's *Mysticall Marriage:* "If [Christ] come not yet into thee, stirre up thy spiritual concupiscence, and therewith let thy soul lust mightily for him."[64] There is a Protestant as well as a Catholic bridal mysticism with a number of queer twists and turns. Homoerotic devotion to Christ crosses generations as well as denominations.

Nineteenth-century construction of Jesus as an example of Greek love

Jeremy Bentham, the founder of the philosophic movement known as Utilitarianism in the eighteenth and nineteenth centuries, believed that sexual acts between adult males should be decriminalized. He argued that Greek love or same-sex practices are more useful than male-female intercourse insofar as they produce pleasure while avoiding the dangers of overpopulation, unwanted offspring, abortion, and infanticide.[65] In his unpublished notes, Bentham becomes an apologist for male-male desire. He published parts 1 and 2 of a manuscript, published as *Not Paul, but Jesus,* in 1823 under the pseudonym of Gamaliel Smith.[66] Bentham attacks the body-hatred of St. Paul. For him, Paul is antiutilitarian, fearing pleasure, and Paul's antisexual asceticism does not accord with the ministry of Jesus. By publishing the first two parts of his notes, Bentham hoped to weaken the puritanical strands that dominated English Christianity. *Not Paul, but Jesus,* attempts to prove that Paul's connection to the apostles and Jesus was tenuous. Jesus took an antiascetic stance in contrast to Paul and to John the Baptist. He rejected fasting, breaking the Sabbath laws with his drinking and feasting. Crompton comments, "What emerges in Bentham's notes of 1818 is not just an anti-ascetic Christianity or an antinomian Christ similar to the portrait William Blake was elaborating at almost exactly the same time in his unfinished poem, 'The Everlasting Gospel.'"[67]

Writing in his unpublished manuscript in 1814, Bentham commented:

Jesus from whose lips not a syllable favorable to ascetic self-denial is by any of his biographers presented as having ever issued, Jesus

64. Ibid., 5.

65. See Crompton's analysis and description of Bentham's unpublished notes in Louis Crompton, *Byron and Greek Love: Homophobia in Nineteenth-Century England* (Berkeley: University of California Press, 1985), 250–83.

66. Gamaliel Smith, *Not Paul, but Jesus* (London, Printed for John Hunt, 1823).

67. Crompton, *Byron and Greek Love,* 274.

who among his disciples had one to whom he imparted his authority, and another on whose bosom his head reclined and for whom
he avowed his love — Jesus, who in the stripling clad in loose attire
found a still faithful adherent after the rest of them had fled —
Jesus, in whom the woman taken in adultery found a successful advocate, Jesus has on the whole field of sexual irregularity preserved
an uninterrupted silence.[68]

For Bentham, Jesus identified the sin of Sodom in the Q sayings,
Matthew 10:14–15 and 11:24 and Luke 10:12, with inhospitality. His
interpretation of Genesis 19 and Jesus' Q sayings is compatible with
the most recent biblical interpretations of the sin of Sodom by Bailey,
McNeill, and Boswell.[69]

Jeremy Bentham argued not only that Christ tolerated sexual activity
between males but also that he himself may well have been a subject of
male-male desire. He focused on the passages on the Beloved Disciple
in the Gospel of John. He speculated on the love that Jesus and the
Beloved Disciple shared:

> If the love which in these passages Jesus was intended to be rep-
> resented as bearing toward John was not the same sort of love as
> that which appears to have had place between David and Jonathan,
> the son of Saul, it seems not easy to conceive what can have been
> the object in bringing it to view in so pointed a manner accom-
> panied with such circumstances of fondness. The sort of love of
> which in the bosom of Jesus Saint John is here meant to be repre-
> sented as the object of a different sort from any of which any of the
> other of the apostles was the object is altogether out of dispute.
> For this sort of love, whatever sort it was, he and he alone in these
> so frequently recurring terms maintained as being the Object.
>
> As to any superiority of value in his service in relation to preach-
> ing of the Gospel, no such foundation could the distinction have
> had: for of this nothing is to be found in Saint John by which he
> can stand in comparison with Saint Peter, and on no occasion is

68. Ibid., 260.
69. Bentham was the first interpreter, well before Derrick Bailey and John Boswell, to
note that the sin of Sodom and Gomorrah in Genesis 19 and Jesus' sayings about the
destruction of Sodom refer to the sin of inhospitality. For Bentham, mass rape violated
the laws of hospitality of primitive societies. See Crompton, *Byron and Greek Love*, 275.
Compare with Derrick Sherwin Bailey, *Homosexuality and the Western Christian Tradition*
(Hamden, Conn.: Archon Books, 1975), 8; John Boswell, *Christianity, Social Tolerance, and
Homosexuality*, 92–94.

the rough fisherman to be seen "leaning in the bosom of Jesus" or "lying on his breast."[70]

Bentham comprehends David's "love surpassing the love of women" for Jonathan as sexual.[71] In the above passage, he understands the love shared by Jesus and the Beloved Disciple as sexual as well. Another passage that played on the erotic imagination of Bentham was Mark 14:50–52, where all the disciples flee and where an unnamed young man (*neaniskos*) runs off naked and leaves his linen cloth. Bentham preferred the translation of *neaniskos* as "stripling" and understood him as a boy prostitute who may have been a rival with the Beloved Disciple for Jesus' sexual love.[72] For Bentham, Jesus neither condemned nor found the boy prostitute offensive. The nineteenth-century reformer built a case that Jesus represented Greek love, the male-to-male sexual love much like that of Achilles and Patroculus.

The nineteenth-century Anglican clergy Edward Carpenter wrote about homogenic love in a democratic society. Carpenter refused to use the newly coined word "homosexual," taking the sexual out of the word to desensationalize the word and concept.[73] He believed that Jesus had romantic relations with his male disciples and the Beloved Disciple: "Women break their alabaster caskets, kiss and anoint thy feet, and bless the womb that bare these. While in thy bosom with thee, lip to lip, thy younger comrade lies."[74] For Carpenter, Jesus' crucifixion becomes "the prototype of all men misunderstood and persecuted because they love other men."[75] Like Bentham before him, Carpenter views Jesus as a model of homogenic love with the added difference of Carpenter's notion of Jesus as androgynous. Jesus as an androgyne provides him with a means of speaking of Christ's female soul in a male body, and this enables Carpenter to subvert or, in modern vernacular, queer Victorian gender codes. Frank Leib writes, "For him [Carpenter], the sexuality of Christ fully means a rediscovery of the sacredness of human sexuality."[76] Sacred eroticism may well be the antidote to a history of Christian erotophobia.

---

70. Crompton, *Byron and Greek Love*, 278–79.

71. Ibid., 276–77.

72. Bentham, Crompton mentions, had read in the *Monthly Magazine* an anonymous piece suggesting that the youth was a *cinaedus*, a boy prostitute (ibid., 281).

73. Leib, *Friendly Competitors, Fierce Companions*, 13–14.

74. Cited in ibid., 60–61.

75. Ibid.

76. Ibid., 189.

Contemporary gay constructions

The Anglican canon Hugh Montefiore created quite a stir in suggesting that Jesus had homosexual tendencies.[77] Montefiore offered this solution to the Christian tradition that Jesus never married. That Jesus did not marry because he wished to be absolutely free to do the will of God without encumbrances offers a credible explanation for the public ministry but not for his private life. Montefiore points out the unusualness of a Jewish male remaining unmarried and raises the question whether he was sexually attracted to women. For Montefiore, the possibility of Jesus' homosexuality gives insight into God:

> If Jesus were homosexual in nature, then this would be further evidence of God's self-identification with those who are unacceptable to the upholders of "The Establishment" and social conventions. The character of Jesus here discloses an important aspect of the nature of God, befriending the friendless, and identifying with the underprivileged.[78]

Montefiore's argument anticipates my own queer christology that I first developed within *Jesus ACTED UP*. There I argued that Jesus becomes the Queer Christ on Easter in his identification with all outsiders and, in particular, queer outsiders. That argument was born out of my own homoerotic experience of Jesus the Christ and the realization of the traces of erotic grace within my own homoerotic longings for Christ.

The late Robert Williams wrote that Jesus was "an earthy, lusty, passionate radical."[79] Williams asserts that Jesus was gay. He cites a fragment from the Secret Gospel of Mark when the youthful Lazarus is restored to health. Reading the fragment of Secret Mark, Williams then identifies Lazarus as the Beloved Disciple in the Fourth Gospel and the passionate lover of Jesus. In an unpublished manuscript, "The Beloved Disciple," Williams details his earlier assertions in a fictionalized story about Jesus and his passionate love of Lazarus.[80] In very erotic but sensitive love scenes, Williams portrays Jesus and Lazarus in sexual embrace and intercourse. Jesus is sexually versatile in Williams's imagination, and the Beloved Disciple penetrates Jesus in anal intercourse in the Garden of Gethsemane prior to his arrest.

---

77. Hugh Montefiore, "Jesus: The Revelation of God," in *Christ for Us Today*, ed. W. Norman Pittenger (London: SCM Press, 1968), 101–17.

78. Ibid., 110.

79. Robert Williams, *Just as I Am* (New York: Crown Publishers, 1992), 215.

80. Williams's manuscript has been left to the executor of his estate.

Gay priest and writer Malcolm Boyd takes the critical position that we have no documentation of Jesus' personal life regarding his sexuality. There are indications that Jesus spent his life in the company of men and that his relations with women were open, sensitive, and honest. Arguing from the doctrine of the incarnation as the embodiment of God, Boyd comprehends human sexuality as healthy, vital, and good. While examining a range of gay, lesbian, and bisexual perceptions of Jesus' sexuality, Boyd concludes that Jesus exemplifies God's embodied love and thus provides a role model for gays and lesbians.[81] In an interview, Boyd further refines his earlier position by envisioning the Christ as a gay archetype:

> But in Christ, I find more gay qualities: vulnerability, sensitivity, someone who emptied himself of power, who lived out as a gentle but as strong person that also broke many social taboos and found sterling qualities in a number of people who were despised by the society they lived in. He is very much a gay archetype in understanding of what being gay means.[82]

Joseph Kramer takes the love mysticism of Jesus and expands it to a physical knowing and loving of the body of Christ. In his description of Jesuit seminary life, Kramer speaks of the erotic connectedness he found within his Jesuit community:

> There was an older brother in the seminary to whom I just opened my heart, and he took me under his wing. Eventually that flowed into a night of wrestling and play, eroticism and ejaculations. I've known him ever since then; he's a wonderful man. At least half of the students who were there had sexual encounters with one another. But none of this was compulsive; it was an expression of a deep connection — spiritual, emotional, and physical. We were so close in many ways that it seemed right for our bodies to touch and to sear. We were the body of Christ.[83]

Kramer experiences the body of Christ in the bodies of other men. His sense of identity with Christ is on the level of bodily knowing, experiencing, and loving. Kramer's experience has many of the same descriptive

---

81. Mark Thompson, *Gay Soul: Finding the Heart of Gay Spirit and Nature* (San Francisco: HarperSanFrancisco, 1994), 233. See also Malcolm Boyd, "Was Jesus Gay?" *The Advocate* 565 (December 4, 1995): 90.
82. Boyd, "Was Jesus Gay?" 90.
83. Cited in ibid., 172.

patterns of bodily knowing and loving that medieval woman like Hadewijch and other female mystics experienced. In a conversation with
myself, Joe notes that his prayer is not visual but auditory and definitely
tactile: "Every time Jesus met someone, he touched them. . . . My connection with Jesus is a physical thing. Your body is the body of Christ, your
hands touch the body of Christ."[84] In his interview with Mark Thompson,
Kramer elaborates upon this physical identity and union with Christ: "I
believe that my spirituality is skin — and deep. That's it about the body
as gateway. Jesus didn't say 'This is my mind, these are my thoughts. This
is my body; this is my blood. If you want to be in communion with me,
eat my body, drink my blood.' "[85]

Kramer's vision expands from specific male bodies to an erotic body
of Christ in training men to experience the sacredness of physical touch
and intimacy. His sacred intimate training attempts to bring men in
touch with their erotic energies and capacities for pleasure within a
spiritual environment. For Kramer, an erotic community provides the
environment for the cultivation and the integration of sexuality and spirituality.[86] His notion of erotic community, ritual, and contemplation may
well be a contemporary rearticulation of the homoaffectual friendship
preached by Aelred of Rievaulx to his monks. The difference between
the two is that Kramer is more explicit in his articulation of the bonds
of erotic love, ritual, and contemplation that united the erotic body of
Christ.

Michael Kelly, a former Franciscan, presents a six-volume video series, *The Erotic Contemplative,* where he voices the Catholic tradition of
erotic contemplation of nuptial mysticism, merging it with explicit physical love-making.[87] While Kelly maintains that we do not know much
about Jesus' sexuality, he notes that Jesus was a man "who lived with
passionate freedom and who loved fearlessly and without regard for
cultural norms."[88] Catholic erotophobic practice castrated the power
of the metaphor of love-making with God, removing its passion and
its eroticism. Kelly restores passion and eroticism to the nuptial mysticism of the lover and the beloved, articulating the tradition of being
"kissed by Christ and kissing Christ." Physical and spiritual love-making
are united, not kept apart as in traditional Catholic erotophobic the-

84. Ibid.
85. Ibid., 177.
86. Ibid., 107.
87. Michael Kelly, *The Erotic Contemplative,* 6 vols. (Oakland, Calif.: EroSpirit, 1994).
88. Michael Kelly, "Could Jesus Have Been Gay?" (*http://rainbowsashmovement.org/gayjesus.html*).

ology. Kelly is quite explicit in recovering the social shame of anal intercourse as the point of gay male communion with Christ. Christ is within gay men's semen, entering the body of another man, being absorbed by the body, and transforming the shameful stigma of anal intercourse into divine love-making. Gay men enter into the body of Christ, and Christ penetrates gay men in anal intercourse. Gays, forbidden to love, are invited by God to become Christ's lover. But perceiving Jesus as a penetrated male subverts penetrative, heterosexist masculinity that eschews mutuality for self-pleasure and power. The penetrated Christ provides gay bottoms with an icon of alternative masculinities, subverting heterosexual phallocentrism.

Conclusion

One of the most recent homoerotic portrayals of Jesus is Terrence McNally's play *Corpus Christi,* where McNally tells the story of young Joshua, a thinly disguised Jesus, who is a victim of abuse by homophobic youths in a Texas high school. Fundamentalist Christian protests and conservative Catholic outcries against McNally's play center on Joshua's sexual intimacy with his male disciples. Fundamentalists are obsessed with maintaining a sexless (or a heterosexually celibate) Jesus and fail to recognize the poignant theology of McNally's play by their refusal to read or view it. Joshua is every queer who has undergone homophobic violence, struggled to come out, and discovered the original blessing of his sexual desires and love-making. Many gay men experience *Corpus Christi* with vivid memory of the murder of Matthew Shepard and their own experiences of homophobic violence. In his preface, Terrence McNally makes it quite explicit: "Jesus Christ did not die in vain because his disciples lived to spread his story. It is this generation's duty to make certain Matthew Shepard did not die in vain. We forget the story at the peril of our very lives."[89] While McNally makes every effort to link homophobia with the persecutions endured by Jesus and a dramatic plea for acceptances of queers within the churches, the conservative Christian backlash reveals how profound the linkage of Christian erotophobia and homophobia is and how invested it is in maintaining a heterosexual Jesus. The Catholic need to keep Jesus ideologically

---

89. McNally, *Corpus Christi,* vi. See also Raymond-Jean Frontain, "All Men Are Divine: Religious Mystery and Homosexual Identity in Terrence McNally's *Corpus Christi,"* in *Reclaiming the Sacred: The Bible in Gay and Lesbian Culture,* ed. Raymond-Jean Frontain, 2d ed. (New York: Harrington Park Press, forthcoming).

sexless and the fundamentalist Protestant need to keep Jesus ideologically heterosexual prevent Christians from seeing the moments of grace
within *Corpus Christi*. They fail to understand the message of Jesus' parable of the sheep and goats (Matt. 25:31–46): "Just as you did not do to
the least of these, you did not do it to me"(v. 45).

Some Christian erotophobes would claim that my above genealogical
analysis of homoerotic constructions of Jesus is perverse or obscene.
I would counter their homophobic judgments by saying that we find
traces of erotic grace in these passionate constructions of Jesus. They
have been lifelines for pious Christian men attracted to the same sex,
helping them to find meaning from their prayer closets and perhaps a
limited self-acceptance of their sexual attractions to men and Christ. For
two millennia, many Christian men have read the story of Jesus with a
homoerotic gaze and devotion. For them, Jesus remained a cipher for
homoerotically connecting with God and accepting themselves. They
have long recognized Jesus as one of their own. He is claimed as a
penetrated male, a bottom violating the masculine code of penetration
and phallic domination. He is an outsider, transgressing the normative
borders of heteronormativity and experiencing forbidden love between
men. The dynamics of McNally's play can be seen as the latest attempt to
read his homoerotic life with textual fragments of information in Jesus'
relationship with the Beloved Disciple.

Many gay Christians have imaginatively constructed a Jesus whom they
found attractive. In the essay "Tongues Untied: Memoirs of a Pentecostal
Boyhood," queer cultural critic Michael Warner writes, "Jesus was my first
boyfriend. He loved me, personally, and told me I was his own."[90] Many
Catholic gay youth have grown up on their knees, gazing erotically at
the crucified Jesus with his genitals covered and secretly wanting to lift
off the loincloth and gaze erotically at those genitals. I trace my first
unspoken words of physical attraction to the crucified Jesus, wanting to
strip off his loincloth to gaze at his genitals. As a young prepubescent
child, I remember trying to take off the loincloth on a crucified Jesus.
As I reached puberty, I gazed erotically at Michelangelo's *Risen Christ,* a
nude sculpture in an art book in the library. I lusted after the figure of
Christ, imagining him as the bearded hunk depicted by Michelangelo.
Christ was an utterly desirable, bearded hunk, naked on the cross, and I
entered the seminary to find union with him and make love with him. He
was penetrated by a Roman centurion, fueling taboo Catholic fantasies

---

90. Michael Warner, "Tongue Untied: Memoirs of a Pentecostal Boyhood," *Village Voice
Literary Supplement* (February 1993): 14.

for a boy coming to grips with his sexual feelings about men. For me, this became transformed through contemplative prayer from erotic fantasies to imaginative moments of grace and divine love. In the movie *Priest*, the gay priest agonizes over his vocation to the priesthood because of his homosexual attraction: "I sit in my room sweating. I turn to him for help. I see a naked man, utterly desirable. I turn to him for help, and he just makes it worse."[91] I and many other Catholic men, priests and laymen, have found the naked Jesus utterly sexually desirable, calling us to pursue a relationship, and many of us have discovered that we were utterly desirable to Jesus.

91. See Rambuss, *Closet Devotions*, 65.

SEVEN

FROM CHRIST THE OPPRESSOR
TO JESUS THE LIBERATOR

It's not a matter of emancipating truth from every system of power (which
would be a chimera, for truth is already power) but of detaching the power
of truth from the forms of hegemony, social, economic, and cultural within
which it operates at the present. — Michel Foucault[1]

Christianity aspires to meaning for all people, at all times. Christian
theology, however, is the product of people with power and privilege,
influence and wealth. This gives their theology a partisan bias that renders it meaningful to only a limited audience, particular not universal.
This partisan bias must be unmasked. The theology of Jesus the Christ
must expand to include the reality of gay and lesbian oppression.

My intention in this chapter is not to offer a detailed analysis of
the various forms of christology over the last two thousand years, but
rather to focus on the effects of contemporary christology and its impact
on homophobic discourse and practice. I intend to practice genealogical criticism to deconstruct contemporary christology. Genealogical
deconstruction is a way of keeping questions radically open, examining heterodoxy rather than orthodoxy. It is a negative hermeneutics or
interpretative framework that appears to be lack of piety to orthodox,
practicing Christians. It is the practice of critically questioning christologies, their truth-claims, and their alignments with power. A queer

---

Editorial note: When I first wrote this chapter in *Jesus ACTED UP,* I was hesitant to use the
term "lesbian" in addition to "gay" for fear of false inclusion. I decided to use "gay/lesbian"
but with the condition of letting lesbian voices speak for themselves as often as possible.
At the time, I was also hesitant to include bisexual and transgendered voices because of
false inclusion. This chapter does not include bisexual and transgendered voices explicitly
though it has been used by bisexuals and transgendered Christians to begin to articulate
their theological voices. When I facilitated a panel titled "What Is the BT in GLBT Theology?" at the "Claiming Our Faith: Celebrating the Spiritual in Our Lives" Conference at
Harvard Divinity School in 1999, I found the bisexual and transgendered panelists using
the principles articulated in this chapter.

1. Michel Foucault, *Power/Knowledge* (New York: Pantheon Books, 1980), 133.

genealogical criticism attempts to unearth alternatives within christo-logical discourse by investigating the seams, hesitations, contradictions, and resistances in that discourse. Genealogical criticism contests the norm by drawing to the surface oppositions to that norm, exposing the process whereby one of the terms controls or dominates the other. It disrupts traditional Christian theology by an inversion, an overthrowing of the dominant term with its opposite. In other words, it redirects the terms of Christian theology against themselves.

In his essay "Nietzsche: Genealogy, History," Foucault takes a trans-gressive stance toward social rules; he encourages a genealogical strategy of turning social rules against themselves and their rulers:

> Rules are empty in themselves, violent and unfinalized: they are im-personal and can be bent to any purpose. The successes of history belong to those who are capable of seizing these rules, to replace those who have used them, to disguise themselves so as to pervert them, invert their meaning, and redirect them against those who had initially imposed them: controlling this complex mechanism, they will make it function so as to overcome the rulers through their own rules.[2]

The strategy of genealogical criticism liberates discourse from its former power relations and redeploys it within new formations of truth/power. It contributes to a transgressive or dissident truth. Our disqualified queer knowledge arises out of our experience of homophobic oppression.

Queer criticism deconstructs christology as universal truth-claims, locating it within the shifting cultural systems of which it is a part. It constructs a contextual christological discourse that is born from gay/lesbian social experience. It looks beneath and outside the dom-inant meaning of christological discourse for absent gay/lesbian voices. Queer criticism uses biblical criticism to discover the dangerous memory of Jesus lost beneath nearly two millennia of patriarchal and ecclesial for-mulations. Queer criticism considers the alternative meanings, hidden or disqualified, such as sexuality and pleasure. Traditional christologies usually encode a system of oppositions, divine and human, male and female, asexual and sexual, heterosexual and homosexual. Traditional christological discourse evaluates one term of opposition over another.

Queer criticism is perilous. It intends to exacerbate conflict with institutional ecclesial discursive practices that insist on a particular

---

2. Michel Foucault, *Language, Counter-memory, Practice* (Ithaca, N.Y.: Cornell University Press, 1977), 151.

authoritative reading of christological discourse. By focusing on the challenge of gay/lesbian discursive practice, queer criticism overturns the hierarchical opposition of terms in traditional christologies. It asserts the value of the human, the equality of male and female, sexuality, and the queer.

The queer criticism in this chapter will provoke an ecclesial reaction. To deconstruct ecclesial authority in the creation of a queer christology is to discover how particular ecclesial conceptual discourses restrain gay/lesbian knowledge of christology. Ecclesial authority is a specific form of heterosexist privilege, which silences queers. For Foucault, authority within a specific discursive field is aligned with a particular set of power relations and deployment of rules. These have a disciplinary and regulating function. Ecclesial authority has power over the discursive field of Christianity. It has the power to silence and exclude; it has exercised its authority in a terroristic fashion to silence critics from speaking and exclude them from teaching. Ecclesial authority over the discursive field of Christianity can affect other fields as well. It can use Jesus the Christ or biblical doctrines to bless homophobic practices, discrimination, or governmental policies. It often legitimizes homophobia and homophobic social practices.

Christian churches speak for a certain understanding of historical truth and christological meaning. They claim authority to determine the truthfulness of christological discourse. Our genealogical challenges endanger their ownership of discursive practices and all other connected forms of institutional discourse. Other homophobic institutional practices have depended on homophobic Christian discourse, that is, christological discourse, for their legitimacy. Queer critical practice endangers institutional Christian control and threatens ecclesial authority with what Foucault calls the "insurrection of subjugated knowledges." In this particular context, the subjugated knowledges are queer knowledge, writings, and practices that have been dismissed by mainstream heterosexist/homophobic society. The insurrection of queer knowledge is the foundation of a thoroughly queer theology.

The deconstruction of christology

The notion that Jesus was conceived by the Holy Spirit in a virgin was a late tradition in gospel formation.[3] This notion was transformed into

---

3. Raymond E. Brown, *The Birth of the Messiah* (New York: Doubleday, 1977); Eta Ranke-Heinemann, *Eunuchs for the Kingdom of Heaven* (New York: Doubleday, 1990).

an antisexual rhetoric as Christianity evolved in the Hellenistic world. As Christianity became part of the mainstream of the Roman Empire, its discourse and practice were altered. Hostility to pleasure/desire and the body was the Greco-Roman legacy to Christianity. A growing philosophical and Gnostic-ascetic elision of pleasure/desire was accepted into Christian social practices. Classical Hellenistic techniques of self-mastery were transformed into Christian techniques for controlling the self and eliminating pleasure/desire. By the end of the second century, non-Christians and Christians vied with each other in heaping abuse on the body. Non-Christian authors advocated sexual restraint, and Christian asceticism was derived in part from older Hellenistic, Jewish, and Gnostic ascetic practices. Contempt for the human condition and hatred of the body were culturally widespread, and some of the most extreme manifestations were found in Gnostic and Christian religious practices: "Classical techniques of austerity were transformed into techniques whose purpose was the purification of desire and the elimination of pleasure, so that austerity became an end in itself."[4] Christian discursive practice that was once focused on resistance to the Roman state shifted to preoccupation with the control of sexuality. Suffering had earlier been lionized in Christian discursive practice: now ascetic pain and suffering replaced the notion of pleasure.[5]

An emerging Christian sexual discourse accented the negative importance of desire/pleasure in order to exclude it from social practice.[6]

4. Hubert Dreyfus and Paul Rabinow, *Michel Foucault: Beyond Structuralism and Hermeneutics* (Chicago: University of Chicago Press, 1983), 255. Christian discourse between the second and fourth centuries gave a lot of attention to sexual desire/pleasure. First Corinthians 7:1 and 8 recommend refraining from sex because the end is near. *The Acts of Paul and Thecla*, an enormously popular text in the early Christian movement, maintains that only virgins will be resurrected. See Elaine Pagels's discussion of Thecla in *Adam, Eve, and the Serpent* (New York: Random House, 1988), 18–20. See also Ranke-Heinemann, *Eunuchs*, 18–20; Michel Foucault, *History of Sexuality* (New York: Vintage Books, 1990), vol. 3; E. R. Dodds, *Pagan and Christian in an Age of Anxiety* (Cambridge: Cambridge University Press, 1965), 32–33; James A. Brundage, *Law, Sex, and Christian Society in Medieval Europe* (Chicago: University of Chicago Press, 1987), 60–76; Peter Brown, *The Body and Society* (New York: Columbia University Press, 1988), 65–209.

5. Samuel Laeuchli, *Power and Sexuality: The Emergence of Canon Law at the Synod of Elvira* (Philadelphia: Temple University Press, 1977), 56–113; Beverly Harrison and Carter Heyward, "Pain and Pleasure: Avoiding the Confusions of Christian Tradition in Feminist Theory," in *Christianity, Patriarchy, and Abuse*, ed. Joanne Carlson Brown and Carole Bolin (New York: Pilgrim Press, 1989), 150–66.

6. Foucault observes, "These two options, that sex is at the heart of all pleasure and that its nature requires that it should be restricted and devoted to procreation, are not of Christian but of Stoic origin; and Christianity was obliged to incorporate them when it sought to integrate itself in the State structure of the Roman Empire in which Stoicism was virtually the universal philosophy. Sex then became the code of pleasure" (Michel Foucault, "On Genealogy," in *Michel Foucault*, ed. Hubert Dreyfus and Paul Rabinow [Chicago: University of Chicago Press, 1985], 242). See also Elizabeth A. Clark, "Foucault, the

Christian discourse emphasized purification or the removal of desire/ pleasure rather than mere self-regulation, as in Greco-Roman philosophy. It exalted sexual abstinence as the ideal. Christian discourse, thus, provided social legitimation for its rejection and disapproval of desire/sexual pleasure, celibate practice, and the exclusion of women from Christian ministry: "Christianity did not invent this code of sexual behavior. Christianity accepted it, reinforced it, and gave to it a much larger and more widespread strength than it had before."[7] It is within this crucible of late Greco-Roman ideas of sexual restraint and Stoic self-mastery, neo-Platonism, and conflict with libertarian Gnostic groups that Christian antisexual/antidesire discursive practices were forged.

The elision of pleasure/desire in Christian social practices shaped and accented the image of the celibate Jesus.[8] Christology became an interpretative construction of Jesus and his bodily practices. The more that Jesus the Christ was Hellenized, ontologized, spiritualized, depoliticized, and ecclesialized, the more the human person, Jesus, was neutered. His sexuality diminished into celibate asexuality. In this elision of pleasure/desire, Christian discursive practice incorporated interlocking misogynist and homophobic power relations.[9] Christian discursive practice became anti-erotic/anti-pleasure. Pleasure, subsequently, has rarely been successfully integrated into Christian discursive practice.[10]

Fathers, and Sex," *Journal of the American Academy of Religion* 56, no. 4 (1989): 619–41. For a summary of the incorporation of Stoicism into Christian discourse on human nature, see John McNeill, *The Church and the Homosexual* (Kansas City, Mo.: Sheed Andrews and McMeel, 1976), 89–107. See also Brown, *Body and Society*, 122–37.

7. Foucault, *Power/Knowledge*, 191. See also Foucault, "Sexuality and Solitude," in *On Signs*, ed. Marshall Bosky (Baltimore: Johns Hopkins University Press, 1985), 369.

8. W. E Phipps, *Was Jesus Married? The Distortion of Sexuality in the Christian Tradition* (New York: Harper & Row, 1970), 120–63; see also Dodds, *Pagan and Christian*.

9. Beverly Harrison notes that misogyny and homophobia are sustained by the depth of anti-body, antisensual discourse in dominant Christianity. The fear of eroticism as foreign and evil permeated Christianity from the early second century. Misogyny is reflected in the phobic projection of female stigma onto any males who need to be distanced from dominant norms of manhood, such as men attracted to same-sex practices. See Beverly Harrison, "Misogyny and Homophobia: The Unexplored Connections," in *Making the Connections*, ed. Carol Robb (Boston: Beacon Press, 1985), 135–51. Rosemary Ruether similarly connects homophobia and heterosexism in Christian history; see Ruether, "Homophobia, Heterosexism, and Pastoral Practice," in *Homosexuality in the Priesthood and Religious Life*, ed. Jeannine Gramick (New York: Crossroad, 1990), 21–35. See also James B. Nelson, *Embodiment: An Approach to Sexuality and Christian Theology* (Minneapolis: Augsburg Press, 1979), 37–69; and McNeill, *Church and the Homosexual*, 189.

10. In his detailed study *Law, Sex, and Christian Society*, James Brundage documents hostility to sexual pleasure in Christianity's discursive and nondiscursive practices from its origin to the Reformation. Peter Brown, in *Body and Society*, examines Christianity's anti-body and antisexual perspective from its enculturation into the Hellenistic world to the early Middle Ages. Thomas Aquinas appeared to acknowledge pleasure as a positive value. He said, "Pleasure is the perfection of activity" (quoted by Matthew Fox, *Sheer Joy*

Along with the elision of pleasure/desire, Christian discourse about God incorporated from Greco-Roman philosophy a similar elision of passion (*patheia*). It accepted the Greek notion of *apatheia*.[11] God became apathetic — that is, without passion, unable to suffer, be affected, or be acted upon. Tertullian's description of God is a virtually Stoic exaltation of *apatheia*. Augustine took the critical Stoic opposition of reason against passion, and he defined passion (*passio*) as a "commotion of the mind and contrary to reason." Thus, he believed that it was an inappropriate attribute for God.[12] The Christian God became apathetic in Christian theological discourse.[13] God became totally other, removed, unchanged. God's love (*agape*) became passionless. This stood contrary to the passionate tribal God of Hebrew Scriptures and the loving parent figure, the God of Jesus, who lives, becomes, changes, speaks, acts, suffers, and dies. It stood in stark contrast to the biblical doctrine of a God who loves or is passionate for justice. A God who is unable to suffer or to feel passion is a loveless God.[14]

Tertullian used Jesus as an example of virginity: "Christ was himself a virgin in the flesh in that he was born of a virgin's flesh."[15] Tertullian's revulsion for sexual passion led him to renounce sexual relations with his wife because sexual desire had no place in the life of a Christian. Christian discourse of the second and third centuries ranked unbridled sexual passion with idolatry among the gravest offenses. By the time of Jerome and Augustine, a definite antisexual discourse and practice

---

[San Francisco: HarperSanFrancisco, 1991], 34). Thomas stood against the Augustinian tradition in this regard. However, his view of female sexuality remained narrow. See Fox's discussion, 37–45. I would include Aquinas's statements on same-sex practices as well. It is bizarre for Catholic hierarchs and theologians to canonize an outdated view of sexuality.

11. Dorothee Soelle speaks about *apatheia*, "literally nonsuffering....Apathy is a form of the inability to suffer. It is understanding as a social condition in which people are dominated by a goal of avoiding suffering that it becomes a goal to avoid human relationships and contacts altogether" (Soelle, *Suffering* [Philadelphia: Fortress Press, 1975], 36). Jürgen Moltmann asserts, "In the physical sense, *apatheia* means unchangeableness; in the psychological sense, insensitivity; and in the ethical sense, freedom" (Moltmann, *The Crucified God* [New York: Harper & Row, 1974], 267). Literature on the theme of God's passibility/impassibility: J. K. Mozley, *The Impassability of God* (London: Cambridge University Press, 1926); Terrence Fretheim, *The Suffering of God: An Old Testament Perspective* (Philadelphia: Fortress Press, 1977); S. Paul Schilling, *God and Human Language* (Nashville: Abingdon Press, 1977); Warren McWilliams, *The Passion of God* (Macon, Ga.: Mercer University Press, 1985).

12. Augustine, *City of God*, 8.17. Passion is identified with demons and the pagan gods; rationality is associated with the Christian God.

13. The Christian apologists synthesized the biblical God with Stoic philosophy. The Hebrew God was transformed into the Stoic, apathetic God. Thus, the Hebrew God lost both compassion and passion for justice-doing.

14. Carter Heyward, *The Redemption of God: A Theology of Mutual Relation* (Washington, D.C.: University of America Press, 1989), 12; Moltmann, *Crucified God*, 222, 248.

15. Tertullian, *On the Flesh of Christ*, 20. See Brown's discussion, *Body and Society*, 76–79.

had emerged within Christianity. It reflected three centuries of Christian assimilation into the Greco-Roman world and the struggles with various Gnostic groups. Jerome attacked the British monk Jovinian, who preached that marriage, like the celibate state, could equally be a means for growing in the knowledge of God: "He [Jovinian] put marriage on a level with virginity, while I make it inferior; he declares that there is little or no difference between the two states; I claim that there is a great deal. Finally... he has dared to place marriage on an equal level with perpetual chastity."[16] Jerome believed that too much sexual pleasure in marriage was a form of adultery. Other Christian patriarchs such as Gregory of Nazianzus, Gregory of Nyssa, John Chrysostom, and Ambrose praised virginity. They looked with horror at sexual pleasure.[17]

For Augustine, sexual pleasure/desire was what carries original sin from generation to generation. Augustine considered sexual intercourse undertaken for anything but procreation to be sinful.[18] He codified sexual acts that were necessary in marriage for the preservation of the human race and submitted them to ecclesial control. Such acts were neutral, not sinful, only when they were prompted not by desire/pleasure but for the purpose of procreation. Marriage was good insofar as sexual pleasure was controlled. Augustine connected concupiscence with sexual intercourse: "Everyone who is born of sexual intercourse is in fact sinful flesh."[19] Christ was born without libido or concupiscence since he was born without the intervention of semen. Foucault offers this reading of Augustine:

---

16. Jerome, *Letter 48, to Pammachoius*, 2, quoted in Elaine Pagels, *Adam, Eve, and the Serpent*, 95. Ambrose and Augustine also condemned Jovinian for his heresy. See Pagels's description of the dispute between Jerome and Jovinian, 91–96. See Brown's treatment of Jerome, *Body and Society*, 366–86.

17. Reay Tannahill, *Sex in History* (New York: Stein and Day, 1980), 136–53; Brown, *Body and Society*, 285–322, 341–65.

18. Augustine's legacy has been fifteen hundred years of hostility to sexual pleasure. He maintains that in Eden the connection between man and woman is asexual (*De gen. contra Manichaeos*, 1.19). Sexual pleasure was considered an evil (*City of God*, 22.24; *Against Julian*, 5.9, 5.46; *De homo conjugali*, 3.3, 8.9, 17.9). In *Epistles* 262.4, Augustine advises a woman, "Your husband does not cease to be your spouse because of joint abstinence from carnal relations. You will remain all the more devout as spouses the more you keep this resolution." Virginity thus was a higher state of holiness than marriage with sexual relations: abstinence from pleasure and lust-inspired sexual actions became a preoccupation for Christianity into the modern era. On Augustine and sexuality, see Pagels, *Adam, Eve, and the Serpent*, 98–150; Margaret Miles, *Augustine on the Body* (Missoula, Mont.: Scholars Press, 1979), 41–72; Brown, *Body and Society*, 387–427.

19. *On Marriage and Concupiscence*, 1.13. "That semen itself," Augustine argues, "already 'shackled by the bonds of death,' transmits the damage incurred by sin." Hence, Augustine concludes, "Every human being ever conceived through semen is born contaminated with sin." Pagels summarizes the concept of flesh and sin in *City of God* 13.14 (Pagels; *Adam, Eve, and the Serpent*, 109).

The famous gesture of Adam covering his genitals with a fig leaf is, according to Augustine, not due to the simple fact that Adam was ashamed of their presence, but to the fact that his sexual organs were moving by themselves without his consent. Sex in erection is the image of man revolted against God. The arrogance of sex is punishment and consequence of the arrogance of man. His uncontrolled sex is exactly the same as what he has been toward God — a rebel.[20]

Foucault maintains that Augustine read the biblical text of Adam's rebellion against God as the interpretative framework for understanding the relationship of sex and the Christian construction of the ascetic self.[21] The ascetic's task was "perpetually to control one's thoughts, examining them to see if they were pure, whether something dangerous was not hiding in or behind them; if they were not conveying something other than what primarily appeared, if they were not a form of illusion and seduction."[22] This spiritual struggle of the self against rebellious sexual pleasure has continued to remain normative in Christian discourse through recent times.

For Augustine and other church patriarchs, Jesus the Christ embodied the antipleasure principle that generated multiple discursive practices supporting the construction of the ascetic self and the social position of a male celibate clergy. Jesus was born without libido, according to these patriarchs; traditional Christian discourse, therefore, castrated Jesus, making him an asexual eunuch. It absolutized Jesus' maleness. It drew social attention from bodily existence with all its drives, passions, and desires toward the realm of the spiritually constructed self. It glorified the apathetic self, the ascetic self-mastery over passion. It was necrophilic practice, obsessive social preoccupation with what is dead, unfeeling, regulated, controlled, stripped of passion.[23]

20. Foucault, "On Genealogy," 370; Pagels, *Adam, Eve, and the Serpent*, 110–12.

21. Foucault defines self-technology: "In every culture, I think, this self-technology implies a set of truth obligations: learning what is truth, discovering the truth, being enlightened by the truth, telling the truth. All these are considered important either for the constitution or for the transformation of the self" (Foucault, "On Genealogy," 367). See Michel Foucault, "Technologies of the Self," in *Technologies of the Self*, ed. Luther Martin, Huck Gutman, and Patrick Hutton (Amherst: University of Massachusetts Press, 1988), 16–49; Foucault, "The Political Technology of Individuals," in *Technologies of the Self*, 145–62.

22. Foucault, "On Genealogy," 371.

23. Dorothee Soelle, *Death by Bread Alone* (Philadelphia: Fortress Press, 1978), 9–10. Anti-body dualism emerged in Christian discourse and practice from the basic assimilation of cultural/philosophical misogyny. The basic hatred and fear of women were incorporated into the Christian social production and distribution of a complex web of antisexual,

Jesus' asexual maleness continued to exercise a normative function, excluding women from full ministerial participation in the church and continuing to legitimize antipleasure and misogynist practices. The notion of two natures of Jesus the Christ, defined by the Councils of Nicea and Chalcedon, was an unsuccessful attempt to overcome the Christian incorporation of the divine *apatheia*. The Chalcedonian declaration of Jesus as "true God" and "true man" attempted to balance christological discourse within the binary poles of divine and human. However, a close reading of the declaration underscores that Jesus the Christ is the divine apathetic person, who, nevertheless, possessed a human nature. Divine apathy triumphed over the human and the historical. The apathetic divine superseded the sexual human: the asexual male stood above the sexual female. Maleness was assimilated into the divine essence (*homoousia*), justifying misogynist and homophobic Christian discourse.

This notion of an apathetic God and "his" asexual Christ was fundamental to the social practices of patriarchy, the family, the church, and politics in Christianity from Constantine through the Reformation. The maleness that had been assimilated into the divine essence became normative for the social construction and legitimation of patriarchal power relations. Maleness was associated with superior rationality, spirituality, and authority, whereas femaleness was considered inferior and associated with emotions, embodiedness, and sensuality. Prohibitions against same-sex practices were grounded in the interests of a hierarchical male, celibate, and clerical church in preserving itself against passion and pleasure. Medieval Christianity was male, hierarchical, clerical, authoritarian, highly discriminatory, and exclusivist. The maleness of God supported male privilege. The maleness of the asexual Christ supported the gender politics of Christianity's subordination of women and their exclusion from social power and from orders. Male celibates used the church just as their secular counterparts used women. Jesus' maleness was used to justify rampant ecclesial and social misogyny.

Throughout the medieval era, Christian discourse centered on an apathetic God and the asexual Christ, but Renaissance artists boldly portrayed Jesus in his full genitality.[24] In his study of Renaissance images of

---

misogynist, and homophobic power relations. Maleness was asserted as superior to femaleness: it became a rejection of the body with all its pleasures. See Harrison, "Misogyny and Homophobia," 136–51. See also Nelson, *Embodiment*, 37–69.

24. Leo Steinberg presents compelling evidence of the Renaissance shift toward the sexuality of Jesus: Leo Steinberg, *The Sexuality of Christ in Renaissance Art and in Modern Oblivion* (New York: Pantheon Books, 1983), 1.

Jesus, art historian Leo Steinberg notes that "the evidence of Christ's sexual member serves as the pledge of God's humanation."[25] James Nelson summarizes Steinberg's study:

> In the great cathedrals hung paintings of the Holy Family in which Mary herself deliberately spreads the infant's thighs so that the pious might gaze at his genitals in wonder. In other paintings the Magi are depicted gazing intently at Jesus' uncovered loins as if expecting revelation. In still others Jesus' genitals are being touched and fondled by his mother, by St. Anne, and by himself. So also in the paintings of the passion and crucifixion, the adult Jesus is *depicted* as thoroughly sexual. In some, his hand cups his genitals in death, in others the loincloth of the suffering Christ is protruding with an unmistakable erection.[26]

The Renaissance movement to depict Jesus' genitals affirmed not only his humanity but also his sexuality. The Christ became sexual within popular imagination, signifying a shift within christological and sexual discourse.

Reformation discourse affirmed the essential goodness of nature and salvation by grace. The reformers lifted marriage and, in turn, sexual desire (in marriage) to the level of a more positive affirmation. Companionship and the restraint of sexual desire, rather than procreation, started to *emerge* as positive values in the reformers' theologies of marriage. Luther and Calvin did not overcome the spiritualistic dualism of earlier Christian practice, but they did shift it toward a more positive understanding. Luther understood the restraint of desire no longer in terms of religious life, but in terms of marriage. He confined the raging power of lust/pleasure to lawful expressions within marriage.[27] John Calvin, on the other hand, stressed the companionship of marriage.[28] The Protestant reformers undermined the celibate ideal of dominant Christian discourse and practice, and they advanced Christian discursive practice toward a positive affirmation of human sexuality. The reformers

25. Ibid., 13. See also Arnold Davidson, "Sex and the Emergence of Sexuality," in *Forms of Desire*, ed. Edward Stein (New York: Routledge, 1992), 102–10.

26. James B. Nelson, *The Intimate Connection* (Philadelphia: Westminster Press, 1988), 106.

27. Luther refers to sexual desire and union as instances of shame and disgust; see Luther, "Lectures on Genesis," in *Luther's Works*, ed. Jaroslav Pelikan (St. Louis: Concordia, 1968), 1:62–63, 71, 105. On the other hand, Luther affirms the goodness of marriage and sexuality; see Luther, "Estate of Marriage," in *Luther's Works*, 45:17, 36–37.

28. John Calvin, *A Harmony of the Gospels* (Edinburgh: St. Andrew Press, 1972), 2:249.

could not quite accept sexual pleasure as a complete good; they limited
themselves to affirming Jesus' male humanity and erotic feelings. This
reinforced the church's emphasis on family order and marriage and was
still used to justify the subordination of women to men and their exclusion from leadership within churches. The Reformation churches were
still in the grip of an antisexual, misogynist, and homophobic discursive
field even though they made significant modifications.

Reformation discourse effected a shift — albeit a slight shift — in
Roman Catholic discourse on sexuality and the family. Marriage and
family remained in a secondary position to the state of celibacy among
priests and religious. However, Catholic discourse began to recognize in
a limited fashion the unitive purpose of sexuality in marriage. It was only
with Vatican II and its aftermath that the Roman Catholic Church began
to shift its discursive focus toward the family. It followed the Protestant
vector of discovering Jesus' sexuality and then using his maleness to
justify the dominance of a male, celibate clergy.[29] Like most of the Protestant churches, the Catholic Church remains in the grip of antisexuality,
misogyny, and homophobia.

Sexuality and christology

Jesus' celibacy has been used by Catholic doctrine and practice to but-
tress control of the church by celibate men. As a symbol of asexuality,
the ecclesial portraits of Jesus promoted a moral/political dualism that
subordinated women and denigrated sexual pleasure. Misogyny and
homophobia were, therefore, the natural consequences of such asexual
readings of the biblical traditions.

There has been some movement to discuss Jesus' sexuality in contemporary theology. Tom Driver observes:

> The absence of all comment in them [the Gospels] about Jesus'
> sexuality cannot be taken to imply that he had no sexual feelings.
> ... It is not shocking, to me at least, to imagine Jesus moved to
> love according to the flesh. I cannot imagine a human tenderness,
> which the Gospels show to be characteristic of Jesus, that is not fed
> in some degree by the springs of passion. The human alternative

---

29. John Paul II in *Familiaris Consortia* praises periodic continence in marriage through
the use of the rhythm method of birth control. He maintains married (opposite-sex) sexual
actions may serve procreation or abstinence. In John Paul's gospel of continence, birth
control would allow unbridled pleasure/lust.

to sexual tenderness is not asexual tenderness but sexual fear. Jesus lived in his body, as other men do.[30]

Driver's theological comments were preceded by earlier literary attempts at reconstructing a sexual Jesus. D. H. Lawrence, in *The Man Who Died,* originally titled *The Escaped Cock,* attempted to revise the Christian perspective of antisexuality and give an example of sexual integration. Jesus' bodily resurrection provided Lawrence with the symbolism to explore Jesus coming to sexual wholeness through a priestess of Isis. The celibate Jesus who never had an erection comes to full sexual knowledge. Lawrence comments: "If Jesus rose in full flesh, He rose to know the tenderness of a woman, and the great pleasure of her, and to have children by her."[31] Similarly, Nikos Kazantzakis takes up the question of Jesus and sexuality in his *The Last Temptation of Christ.* The movie version of Kazantzakis's novel, depicting Jesus' struggle with sexual temptation, created an uproar with Christian fundamentalists when it was released. The asexual image of the Christ prevalent in fundamentalist groups will not entertain even the suggestion of the sexual temptation of Jesus.

As noted earlier, William Phipps takes up the question of Jesus' sexuality in his book *Was Jesus Married?* Phipps argues that antisexual rhetoric in early Christianity distorted the picture of Jesus into the celibate Christ. He argues that Jesus was married. Phipps's argument has merit against the strong residual antisexual discourse of Christianity. However, he desperately wants Jesus to be a social construction of heterosexuality.[32] Phipps's unnuanced use of scriptural evidence is not the issue here.[33] The point is that his raising the question indicates a paradigm shift has taken place in the Christian valuation of sexuality.

Within Protestant and more recent Roman Catholic christological discourse, Jesus the Christ becomes a model of heterosexuality, a foundation for legitimizing heterosexist Christian truth and social constructions on marriage and the family.[34] The heterosexual Christ remains, nonetheless, celibate and does not go as far as the fictional reconstructions

30. Tom R. Driver, "Sexuality and Jesus," *Union Seminary Quarterly Review* 20 (1965): 240, 243.

31. D. H, Lawrence, *The Later D. H. Lawrence* (New York: Knopf, 1952), 391.

32. Phipps, *Was Jesus Married?* See also William Phipps, *The Sexuality of Jesus* (New York: Harper & Row, 1975).

33. John Meier disputes Phipps's use of the scriptural evidence to argue for a married Jesus and instead assumes the traditional position of Jesus' celibacy; see Meier, *A Marginal Jew: Rethinking the Historical Jesus* (New York: Doubleday, 1991), 1:332–45.

34. Tom Driver argues against the current Christian practice of keeping Jesus the Christ as a centrist model. Such a centrist model leads to normative practices that are exclusive; see Driver, *Christ in a Changing World: Toward an Ethical Christology* (New York: Crossroad, 1981), 32–56.

of Lawrence and Kazantzakis. Jesus the heterosexual male Christ continues the moral/political dualism that subordinates the social position of women in the church and in society and that excludes sexual variation. Jesus the Christ becomes the cultural force for legitimizing compulsory heterosexuality.

Contemporary heterosexist Christian theology proclaims a heterosexist Christ: this results in a homophobic creationism. Homophobic creationism is the practice of using the creation accounts in Genesis 1–3 and Genesis 19 to justify heterosexual practice as normative because it is rooted in creation. Fundamentalist Christian ex-gay/ex-lesbian organizations that convert gay men and lesbians to heterosexuality in order to save them usually support their homophobic practice by pointing to the creation accounts. Likewise, the Vatican documents on homosexuality promote compulsory heterosexuality as normative of creation. The Vatican notion of homosexual orientation as "intrinsically evil" and "objectively disordered" manifests homophobic creationism.

Heterosexist Christian interpretations of the Genesis creation accounts legitimize a dominant male god, patriarchal power relations of men over women, and gender differentiations. The male God creates man (Gen. 2:7); woman is created as a helpmate to man (2:18–23); woman is created from the rib of man and is dependent upon him (Gen. 2:21–23); man names woman and has power over her (Gen. 2:23); woman's desire for man keeps her submissive (Gen. 3:16); God gives man the right to rule over woman (Gen. 3:16). According to heterosexist/homophobic creationism, God's creation is distorted by the sin of woman and later the sin of Sodom.[35] These biblical interpretations maintain the normalcy of the domination of male over female and the heterosexual sexual practices over same-sex practices. They contribute to the social organization and legitimation of homophobia.

In *God and the Rhetoric of Sexuality*, Phyllis Trible provides a fresh interpretation of the creation accounts. She tries to deconstruct misogynist readings by pointing out that metaphors and images for God as masculine are only partial. Trible translates Genesis verses in a way that stresses the notion of the image of God as both male and female: "and God created humankind in his image; / in the image of God created he him: / male and female created he them."[36] For Trible, the deconstruction of biblical misogyny is performed through restoring the balance of the fe-

---

35. George Edwards, "A Critique of Creationist Homophobia," in *Homosexuality and Religion*, ed. Richard Hasbany (New York: Harrington Park Press, 1989), 95–118.
36. Phyllis Trible, *God and the Rhetoric of Sexuality* (Philadelphia: Fortress Press, 1978), 12.

male images of God.[37] It critiques the entrenched patriarchy of biblical criticism.

Recently feminist theologians have deconstructed the maleness of Christ within christological discourse in a similar manner. They have reconstructed an inclusive christological discourse by not limiting the figure or meaning of Christ exclusively to the male Jesus. They widen the meaning of Christ to include feminine social practice.[38] Elisabeth Schüssler Fiorenza attempts to shift the burden of christological discourse to the *basileia* vision and practice of Jesus.[39] Other feminist theologians have placed christology in the practices and struggles of women. The term "Christa" refers to a female Christ-figure on the cross, as with the crucifix hanging for a time in the Cathedral of St. John the Divine in New York City.[40] Rita Nakashima Brock uses the term *Christa* to pioneer a christology not centered on Jesus but on the community.[41] Brock asserts:

> Jesus participates centrally in this Christa/Community, but he neither brings erotic power into being nor controls it. He is brought into being through it and participates in the cocreation of it. Hence Christa/Community is a lived reality expressed in relational images in which erotic power is made manifest. The reality of erotic power within connectedness means it cannot be located in a single individual. Hence what is truly christological, that is, truly revealing of divine incarnation and salvific power in human life, must reside in connectedness and not in single individuals. The relational nature of erotic power is as free during Jesus' life as it is after his death. He neither reveals nor embodies it, but he participates in its revelation and embodiment.[42]

Brock extends christology beyond the historical Jesus to the feminist community. Likewise, Carter Heyward uses the concept of Christa to embody erotic energy: "In the context of sexist, erotophobic patriarchy, Christa, unlike the male Christ, is controversial because her

---

37. Norman Gottwald shares Trible's conclusions; see Gottwald, *The Hebrew Bible: A Socio-literary Introduction* (Philadelphia: Fortress Press, 1985), 239.

38. Patricia Wilson-Kastuer, *Faith, Feminism, and the Christ* (Philadelphia: Fortress Press, 1983); Rosemary Ruether, *To Change the World: Christology and Cultural Criticism* (New York: Crossroad, 1981); Elisabeth Schüssler Fiorenza, *In Memory of Her* (New York: Crossroad, 1989).

39. Schüssler Fiorenza, *In Memory of Her*, 118–54.

40. The sculpture by Edwina Sandys was on display during Lent in 1984. See Carter Heyward, *Touching Our Strength* (San Francisco: Harper & Row, 1989), 114.

41. Rita Nakashima Brock, *Journeys by Heart* (New York: Crossroad. 1991), 113.

42. Ibid., 52.

body signals a crying need for woman-affirming (nonsexist), erotic (non-erotophobic) power that, insofar as we share it, will transform a world that includes our own personal lives in relation."[43] For feminist theologians, Jesus is retrieved in relation to the struggles of women for justice.

Similarly, the practice of a queer criticism radically questions contemporary heterosexual or past asexual constructions of christological discourse. It unpacks sexual oppositions that have been glossed over in totalizing truth-claims of Christian discourse. It uses feminist reconstructive practice against misogyny as part of its discourse. It employs its own critical practice against homophobia, but it also constructs queer bodies, queer selves, and queer sexuality. In feminist and queer critical practice, the erotic self is embodied over and against the apathetic self. The recovery of bodily connectedness and the affirmation of the erotic goodness of the body provide a corrective to an Augustinian severity that has long dominated Christian discourse. The contemporary recovery of embodied sexuality as a positive value is important for shaping a christology sensitive to the struggles of queer Christians.

Queer criticism recognizes christological discourse as historically constructed through misogyny, antisexuality, and homophobia. A queer christology starts with Jesus' practice and death and reconstructs the claims of Easter within queer critical practice.

The retrieval of Jesus' **basileia** *practice*

Jesus used the symbol of God's reign (*basileia*) to speak of liberating activity of God among people.[44] The symbol of Jesus' reign was the organizing symbol of his message and his practices. For Jesus, God's reign was socially provocative and politically explosive.[45] It was socially provocative in that its coming belonged to the least, those like children (Matt. 18:4; Mark 10:15), the destitute (Luke 6:20), the perse-

---

43. Heyward, *Touching Our Strength*, 114.

44. Norman Perrin, *Jesus and the Language of the Kingdom* (London: SCM, 1976); J. D. Crossan, *In Parables* (San Francisco: Harper & Row, 1973); Bruce Chilton and J. L. H. McDonald, *Jesus and the Ethics of the Kingdom* (Grand Rapids, Mich.: William B. Eerdmans, 1987).

45. Some good treatments of the historical Jesus: E. P. Sanders, *Jesus and Judaism* (Philadelphia: Fortress Press, 1987); Richard Horsley, *Jesus and the Spiral of Violence: Popular Jewish Resistance in Roman Palestine* (San Francisco: Harper & Row, 1987); Marcus Borg, *Jesus: A New Vision* (San Francisco: Harper & Row, 1987); J. D. Crossan, *The Historical Jesus: The Life of a Mediterranean Jewish Peasant* (San Francisco: HarperSanFrancisco, 1991); Paul Hollenbach, "Liberating Jesus for Social Involvement," *Biblical Theology Bulletin* 15 (1985): 151–57.

cuted (Matt. 5:10), and the outcasts (Matt. 21:31). God's reign was also politically explosive. Jesus practiced liberation in his siding with the humiliated and oppressed of Jewish society. He gave them hope and the courage to resist the domination politics of first-century Palestine.

The symbol of God's reign was polymorphous. It could take the metaphorical shape of a physical object (a mustard seed, leaven, a treasure), particular actions (healing, exorcisms, table association, the Temple demonstration), or visionary words. God's reign could be represented in parables, or it could be performed in action. The performed symbol of God's reign could open human communication to new dimensions and possibilities within social and political experience. Jesus and his group of disciples performed these social actions as if they represented God's coming reign.[46]

Jesus was a practitioner of God's reign unfolding in first-century Palestine. His *basileia* praxis was social; it had symbolic configurations with definite actions, particular social forms, and specific political goals. In his parables, the image of God's reign is often shocking and provocative: the good Samaritan (Luke 10:29–37), the prodigal son (Luke 15:11–32), the vineyard workers (Matt. 20:1–13), and the great banquet (Luke 14:16–23; Matt. 22:1–10). In the first century, the term "good Samaritan" was as shocking as the term "queer Christians" is to fundamentalist Christians today. The image of the father in the parable of the prodigal son breaks patriarchal stereotypes in his surprising actions toward his two sons. The egalitarian vision of God's reign in the parables of the vineyard workers and the great banquet undermines exclusive, privileged, and hierarchical attitudes of social power.

Jesus' *basileia* message and praxis signified the political transformation of his society into a radically egalitarian new age, where sexual, social, religious, and political distinctions would be irrelevant. Jesus struggled for *basileia* liberation in his siding with the humiliated, the oppressed, and the throwaway people of first-century Jewish society. He welcomed them at table and healed them of their social wounds. Jesus gave instructions on how to invite guests to a dinner (Luke 14:11–14). His meals did not create social distinctions but bridged them by including the outsider. His meals are inclusive metaphors for God's reign and its openness.[47] Jesus emphasized a generalized reciprocity, a giving without expecting a return (Luke 6:35). It is a form of giving that frees other people to give in return.

---

46. Chilton and McDonald, *Jesus*, 110–54.
47. Norman Perrin, *Rediscovering the Teachings of Jesus* (New York: Harper & Row. 1967), 1028; Crossan, *Historical Jesus*, 261–64, 341–44.

John Dominic Crossan maintains that the heart of Jesus' ministry was a "shared egalitarianism of spiritual and material resources," an unbrokered reign of God.[48] The discipleship of equals became a form of egalitarian relating between men and women.[49] This discipleship was marked by the sharing of goods, the equality of male and female disciples, an inclusiveness at table, and loving service at the table.[50] Jesus pointed out,

> The kings of the Gentiles exercise lordship over them; and those in authority over them are benefactors. But not so with you; rather let the greatest among you become as the youngest, and the leader as one who serves. For which is the greater, one who sits at table, or one who serves? Is it not the one who sits at table? But I am among you as one who serves. (Luke 22:24)

In his own words, Jesus modeled God's reign as one who serves at table and who washes the feet of his disciples. He asked his disciples to imitate these *basileia* actions. His *basileia* practices at table also criticized domination politics — the politics of Jewish aristocracy and Temple leadership, Herod Antipas, Pilate, and the Roman imperial system.

Jesus' liberative practice of God's coming reign depicted a critical alternative vision of social and political relations. It moved social and political relations in the direction of freedom, justice, and love. What Jesus practiced was meant to communicate to others the social presence of God's reign. God was socially present in *basileia* actions. God was available in the struggles and practices for human liberation.

The critical alternative in Jesus' *basileia* vision was not oppressor and oppressed exchanging roles. The cycle of abusive power, whereby an oppressor is vanquished by a former victim who then becomes oppressor, would come to a halt. God's reign would belong to the poor but not in the counterviolence of the Jewish resistance movement. God's reign would belong to the poor and oppressed who practiced loving service, not dominating power. Service at table would become the political infrastructure of God's new society. Thus, Jesus' basic *basileia* message and practice questioned power that victimized and oppressed people. Without compassion, all religious, economic, social, and political authority became oppressive. The power to dominate was embedded in the

---

48. Crossan, *Historical Jesus*, 341, 346.
49. Schüssler Fiorenza. *In Memory of Her*, 140–50.
50. Douglas Oakman, *Jesus and the Economic Questions of His Day* (Lewiston, N.Y.: Edwin Mellen Press, 1986), 213–15: Halvor Moxnes, *The Economy of the Kingdom* (Philadelphia: Fortress Press, 1988), 157–59.

motivations behind the extremism of piety, in the inflexibility of fundamentalists and literalists, in economic divisions, and in the legitimations
of political control.[51] He gave people hope and the courage to resist
domination politics manifested in social and economic inequalities.

Jesus confronted the systemic injustice of the imperial Roman control in which Jewish peasants found themselves. Jewish peasants were
squeezed by a religious and political system of economic extraction.
Bread and indebtedness were survival issues they faced every day. In
the Abba prayer Jesus addressed these needs: "Give us this day our daily
bread, and forgive us our debts as we forgive our debtors," he prayed. As
one contemporary theologian puts it, "Indebtedness disrupts the ability of a social order to supply daily bread. God is petitioned to remove
the oppressive power of debt in people's lives."[52] Waging conflict and
negating the existing structures of socioeconomic and political domination were part of Jesus' liberative praxis. He did not hesitate to criticize,
dispute, reject, condemn, and resist power relations and practices that
oppressed. These were liberative skills used in fighting for and actualizing God's compassion and justice. Jesus' kingdom praxis fundamentally
symbolized and actualized freedom.

The irruption of God's reign into the present called for a change of
direction or a new path. The practice of Jesus made clear the radical
freedom from which he acted. His praxis encompassed the political tensions that were realities in first-century Palestine. However, Jesus' praxis
contradicted the logic of an oppressive system imposed upon the poor,
the socially dysfunctional, the unclean, and the outsider in Palestine. His
radical freedom was measured precisely by his ability to participate in
their world and point to the innovative social network of God's reign. His
basileia practice of solidarity was his compassionate identification with
the oppressed and his active commitment to social change. The practice
of solidarity is what I include in the term *love-making:* it is vital to justice-

51. For a good picture of first-century Judaism, see Richard Horsley and John Hanson,
Bandits, Prophets, and Messiahs (San Francisco: Harper & Row, 1985); Horsley, *Jesus and
the Spiral;* Oakman, *Jesus and the Economic Questions;* Gerd Theissen, *The Sociology of Early
Palestinian Christianity* (Philadelphia: Fortress Press, 1988); Anthony Saldarini, *Pharisees,
Scribes, and Sadducees* (Wilmington, Del.: Michael Glazier, 1988); Crossan, *Historical Jesus;*
Martin Goodman, *The Ruling Class of Judea: The Origins of the Jewish Revolt against Rome
A.D. 66–70* (Cambridge: Cambridge University Press, 1987); Sheldon Isenberg, "Power
through the Temple and Torah in Greco-Roman Palestine," in *Christianity, Judaism, and
Other Greco-Roman Cults,* ed. Jacob Neusner (Leiden: E. J. Brill, 1975), 24–52.

52. Oakman, *Jesus and the Economic Questions,* 155. See also Horsley, *Jesus and the Spiral,*
246–84; John Kloppenborg, "Alms, Debt, and Divorce: Jesus' Ethics in Their Mediterranean Context," *Toronto Journal of Theology* (1990): 182–200; Crossan, *The Historical Jesus,*
294.

doing. Jesus proclaimed and practiced God's reign, a just and loving society where God would be socially in the midst of human interactions.

Jesus' *basileia* actions were political activities, oriented toward the radical transformation of the Jewish community. Jesus' *basileia* actions presented a critical alternative to the domination politics of the clerical aristocracy and the Roman imperium. He created a political community that mirrored the social presence and compassion of God. Jesus' *basileia* praxis was performed in specific social situations with specific intention. He engaged his social situation in its entirety with a continuous stream of kingdom actions, always trying to perform God's reign within any given social situation.

The politics of the cross

It was not God's will that Jesus died to ransom those with sin. This was a Christian interpretation of the death of Jesus. Rather, the cross symbolized the violent and brutal end of Jesus in the context of his political praxis for God's reign. Jesus was executed by the political infrastructure of Jewish Palestine as a political insurgent. The Jewish religious aristocracy and their Roman rulers perceived Jesus' message and practice of God's reign as a threat to the political order. The cross was a political tool used by Roman landowners to control slaves and by the Roman military to control native populations. It symbolized political terror, the mechanism of social control and oppression. In commitment and trust, Jesus died for God's coming reign. His death embodied his own vision and commitment to practice God's reign to the very end.

Jesus did not accept political legitimacy based on control of the Temple and social exploitation. Nor did he accept the logic of social and political hierarchies built on a foundation of wealth, privilege, status, power, and force. Jesus developed a practice in service to God's reign. The logic of God's reign was the logic of an abundance that is shared. It was characterized by reciprocal sharing of economic, religious, and social resources. The logic of the *basileia* was not the exercise of power to oppress. It was the exercise of power in the form of service, waiting on table and washing guests' feet. Hierarchical relations and social divisions were reduced to unbrokered egalitarian social relations in God's coming reign.

Because of his message and practice of God's coming reign, Jesus came into lethal conflict with the powerful. Jesus died because his *basileia* praxis was politically provocative. It suggested liberation from oppression, poverty, and extremism. God's reign meant liberation from the

"Gentile rulers who lord over." It meant liberation from exploitation resulting in indebtedness, slavery, and starvation. It meant liberation from the particular holiness ideologies that excluded people because of illness, sin, or social status from the covenant community.

Jesus' provocation in the Temple demonstration and his active campaign against the Temple aristocracy proved to be lethal.[53] Jesus performed a Stop the Temple action in overturning the money changers' tables, preventing the sale of sacrificial animals, and stopping anyone from carrying anything through the Temple precincts. By challenging the Temple leadership, he challenged the Roman imperial system, since the Jewish high priests were appointed by Roman prefects in Jerusalem. It was inevitable that Jesus' revolutionary vision and praxis of God's reign resulted in his political execution. He appeared to the chief priests, the Jerusalem aristocracy, and the Romans as a messianic pretender who threatened the established political order of Palestine. He was murdered by the structures of social control and political repression because he refused to be silent.

Jesus' teachings and practice of the egalitarian, unbrokered reign of God threatened the position of the privileged and the balance of political power that rested in their favor. Wealth was unjustly distributed because political power was in the hands of less than 2 percent of the population of Jewish Palestine. Jesus spoke of a God who sided not with the wealthy, the privileged, and the powerful but with the poor, the oppressed, the weak, the outsider, and the undesirable. Jesus' practice symbolized God's reign for the poor, a new economics of shared resources and a new politics of service. With his message of God's solidarity with the oppressed and a commitment to justice-doing, Jesus threatened the political order established by the Romans and the co-opted Jewish aristocracy. His action in the Temple was a visible symbol of unbrokered egalitarian relations of God's coming reign.

Jesus' sentence of death was handed down and executed by Romans. Jesus was put to death on the cross for political rebellion. The cross symbolized the cruelty of the Roman imperial system, patriarchal violence and privilege, the political infrastructure of the co-opted aristocracy and Temple leadership, a compromised sacerdotal aristocracy, and ultimately ruthless human behavior. Crucifixion awaited both the charismatic prophet and the revolutionary. It was the ultimate

---

53. E. P. Sanders recognizes the lethal consequences of Jesus' action in the Temple, yet he does not realize the full political implications of the action. Horsley does recognize the political implications, see Sanders, *Jesus and Judaism*, 75, 296–306; Horsley, *Jesus and the Spiral*, 297–317.

deterrent of the Roman political system for keeping revolutionaries and would-be messiahs in check. Crucifixion was the consequence of Jesus' commitment to *basileia* praxis and its conflictual nature.

Easter: the Queer Christ

On Easter, Jesus became God's Christ, that is, God's power of embodied solidarity, justice, love, and freedom. Despite prevalent heterosexist christological discourse, it is not Jesus' maleness that made him the Christ. It is his *basileia* practice of solidarity with the oppressed, his execution, God's identification with his crucifixion, and God's raising him from the dead that made Jesus the Christ. In his *basileia* practice, Jesus asserted God as the saving reality of solidarity and justice for the oppressed. Through the resurrection God affirmed the validity of Jesus' *basileia* message of the end of domination; by raising Jesus, God said no to human oppression. Francis Schüssler Fiorenza asserts, "Belief in Jesus' resurrection is belief in God's justice that vindicated the life and praxis of Jesus and had the effect of affirming that life and that praxis."[54] For queer Christians, the risen Jesus stands in solidarity with oppressed gay men and lesbians. The risen Jesus is the hope for justice.

Easter was God's embodied action of solidarity and justice; God identified with the murdered Jesus' practice of solidarity. The Easter action of God turned Jesus into a parable, a parable about God. God was revealed as the compassionate power of justice that saved Jesus from death. Easter became the event of God's liberative practice, God's truth for justice. God stood in solidarity with the crucified Jesus. God did not negate the brutal death of Jesus; it was real, violent, and cruel. But God identified with the crucified Jesus. God was there in the midst of brutal human violence. God genuinely embraced the total flesh of Jesus in suffering and death. On Easter, God asserted that the oppressive political system would not triumph in the death of Jesus and that the tragedy of Jesus' death in service to God's reign would not be the last action. God asserted that the kingdom would triumph over human oppression.

God's liberative praxis on Easter does not negate the real tragedies of human history, the monstrous cruelties, and the forgotten deaths of innocent victims. Rather, the depths of human suffering are met with the solidarity of Jesus. Jesus becomes the Christ. He is a parable of God's strong assertion that human barbarism, political oppression, and dominating power relations will not triumph. This includes the oppressive

---

54. Francis Schüssler Fiorenza, *Foundational Theology* (New York: Crossroad, 1986), 45.

political systems that have persecuted and executed men and women with same-sex attraction, that murdered gay men and lesbians in the Nazi death camps, that blocked effective and compassionate responses to gay men with HIV infections, and that promote homophobic violence and oppression. God is concealed and murdered; God is there in every death of a gay man or a lesbian woman. God will remember innocent gay and lesbian people, and Easter justice will triumph.

On Easter, God raised Jesus to the level of a discursive symbol and praxis, and Jesus became the Christ, the liberative praxis of God's compassion in the world. God's liberative praxis included the symbolics of Jesus' *basileia* practices. It took the political shapes of Jesus' *basileia* praxis of empowering hope, love, solidarity, and human freedom. It now takes on the form of real solidarity with the suffering and the poor. God's social praxis is power with the transformative capacity to reach out for freedom, love, and justice. It stands in direct contrast and opposition to the production, circulation, and use of power for domination. The power of God's freedom remains an integral part of the human practice of freedom.

What Easter communicates is the practical correlation of Jesus' *basileia* praxis and God's liberative praxis. Easter empowers the faith that God was configured in Jesus' social activities, in particular, his social practices of solidarity and justice. Easter announces that Jesus' *basileia* praxis actualized God's praxis. The message of Easter is the hope of God's universal solidarity with the oppressed. The hope of resurrection is the faith that God's power will continue to transform the reality of oppression and death into life and freedom. God's Christ continues to be politically configured in solidarity with the poor and the weak, the socially deviant and the outsider. God's Christ is socially in the midst of interactions that empower, that liberate people in the direction of justice, freedom, and love. God's Christ is in the midst of political struggle for liberation. Political liberation is God's insurrection against the political horrors and atrocities of human history, against the misuse and abuse of political power. God's Christ is in the midst of gay and lesbian political struggles: this is the practice of God's justice.

Jesus' *basileia* message is grounded in his political praxis; it provides for alternative, critical, resistant, and conflictual forms of human action. It means that *basileia* praxis is always socially situated, that is, dialectical and symbolic social and political activity. It is political activity that symbolizes the *basileia* interests and is practiced with a critical edge. The growth of God's reign is a historical process of struggle for social and political liberation. *Basileia* liberation requires the communicative idiom of political discourse and practice to present a critical alternative to dominating political relations, networks of oppressive power, and systems of exclusion. It critically engages all oppressive and dominating activity, always very conscious of those who are oppressed and dominated by such activity. *Basileia* liberation expresses and practices novel patterns of nonabusive and nonoppressive power relations. It consciously symbolizes the social alternative of political liberation. It practices solidarity with the poor, the weak, and the vulnerable. *Basileia* activity expands the critical and analogical potential of Jesus' *basileia* symbol system into new economic, social, political, historical, and cultural situations.

God's praxis is not enslaving or oppressive; it is compassionate and liberative. God is "the event of suffering, liberating love."[55] The resurrection of the crucified Jesus constitutes liberating power. God is configured to the suffering and death of Jesus; God dies with Jesus. According to Dorothee Soelle, God's insurrection against human injustice is Jesus' resurrection.[56] God rejects the political sanctioning of injustice, oppression, and exploitation of the innocent. God stands in solidarity with the innocent and the oppressed of history. God's liberative praxis takes the specific contours of justice and the practices of Jesus: healing and exorcism; table fellowship; a Torah of compassion; the founding of social groups to practice the new social relationships of God's reign in advance; solidarity with the poor and the weak; active resistance and critical engagement of domination politics and holiness discourses; reciprocal sharing of goods and mutual service in love; critical challenge, conflict, and martyrdom; the quest for freedom and final liberation. In other words, God takes the role and perspective of Jesus in his solidarity with the oppressed.

What Easter affirms is the total liberative compassion and justice of God in Jesus the Christ. God's creative freedom is the production and circulation of networks of nonoppressive power relations. It is the creative production of power that allows for the novel, new possibilities, and freedom. The oppressed and the oppressor designate concrete political realities. The oppressed are involved in a social relationship of dependence in which their status, power, and economic livelihood are diminished. God's liberative praxis transforms this social reality so that it is no longer characterized by *dependence* or by negativity. God's liberative praxis becomes specific forms of political interaction, specific forms of nonoppressive power that are oriented toward critical change. These

---

55. Moltmann, *Crucified God*, 252.
56. Dorothee Soelle, *The Strength of the Weak* (Philadelphia: Westminster Press, 1984), 71–76.

forms of nonoppressive power include strategic modes of social transformation; they include resistance, struggle, reform, conflict, and social
transgression.

God's liberative praxis challenges the ideologies that sanction a status
quo of oppression, domination, and exploitation. It struggles with the
concentration of valued scarce resources — power, wealth, status — in the
hands of the few. It moves to an equitable sharing of economic and valued
resources. God's social praxis challenges political hierarchies and moves
toward a *basileia* egalitarianism. It conflicts with ideologies and practices
that absolutize social symbols, interactions, structures, and systems. All
"isms" absolutized are shattered by God's liberative praxis.

God's liberative praxis is an ongoing dynamic movement that includes
conflict, negation, and the emerging possibilities of the new. In particular, it conflicts with all that is not yet *basileia*, that is, what remains under
the politics of homophobic domination and heterosexist exploitation.
However, it negates all exploitative human actions, all infrastructures
of political domination, and all social stratifications with symbolic and
political acts of the emerging reign of God. It negates the social systems and political structures that lead to the executions of Jesus and
countless others. It judges those social structures, those discursive and
nondiscursive practices, as not the *basileia*.

Practical implications of a queer christology

A queer christology begins with the experience of homophobic oppression and gay/lesbian reverse discursive experience. It is discourse rooted
in gay/lesbian practice. This is the practice of christology constructed
in the midst of human suffering and real oppression: it stands contrary
to the practices of ecclesial christology.

As discussed earlier, Episcopal priest and writer Malcolm Boyd was
not the first to raise the question of Jesus' homoerotic feelings. In the
late 1960s, Hugh Montefiore, an Anglican canon, suggested that Jesus
may have had same-sex inclinations.[57] However, Boyd argues for a gay-
sensitive Jesus for queer Christians:

---

57. *Newsweek*, August 7, 1967, 83; Hugh Montefiore, *For God's Sake* (Philadelphia: Fortress Press, 1969), 182. Phipps argues that if Montefiore's speculations are perceived as
plausible, it may be due to the effeminate way that artists represented Jesus. He notes that
artists frequently used women as models to capture Jesus' tender qualities; see Phipps, *Was
Jesus Married?* 7. Phipps wants a total heterosexual construction of Jesus' sexual practices.
He demonstrates heterosexist stereotypic understanding of people inclined to same-sex
practices as effeminate.

Gay spirit, as we have come to understand it, fits Jesus easily. He appears to us as an androgynous man. Jesus shared his feelings, empathized with those of others, and was not afraid of intimacy. He was sensitive and vulnerable, consented to his own needs, knew how to receive as well as give to another. Jesus exalts the spiritual dimension inherent in a truly liberated expression of sexuality.[58]

As I've noted, Robert Williams also has raised the question of a queer Jesus. He speculates, "Jesus was the passionate lover of Lazarus, a young man who became his disciple. When the two of them met, there was that electricity we have learned to call limerence, or love at first sight."[59] Many queer Christians feel comfortable with the affection that Jesus had for Lazarus, for Mary Magdalene, and for the Beloved Disciple. They feel at home with the affectional ease of Jesus with both men and women. Jesus broke many of the gender patterns and hierarchies of patriarchal power.[60] Thus, the gay and lesbian community has raised the question of Jesus' sexual intimacy, claiming Jesus as one of their own. This is hardly a strange social phenomenon. African American Christians have claimed the black Christ for their liberator, and some feminists speak of the Christa.[61] It is only natural for queer Christians to reclaim Jesus as gay/lesbian-sensitive and construct a queer Christ.

Rosemary Ruether calls for restoring sexuality to the traditional image of Jesus. She claims that Jesus "appears to be neither married nor celi-

58. Malcolm Boyd, "Was Jesus Gay?" *The Advocate* 565, December 4, 1990, 90. Boyd also quotes the Rev. Sandra Robinson, dean of Samaritan College: "I never knew how to separate my spirituality from my sexuality. . . . Sleeping with a woman was both natural and fulfilling. It's unthinkable to me that Jesus could be uncomfortable with my lesbianism. He understands fully that being lesbian or gay isn't simply a matter of genital behavior but is a whole way of being. Jesus was just as queer in his time as we are in ours. What a gift."

59. Robert Williams, *Just as I Am: A Practical Guide to Being Out, Proud, and Christian* (New York: Crown Publishers, 1992), 122. See Williams's full reconstruction of Jesus as gay and sexual, 116–22. I had the privilege of reading Williams's manuscript *The Beloved Disciple*. As I noted earlier, in that work, Williams reconstructs a fictional story of Jesus and Lazarus as lovers. One of the many valuable aspects of the work is the vivid description of the love-making between Jesus and Lazarus. *The Beloved Disciple* directly confronts the sexphobic and homophobic attitudes of Christians regarding Jesus, and at the same time, it expresses the widespread intuition shared by many gay Christians about Jesus.

60. Rosemary Ruether, "The Sexuality of Jesus: What the Synoptics Have to Say," *Christianity and Crisis* 38, no. 8 (1978): 136–37.

61. The reclamation of Jesus as black has been an empowering resource for African Americans' liberation practice. See James Cone, *A Black Theology of Liberation* (Philadelphia: J. B. Lippincott, 1970), 212–19; Cone, *God of the Oppressed* (New York: Seabury Press, 1975), 133–37. Some feminist theologians have started to speak about the Christ/a as the woman-affirming experience of Jesus the Christ; see Heyward, *Touching Our Strength*, 114–18; Brock, *Journey by Heart*, 52–53, 67–70.

bate. If there is anything at all to be said about the sexuality of Jesus, it is that it was a *sexuality* under the control of friendship. He could love John and Mary Magdalene, physically embrace and be embraced by them because first of all he knew them as friends, not as sexual objects."[62]

Jesus' relationships were "controlled not by sexuality, but by friendship." Such attempts by Boyd, Williams, and Ruether to restore the sexuality of Jesus affirm and uplift the sexually oppressed.[63] However, they say nothing about the historical Jesus' particular sexual practices. That information has been lost to biblical sources and history.[64] Yet we have access to some of Jesus' embodied actions for the *basileia*, and there we glimpse some nonheterosexist and nonhomophobic sexual patterns.

Jesus is liberated from the christological constructions that emerge from Christian homophobic discourse and the oppression of lesbian/gay people. Christology is a matter of proclaiming God's solidarity and justice-doing, which cannot be separated from the reign of God. God's solidarity and justice-doing form the basis of Jesus' *basileia* practice, and with them Jesus is revealed in the Easter event. The churches have made Christ into a symbol of homophobic oppression and violence. Jesus' crucifixion has been transformed into an abstract norm for Christian sexist power relations. Early in Christian history, Jesus' crucifixion was stripped of its political reality, transformed and spiritualized into the event of asexual salvation. It lost its social embeddedness; it was disembodied, abstracted, and spiritualized. A queer reclamation of Jesus retrieves the socially embedded Jesus and the political dimensions of his crucifixion. It was a brutal political death at the hands of a repressive political infrastructure.

It was not God's will that Jesus die. This abstraction of Jesus' crucifixion as God's will forms the basis for the nonsexual practice of

---

62. Ruether, "Sexuality of Jesus," 136, 137.

63. See Clark's reconstruction of a gay-sensitive Jesus. J. Michael Clark, *A Place to Start: Towards an Unapologetic Gay Liberation Theology* (Dallas: Monument Press, 1987), 108–17. E. M. Barrett argues for an embodied, sexual Jesus; see Barrett, "Gay People and Moral Theology," in *The Gay Academic*, ed. Louin Crew (Palm Springs, Calif.: ETC Publications, 1978), 329–34.

64. The Jesus traditions in the Bible do not provide us with any information on the sexual practices of Jesus, whether those practices were opposite-sex or same-sex or nonexistent. The silence of the biblical sources and the idealization of celibate practice by the later church do not prove that Jesus was celibate. The question of Jesus' sex practice remains unanswerable. However, Jesus broke gender lines and roles of his first-century society in his relationships with women disciples. His washing the feet of his disciples was a function frequently performed by a wife for her husband or a servant for his master. Jesus had a great deal of social freedom that appeals to gay/lesbian Christians.

power.[65] It legitimizes the construction of the ascetic self, purified of desire/pleasure.

In his message and practice of the coming reign of God, Jesus embodied a preferential option for the oppressed. In his social practices, he modeled a new *basileia* network of social relations that were nonexploitative, nonhierarchical, and nonoppressive. Men and women found hope in new forms of *basileia* relating. Jesus was radical in his practice of solidarity with oppressed men and women. His was a commitment aware of the political risks. Jesus' death is a tragic death at the hands of an oppressive political structure in first-century Palestine. The cross is God's invasive identification with the oppressed. The oppressed now include the sexual oppressed, those oppressed because of their sexual preference or identity.

Jesus the Christ belongs to queer practice of liberation. We need a christology that is rooted in gay and lesbian liberative practice, in our struggle for sexual liberation. For centuries, the crucifixion of Jesus represented the death of sexuality. The crucifixion stripped Jesus of his sexuality, his humanity, and the sociopolitical reality of his death. Christian discursive and nondiscursive practices have repeated Jesus' crucifixion. They remain acts of violence against the sexually oppressed. However, God's revelation on Easter aims to bring an end to crucifixions, not perpetuate them in the deployment of oppressive power relations.

The gay and lesbian reclamation of Jesus and his *basileia* practice becomes the generative matrix for reinterpreting Jesus' death and the Christ event in a nonhomophobic, nonheterosexist, and nonoppressive context. For us, the political death of Jesus reveals homophobic/ heterosexist power at its fullest. The cross symbolizes the political infrastructure of homophobic practice and oppression. It symbolizes the terror of internalized homophobia that has led to the closeted invisibility of gay and lesbian people. It indicates the brutal silencing, the hate crimes, the systemic violence perpetuated against us. The cross now belongs to us. We have been crucified. We have been martyred. We

---

65. An early Christian apologetic to shift blame from Pilate and the Romans to the Jewish leadership takes place in the formation of the passion accounts of the four Gospels. The fact of Jesus' crucifixion presented problems to citizens in the Greco-Roman world. Paul encountered obstacles in preaching a crucified messiah (1 Cor. 1:23). There was no more heinous crime than political revolution. If Jesus was regarded as a political revolutionary (*lestes*), then his whole movement came under suspicion. The depoliticizing of Jesus and his death and the subsequent spiritualizing of the Christ led to an inculturation of Christian discourse within Greco-Roman philosophy. Depoliticizing, spiritualizing, and the idealization of celibacy are integrally woven in Christian discourse on God, Christ, and sexuality.

have been nailed to that cross by most of the Christian churches. They continue to legitimize, bless, and activate violence against us.

Jesus was put to death for his *basileia* solidarity with the poor, the outcast, the sinner, the socially dysfunctional, and the sexually oppressed. Jesus died in solidarity with gay men and lesbians. His death becomes a "no" to closeted existence, to gay/lesbian invisibility and homophobic violence. The cross has terrorized gay men and lesbians. It has been a symbol of lethal sexual oppression, but Jesus' death shapes the cross into a symbol of struggle for queer liberation. From the perspective of Easter, God takes the place of the oppressed Jesus on the cross. God identifies with the suffering and death of Jesus at the hands of a political system of oppression. For gay and lesbian Christians, Easter becomes the event at which God says no to homophobic violence and sexual oppression. God says no to the stripping away of Jesus' sexuality by Christian discourses that deny his embodied *basileia* practice. Jesus the Christ symbolizes God's practice of solidarity with us, the sexually oppressed or dissident (*anawim*). The *anawim* represent the biblical poor and powerless, a class of socially oppressed people. In the Hebrew Scriptures, God is partial to the poor (*anawim*), the powerless, and the undesirables. We may expand the meaning of *anawim* to include all those who are oppressed because of the politics of gender or sexual practices. The *anawim* become for us all people who were discriminated against, oppressed, tortured, and killed because of their sexual practices or because of their deviation from gender roles. The *anawim* represent the sexually different or the sexually oppressed.

Easter becomes the hope of queer sexual liberation. The queer struggle for sexual liberation will triumph; this is the promise of Easter. When God raised Jesus from the dead, Jesus became God's Christ, God's practice of compassion, solidarity, and justice in the world. "Christ" is a relational term: it brings together Jesus' *basileia* practice and God's liberative practice. Jesus' *basileia* practice participates in God's liberative actions. To experience Jesus the Christ is to do God's justice: it is to live justice. God's liberative power claims Jesus' *basileia* practice of solidarity with the oppressed; it becomes God's justice for the oppressed.

On Easter, God made Jesus queer in his solidarity with us. In other words, Jesus "came out of the closet" and became the "queer" Christ. Jesus the Christ becomes actively queer through his solidarity with our struggles for liberation. Jesus becomes gay/lesbian rather than gay because of his solidarity with lesbians as well. This is not to deny the maleness of Jesus but to point out the innate human capacity of both men and women to stand in solidarity with one another. It, however, does deny the political gender identifications of Jesus with masculinity and the subsequent ecclesial violence to women in history. Therefore, Jesus the Christ is queer by his solidarity with queers.

The Queer Christ is an attempt to construct a christological discourse that interprets Jesus' embodied practices in a positive, queer-affirming theological discourse. To say Jesus the Christ is queer is to say that God identifies with us and our experience of injustice. God experiences the stereotypes, the labeling, the hate crimes, the homophobic violence directed against us:

> Three assailants harassed two gay men outside a gay bar and slashed the bar doorman's throat with a knife when he attempted to stop the harassment. Leaving the bar, they approached a gay man waiting for a bus and said to him, "We're going to teach you faggots a lesson." They stabbed the victim, puncturing his lung.[66]

To affirm that Jesus the Christ is queer is to politically identify Christ with the two gay men slashed. Jesus the Christ is "queer-bashed." Here modern Roman soldiers of homophobic violence pierce the gay/lesbian Christ with a knife. The Queer Christ is politically identified with all queers — people who have suffered the murders, assaults, hate-crime activities, campus violence, police abuse, ecclesial exclusion, denial of ordination and the blessing of same-sex unions, harassment, discrimination, HIV-related violence, defamation, and denial of civil rights and protections. Jesus the Queer Christ is crucified repeatedly by homophobic violence. The aim of God's practice of solidarity and justice-doing and our own queer Christian practice is to bring an end to the crucifixions in this world.

If Jesus the Christ is not queer, then his *basileia* message of solidarity and justice is irrelevant. If the Christ is not queer, then the gospel is no longer good news but oppressive news for queers. If the Christ is not queer, then the incarnation has no meaning for our sexuality. It is the particularity of Jesus *the* Christ, his particular identification with the sexually oppressed, that enables us to understand Christ as black, queer, female, Asian, African, a South American peasant, a Jewish transsexual, and so forth. It is the scandal of particularity that is the message of Easter, the particular context of struggle where God's solidarity is practiced. God and the struggle for sexual justice are correlated in practice in a queer christology.

---

66. National Gay and Lesbian Task Force Policy Institute, *Anti-Gay/Lesbian Violence, Victimization, and Defamation in 1990* (Washington, D.C.: NGLTFPI, 1991), 13.

Easter becomes God's sociopolitical unfolding of what *basileia* praxis symbolizes. It is a conscious political transformation of the world; it is making God's nearness real in the world. It is the creative transformation of socially embedded men and women in the direction of human and political freedom. God's liberative praxis is necessarily embedded in the social and political situation of gay and lesbian people. It is, thus, impossible to separate the history of God's social praxis from queer social praxis. God's praxis is found socially in the midst of the liberative praxis of the gay/lesbian community. It is the heart of our critical and liberative practice for justice and freedom.

EIGHT

EXPANDING CHRIST'S
WARDROBE OF DRESSES

Historically, obscene Christs have appeared when people want to uncover the graceful pretences of current christologies. The Christ of Black theology was obscene because it uncovered racism under the guise of the white Jesus.... The Christa is another example of obscenity. It undresses the masculinity of God and produces feelings and questionings which were suppressed by centuries of identificatory masculine processes with God.

— Marcella Maria Althaus-Reid[1]

Since I first wrote about the Queer Christ, I have attempted to understand the full contours and shapes of a queer christology. Many churches have used the heterosexual Christ for queer bashing and all sorts of systematic violence directed at translesbigays, from promoting the ex-gay movement to restore queer folks to heterosexuality, to supporting the ex-trans movement to restore gender-variant folks to their original gender, to backing legislative initiatives to exclude queers from the human right to intimacy. In the previous chapter, written over a decade ago, I identified the Queer Christ with the embodied praxes of gay and lesbian Christians, including their love-making and justice-doing. That was liberating at the time when I first proposed a queer christology, but now it is too limiting in its failure to include bisexuals, transgendered folks, and heterosexual queers. In this essay, I want to expand further the dimensions of the Queer Christ to include the Bi/Christ and the Trans/Christ. Marcella Althaus-Reid provides a dialogue partner for my expansion of queer christology.[2]

First, I want to engage Althaus-Reid's hermeneutics of obscenity and her model of the Bi/Christ by way of an exploration of Judith Butler's notion of gender as performance. Then, I want to ask if Althaus-Reid's

---

1. Marcella Althaus-Reid, *Indecent Theology: Theological Perversions in Sex, Gender, and Politics* (New York: Routledge, 2001), 111.
2. Judith Butler, *Gender Trouble* (New York: Routledge, 1990).

Bi/Christ sufficiently expands the contours of queer christology, using the case of transgendered folks. I am an "out-of-the-closet theologian" who believes, along with Althaus-Reid, that personal narrative is woven within theological explorations. Perversion and obscenity are the theological tools for engaging Christianity from Althaus-Reid's social location as a Latina, bisexual, feminist liberation theologian. The obscene attracts me because it transgresses the heteronormative and challenges ecclesial erotophobia.[3] Obscenity "does not renounce the viscosity of materiality," and, in fact, Althaus-Reid asserts it leads to a "dis-covering of grace," both by undressing the economy of heteronormativity and surfacing alterity.[4] Althaus-Reid proposes that the Bi/Christ is "Obscenity no. 1."[5] Though she moves christology into more fluid and expansive categories with the Bi/Christ, I would like to engage the notions of gender as drag performance and expand what I find implicit in her model of the Bi/Christ.

Let me first explore three queer representations of Christ — labeled blasphemous, obscene, and perverse; discuss the Bi/Christ, its strengths and weaknesses; and make suggestions for a postmodern Queer Christ, a Bi/Transvestite Christ.

•

As I discussed earlier, the off-Broadway play *Corpus Christi* written by popular playwright Terrence McNally produced a firestorm of protest.[6] McNally produces his own gay version of the greatest story ever told. In the play, Joshua is a gay teenager whose love for opera, poetry, and chess and whose participation in high school musicals are disparaged by his mother and classmates as feminine. He is battered at a high school dance when two gay-bashers attempt to flush his head in a urinal. Joshua, a thinly disguised Jesus, blesses a same-sex union and thus institutes it as a sacrament while a Catholic priest refuses to perform the rite. The most blasphemous aspect of the play is McNally's portrayal of Joshua as sexually intimate with his male disciples. By offering his body and blood for the salvation of humanity, Joshua preaches the sacramental nature of human sexuality, including queer sex. McNally writes in his preface:

> Very few Christians are willing to consider that their Lord and Savior was a real man with real appetites, especially sexual ones.

---

3. See Robert E. Goss, "The Insurrection of Polymorphously Perverse: Queer Hermeneutics," in *A Rainbow of Religious Studies,* ed. J. Michael Clark and Robert E. Goss (Las Colinas, Tex.: Monument Press, 1996), 9–31.

4. Althaus-Reid, *Indecent Theology,* 111.

5. Ibid., 112–20.

6. Terrence McNally, *Corpus Christi* (New York: Atlantic/Grove, 1999).

To imagine that he was not only sexually active but a homosexual
as well is gross blasphemy. And they would deny others the right
to conceive him as such. They do not understand that a good
part of our humanity is expressed through our sexuality and is not
exclusive of it.[7]

Christian reaction to staging *Corpus Christi* has been vehement, with
threats of personal violence to theater staff and cast and threats of arson
for the Manhattan Theater Club. The Catholic League for Religious and
Civil Rights, a traditionalist group, led a campaign of protest against
the play. The play received national attention from organizations of the
Christian right such as the Family Research Council and others as a
"militant homosexual assault" on Christianity and blasphemous assault
on Jesus.

•

In Europe, the Swedish photography exhibition *Ecce Homo* produced a
flurry of fundamentalist protests and letters. Attracting over twenty thousand visitors, the photo exhibit included a homosexual Jesus in black
stiletto heels surrounded by muscular leather men and transvestites;
drag queens replacing the disciples in a version of Leonardo da Vinci's
The Last Supper; and a version of the conception of Jesus in which Mary
is portrayed as a lesbian who is handed a test tube for artificial insemination by an angel. In an interview, Swedish artist Elizabeth Ohlson stated,
"My aim is to show a loving God. One who loves, above all, when there
is love."[8]

•

The short film *Cowboy Jesus* screens Jesus as a black lesbian who rides a
Harley-Davidson motorcycle. The film opens with a picture of a nude
black woman on the cross. Mary Magdalene is attacked by a group of
hoodlums, and Jesus steps in to save her, beginning an interracial love relationship. Neo-Nazis interrupt and attack the women's group at the Last
Supper because Jesus and Magdalene are an interracial lesbian couple.
After Jesus the lesbian is crucified, she is resurrected and rides off into
the sunset with Magdalene.[9]

•

7. Ibid., v.
8. Cited in Abigail Schmelz, "Homosexual Jesus Raises Eyebrows at Gay Festival,"
Reuters, July 23, 1998.
9. Sylvia Moreno, "Public Airwaves, Private Opinions: Film on Arlington Cable
Channel Assailed," *Washington Post,* November 15, 1998.

Protestant fundamentalists have identified salvation with heterosexuality within the ex-gay movement, using Jesus as a template for compulsory heterosexuality or what Althaus-Reid identifies as "Jesus = Penis" discourse.[10] The Catholic position follows a similar trajectory that Jesus was certainly perfect and celibate in his dedication to God's reign. If he was perfect, then his sexuality could never be "intrinsically evil, objectively disordered." The heterosexual economy is "intrinsically good, objectively ordered," part of the natural order and thus divinely bestowed. The official Catholic construction of Jesus promotes an ideology of heteronormativity and masculinist privilege, though chapter 6, above, which explores the history of Christian homodevotionalism, undermines the position that heteronormativity has been the only voice in history. It has just been the dominant voice in recent centuries.

Althaus-Reid writes, "Jesus' sexuality belongs to something intuitively recognized in him by Queer people: a disorder, a Christ painted in the permanent exposure outside the normative borders and a Jesus of a corruptible nature."[11] Queer people outside of heterosexuality provide the seeds for a larger Christ outside of binary categories; queer constructions of Christ question the heterosexual economy that has dressed Jesus as a "heterosexually oriented (celibate) man."[12] Althaus-Reid wants to undress Christ from heterosexuality and redress Christ in postmodern sexualities, genders, and economic locations:

> Christ can be represented very movingly as a young woman holding another woman tightly, as they stand at the closed door of a church amidst voices within the church shouting "stay out" to the young lesbian.... Or we can envisage a transgendered Christ, taking on the Christself the oppression and injustice that a person suffers when gender and sexuality are dislocated. The Bi/Christ takes it all into his life: economic deprivation and social marginalization, exacerbated by a kind of heterosexual excommunication from God.[13]

Christ is not only outside the gates of the churches but also outside the boundaries of heterosexuality. Althaus-Reid is committed to a larger Christ, encompassing those excommunicated from a heterosexually

---

10. Althaus-Reid, *Indecent Theology*, 106.
11. Ibid.
12. Ibid., 114.
13. Ibid., 116. Althaus-Reid refers here to Elizabeth Stuart, *Religion Is a Queer Thing* (Cleveland: Pilgrim Press, 1997), 23.

violent God, those suffering from economic deprivation, and those
socially marginalized.

For Althaus-Reid, bisexuality offers a way of sexual thinking that refuses to take heterosexual categories into consideration.[14] Bisexuality
is often understood as a confusion of categories; it is undoubtedly a
disruptive category for heteronormativity. Her model of the Bi/Christ
represents a nomadic category that disturbs the exclusive heterosexual
identity template and allows for such obscene and queer representations
of Christ as the three above-mentioned postmodern illustrations while
including all unnamed and noncatalogued sexualities deviating from
heteronormativity. Building on bisexual writers, Althaus-Reid argues
for deconstructing the heterosexual economy that is obsessed within
fixed sexual identity categories, controlling boundaries, and thinking
hierarchically in binary categories. Feminist and queer liberation theologies have enlarged Christ beyond the heterosexual economies of
the churches.[15] Since bisexuality represents the fluidity of sexual templates, Althaus-Reid develops an indecent christology to reach people
outside the gates of heterosexuality and the church. The theological
category of bisexuality erases what Brian Loftus designates as "the sexual marking in the establishment of hierarchy and power distribution."[16]
Althaus-Reid notes that Loftus refuses to make bisexuality into another
sexual category like heterosexuality or even homosexuality with its ideological categories. She wants to disrupt the tendencies toward sexual
fixed categories with more fluid, nomadic categories, and she wants to
disrupt heteronormative christologies. Fixed categories of sexuality and
gender can be as violent as fixed christologies. Sexual and gender fluidity along with christological fluidity, I believe, are the vital contours for
constructing an inclusive christology.

One of the beautiful and elegant pieces of theological writing in
Althaus-Reid's work occurs in reference to the Bi/Christ and the notion
of "pitching of tent" in John's prologue:[17]

> Only a Bi/Christ category which happens to be so unsettled, that
> no mono-relationship could have been so easily constructed with

---

14. Althaus-Reid, *Indecent Theology*, 117.

15. Lisa Isherwood, *Liberating Christ: Exploring the Christologies of Contemporary Liberation Movements* (Cleveland: Pilgrim Press, 1999).

16. Althaus-Reid, *Indecent Theology*, 113.

17. The Greek *skenoun* is related to *skene*, pitching a tent. There is an implication of localizing the presence of God. Raymond Brown holds that behind this phrase there is a notion of Jesus as the Shekinah of God. See Raymond Brown, *The Gospel according to John, I–XII* (Garden City, N.Y.: Doubleday, 1966), 32.

it. Bi/christology walks like a nomad in lands of opposition and exclusive identities, and does not pitch its tent forever in the same place. If we considered that in the Gospel of John 1:14, the verb is said to have "dwelt among us" as a tabernacle (a tent) or "put his tent amongst us," the image conveys Christ's high mobility and lack of fixed space or definitive frontiers. Tents are easily dismantled overnight and do not become ruins or monuments; they are rather folded and stored or reused for another purpose when old. Tents change shape in strong winds, and their adaptability rather than their stubbornness is one of their greatest assets.[18]

Althaus-Reid correlates the nomadic category of pitching a tent with bisexuality to construct a christology, for such a correlation provides new ways to look outside gender/sexual binarism and hierarchy. The construction of Christ need not be exclusive, for fluid categories enable Jesus to become the Drag Christ, the Leather Christ, the Heterosexual Christ, the Gay Christ, and the Lesbian Christ. But is the Bi/Christ fluid enough? Is it queer enough to be inclusive?

Earlier in *Indecent Theology,* Althaus-Reid explores Mary the Drag Queen or Jesus as a cross-dresser in the figure of Santa Librada — the crucified Woman Christ of the poor.[19] Santa Librada is a divine cross-dresser, displayed as statues and stamps by the Santerias of Buenos Aires. Althaus-Reid acknowledges that the popular image of Santa Librada during carnivals is an unstable cross-dressing of Mary and Jesus. She writes:

> [W]e do not know who is who and that instability is part of a transvestite epistemology, which by doubting the binary pair in religious opposition (Mary/woman and Jesus/man) succeeds in doubting the stability of the whole theological gender system.... It [Librada] makes of Christ a Christ dressed as Mary, and of Mary, a woman occupying the male divine space of the cross.[20]

Santa Librada, as ambiguous drag queen or drag king, blurs the gender boundaries that patriarchal culture and Christianity need to see as fixed, ontological, naturalized, and divine. Poor migrant workers worship Santa Librada, and during the dictatorial times in Argentina, the figure stood as a critique of the repressive politics of dress, sexuality, and conformity. The transvestite Santa Librada expresses the liberative

---

18. Althaus-Reid, *Indecent Theology,* 119–20.
19. Ibid., 80.
20. Ibid., 80–82.

potential of sexual and political transgressions as she is carried through the streets while the celebrating poor sing songs of political criticism.

Althaus-Reid's intention in her obscene model of the Bi/Christ is to create a "diverse Ultra Christ, incarnated (located) in our specific time and communities."[21] Is the Bi/Christ expansive enough a model to incorporate the alternative representations of Jesus that I raised in the above examples?

Definitely the Bi/Christ destabilizes the sex/gender system embedded in heteronormative christologies and used to legitimize oppressive heterosexual networks of power.

What if we understand the above postmodern representational strategies of Jesus/Christ as parodic performances? Those parodies would critique dominant theological constructions of Jesus/Christ as asexual, male, and even heterosexual by demonstrating how dominant representations of Jesus/Christ are also constructed within a patriarchal sex-gender-desire system claiming universal significance within a postmodern world. The South American carnival, likewise, elevates the parodic to a communal performance.

I would like to accessorize Marcella Althaus-Reid's obscenity of the Bi/Christ with the modification of the Bi/Transvestite Christ. It is not undressing her model but accessorizing her model a bit, sort of adding those "motorbike boots" (of which she speaks fondly). If I image the Christ in the protean images of the pop singer Madonna, a queer cultural icon, from my own social location, what does that do to Althaus-Reid's obscene model of the Bi/Christ? Madonna represents a nomadic category that Althaus-Reid attempts to develop in the Bi/Christ. When I add queer theory to the mixture, that is, Judith Butler's notion of gender performativity, the Bi/Christ becomes a fluid model. Butler's notion of gender as performative like drag becomes a critical lens for comprehending Madonna as an example of the fluid, ever-changing, and nomadic category that Althaus-Reid attempts to model with the Bi/Christ and from her social location of transgressive carnivals.

Madonna and queer performance

Judith Butler, one of the pioneers in queer theory, argues that gender is an act, a performance, a set of manipulated codes, costumes, rather than a core aspect of essential identity. Butler's main metaphor for gender is "drag," performative cross-dressings. Performance describes how the

---

21. Ibid., 117.

body provides a surface upon which various acts and gestures accrue gendered meanings. All gender is a form of "drag," for there is no "essential" core for gender to signify.[22] Gender is thus a fantasy construct. Drag performances are parodic replayings of gender in order to subvert its meanings in a heterosexist society, and in principle, drag has the virtue of showing that gender is an imitative structure. Parodic repetitions of gender become subversive because they destabilize received notions of gender as natural. Gender parodies become subversive acts by displacing and blurring the reproduction of the cultural differences between man and woman.

For many young queers, Madonna comes as close as any media star to being a queer icon. Though young American queers do not experience the economically injurious conditions of poverty, they remain socially marginalized and practice their carnivals in clubs and at Pride festivals. In queer culture, Madonna remains an icon whose prosex sensibilities and whose gender parodies resonate with translesbigay imaginations and lives. I use Madonna and her videos to teach Judith Butler's *Gender Trouble* and queer theory to undergraduates.[23] Madonna crosses the margins of sexual/gender differences with impunity and style. Over the years, queers watched her constant image changes from a material girl, to a parody of Marilyn Monroe, to her assertion of female power and sexuality, to her appropriation of queer culture. Madonna is an ever-fluid icon of change, with protean persona changes — little girl, vulnerable lover, the sexual virgin, the blonde bombshell, bad girl, sexual outlaw, Eva Peron, cross-dresser, fluctuator of sexual identities, victim and victor, top and bottom, mother and wife. She is sexy, flamboyant, transgressive, obscene, and courageous. Her plasticity of changing performances and fluid identities embodies the arguments of Judith Butler's notion of sex/gender identity as parodic performance. In fact, Madonna is the queen of parodic critique, equally mocking femininity and masculinity as masquerades. Her subversive identities and performances reveal the discontinuity between the sex/gender system and anatomy as well as expose the normative as socially constructed.

A central element of Madonna's sexual politics is female empowerment and the freedom to express female sexuality. In the video *Music*, she takes on a "butch" role in the sense that she reappropriates the role of a male pimp, repeating masculine mechanisms used to control women but reversing those mechanisms to control men and flirt with

---

22. Butler, *Gender Trouble*, 134–50.
23. See Reena Mistry, "Madonna and Gender Trouble" (*www.theory.org.uk/madonna.htm*).

women.[24] Madonna challenges the notion of women as passive sex objects by reversing the gender roles and performing simulated sexual
acts on her male dancers. She usurps the male "top" position. Her displacement of the male role opens gender to new resignifications and
recontextualizations. Therefore, Madonna claims, "I can be a sex symbol, but I don't have to be a victim."[25] Her admission becomes the truth
of many queers in their sexual and gender transgressions.

Madonna has pushed the cultural limits of the sexually acceptable
even further. Her "Blond Ambition" tour was censored in many cities. In
her video *Like a Prayer* Madonna broke the race/sex barrier, exposing
American unease with interracial relationships and negative attitudes
about race. She kisses a statute of a black saint who is attired as Jesus and
who, later in the video, is replaced by a black man unjustly arrested for
the murder of a white woman. The Catholic Church and fundamentalists
criticized the video (forcing Pepsi to withdraw excerpts of the video as
a commercial) and discredited her for blasphemous use of icons — her
name, wearing a cross, the burning of a cross, the use of the altar, and the
stigmata she receives imaging Christ's suffering. Many queers danced in
solidarity at the clubs to *Like a Prayer,* welcoming her rebellion against
the censorships of Jesse Helms and his religious counterparts.

MTV refused to show Madonna's video *Justify My Love,* which depicts
her in a sexual encounter with Tony Ward, a gay porn movie star. Later,
other figures enter the scene, many androgynous; one of them engages
in an open kiss with Madonna. It is impossible to tell whether it is a
male or female. Madonna's earlier flirtations with lesbian desire and her
ambiguous connection with Sandra Bernhard played on queer imaginations and gossip. Displacement is at the core of the video's transgression.
Two men facing each other replace Madonna and her companion. In
the infamous bedroom scene, multiple androgynous bodies intersect
and shift in a series of displacements. The camera ranges over bodies, undisturbed by substitutions. *Justify My Love* blurs the boundaries
between sex, gender, and desire, demonstrating their plasticity and
fluidity.

At a Pride festival, I saw a young lesbian wearing a T-shirt with a *Justify
My Love* logo. I just had to have one, and I bought a *Justify My Love*
T-shirt to be in solidarity with Madonna's rebellion against society and
the church. For me, Madonna has been not only a queer icon but also

---

24. Beverly Skeggs, "A Good Time for Women Only," in *Deconstructing Madonna,* ed.
Fran Lloyd (London: Batsford, 1993), 67.
25. Pamela Robertson, *Guilty Pleasures: Feminist Camp from Mae West to Madonna* (New
York: I. B. Taurus, 1996), 127.

a Christ icon who has dissolved the boundaries between queer culture and queer faith communities. I refused then and even now to justify anything queer to the ecclesial erotophobes.

Much of what Madonna does on stage and in her videos can be read in terms of Judith Butler's notions of subverting the categories of gender/sex. Madonna's play with gender/sex categories prevents identification with any constant image. She skillfully adopts one mask after another, continually inventing protean personas to expose that there is no essential category of gender/sex. The displacement in drag, as theorized by Judith Butler and performed by Madonna, suggests a fluidity of identities open to resignification and recontextualization through what conservative Christian culture deems obscene. In *Like a Virgin,* Madonna appropriates the role of a female Christ, a Christa with stigmata, whose erotic relationship with a black saintly figure helps her to understand a solidarity with the black man falsely charged for a crime that he did not commit. Madonna's parodic performances offer us a subversive and transgressive paradigm for resignifying the resurrected Christ into the liminal borders of the indecent. In a forthcoming text, I have completed the chapter on queer christology: "What If Christ Came Back as Madonna?"[26]

The Bi/Transvestite Christ

There are parallels between the three obscene representations of Jesus mentioned earlier and Madonna's performances. In the three representations of Jesus, there is a movement to deliteralize the heterosexual and patriarchal constructions of Christ. Likewise, Madonna deliteralizes her role as female through camp, parodic performances, role inversions, and displacements. Althaus-Reid uses Marjorie Garber's analyses of cross-dressing, pointing out that cross-dressing emigrates beyond sexual binarism and creates a third alternative. Althaus-Reid notes, "A transvestite has a clear gender location, but not a sexual one. Transvestites can be heterosexual married men, lesbians trapped in male bodies, or any intersection between two different things, sexual attraction and gender construction."[27] While the Bi/Christ model can be fluid enough for a variety of sexual configurations, it does not have the fluidity to extend gender into the border regions of Santa Librada or the

26. See Robert E. Goss, "What If Christ Came Back as Madonna? From the Asexual Christ to the Polymorphously Sexual Christ," in *Jesus Came Out: The Challenge of Postmodern Sexualities* (forthcoming).

27. Althaus-Reid, *Indecent Theology,* 81.

Gospel Girls, drag queens who perform gospel tunes on Sundays in an Atlanta gay bar.[28] Althaus-Reid recognizes that sexual attraction and gender constructions are two different things. The Bi/Christ addresses sexual attraction but not gender constructions. The model, as I perceive it, leaves out gender conformists and gender transgressors. For me this becomes more poignant with the emergence of contemporary transgendered theologies.[29]

In *Omnigender,* Virginia Mollenkott comes out as a masculine female, identifying with transgendered folks. She points out in her survey of transgendered imagery in the Christian Scriptures that in Ephesians 5, the male Christ has a female body, the church. The collective body is the bride of Christ (Eph. 5:25–27) while Christians are comprehended as members of Christ's body (Eph. 5:30). Mollenkott concludes, "If the body of Christ is assumed to be a male body, then Christian women, by putting on Christ like a garment, are imagined as either androgynous he/she or as transvestites."[30] Putting on Christ or the identification of Christ with diversely gendered folks with a wide variety of sexual attractions indicates the limitations of the Bi/Christ. The Bi/Christ needs to add a gender-performative dimension to be gender-inclusive.

Feminist theologian Eleanor McLaughlin develops a paradigm of cross-dressing suggested by Marjorie Garber's *Vested Interests* to develop a transvestite christology.[31] McLaughlin views cross-dressing as a means to preserve "embodiment beyond androcentricity." Transvestites provide a critique of binary cultural categories by revealing the cultural construction of gender categories:

> Transvestites blur and make ambiguous that which the culture believes it needs to see as a clear and fixed buffer against unwonted social change. Transvestites arouse anxiety which comes from encountering people or things in the wrong place.... Jesus acts as a a transvestite when he takes a drink from the religiously outcast Samaritan woman or kneels like a slave girl to wash his disciples' feet. Cross-dressing is to indulge in socially taboo behavior. It vio-

---

28. Edward R. Gray and Scott Lee Thumma, "Amazing, Grace! How Sweet the Sound! Southern Evangelical Religion and Gay Drag," in *A Rainbow of Religious Studies,* 33–53.

29. Virginia Ramey Mollenkott, *Omnigender: A Trans-religious Approach* (Cleveland: Pilgrim Press, 2001).

30. Ibid., 110.

31. Eleanor McLaughlin, "Feminist Christologies: Re-dressing the Tradition," in *Reconstructing the Christ Symbol: Essays in Feminist Christology,* ed. Maryanne Stevens (New York: Paulist Press, 1993), 118–49.

lates structures and expectations. It de-stabilizes and questions the categories, especially the fundamental duality, male/female.[32]

McLaughlin notes that Marjorie Garber describes cross-dressing as a "disruptive act of putting into question" essences and dualities.[33] Christ becomes the trickster with transvestite sensibilities, for like many cross-dressers, he breaks the binary cultural categories of pure/impure and male/female.

Christ is a performative "drag queen" or "drag king" whose appeal may cross gender and sexual boundaries indiscriminately and hold out the eschatological hope of obscene inclusivity. McLaughlin writes,

> The transvestite Jesus makes a human space where no one is out of place because the notions of place and gender have been transformed. Yes human, yes God, yes woman, yes man, yes black, yes yellow, yes friend, yes stranger...yes, yes, yes, yes.[34]

I would add to McLaughlin's above quotation many other obscene and queer configurations unimagined by her: the leather Christ, Christ the bottom, Christ the lesbian boy, Christ the drag queen, and so on. McLaughlin's notion of the transvestite allows for the Christ's protean solidarity with all peoples, all economic and political locations, all genders, and all sexual orientations.

In speaking about the Christ, Vanessa Sheridan builds on male and female stereotypes to argue that to become Christlike involves social markers from masculine and feminine genders. She comprehends transgendered Christians as crossing the lines of restrictive gender codes and imitating the gender-variant social and spiritual characteristics of Jesus. Sheridan describes McLaughlin's model of Christ the transvestite as a "bold, transformative, and liberating new image of Christ."[35]

McLaughlin converges in the direction intended by Althaus-Reid's Bi/Christ to break boundaries of compulsory heterosexual constructions of Jesus the Christ. Jesus the Christ is a liminal figure, and queer postmodern representational strategies reclaim the sexuality of Jesus/Christ and play with fluid gender constructions intersected with diverse sexual attractions. The mixing and matching of signifiers of gender difference and sexual difference in representational strategies of the Christ

32. Ibid., 138–39.
33. Marjorie Garber, *Vested Interests: Cross-Dressing and Cultural Anxiety* (New York: HarperPerennial, 1993), 13.
34. McLaughlin, "Feminist Christologies," 144.
35. Vanessa Sheridan, *Crossing Over: Liberating the Transgendered Christian* (Cleveland: Pilgrim Press, 2001), 96.

provide an alternative way of envisioning the Christ as having liberating significance for the queer community. Our queer exploration cuts the Christ from the moorings of dominant, heterosexist and patriarchal theologies while rearticulating the Christ within diverse sexualities and diverse theologies that affirm sexual and gender alterities. The Queer Christ is impelled by dogmatic constructions that refuse to recognize that all women, gender-variant folks, and sexual minorities image the Christ. The silence has been a core construction that allows church violence to be directed against us and against many others.

The Ultra Christ that Althaus-Reid envisions needs a larger wardrobe to cross-dress to depict the diverse peoples and pluralistic social locations of the postmodern world. The Ultra Christ includes not only the Bi/Christ to express sexual fluidity but also the Transvestite/Christ to express gender fluidity. That, I would contend, is more faithful to the metaphor of God pitching a rainbow tent among us and reflecting gendered and sexual diversity within the risen Christ.

PART 3

QUEERING THE BIBLE

NINE

HOMOSEXUALITY, THE BIBLE, AND THE PRACTICE OF SAFE TEXTS

[N]o credible case against homosexuality or homosexuals can be made from the Bible unless one chooses to read Scripture in a way that sustains the existing prejudice against homosexuality and homosexuals. . . . The "problem," of course, is not the Bible, it is the Christians who read it.

—Peter Gomes[1]

For the last several years, I have lectured on homosexuality and Christianity to some twenty community groups, churches, and universities per year. It is a personal commitment to end homohatred in the United States. In a daily gay listserv to which I subscribe, there is not nearly a day without homophobic letters to the editor that cite a small group of biblical verses to justify their homohatred and opposition to translesbigay marriage, adoption, and civil rights. When I spoke at the University of Central Arkansas, my talk could not be publicly advertised to the greater university because there were administrative concerns about the negative reactions from predominantly conservative Christians in Conway. When I spoke at Georgetown University, posters announcing my lecture were consistently torn down or vandalized. Religious homohatred does not seem to recede but becomes more virulent in Protestant or Catholic enclaves of higher education where academic freedom has been traditionally espoused. However, religious homohatred is being challenged from the emerging body of scholarly evidence about the very biblical texts often used to justify that hatred.

Recently I have been reflecting on the ACT UP slogan: "Silence = Death." I was the target of a hate crime, a minor annoyance in comparison to the murders of Matthew Shepard or Billy Jack Gaither and the violent harassment experienced by many translesbigays. Someone broke

---

1. Peter Gomes, *The Good Book: Reading the Bible with Mind and Heart* (New York: William Morrow, 1996), 147, 162.

into my university office, tore the book cover of *Jesus ACTED UP* from the door of my office, and posted biblical quotes with the word "faggot." The homophobe took the hardcover of the book from my shelf, carved out the pages of the book, stuffed rotting meats in the book, and replaced the book within my bookshelf. It was an act directed at myself for being openly gay and at my vision of a queer Christianity; such queer visions provoke a heated and often virulent reaction from heterosexist Christianity. Heterosexist Christianity cannot tolerate any heresy from compulsory heterosexuality.

Patricia Beattie Jung and Ralph Smith define heterosexism as "a reasoned system of bias regarding sexual orientation. It denotes prejudice in favor of heterosexual people and connotes prejudice against bisexual and, especially, homosexual people. . . . It is rooted in a largely cognitive constellation of beliefs about human sexuality."[2] This bias holds heterosexuality as normative for judging all forms of human sexuality. Over the last several years several heterosexist evangelical authors have published a number of books on the texts often applied to homosexuality.[3] While some of these authors may engage the developments in critical, historical-biblical scholarship, most do not. Even those evangelical scholars who engage and read the scholarship of the last two decades spend time refuting that body of critical scholarship and repackage the same old exegesis of these texts, promoting theological hatred and spiritual abuse. They are disingenuous in claiming that their readings are the plain meanings of the text, for they fail first to understand their own heterosexist biases and second to appropriate critical cultural studies on gender and sexuality. In addition, these conservative scholars take pains to depict homosexual life as loathsome, depressing, lonely, and dangerous. These stereotypes are false caricatures, pointing to the failure of these scholars to engage queer communities of faith such as the MCC (Metropolitan Community Church). These scholars reflect the biases of their own church communities and their social practice of violence and exclusion of "practicing homosexuals."

When I assert that the Jewish and Christian Scriptures say nothing whatsoever about homosexuality as an orientation or a modern identity template, it is not an empty mantra. Behind such a statement stands a large body of contemporary literature from cultural and gender studies

---

2. Patricia Beattie Jung and Ralph F. Smith, *Heterosexism: An Ethical Challenge* (Albany: State University of New York Press, 1993), 13.

3. Ibid., 14.

about the social construction of gender and sexuality, largely ignored by homophobic Christians and scholars.[4] "Homosexuality" and "heterosexuality" are modern concepts coined in German psychiatric practice in 1870 to describe emerging modern identities. The 1909 *Merriam-Webster's New International Dictionary* defined "homosexuality" as a medical term, referring to "morbid sexual passion for one of the same sex," while the 1923 edition defined heterosexuality as the "morbid passion for one of the opposite sex."[5] It was only in the 1934 edition of Webster's dictionary that "heterosexuality" was changed to mean "manifestation of sexual passion for one of the opposite sex."[6]

Despite claims by religious extremists, there are no biblical words that can be translated by the word "homosexual" because the concept of sexual orientation was totally absent in the ancient Mediterranean world. The Bible speaks neither about sexual orientation nor about sexual identity nor about the modern subjectivities of heterosexuality, homosexuality, bisexuality, and transgendered identity. These identities are absent from the biblical worldview. The apostle Peter did not think of himself as heterosexual, and Paul did not view himself as homosexual because such concepts were alien to their thinking about sexuality in the ancient Near Eastern cultures and first-century Greco-Roman world. What the Bible does speak about is a cultural understanding of sexuality and gender from masculinist ideology, or what I term the code of the penetrator.

Modern heterosexist scholars fail to understand the ancient Mediterranean "insistence on understanding sexual difference as matter of degree, gradations of one basic male type."[7] They are already invested in an ideological and rigid gender system that privileges heterosexual masculinity over femininity and other variations of sexuality. Their ideological blinders motivate them to claim the "plain truth of text" that privileges heterosexuality over all other sexual variations. Theological ethicist Beverly Harrison reminds us that homophobia is embedded in

---

4. For gender studies, see for example, Elisabeth Schüssler Fiorenza, ed., *Searching the Scriptures: A Feminist Introduction* (New York: Crossroad, 1995), and *Searching the Scriptures: A Feminist Commentary* (New York: Crossroad, 1994). For cultural studies on sexuality, see David Halperin, *One Hundred Years of Homosexuality: And Other Essays on Greek Love* (New York: Routledge, 1990); Edward Stein, ed., *Forms of Desire: Sexual Orientation and the Social Constructionist Controversy* (New York: Routledge, 1992); Eve Kosofsky Sedgwick, *Epistemology of the Closet* (Berkeley: University of California Press, 1990).

5. Jonathan Katz, *The Invention of Homosexuality* (New York: E. P. Dutton, 1996), 93.

6. Ibid.

7. Thomas Laqueur, *Making Sex: Body and Gender from the Greeks to Freud* (Cambridge, Mass.: Harvard University Press, 1992), 5.

misogyny, the hatred of women.[8] Harrison's insight has remained a key for me in comprehending the masculinist model of sexuality reflected in the ancient cultures of the biblical texts.

The Greco-Roman cultures understood gender differently from our own culture. In *Making Sex,* Thomas Laqueur demonstrates how the ancient world constructed sexuality not within our contemporary two-sex model but within a one-sex model:

> Thus the old model, in which men and women were arrayed according to their degree of metaphysical perfection, their vital heat, along an axis whose *telos* was male, gave way by the late eighteenth century to a new model of radical dimorphism, of biological divergence. An anatomy and physiology of incommensurability replaced a metaphysics of hierarchy in the representation of woman in relation to man.[9]

Ancient Near Eastern and Greco-Roman cultures perceived the two genders within a continuum of and range of maleness. The male-female continuum was always hierarchical, with females as lesser males on the one-gender scale.

Ancient sexuality codes find their basis in status: sex is most often viewed as an act between the active partner, the partner of a higher social status, who assumes the role of the penetrator, and the passive partner, a female or male partner of inferior social status, who takes on the penetrated position. Sex is comprehended within the model of active/passive or insertor/insertee or what colloquial language terms top/bottom. Men in the ancient Greco-Roman world were catalogued according to their social status (and thus power). Free men or citizens were expected to play the insertive role in sex with either female or male. Sex is essentially penetration of a person of lesser status — whether it is a female, a lesser male, or a youth. Penetration establishes or expresses a superior status over the penetrated. Sexual penetration includes penile-vaginal, penile-anal, and penile-oral. Roman scholar Craig Williams notes:

> In Roman terms they [males] were either men (*viri*), who might seek to penetrate females vaginally (*fututores,* to use the coarse Roman vocabulary), to penetrate either males or females anally

8. Beverly Harrison, "Misogyny and Homophobia: The Unexplored Connections," in *Making the Connections,* ed. Carol Robb (Boston: Beacon Press, 1985), 135–51.

9. Laqueur, *Making Sex,* 5–6.

(*pedicones*), or to penetrate either males or females orally (*irruma-tores*), or any combination of these three; or they were ridiculed as *non-men*, who might befoul their mouths by giving others pleasure (*fellatores* or *cunnilingi*), or who might abrogate their masculinity by being anally penetrated (*pathici* or *cinaedi*).[10]

A Roman man engaged in sexual relations with free Romans other than his wife could retain his masculine status as long as he maintained the active role of the penetrator. He could freely seek sexual partners from prostitutes, free persons or slaves of either sex, or his own slaves of either sex. No one ever questioned his Roman's masculine status as long as he was a penetrator in oral, vaginal, or anal sex. The free-born man who was passive in sexual relations with other men was viewed with contempt and derision. Even today, North African men in Islamic cultures like to penetrate all kinds of human beings — women, boys, and men. The active male in no way endangers his male identity or social status by penetrating another male, whereas penetrated males cannot be conceptualized as men. Adult male prostitution is regarded as shameful because it feminizes the passive male.

There are seven texts used or rather misused as texts of terror, as weapons against translesbigay people: Leviticus 18:22 and 20:13; Genesis 19; Judges 19; 1 Corinthians 6:9; 1 Timothy 1:10; and Romans 1:26–27. These texts, misused by some, reflect a model of sexuality and gender codes different from those in our postmodern world. The key issue be-hind these biblical texts traditionally applied to homosexuality does not concern same-sex behaviors but deals with phallic violence and gender transgressions.

Leviticus 18:22 and 20:13

The only direct reference to male homoeroticism in the Hebrew Scriptures appears in Leviticus 18:22 and 20:13. Orthodox Jews and fun-damentalist Christians take the verses as a blanket condemnation of all homosexual practices. Leviticus 18:22 and 20:13 speak of a man who "lies the lying down of a woman." What do these verses really prohibit? Lying down is a euphemism for a sexual act, and the meaning of "the ly-ing down of a woman" (*miskab issah*) is not obvious to a modern reader. In our culture, we speak of going to bed with someone, but our phrase is ambiguous. It tells us nothing of what happens in bed or who does

---

10. Craig A. Williams, *Roman Homosexuality: Ideologies of Masculinity in Classical Antiquity* (New York: Oxford University Press, 1999), 227.

what to whom in bed. Does the Hebrew phrase denote oral, vaginal, or anal sex? It can include all of the above or none of the above. The most persuasive arguments is that it refers to male-to-male anal intercourse.

Saul Olyan, a biblical scholar at Brown University, deciphers the meaning of "the lying down of a woman" in parallel uses of the idiom "the lying down of a male" (*miskab zakar*) within the Hebrew Bible. He concludes that the phrase "the lying down of a male" must mean male vaginal penetration.[11] Olyan speculates that "the lying down of a woman" means "something like the act or condition of a woman's being penetrated, or more simply, vaginal receptivity, the opposite of vaginal penetration."[12] In sexual intercourse, a woman experiences male penetration and offers her male partner vaginal receptivity. Olyan concludes, "the male-male sex laws of the Holiness Source appear to be circumscribed in their meaning; they seem to refer specifically to intercourse and suggest that anal penetration was seen as analogous to vaginal penetration on some level, since the 'lying down of a woman' seems to mean vaginal receptivity."[13] Other interpreters, such as Thomas Thurston and Daniel Boyarin, also concur that the issue is anal intercourse.[14] In other words, Leviticus 18:22 and 20:13 do not prohibit male oral sex, masturbation, or intercrural sex (intercourse in which a male's genitals rub between the thighs of his partner). They are totally silent about the range of female-to-female sexuality. Nor do they prohibit a bisexual male engaging in group sex as long as he does not penetrate another man and is not penetrated by another.

Olyan takes "the lying down of a woman" (*miskebe issa*) to mean that "receptivity is bounded on the side of biological sex; it is constructed as appropriate exclusively to females; it is gendered as feminine."[15] Martti Nissinen notes that some of the provisions of Middle Assyrian laws indicate that male receptivity or passivity in freeborn men, either coerced or consensual, disgraced the passive male by categorizing him with slaves and females.[16] Here the Leviticus text objects to a male who becomes

11. Saul M. Olyan, "'And with a Male You Shall Not Lie the Lying Down of a Woman': On the Meaning and Significance of Leviticus 18:22 and 20:13," *Journal of the History of Sexuality* 5 (1994): 185.

12. Ibid.

13. Ibid., 185–86.

14. Thomas Thurston, "Leviticus 18:22 and the Prohibitions of Homosexual Acts," in *Homophobia and the Judaeo-Christian Tradition*, ed. Michael L. Stemmeler and J. Michael Clark (Dallas: Monument Press, 1990), 7–24; Daniel Boyarin, "Are There Any Jews in 'The History of Sexuality,'" *Journal of the History of Sexuality* 5, no. 3 (1995): 333–55.

15. Olyan, "And with a Male," 188.

16. Martti Nissinen, *Homoeroticism in the Biblical World: A Historical Perspective* (Minneapolis: Fortress Press, 1998), 20–28.

a substitute for a female. It calls a man functioning as a woman an abomination (*to'eba*), what Olyan has rendered as "the violation of a socially constructed boundary" or perhaps a taboo. "Abomination" occurs six times in chapters 18 and 20 of the Holiness Code, referring to ritual impurity; it occurs nowhere else in Leviticus. Therefore, Leviticus 18:22 only condemns anal intercourse, not proscribing all male-to-male sexual acts. For Olyan, the misuse of male semen, not the act of anal intercourse, generates the ban in Leviticus.

There is one problem with Olyan's interpretation, for nowhere is there condemnation of male-to-female anal intercourse in the Holiness Code in Leviticus. It is not the mixture of semen and excrement that generates the ban and imputation of ritual impurity for male-to-male anal intercourse. Rather there is another type of mixture that generates impurity. Martti Nissinen points out that two men engaged in anal intercourse mirrored the male and female roles. Because the penetrated lost his manly honor, the transgression is a confusion of gender roles. Ancient Near Eastern sources were concerned about confusing or mixing gender roles, and the Hebrews in particular were concerned about mixing their gender roles, something that becomes clear in the prohibitions against cross-dressing (Deut. 23:2), against eunuchs, and against any sort of third-gender roles comparable to those of castrated male devotees to the Mesopotamian goddesses.[17]

Jewish scholar Daniel Boyarin provides Talmudic arguments to support the insight of Nissinen on the mixing of genders. While the Talmudic interpretation is historically much later than the social context of Israel's Holiness Code, it provides a coherent reading consistent with the gender codes of the earlier period:

> There was something pathological and depraved, however, in the spectacle of an adult male allowing his male body to be used as if it were the body of a person of penetrable status, whether the man did so for pleasure or for profit. It is sex-role reversal, or gender deviance, that is problematized here. . . . I suggest also penetration of a male constituted a consignment of him to the class of females . . . a degradation of status; this constituted a sort of mixing of kinds, a general taboo occurrence in Hebrew culture.[18]

For Boyarin, the mixing (*tebhel*) is akin to the taboo of cross-dressing: "The woman shall not wear that which pertains unto a man, neither shall

---

17. Ibid., 43–44.
18. Boyarin, "Are There Any Jews," 341.

a man put on a woman's garment" (Deut. 22:5). The priestly Holiness Code reflects the creation theology of Genesis 1:27, where God created male and female as separate creatures. The kinds are to be kept separate, not blurred or mixed: "it is 'use' of a male as female that is *to'ebha,* the crossing of a body from one God-given category to another, analogous to the wearing of clothes that belong to the other sex."[19]

Boyarin notes that the Hebrew word for female (*neqeba*) means "orifice bearer."[20] The female represents the category of penetrative receptivity. He concludes, "Men penetrate, women are penetrated; so for a man to be penetrated constitutes a 'mixing of kinds' analogous to cross dressing."[21] Male-to-male anal intercourse mixes gender roles by relegating one partner to the role of a receptive woman. The receptive partner is condemned as well because the male penetrator causes his partner to cross gender boundaries and become like a woman. Sexuality is understood as penetrative sex — male penetration of women or of lesser males who become women. This explains why there is no condemnation of female homoeroticism — it was impossible for the ancient Israelites to conceive of two women having sex within the penetrative model of sexuality.

The foremost scholar on Leviticus, Rabbi Jacob Milgrom, advances the notion that if the Holiness Code is so bound to the holy land of Israel, then Leviticus 18:22 and 20:13 are not applicable to female, Gentile, or Jewish same-sex relations outside of Israel. It applies only to Jewish homoeroticism within the land of Israel. Jacob Milgrom concludes, "The ban on homosexuality is limited to male Jews and inhabitants of the holy land. The basis for the ban . . . is the need for procreation which opposes, in biblical times, the wasting of seed."[22] Milgrom's line of thinking upsets those critics who want to make these verses a blanket condemnation of both female and male homoeroticism. He takes seriously the opening verses of Leviticus 18 that explicitly state why the Egyptians and the Canaanites lost the land — because of their violations of purity.

Genesis 19 and Judges 19: male rape

Genesis 19 shares a history of narrative development with its parallel story in Judges 19. However, there is no clear scholarly consensus on the

---

19. Ibid., 343.

20. Ibid., 345.

21. Ibid., 347.

22. Jacob Milgrom, "Does the Bible Prohibit Homosexuality?" *Biblical Review* (December 1993): 48ff. See Milgrom's expanded argument in *Leviticus 17–22: A New Translation with Introduction and Commentary* (New York: Anchor Bible, 2000), 1785–90.

dependence of one story on another or a core narrative that branched into narrative traditions. Gender codes of honor, shame, and sexual property are equally operative in both stories.

The centuries-long Christian tradition that relates Genesis 19 to same-sex practices has given us the term "sodomy," coined in medieval Christianity.[23] It is the story most frequently cited by homophobic Christians for their hatred of translesbigays. Sodom has become the image of human depravity and moral decay, but the story in Genesis 19 has nothing to do with same-sex sexuality; it has to do, rather, with male rape.

The story of the destruction of Sodom-Gomorrah has been incorporated into the Abraham saga. Chapters 18–19 of Genesis form a literary unit that many fundamentalist and evangelical interpreters fail to analyze as a whole. When chapter 19 is read with chapter 18, the inhospitality of Sodom is contrasted with the rural social code of hospitality. Hospitality is part of the cultural code and the editor's theological motif operative in Genesis 18–19. It is introduced in chapter 18 when Abraham welcomes and entertains the messengers from God. In a similar fashion, Lot welcomes the messengers in Sodom. The editor contrasts the rural, pastoral welcoming of strangers with the urban hostility to them. The messengers are foreigners within the city, and the men of Sodom surround the house and insist that "we might know them (*yadha*)." The Hebrew word to "know" (*yadha*) is occasionally used as a euphemism for sexual intercourse, and here in this chapter and Judges 19, *yadha* needs to be translated and contextualized in the sexual codes of the penetrator and the penetrated in the ancient world. A more apt colloquial translation would be to "womanize, make into a woman." In the context, it suggests "penetrating a male like a woman," or anal intercourse. Ancient Near Eastern societies subjected those they had conquered, enemies, strangers, and trespassers to phallic anal penetration to indicate their subordinate status.

Lot's offer of his daughters to the mob is shocking to readers. He owns his daughters; they are his sexual property for his disposition. He is willing to let his daughters suffer gang rape rather than allowing the messengers to suffer such collective violence, gender denigration, and humiliation. Few homophobic interpreters ever raise an outcry at the nonconsensual offer of Lot's daughters to the mob but focus their attention on the rejection of the daughters to indicate that homosexuality is the center of the incident. The mob has rejected women for the male messengers as gay men have rejected heterosexuality for other men.

23. Mark Jordan, *The Invention of Sodomy* (Chicago: University of Chicago Press, 1996).

Yet Lot's offer dispels any identification with what modern society designates as homosexuality. The crowd is out to inflict the collective violence
of rape and thus remove the threat of the strangers. The crowd is no
more representative of homosexuality than a local urban street gang
who attacks and rapes a stranger coming into their territory.

But hospitality interpreters such as John Boswell and John McNeill
bracket out some vital interpretative elements: phallic violence and patriarchal gender codes of domination/subordination and honor/shame.[24]
As heterosexist interpreters, their hospitality analysis suffers from a similar lack of gender analysis. Much of their interpretation is based on
taking the verb to know (*yadha*) as knowing and not as a sexual act. In
the Talmud, the rabbis took the offense of the men of Sodom as sexual.[25]

Recent exegesis of this text has helped some churches to acknowledge that Genesis 19's primary concern is not homoerotic relations but
violent sexual abuse of outsiders. But heterosexist interpreters still focus
not on the threat to the daughters but on the attempted male-to-male
rape. Many churches contextualize the sin of Sodom as rampant homosexuality. If they address issues of phallic violence and hospitality, they
localize the sin as homosexual rape and the vilest act of inhospitality.
Heterosexist interpreters neglect the violence to women, and this fact
slides into the background of their church documents and policies
against homosexuality. They are unable to comprehend the connections
between misogyny and homophobia.

Biblical scholar George Edwards supplements the hospitality interpretation by underscoring the phallic violence and the prophetic cry
for justice. The "outcry" (*zecaqa*) against Sodom in Genesis 18:21 and
19:3 is a technical word for oppression and injustice, not sexual sin.[26]
In his commentary on Genesis, the German biblical scholar Gerhard
Von Rad describes the term as signifying "the cry for help which one
who suffers great injustice screams."[27] Gary Comstock reads the story
as patriarchal propaganda, the "latest macho, sexist, rape-and-pillage,
straight-from-hell video rental."[28] He compares the patriarchal violence
of the story to the attitudes of gay-bashers. These readings rightly shift

24. John McNeill, *The Church and the Homosexual* (Kansas City, Mo.: Sheed, Andrews,
McMeel, 1976), 68–75; John Boswell, *Christianity, Social Tolerance, and Homosexuality*
(Chicago: University of Chicago Press, 1980), 92–98.

25. Boyarin, "Are There Any Jews," 350.

26. George Edwards, *Gay/Lesbian Liberation: A Biblical Perspective* (New York: Pilgrim
Press, 1984), 42–46.

27. Gerhard Von Rad, *Genesis: A Commentary*, trans. J. H. Marks (Philadelphia: Westminster Press, 1972), 211.

28. Gary Comstock, *Gay Theology without Apology* (Cleveland: Pilgrim Press, 1993), 41–42.

reader attention from the violation of hospitality to patriarchal violence to male strangers and to the daughters, "the other" inscribed within the biblical text.

Leland White and several other scholars expand the interpretative framework to weave the themes of hospitality and sexual violence within the Hebrew cultural script of honor/shame.[29] The honor-oriented cultures of the ancient Near East comprehend hospitality not within an individualist, modern perspective but within a collective perspective of families, clans, villages, cities, and people. Hospitality is enjoined by many ancient codes where such a virtue often entails a life-and-death situation. When the messengers enter into Sodom as strangers, they have no legal status. The men of Sodom assess the threat and decide to make them symbolically women and thus physically submissive. They intend to violate their bodily integrity to remind them that their status is comparable to women. Lot, as a patron, extends hospitality to the strangers, and their acceptance of his hospitality indicates their subordination to him. The Sodomites' assault is an affront on Lot's honor because they threaten his control over his home. By standing in the doorway and intervening, Lot symbolically asserts his right over his household and his right to offer hospitality to the messengers in Sodom.

The laws of hospitality are fused with the patriarchal gender code that privileges males over females. That code requires that Lot protect male honor over female honor. In other words, it is better to shame a woman than a man. So Lot offers the sexual capital of his household, his virgin daughters, in exchange for preserving the honor of the strangers. The mob rape would dishonor not only the messengers but also Lot, his household, all his clan, and all those people associated with him. Nissinen writes:

> In a patriarchal society, manly honor largely is equivalent to human value, to offend is a grave shame. Gang rape of a man has always been an extreme means to disgrace one's manly honor, to reduce one to a woman's role....It is not a matter of exercising one's homosexual orientation or looking for erotic pleasure but simply of protecting or threatening one's masculinity. Rape — homosexual or heterosexual — is the ultimate means of subjugation and domination.[30]

---

29. Leland J. White, "Does the Bible Speak about Gays or Same-Sex Orientation? A Test Case in Biblical Ethics: Part I," *Biblical Theology Bulletin* 25, no. 1 (spring 1995): 14–23; Ken Stone, "Gender and Homosexuality in Judges 19: Subject-Honor, Object-Shame?" *Journal for the Study of the Old Testament* 67 (1995): 87–107.

30. Nissinen, *Homoeroticism in the Ancient World,* 48.

Genesis 19 can be read as a male contest of honor, or contest of testosterone, between Lot and the men of Sodom, and the resolution of the honor contest occurs in the blinding of the Sodomites. The editor of Genesis uses this story to enhance Israelite honor in the confrontation with non-Israelite city life. The Sodomites are engaging social violence and oppression in their attempt at male rape, and Sodom became a symbol of injustice and oppression within the Hebrew scriptural tradition. In numerous biblical texts, there are no indications of the sin of Sodom as referring to same-sex behaviors. In Isaiah 1:9–10, injustice, insincere sacrifice, and oppression are the sins of Sodom. The prophet Ezekiel comprehends the sin of Sodom as a sin of injustice; he writes, "This was the sin of your sister Sodom: she did not support the poor and the needy. They were haughty, and did abominable things before me" (Ezek. 16:49–50). Other examples are Jeremiah 23:14, which designates adultery and hypocrisy as the sin of Sodom, and Wisdom of Solomon 19:13–14, which identifies the sin as the violation of hospitality. When Jesus says that it will be more tolerable for Sodom than for those not hearing God's messengers, he has in mind not the Sodomites' sexual practices but their inhospitality (Matt. 10:14–15; 11:20–24; Luke 10:10–12). It is the refusal to hear God's messengers. The Hebrew biblical authors and Jesus were at home with the interpretation of the Sodom story as a crime of violence, inhospitality, and social oppression.

Judges 19 brings into sharper relief than Genesis 19 the relationship of the gender codes and male violence. The Levite's wife asserts her independence and returns to her father's household. In ancient Hebrew patriarchy, women are sexual property, belonging to their fathers, brothers, and husbands. By leaving her husband, the woman threatens the gender code. The Levite follows her to his father-in-law's household to reclaim his property. His father-in-law, however, tries to persuade the Levite to remain in his household by wining and dining him for days. He stays in his father-in-law's household, remaining subordinate to another male's protection and giving up his autonomy like a woman.

On the return trip, the Levite and the woman find shelter in an old man's house in Gibeah. A mob of men surrounds the house, demanding, "Bring out the man who came into your house that we may have intercourse with him" (Judg. 19:22). The old man offers the mob his virgin daughter and the Levite's woman for ravishing. The mob declines the offer, and the Levite seizes his woman and pushes her out the door for their violent pleasure. The mob brutally rapes the woman, torturing her through the night and leaving her for dead in the morning. The escalating violence, however, does not end there. The Levite discovers the woman on the doorstep and tells her to "get up" so that they can continue their journey. The text records her silence, implying her death. The Levite proceeds to dismember her body into twelve parts, burying her in the territories of the twelve tribes. This leads to tribal revenge and war against the men of Gibeah.

The men of Gibeah want the Levite, but they get a woman. The two impulses seem narratively to be at odds. The host promotes an androcentric ideology of deflecting the violence from the male guest: "Do it to the women, not to the male." The men of Gibeah want to humiliate the Levite in the most degrading way by womanizing or penetrating him through anal intercourse. But when we now read the story, we need to unmask how the honor/shame code surrounding hospitality to strangers is closely wedded to patriarchal ideology of gender and sexuality. Male penetrative sexuality is used as a social expression of subordinate status of women and a weapon to shame men.

When we examine the Hebrew Scriptures, we find no identifiable notions of homosexual orientation. We do find several particular forms of same-sex representations of rape and gender-code violations. We do not consider heterosexual rape as a form of heterosexual sexual expression; neither can we designate homosexual rape in Genesis 19 as homosexual sex: "The generalized application of the rapists of the Genesis 19 story to modern gay/lesbian sexual practices is inappropriate reconstruction; there is a fallacy equating rape with consensual same-sex practices in Christian fundamentalist reading of the text."[31] No sensible heterosexual person would characterize rape as sexuality; it is violence, not sex. The real act of sodomy is the particular application of the story to translesbigays and the translation of textual violence into social violence.

The Christian Scriptures

There are no sayings of Jesus against same-sex relationships. Jesus inclusively accepted people; he had little to say about sexuality except for those few occasions where he condemned exploitation or double standards. If the churches spent as much time as Jesus did on sexuality, there would be a lot healthier congregations welcoming and not excluding folks based on sexual orientation. Jesus' focus in his ministry was on justice, love, and inclusion. He saw hypocrisy and injustice as far greater threats to the realm of God.

---

31. Robert E. Goss, *Jesus ACTED UP: Gay and Lesbian Manifesto* (San Francisco: HarperSanFrancisco, 1993), 92.

Paul, however, continues to present a problem for many translesbigays. Some mainline churches and the religious right have used Paul to justify (1) exclusion from churches and denial of ordination of "practicing homosexuals," (2) reparative therapies that attempt to change sexual orientation or gender transitions, (3) legal discrimination in housing, employment, and the right to marry. We need to investigate the words in 1 Corinthians 6:9 wrongly translated for "homosexual": sodomite, pervert, or some abusive derivative; and we need to uncover what the real issue is in Romans 1:26–27. Christian churches have used 1 Corinthians 6:9, 1 Timothy 1:10, and Romans 1:26–27 to maintain that translesbigays will be eternally damned.

1 Corinthians 6:9

In 1 Corinthians 6:9, Paul writes, "Do not be deceived: neither the immoral, nor idolaters, nor adulterers, nor homosexuals (*oute malakoi oute arsenokoitai*), nor thieves, nor the greedy, nor drunkards, nor revilers, nor robbers inherit the kingdom of God." Most commentators accept the fact that Paul incorporated his vice list from already existing vice lists in Hellenistic Judaism. Paul's contemporary Philo of Alexandria uses lists of vices over a hundred times in his writings.

John Boswell was one of the first scholars to point out the multiple mistranslations of two words applied to homosexuality: *malakos* and *arsenokoites*.[32] *Malakos* literally means "soft." Biblical scholar Robin Scroggs links the term *malakos* to an "effeminate call boy," to the one who is penetrated in anal intercourse.[33] There have been times fundamentalist Christians have applied the word *malakos* or "effeminate" to condemn transsexuals as well. The word *malakos* stresses softness against the hardness of masculinity. During the first century C.E., the masculinist ideology of the Greco-Roman world may have associated "softness" or "effeminacy" with men who submitted to passive anal intercourse in the gender roles of women. Yet there may have been other associations in the ancient world lost to careless mistranslations and the equation to contemporary homosexuality.

Yale biblical scholar Dale Martin has provided the most conclusive evidence in arguing that the term referred to the entire complex of

---

32. Boswell, *Christianity*, 338.
33. Robin Scroggs, *The New Testament and Homosexuality* (Philadelphia: Fortress Press, 1983), 62–64.

femininity and that effeminacy had no relation to male-to-male sexuality in the Greco-Roman world. He cites Pseudo-Aristotelian's *Physiognomy,* which describes the *malakos* as "delicate-looking, pale-complexioned and bright-eyed: their nostrils are wrinkled and they are prone to tears. These characters are fond of women and inclined to have female children."[34] Martin concludes, "In fact, *malakos* more often referred to men who prettied themselves up to further heterosexual exploits."[35] It was often used as an epithet of insult for men who loved women too much and were sex addicts. They became effeminate by too much association with and their love for women.

The second term, *arsenokoites,* is a Greek compound noun, composed of *arseno,* literally "man," and *koites,* meaning "sleeping." One of my colleagues translates it as "couch potato." The problem with this term is that it is used only twice in the Christian Scriptures (1 Cor. 6:9; 1 Tim. 1:10) and that it ultimately remains obscure in its meaning within the Christian Scriptures. There is outside use of the word that allows some limited speculation on its possible meaning. In the *Sibylline Oracle* 2, "Do not steal seeds.... Do not *arsenokoitein,* do not betray, do not murder," the term occurs in what Martin calls "economic sins, action related to economic injustice or exploitation."[36] Martin observes that *arsenokoitein* does not appear elsewhere in the text except where sexual sins are denounced. He finds a similar usage of *arsenokoites* in the *Acts of John,* where it is listed among sins related to economic injustice. In his *Refutation of All Heresies,* Hippolytus narrates how the evil angel Nass commits adultery with Eve and takes Adam as his slave boy. Hippolytus uses the word *arsenokoitia* to denote Nass's relationship with Adam, implying that this is a coercive and unjust use of another person sexually. Martin concludes from his survey of Greco-Roman and early Christian literature that *arsenkoites* refers to "a particular role of exploiting others by means of sex, perhaps but not necessarily by homosexual sex."[37] For nearly a thousand years, Christians have committed violence against people attracted to the same sex and still brutalize them over the mistranslations of these words with obscured usages and meanings.

---

34. Dale Martin, *The Corinthian Body* (New Haven: Yale University Press, 1995), 33.

35. Dale Martin, "*Arsenokoites* and *Malakos*: Meanings and Consequences," in *Biblical Ethics and Homosexuality: Listening to Scripture,* ed. Robert L. Brawley (Louisville: Westminster John Knox, 1996), 126.

36. Ibid., 120.

37. Ibid., 123.

Romans 1:26–27

In Romans 1:26–27, Paul speaks about the exchange (*metallsasso*) of natural for unnatural female and male homoerotic relationships. These verses form part of Paul's larger argument on Roman idolatry and function as a prelude for arguing against judgmental Jewish critics. Paul uses the examples of the exchange of natural relations for his argument of idolatry and the consequences of changing the created order for disorder. In Paul's thinking, the exchange (*metallaxan*) of the Creator for a creature leads to women exchanging (*metallaxan*) natural intercourse (*ten physiken khresin*) for unnatural (*para physin*) and men likewise giving up natural relations (*ten physiken khresin*) with women. For Paul, Gentiles have exchanged God for created things, resulting in disordered sexuality.

While many scholars believe that the exchange of natural sexual intercourse for unnatural intercourse refers in Romans 1:26–27 to some form of homoerotic relationships, some argue that the exchange refers to heterosexual "sexual perversion." John Boswell argues that heterosexually oriented people engage in homosexual acts. His use of modern sexual-identity templates has been criticized for their anachronistic application to ancient sexuality.[38] James Miller claims that the exchange refers to unnatural heterosexual oral or anal intercourse because Paul's culture did not have a linked concept of male and female homoeroticism.[39] Tom Hanks follows Miller's reading that Romans 1:26 refers to women engaging in anal sex with men to avoid procreation, but he sees that verse 1:27 is built on the Leviticus prohibitions against male-to-male, unprotected anal sex.[40]

In a different interpretative trajectory, Robin Scroggs comprehends the exchange as referring to relationships between an older man and a youth. While providing an excellent study of cultural pederasty in the Greco-Roman world, Scroggs's model fails to account fully for the verses on female homoeroticism and adult-male-to-adult-male homoeroticism.[41] He notes the rare mention of female homoeroticism within Jewish and Greco-Roman sources but fails to comprehend female homoeroticism within Paul's gender codes. L. William Countryman and Daniel Helminiak attempt to understand Romans 1:26–27 within the

---

38. Boswell, *Christianity*, 108–10.
39. James E. Miller, "The Practices of Romans 1:26: Homosexual or Heterosexual?" *Novum Testamentum* 35 (1995): 1–11; Miller, "Pederasty and Romans 1:27: A Response to Mark Smith," *Journal of the American Academy of Religion* 65, no. 4 (1997): 861–65.
40. Tom Hanks, *The Subversive Gospel* (Cleveland: Pilgrim Press, 2000), 90–91.
41. Scroggs, *The New Testament and Homosexuality*, 85–98.

purity codes of Judaism. For Countryman, the homoerotic acts are an unclean part of Gentile culture, now insignificant in Christ. These homoerotic acts are not accorded Paul's judgment of deserving death (Rom. 1:32).[42] They are rhetorical means for articulating Gentile idolatry and uncleanliness while later unpacking Jewish sinfulness. Paul affirms at the end of his letter: "I know and am persuaded in Lord Jesus nothing is unclean in itself, but is unclean for anyone who thinks it is unclean."

Helminiak wants to understand *para pysin* as "beyond nature," and he explores whether the verses in Romans might refer to heterosexual nonprocreative sex acts such as heterosexual intercourse during menstruation, having intercourse standing up, and oral or anal sex.[43] "Beyond nature" becomes unusual, out-of-the-ordinary sexual acts. Ultimately, Helminiak falls back to Countryman's purity thesis of homogenital acts as impure but not ethically wrong, but Paul uses this rhetorical structure to get past Jewish sensibilities of religious purity and superiority over Gentile impurity. For the above authors, Paul is trying to heal the split of Jewish and Gentile Christians in Rome; these theses are meant to rehabilitate Paul for the queer community.

Bernadette Brooten has convincingly argued that the issue of female homoeroticism is connected with Paul's perspective on gender codes. Her gender analysis undercuts the above male perspectives on Romans 1:26–27 and does not rehabilitate Paul. What Paul means by "exchanged natural relations for unnatural relations" is that "women exchanged the passive, subordinate sexual role for an active autonomous role."[44] Martti Nissinen, likewise, affirms, "It was woman's active sexual role that was regarded as truly contrary to nature."[45] Such a change constitutes that men take a passive, subordinate sexual role like women in exchange for the normal role of the male penetrator. In the dominant Greco-Roman culture of the first century C.E., the penetrator and penetrated constitute foundational categories for the model of sexuality, and they are intertwined with the cultural gender codes.

Brooten comprehends the violations of female and male homoeroticism in light of 1 Corinthians 11:2–16, where Paul describes a natural hierarchy: God, Christ, man, woman. He requires strict gender differentiation with hairstyle and headdress. Women are not to cut their

---

42. L. William Countryman, *Dirt, Greed, and Sex: Sexual Ethics in the New Testament and Their Implications for Today* (Philadelphia: Fortress Press, 1988), 109–23.

43. Daniel Helminiak, *What the Bible Really Says about Homosexuality* (San Francisco: Alamo Square Press, 2000), 83, 87.

44. Bernardette Brooten, *Love between Women: Early Christian Responses to Female Homoeroticism* (Chicago: University of Chicago Press, 1996), 63.

45. Nissinen, *Homoeroticism in the Ancient World*, 108.

hair short like men, while men are not to wear their hair long like women. Women's long hair is insufficient for marking gender difference. Paul requires the veiling of women's heads as well. Nissinen notes, "This hierarchical pattern was not invented by Paul but belonged to his culture. Gender role categories in the eastern Mediterranean, with culturally defined concepts of maleness and femaleness, masculinity and effeminacy,... are not determined by anatomical sex only but also by an appropriate self-presentation and conformity to established gender roles."[46] Paul accepted the gender ideologies without question, and these were drawn from Hellenistic Judaism.

The issue at the heart of Romans 1:26–27 is the rigid gender codes Paul grew up with as a Pharisaic Jew and perhaps his own fears about his sexual drives. Paul is anxious about men with long hair and women with short hair because this confuses his rigid cultural understanding of maleness and femaleness. Paul fears a man who will be penetrated like a woman by another man. That man has betrayed his male status and privilege. Nissinen argues that Paul was familiar with *tribades,* women who have usurped the male position as penetrator or as top. Greco-Roman folklore had these women grow their clitoris into a penetrative phallus because the people could not conceive sex outside of the penetrator/penetrated model. These women's transgressions involve their attempts to be like males, to be penetrators of women; thus, they have usurped a male social role. These transgressions confuse the created gender codes of males as active penetrators and women as passive receptors. These are Paul's personal opinions woven into his pastoral letter to the Romans. Many Christians no longer condone his acceptance of slavery nor his statements about women.

Conclusion

At the heart of these texts misapplied to translesbigay folks is a deep misogyny, the hatred and fear of women. Contemporary homophobia is embedded in ancient misogynist gender codes that many of us no longer hold. The passive role of a male in anal intercourse was identified with the female role. Because of the view of women as sexual property and the dominant view of asymmetrical sexual relationships, a woman in an active role was culturally offensive. Both defied cultural codes of natural order, for it was natural in the Greco-Roman world for a free male to penetrate a boy, a male of lesser status, a slave, or a woman. It

---

46. Ibid., 107.

was unnatural for a free man to be penetrated by another free man or for a male of lesser status or for a woman, without a penis or semen, to be penetrated by another woman. These cultural ideas were fused with a natural, creation theology within Hellenistic Judaism and later Christianity.

The Hebrew Scriptures do not speak of anything remotely like female homoeroticism; nor do they mention male/female masturbation or male/female oral sex. There are only references to male-to-male anal intercourse in Leviticus 18:20, 22:13, and the violation is a gender transgression, a betrayal of the privilege of male status within a patriarchal culture that valued the male over the female. Nor does male rape have any of the features of contemporary gay male sexuality, relationality, mutuality, or love.

For many conservative Christians, Paul has been used as the final word on homosexuality. Many churches have used these mistranslations of *arsenkoites* and *malakos* to justify the exclusion of translesbigays from their congregations, to deny them ordination, and to refuse to bless and recognize their unions. The sin of Sodom has been magnified by such blatant and cruel inhospitality within many churches, and the mistranslations have mutated into social policies of public discrimination and legitimizing a climate of public violence.

Many contemporary Christians object to Paul's views on women and his support of slavery in the Greco-Roman world. They have rejected his opinions on women and slavery as the word of God, realizing that these are his opinions, holding little weight in our contemporary Christian practices. Why many still cling to Paul's cultural opinions expressed in Romans 1:26–27 and ignore sound biblical interpretations of scholars has less to do with theological or biblical reasons and more to do with prejudicial motivations and homophobic reactions and hatred best left to the psychologist or therapist to explain.

TEN

OVERTHROWING HETEROTEXTUALITY — A BIBLICAL STONEWALL

With the rise of postmodernism we have seen a shift in biblical hermeneutics that considers the role of the reader in assigning meaning to the biblical text. Not only have we come to realize that readers make meaning of texts, but readers also bring a particular "self" to the text which is shaped by a variety of factors such as race, ethnicity, gender, class, religious affiliations, socioeconomic standing, education, and we would add, sexual orientation.
— Robert E. Goss and Mona West[1]

The cultural "myth" of the heterosexual insider is a modern insidious myth because it depends on the binary notions of the "insider/outsider." Anthropologist Mary Douglas has noted how social groups become self-defined enclosures, protecting the boundaries of entry and exit.[2] Thus, social groups set up categories of insiders and outsiders. The most scandalous boundary crossings are directly related to gender, race, class, and sexuality. Generations of judges, church and synagogue leaders, politicians, theologians, military leaders, scientists, and even families have formed homophobic interpretative communities, justifying the punishment of sexual outsiders who were persecuted because they claimed to possess a dangerous truth threatening particular mythic visions of a heterosexual cosmos. Patricia Beattie Jung and Ralph F. Smith describe heterosexism as "a reasoned system of bias regarding sexual orientation. It denotes prejudice in favor of heterosexual people and connotes prejudice against bisexual, and especially, homosexual people."[3] It is a pervasive attitude whereby individuals and cultural institutions are conditioned to live and act as if everyone is heterosexual. Heterosexism is

---

1. Robert E. Goss and Mona West, eds., introduction to *Take Back the Word: A Queer Reading of the Bible,* ed. Goss and West (Cleveland: Pilgrim Press, 2000), 4.
2. Mary Douglas, *Purity and Danger* (London: Routledge & Kegan Paul, 1966).
3. Patricia Beattie Jung and Ralph F. Smith, *Heterosexism: An Ethical Challenge* (Albany: State University of New York Press, 1993), 13. See also Dale Martin, "Heterosexism and the Interpretation of Romans 1:18–32," *Biblical Interpretation* 3, no. 3 (1995): 332–35.

analogous to sexism, racism, and other "isms" that judge and discriminate against people as "other." Heterosexism has silenced and erased the lives of translesbigay people by creating cultural images of heterosexual normalcy and by pathologizing all deviancies from those images. It has also pervaded and dominated the particular reading strategies of Jewish and Christian communities, or what Stanley Fish has described as "interpretative communities."[4] Religious interpretative communities are specific social groups that read the scriptural texts from the authoritative lens of their own particular theological biases and traditions. These communities may be qualified by such specific attributes as denomination, race, gender, ethnicity, class, and even sexual orientation.

The integral strategy of heterosexist interpretative communities is to convince us of their line of biblical interpretation: that the texts condemn us as queers and that there are textual silences about us. These communities are convinced that the Bible is rampant with heterosexuality, except in certain passages that condemn particular homoerotic sexual acts. Thus, the temptation is to follow heterosexist scripts that either pathologize us as the evil "other" or closet homoeroticism in Jewish and Christian Scriptures. Many translesbigays have thus been abused, excluded from their synagogues and churches, the subjects of hate campaigns to demonize them and the targets of social violence. Suffering from biblical abuse, many queers are convinced that the Bible is their enemy, or they have abandoned their churches or been excluded. However, these reading strategies of heterosexist interpretative communities have the undesirable effect of producing queer interpretative communities. Initially gay/lesbian Jews and Christians formed interpretative communities to read the biblical texts to protect themselves from religiously sanctioned violence, yet they also brought their theological grid of affirming lesbian/gay lives to take back the word in a cultural war over the Bible. The Bible has become a hotly contested book in the cultural war between the religious right and queers.

What I would like to explore is how queers as a collection of interpretative communities approach biblical texts. There are several textual strategies of reading that have emerged within the post–Stonewall era: (1) deflecting textual violence, (2) outing the text, (3) and befriending the text, or discovering queer subjectivity within the text. All three reading strategies represent forms of "apologetics," a style of rhetorical discourse designed to critique the truth-claims of one interpretative

---

4. See Stanley Fish, *Is There a Text in the Class? The Authority of Interpretative Communities* (Cambridge, Mass.: Harvard University Press, 1980). See also Virginia Mollenkott, *Sensuous Spirituality: Out from Fundamentalism* (New York: Crossroad, 1993), 167ff.

community while promoting one's own truth-claims. The first interpretative strategy consists of a "negative" apologetics, aiming to critique the heterosexist interpretations of texts applied to homosexuality and deflect the resulting social violence. This negative apologetics has consumed gay/lesbian Christians and Jews for nearly thirty years. The second and third reading strategies consist of forms of a positive apologetics, promoting queer reading strategies over the heterosexual erasures of homoeroticism from the text and discovering queer subjectivity within the text. Whereas negative apologetics engage in defensive strategies to undermine the argumentation of another interpretative community, positive apologetics remain offensive in promoting their truth-claims. I would maintain that each of these apologetic reading strategies takes the authority of the biblical text serious while critiquing heterosexist interpretative strategies and promoting queer readings of the text.

Deflecting textual violence

In *Jesus ACTED UP*, I appropriated and widened the usage of Phyllis Trible's "texts of terror" from its initial application to women to how churches have used scriptural texts against queers.[5] Many gay and lesbian scholars have expended energy in battling biblical terrorism. I want to address only gay/lesbian scholars and exclude heterosexual scholars such as Victor Furnish, Robin Scroggs, Jacob Milgrom, Walter Wink, Martti Nissinen, and George Edwards who have been queer-friendly in their exegesis of the texts of terror and against the homophobia of ecclesial interpretative communities.[6] They have worked to diffuse textual violence and homophobia within many mainline churches.

John McNeill's *The Church and the Homosexual* (1976), Virginia Mollenkott and Letha Scanzoni's *Is the Homosexual My Neighbor?* (1978), Tom Horner's *Jonathan Loved David* (1978), and John Boswell's *Homosexuality, Christianity, and Social Tolerance* (1980) are queer classics that pioneered

---

5. Robert E. Goss, *Jesus ACTED UP: A Gay and Lesbian Manifesto* (San Francisco: HarperSanFrancisco, 1993), 88–94.

6. Victor Furnish, *The Moral Teaching of Paul* (Nashville: Abingdon Press, 1979); Robin Scroggs, *The New Testament and Homosexuality* (Philadelphia: Fortress Press, 1983); Jacob Milgrom, "Does the Bible Prohibit Homosexuality?" *Biblical Review* (December 1993); Walter Wink, "Biblical Perspectives on Homosexuality," *Christian Century*, 96, no. 36, November 7, 1979, 1082–86; Martti Nissinen, *Homoeroticism in the Biblical World: A Biblical Perspective* (Minneapolis: Fortress Press, 1998); George Edwards, *Gay/Lesbian Liberation: A Biblical Perspective* (New York: Pilgrim Press, 1984).

exegesis to deflect social and cultural violence.[7] For the late 1970s and the early 1980s, these authors provided excellent exegesis of the biblical texts of terror and spurred tremendous counterattacks from heterosexist scholars and church leaders. Boswell's work initiated serious scholarly discussion of the social context of the biblical texts of terror but was generally ignored by church leaders. What Boswell and the other authors precipitated was an apologetic battle for the interpretative control of the biblical text. They challenged the mainstream of heterosexist interpretation and control of the text, critiquing its cultural biases and arguing for a closer reading of the text within its own social context. They also initiated intense debate within synagogues and churches on the issue of homosexuality and specific biblical texts. Perhaps their most important contribution was that they initiated a "biblical Stonewall" rebellion against heterosexist interpretative communities and strengthened the emerging gay/lesbian denominational groups and churches as interpretative communities. They stood up against the long-standing tradition of textual abuse with cogent arguments of historical criticism and constructions of the ancient codes of sexuality and gender.

Since the 1970s, a critical mass of gay/lesbian scholarship on same-sex affectional preferences has countered oppressive biblical readings supported by interpretative communities that were heteropatriarchal and oftentimes misogynist. I number some of the negative apologists: William Countryman, Gary Comstock, Peter Gomes, Daniel Helminiak, Deirdre Good, Michael Vasey, Dale Martin, Saul Olyan, Ken Stone, Bernadette Brooten, and myself.[8] Influenced by the writings of Michel

7. John McNeill, *The Church and the Homosexual* (Kansas City, Mo.: Sheed Andrews and McMeel, 1976); Virginia Mollenkott and Letha Scanzoni, *Is the Homosexual My Neighbor?* (San Francisco: Harper & Row, 1978); Tom Horner, *Jonathan Loved David* (Philadelphia: Westminster Press, 1978); John Boswell, *Homosexuality, Christianity, and Social Tolerance* (Chicago: University of Chicago Press, 1980).

8. L. William Countryman, *Dirt, Greed, and Sex: Sexual Ethics in the New Testament and Their Implications for Today* (Philadelphia: Fortress Press, 1988); Gary Comstock, *Gay Theology without Apology* (Cleveland: Pilgrim Press, 1993); Peter Gomes, *The Good Book: Reading the Bible with Mind and Heart* (New York: William Morrow, 1996); Daniel Helminiak, *What the Bible Really Says about Homosexuality* (San Francisco: Alamo Square Press, 2000); Dierdre Good, "Reading Strategies for Biblical Passages on Same-Sex Relations," *Theology and Sexuality* no. 7 (1977): 70–82; Michael Vasey, *Strangers and Friends: A New Exploration of Homosexuality and the Bible* (London: Hodder & Stoughton, 1995); Dale Martin, "*Arsenokoites* and *Malakos*: Meanings and Consequences," in *Biblical Ethics and Homosexuality: Listening to Scripture*, ed. Robert L. Brawley (Louisville: Westminster John Knox, 1996), 117–36; Saul M. Olyan, " 'And with a Male You Shall Not Lie the Lying Down of a Woman': On the Meaning and Significance of Leviticus 18:22 and 20:13," *Journal of the History of Sexuality* 5 (1994): 179–206; Ken Stone, "Gender and Homosexuality in Judges 19: Subject-Honor, Object-Shame?" *Journal for the Study of the Old Testament* 67 (1995): 87–107; Bernadette Brooten, *Love between Women: Early Christian Responses to Female Homoeroticism* (Chicago: University of Chicago Press, 1996).

Foucault, queer studies produced by David Halperin, John J. Winkler,
Robert Padgug, and others have further rendered unstable the categories of "homosexuality" and "heterosexuality" in their application to
ancient Near Eastern and Mediterranean sexualities.[9] As discussed earlier, homosexuality and heterosexuality are modern concepts coined in
German psychiatric practice in 1870. These modern sexual templates
are inapplicable to ancient identities.

Saul Olyan provided the most cogent exegesis of Leviticus 18:22,
20:13, while Dale Martin has provided the most persuasive translations
of *malakos* and *arsenokoites* in 1 Corinthians 6:9. Gay and lesbian scholars
have employed one of two rhetorical reading strategies, either arguing
the inapplicability of the texts of terror to contemporary gay/lesbians or
considering the texts as cultural condemnations of same-sex eroticism
but superseded by other biblical warrants. Such evangelical scholars as
Marion Soards, Thomas Schmidt, and Richard Hayes have conceded the
Hebrew biblical texts in their counterattacks against gay/lesbian rhetorical arguments over the biblical texts of terror but have drawn a last
line of defense around the creation accounts in Genesis and around
Romans 1.[10] Bernadette Brooten's *Love between Women: Early Christian Responses to Female Homoeroticism* (1996) has nearly ended the battle over
Romans 1 by employing complex feminist and class social analysis. It
also eroded earlier gay male and heterosexist exegesis.

The tide of queer scholarship has overturned these texts of terror in
many mainline, denominational churches. Evangelical, fundamentalist,
and neoconservative groups of mainline denominations, however, continue to cling to noncritical, heterosexist, and misogynist interpretations
of the texts of terror. The next stage in negative apologetics would be
to engage these groups in their methods of argumentation and epistemological criteria of knowledge. This may provide an even greater
challenge for queer scholars, demanding that they abandon historical,
literary, and cultural criticism for such an engagement and try novel attempts to engage evangelical Christians on their own terrain. The battle

9. David M. Halperin, *One Hundred Years of Homosexuality* (New York: Routledge, 1990);
David M. Halperin, John J. Winkler, Froma I. Zeitlin, eds., *Before Sexuality: The Construction
of Erotic Experience in the Ancient Greek World* (Princeton, N.J.: Princeton University Press,
1991); John J. Winkler, *The Anthropology of Sex and Gender in Ancient Greece* (New York: Routledge, 1990); Robert Padgug, "Sexual Matters: On Conceptualizing Sexuality in History,"
Radical History Review 20 (1979): 3–23.

10. Marion Soards, *Scripture and Homosexuality: Biblical Authority and the Church* (Louisville: Westminster John Knox, 1995); Thomas Schmidt, *Straight and Narrow* (Downers
Grove, Ill.: InterVarsity, 1995); Richard Hays, "Awaiting the Redemption of Our Bodies:
Drawing on Scripture and Tradition in the Church Debate on Homosexuality," *Latimer*
110 (June 1992): 20–30.

has just begun over the biblical texts. In her summary article, "Battling for the Bible," Deryn Guest notes that choosing between conflicting readings will require nonviolent arguments of persuasion by queer academics and queer communities of faith like UFMCC.[11] She ends with an apocalyptic scenario detailed by Elizabeth Stuart in which the churches for years are debating, and they begin to hear a distant rumbling:

> Should they ignore hoping it will pass, open the door and let in or barricade themselves against it? But everyone suspects that this rumble on the horizon has the potential to sweep them off their feet, scatter their papers, overturn their table and change the familiar landscape in which they have been working. The rumble on the horizon is queer theology and what it threatens to disrupt is the debate on "homosexuality" which continues to occupy the minds of the churches as it has, on and off, for the last thirty years.[12]

This apocalyptic rumble, prophesied by Stuart, is taking place in the shift from negative apologetics over the biblical text to positive appropriations of the biblical texts from a queer perspective. Guest writes, "in the future queer theology will exercise a profound impact, and queer readings that move beyond the current boundaries of 'legitimate' interpretations will proliferate. This will radically reshape the terrain on which the debate takes place."[13]

In an article titled "Gay/Lesbian Interpretation" in the *Dictionary of Biblical Interpretation,* Ken Stone concludes, "While a great deal of light has been shed on biblical attitudes towards sexual practice, much less work has been done on the production of readings of biblical texts from explicitly lesbian, gay, or bisexual reading locations."[14] I would add to Stone's list the emerging social location of transgendered voices reading the biblical text and claiming their voice within it.

Outing the text

Like feminists and African Americans, queer readers have had to live with a violent literary tradition, one that condones violence against people attracted to the same sex. They have adopted similar reading

---

11. Deryn Guest, "Battling for the Bible: Academy, Church, and Gay Agenda," *Theology and Sexuality* 15 (2001): 90.

12. Ibid., 91.

13. Ibid., 66.

14. Ken Stone, "Gay/Lesbian Interpretation," *Dictionary of Biblical Interpretation,* ed. John H. Hayes (Nashville: Abingdon Press, 1999), 433.

strategies to feminists and to African Americans to deflect the heteropatriarchal interpretations and textual violence. Many queers, likewise,
are resistant readers who struggle against heterocentric privilege that
erases them from the text, and they have countered heterosexist usage
of the Bible as a source of oppression and exclusion with a strategy
of "outing the text" or discovering queer voices within the text. This
comes from the resistant practices of hearing the heterosexual presump-
tive interpretations of the text from the pulpit and attempts to insert
themselves into the text.

Gay evangelical author Michael Vasey echoes a hard-fought insight
for many queers when he writes, "The Bible is not a weapon in a cultural war, but a source of wisdom offered by a gracious God to people
who easily get the wrong end of the stick."[15] When queer Christians have
looked to the biblical text, many have not found themselves or their lives
reflected in the texts of terror such as those about the "rapists" in Genesis 19, the "abominations" in Leviticus 18, or the "unnatural sinners" in
Romans 1:25–27. Initially, they have struggled with the textual violence
of various interpretative communities who abusively applied these texts
of terror to them, but they have not willingly seen themselves within
these texts. As queer denominational groups, churches, and synagogues
formed in the 1970s, they created new interpretative communities engaging the scriptures not as enemy but as "friend." Yet many queer
Christians, who journeyed into exile communities, found that they had
to recover from the years of religious and homophobic abuse from their
previous churches. The writings of queer scholars have provided invaluable pastoral tools for clergy in explaining away the biblical texts of
terror for abused Christians.

Queer Christians found themselves reflected in stories of Ruth and
Naomi, Jonathan and David, and Jesus and the Beloved Disciple. The
pastoral practice of those churches, synagogues, and denominational
groups have used these texts as liturgical readings in the blessings of
same-sex unions and providing legitimacy to their unions.[16] These wor-

---

15. Vasey, *Strangers and Friends,* 138.

16. Two popular gay/lesbian ritual books, *Daring to Speak Love's Name,* by Elizabeth Stuart, and *Equal Rites,* coedited by Kittredge Cherry and Zalmon Sherwood, use the classical
texts of Ruth 1:16–17; 1 Samuel 18:3; and 2 Samuel 1:26. If John Boswell is correct, contemporary queer Christian praxis around the same-sex coupling of Ruth and Naomi and
Jonathan and David finds its antecedents in same-sex blessings in early medieval Christianity. See Elizabeth Stuart, *Daring to Speak Love's Name* (London: Hamish Hamilton, 1992),
54; Kittredge Cherry and Zalmon Sherwood, eds., *Equal Rites* (Louisville: Westminster John
Knox, 1995), 100; John Boswell, *Same-Sex Unions in Premodern Europe* (New York: Villard
Books, 1994), 136–38.

ship practices initially outed the homoerotic within the biblical text through communal imaginative readings.

"Outing" is a transgressive strategy that publicly reveals a person's sexual orientation. It breaks the conspiracy of silence, forcing queers out of the closet by speaking the unspeakable and disrupting the codes of silence. Generally, outing has been a divisive issue within the queer communities.[17] It has been less controversial with historical figures long dead such as King James II of England or Isaac Newton. Nancy Wilson, lesbian elder of the UFMCC, breaks the heterosexist presumption of "compulsory heterosexuality" over biblical figures by outing them:

> It is time boldly to liberate some biblical gay, lesbian, and bisexual characters and stories from ancient closets. It may seem unfair to "out" these defenseless biblical characters, but I'm tired of being fair. Centuries of silence in biblical commentaries and reference books have not been fair.[18]

Wilson counters pervasive biblical heterosexism by outing "eunuchs" and "barren women," Ruth and Naomi, Jonathan and David, the gay centurion, Lydia in Acts, and Jesus as bisexual. Wilson wants to move the queer community from its experience of religious abuse and exclusion to a positive interpretation of the Bible. In other words, she is reclaiming the text for the queer community when she writes, "The Bible must be a holy text for gays and lesbians because we are truly human, created by the God who created heaven and earth."[19] Queer folks have the right to be included because they are made in the image of God and thus must be included within the text. Wilson articulates a tribal hermeneutic for gays and lesbians, reading eunuchs and barren women as gay, lesbian, and bisexual antecedents.[20] She also includes Jesus in her list of eunuchs within the biblical text, noting the parallels between, on the one hand, Jesus' alienation with his family and his itinerancy and, on the other, the lives of gays/lesbians.[21]

Wilson is not alone in reading the text from such a positive perspective of outing biblical figures. I also include heterosexual people like Bishop Spong and the German biblical scholar Gerd Theissen in outing

---

17. See Goss, *Jesus ACTED UP*, 41–42; Richard Mohr, *Gay Ideas: Outing and Other Controversies* (Boston: Beacon Press 1994), 11–48.

18. Nancy Wilson, *Our Tribe: Queer Folks, God, Jesus, and the Bible* (San Francisco: HarperSanFrancisco, 1995), 112.

19. Ibid., 75.

20. Ibid., 120–31.

21. Ibid., 134–39.

St. Paul as a repressed homosexual.[22] In the final volume of his trilogy, *Freedom, Glorious Freedom,* John McNeill interprets the Q story of the centurion and his boy (Matt. 8:5–13; Luke 7:10). McNeill speaks of the gay centurion and his beloved boy: "Here we have the most direct encounter of Jesus Christ with someone who today would be pronounced 'gay' and Christ's reaction is acceptance of the person without judgment and even eagerness to be of assistance to restore the *pais* (boy) to health."[23]

Evangelical biblical scholar Tom Hanks labels both the apostle Paul and the evangelist Matthew as gay.[24] In *The Subversive Gospel,* Hanks adopts this strategy, attempting to break up the heterosexist readings of the Christian Scriptures with close attention to the diversity of voices within the text.[25] From his own perspective, Hanks attempts to use evangelical Christians' style of interpretation to widen their narrow readings but ultimately wants to surrender authority to the text. Thus, he wants to provide credible interpretations of biblical texts and persons to persuade elements of evangelical Christianity that find the biblical text authoritative.

Following in the tradition of John Boswell, the late Robert Williams uses "gay" indiscriminately and essentially as a sexual identity continuous throughout history. He writes, "We can find traces of our people in the Bible only by employing approaches that are radical, revisionist, and reconstructionist."[26] Williams makes use of Dorothee Soelle's notion of *phantasie* as a "creative imagining,... [an] active imaging of faithful possibilities" as a supplement to historical criticism.[27] Williams's notion of queer imagination provides a creative means of counterreading the biblical text from the presumptions of normalizing heterosexuality. His use of creative imaging has striking similarities to Elisabeth Schüssler Fiorenza's "hermeneutics of creative actualization" or "biblical imagination" to reclaim the dangerous voices of women within the scriptures:

---

22. See Gerd Theissen, *Psychological Aspects of Pauline Theology* (Philadelphia: Fortress Press, 1987); John Shelby Spong, *Living in Sin: A Bishop Re-thinks Human Sexuality* (San Francisco: Harper & Row, 1988), 151.

23. John McNeill, *Freedom, Glorious Freedom* (Boston: Beacon Press, 1996), 132.

24. Thomas Hanks, "A Family Friend: Paul's Letter to the Romans as a Source of Affirmation for Queers and Their Families," in *Our Families, Our Values: Snapshots of Queer Kinship,* ed. Robert E. Goss and Amy Adams Squires Strongheart (New York: Harrington Park Press, 1997), 137–50; Hanks, "Matthew and Mary of Magdala: Good News for Sex Workers," in *Take Back the Word: A Queer Reading of the Bible,* ed. Robert E. Goss and Mona West (Cleveland: Pilgrim Press, 2000), 185–95.

25. Thomas Hanks, *The Subversive Gospel* (Cleveland: Pilgrim Press, 2000).

26. Robert Williams, *Just as I Am* (New York: Crown Publications, 1992), 55.

27. Ibid., 56. See also Dorothee Soelle, *Beyond Mere Obedience* (Minneapolis: Augsburg Press, 1970), 30ff.

a hermeneutics of liberative vision and imagination seeks to actualize and dramatize biblical texts differently. The social function of imagination and fantasy "is to introduce possibilities,... [for] we can work toward actualizing only that which we have first imagined." Creative re-imagination employs all our creative powers to celebrate and make present the suffering, struggles, and victories of our biblical foresisters and foremothers.[28]

Williams's use of imaginative readings to discover the homoerotic within the scriptural text mirrors one element of Schüssler Fiorenza's complex critical feminist interpretation. It also delineates the future development of reading the biblical text from queer social locations.

Real textual subversion, however, takes place when queer churches, synagogues, and groups decenter heterosexual presumptions and readings that often suppress diversity, gender, race, class, ethnicity, and sexual alternatives. The scriptures are not the privileged possession of heterosexuals but belong to all Jews and Christians of faith, including queer Jews and Christians. Outing has been a positive apologetic for queer readings of the biblical text and for reading themselves into the biblical texts, claiming certain narrative figures as their own.

My objection is not to the use of "outing" or queer imagining as reading practices to disrupt interpretative silences of textual evidence of homoeroticism, but I object to the anachronistic labeling of specific characters as gay, lesbian, bisexual, or even heterosexual. The cognitive content of sexual-identity templates is thoroughly modern, for, as I have discussed earlier, ancient Jews, Greeks, and Romans did not understand themselves as gay, lesbian, bisexual, transgendered, or heterosexual.[29] They thought of themselves as Jew, Greek, or Roman; male or female; freed or slave. They understood their status within the male code of the penetrator and the penetrated; the penetrator had greater status than the penetrated. There are no biblical words that denote heterosexual, bisexual, transgendered, or homosexual orientations; thus, these modern identity templates remain anachronistic when applied to specific biblical characters. For example, Gerd Theissen and Bishop Spong call St. Paul a "closeted homosexual" because his personality and psychological repression meet what our culture designates as closetedness, but it would be a mistake to impose our cultural definitions of closetedness upon an ancient culture. It is anachronistic to impose these modern

---

28. See Elisabeth Schüssler Fiorenza, *Bread Not Stone* (Boston: Beacon Press, 1984), 21; Schüssler Fiorenza, *But SHE Said* (Boston: Beacon Press, 1992), 26–28.

29. Jonathan Katz, *The Invention of Heterosexuality* (New York: Dutton, 1995).

identity templates on ancient persons and texts.[30] Granted that Paul fits the personality profile of a gay closeted man, suffering from internalized homophobia; and granted that he did suffer from fear of his sexual attractions to men; still, to call Paul a closeted homosexual is as anachronistic as it is to read the texts from the presumption of heterosexuality. The question that remains for queer interpretive communities is whether we can see ourselves reflected in biblical narratives without these modern identity templates.

A second critique of the "outing" strategy is that it does not move very far from the interpretative strategies or negative apologetics to deflect textual violence against queers. Outing, like textual deflection, grants to the Bible too much power to authenticate our lives as queers. Both interpretative strategies look to the scriptures to authorize our sexual behaviors and to find an outside "divine" word to validate our erotic selves. If we come to the text with the purpose of finding validation for our erotic lives, then we limit our encounters with the text of scripture because we place authority entirely in the text as a parent. There is no dialogue, for validation of queer erotic lives must first originate from within queer lives, realizing the goodness and original blessings of queers' sexualities. That such validation is a priori means that queer folks need to come out and recognize the blessing of their sexualities before they engage the biblical text. Theologian Gary Comstock writes,

> Instead of making the Bible into a parental authority, I have begun to engage with it as I would a friend — as one to whom I have made a commitment and in whom I have invested dearly, but with whom I insist on a mutual exchange of critique, encouragement, support, and challenge.[31]

Queer reading requires not surrendering to biblical authority as a parent but engaging the text as an equal, and in the encounter as friend, readers bring their own queer social context to the text. The authority of the text remains in the back-and-forth encounter of equals.

Befriending texts

It is insufficient to dismantle homophobic interpretations of the texts of terror or to just out the text, for it is necessary to bring the biblical

---

30. Tarachow presents the most cogent analysis of Paul's sexual attraction to men; see Sidney Tarachow, "St. Paul and Early Christianity: A Psychoanalytic and Historical Study," *Psychoanalysis and the Social Sciences* 4 (1955): 223–81.

31. Comstock, *Gay Theology without Apology,* 11.

texts into dialogue with the contexts of queer lives. The text of queer lives must interact with the text of scripture. In 1993, I wrote,

> A critical gay and lesbian interpretation seeks to make the reading of the text an experience of liberation. It becomes a practice of solidarity with the non-persons of the text, surfacing the oppositional conflict between religious-political power and the non-person.... A queer hermeneutics of critical engagement becomes a hermeneutics of solidarity in appropriating the past meaning of the biblical texts. Solidarity is the compassionate identification with the oppressed.[32]

Queer critical readings of the scriptures transform texts into "narratives of resistance," whereby queer Christians can hear the resonances of their voices and lives within the text.[33] When I use "queer," I no longer mean just gay and lesbian, but I also include bisexual and transgendered. My "queerness" is a priori before my reading a biblical text, and it is the horizon or social location from which I enter into the text, queer it, and bring it into my own queer world of meaning and empowered Christian practice. Because of their experience of exclusion from the churches and continued homophobic discrimination, queers can feel a sense of solidarity or an affinity with the nonpersons, the poor, the marginal, the lepers, the gender-benders, the strangers or foreigners, the sexual nonconformists such as eunuchs or barren women, or the boundary-breakers in biblical narratives.

Queer marginality gives a particular insight and advantage in reading the scriptural text over nonmarginalized folks but does not privilege queer readings over the readings of other marginalized and oppressed groups. In other words, queer readers can become the subject of these narrative texts, discovering within them their voices and agency. They can reconfigure the texts or biblical figures imaginatively within their lives because they already have come out and have found their sexuality as an original blessing from God.

Gary Comstock, naturally weary about the scriptures as a patriarchal document, finds a few narrative figures such as Jonathan and Vashti whom gay men can appropriate as models of the unconventional nurturer.[34] Comstock reads the tale of Queen Vashti in the Book of Esther as a model for gay resistance; he queers the text, transgressing gender codes to appropriate the resistance voice of a feisty queen

---

32. Goss, *Jesus ACTED UP*, 104–5.
33. Ibid., 105.
34. Comstock, *Gay Theology without Apology*, 79–90.

as a model for contemporary gay men.[35] More significantly, Comstock does not surrender to the authority of the text but relates to the text through conversation and dialogue. By engaging the text, not as authority but as guide, Comstock allows queerness of lives to provide a critical interpretative role in discovering authority in our own experiences.

On the other hand, Richard Cleaver, indebted to Latin America liberation theologies, provides a consistent gay reading of the scriptures that moves beyond outing and in fact reclaims the text.[36] While Comstock undertakes to befriend the text, Cleaver in *Know My Name* provides a gay reading of biblical texts. However, what troubles me in reading Cleaver is not his interpretation of the text but his engagement. It is rich on the side of textual interpretation, but it is too flat a reading from a gay social context. There is so much from contemporary gay politics and culture missing from his dialogue: the fight for civil rights, the right to intimacy, the numerous ballot initiatives targeting queer people, and the exclusion of bisexual and transgendered voices.

While Cleaver's reading of texts is flat, Roland Boers reads the Saul and David saga from the lens of queer culture. The action hero and the villain struggling to the death in a homoerotic conflict provides the matrix for his interpretation of "David the cock collector."[37] Boers uses Keanu Reeves to interpret the ambiguously active and passive behaviors of David as Saul's boy, his versatility with Jonathan, and ultimately his role as Yahweh's boy. Reeves provides a queer template for David's ambiguous activeness and passivity in several films. David represents "the best facsimile of all that gay men desire: an action man with gripping hands and eager, come-fuck-me eyes."[38]

Mona West, the senior pastor at the Cathedral of Hope, speaks of this process of queer self-discovery within the biblical narratives as "befriending the text": "the point of reference for a queer reading of scripture is the notion that the Bible is our friend. When we approach the Bible as a friendly text, as a text that 'does no harm,' the terror of the scriptures is transformed into the life giving word of God. We are able to find our story within it."[39] Likewise, lesbian theologian Elizabeth Stuart writes, "Reading the Bible with queer eyes turns the Bible from being

---

35. Ibid., 51–60.

36. Richard Cleaver, *Know My Name* (Louisville: Westminster John Knox, 1995).

37. Roland Boer, *Knockin' on Heaven's Door: The Bible and Popular Culture* (New York: Routledge, 1999), 22–32.

38. Ibid., 20.

39. Mona West, "Reading the Bible as a Queer American: Social Location in Hebrew Scriptures," *Theology and Sexuality* 10 (March 1999): 35.

an enemy to being a friend."[40] Befriending the text is the imaginative reading from a queer social location. It does not exclude a hermeneutics of suspicion but includes a hermeneutics of queer solidarity with the marginal and perhaps more importantly a hermeneutics of queer imagination. It can include a hermeneutics of queer eroticism, as just illustrated by Roland Boer's reading of the David saga. We need to read the text with a suspicion not only of patriarchy but also of compulsory heterosexuality. Patriarchy is not a divinely created order but a cultural matrix that mediated a communal engagement of revelation of God. Modern church leaders and scholars, reading from presumptions of heteronormativity, exclude diverse voices within the texts. Postmodern queers are resistant readers, reading from the position of the sexually excluded and the gender abjected.

As queer readers, we want to befriend the scriptures, to find our voices, and to surface subversive memories of God's insurrection against human oppression and the promise of liberation. What does this entail? First, it requires coming out — to self, families, friends, and God. Coming out requires coming into our original blessing of our erotic lives and coming out into a community. Once we recognize our giftedness, then we can approach the text with positive subjectivity. Mona West notes that there are four overarching concerns that shape queer readings of the text: inclusiveness, hospitality, coming out, and families.[41] West gives numerous examples of all four concerns in her essay "Reading the Bible as a Queer American."[42] I would add to her list liberation or human freedom.

Translesbigay readers align themselves with the scriptures so that a hermeneutical dialogue results between the text and the contexts of their lives. It allows interplay, an open dialogue between text and queer imagination, whereby queers can envision God's transformatory action in their lives and communities. Translesbigays bring the context of their lives to the text and, in turn, reconfigure the text into the social world of their lives. Timothy Koch, as mentioned previously, speaks of cruising as a method in approaching the scriptures:

> cruising is the name we give to using our own ways of knowing, our desire for connection, our own savvy and instinct, our own re-

---

40. Elizabeth Stuart, "Prophets, Patriarchs, and Pains in the Neck: The Bible," in *Religion Is a Queer Thing*, ed. Elizabeth Stuart et al. (Cleveland: Pilgrim Press, 1997), 45.

41. West, "Reading the Bible," 36. When you read West's essay, you will understand my critique of Cleaver's work as flat from the position of social context. He does not allow his social context to sufficiently shape his reading of the biblical text.

42. West, "Reading the Bible," 35–39.

sponse to what attracts us and compels us. To cruise the scriptures means to treat these women and men as we would any heterogeneous group, recognizing that there will be some friends, some enemies, a lot who either don't care one way or other or else don't really do anything for me, and a few really hot numbers! Cruising requires keeping our eyes and ears open, maintaining our awareness that attackers may lurk, recognizing that not all of our efforts will result in anything remotely resembling success — yet all the while participating actively to create the possibilities of life-enhancing, thrilling contact with these texts![43]

Koch speaks of using "gay radar" or "gaydar" when approaching the text. I believe that Koch's approach is innovative and erotically titillating, but what is significant is that he brings his life experience as an out gay man to engage the text by cruising and finding characters who enrich his life in this erotic encounter. He reads Elijah as a "hairy leather-man" in 2 Kings 1:2–8 and reads other biblical figures in similar fashion.[44] Koch's reading is less anachronistic, though there are some hints of anachronism in his interpretation. He contextualizes Elijah within the idea of the holy man attracted to men, wrapped in goat skins, a scenario Judy Grahn writes about.[45] Koch's a priori erotic, albeit queer encounter with the text presupposes (1) bringing his world of experience to the text, (2) cruising, or the encounter with the text, and (3) his life enriched or transformed from the erotic encounter with the text. The image of cruising the scriptures allows for the interplay and play of queer imagination with all its potential for camp and parody, and with critical tools for overturning gender hierarchies and sexual fixity. For Koch, the orgasmic consummation of cruising the text provides the motivation for queer interplay.

Mona West and I undertook a book project now published as *Take Back the Word: A Queer Reading of the Bible*, an anthology of translesbigay Jews and Christians reading the biblical texts from their own particular

---

43. Timothy Koch, "Cruising as Methodology: Homoeroticism and the Scriptures," in *Queer Commentary and the Hebrew Bible*, ed. Ken Stone (Sheffield: Sheffield University Press, 2001), 175.

44. Koch reads Lydia the Shrewd (Acts 16:11–15), Jehu the Zealous (2 Kings 10:12–17), and Ehud the Erotic (Judg. 3:12–26) with his cruising method. See ibid., 176–80.

45. Koch uses the goat-skinned, leather god. See Judy Grahn, *Another Mother Tongue: Gay Words, Gay Worlds* (Boston: Beacon Press, 1984), 95ff. As an essentialist, Grahn believes that gay identity can be found throughout history. Koch borders on an essentialist interpretation. However, I would argue that there has been gender-bending, homoeroticism, and bi-eroticism in all ages. People did not self-identify themselves as gay, lesbian, bisexual, transgendered, or heterosexual.

social contexts. It originated from a joint workshop at the 1995 Atlanta UFMCC General Conference, where we proposed a queer method of approaching the biblical texts. We began to canvas and recruit contributors from all sorts of translesbigay social locations and invited them to contribute to the project. Our reading strategy as a collection of contributors was to read from our particular social locations:

> It is a strategy that "outs" the Queer community by articulating the community's lived experience in and beyond the closet as well as its particular concerns when encountering and appropriating the biblical text. It is a strategy that attempts to take back the Bible as the word of God for our community, instead of a club. It is a strategy that takes into account the multifaceted nature of our community as gay men, lesbians, transsexuals, and bisexuals with different ethnicities, socioeconomic standings, and religious communities.[46]

All the contributors are trained readers, representing a limited cross-section from academic and particular interpretative communities. In the preface, biblical scholar Mary Ann Tolbert writes:

> In the case of queers . . . the fact that all texts, including the biblical texts, are generally ambiguous and indeterminate, thus requiring readers to refine and complete their meaning, is something of a two-edged sword. Since reading is always and inevitably a process in which the commitments, views, and cultural and social location of each reader profoundly influence the way those ambiguities and indeterminacies are decided, readers of texts become the co-creators of their meanings.[47]

Tolbert recognizes that authoritative readings come not from the biblical text itself but from the assumptions that translesbigay (and other) readers bring to the text. The queer contributors foreground themselves as real flesh-and-blood readers, variously situated as they transgress heterosexist boundaries and even the sexual orthodoxies of gay and lesbian to include bisexual and transgendered contributors. Transgressing boundaries of dominant interpretative communities is a rebellious act that breaks the conceptual categories, and when it is applied to textual readings, queer readers provide a creative rebellion, driven by the

---

46. Goss and West, eds., *Take Back the Word*, 4.
47. Mary Ann Tolbert, "What Word Shall We Take Back?" in *Take Back the Word*, x.

diversity of our imaginations and our commitments to justice and inclusion. Our Stonewall has been realized in our overthrow of biblical heterotextuality by destabilizing the text — eroticizing, tricking, allegorizing, using camp or laughing at the text. Perhaps the greatest offense of these queer reading strategies of befriending the text is our affirmations: (1) we too have been graciously invited to God's inclusive table; (2) our interpretative communities are spiritually maturing to produce their own readings of the scriptures; and (3) we are taking back the word as we take back our Christian practices.

Take Back the Word is certainly not inclusive enough of all queer social locations, but it is a beginning, followed by Ken Stone's *Queer Commentary and the Hebrew Bible* and a massive queer commentary on all the books of the Bible.[48] *Take Back the Word* is a positive reading of the Hebrew and Christian Scriptures. The coeditors chose "take back the word" after playing around with a number of titles. "Taking back the word" indicated not only our queer reclamation of the biblical text for ourselves but also our Christian activist inclinations.

---

48. Stone, ed., *Queer Commentary and the Hebrew Bible*. Deryn Guest, a Hebrew Scripture scholar at the University of Birmingham (UK), Mona West, Hebrew Scripture scholar and director of spiritual development at the Cathedral of Hope, and myself have recruited translesbigays from all over the world to work on commentaries on each of the books of the Hebrew and Christian Scriptures from a queer perspective.

--- PART 4 ---

QUEERING THEOLOGY

ELEVEN

TRANSGRESSION AS A METAPHOR
FOR QUEER THEOLOGIES

*Theology in the United States, therefore, has undergone a shift from using
a melting pot model, in which theology as officially understood sought a
dominant or common human experience, to a model that values the collage
of different faces, voices, styles, questions, and constructs. Black theologies, Asian-American theologies, feminist theologies, womanist theologies,
theologies from gay men and lesbian women, and theologies offered from
the perspectives of the disabled are all present on the scene today. Where
once such differences were either ignored or belittled as "special interests,"
theology today is increasingly understood as having its vitality only insofar
as its traditional sources embrace new voices and their differences.*

—Rebecca Chopp and Mark Taylor[1]

Queer theory emerged in the 1980s from AIDS activism and a new
wave of political activism to counter the backlash of the new right
under the Reagan and Bush presidencies. The radical politics of difference — influenced by the French postmodernists such as Lacan,
Derrida, and Foucault — challenged the politics of gay and lesbian identities. A gay/lesbian academic conference, the Politics of Pleasure, held
at Harvard University in 1990, brought AIDS activists and gay/lesbian
academics together. The debate over whether gay and lesbian identities were essential or socially constructed was nearing its conclusion,
and the social constructionists gained prominence as the popularity of
Michel Foucault was on the rise. There was a synergy at the conference
between street activists and academics, for queer theory was undergoing its birth pangs. The deans of queer theory — Eve Sedgwick, David
Halperin, and Judith Butler — shaped its birth, giving it a contentious
edge in deconstructing the ethnic model of identity politics that was
shaped by Stonewall and that continued into gay/lesbian activism in

---

1. Rebecca S. Chopp and Mark Lewis Taylor, *Reconstructing Christian Theology* (Minneapolis: Fortress Press, 1994), 4.

the 1980s. Queer theory was an academic and political Stonewall whose significance continues to impact translesbigay academics and politics. It also challenges and will change theology.

Heteronormativity, a neologism, was coined as a new category when queer theory defined itself as an academic-cultural movement. It became a term to describe the dominant sex/gender system that privileges heterosexual males while it subordinates women and disprivileges gender/sexual transgressors. For many people, gender and sexuality are only intelligible within a heterosexual matrix. This heteronormative understanding creates a gender/sexual fundamentalism that pathologizes gender and sexual differences and fails to accept the fluidity of gender and sexual identity.

The ethnic model of the gay/lesbian movement split into two directions, typified by the publication of Andrew Sullivan's *Virtually Normal* and Urvashi Vaid's *Virtual Equality*.[2] Sullivan subscribes to heteronormative thinking, replicating an assimilationism by articulating a homonormativity that ignores cultural, gender, sexual, and racial differences. Conservative gays and lesbians try to assimilate into society. Thus, there are good gays who fit into society and outrageous gays who break the homonormative code. Urvashi Vaid, on the other hand, moved from an ethnic model of gay/lesbian identity to an inclusive model of gender, sexual, cultural, racial, and ethnic differences within a moral vision of creating a more just society. Her model allows for queer fluidities and differences to be mainstreamed.

Heteronormative theology is not the only orthodoxy. Lesbian and gay theologies a decade ago seldom mentioned bisexuals and never even addressed the transgendered. In the American Academy of Religion, the largest professional association of religious scholars, the Lesbian Feminist Issues Group in Religion and the Gay Men's Issues Group in Religion were formed to promote gay and lesbian voices in religion. During the last ten years, many of the major lesbian and gay theological books arose from papers delivered at the annual conferences each November. These lesbian and gay theologies have underscored their struggles against the hetero/homosexual categories, making significant scholarly contributions and critiques based upon affirmative lesbian and gay identities.

Many gay and lesbian theologians have, however, fallen into a trap that makes hetero/homo sexual preferences the exclusive metacate-

---

2. Andrew Sullivan, *Virtually Normal* (New York: Alfred A. Knopf, 1995); Urvashi Vaid, *Virtual Equality* (New York: Doubleday, 1995).

gories of sexual identity. There are other homosexuals who do not fit into the categories of heterosexual, lesbian, and gay. The idea of a unitary gay or lesbian identity has been fundamental to the formation of gay/lesbian theologies. But these theologies have framed identity on the assumption that gays are like an ethnic group; we have minoritized our identity based on our homoerotic desires and attractions. But do our sexual attractions to men unite us like an ethnic group? Or as we probe beyond this surface of ethnicization of sexual desire, do we find a great deal of difference and hybridity?

Cultural critic Steven Seidman notes recent critique of the ethnic model:

> The dominant ethnic model of identity and community was accused of reflecting a narrow white middle-class, Eurocentric experience. The very discourse of liberation, with its very notion of a gay subject unified by common interests, was viewed as a disciplining social force oppressive to large segments of the community in whose name it spoke.[3]

The minoritization of male sexual identity does not neatly fold into the categories of gay normativity. Neither bisexual men nor female-to-male transsexuals nor the intersexed fit neatly into our gay template. Elias Farajaje-Jones speaks of an "in-the-life" identity for a range of African American males attracted to the same gender or both genders.[4] Hispanic American, Asian American, and Native American men have social constructions of identity that may not easily be subsumed under the category of gay since it is frequently constructed as white, middle-class male. Gay identity can be as confining as "closetedness" in its minoritization and elision of the social-cultural differences of same-sex desire while privileging white gay males.

While gay/lesbian theological works have concentrated mainly on questions of homosexuality, queer theory has expanded its realm of investigation to sexual desire, paying close attention to cultural construction of categories of normative and deviant sexual behavior. Queer theory expanded the scope of its queries to all kinds of behaviors linked to sexuality, including gender-bending and nonconventional sexualities.

---

3. Steven Seidman, "Identity and Politics in a Postmodern Gay Culture: Some Conceptual and Historical Notes," in *Fear of a Queer Planet,* ed. Michael Warner (Minneapolis: University of Minnesota Press, 1993), 125.

4. Elias Farajaje-Jones, "Breaking Silence: Toward an In-the-Life Theology," in *Black Theology,* ed. James H. Cone and Gayraud S. Wilmore (Maryknoll, N.Y.: Orbis Books, 1993), 2:139–59.

It analyzed sexual behaviors, all concepts of sexual identity, and categories of normative and deviant. These formed sets of signifiers, which created constructed social and cultural meanings. Queer theory is a set of ideas based around the notion that identities are not fixed and do not entirely determine who we are. As a field of inquiry, queer theory shifts the emphasis away from specific acts and identities to the myriad ways in which gender and sexualities organize and even destabilize society.

Queer theory claims that sexual categories shift and change. It differs from earlier gay/lesbian identity politics by arguing that sexual identity and even the gender templates are not fixed but rather elastic. Here are some examples that threaten identity categories:

> A woman marries a man, but years later she realizes her deep attraction to women and then comes out as a lesbian. Several years later she realizes that she is bisexual and comes out again.

> A colleague of mine came out in divinity school as a lesbian. Now she and her lesbian lover of many years are gaytrans males. Butch dykes are now identifying as transmales. There are lesbian leather boys and lesbian daddies who perform a wider range of masculinity than heterosexual males.

> In Tony Kushner's *Angels in America,* Roy Cohn describes himself to his doctor as a heterosexual man who has sex with guys.[5] There are many ethnic men who do not identify as gay or bisexual because they take on the penetrator role in sexual intercourse with other men. They self-identify as heterosexual. Or the group of married men, who identify themselves as heterosexual, get together for sex.

> A queer man who loves men may sleep with a close woman friend to conceive a child or just because they are close. They maintain joint custody and raise the child together. Or the British journal *Gay Times* announced, "Sex between gay men and lesbians is coming out of the closet.... Now people talk openly of their opposite sex-same sexuality lovers."[6] If self-identified lesbians and gays are partnered sexually, how do they then define themselves?

---

5. Tony Kushner, *Angels in America: A Gay Fantasia on American Themes, Part One: Millennium Approaches* (New York: Theatre Communications Group, 1992), 45.

6. Quoted in Marjorie Garber, *Bisexuality and the Eroticism of Everyday Life* (New York: Routledge, 2000), 46.

There are heterosexual women who identify as gay men. They dress in gay fashion and date men. The trendy gay male ghetto culture has become less about sexual liberation than brand-name and cultural style.

Postmodern sexualities demolish the neat social categories of sexuality and gender with multiple subjectivities and fluid desires. Gay, lesbian, bi, trans, and hetero do not have the stretch to comprehend the fluidity of desires and identities. Carol Queen and Lawrence Schimel have produced *Pomosexuals: Challenging the Assumptions,* a volume on postmodern sexualities, inclusive of "multiple subjectivities" and fluid desires. None of the contributors fits into neat gender or sexual categories. The editors comment, "Pomosexuality (postmodern sexuality) lives in the space in which all other nonbinary forms of sexual and gender identity reside — a boundary-free zone in which fences are crossed for the fun of it, or simply because some of us can't be fenced in."[7]
People change their sexual identities over the course of a lifetime. Bodies draw on a wide variety of gender performativity. Some change gender without changing embodiment while others later change their embodiment. Some queer folks disrupt the gendered meaning of their genitals by mapping out a new terrain of gendered performativity by decoupling gender from their genitals, while others couple their performativity to a change of genitals. Transgendered people may often feel themselves in contrast to their physical bodies and genitals.

Many folks refuse to be categorized into a sexual identity while others have accepted their narrative identities. People cross from normative spaces into "queer" ones when they do not line up in expected ways — when a man wears a dress or desires men. Provincetown annually celebrates a weekend of heterosexual transvestite men and their partners. Bisexuality destabilizes the notion of sexual identity as fixed while transgendered identities render gender instable as a category of citation. Thus, sociologist Steven Seidman observes, "Queer theory, the aim is not to abandon identity as a category of knowledge and politics but to render it permanently open and contestable as to its meaning and political role."[8]

---

7. Carol Queen and Lawrence Schimel, eds., *Pomosexuals: Challenging Assumptions about Gender and Sexuality* (San Francisco: Cleis Press, 1997). See also C. Jacob Hale, "Leatherdyke Boys and Their Daddies: How to Have Sex without Women or Men," *Social Text* 15, nos. 3 and 4 (fall–winter 1997): 223–39.

8. Steven Seidman, ed., *Queer Theory/Sociology* (Cambridge: Blackwell, 1996), 12.

Queer studies

Queer studies thus represent a paradigm or discursive shift in the way some scholars view sexual identity. Queer studies attempt not to abandon identity as a site for knowledge and politics but to problematize fixed and hegemonic notions of identity:

> Queer theory is suggesting that the study of homosexuality should not be a study of a minority — the making of the lesbian/gay/bisexual subject — but a study of those knowledges and social practices that organize "society" as a whole by sexualizing — heterosexualizing or homosexualizing — bodies, desires, acts, identities, social relations, knowledges, culture, and social institutions.[9]

Queer theorists argue that identities are always multiple, hybrid, provisional, or composite and that an infinite number of identity markers can combine to form new sites of knowledge. For queer theorist Michael Warner queer is a transgressive paradigm, representing "a more thorough resistance to the regimes of the normal."[10] Likewise, David Halperin states, "Queer, then, demarcates not a positivity but a positionality vis-à-vis the normative — a positionality that is not restricted to lesbians and gay men but is in fact available to anyone who is or who feels marginalized because of her or his sexual practices."[11] Michael Warner, David Halperin, Judith Butler, Eve Kosofsky Sedgwick, and other theorists perceive the queer paradigm as resistance to normativity, including heteronormativity and gay and lesbian normativities.[12]

Queer is often understood as critically nonheterosexual, transgressive of all heteronormativities and, I would add, homonormativities. "Queer" turns upside down, inside out, and defies heteronormative and homonormative theologies.[13] I use "queer" theologically, not only as an identity category but also as a tool of theological deconstruction, for

---

9. Ibid., 13.

10. Michael Warner, introduction to *Fear of a Queer Planet*, xxvi.

11. David M. Halperin, *Saint Foucault: Towards a Gay Hagiography* (New York: Oxford, 1995), 62.

12. See Warner, ed., *Fear of a Queer Planet;* Steven Seidman, ed., *Queer Theory/Sociology;* Judith Butler, *Bodies That Matter* (New York: Routledge, 1993).

13. For a sampling, see the following authors' discussion of queer: J. Michael Clark, *Defying the Darkness: Gay Theology in the Shadows* (Cleveland: Pilgrim Press, 1997), 6; Robert E. Goss, *Jesus ACTED UP* (San Francisco: HarperSanFrancisco, 1993), xix, 55–57; Goss, "Insurrection of the Polymorphously Perverse: Queer Hermeneutics," in *A Rainbow of Religious Studies*, ed. J. Michael Clark and Robert E. Goss (Las Colinas, Tex.: Monument Press, 1996), 16–19; Warner, introduction, xxvi; Halperin, *Saint Foucault*, 60–66.

"queer" as a verb means "to spoil or to interfere." Heteronormative theologies exclude me except in their hermeneutics of abomination while gay/lesbian normative theologies exclude those who do not neatly fit into the categories. When I queer or spoil an already spoiled hetero- or gay-normative theological discourse, I have transgressed the boundaries of normativity that are embedded in particular discourses and practices. In traditional theological language, queering has a prophetic edge in its critiques.

I want to address the hermeneutical role of normative transgression in emerging queer theologies and for the future development of hybrid queer theologies. In other words, I want to queer the template of gay normativity. In *The Mythology of Transgression,* cultural critic Jamake Highwater describes several negative metaphors for transgression: as abomination, deformity, and science. He perceives some positive metaphors of transgression, such as sensibility, culture, and revelation. The commonplace understanding of transgression is a violation of morality. Highwater asserts:

> [T]he word "transgression" is generally understood to mean an action that is morally subversive. A transgression is closely associated with the religious idea of damnation. Therefore, we do not admire those who transgress. We reproach them as sinners. And the more "terrible" the transgression, the more we reproach them. We may ridicule them, disdain them, beat them, imprison them, or we may even kill them. But the worst of all punishments is doubtlessly our attempts to redeem them, to change them from their sinful ways to our blessed ways.[14]

The Latin *transgredior* means "to pass over, to go beyond, or to advance." *Transgredior* is an action that carries a person across fixed boundaries or beyond borders. Transgression destroys traditional boundaries or undermines established paradigms by revealing their fragility and instability. It challenges modes of regulating discourse: Who is canonically allowed to speak? Who is allowed entry? Who is denied access? Who can speak for me?

Michel Foucault understood transgression as resistance to normalizing practices of master narratives. Foucault said in an interview, "To resist is not simply a negation but a creative process."[15] Transgression

---

14. Jamake Highwater, *The Mythology of Transgression: Homosexuality as Metaphor* (New York: Oxford University Press, 1997), 42.
15. Quoted in Halperin, *Saint Foucault,* 60.

is not merely a rebellious act but a Foucaultian liberative action driven by the imagination of alternative possibilities and hopes. Along with Highwater, I comprehend transgression primarily as "an act that brings about transformation."[16] Transgression is essential to the hermeneutical development of queer theologies and queer hybrid theologies.

I am going to focus on the need for transgressing or queering my own normativity as a white, gay male who writes queer theological discourse from a privileged, middle-class location in a midwestern U.S. university. I propose that future queer theologies not only will transgress the binary divisions of hetero/homo, gay/lesbian, and male/female but will develop new hybrid sexual theologies that free the signifiers from the tyranny of normative signifieds. I want to transgress even my own signifiers from the logic of gay normative identity. Mine becomes one queer site among many others for constructing theology and requires dialogue with other sites of identity.

Queering gay boundaries

Michel Foucault's treatment of homosexuality as a strategic positionality instead of a psychological essence initially inspired queer studies. Foucault suggested that gays should resist categorization and undermine all reifications of sexual identity. David Halperin observed, "Foucault's approach also opens up, correspondingly, the possibility of a queer politics defined not by the struggle to liberate a common, repressed, preexisting nature but by an ongoing process of self-constitution and self-transformation — a queer politics anchored in the perilous and shifting sands of non-identity, positionality, discursive reversibility, and collective self-intervention."[17] Foucault's legacy is a constant, postmodern subversion of the paradigm(s) into ever-widening margins of conversation. "Queering" or transgressing the queer is concerned to include everyone and to speak for no one in particular. Let me further problematize gay identity with two concrete examples.

One of my undergraduate students at Webster University had announced to a gay group that he was a "bisexual gay." A veteran gay activist who had grown up in the Stonewall era told him emphatically, "You can't be both. You got to be one or the other." For that veteran activist, my student was uttering sheer nonsense, messing up his conceptual category of gay identity. My student muddied the category of "gay"

16. Highwater, *Mythology of Transgression*, 43.
17. Halperin, *Saint Foucault*, 122.

with its fixed markers and normative boundaries by not conceptualizing in either/or dichotomies but affirming his identity within "both/and" categories of bisexual and gay. His inclusive queerness questioned established gay boundaries; it transgressed fixed identity templates of straight, bisexual, and gay. Is identity so easily confinable to fixed markers that frame the self, body, desire, and actions? Or may it be more fluid, hybrid, or contestable than we ever imagine? Can ambiguity, liminality, and diversity be included in a new queer discursive shift and subsequently in a queer theological discourse?

Another example that subverts my own identity categories concerns a lesbian bouncer at a gay bar. I came to know her as a butch lesbian who dates women. She questioned her identity as a woman and as a lesbian, realizing first that she was male-identified and that she was a male trapped in a female body. But her crossover from female to male may not end where I might first anticipate, for she became a gaytrans male dating gay males. He now lives on the border regions of gender categories and sexual identity, an immigrant transgressing a culture of gendered and sexual citizenships. My attempts to understand her transition within the logic of binary gender were short-circuited like a Zen koan. Understanding emerges from the narrative histories of transsexuals themselves.

Transgendered writers Leslie Feinberg and Kate Bornstein have critically interrogated our gendered categories, suggesting that much of our gender difficulty is comprehending gender as a reified essence, with a limited range of normative expressiveness.[18] They trouble our gendered conceptions with fluid possibilities and new potentialities of transgendered by living in interstitial cultural spaces. They denounce the binary logic of heterosexist and gay/lesbian constructions of gender, abandoning the talk of gender boundaries.

Postmodern sexualities complicate even the identity of heterosexuality. Yale professor Laurie Essig speaks of "heteroflexibility," the newest variation of heterosexual identity. It is a semantic strategy adopted by college students to keep their sexual options open. She describes the heteroflexibility of her students:

This means that the person has or intends to have a primarily heterosexual lifestyle, with a primary sexual and emotional attachment to someone of the opposite sex. But that person remains

---

18. Leslie Feinberg, *Transgendered Warriors* (Boston: Beacon Press, 1994); Kate Bornstein, *Gender Outlaw: On Men, Women, and the Rest of Us* (New York: Vintage Books, 1994).

open to sexual encounters and even relationships with persons of the same sex. It is a rejection of bisexuality since the inevitable question that comes up in bisexuality is one of preference, and the preference of the heteroflexible is quite clear.[19]

Here postmodern heterosexuals can envision indulging in homosexual sex. Essig divides society into the categories of heteroflexibility and heterorigidity and homoflexibility and homorigidity. Such a grid is a reworking of the essentialist and constructionist debates around sexual identity. Essig envisions a postmodern, queer world beyond the mire of the rigid binaries of "hetero" and "homo" with multiple subjectivities and fluid sexual desires.

These examples trouble heterosexuals as well as many gays/lesbians who think in reified binary constructions of gender and sexual orientation. They upset residual essentialist understandings of gender. They also upset those binary thinkers in religious discourse — whether Jewish, Christian, or Islamic — who are already grounded in all-encompassing religious narratives that are used to sustain a regime of compulsory heterosexuality and fixed, hierarchical gender relations. Postmodern thinkers have been welcomed in the academy without much turmoil, but queer postmodern theologians are marginalized because they threaten the very gender and sexual codes upon which those master narratives have been constructed. I want to look at postcolonial theory that advances beyond the aesthetics of postmodern deconstruction for a thorough queer discourse as the basis for future queer sexual theologies.

Some postcolonial theorists introduce a notion of hybridity that undermines the normative categories of modernity and postmodernity of the First World. Homi Bhabha writes about hybridity:

> The stairwell as liminal space, in-between the designations of identity, becomes the process of symbolic interaction, the connective tissue that constructs the difference between upper and lower, black and white. The hither and thither of the stairwell, the temporal movement and passage that it allows, prevents identities at either end of it from settling into primordial polarities. This interstitial passage between fixed identifications opens up the possibility of a cultural hybridity that entertains difference without an assumed or imposed hierarchy.[20]

19. Laurie Essig, "Heteroflexibility," *Salon Magazine*, November 15, 2000.
20. Homi K. Bhabha, *The Location of Culture* (New York: Routledge, 1994), 4.

Bhabha's notion of cultural hybridity and interstitial space allows for liminal spaces in which cultural differences can be articulated. When applied to the categories of gender and sexual orientation, hybridity and interstitial space allow for the movements between fixed categories of sexual orientation and gender as well as admitting the tensions between cultural identity markers. Hybridity becomes conscious practice, allowing for interaction between identity categories and markers. The notion permits the emergence of new identities from cultural disidentifications and the emergence of sexualities that rigid gender- and sexual-orientation stereotypes prohibit.

For theology, queering becomes a productive style of theological practice and discourse that can disorganize our normative categories. Queer desire crosses all identity and gender boundaries; it is ineffable, an ever-shifting transgressiveness that uncovers ever-new hybrid identities. For example, asserting an African American "in-the-life" or Native American "two-spirited" identity does not adequately articulate the differences that have to do with religion, geography, relation to gay, white males, gender, class, age, ability, education, and so on. Frank Browning's latest book, *A Queer Geography*, investigates how geography shapes homoerotic desires and identities, demonstrating what anthropologists and cultural historians have argued for some time how cultures organize structures of sexual identity.[21]

Queer theory has deconstructed the colonial category of "gay" as white, North American, middle-class, late-capitalist, and even middle-aged. Gay identity seems too hardened, too mainstream a category for adequate queer theological reflection, and too inflexible for developing a full queer politics of difference. It is the same critique that I would make of heteronormative theologies and postmodern theologies. Queer has widened my self-definitions by navigating me into uncharted waters where I engage in conversations with people whose identities are shaped by particular markers and personal experiences quite different from my own. These experiences are challenging, engaging, and ever-widening. I find myself theologically committed to engage and learn from different worlds, cultures, histories, and communities. Queering is

---

21. Frank Browning, *A Queer Geography: Journeys towards a Sexual Self* (New York: Crown Publishers, 1996); Rudi C. Blyes, *The Geography of Perversion* (New York: New York University Press, 1995); Stephen O. Murray and Will Roscoe, eds., *Islamic Homosexualities: Culture, History, and Literature* (New York: New York University Press, 1997); Arno Schmitt and Jehoeda Sofer, *Sexuality and Eroticism among Males in Moslem Societies* (New York: Harrington Park Press, 1992); David E. Greenberg, *The Construction of Homosexuality* (Chicago: University of Chicago Press, 1988).

ultimately opening space to new immigrant identities to articulate their own perspectives, quite radical and even challenging to my own.

I am prepared to argue that my own theological positions, like identity categories, are only tentative and that they need to be subverted from a gay/lesbian paradigm into uncharted territories and geographies of diverse sexual and gender hybridities. If I am to take "queer" as a serious paradigm for theological discourse and practice, I need to engage not only bisexual and transgendered voices but also the voices of the intersexed and of men and women of color who share homoerotic desires. In *Jesus ACTED UP*, I wrote from a queer perspective that was limited to gay and lesbian voices. I remember a bisexual student from Eden Seminary who challenged me, "Where is my bisexual voice?" That comment greatly troubled me while I fumbled for an explanation of my postmodern commitments to particularity and apologetically pointed to the voices that have shaped my queer theological practice. At the 1994 Freedom Celebration in San Francisco, I encountered a transsexual, Victoria Kolakowski, who challenged my gendered categories and ever since has mentored me to an awareness of transsexualism and theological discourse.[22] How many others could raise the same question from social locations of the ethnic, the underclass, the illegal immigrant, or other communities?

In a recently coedited volume, *Our Families, Our Values: Snapshots of Queer Kinship,* my commitment to hybridity led me to recruit multicultural, multigendered, and multisexual voices from Christian, Buddhist, Wiccan, and Jewish perspectives.[23] By no means does this volume exhaust the sexual and gendered fluidities of multicultural and multireligious queer identities. It only begins the process of uncovering sexual and gendered hybridities. Mona West and I were committed to include translesbigay perspectives in our anthology, *Take Back the Word.* Our inclusion of diverse perspectives was good, but not good enough. There is always the need to include other forgotten voices.

My evolving queer perspective is committed to deregulate heterosexual as well as gay hegemony by articulating a variety of gender and sexual differences: lesbians, gays, bisexuals, drag queens, transsexuals, transgendered, leather folk, and even queer heterosexuals. Queer sig-

22. Victoria S. Kolakowski, "Toward a Christian Ethical Response to Transsexual Persons," *Theology and Sexuality* 6 (March 1997): 10–31; Kolakowski, "Eunuchs and Barren Women: Queering the Breeder's Bible," in *Our Families, Our Values: Snapshots of Queer Kinship,* ed. Robert E. Goss and Amy Adams Squires Strongheart (New York: Harrington Park Press, 1997), 35–50.

23. See Goss and Strongheart, eds., *Our Families, Our Values.*

nifies not only those attracted to the same gender or both genders but also anyone who defies the dominant structures of normative sexual templates or even the normative templates of the gender system.

Critiques: new transgressions and hybridity

There is much current debate in and around queer studies; much of the debate revolves around the assimilation of tendencies of segments of the gay community into mainstream culture. Sociologist Steven Seidman, however, criticizes queer theory for "denying the differences by either submerging them in an undifferentiated oppositional mass or by blocking the development of individual and social differences through the disciplining compulsory imperative to remain undifferentiated."[24] Seidman and other critics have raised vital questions whether a liberation movement can build political cohesion based on the violations of normative structures. On the other hand, queer raises questions about the nature of our social identities as multicultural, multigendered, and multisexual. Its critics like Seidman and others fear that queer will elide hard-fought differences. Objections to queer theology find similar criticisms from some lesbian and gay theologians in their failure to engage different notions of postmodern sexualities and genders. While admittedly queer does muddy the distinctions among sexual-identity categories and the differences between men and women, it also raises epistemological questions about the stability of these templates of sexual and gendered identity. It subverts our normative assumptions about identity and gender while articulating the varied particularities of emerging hybrid voices. In its transgressions, queer discursive practice may decolonize our identity and gendered templates because multigendered and multicultural sexual identities navigate us into a radical inclusion of voices that trouble heteronormative- and gay-normative theological discourse. Engaging in what appears to be "Balkan-style," carnivalesque dialogues of diversity subverts our attempts at universal but exclusionary theological discourse. They force us to deal with the plurality of social context and personal narrative histories about sexual desire.

Will queer theologies remain queer, or will queer theologies ultimately transgressively reinscribe themselves into some new hybrids? If queer theologies remain open-ended theological discourses that participate in a creative dialogue with the various hybrid subcultures of

---

24. Seidman, "Identity and Politics," 133. See also Seidman, introduction to *Queer Theory/Sociology*, 1–29.

desire and gender, of outsiders and insiders, of diverse social locations, then new sexual and gendered hybrid theologies will emerge. Let me speculate on some new transgressions. Bisexual theologies will certainly undermine gay/lesbian and heterosexual theological discourse. Both gay/lesbian and heterosexual theologies subscribe to the politics of otherness with an either/or paradigm while bisexual theologies represent a subversive alternative to either/or thinking. They stress a both/and method that undermines either straight or gay methods of theological reflection and promote mediating methods to bridge hetero and gay theological discourses. Veteran gay/lesbian theologians have a difficult time disprivileging their own discourse and allowing the multiple voices to disrupt their discourse.

As we immerse ourselves in the narrative histories and theological discourses of Asian American homosexual men, bisexual womanists, or biracial female-to-male transsexuals, we may learn about sexualities in the plural, their instabilities, and the different social/cultural constructions of hybrid sexual identities. We may also learn about the multidimensional and multicultural perspectives of sexual identity. Hopefully, we may expose all traces of privilege within our own theological discourse, any traces of American white supremacism, centrism, sexism, classism, or biphobia. Thus we may become more responsible in making new hybrid voices accessible.

Transgendered theologies, likewise, raise some profound questions and presumptions about gender. Gender-bending and intersexuality threaten a society that maintains gender rigidity. Transgendered and intersexual activists are only recently raising their voices to further widen the sex and gender liberation movement. While transgendered theology is only in its infancy, we can expect it to undermine heteronormative and gay/lesbian normative constructions of maleness and femaleness with new interstitional gender spaces.

The development of bisexual and transgendered theologies will offend some by their inclusivenesss, moving beyond binary thinking of hetero/homo and deconstructing rigid gender boundaries. Bisexual and transgendered theologies will threaten far more those gays who want to assimilate into mainstream society. There are many ways to be queer, and future queer theologians will connect those ways with the networks of power relationships that shape race, gender, sexuality, ethnicity, religion, class, physical conditions, age, and our relationships to the earth. Rather than assimilate, future queer theologies will mainstream and celebrate sexual/gender diversities, shifting theological practice into uncharted intersections of sexual, gendered identities. During the twenty-first century, queer theologies will undergo profound changes as the contextual translesbigay theologies emerge from postcolonial Asia, Latin America, and Africa, critiquing and disorganizing our queer categories.

Queer theologies, I may conclude, will not ever abandon identity and gender as categories of knowledge or liberative practice but will render them open and contestable to various meanings that promote coalitional politics. Queer discursive practice will challenge our theological discourse based on a narrow regime of sexual and gendered truth by undermining our identity templates of heterosexual/homosexual and gender categories of male/female. Can we meet the challenge of being mentored by new queer voices? The challenge is unsettling, but I find it also thoroughly queer. Let me quote queer theorist Michael Warner:

> Queer politics has not just replaced older modes of lesbian and gay identity; it has come to exist alongside those older modes, opening up new possibilities and problems whose relation to more familiar problems is not always clear. Queer theory, in short, has much to do just in keeping up with queer political culture. If it contributes to the self-clarification of the struggles and wishes of the age, it may make the world queerer than ever.[25]

Queer theory aims not to abandon sexual and gender identity as an epistemological category but to render it more flexible, permanently open to revision, and changeable.

Postscript

Postmodern sexualities and new gender constructions become a paradigm for reconstructing Christian practice and traditional theology. They represent a millennial paradigm shift in theological discourse, or what Michel Foucault has described as the "insurrection of subjugated knowledges."[26] Sexual and gender diversity provides a new paradigm for reinvesting the dead doctrines and practices of an erotophobic, gender-rigid Christianity. Queer sexual theologies have begun to concentrate on several questions: how sexuality and spirituality are connected; the fluidity of sexual identity and gender constructions; sexual relationships; rereading the biblical texts and the Christian tradition from a queer perspective; how spirituality and sexuality affect our attitudes and

---

25. Warner, introduction to *Fear of a Queer Planet*, xxviii.
26. Michel Foucault, *Power/Knowledge* (New York: Pantheon Books, 1980), 82.

practices toward God, self, and neighbor; how the church relates to sexuality/gender in mission, worship, sacraments, and rites. The erotic spiritualities of translesbigays have the potential to revitalize Christianity.

A queer theology can proceed only from critical analysis of the social context that forms our experience, our struggles, and our emergent, innovative, and transgressive sexual practices. Such a theology is an organic or community-based project, including our sexual contextuality, a commitment to radical inclusion, and the realization that our theological arguments are always tentative and open to revision from new contextualities and new emerging voices.

I am grateful to be in a church where queer inclusion is a primary value. Within my church there is a transgendered support group that meets. My learning about transgendered issues has been accelerated by my supervision of one of our clergy's doctoral dissertation on transgendered theology. I am convinced that the only way I can remain faithful to my vocation as a queer theologian is to remain open and to listen to the narrative histories of peoples different from myself. Oppressed, excluded, and marginalized peoples must remain as my mentors while I mentor younger queer theologians to transgress my theology.

TWELVE

FROM GAY THEOLOGY
TO QUEER SEXUAL THEOLOGIES

*And in the last days it shall be, God declares, that I will pour out my Spirit
upon all flesh, and your sons and daughters will prophesy, and your young
men [and women] shall see visions, and your old men [and women] shall
dream dreams.* —Acts 2:17

In attempting to envision what future directions queer Christian praxis
and theology may take in the twenty-first century, I have no particular
clairvoyant gifts to offer. But I can make some reasonable speculations
by examining how the translesbigay Christian movement came into existence, its organizational developments, and directions for theological
growth and practice. At the heart of my speculations is the belief or
rather the hope that queer Christianity may partner with progressive
elements of various Christian denominations to form a new church
committed to a sexual reformation of Christianity and committed to
justice-love.

The lesbian/gay Christian movement developed during the radical
1960s and the revolutionary 1970s to solidify theological growth. Theological growth has accompanied the organizational growth and complex development of the queer movement in the twenty-first century.
Groundbreaking for the emergence of gay theology was Derek Bailey's
Homosexuality and the Western Christian Tradition in the mid-1950s.[1] Bailey, a heterosexual scholar, traced the development of homohatred from
the biblical texts through the formation of Christian practice and theology in the early and late Middle Ages. Homosexual theology started in
the late 1950s with Robert Wood's *Christ and the Homosexual,* followed by
the blossoming of homosexual theology in the 1970s with such works as
Tom Horner's *Jonathan Loved David,* John McNeill's *The Church and the
Homosexual,* and Virginia Ramey Mollenkott's and Letha Scanzoni's *Is the*

---

1. Derek Bailey, *Homosexuality and the Western Christian Tradition* (New York: Longmans,
Green, 1955; repr. Hamden, Conn.: Archon Books, 1975).

Homosexual My Neighbor?[2] These were apologetic works that attempted
to reconcile the opposition of the churches to homosexuality and offer
a theological interpretation of homosexuality. They focused on pastoral
care and inclusion of the homosexual into the life of the church; their
method was to muster psychological, biblical, historical, and psychological data for an argument for the inclusion of gays/lesbians. These classic
books strengthened the nascent formation of denominational groups,
but perhaps more importantly, they empowered a future generation of
queer scholars, including myself, who commit themselves to find the
liberating resources within Christianity to fight against intolerance.

John Boswell's *Christianity, Social Tolerance, and Homosexuality* marked
a development from a theology of homosexuality to the historical
reclamation of gay voices within Christian traditions.[3] Boswell's work
met with general academic acclaim but empowered denominational
gay/lesbian groups in their loyal opposition. Boswell's book initiated
serious discussion of the social context of the biblical texts of terror but
generally was ignored by church leaders. In the 1980s, debate shifted
to an apologetic battle for the interpretative control of the biblical
text. Heterosexual biblical scholars such as Robin Scroggs, Victor Furnish, and George Edwards and openly gay biblical scholar L. William
Countryman contextualized the texts of terror and elaborated upon the
general lines of biblical interpretation initiated by Boswell.[4] The debate still fiercely rages over interpretative control of the biblical texts,
but historical-critical approaches together with the works of identifiable
queer biblical scholars are slowly beginning to prevail in many mainline
denominations.[5]

2. Robert Wood, *Christ and the Homosexual* (New York: Vantage Press, 1959); Tom
Horner, *Jonathan Loved David: Homosexuality in Biblical Times* (Philadelphia: Westminster
Press, 1978); John McNeill, *The Church and the Homosexual* (Kansas City, Mo.: Sheed
Andrews and McMeel, 1976); Virginia Ramey Mollenkott and Letha Scanzoni, *Is the
Homosexual My Neighbor?* (San Francisco: Harper & Row, 1978).

3. John Boswell, *Christianity, Homosexuality, and Social Tolerance* (Chicago: University of
Chicago Press, 1980).

4. Robin Scroggs, *The New Testament and Homosexuality* (Philadelphia: Fortress Press,
1983); George Edwards, *Gay/Lesbian Liberation: A Biblical Perspective* (New York: Pilgrim
Press, 1984); L. William Countryman, *Dirt, Greed, and Sex: Sexual Ethics in the New Testament
and Their Implications for Today* (Philadelphia: Fortress Press, 1988).

5. Robert L. Brawley, ed., *Biblical Ethics and Homosexuality* (Louisville: Westminster John
Knox, 1996); Sally B. Geis and Donald Messer, eds., *Caught in the Crossfire* (Nashville:
Abingdon Press, 1994); Jeffrey Siker, ed., *Homosexuality in the Church* (Louisville: Westmin-
ster John Knox, 1994); Marion Soards, *Scripture and Homosexuality* (Louisville: Westminster
John Knox, 1995); Thomas Schmidt, *Straight and Narrow* (Downers Grove, Ill.: InterVarsity
Press, 1995); Daniel Helminiak, *What Does the Bible Really Say about Homosexuality?* (San
Francisco: Alamo Square Press, 2000); Peter Gomes, *The Good Book: Reading the Bible with
Mind and Heart* (New York: William Morrow, 1996); Martti Nissinen, *Homoeroticism in
the Biblical World: A Historical Perspective* (Minneapolis: Fortress Press, 1998); Bernadette

Gay theology in the 1980s centered on two issues: biblical texts that were used to justify homosexuality as sin and psychological issues of sexual orientation to deconstruct moral theologies based on natural law. It found itself in an apologetic mode attempting to make cosmetic changes within the churches to justify the acceptance of gay/lesbians. Gay theology did not address the issues of sexism; it was unable to make theoretical connections between misogyny and homophobia or connect homophobia to other forms of oppression. The writings of Maury Johnston, Chris Glaser, John McNeill, and John Fortunato among others hardly dialogued with the lesbian theologies of Carter Heyward, Mary Hunt, or Virginia Mollenkott.[6] Gay theology focused on the expulsion of "out" gay male and sometimes lesbian clergy, the denial of ordination to gays/lesbians, and the refusal to bless same-sex unions. Theological anthologies — including gay, closeted-gay, and straight contributors — responded with an apologetic for or against church statements on the issue of homosexuality.[7] These writings remained reactive to church statements about homosexuality but provided little challenge to the authority of the churches.

Gay theology inevitably became problematic in its singular focus on gay male issues, excluding lesbian voices. The theological split along gender lines between gay and lesbian started in the late 1970s with the feminist movement, slowed in the early years of the AIDS pandemic, but resurfaced in the late 1980s and early 1990s. While John Boswell's earlier work was important to the gay/lesbian Christian movement in the 1980s, it had a major shortcoming: almost all the material that Boswell covered regarded male homoeroticism, while the history of female homoerotic relations and desires within Christianity was conspicuously absent. More recently, Bernadette Brooten's *Love between Women: Early Christian Responses to Female Homoeroticism* (1996) provides a correction to the absence of female voices in Boswell's work. A second factor that problematized gay theology was its failure to include bisexual, transgendered, and ethnic/racial voices. The push for inclusion of lesbian, bisexual, and transgendered voices impacted gay theology, expanding

Brooten, *Love between Women: Female Homoeroticism in Early Christianity* (Chicago: University of Chicago Press, 1996); Thomas Hanks, *The Subversive Gospel* (Cleveland: Pilgrim Press, 2000).

6. Maury Johnston, *Gays under Grace* (Nashville: Winston-Derek Publishers, 1983); Chris Glaser, *Come Home* (San Francisco: Harper & Row, 1990); John McNeill, *Taking a Chance on God* (Boston: Beacon Press, 1988); John Fortunato, *Embracing the Exile* (San Francisco: Harper & Row, 1982).

7. For example, Jeannine Grammick and Pat Furey, eds., *The Vatican and Homosexuality* (New York: Crossroad, 1988); Robert Nugent, ed., *A Challenge to Love: Gay and Lesbian Catholics in the Church* (New York: Crossroad, 1983).

beyond its white, middle-class male parameters and addressing issues of gender, patriarchy, class, and race.

The final context, problematizing gay theology, was the ravages of the AIDS pandemic and the escalating social hatred of the churches. Both AIDS and cultural homohatred forced gays into coalition and partnerships with other groups. Translesbisexuals had responded to the AIDS pandemic as it affected gays, beginning a broad coalition based upon HIV health issues and voluntarism in creating major AIDS response organizations in every major city. Many infected by HIV and those affected by HIV have found themselves defensive in affirming that sexuality is a gift of God despite the condemnation of churches. The Reagan years were a period when HIV placed homosexuality in a negative national spotlight nearly on a daily basis. The various groups of the religious right were focused on a wide variety of political issues from abortion to anticommunism. With the end of the Cold War, the religious right turned its attention to the gay/lesbian movement, using it as a mechanism for fundraising and galvanizing its membership against a homosexual menace that threatened families, churches, and the nation.

Coalitions expanded gay concerns from a single issue to a broad range of issues. Gays became concerned with women's issues such as reproductive freedom, sexism, and health because lesbians were there for their HIV-positive gay brothers. AIDS activism and queer activism developed from social violence, apathy, discrimination, and the growing backlash from the religious right. The explosion of activism in the late 1980s and early 1990s also transformed gay theology into queer theology and widened its dialogue partners.

The transformation into Christian queer theology continues, currently revolving around four inclusionary issues: (1) changing the churches or creating a postdenominational church, (2) the challenge of post-Christianity, feminism, and other spiritual paths, (3) queer sexual theology, (4) justice perspectives of other cultural contexts and social groups. These challenges, I believe, will determine the success of the new liberating theologies of the translesbigay Christian movement and will be invaluable for the creation of a postdenominational church of justice-love in the twenty-first century.

Changing the churches or creating a postdenominational church

The erotophobia and homophobia of the churches force the question: How much progress have queer Christians made in the churches in the last three decades? Is church any longer a relevant category for translesbigays? The church has been, at best, an inhospitable social community, refusing to bless their unions and ordain open "practicing" homosexuals. At its worst, the church is as hostile a community as the rapists of Sodom in Genesis 19, committing overt violence against queers. What binds translesbigays to their churches is no longer cultural denominational loyalties in the face of ecclesial violence and exclusion. The continual broadsides of denominational homophobia have forced a number of assimilationist and separatist strategies vis-à-vis the churches. The divisions within American churches, for example, have not raged so intensely since the abolitionist movement against slavery. Kathy Rudy opens her book *Sex and the Church* with this powerful assessment: "The issue of homosexuality threatens to divide Christian churches today in much the way that slavery did 150 years ago."[8] The Lutheran (ELCA), United Methodist, Presbyterian, and Episcopal Churches are deeply divided over the issue of homosexual ordination and the blessing of same-sex unions.

One of the earliest strategies was the formation of denominational groups such as Dignity, Integrity, Affirmation, and Lutherans Concerned as points of loyal resistance to ecclesial homophobia. In existence for nearly a quarter of a century, many of these mainline denominational groups have been generally gay-male dominated and resistant to women's issues. Many translesbigay Christians hoped that these denominational groups would not merely resist the violence and exclusion of their own churches over their sexual orientation but would eventually overcome denominational opposition to themselves. Their vision of church transformation was often limited to the inclusion of themselves, not realizing that the failure to include themselves was symptomatic of deeper problems and exclusions.

How much success have they had in moving their denominations to recognize gay/lesbian ordinations and bless same-sex unions? Some have had more impact than others on their churches by creating a movement of open and affirming congregations. The National Gay and Lesbian Task Force (NGLTF) has organized the Religious Roundtable to bring denominational and national religious groups together to fight the political organization and national campaigns of the religious right against translesbigays. The queer activists within the NGLTF learned through several setbacks in ballot initiatives to realize that they needed to tap the resources of queer faith activists to fight the religious right.

Dignity, once the largest U.S. denominational group, experienced a

---

8. Kathy Rudy, *Sex and the Church* (Boston: Beacon Press, 1997), xi.

period of decline when the Catholic bishops undermined the group, forbidding Catholic priests to celebrate Mass for the group, denying meeting space on Catholic property, and setting up diocesan outreach groups as alternative parishes for homosexuals with a "Don't Ask, Don't Tell" policy. Catholic hierarchical persecution led to the silencing of Sister Jeanine Grammick and Robert Nugent from New Ways Ministry in their pastoral outreach to Catholic homosexuals.

More promising developments occurred in the emergence of More Light, the Reconciling Congregation Program, and Open and Affirming churches. These groups have made efforts to draw translesbigays back into their churches. Some translesbigay Christians have not given up hope of effecting change. Many are happy that individual churches are finally facing their own homophobia, dealing with their own violence before inviting queers into the community. Welcoming back translesbigay Christians, however, means partial inclusion, closeting erotic lives, not blessing queer unions, and not ordaining queers. These welcoming churches are not yet prepared for the full and indiscriminate inclusion envisioned and brokered by Jesus in his table fellowship. They have begun to deal with the issue of homosexuals, but very few have faced bisexuals and the transgendered within their congregations.

When should translesbigays say "enough is enough" and leave their churches? How much pain is necessary before it is time to shake the dust from their feet and move into exile and find a space that is more welcoming and fruitful for their spiritual development? For many translesbigay Christians, their churches have betrayed God's gift of sexuality and continue an erotophobic agenda. Many queer Christians see moving out of their denominational churches as the only way to escape religious abuse and to experience God's liberating grace. To leave and embrace exile takes a commitment of faith. Dan Spencer uses the image of the diaspora church in his discussion of the ecclesia of lesbians and gays.[9] I have used the liberation model of a "base community" from Latin American liberation theology or the queer *ecclesia* to image our creating church and struggling with ecclesial homophobia.[10] Both diaspora and base community are contained in the image of exile space, the fundamental matrix for the development of queer-inclusive, postdenominational church.

In the last two decades, there has been a proliferation of independent churches, imitating their denominational churches: independent

9. Dan Spencer, "Church at the Margins," in *Sexuality and the Sacred,* ed. James B. Nelson and Sandra P. Longfellow (Louisville: Westminster John Knox, 1994), 397–402.

10. Robert E. Goss, *Jesus ACTED UP: A Gay and Lesbian Manifesto* (San Francisco: HarperSanFrancisco, 1993), 123–25.

orthodox and ecumenical catholic churches; evangelical, nondenomi-national, and even fundamentalist churches. These churches frequently duplicate their churches of origin with the one exception of the inclusions of translesbigays.

The queer Christian movement has also witnessed the emergence of postdenominational religious organizations, networks, and churches. In the United States and Europe, Other Sheep, a nonprofit, ecumeni-cal organization, has developed a ministry to sexual minorities in Latin America. It has fostered and developed translesbigay Christian networks in Latin and South America and elsewhere, even fostering connections with queer Christians in Cuba, Africa, and India. In Europe, Protestant and Catholic translesbigay Christians have come together in Jonathan and David communities while in the UK the Lesbian Gay Christian Movement formed to support individual queer Christians across denom-inational lines and to help the churches reexamine their theological positions on sexuality and inclusion. Such global groups have crossed ecumenical, national, and cultural lines to build faith coalitions and jus-tice networks. They have become visible in pre-sessions to International Lesbian Gay Association (ILGA) conferences. Such networks are in their infancy as they organize internationally.

In 1968, Troy Perry founded the Universal Fellowship of Metropolitan Community Churches (UFMCC) as an alternative to the churches.[11] In its early history, the UFMCC understood its existence as temporary until the attitude of the churches changed on homosexuality. The UFMCC grew to become the largest queer church, with over three hundred churches in seventeen countries. The Dallas Cathedral of Hope is a mega–queer church with over thirty-five hundred members, providing extraordinary ministry to the poor of Dallas in such projects as a read-ing literacy program, restoring the houses of the poor, and providing major funding for AIDS outreach within the community. The UFMCC is a postdenominational church, representing and blending the diverse traditions of a number of Christian denominations. Mainline denomina-tional groups place doctrinal adherence at the center of their churches but differ within their denominations in the area of sexual orientation. The UFMCC is postdenominational in that it starts with the principle not of doctrinal adherence but of doctrinal diversity, allowing for a wide range of ecumenical interpretations of doctrine and a blending of a variety of liturgical practices. One challenge to such a queer post-denominational church has been the inclusion of heterosexuals, but its

11. Troy Perry, *Don't Be Afraid Anymore* (New York: St. Martin's Press, 1990).

structural reorganization at its 2001 general conference made it possible to affiliate with other churches in the twenty-first century. I have publicly speculated that the UFMCC will affiliate with the United Church of Christ within the next twenty-five years. It has pursued an aggressive ecumenical-relations program with the National Council of Churches and other faith communities.

Two significant trends during the 1990s were barometers for social change. First, there was the rise of gay/lesbian seminarian groups at many of the major divinity schools and denominational seminaries in the United States. When I was finishing my work in 1990 at Harvard Divinity School, there was a lesbigay caucus. Several years later transgendered students were included in the caucus. By 1990, the American Academy of Religion, the largest professional group of scholars in religion, saw the emergence of gay and lesbian groups. Out scholars began to deliver papers and collaborated in their work. These groups have fostered the professional development and academic recognition of queer studies in religion, resulting in major published books in religion and theology. Professional collaborations have resulted in increased visibility within the academy, new books, and scholars organizing on social and political issues.

These two trends prepared the way for the foundation of the Center for Lesbian Gay Studies in Religion and Ministry at the Pacific School of Religion. The center describes itself as follows: "The Center is dedicated to the encouragement of new, creative scholarship on the interrelations of religion and sexuality/sexual orientation; to the production and dissemination of innovative resources for the academy, faith communities, and the general public; to the development of enlightened leadership around issues of religion and sexuality through education; and to presenting a new public voice in the debate over sexual identity through media outreach and coalition building."[12] I expect the foundation of several other centers at the divinity schools of major research universities and the development of several endowed chairs in queer studies in religion and theology in the near future.

Dismantling barriers of ecclesial homophobia will only take place with pressure from within the churches over the continual scandal of exclusion and violence and with the challenge of inclusive love by translesbigay Christians within mainline denominations and post-denominational churches. Marilyn Alexander and James Preston argue for a combination of insider and outsider "ACT UP" strategies, building

---

12. See the center's website: *www.clgs.org/*.

networks inside and outside denominations as pressure points to change the homophobic exclusion and violence of the churches.[13] The building of interdenominational networks will only increase in the future, crossing international and cultural boundaries. These ecumenical networks will give rise to new postdenominational churches where inclusion of all peoples at the table will be a common mission.

Soulforce, founded by Mel White, is an ecumenical movement of clergy and laity dedicated to the nonviolent principles of Mahatma Gandhi and Martin Luther King Jr. and committed to combat oppression and religious abuse against translesbigays.[14] Over the last several years, Soulforce has staged nonviolent protests, symbolic rituals and vigils, and nonviolent arrest actions against the Roman Catholic bishops at the National Conference of Catholic Bishops, the Southern Baptist Convention, and the Episcopalian, Presbyterian, and United Methodists Church conferences. Joining the transgender affinity group, I participated in Soulforce's 2000 demonstration and arrest action at the Catholic bishops' meeting in Washington, D.C. Soulforce has launched a campaign to withhold tithes from homophobic churches. Whether the overt nonviolent tactics of arrest actions and media challenges will have the capability to organize translesbigay peoples of faith across denominational lines for the creation of a postdenominational network committed to justice and change the hearts of the homophobic churches is yet to be seen.

The challenge of post-Christianity, feminism, and other spiritual paths

As the spirituality of many translesbigays has increasingly become postmodern, it also has become post-Christian. Some post-Christians perceive queer denominational groups and postdenominational churches as rearranging deck chairs on the *Titanic*.[15] Many queers find Christianity irrelevant at best and too often violent and oppressive. Can we create a Christianity that escapes its heritage of violence and erotophobia while addressing the authentic spiritual needs of translesbigays? There is much value in the queer Christian movement and its theologians wrestling with post-Christian theologies, feminist theologies, and other

---

13. Marilyn Bennett Alexander and James Preston, *We Were Baptized Too: Claiming God's Grace for Lesbians and Gays* (Louisville: Westminster John Knox, 1996), 98–100.

14. See *www.soulforce.org*.

15. See Joseph Colombo's review of *Jesus ACTED UP*, in *The Journal of Men's Studies* 4, no. 3 (1996): 318–20.

non-Christian spiritualities and groups that have arisen within the trans-lesbigay community. Meanwhile Soulforce has exercised a prophetic, nonviolent challenge to the violent and homophobic denominations.

A number of queer theologians have moved away from dead doctrines and violent practices of the Christian churches into a post-Christian theology. New post-Christian theologies have no place for christo-logical claims. Post-Christian theologies reflect some currents in the queer community, but there is no defined constituency in particular churches. Thus there is little connection between theological and com-munal practice. This does not mean post-Christian, queer theologies are irrelevant to Christian queer liberation theologies. I would argue that post-Christian theologians maintain a connection to the queer community, whose spiritual practices are countercultural rituals of cir-cuit parties, communal rituals of erotic bonding, and explorations of alternative spiritual practices.

Ron Long's gay indigenous theology, for example, attempts to make a link between gay sex and religious experience.[16] Long disengages gay sex from the question of legitimate, intimate relations and focuses on the religious dimensions of gay sex. He maintains that sex itself constitutes for gay men a religious experience. His phenomenology of gay sexual experience, while questioning Christian constructions and restrictions, provides a dialogue partner for queer Christians. J. Michael Clark, on the other hand, builds on feminist theologies and pushes gay theology into environmental issues.[17] Clark reminds us that the Christian com-plicity in abdicating earthly responsibilities has led to a rampant view of disposability. Christian queer theologians need to give serious con-sideration to the works of Clark, Long, and many others and need to engage those works in dialogue in order to develop their own theolo-gies. Queer Christian theologians need to be immersed within queer culture and totally in touch with its currents.

A second challenge to gay theology is listening to feminist, lesbian-feminist, and womanist concerns. Misogyny is rampant in conservative gay denominational groups and churches, and it is as destructive and insidious as heterosexual misogyny or lesbian separatism. It has often rendered the invisibility of lesbians, submerged lesbian voices beneath gay concerns, and generally been negative to the concerns of trans-

---

16. Ron Long, "Toward a Phenomenology of Gay Sex: Groundwork for a Contemporary Sexual Ethic," in *Embodying Diversity: Identity, (Bio)Diversity, and Sexuality*, Gay Men's Issues in Religious Studies, vol. 6 (Las Colinas, Tex.: Monument Press, 1995).

17. J. Michael Clark, *Beyond Our Ghettoes: Gay Theology in Ecological Perspective* (Cleveland: Pilgrim Press, 1993).

gendered folks. Gay theology and spirituality have recently undergone revision on their way to becoming queer by (1) becoming more aware of women's issues, (2) realizing the interconnections between misogyny, homophobia, race, and class, (3) and dialoguing with bisexual and transgendered people. For instance, Gary Comstock, Richard Cleaver, and Dan Spencer have articulated a gay theology that is feminist-identified, builds upon feminist theologies, is liberation-oriented, and is unapologetic.[18] Both Spencer's and Cleaver's theologies are widening a gay male perspective to engage feminist, lesbian-feminist, and womanist theologies but are certainly not identifiably queer in their tonalities and their political strategies. While feminist-identified in his theological writings, Gary Comstock is implicitly queer in crossing the gender lines by advancing the feisty Queen Vashti in the Book of Esther, who resists patriarchy, as a model for gay men.[19] Gay theology has been transformed into queer theology as it dialogues with feminist theology and aligns itself with feminist analysis into heterosexism and its sex/gender codes.

Finally, the Christian translesbigay theologies need to also engage and dialogue with other spiritualities. Mark Thompson's *Gay Soul* made a significant contribution to the discussion of gay spiritualities in the 1990s.[20] Thompson sought sixteen diverse elders who have pioneered the development of gay spiritualities on such topics as transvestism, s/m, the gay wounded soul, androgynes, embodied and erotic spirituality, AIDS, homophobia, astrology, and gay archetypes. These indigenous gay spiritualities and practices form the matrix for the new queer theologies; they also represent a large segment of the translesbigay population.

Post-Christian theologies, feminist theologies, and non-Christian spiritualities will not be easily dismissed. Nor should they be dismissed as irrelevant. Rather, they will become foundational for reformulating and reenvisioning imaginative Christian queer theologies. They reflect the diversity of translesbigays' quest for spiritual meaning and the integration of their sexualities within diverse non-Christian religious

---

18. Gary Comstock, *Gay Theology without Apology* (Cleveland: Pilgrim Press, 1993); Richard Cleaver, *Know My Name: A Gay Liberation Theology* (Louisville: Westminster John Knox, 1995); Daniel Spencer, *Gay and Gaia: Ecology, Ethics, and the Erotic* (Cleveland: Pilgrim Press, 1997).

19. Comstock, *Gay Theology without Apology*, 51–60. See Ken Stone's analysis in "Biblical Interpretation as a Technology of the Self: Gay Men and the Ethics of Reading," in *The Bible and Ethics of Reading*, ed. Danna Nolan Fewell and Gary Phillips, *Semeia* 77 (1997): 139–53.

20. Mark Thompson, *Gay Soul: Finding the Heart of Gay Spirit and Nature* (San Francisco: HarperSanFrancisco, 1995); Robert Barzan, *Sex and Spirit: Exploring Gay Men's Spirituality* (San Francisco: White Crane, 1995); Randy P. Conner, *Blossom of Bone* (San Francisco: HarperSanFrancisco, 1993).

communities; by engaging in dialogue and sharing practices, queer Christians will develop new, vibrant spiritualities that are connected to sexuality and to the practice of justice-love.

Challenges for queer sexual theologies

The queer revision of gay theology is grounded in strength, no longer in self-hatred, nor in accommodation or apology. Queer theology initially responded to the peril of political violence, the onslaught of the AIDS pandemic, and the emergent anger and activism. Violence made the queer movement "queer." Conservative gays, with postgay dreams and hopes of "fitting in," argue that we are just like straight people. Although such arguments for fitting into straight society ring hollow as social violence escalates, there continue to be strong gay currents for assimilating into heterosexual society.[21] Emerging with AIDS and queer activism, queer liberation theologies have refused to be co-opted into noncritical assimilationism and have taken critical and even transgressive stances to the dominant culture. ACT UP, Queer Nation, Outrage, and other AIDS and queer activist groups have reclaimed the epithet "queer" from cultural homophobic practice to brand our sexual desires and transform them into a postmodern label of political dissidence. It has evolved as a coalitional term for translesbigay people and is inclusive of heterosexual activists who identify with queer sexual dissidence. "Queer" designates transgression, political dissidence, differences, and coalitional diversity. According to *Webster's Third New International Dictionary of the English Language*, "queer" as a verb means "to spoil the effect of, to interfere with, to disrupt, harm, or put in bad light." Queering an already spoiled and exclusive Christianity is to make it more inclusive for translesbigays. Queering is a deconstructive critique of homophobic and heterosexist political theology that already excludes us. It inverts cultural symbols and perverts and disrupts valued theologies and church practices that are already spoiled for us. Queering imaginatively reconstructs theology, spirituality, and church practices in new, inclusive configurations.[22] Queer performances are "prophetic," challenging ecclesial exclusions and hierarchical and gendered power relations. Queer

---

21. Bruce Bower, *A Place at the Table* (New York: Poseidon Press, 1993); Andrew Sullivan, *Virtually Normal* (New York: Alfred A. Knopf, 1995).

22. Jonathan Dollimore uses the notion of "transgressive reinscription" to describe the process of reclaiming "queer." See Jonathan Dollimore, *Sexual Dissidence* (Oxford: Clarendon Press, 1991), 323–24. See also Robert E. Goss, "Erotic Contemplatives and Queer Freedom Fighters," *Journal of Men's Studies* (February 1996): 243–61.

activists are attracted to public performances and demonstrations that have a flare for the dramatic and that confront oppression.

Some of the major publishing houses of religious books broke rank from the conservative houses to tap the gay/lesbian market niche. This resulted in the birth and the mainstreaming of queer theology as a disciplinary field of study in the 1990s. In 1992, Robert Williams's *Just as I Am* pioneered the development of queer theology.[23] Williams, speaking as a gay cleric ostracized from the Episcopal diocese of Bishop John Spong, attempted to forge a queer sexual theology, addressing many of the above challenges to gay theologies. The next year witnessed the publication of Gary Comstock's *Gay Theology without Apology*, J. Michael Clark's *Beyond Our Ghettoes*, and my own *Jesus ACTED UP*. Clark speaks as an HIV-positive theologian, wrestling with ecofeminism to create a liberation theology and an ethic of right living. Comstock's book appealed to mainline Protestant denominations, building on feminist writings and gay readings of biblical texts. *Jesus ACTED UP* drew its audience from marginalized queer Christians within denominations, the UFMCC, and justice-oriented Christians.

Robert Williams, Nancy Wilson, Kathy Rudy, Elias Farajaje-Jones, and I, among others, openly identified our theologies as queer.[24] We developed our theologies in dialogue with the queer street activists and academics in the early 1990s. Queer politics, represented by the multiracial and multiethnic coalitions of translesbigays, became the social context for early Christian queer theologies. Queer theologies represent a new liberation discourse of sexual dissidence and empowerment, deconstructing and reconstructing Christianity from a genuine perspective of marginality, gender differences, multiplicities, and prosex dissidence.

Each author speaks from a particular intersection of political struggle and oppression. Nancy Wilson, a charismatic elder and lesbian pastor of the UFMCC, expands her gay/lesbian theology to include a bisexual dimension. Elias Farajaje-Jones, one of my heroes, is a bisexual queer with a multiracial and multiethnic background who has an uncanny ability to blend profound multi-issue social analysis with liberation discourse and spirituality. None of the above queer authors speaks for all translesbigay voices, but all are aware of wider concerns of other sexual minorities. Farajaje-Jones is one of the first open bisexual theologians to

23. Robert Williams, *Just as I Am* (New York: Crown Publishers, 1992).

24. Williams, *Just as I Am;* Wilson, *Our Tribe;* Rudy, *Sex and the Church;* Elias Farajaje-Jones, "Breaking Silence: Towards an In-the-Life Theology," in *Black Theology,* ed. James H. Cone and Gayraud S. Wilmore (Maryknoll, N.Y.: Orbis Books, 1993), 2:139–59; Goss, *Jesus ACTED UP.*

date who has committed his theology to writing, public lectures, and activist demonstrations. Bisexuality undermines the either/or categories of heterosexual and gay/lesbian, for it represents definitionally a both/and connection to heterosexuality and homosexuality.

Male-to-female Victoria Kolakowski and female-to-male Justin Tanis have pioneered transsexual theological reflection and raise the question of transgendered oppression and inclusion.[25] Transgendered theology promises to destabilize our fundamentalist notions of gender, proposing a wide range of fluid masculinities and femininities. Recently, Virginia Mollenkott has come out as masculine female. Her book *Omnigender* prepares the way for new, exciting theologies of transgendered and intersexed voices, and it has been followed by another transgendered theology, *Crossing Over*, by cross-dresser Vanessa Sheridan.[26] Transgendered activism may have propelled transgendered theology further along than bisexual theology. If you asked me several years ago, I would have thought the reverse. Maybe those trends are due to insufficient biactivism within communities of faith or to bisexuals not experiencing the degree of exclusion and hostility that transgendered folks do.

As bisexual and transgendered voices break silence, queer theologies will evolve to a new sophistication of theological discourse with new sexual particularities, new understandings of genders, and shades of differences. They will flesh out residual biphobia and transphobia, forcing earlier queer theologians, including myself, to engage expanded definitions of sexualities and genders. They will assist us to see sexual and gender oppression from novel perspectives as well as assist in recognizing how the sex/gender binary system is so ingrained in the economics and politics of compulsory heterosexuality.

Queer theologies proceed from critical analysis of the social context that forms our sexual and gender experiences and the web of interlocking oppressions and from our innovative and transgressive practices.

---

25. Victoria S. Kolakowski, "The Concubine and the Eunuch: Queering the Breeder's Bible," in *Our Families, Our Values: Snapshots of Queer Kinship*, ed. Robert E. Goss and Amy Adams Squires Strongheart (New York: Harrington Park Press, 1997), 35–50; Kolakowski, "Throwing a Party: Patriarchy, Gender, and the Death of Jezebel," in *Take Back the Word: A Queer Reading of the Bible*, ed. Robert E. Goss and Mona West (Cleveland: Pilgrim Press, 2000), 103–14; Kolakowski, "Toward a Christian Ethical Response to Transsexual Persons," *Theology and Sexuality* 6 (March 1997): 10–31; Justin Tanis, "Eating the Crumbs That Fall from the Table," in *Take Back the Word*, 43–54.

26. Virginia Ramey Mollenkott, *Omnigender: A Trans-religious Approach* (Cleveland: Pilgrim Press, 2001); Vanessa Sheridan, *Crossing Over: Liberating the Transgendered Christian* (Cleveland: Pilgrim Press, 2001). For an intersexed theology, see Sally Gross, "Intersexuality and Scripture," *Theology and Sexuality* 11 (September 1999): 65–74.

Queer theology is an organic or community-based project that includes our diverse sexual contextualities, our particular social experiences of homo/bi/transphobic oppression and their connections to other forms of oppression, and our self-affirmations of sexual/gendered differences, and it will impact the future developments of liberation theologies.

Queer theologies have an inclusive potential that ghettoized gay theology lacked in the 1980s and the early 1990s. It offends some Christians holding to earlier gay theology because it moves beyond binary divisions of straight/gay and blurs such constructions. Queer theologies comprehend gender, race, homophobia, class, ethnicity, and disability as shaping our sexuality in addition to our sexual desires. All these factors contribute to our constructions and experiences of human sexuality, and no single location is capable of speaking for all other social locations. Queer theologies have the potential to unite people over a range of barriers involving gender, sexual orientation, race, class, physical abilities, and ethnicity. One danger of queer theology is gay theological hegemony and the false exclusion of the voices of translesbisexuals with various shades of contextualities.[27] A new generation is already beginning to speak, write, and develop queer theologies from womanist, Hispanic, and Asian perspectives.[28] These shades, variants, and tonalities in queer theologies will develop in imaginative configurations that will stretch earlier queer theologies and draw them into new sexual contextualities. The new generation of queer theologians, I believe, will mentor the pioneers of queer theology, teaching and instructing us on what was not of immediate concern, visible, or understandable.

The implications of queer theory in the reformulation of a Christian theology of sexuality are profound and exciting. Queer theologies no longer follow the dead-end routes of various Christian theologies of sexuality, but they reconstruct their theologies within a postmodern sexual paradigm, with its sexual and gender diversity. Queer liberation

---

27. Mary Hunt, "Catching Up to Queer Theology," *Frontiers* 10 (September 1993): 59–60; Robert E. Goss, "The Insurrection of the Polymorphous Perverse: Queer Hermeneutics," in *A Rainbow of Religious Studies,* ed. J. Michael Clark and Robert E. Goss (Las Colinas, Tex.: Monument Press, 1996), 9–31.

28. Renee L. Hill, "Who Are We for Each Other? Sexism, Sexuality, and Womanist Theology," in *Black Theology,* 2:345–54; Juan Oliver, "Why Gay Marriage?" *Journal of Men's Studies* 4, no. 3 (1996): 209–24; Irene Monroe, "The Ache Sisters: Discovering the Power of Erotic in Ritual," in *Women at Worship: Interpretations of North American Diversity,* ed. Marjorie Procter-Smith and Janet R. Walton (Louisville: Westminster John Knox, 1993); Monroe, "When and Where I Enter, Then the Whole Race Enters Me: Que(e)rying Exodus," in *Take Back the Word,* 82–91; Patrick S. Cheng, "Multiplicity and Judges 19: Constructing a Queer Asian Pacific American Biblical Hermeneutic," *Semeia* 90/91 (2002): 119–33; Cheng, "God Loves Sex Too (Getting Down with the Spirit)," *DRAGÜN* (2000).

theologies leave behind the bankrupt Christian theologies of sexuality, committed to rigid gender codes and narrow sexual normativities, and they will challenge the churches to recognize their betrayal of God's gift of human sexuality in all its diversity. They have betrayed God's gift of sexuality and gender by not recognizing the original blessing of our sexuality, by refusing to bless our relationships, by refusing to recognize our families, and by denying us ordination. Most churches have an impoverished theology of sexuality that has lent itself to gender and sexual oppression.

Sexualities and new gender constructions become a paradigm for reconstructing Christian practice and traditional theology. They represent a millennial paradigm shift in theological discourse by including sexual and gender diversity and reinvesting the dead doctrines and practices of an erotophobic, gender-rigid Christianity. Queer sexual theologies have begun to concentrate on several questions: how sexuality and spirituality are connected; the fluidity of sexual identity and gender constructions; sexual relationships; rereading the biblical texts and the Christian tradition from a queer perspective; how spirituality and sexuality affect our attitudes and practices toward God, self, and neighbor; and how the church relates to sexuality/gender in mission, worship, sacraments, and rites.

Nancy Wilson, Elizabeth Stuart, Carter Heyward, Michael Kelly, Mary Hunt, and I have made initial contributions to a sexual theology, connecting eros to justice.[29]

The challenge for queer theologies is whether they can integrate sexuality and spirituality. Can our sexual theologies raise questions of justice? Dan Spencer has developed the feminist reclamation of the erotic into a gay ecological framework of justice.[30] Can such a liberation theology transform queers into erotic contemplatives and freedom fighters? Can they continue to expand our vision of justice beyond the blinders of our current commitments?

Sex, relationships, and families are reconstructed into new categories of queer experience. Queers will reclaim family values through new

29. Wilson, *Our Tribe;* Elizabeth Stuart, *Just Good Friends: Towards a Lesbian and Gay Theology of Relationships* (New York: Mowbray, 1995); Carter Heyward, *Touching Our Strength: The Erotic as Power and the Love of God* (San Francisco: Harper & Row, 1989); Michael Kelly, "Christmas, Sex, Longing, and God: Towards a Spirituality of Desire," in *Our Families, Our Values,* 61–76; Hunt, "Catching Up to Queer Theology," 59–60; Goss, "The Insurrection of the Polymorphous Perverse," 9–31; Goss and Strongheart, eds., *Our Families, Our Values.*

30. Daniel Spencer, *Gay and Gaia: Ethics, Ecology, and the Erotic* (Cleveland: Pilgrim Press, 1996).

patterns of community and new families of choice.[31] Elizabeth Stuart embeds our sexual relationships within a retrieved Christian tradition of friendship while I queer the procreative privilege of heterosexist theology, arguing for a reconstructed procreativity inclusive of the reality of our relationships and our families.[32] Nancy Wilson develops a Sabbath sexual theology, paraphrasing the Sabbath saying of Jesus: "Humans were not made for sexuality, but sexuality was made for humans." Wilson's sexual theology weaves pleasure and bodily hospitality into a promising framework for further ethical refinement.[33]

Sex can open us to a spiritual dimension of meditative practice. Michael Kelly reclaims the Christian heritage of scriptures and medieval spiritual writings, predominantly homoerotic and bisexual in their meditative envisioning, as resources to reembody our sexuality and spirituality, and he does it very well in a series of video talks entitled *The Erotic Contemplative*.[34] In "Revisioning Sexuality" (vol. 2), Kelly proposes that deep spiritual experience draws us to sexuality and that deep sexual experience draws us into spirituality. Kelly's proposal is not really revolutionary, for Christian mystics have always been drawn to use erotic metaphors found in the Song of Songs to describe their union with Christ. It is God who draws us from spirituality to sexuality and from sexuality to spirituality, for God is the source of the longing for physical and spiritual union. For most of its history, Christianity barely tolerated sexuality or tolerated it only within heterosexual marriage. Queer Christians, when awakened to God in our sexual love-making, embark upon a transformative journey that includes a journey into the desert where we taste exile, rejection, and stigmatization. In the video "Liberation" (vol. 5), Michael Kelly notes that there is a turning point on our spiritual journey toward liberation where we are asked to make love to God. For Kelly, it is in making love with the crucified Christ that we learn to be sexually receptive to God as divine lover, become bottoms to God who has modeled being a bottom in Christ, and learn solidarity with all suffering peoples. Thus, we who have been forbidden love by our

---

31. Mark Kowalewski and Elizabeth Say, *Gays, Lesbians, and Family Values* (Cleveland: Pilgrim Press, 1998). For more radical reconstructions, see Kathy Rudy, "Where Two or More Are Gathered: Using Gay Communities as a Model for Christian Ethics," in *Our Families, Our Values,* 197–218; Mary Hunt, "Variety Is the Spice of Life: Doing It Our Ways," in ibid., 97–108.

32. Stuart, *Just Good Friends.*

33. Wilson, *Our Tribe,* 231–80.

34. Michael Kelly, *The Erotic Contemplative,* 6 vols. (video series) (Oakland, Calif.: EroSpirit Institute, 1994).

churches are asked by God to become the lover. From this love-making with the crucified Christ we embark on building God's reign.

Heterosexist hegemony in the biblical academy has prevented imaginative interrogation of the biblical traditions. Much of gay scholarship has expended too much energy in deconstructing the biblical texts of terror that have been used to justify violence against us. New queer hermeneutics may reclaim those texts as part of our erotic history, shifting its hermeneutical gaze from reacting to homophobic biblical interpretations to reading the biblical texts from translesbigay perspectives. In chapters 9 and 10 in this volume, I traced the overthrow of heterotextuality by queer scholars who first battled over the texts to deflect textual violence and then have befriended the biblical text to provide imaginative queer readings. This is a cornerstone for the coming Sexual Reformation of Christianity.

Justice perspectives

The seeds of queer theologies planted at the end of the twentieth century will blossom in this century. The theological task of queer theologies will continue to be determining the implications of God's revelation through a community primarily consisting of queer Christians and determining what this means for life and ministry to the mainline churches and the world. Queer theologies espouse an ecumenical vision of community, doctrine, human sexuality, prophetic ministry, and human liberation. Queer theologies aim for the sexual reformation of the mainline, evangelical, and fundamentalist churches.

The greatest challenge to queer theologies will be to develop comprehensive social analyses to delineate interlocking networks of oppression. One of the most successful efforts in this regard is Marvin Ellison's *Erotic Justice,* developing a gay/lesbian social analysis linking homophobia, sexism, racism, and ablism.[35] I use his book to train future MCC clergy in a class on sexual theology meant to assist them in making the connections between their love-making in the bedroom and justice in the world. Future queer, multi-issue social analyses will further develop the connections between sexual theologies and social ethics. Future queer theologians will help our communities to end the privileging of our oppression, involve them in wider issues of global justice, and build international justice networks across interreligious lines.

---

35. Marvin Ellison, *Erotic Justice: A Liberating Ethic of Sexuality* (Louisville: Westminster John Knox, 1995).

During the twenty-first century, queer theologies will undergo profound changes as the contextual translesbigay theologies emerge from eastern Europe, Asia, South America, and Africa. The development of bisexual and transgendered theologies will offend some by their inclusivenesss, moving beyond binary thinking of hetero/homo and deconstructing rigid gender boundaries. Bisexual and transgendered theologies will threaten those who want to assimilate into society and present the queer community in sanitized categories, not the messy bisexual and transgendered templates that upset gay/lesbian orthodoxy. Marcella Althaus-Reid's *Indecent Theology* pioneers a Latina, queer bisexual theology, making uncanny connections between gender, sexual orientation, class, and economic and political analyses.[36] There are many ways to be queer, and future queer theologians will connect those ways with the networks of power relationships that shape race, gender, sexuality, ethnicity, class, physical conditions, age, and our relationship to the earth. Rather than assimilate, future queer theologies will mainstream and celebrate diversities, promoting issues of global justice and sexual/gender freedom. Will they remain queer, or will queer theologies ultimately transgress themselves and reinscribe themselves into something entirely new?

Already the postdenominational UFMCC requires a course in sexuality theology for all future and transfer clergy. Such a course promotes the diverse voices of translesbigays and their views on sexuality and gender, and it addresses how to do theology from our diverse sexualities and genders, how to integrate sexuality and spirituality, and how to connect sexuality to justice. New generations of erotic contemplatives, theologians, and freedom fighters will have the tools to widen their theological discourse and practice as they encounter the emergent theologies of translesbigay Christians in other cultural contexts. Such courses need to be introduced into all the mainline seminaries, equipping the next generations of clergy for ministry, ecumenical collaborations, ending global violence, and fighting for the survival of the biosphere.

These sexual theologies will prepare queer Christians for the twenty-first century and their mission to become theological troublemakers or prophets who will shake the theological roots of other Christian communities and challenge them to undertake a more inclusive theology of sexuality and justice-based sexual theology. This will be a Sexual

---

36. Marcella Althaus-Reid, *Indecent Theology: Theological Perversions in Sex, Gender, and Politics* (New York: Routledge, 2000).

Reformation, changing the paradigm for theological reflection as the Protestant Reformation did during the sixteenth century.

Queer sexual theologies will remain troublesome and even provocative for churches with their impoverished theologies of sexuality. Can our churches become "open and affirming" of heterosexuals without the tokenism that many queers now experience in many open and affirming congregations? Can we envision the full inclusion of heterosexuals at our table? Can we assist the churches in overcoming their erotophobia?

Our vision and mission of justice involve healing the split between sexuality and spirituality within the Christian churches and assisting those churches to rediscover God's gift of diverse sexualities/genders. Our mission is the sexual and gender reformation of the churches and the forging of a new Church of Christ, a Church of Justice-Love. But is that enough to meet the challenges of the twenty-first century? Can such a postdenominational church forge affiliations and combine resources to create a worldwide network of peoples of all faith to work for global and environmental justice?

Is it so queer to dream of liberation in its entirety? Or is it queerer to accomplish the full liberation of oppressed and oppressor alike as well as the earth in future generations?

INDEX

Related titles available from The Pilgrim Press:

BETWEEN TWO GARDENS
Reflections on Sexuality and Religious Experience
James B. Nelson

Nelson discusses men's liberation; sexuality in Jewish, Catholic, and Protestant interpretations; religious and moral questions of professionals counseling homosexuals; the singleness of the church; the family; and various attitudes toward abortion. The result is a healthy connection between human sexuality and a life of faith.

ISBN 0-8298-0681-4; Paper, 194 pages; $12.95

COMING OUT THROUGH FIRE
Surviving the Trauma of Homophobia
Leanne McCall Tigert and Timothy Brown, eds.

A book for lesbians, gays, bisexuals, and transgendered persons seeking to move through the trauma of homophobia with the passion and power of transformation. Also useful for pastors, therapists, and other helping professionals who seek to confront prejudice and fear and further the process of healing and recovery in the church and the wider community.

ISBN 0-8298-1293-8; Paper, 148 pages; $12.95

COMING OUT TO PARENTS
A Two-Way Survival Guide for Lesbians and Gay Men and Their Parents
Revised and Updated
Mary V. Borhek

For gays and lesbians, this book explores the fears and misgivings accompanying their revelation to their parents and offers suggestions on how and when to come out, what reactions to expect, and how to deal with ensuing awkwardness. For parents, it guides them through natural feelings of grief and loss and shows how understanding, compassion, and insight can lead to deeper love and acceptance.

ISBN 0-8298-0957-0; Paper, 310 pages; $16.00

COMING OUT WHILE STAYING IN
Struggles and Celebrations of Lesbians, Gays, and Bisexuals in the Church
Leanne McCall Tigert

Tigert reflects upon her own personal struggle with the church as a source of pain, alienation, support, and spiritual renewal, and shares others' struggles with the church in the hope of opening the doors to change, healing, and liberation for GLBT individuals.

ISBN 0-8298-1150-8; Paper, 182 pages; $15.00

COMING OUT YOUNG AND FAITHFUL
Leanne McCall Tigert and Timothy Brown, eds.

This groundbreaking collection comes from gay, lesbian, bisexual, transgender, and questioning teens who share their experiences in their communities and churches. Includes resources for ministry and advocacy to help open the doors of affirmation, love, and commitment to the needs of GLBT youth and young adults.

ISBN 0-8298-1414-0; Paper, 112 pages; $13.00

COURAGE TO LOVE
Liturgies for the Lesbian, Gay, Bisexual, and Transgender Community
Geoffrey Duncan

An exceptional collection of worship and other liturgical resources inclusive of and sensitive to the LGBT community for both clergy and lay people. Beneficial for relationships with families, church, and community. Includes liturgies for the Eucharist and same-sex marriages.

ISBN 0-8298-1468-X; Paper, 384 pages; $23.00

CROSSING OVER
Liberating the Transgendered Christian
Vanessa Sheridan

Using tenets of liberation theology, transgendered author Vanessa Sheridan shares honest portrayals and dispels myths about transgendered people, offering encouragement and hope to strengthen the struggle for justice in the church as well as the larger community.

ISBN 0-8298-1446-9; Paper, 160 pages; $16.00

THE ESSENTIAL GAY MYSTICS
Andrew Harvey, ed.

From Sappho to Whitman, Vergil to Audre Lorde, a collection of mystical writings covers the period from early Greek writers to the twentieth century. Contains over sixty selections celebrating those who love others of the same sex.

ISBN 0-8298-1443-4; Paper, 304 pages; $18.00

GAY THEOLOGY WITHOUT APOLOGY
Gary David Comstock

A case for the acknowledgment of varied expressions of humanity. Comstock presents essays that express a specific gay theology, which is an understanding of his personal concern — for all people to recognize that there is a true benefit to fully appreciating gayness as a part of being both human and Christian.

ISBN 0-8298-0944-9; Paper, 184 pages; $15.95

TAKE BACK THE WORD
A Queer Reading of the Bible
Robert Goss and Mona West, eds.

A point of reference for gay, lesbian, bisexual, and transgender persons to define and affirm themselves in the social environment of the Bible. Contains essays from gay, lesbian, bisexual, and transgender scholars and clergy who rewrite exclusive and oppressive conventional thinking.

ISBN 0-8298-1397-7; Paper, 240 pages; $20.00

MY ROSE
An African American Mother's Story of AIDS
Geneva E. Bell

A mother's moving story of her gay son and his struggle with AIDS, and her devastation, shame, and anger at God. But it is also a witness to the deep faith that enabled the author to come to terms with this tragedy, as well as a record of how a family, a community, and a church were transformed by God's love.

ISBN 0-8298-1160-5; Paper, 86 pages; $13.00

RELIGION IS A QUEER THING
A Guide to the Christian Faith for Lesbian, Gay, Bisexual, and Transgendered Persons
Elizabeth Stuart with Brounston, Edwards, McMahon, and Morrison, eds.

Queer theology is a generic term for a theology that embraces and encompasses a whole set of theologies — gay, lesbian, bisexual, and transgendered. This is an ongoing developing theology accessible to the general audience.

ISBN 0-8298-1269-5; Paper, 152 pages; $15.95

QUEER COMMENTARY AND THE HEBREW BIBLE
Ken Stone, ed.

Seven "queer readings" of the Hebrew Bible followed by three responses form the body of this book, embodying the tenets of queer theory applied to biblical commentary.

ISBN 0-8298-1447-7; Paper, 256 pages; $28.00

OMNIGENDER
A Trans-Religious Approach
Virginia Ramey Mollenkott

Winner of a Lambda Literary Award and a PMA Benjamin Franklin Award, *Omnigender* is a proposal for a new paradigm to undo the oppressive aspects of the binary construct of gender identity and other harmful roles inflicted on individuals. Offers fresh ways of thinking about gender in our society.

ISBN 0-8298-1422-1; Hardcover, 208 pages; $18.00

OUR DAUGHTER MARTHA
A Family Struggles with Coming Out
Marcy Clements Henrikson

Combining her experience with excerpts from her daughter's journal, author and laywoman Henrikson takes us on her journey to accepting her lesbian daughter and her active role in support of gay and lesbian rights in the church and society. Ideal for families and congregations with gay and lesbian members.

ISBN 0-8298-1432-9; Paper, 112 pages; $10.00

MY SON ERIC
A Mother Struggles to Accept Her Gay Son and Discovers Herself
Revised and Expanded
Mary V. Borhek

When *My Son Eric* was originally published in 1979, the world was a much different place than it is today for lesbians and gay men. Borhek has spent twenty years at the center of many advancements in lesbian and gay life, and this book continues to sound the trumpet for love and acceptance.

ISBN 0-8298-1427-2; Paper, 176 pages; $14.00

OUT ON HOLY GROUND
Meditations on Gay Men's Spirituality
Donald L. Boisvert

Author Boisvert presents his own meditations through the context of theology, myths, rituals, symbols, and spiritual culture in order to create a compelling portrait of gay spirituality as a serious yet perceptive and provocative cultural expression in North America.

ISBN 0-8298-1369-1; Paper, 148 pages; $19.95

To order these or any other books
from The Pilgrim Press, call or write:

The Pilgrim Press
700 Prospect Avenue East
Cleveland, OH 44115-1100

Phone orders: 800.537.3394 (M-F, 8:30am–4:30pm ET)
Fax orders: 216.736.2206

Please include shipping charges of $4.00 for the first book
and 75¢ for each additional book.

Or order from our web sites
at www.pilgrimpress.com

Prices subject to change without notice.